HOME
AFTER
DARK

HOME AFTER DARK

A NOVEL

DAVID SMALL

LIVERIGHT PUBLISHING CORPORATION

A Division of W. W. Norton & Company

Independent Publishers Since 1923

New York • London

Printed in the United States of America
First Edition

For information about permission to reproduce selections from this book, write to Permissions, Liveright Publishing Corporation, a division of W. W. Norton & Company, Inc., 500 Fifth Avenue, New York, NY 10110

For information about special discounts for bulk purchases, please contact W. W. Norton Special Sales at specialsales@wwnorton.com or 800-233-4830

Manufacturing by LSC Communications, Harrisonburg
Production manager: Anna Oler

Library of Congress Cataloging-in-Publication Data

Names: Small, David, 1945– author, artist.
Title: Home after dark : a novel / David Small.
Description: First edition. | New York : Liveright Publishing Corporation, [2018] | Summary: Thirteen-year-old Russell Pruitt, abandoned by his mother, follows his father to dilapidated 1950s Marshfield, California, where he is forced to fend for himself against a ring of malicious bullies.
Identifiers: LCCN 2018015021 | ISBN 9780871403155 (hardcover)
Subjects: LCSH: Graphic novels. | CYAC: Graphic novels. | Adolescence—Fiction. | Self-esteem—Fiction. | Family life—Fiction. | Bullying—Fiction.
Classification: LCC PZ7.7.S556 Ho 2018 | DDC 741.5/973—dc23
LC record available at https://lccn.loc.gov/2018015021

Liveright Publishing Corporation, 500 Fifth Avenue, New York, N.Y. 10110
www.wwnorton.com

W. W. Norton & Company Ltd., 15 Carlisle Street, London W1D 3BS

1 2 3 4 5 6 7 8 9 0

TO MIKE KLEIMO, KEVIN BRADY, MARK QUIN, AND BRAD ZELLAR
FOR THEIR MEMORIES,
AND, AS EVER,
TO MY WIFE, SARAH,
FOR HER LOVE, HER PATIENCE, AND HER ENDURANCE.

HOME AFTER DARK

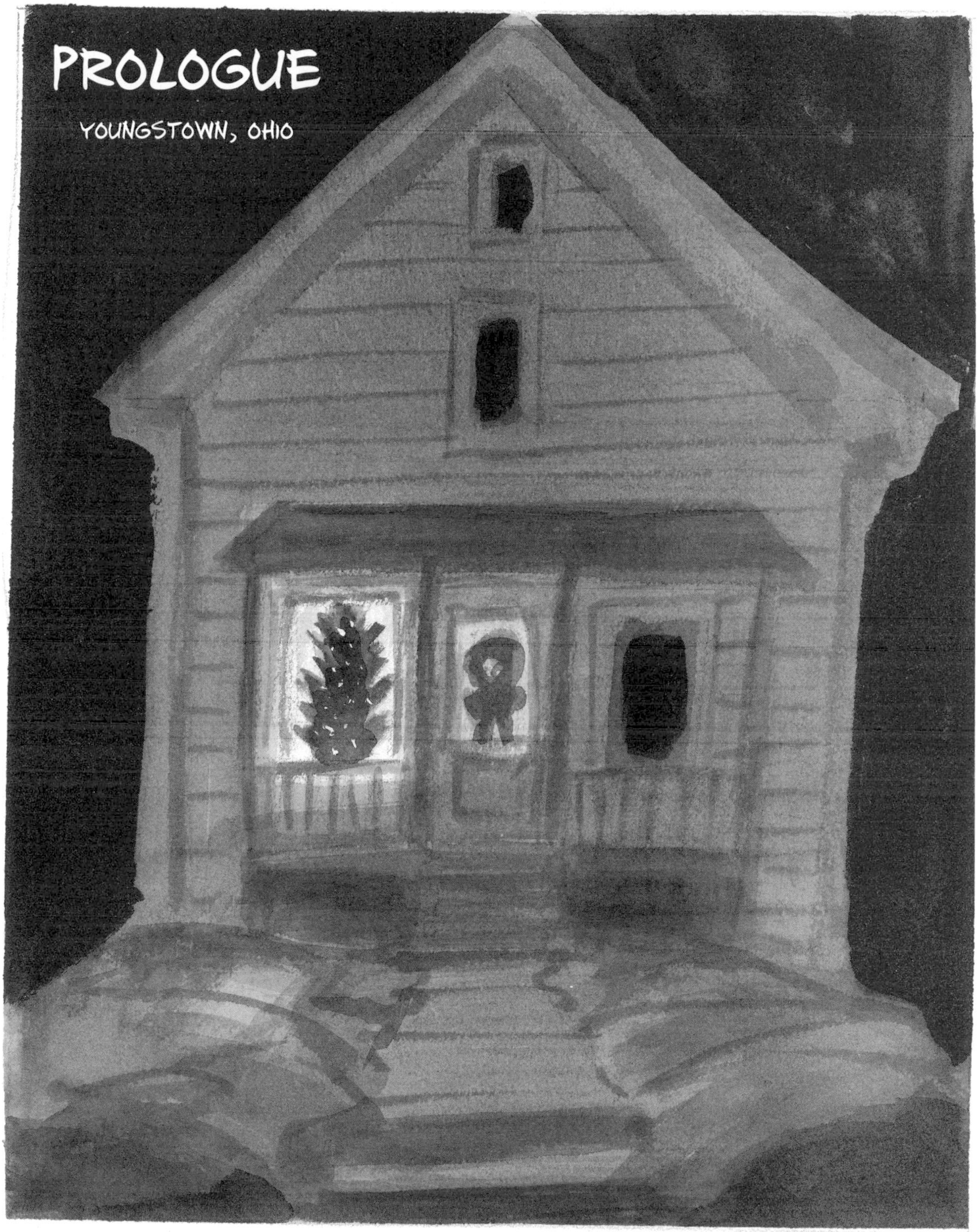
PROLOGUE
YOUNGSTOWN, OHIO

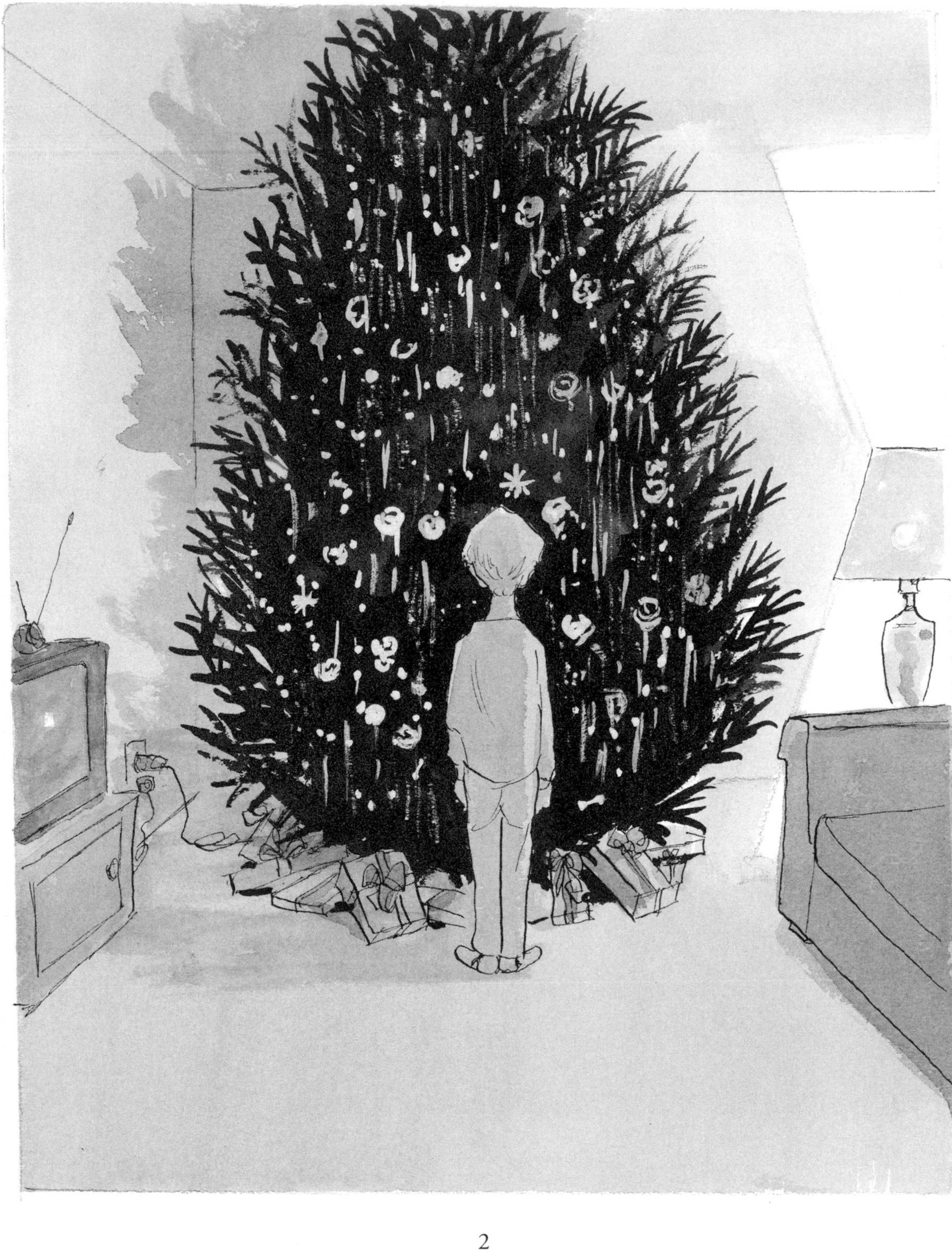

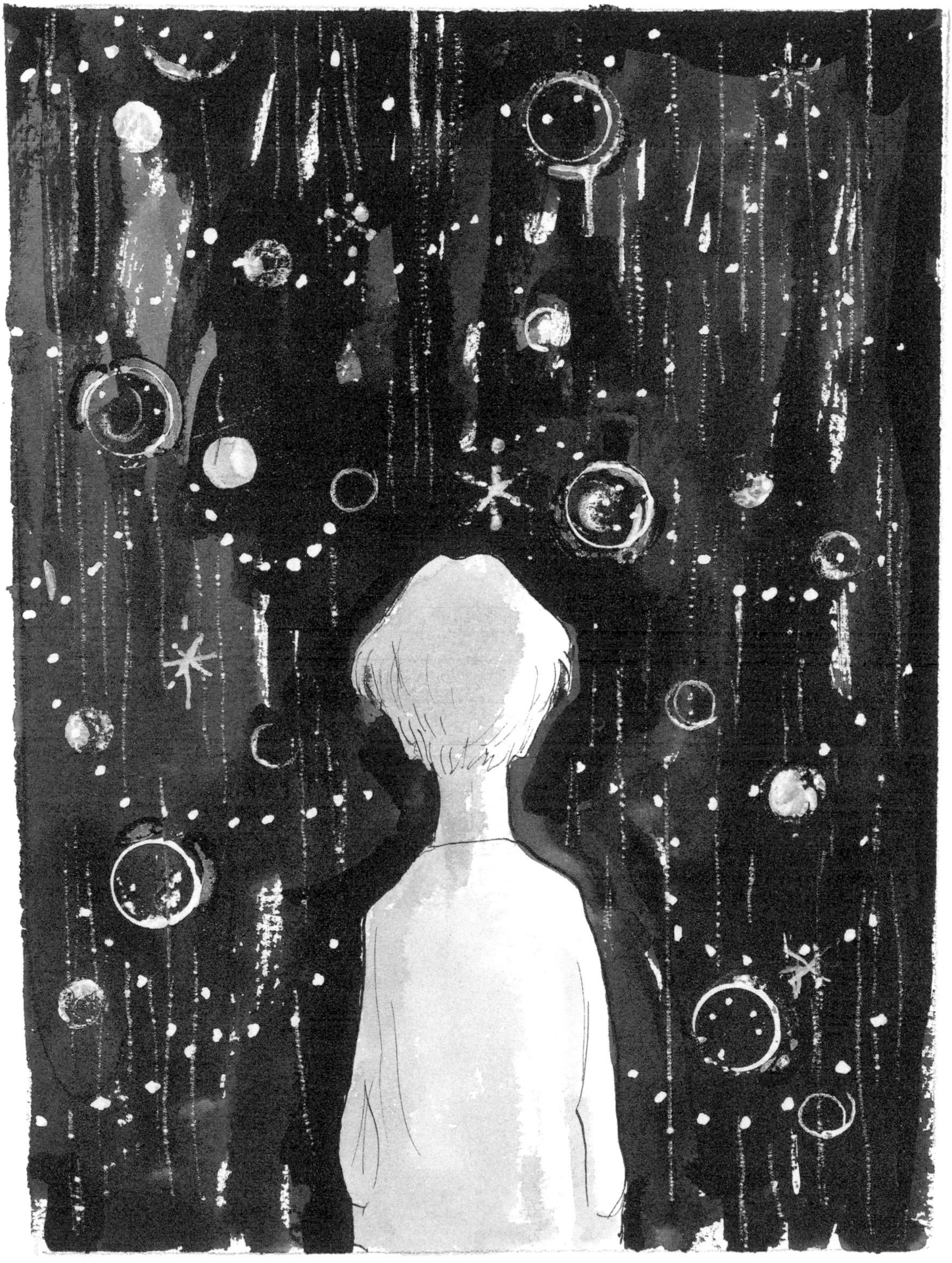

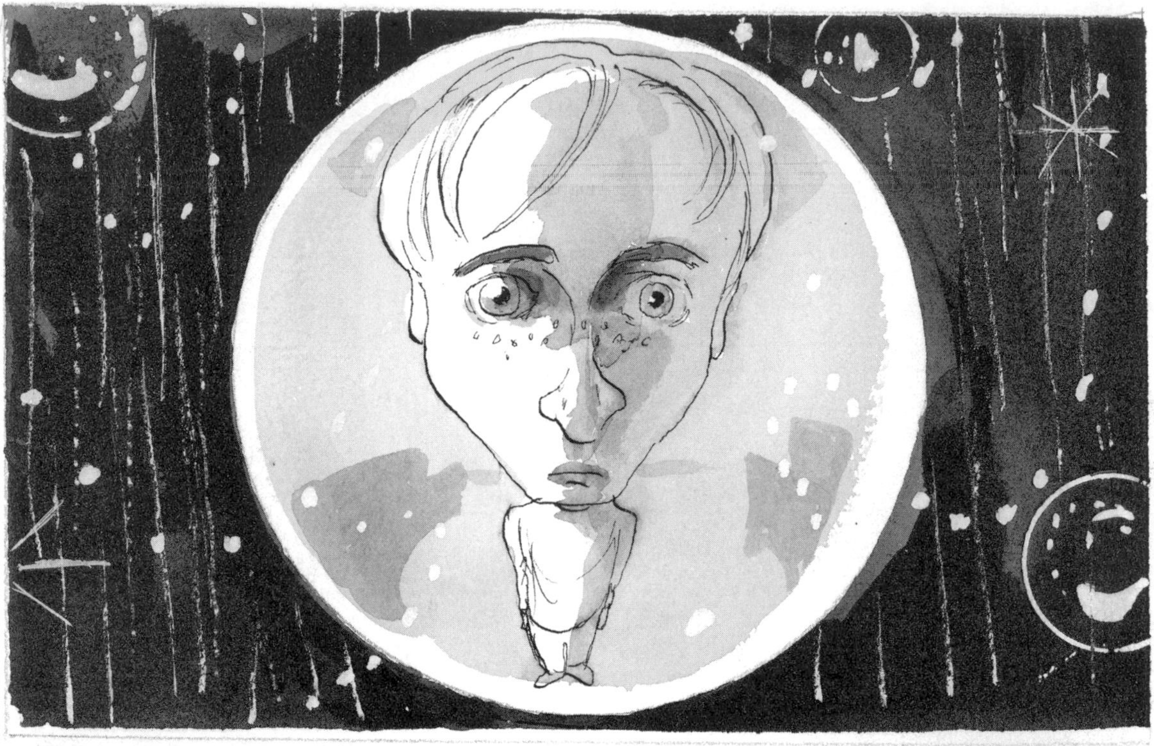

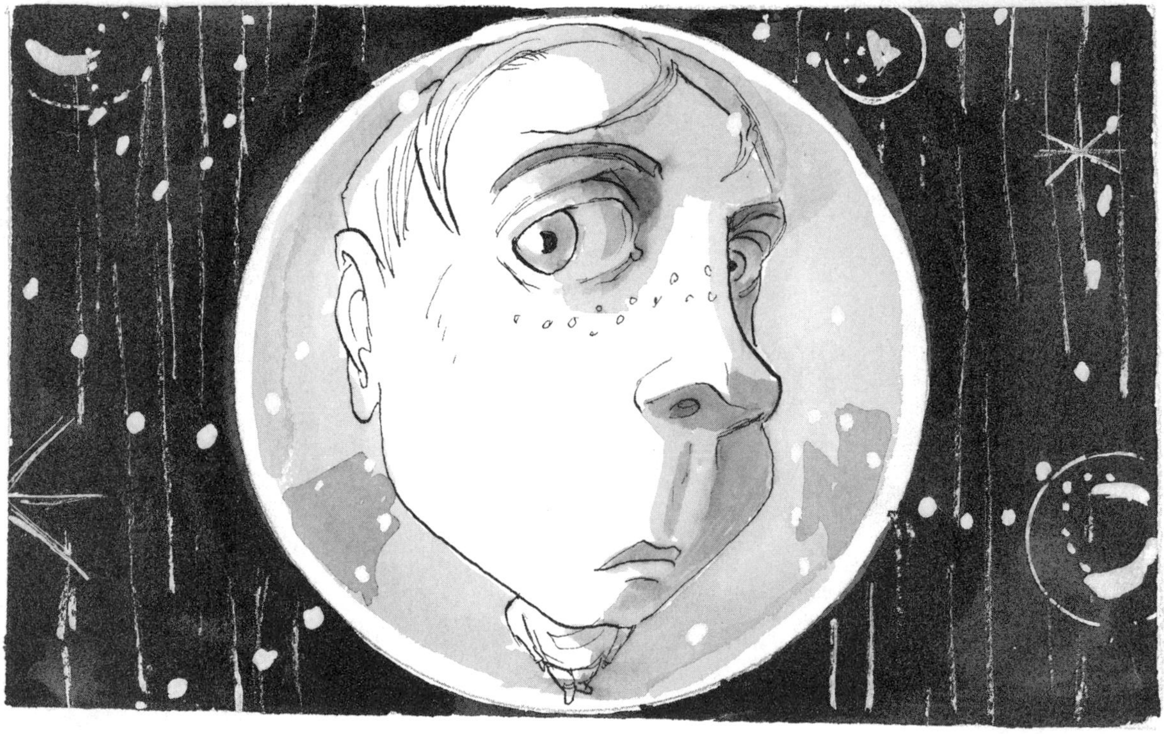

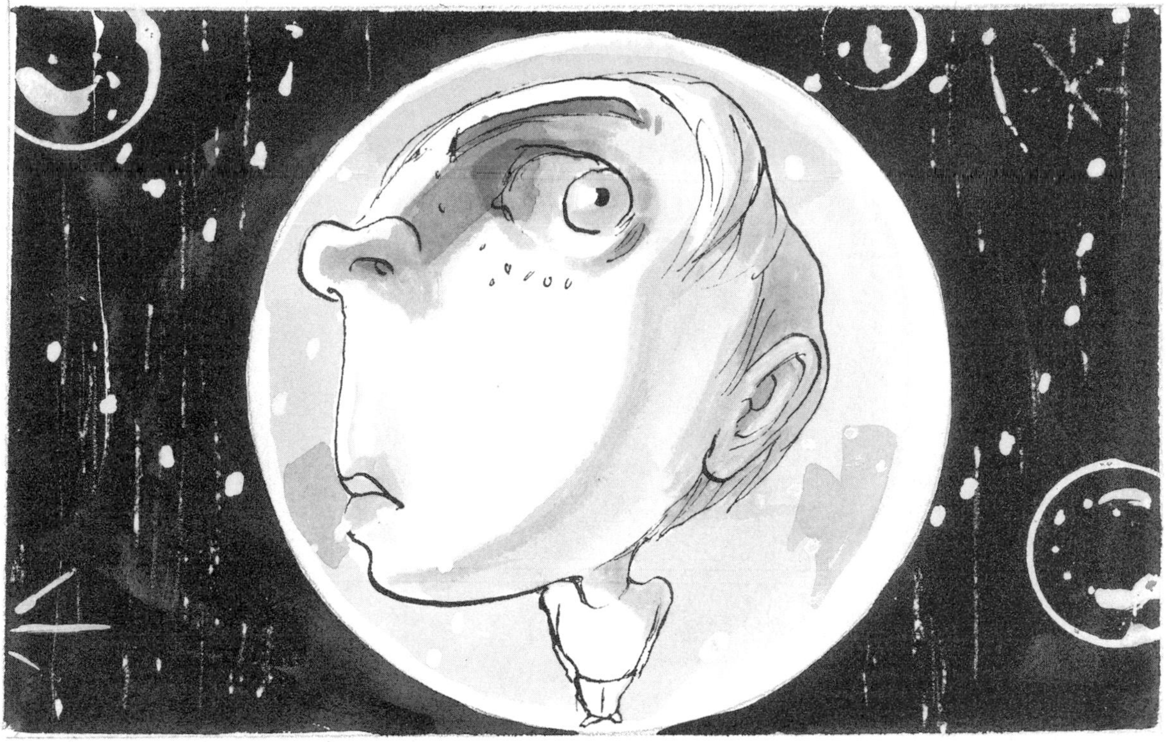

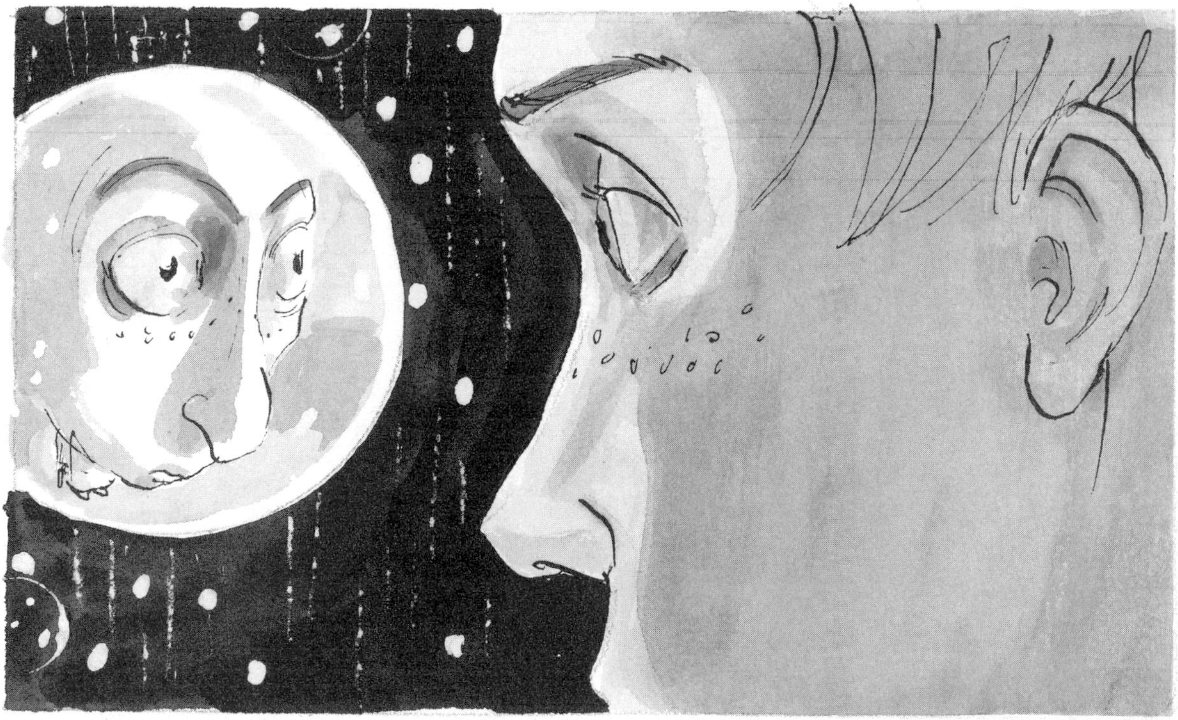

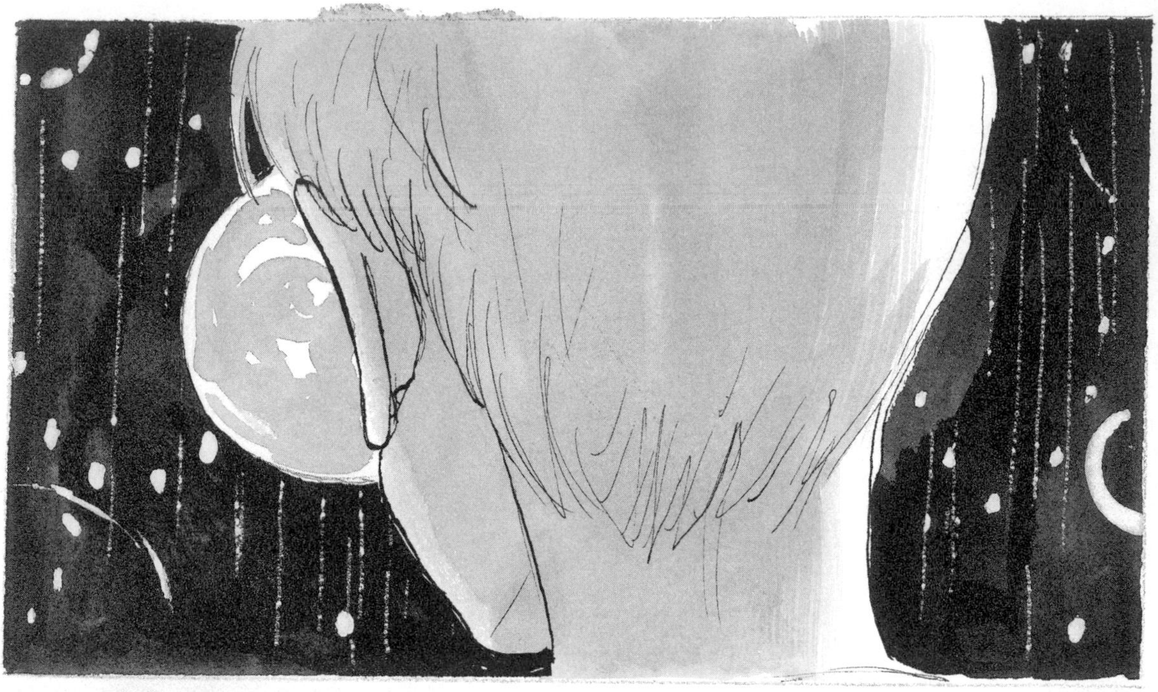

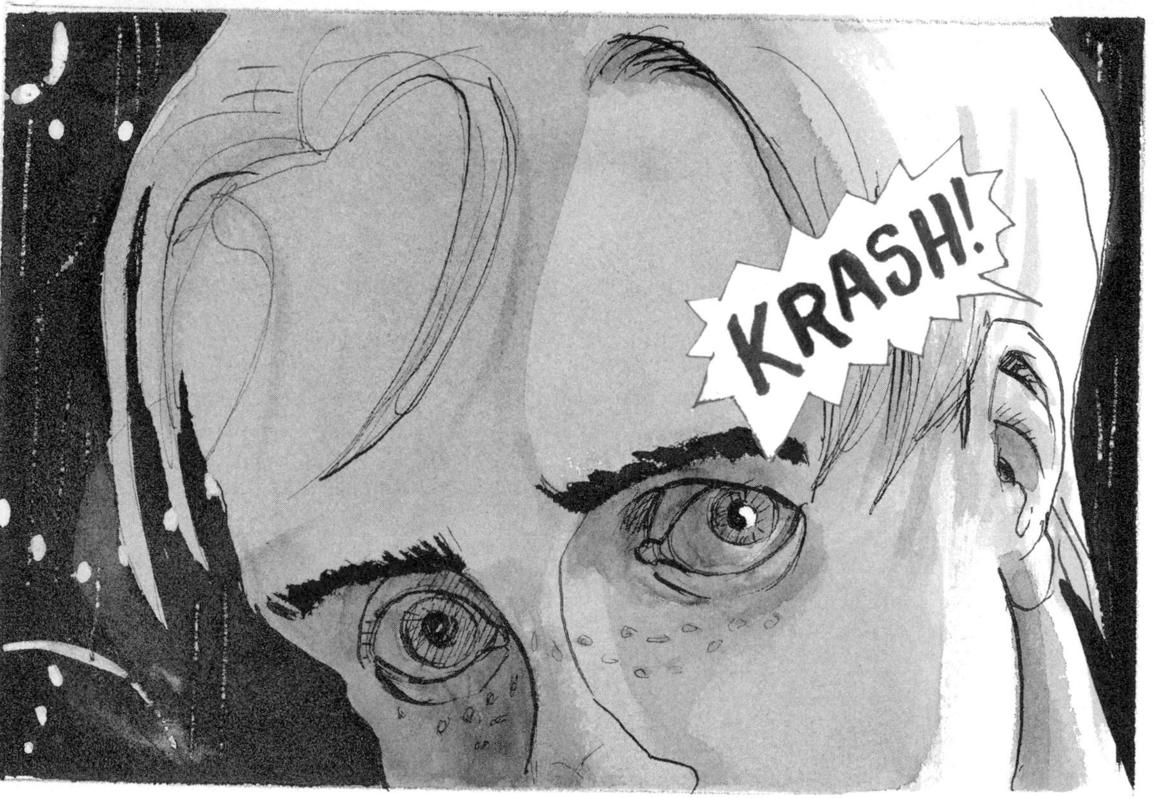
KRASH!

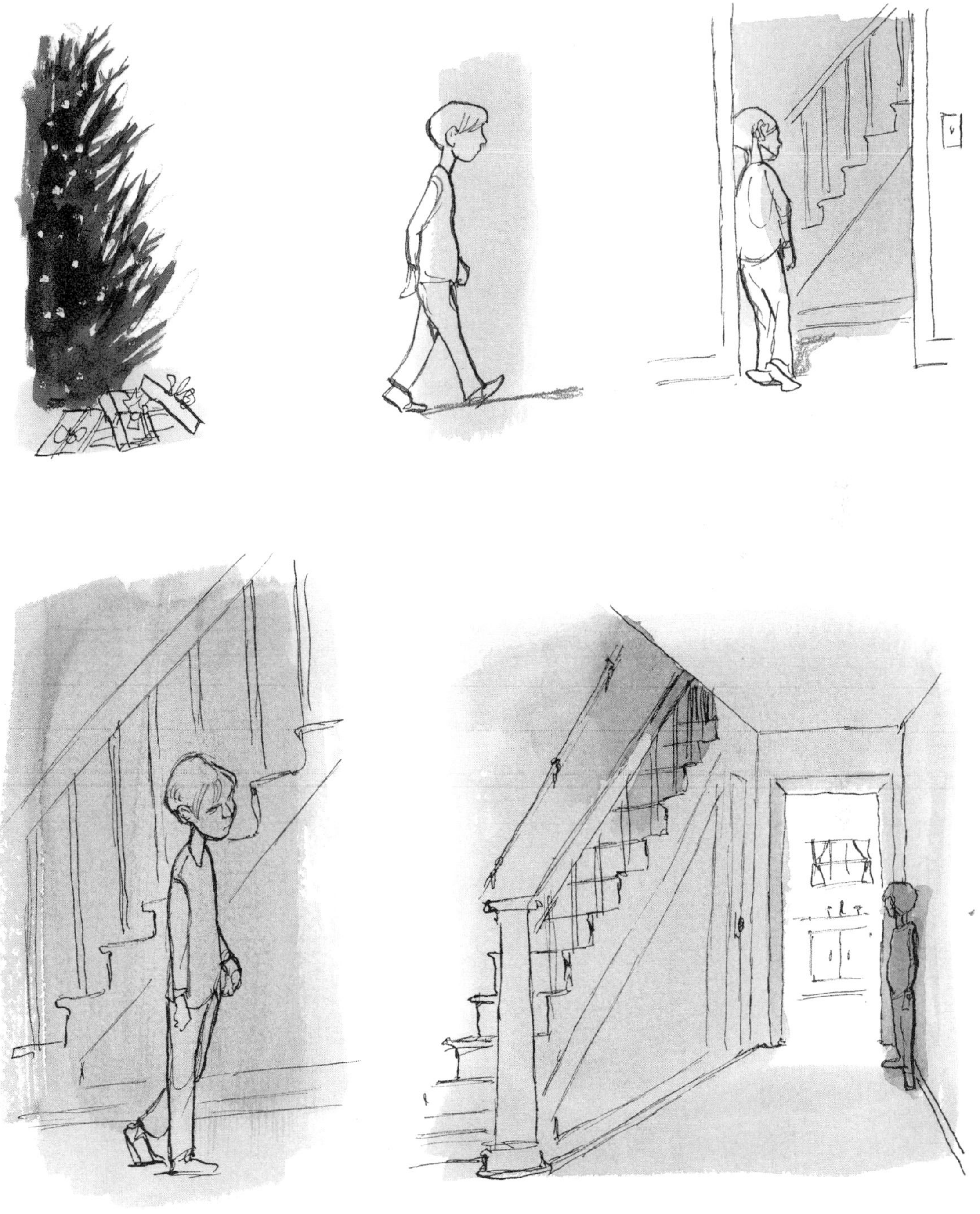

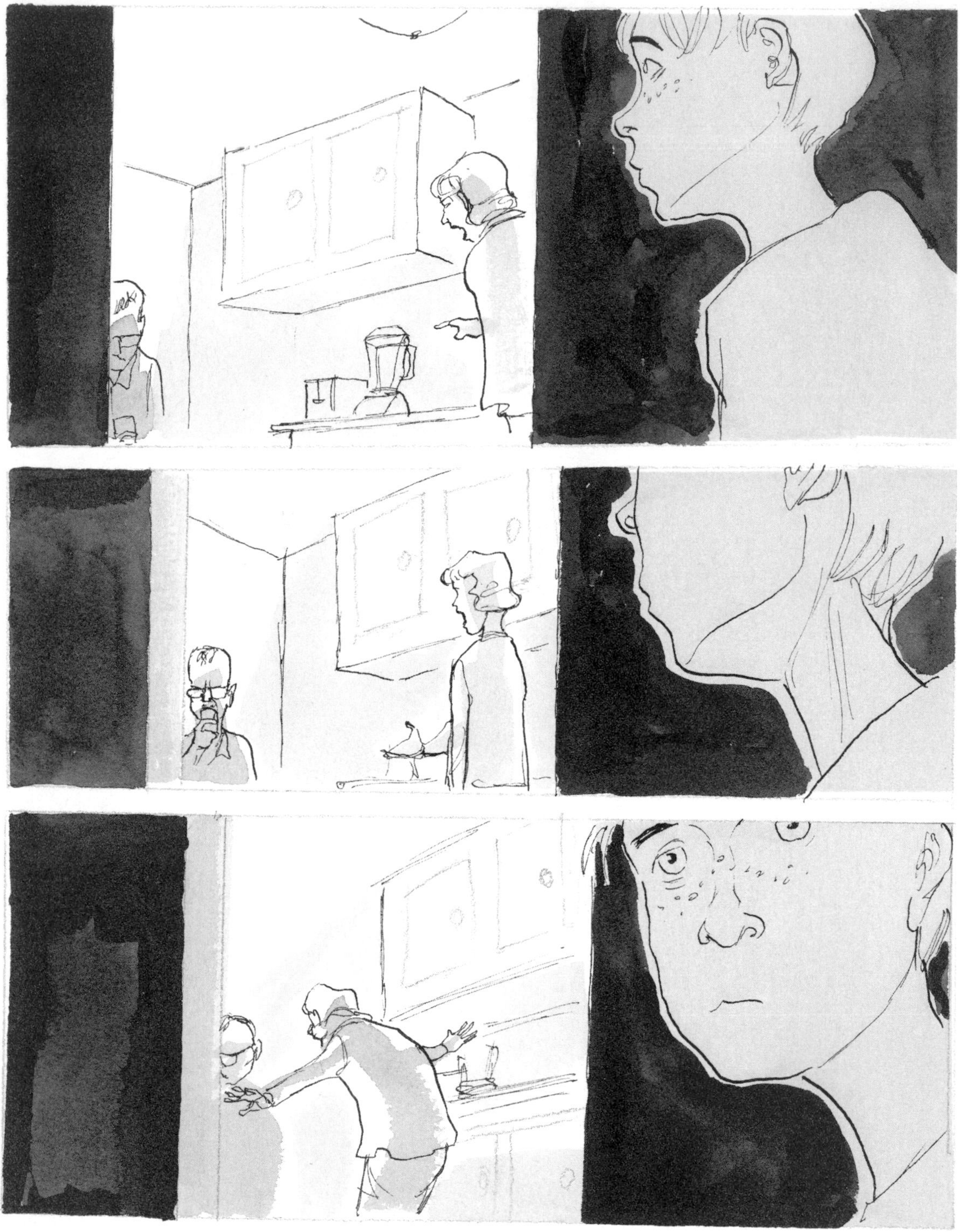

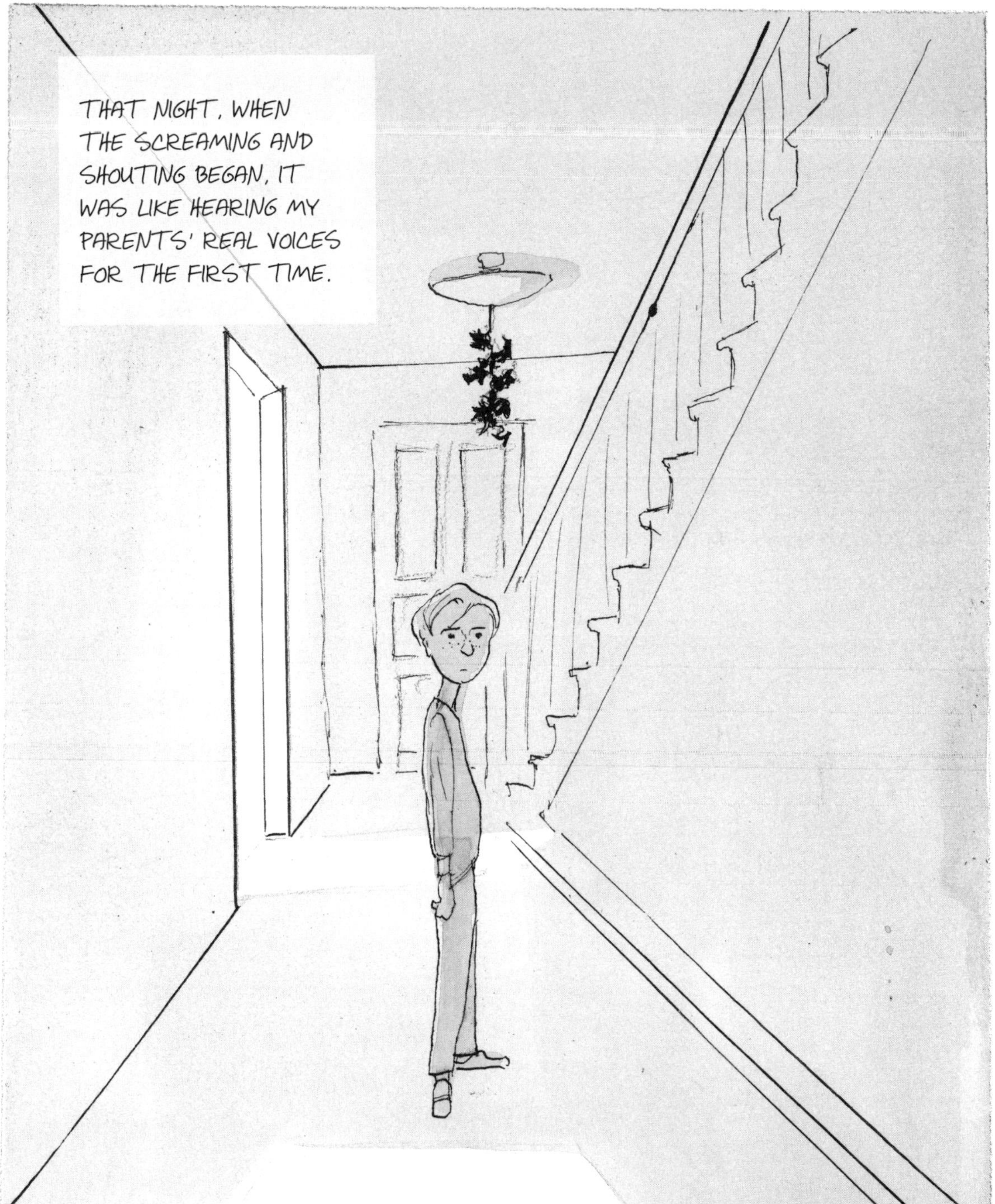
THAT NIGHT, WHEN THE SCREAMING AND SHOUTING BEGAN, IT WAS LIKE HEARING MY PARENTS' REAL VOICES FOR THE FIRST TIME.

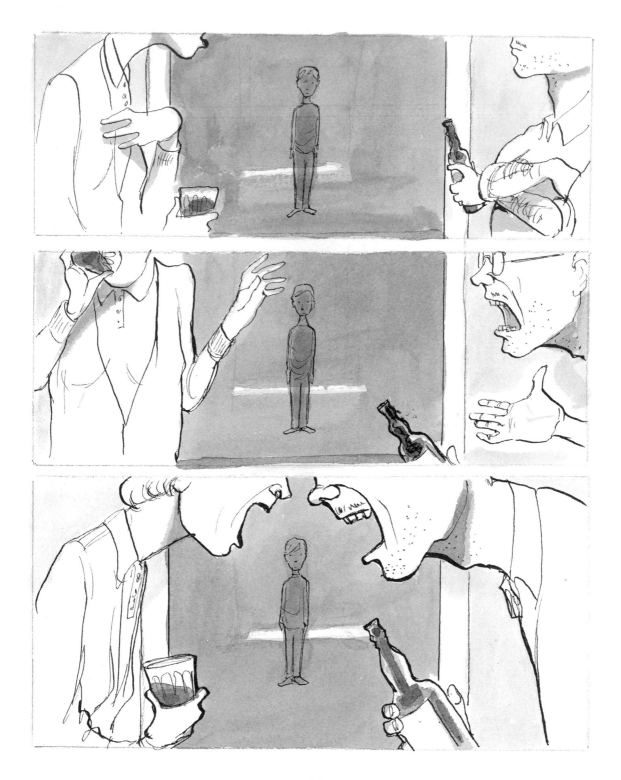

THAT SUMMER, MOM RAN
AWAY WITH OLLIE JACKSON
(KNOWN ON THE FOOTBALL
FIELD AS "ACTION JACKSON"),
DAD'S BEST FRIEND.

DAD DECIDED TO MOVE US TO CALIFORNIA.

AFTER HIS STINT IN THE KOREAN WAR, THEN THE DIVORCE, I GUESS ALL HE COULD THINK OF WAS THAT DREAM OF SUN, SAND, AND GOLDEN BODIES.

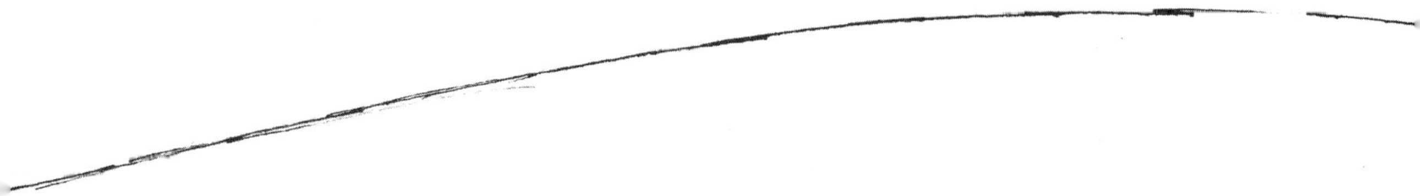

CHAPTER ONE

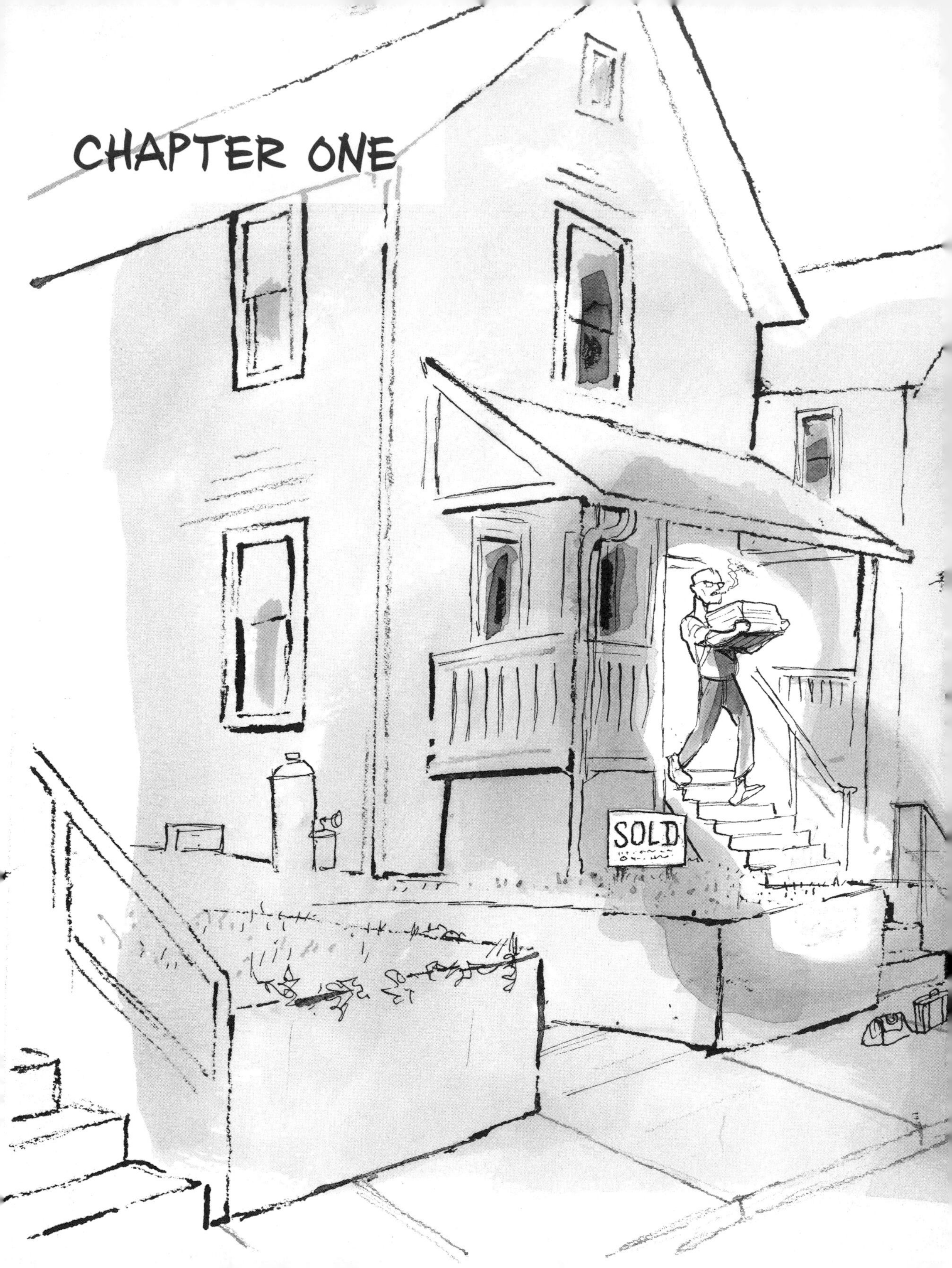
SOLD

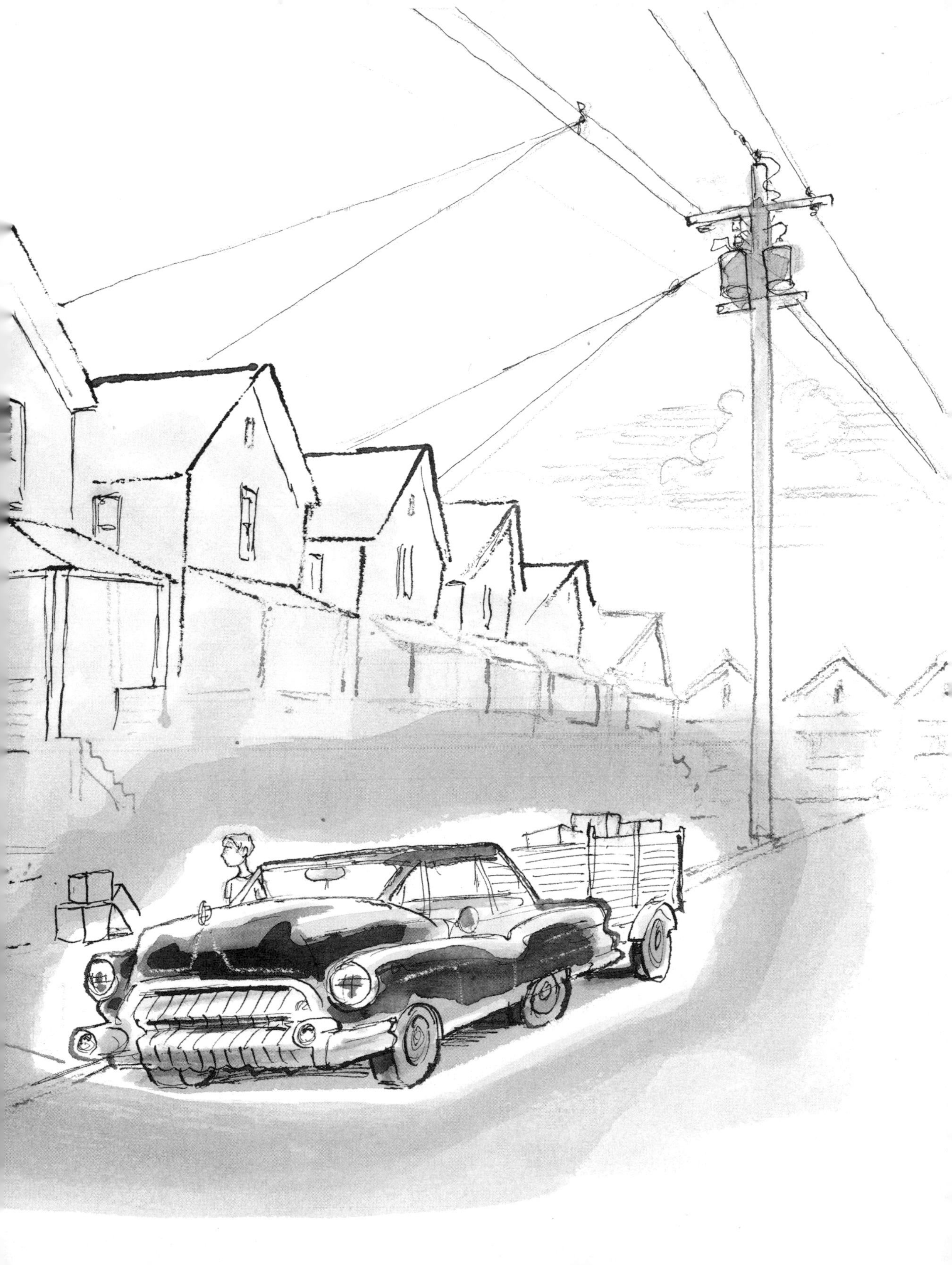

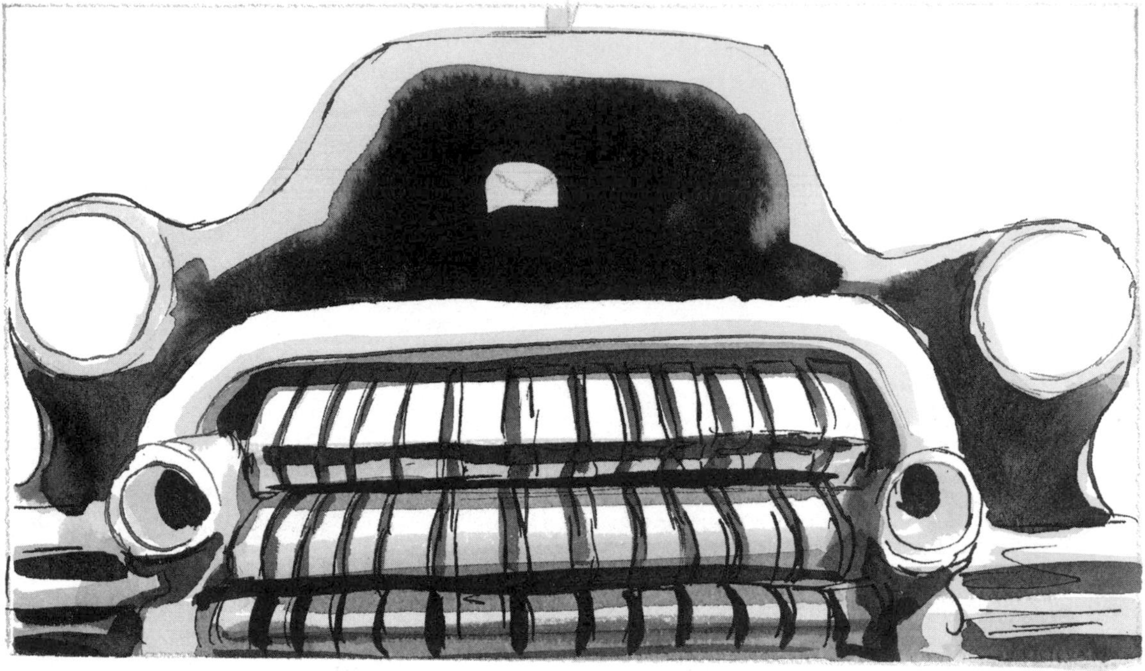

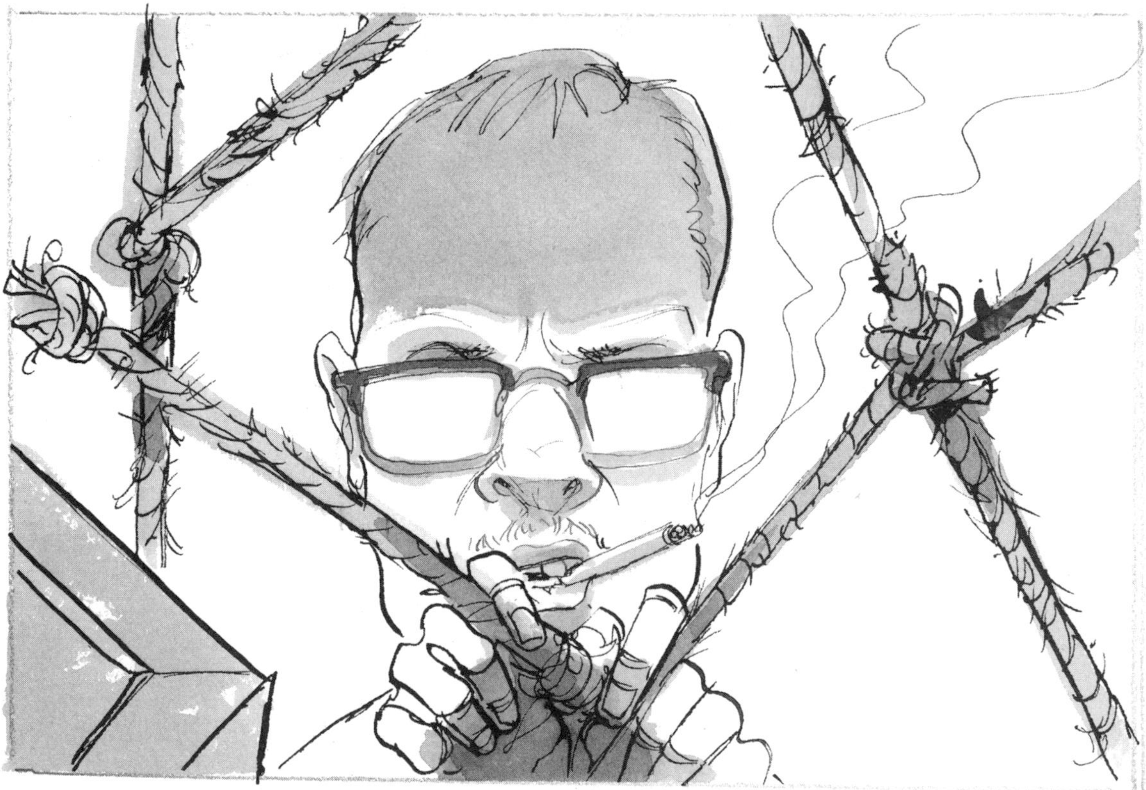

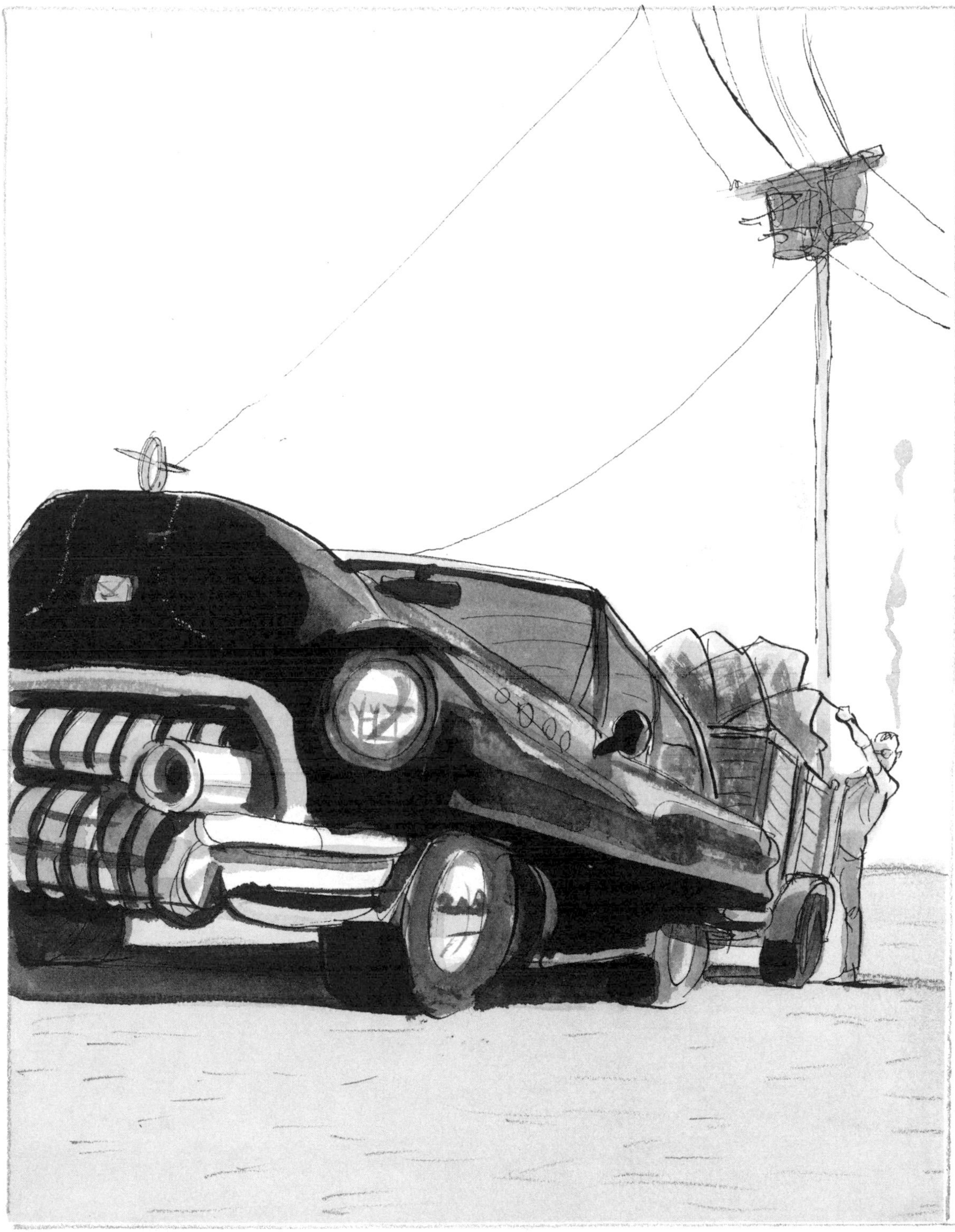

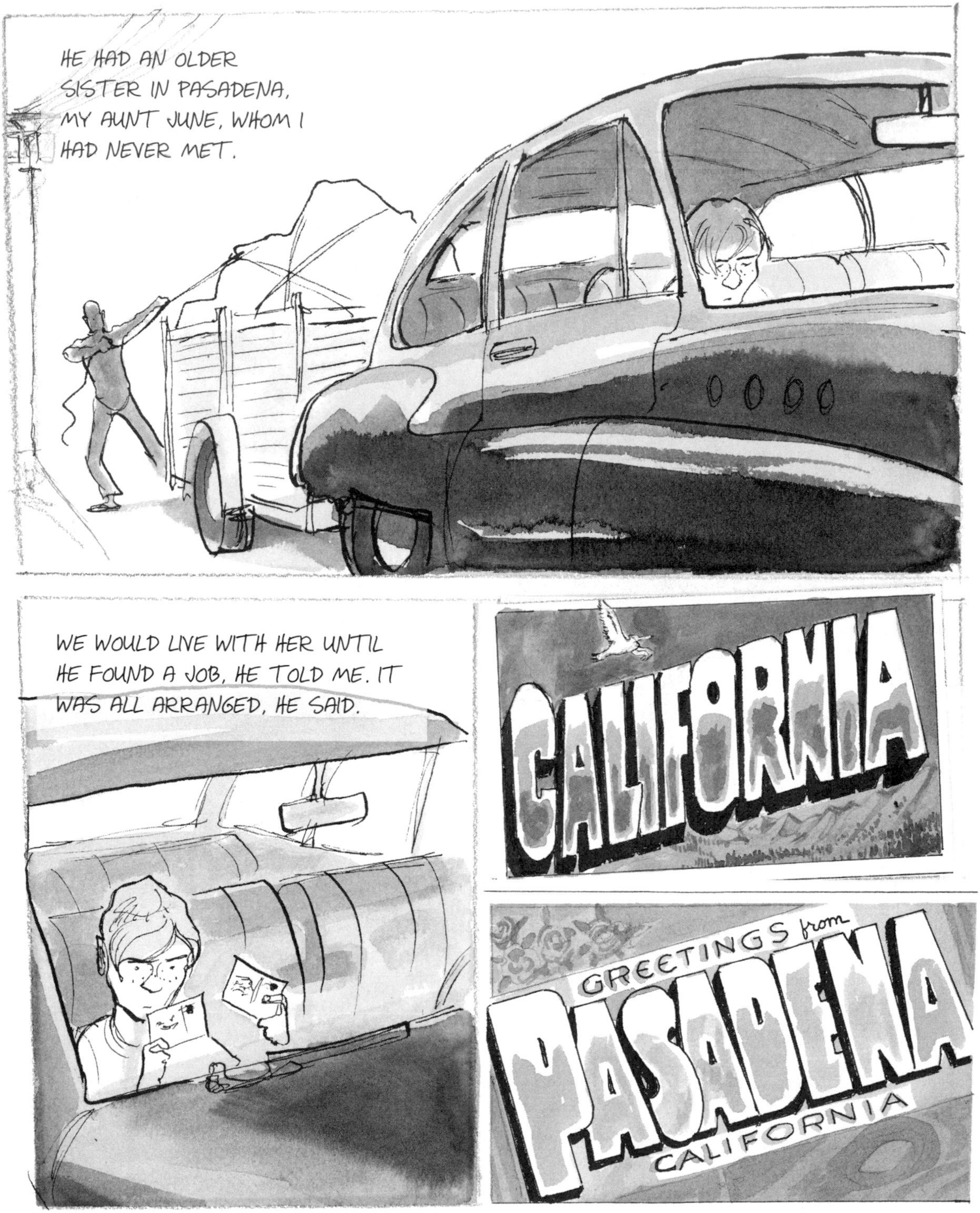
HE HAD AN OLDER SISTER IN PASADENA, MY AUNT JUNE, WHOM I HAD NEVER MET.
WE WOULD LIVE WITH HER UNTIL HE FOUND A JOB, HE TOLD ME. IT WAS ALL ARRANGED, HE SAID.
CALIFORNIA
GREETINGS from
PASADENA
CALIFORNIA

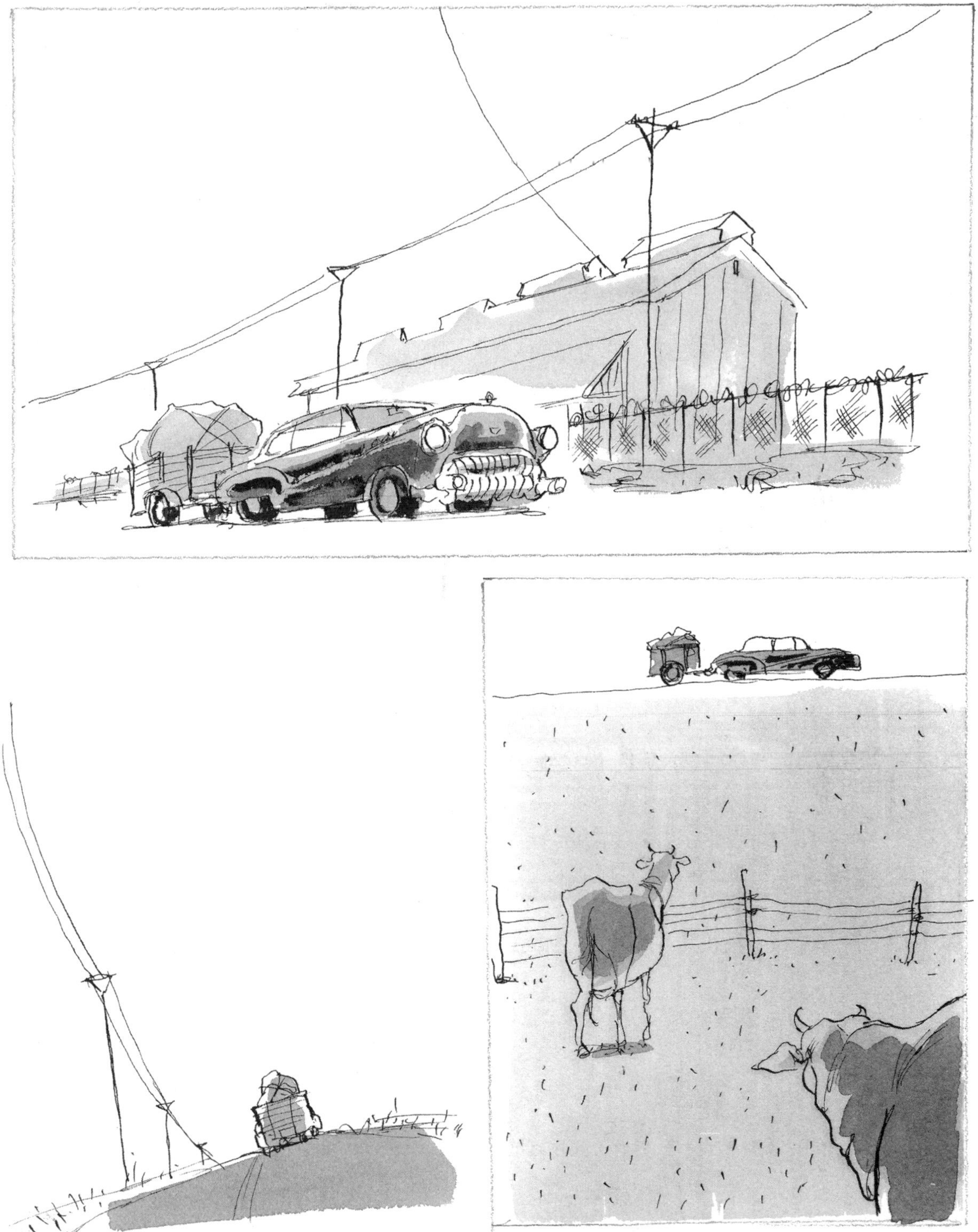

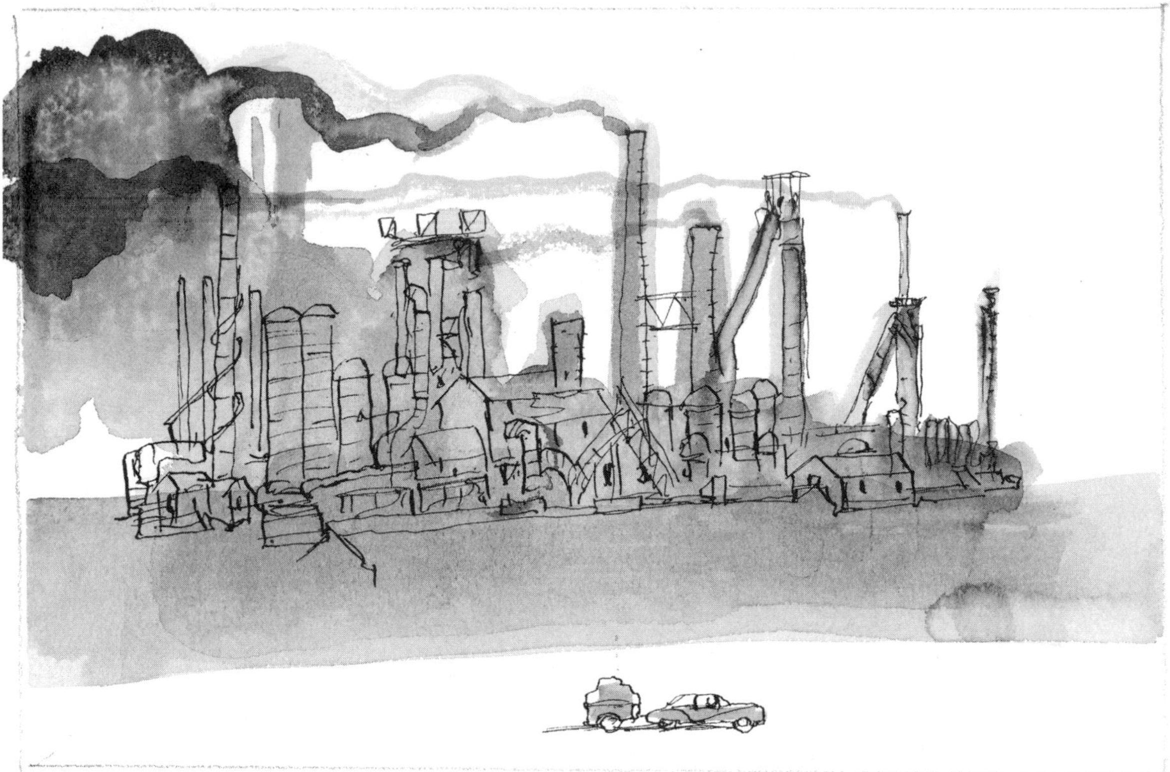

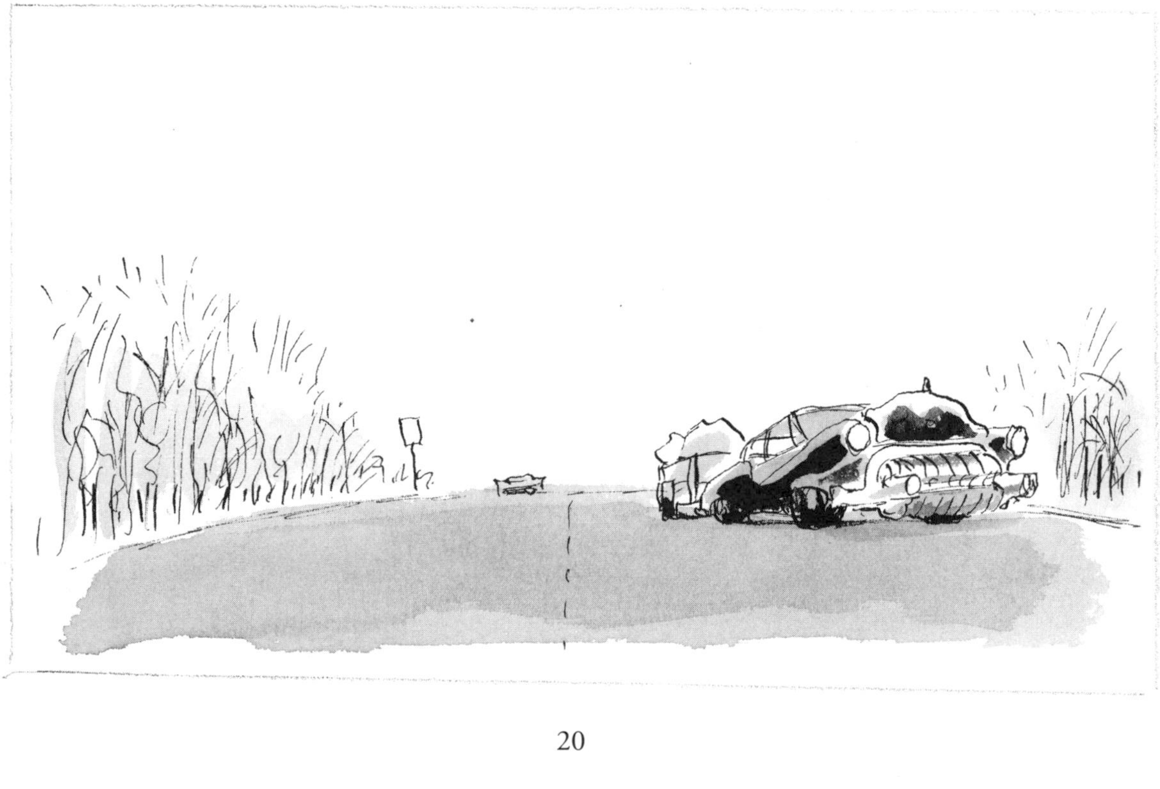

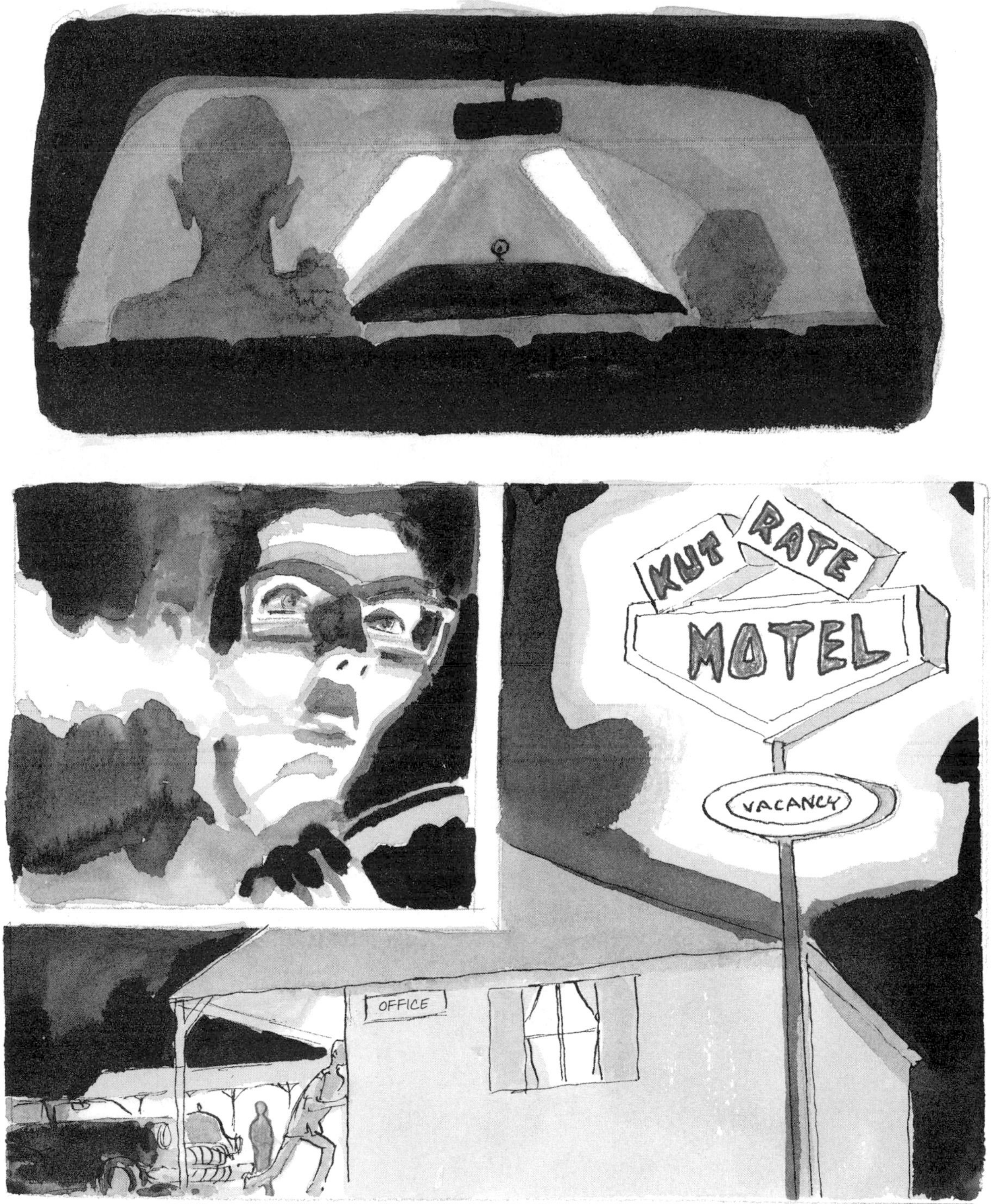
KUT RATE
MOTEL
VACANCY
OFFICE

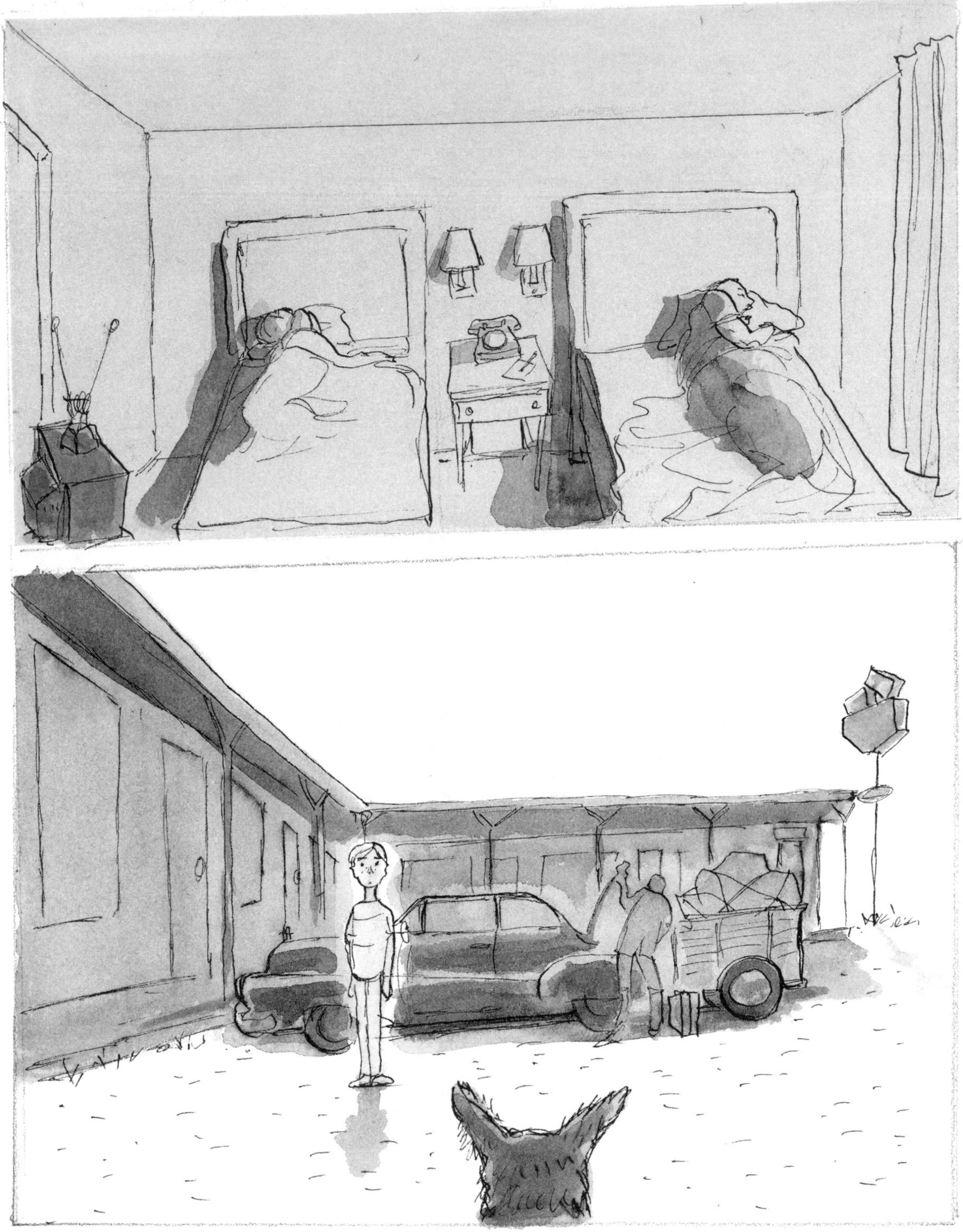

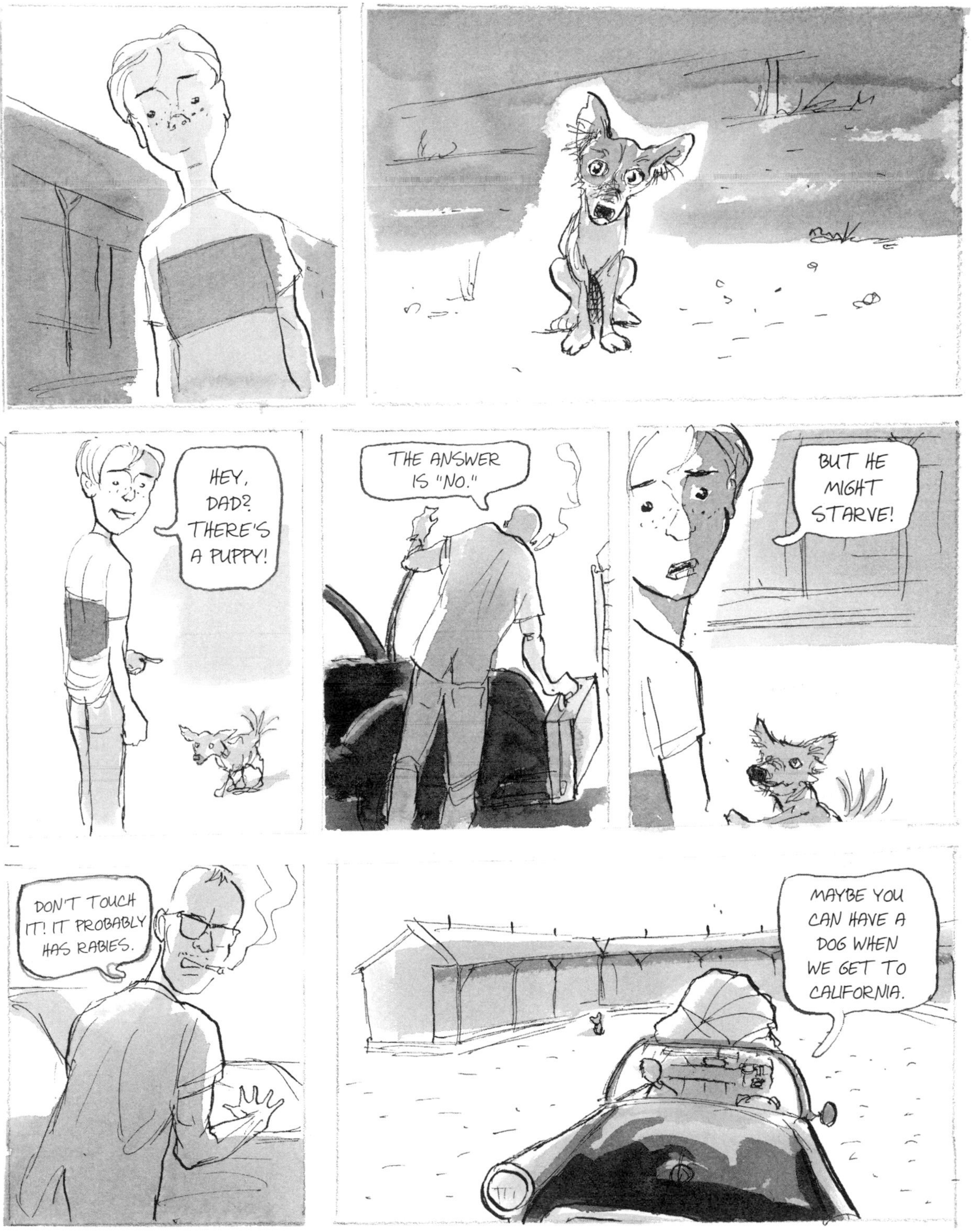
HEY, DAD? THERE'S A PUPPY!
THE ANSWER IS "NO."
BUT HE MIGHT STARVE!
DON'T TOUCH IT! IT PROBABLY HAS RABIES.
MAYBE YOU CAN HAVE A DOG WHEN WE GET TO CALIFORNIA.

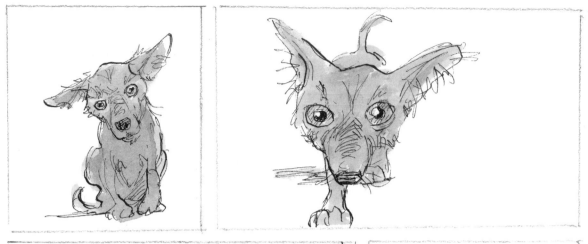

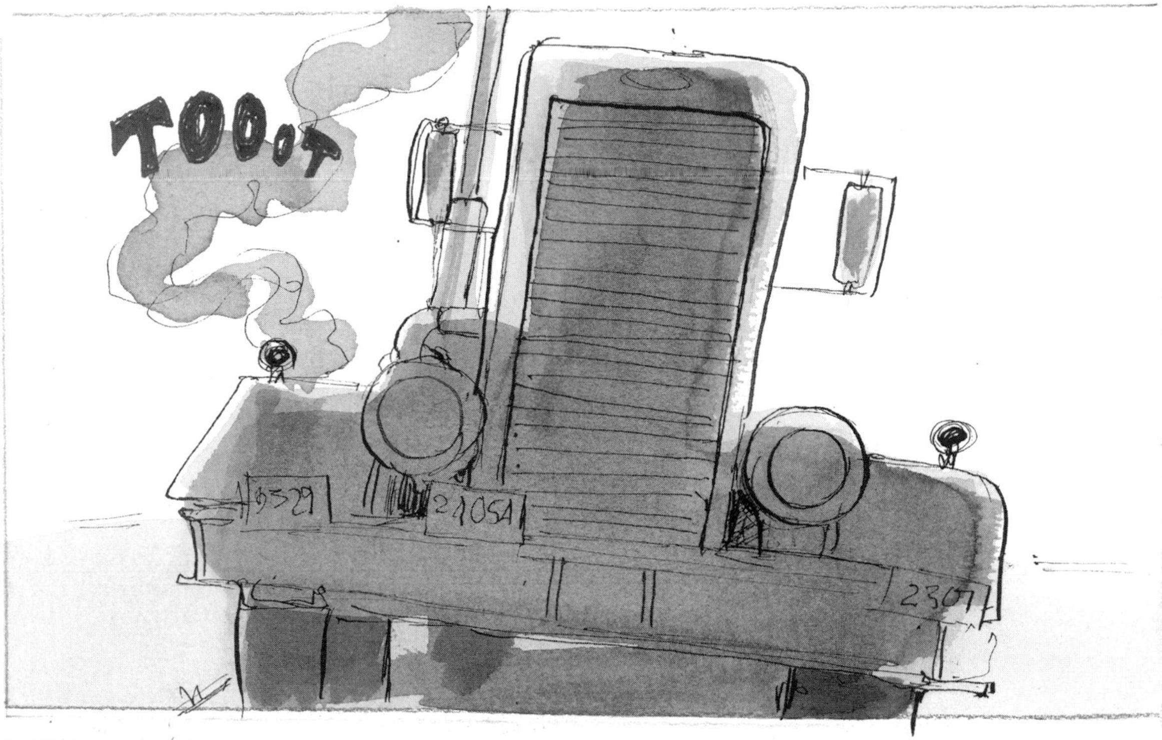
TOOOT
0529
24054
2307

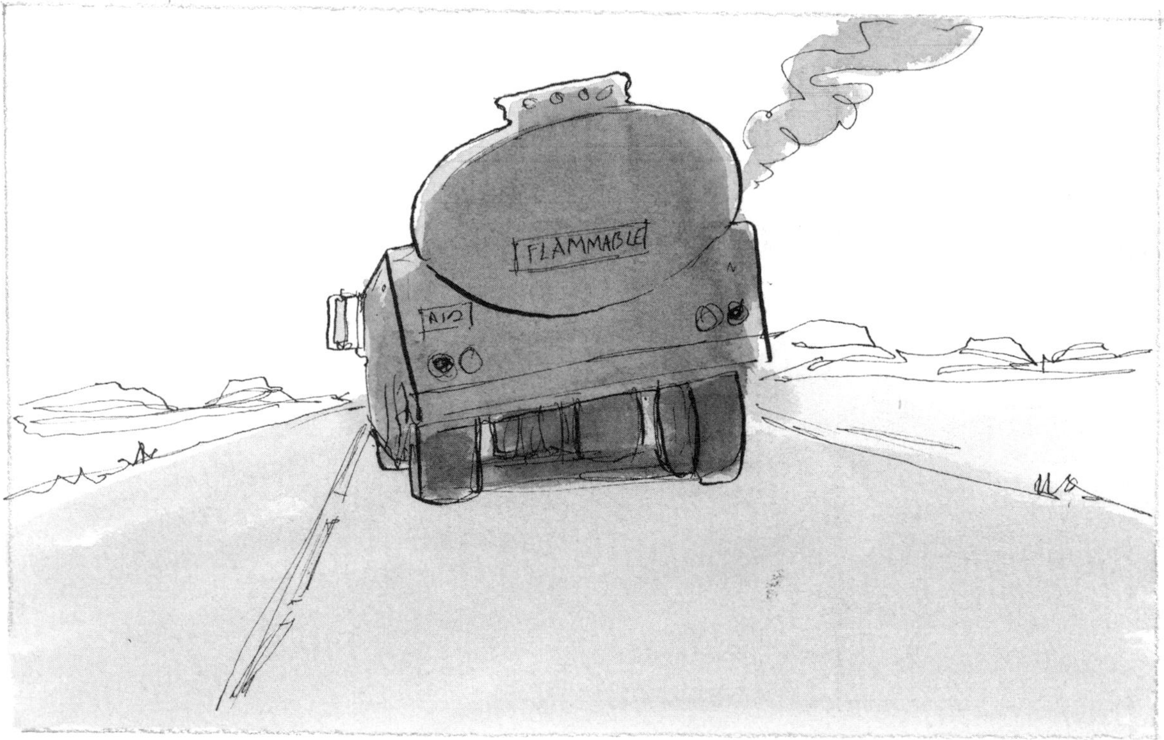
FLAMMABLE

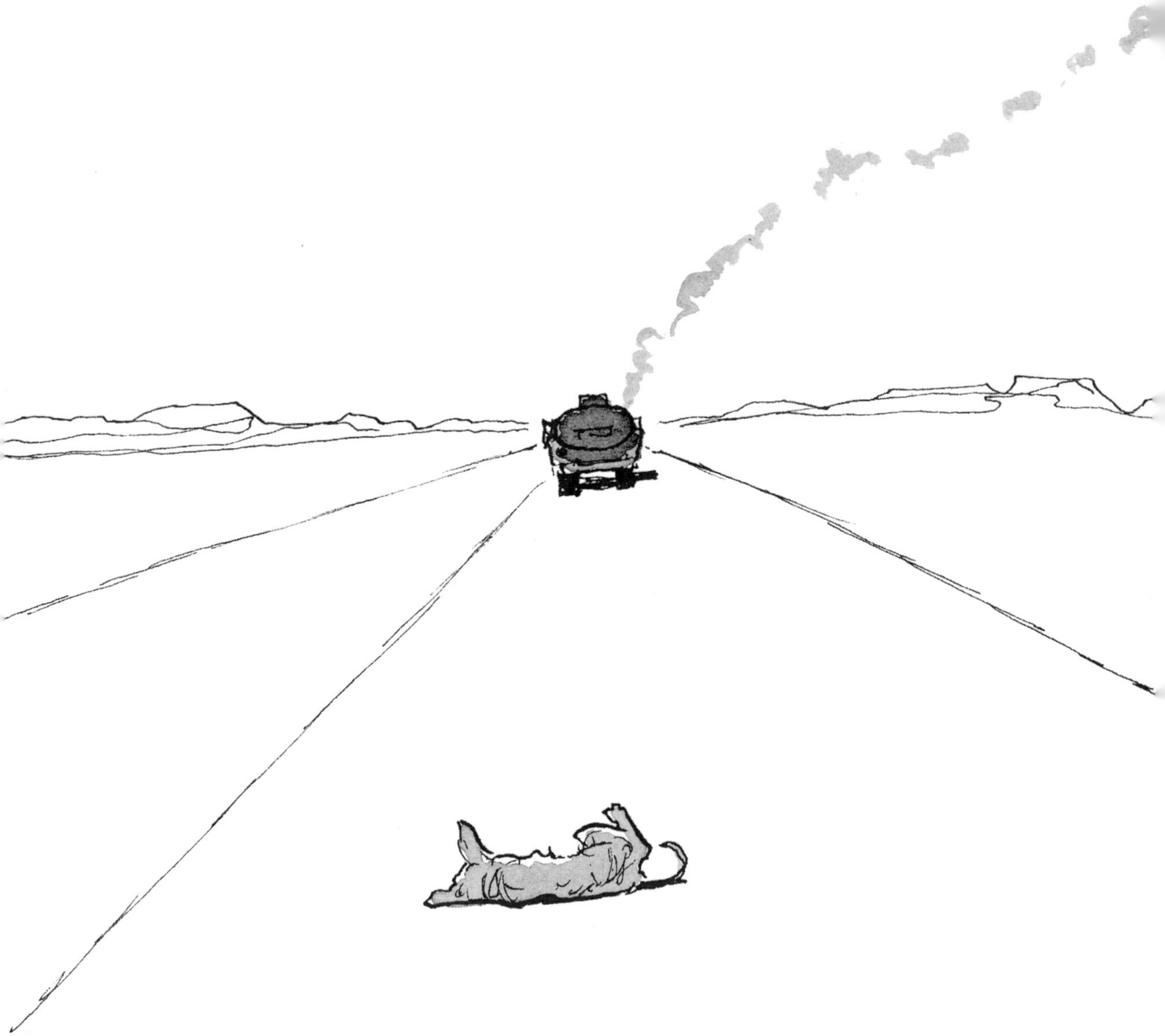

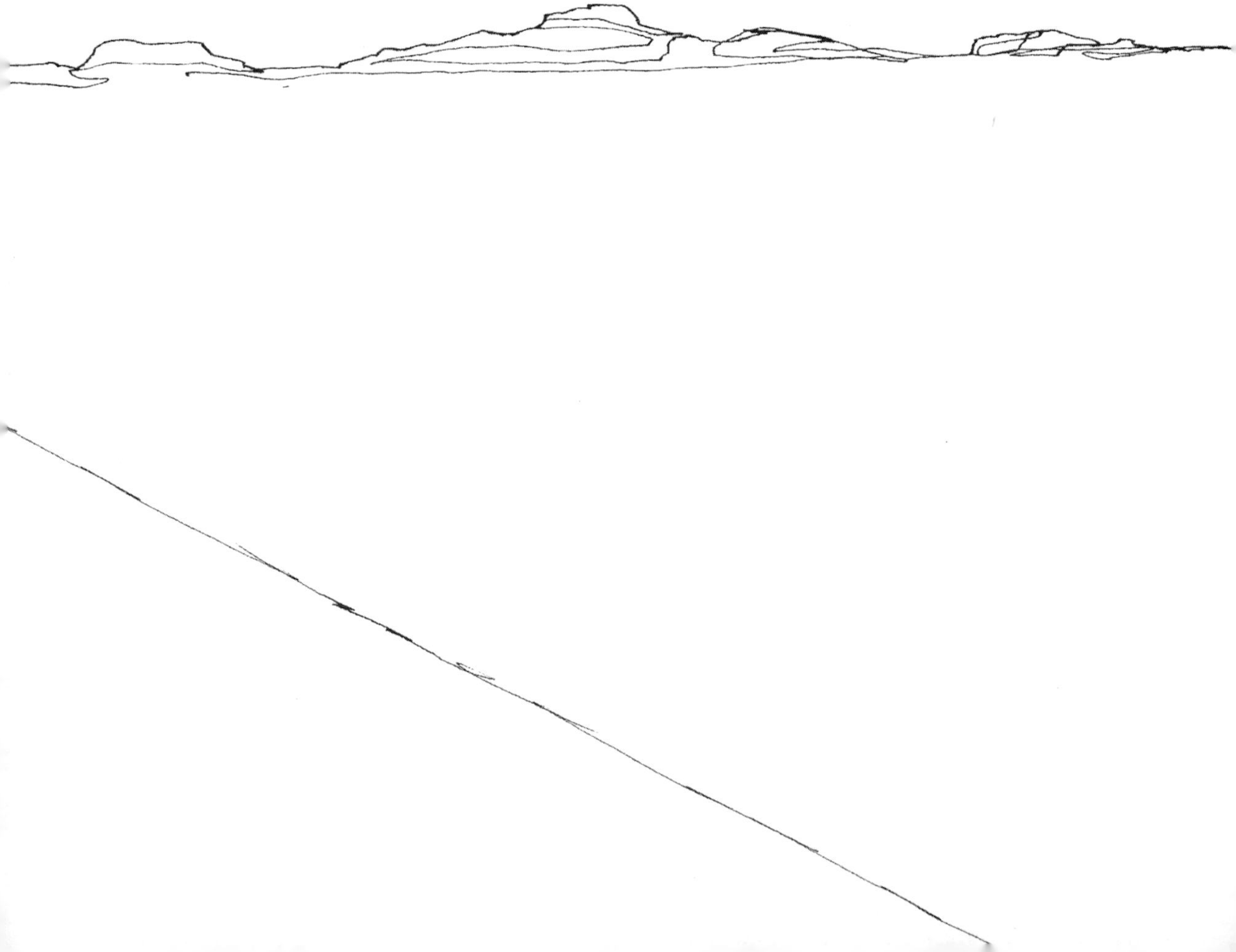

CHAPTER TWO

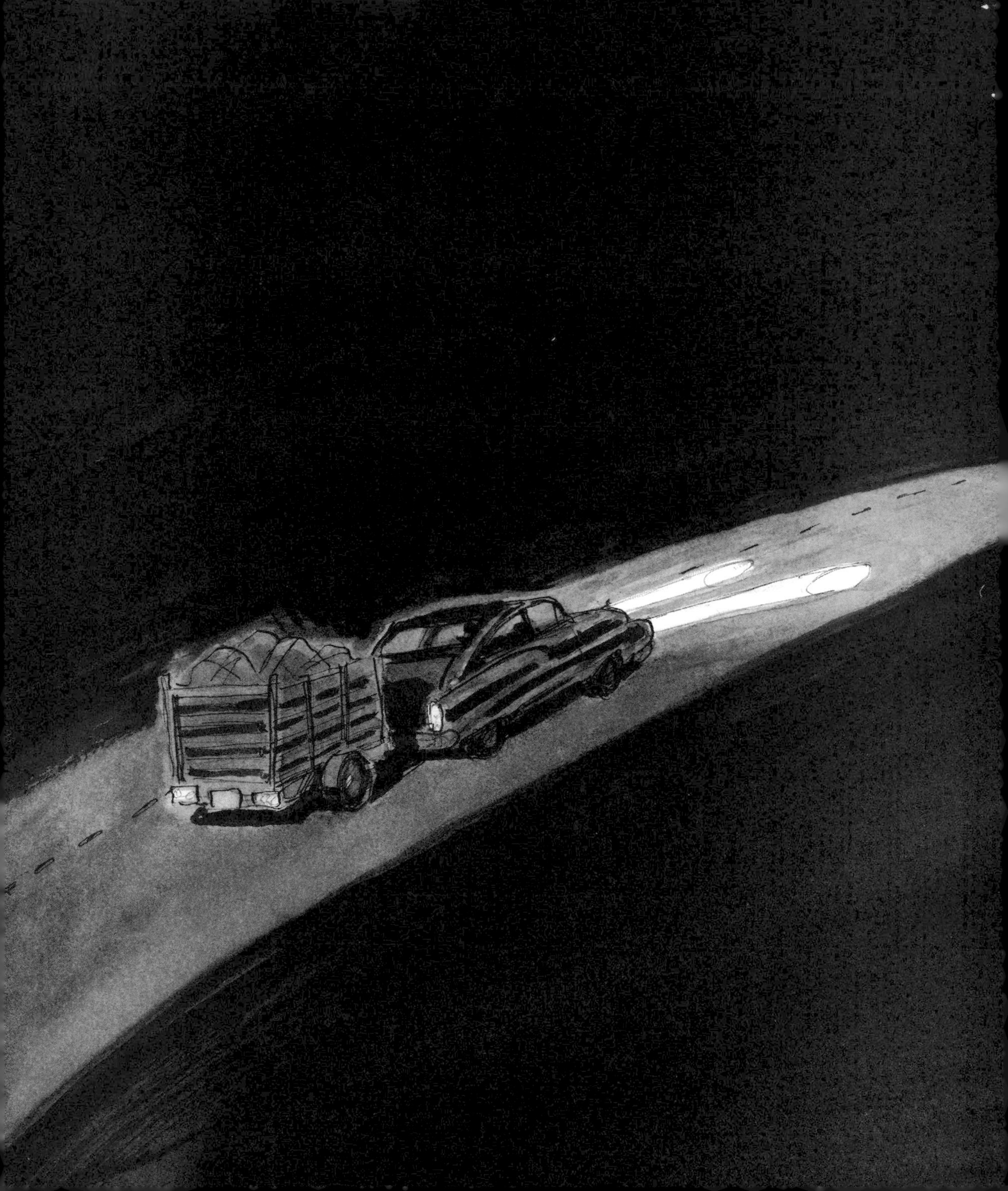

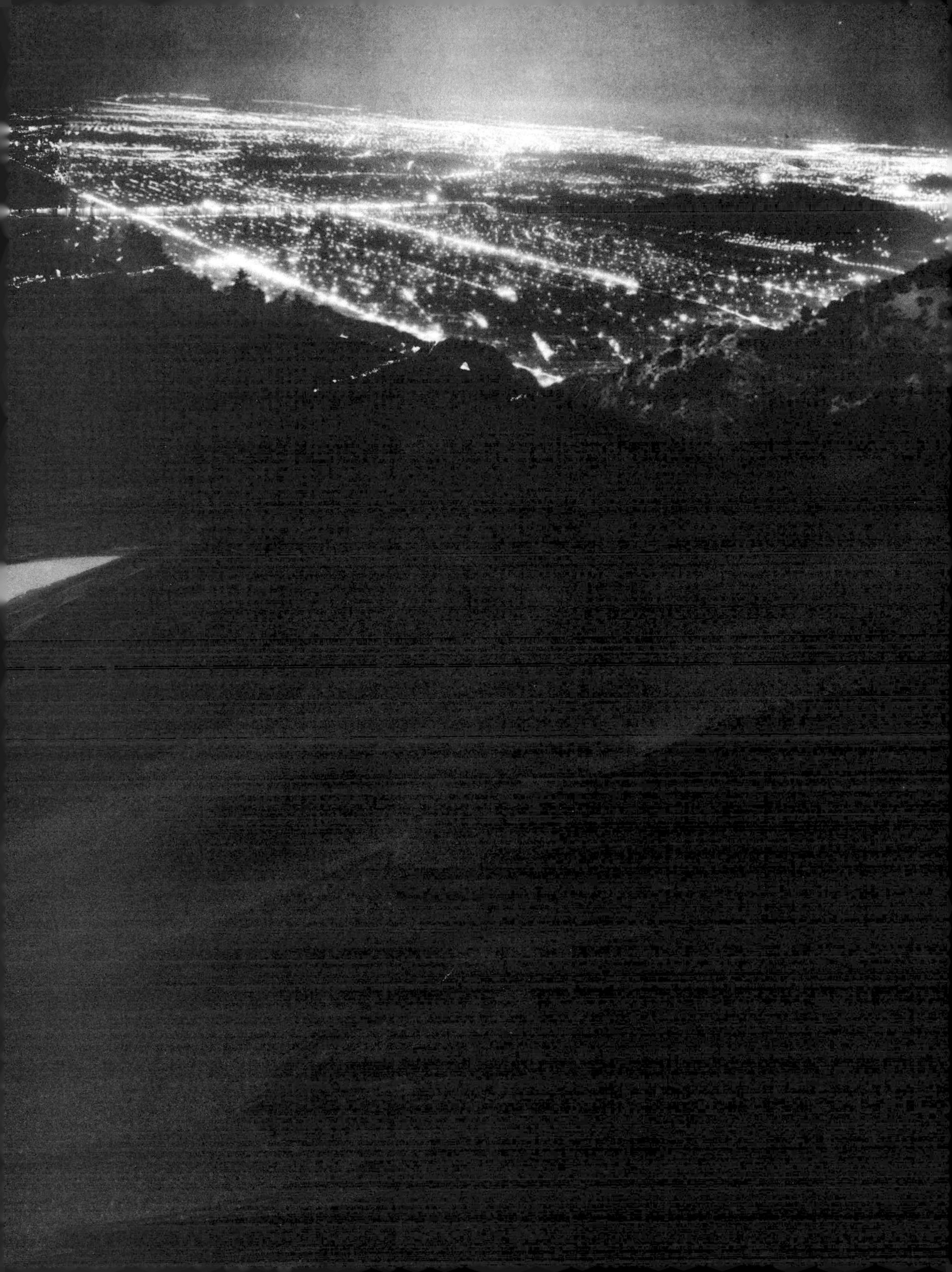

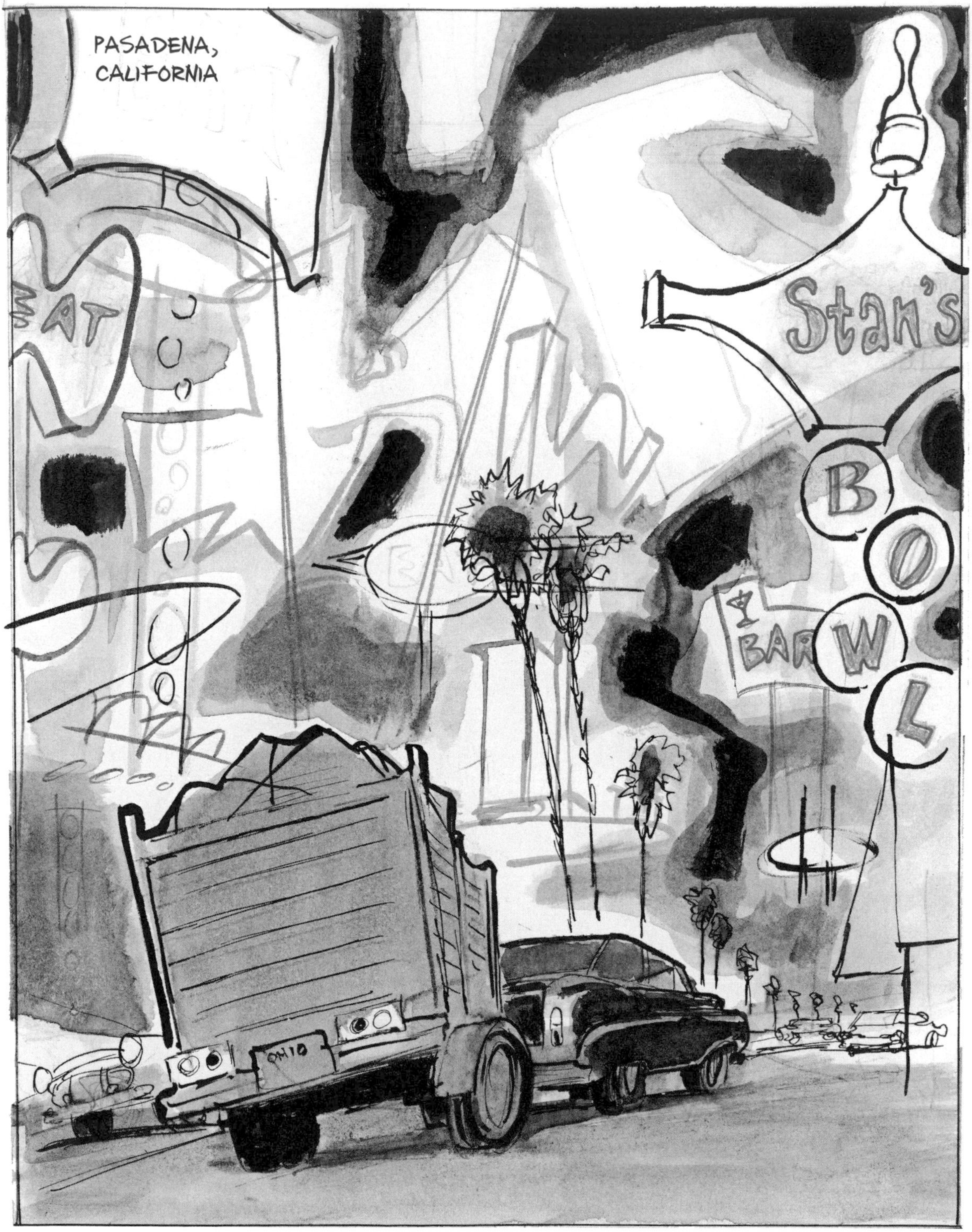
PASADENA,
CALIFORNIA
Stan's
BOWL
BAR
OHIO

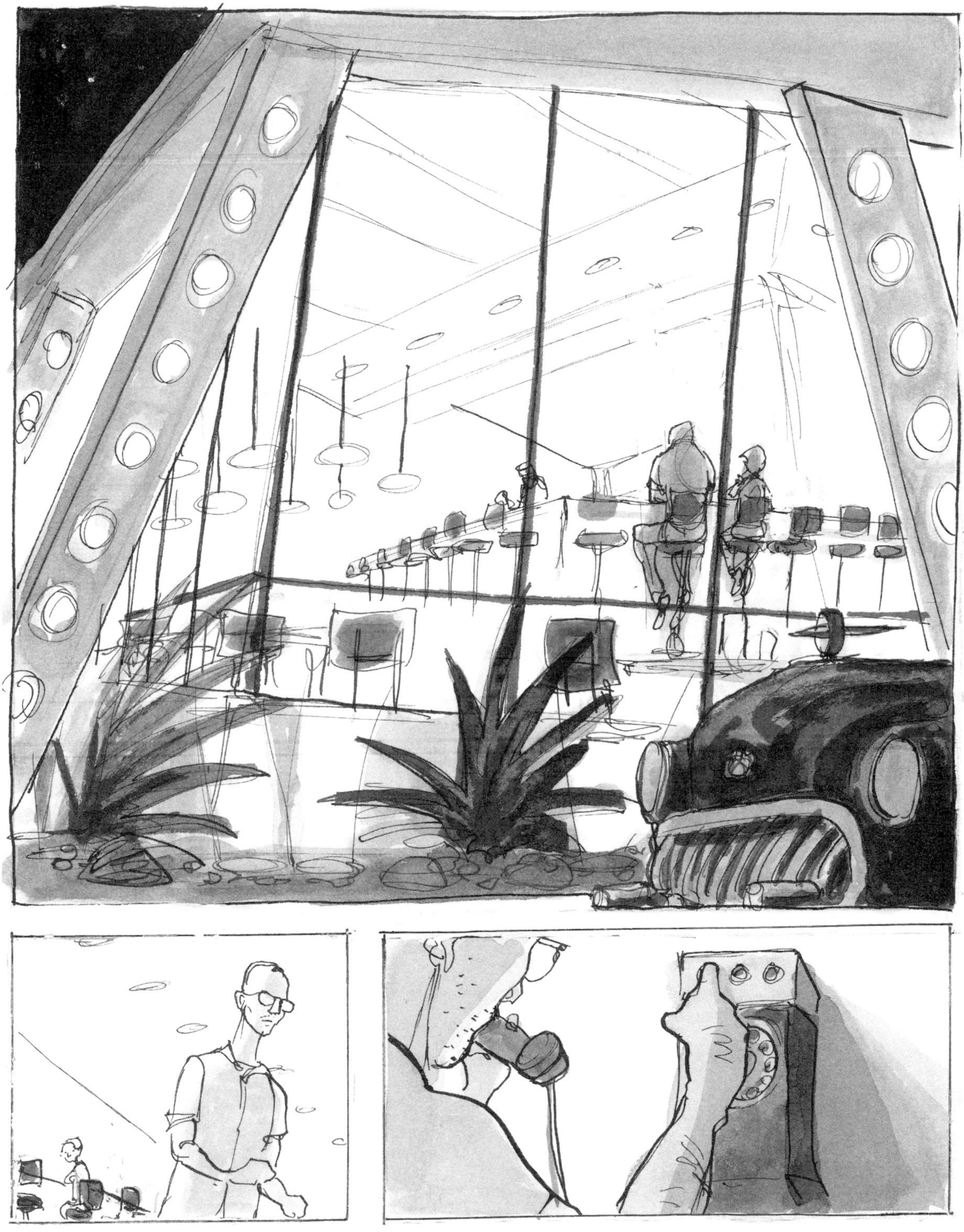

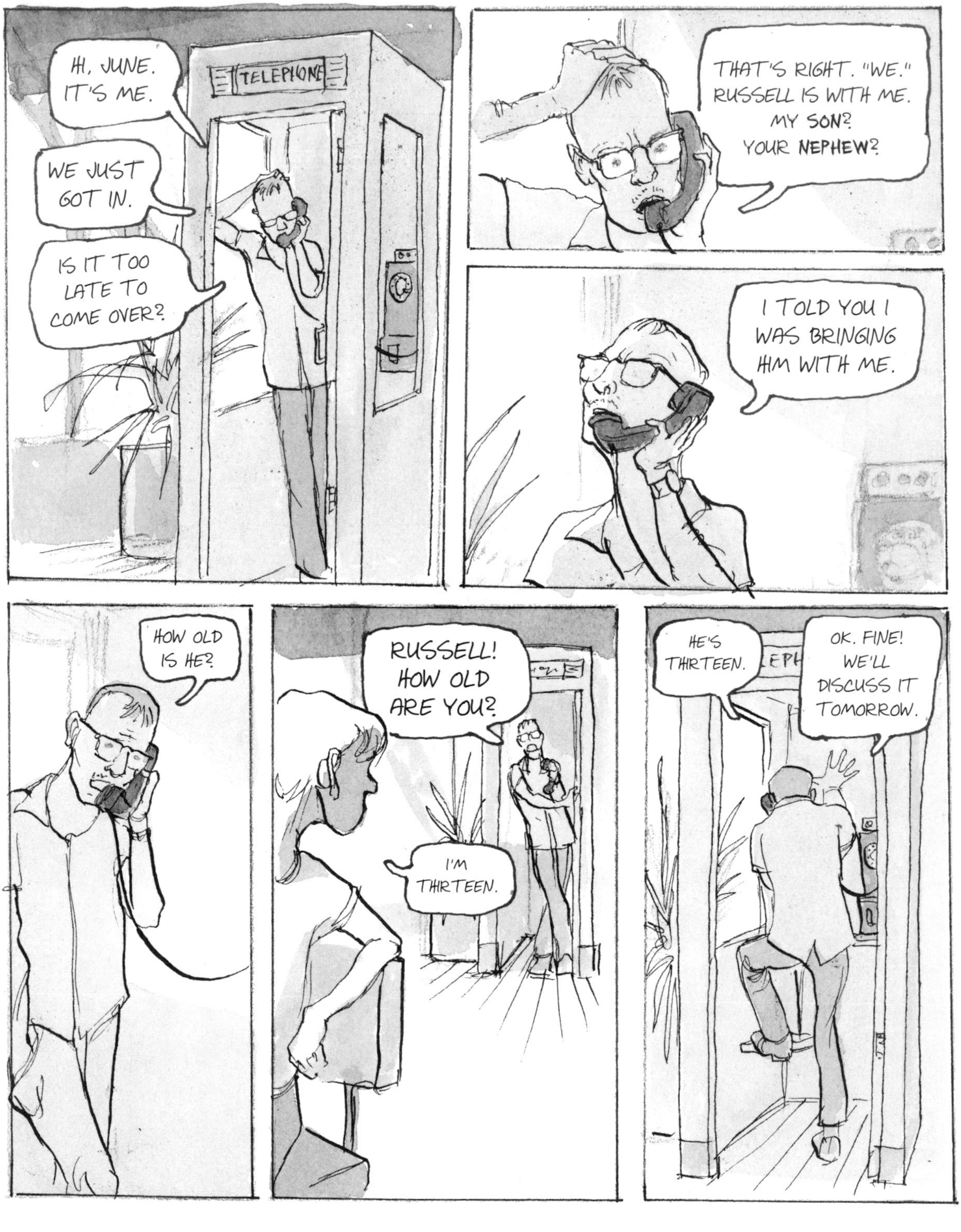
HI, JUNE. IT'S ME.
WE JUST GOT IN.
IS IT TOO LATE TO COME OVER?
TELEPHONE
THAT'S RIGHT. "WE." RUSSELL IS WITH ME. MY SON? YOUR NEPHEW?
I TOLD YOU I WAS BRINGING HIM WITH ME.
HOW OLD IS HE?
RUSSELL! HOW OLD ARE YOU?
I'M THIRTEEN.
HE'S THIRTEEN.
OK. FINE! WE'LL DISCUSS IT TOMORROW.

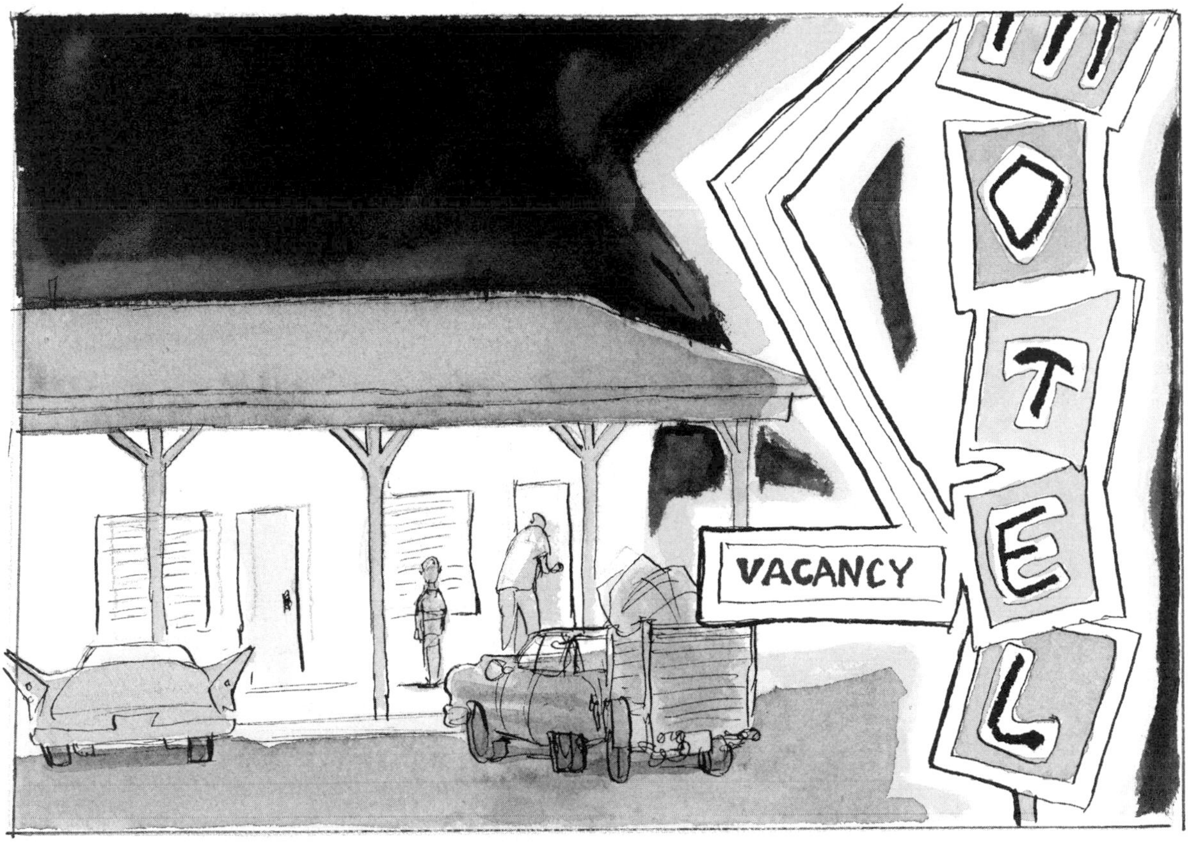
MOTEL
VACANCY

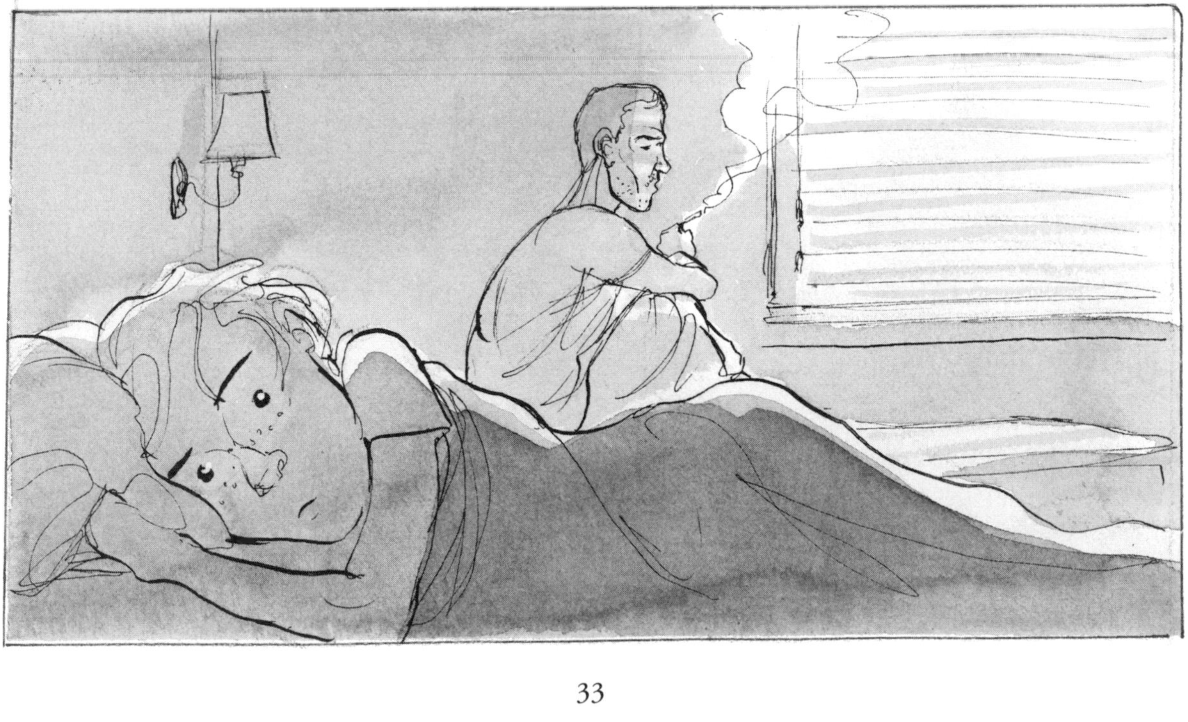

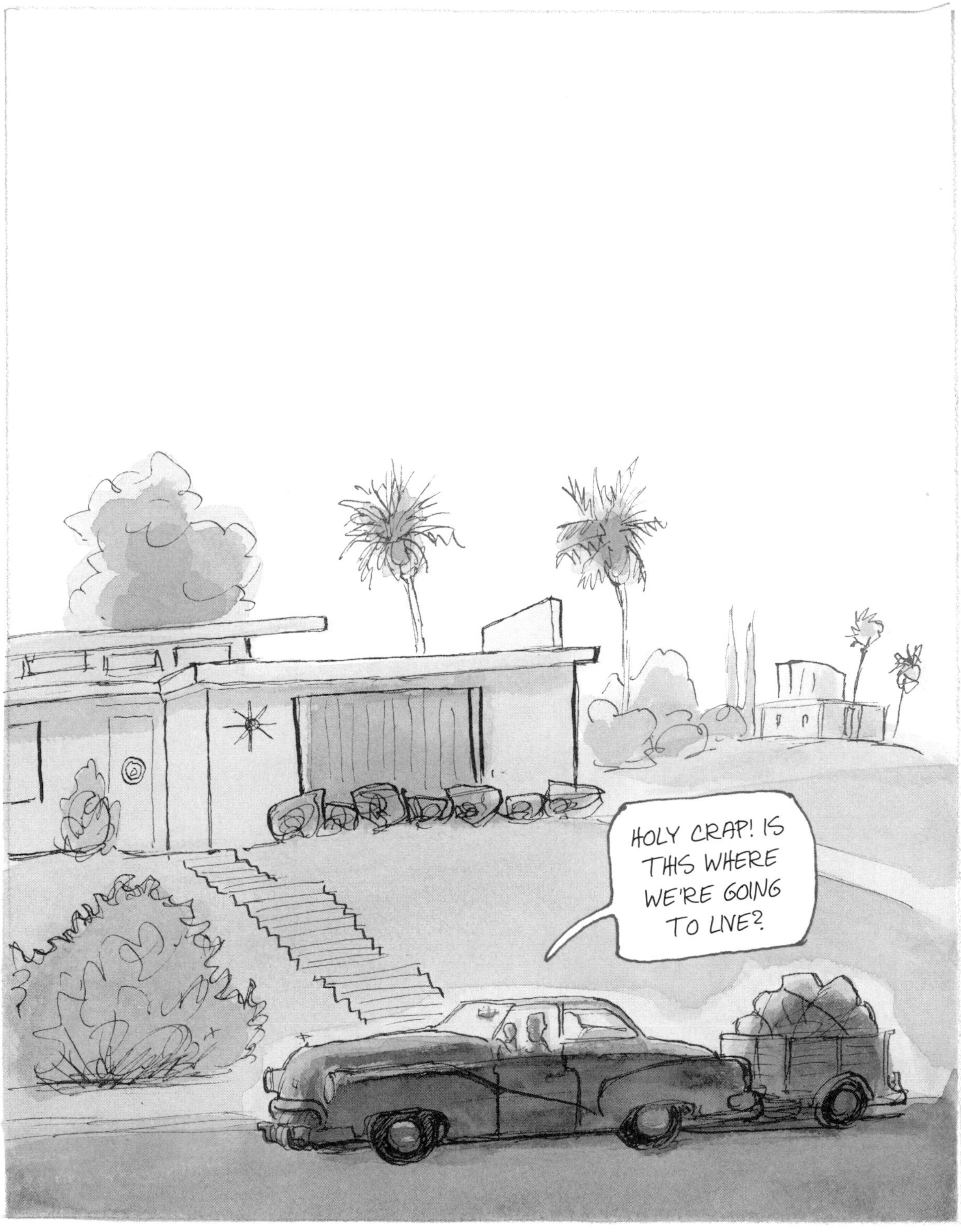
HOLY CRAP! IS THIS WHERE WE'RE GOING TO LIVE?

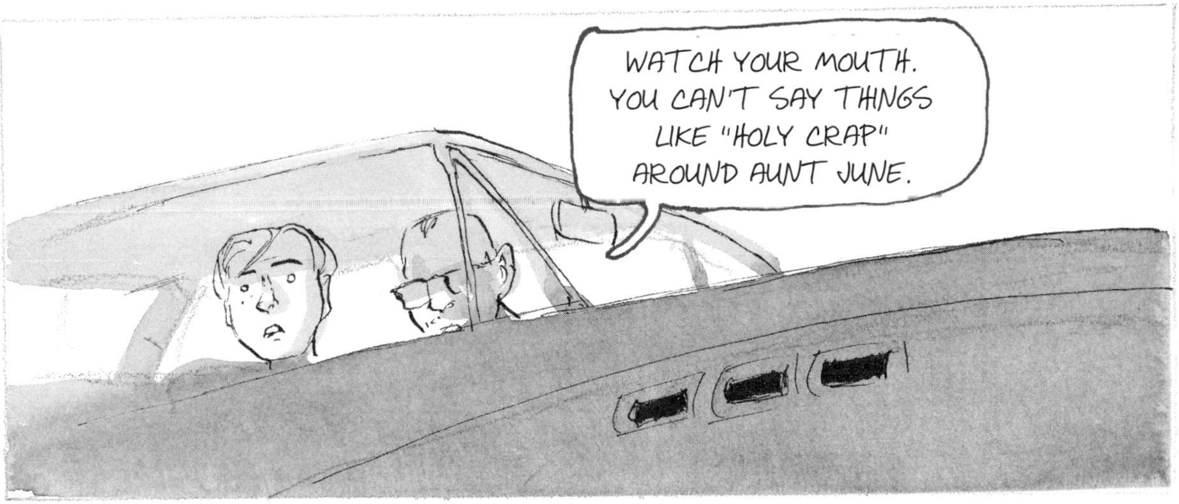
WATCH YOUR MOUTH. YOU CAN'T SAY THINGS LIKE "HOLY CRAP" AROUND AUNT JUNE.

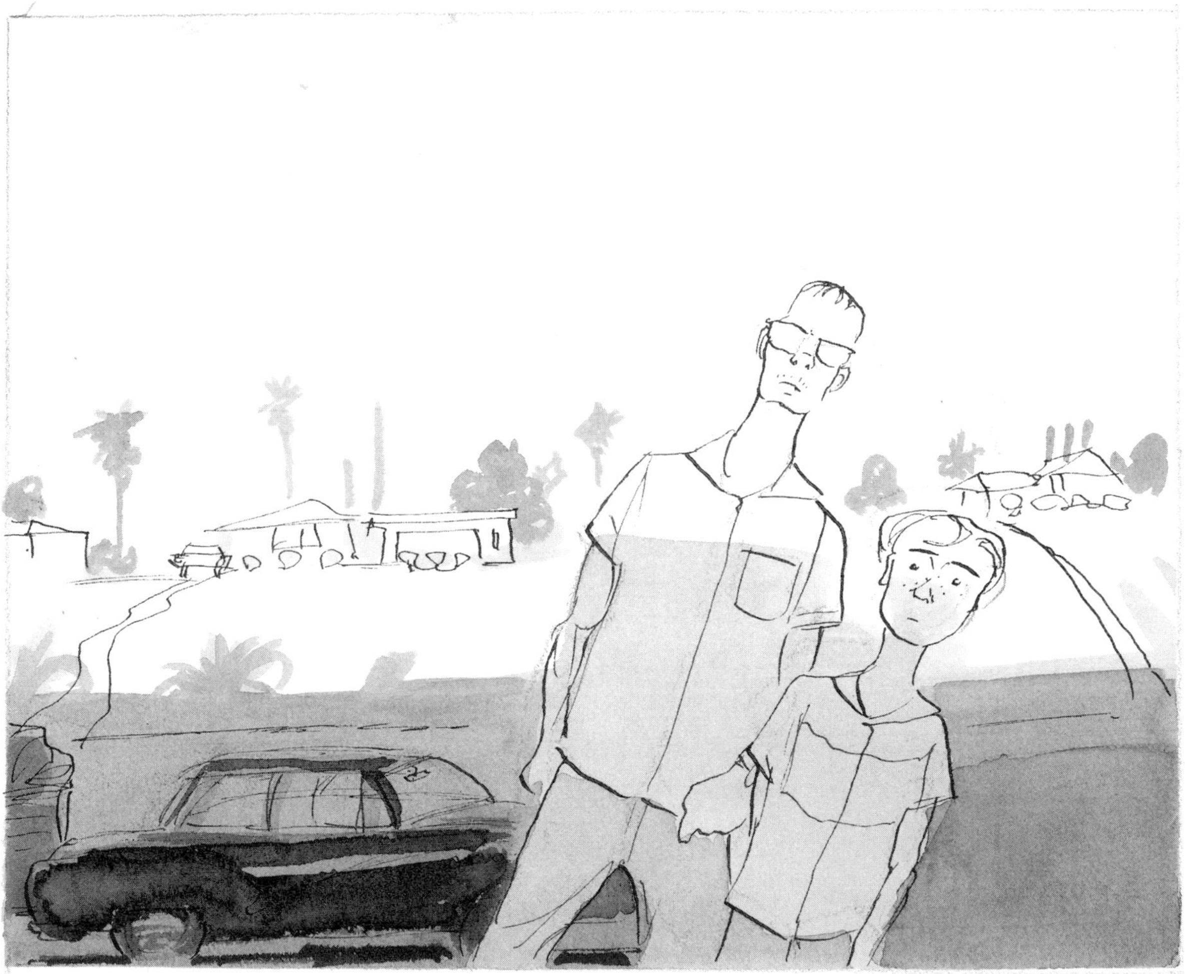

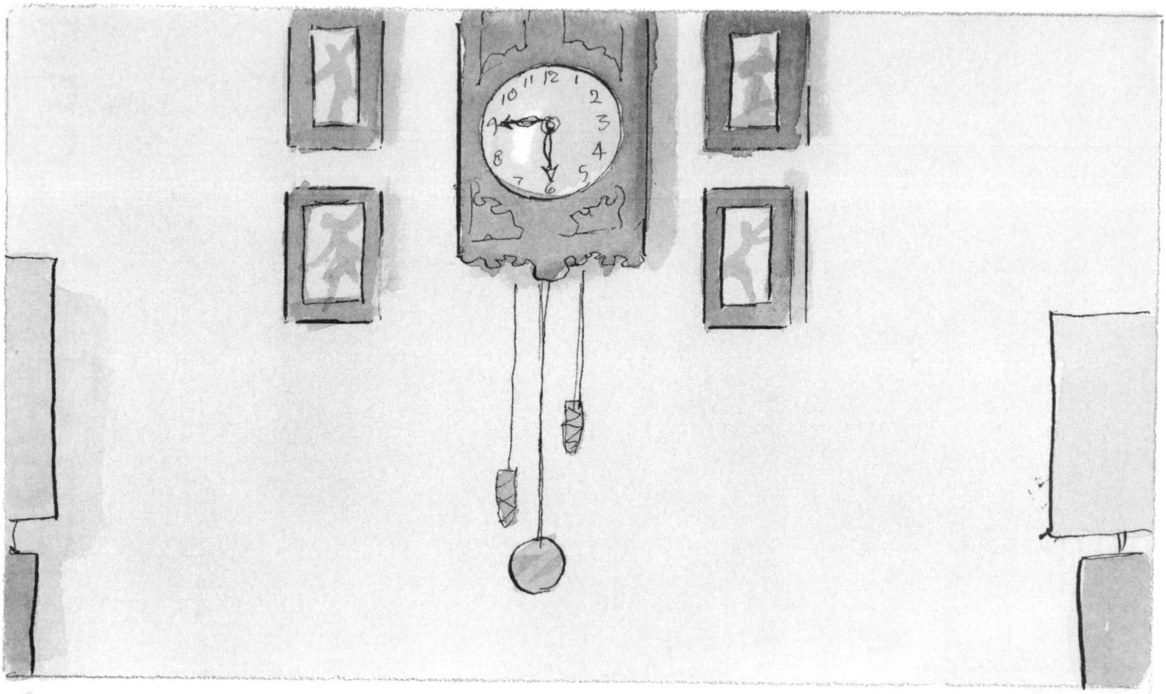

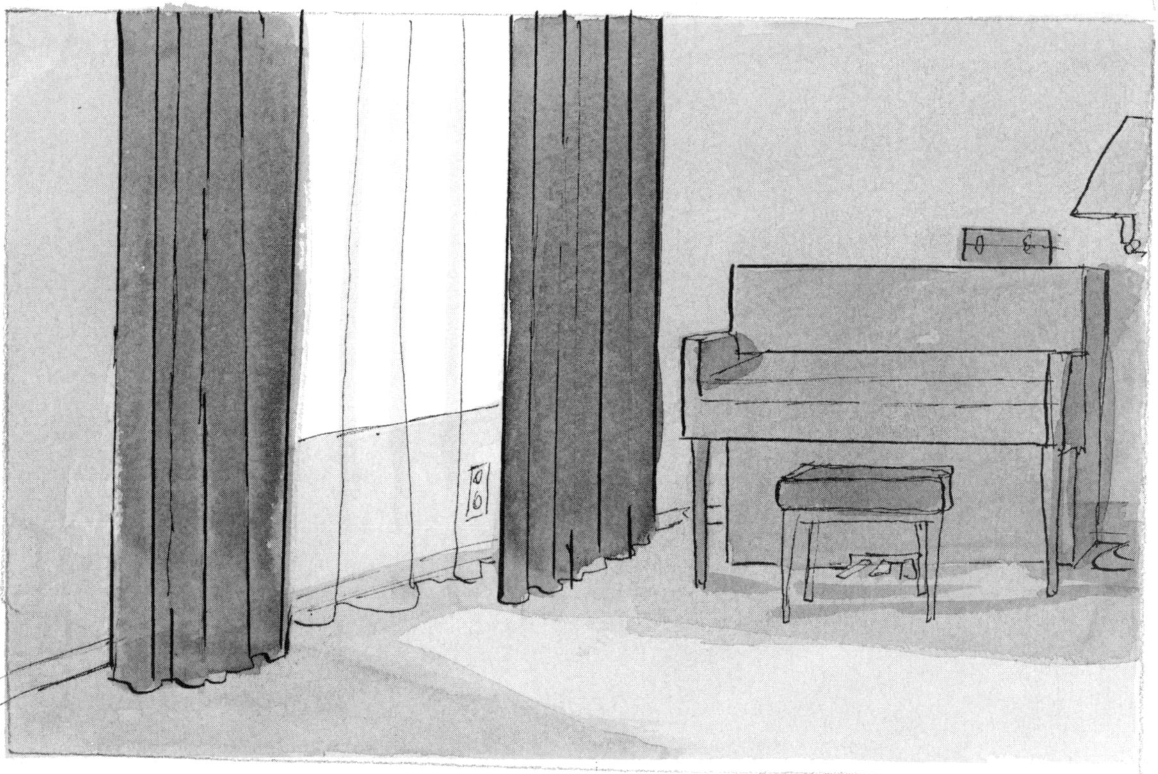

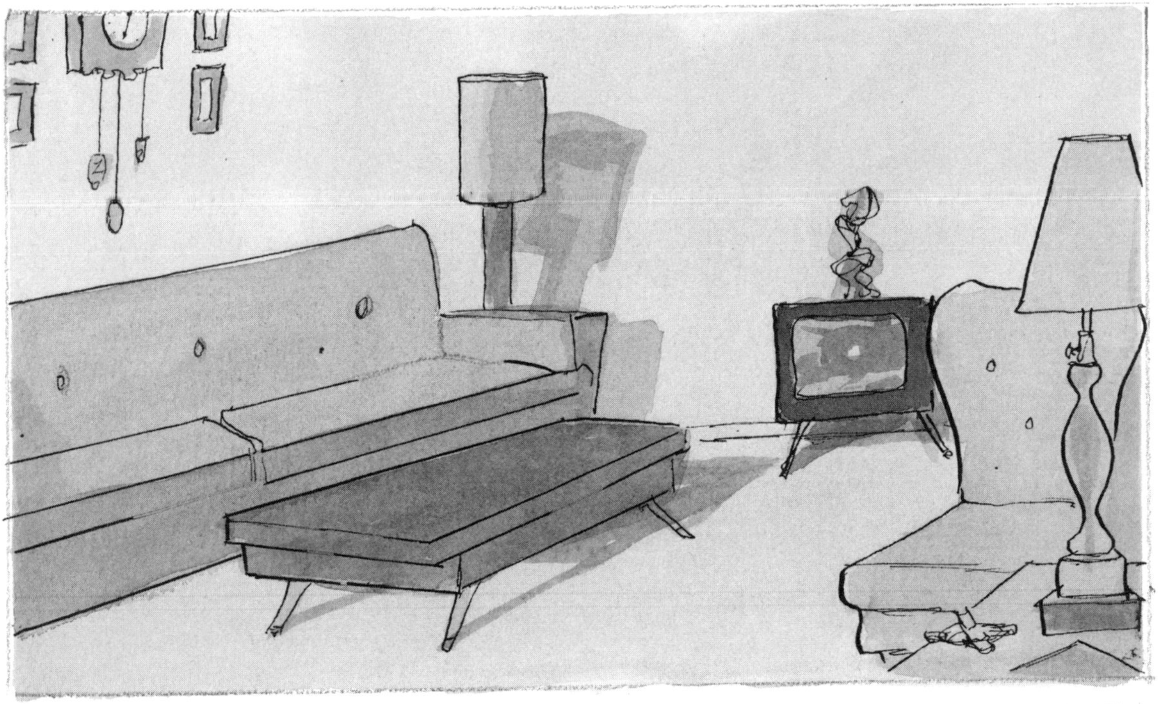

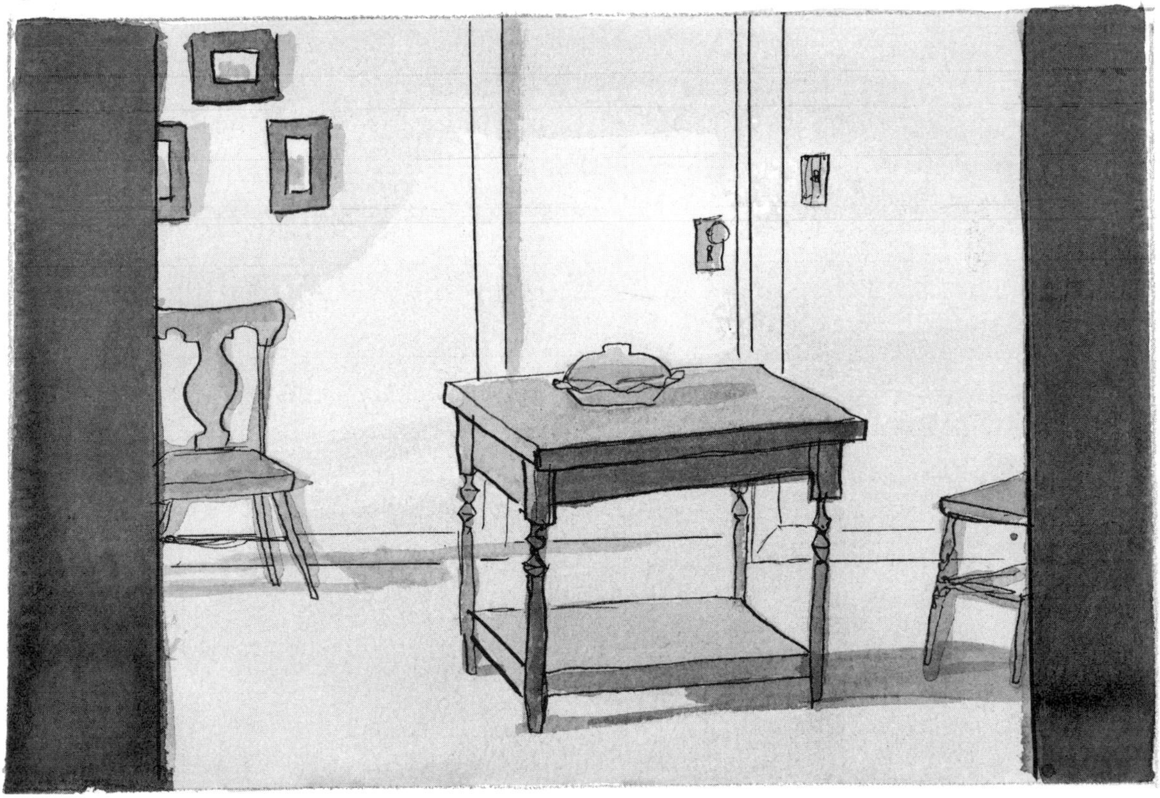

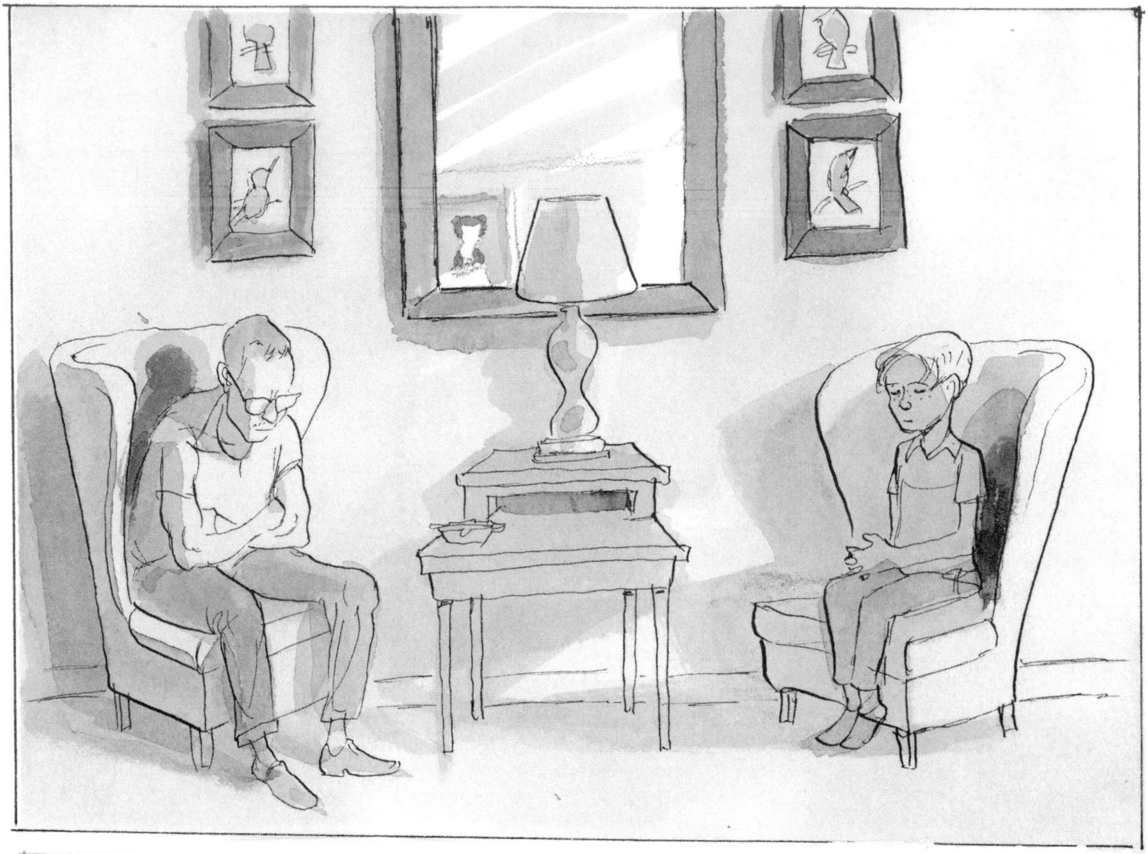

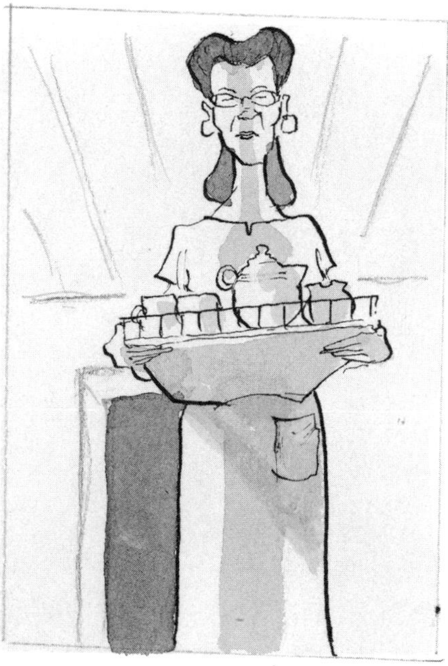

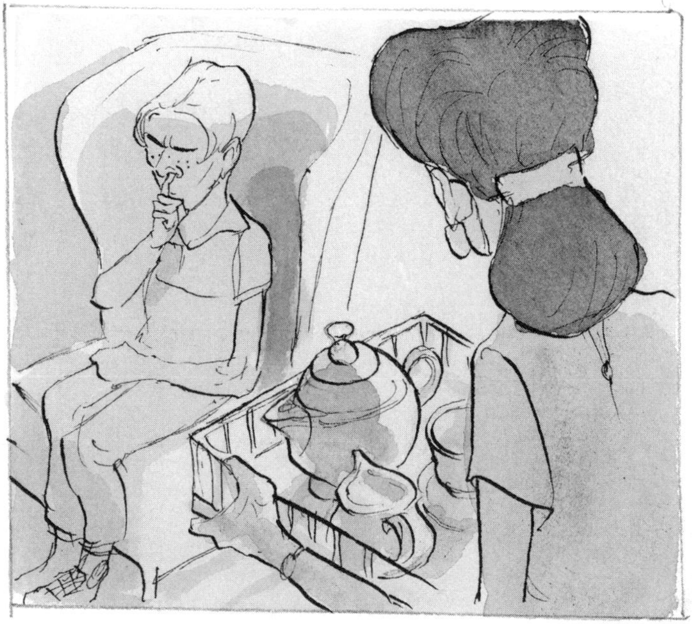

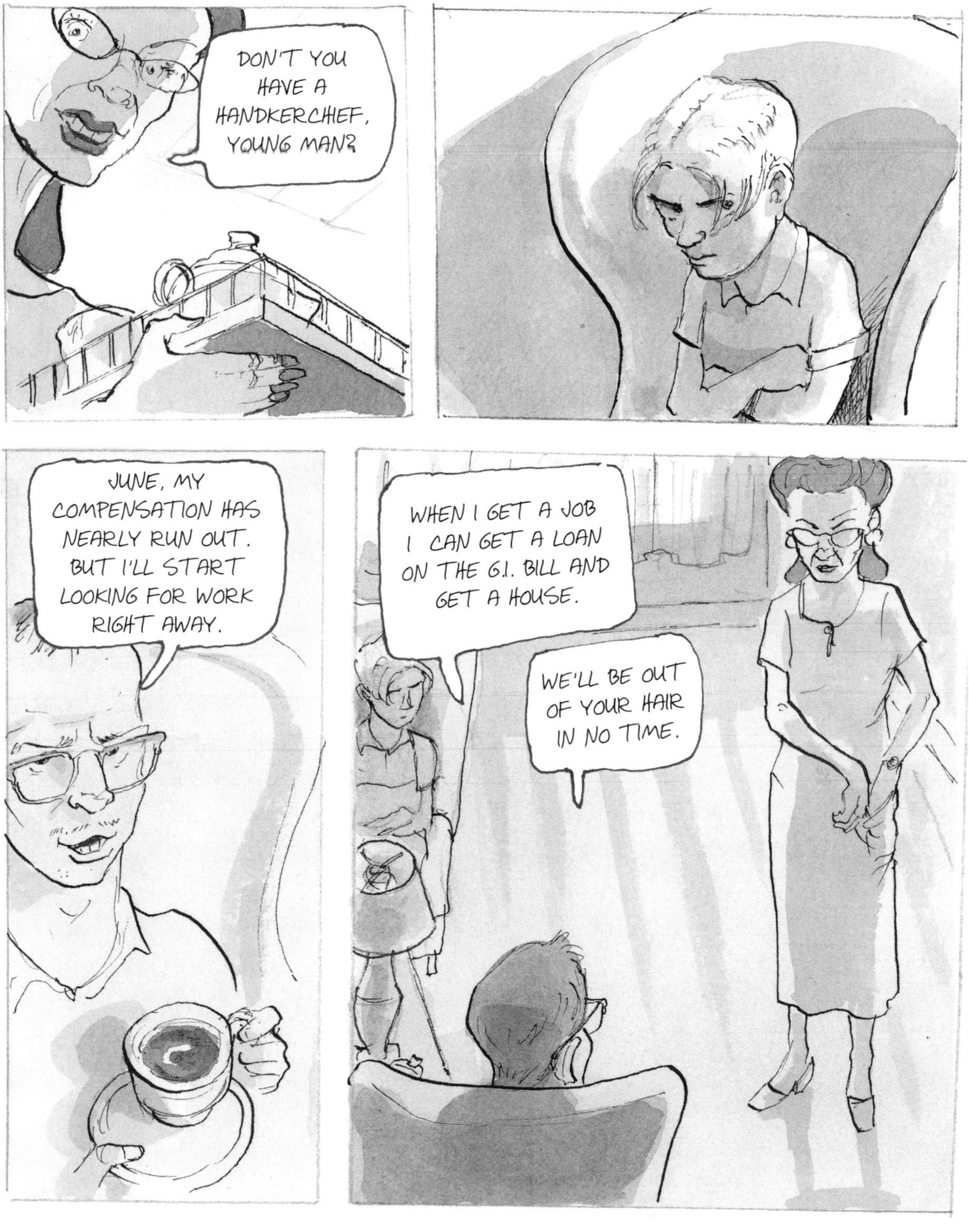
DON'T YOU HAVE A HANDKERCHIEF, YOUNG MAN?
JUNE, MY COMPENSATION HAS NEARLY RUN OUT. BUT I'LL START LOOKING FOR WORK RIGHT AWAY.
WHEN I GET A JOB I CAN GET A LOAN ON THE G.I. BILL AND GET A HOUSE.
WE'LL BE OUT OF YOUR HAIR IN NO TIME.

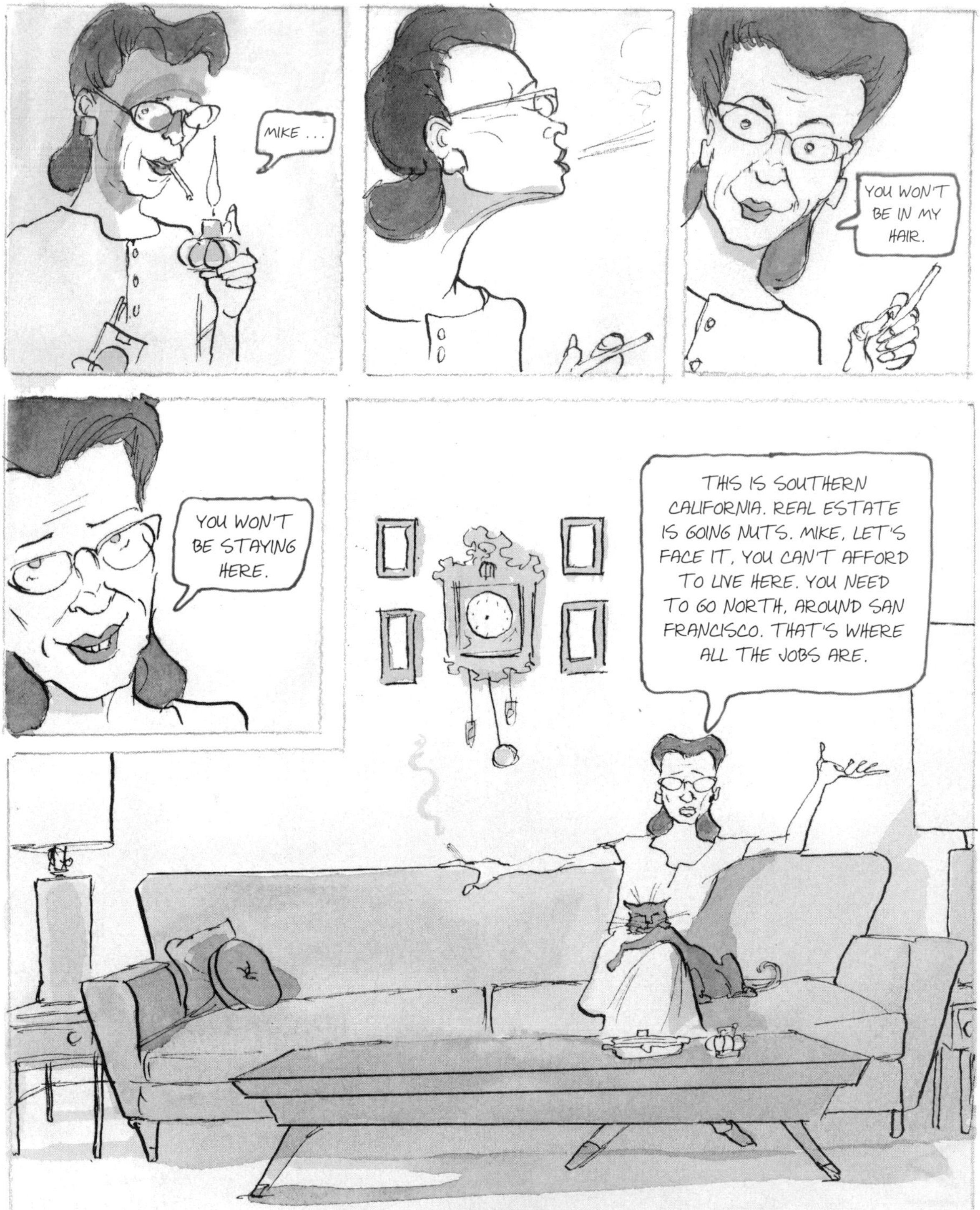
MIKE . . .
YOU WON'T BE IN MY HAIR.
YOU WON'T BE STAYING HERE.
THIS IS SOUTHERN CALIFORNIA. REAL ESTATE IS GOING NUTS. MIKE, LET'S FACE IT, YOU CAN'T AFFORD TO LIVE HERE. YOU NEED TO GO NORTH, AROUND SAN FRANCISCO. THAT'S WHERE ALL THE JOBS ARE.

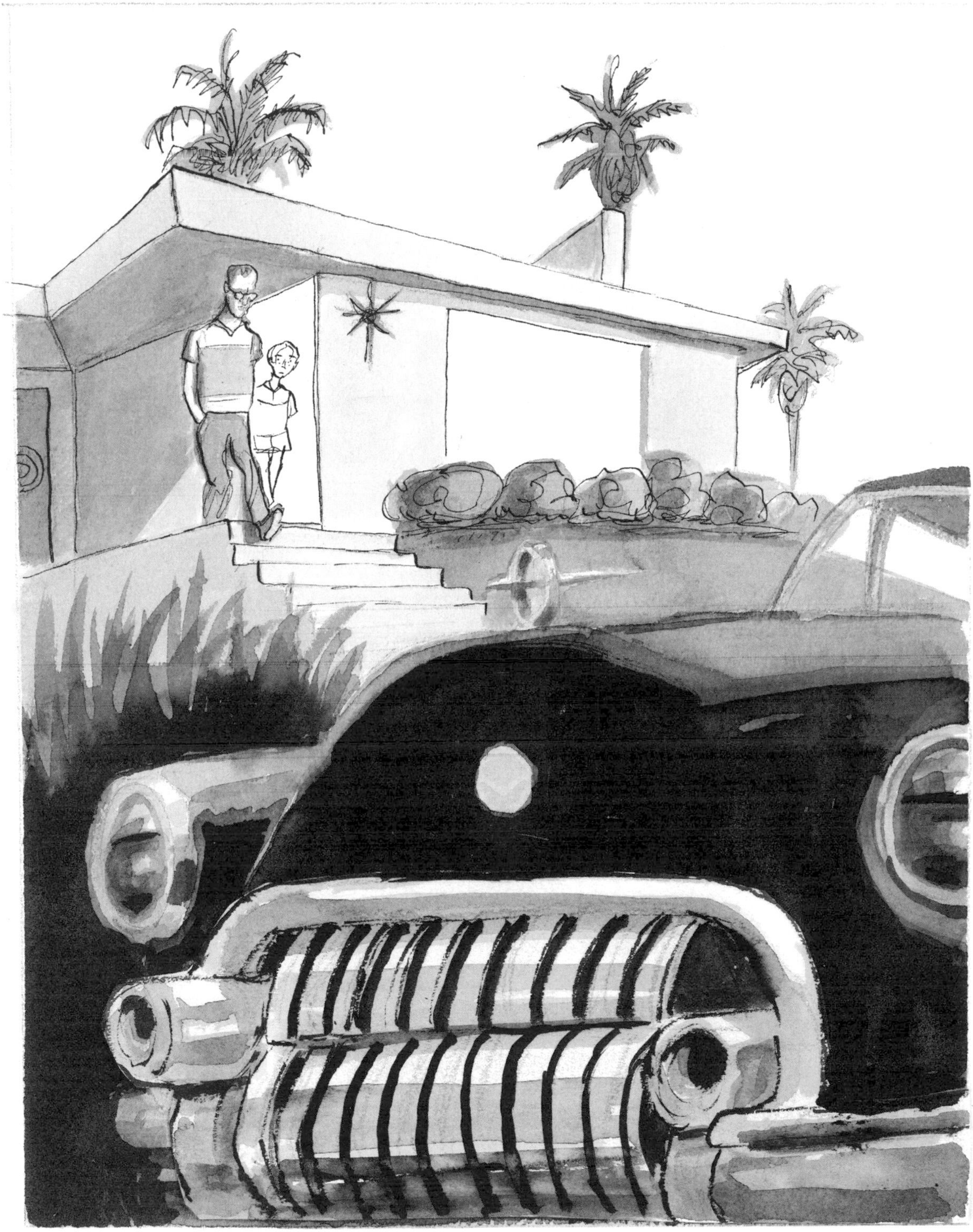

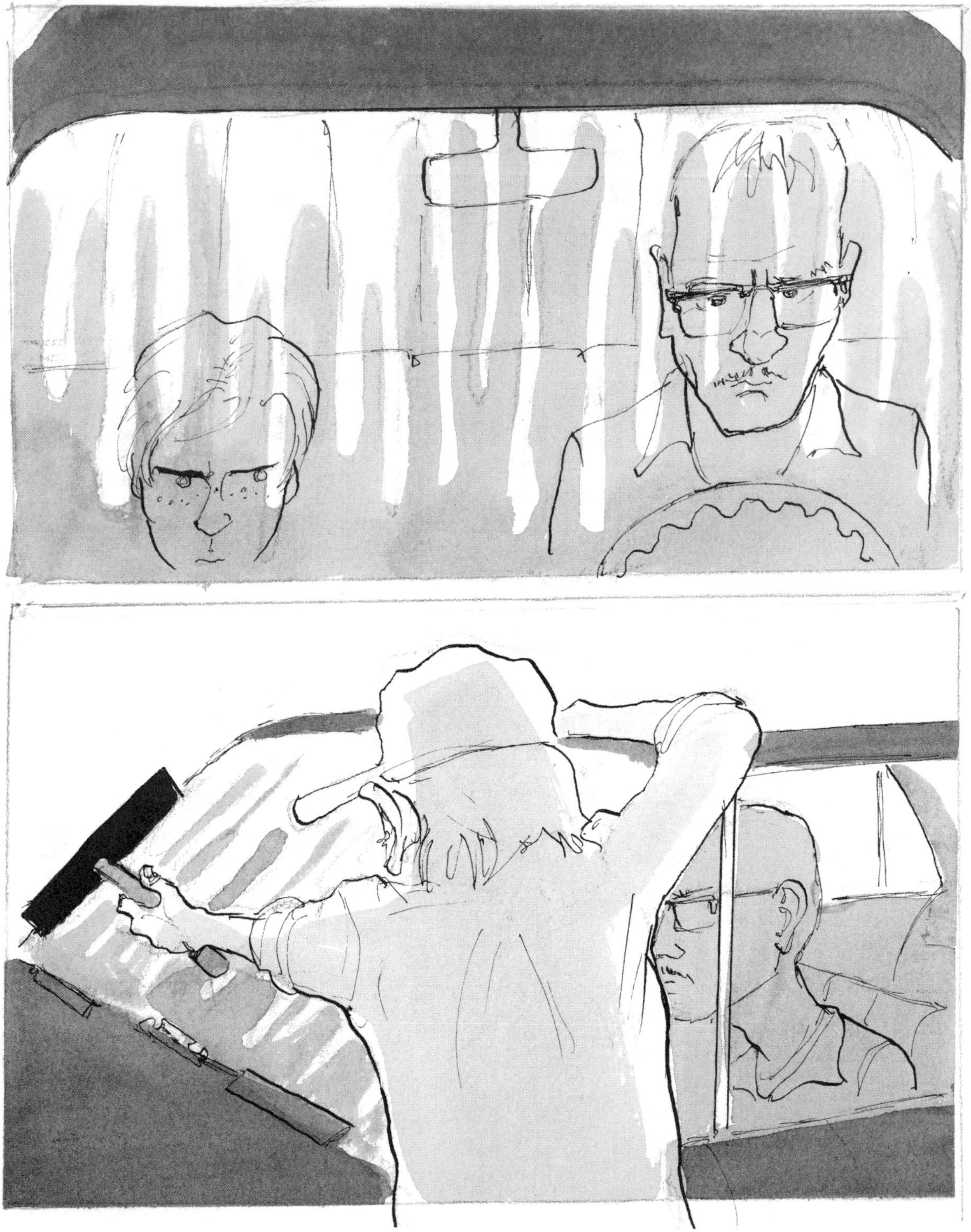

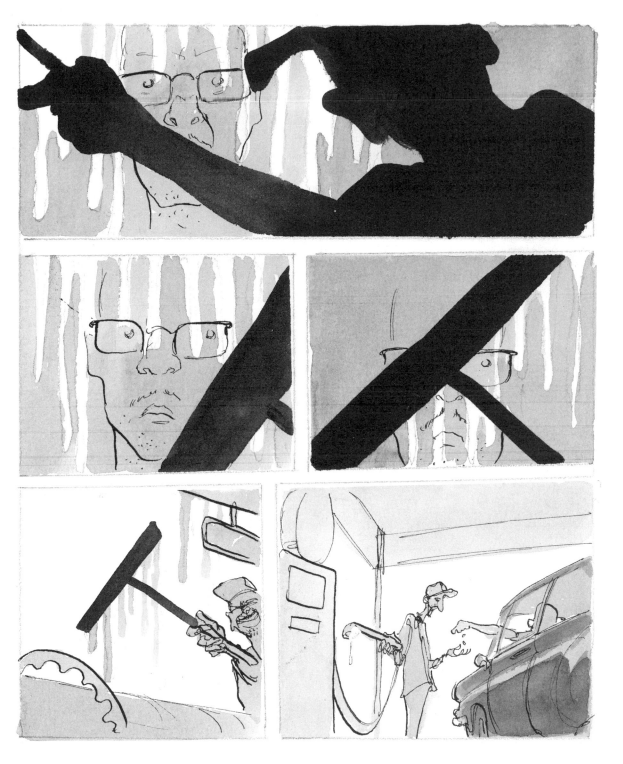

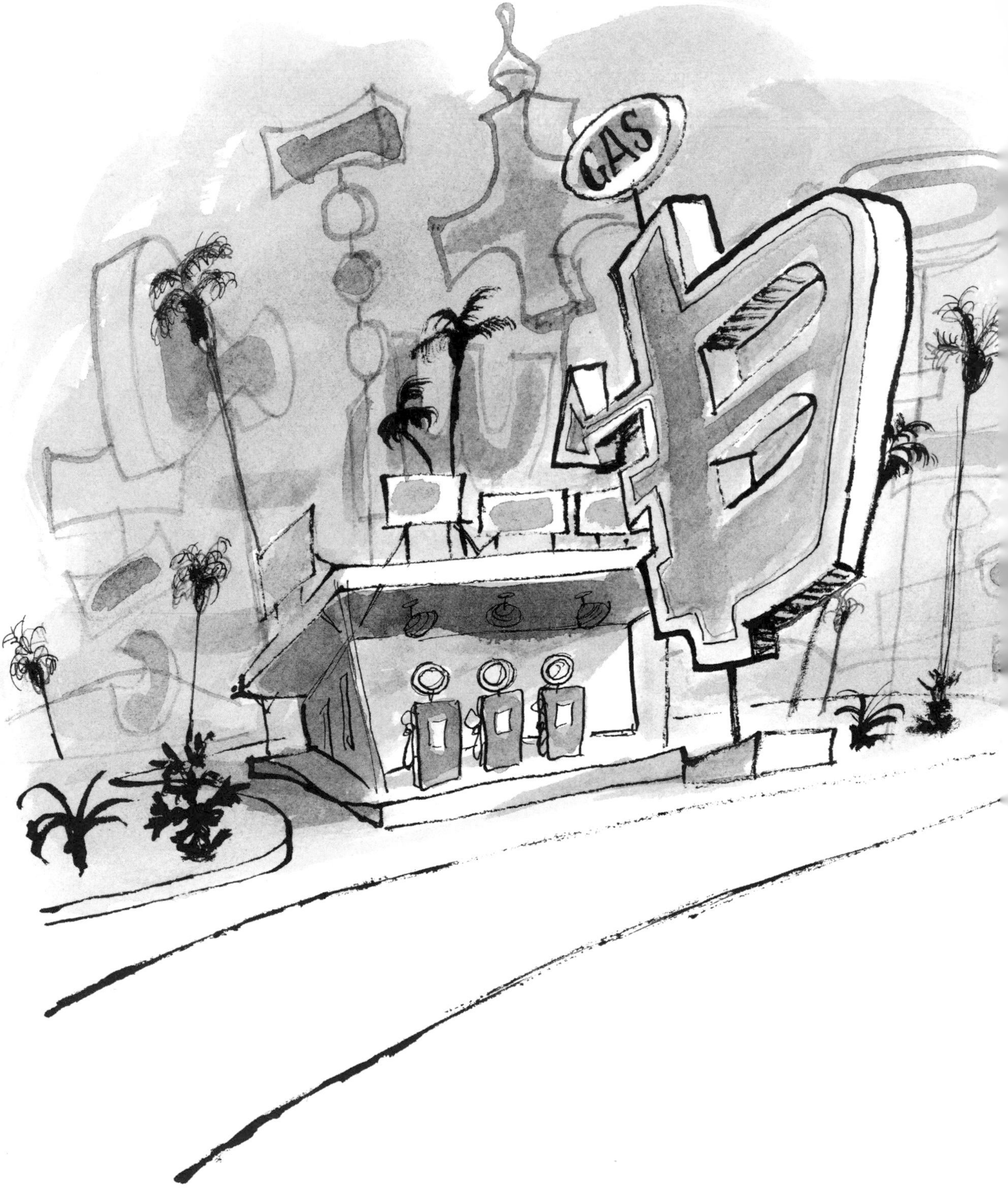
GAS

CHAPTER THREE

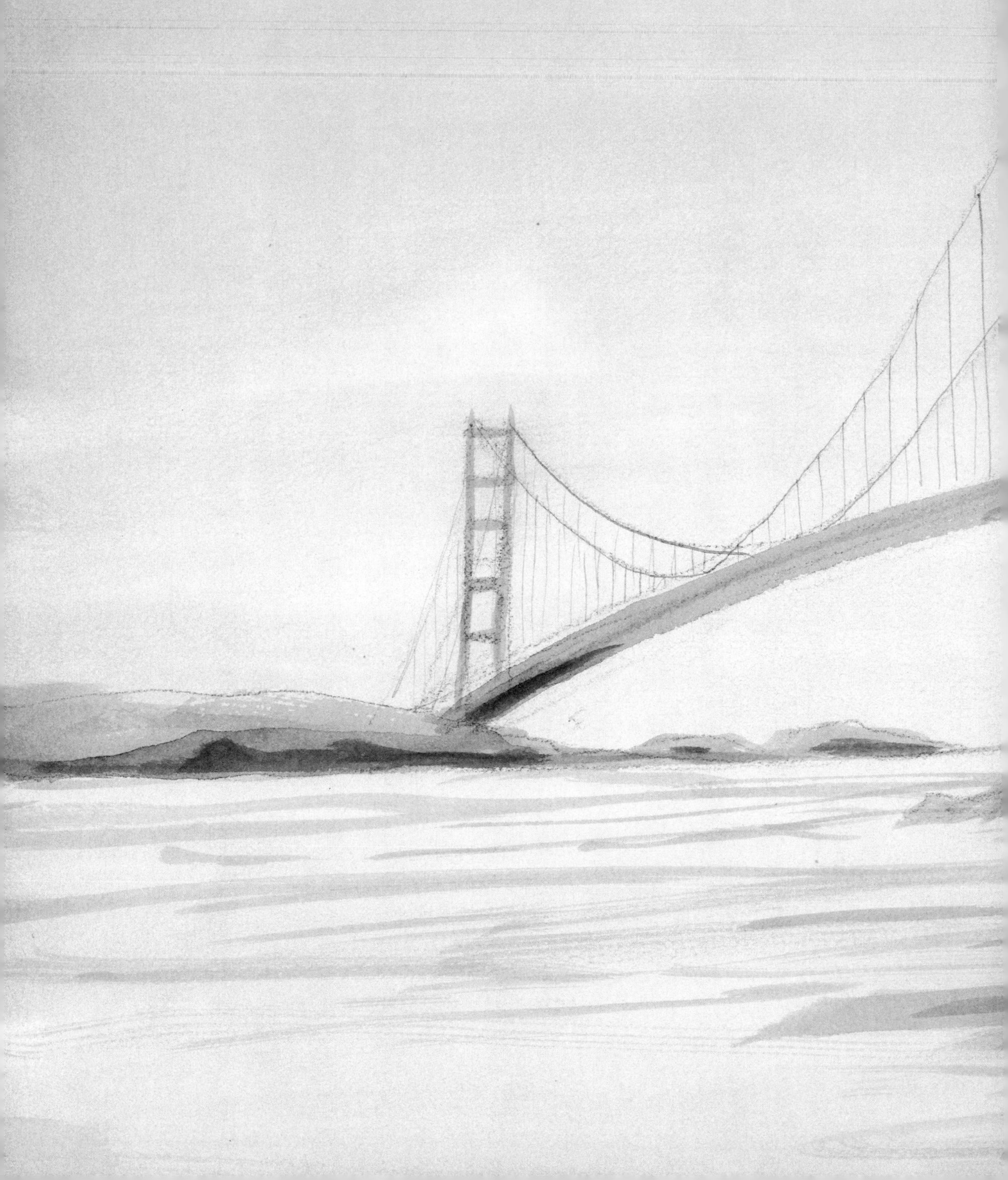

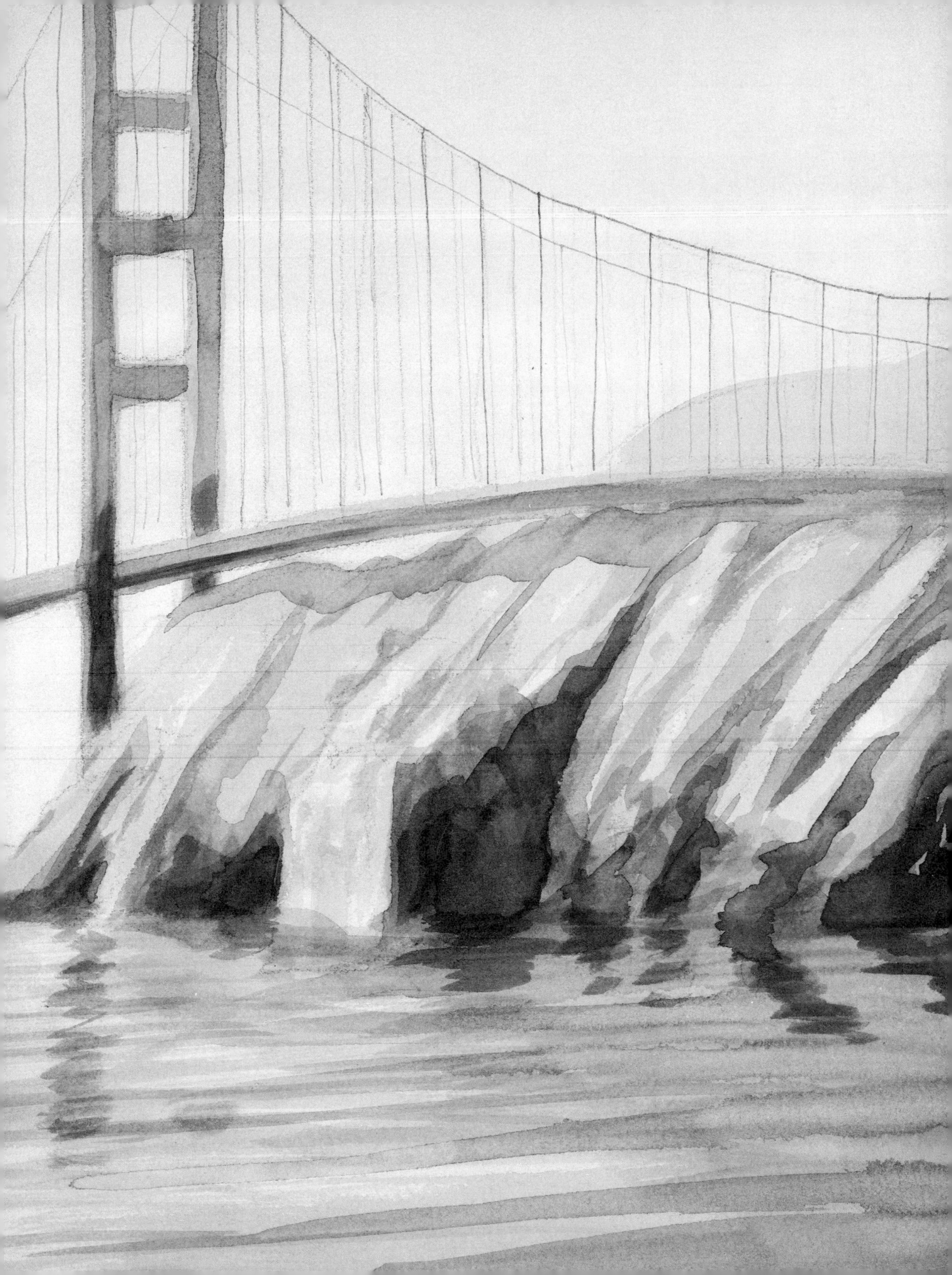

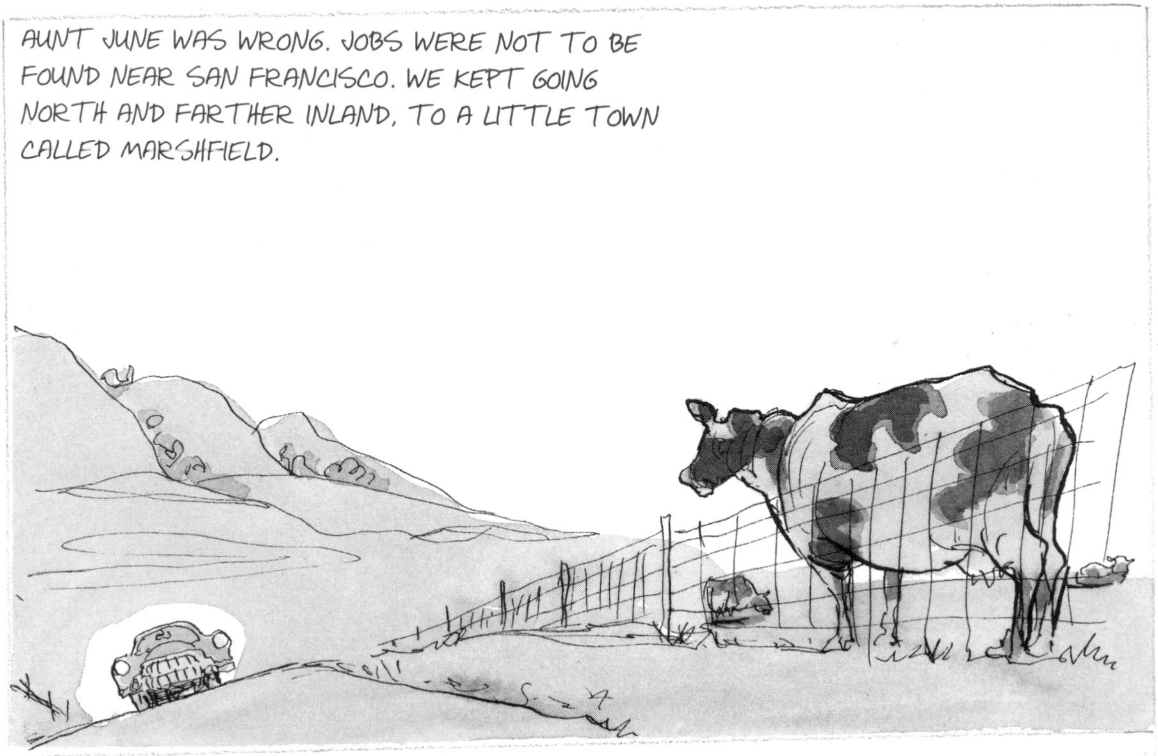
AUNT JUNE WAS WRONG. JOBS WERE NOT TO BE FOUND NEAR SAN FRANCISCO. WE KEPT GOING NORTH AND FARTHER INLAND, TO A LITTLE TOWN CALLED MARSHFIELD.

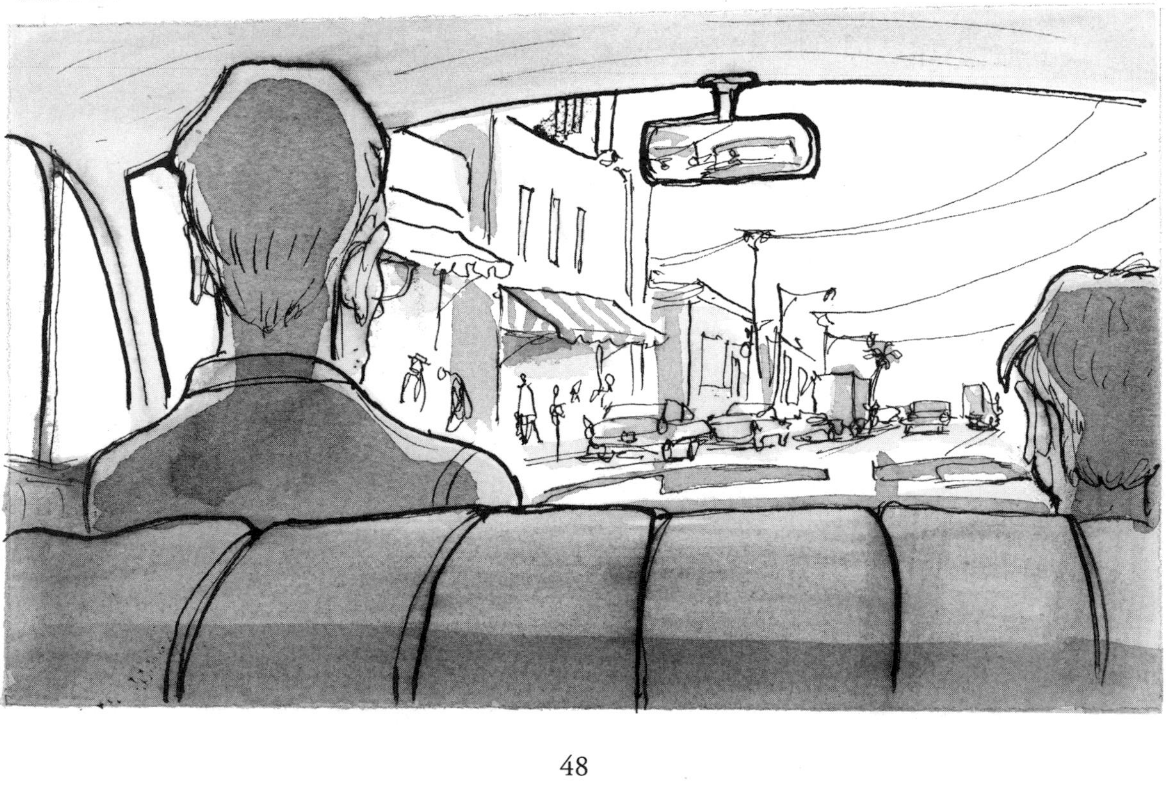

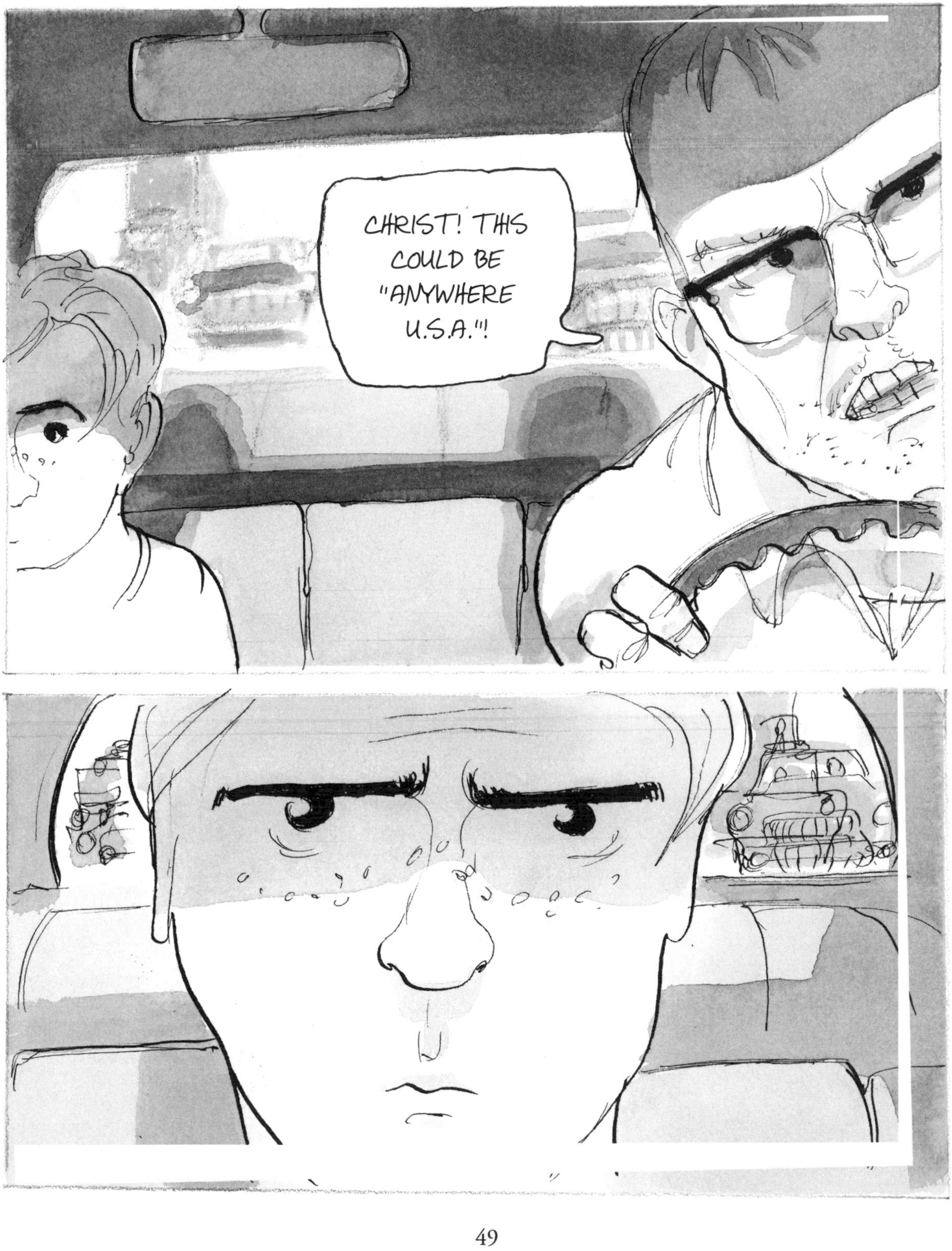
CHRIST! THIS COULD BE "ANYWHERE U.S.A."!

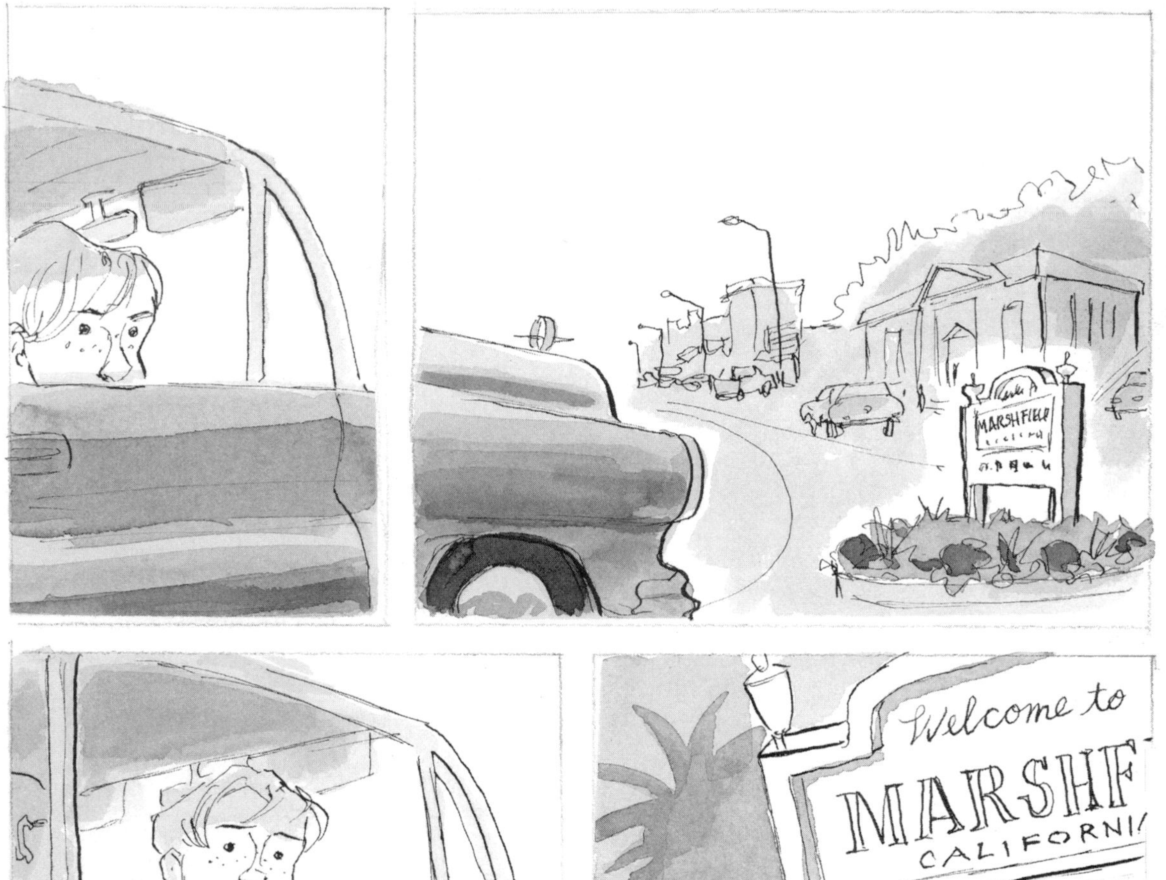
Welcome to
MARSHF
CALIFORNI
LIONS
L
INTERNATIONAL
G

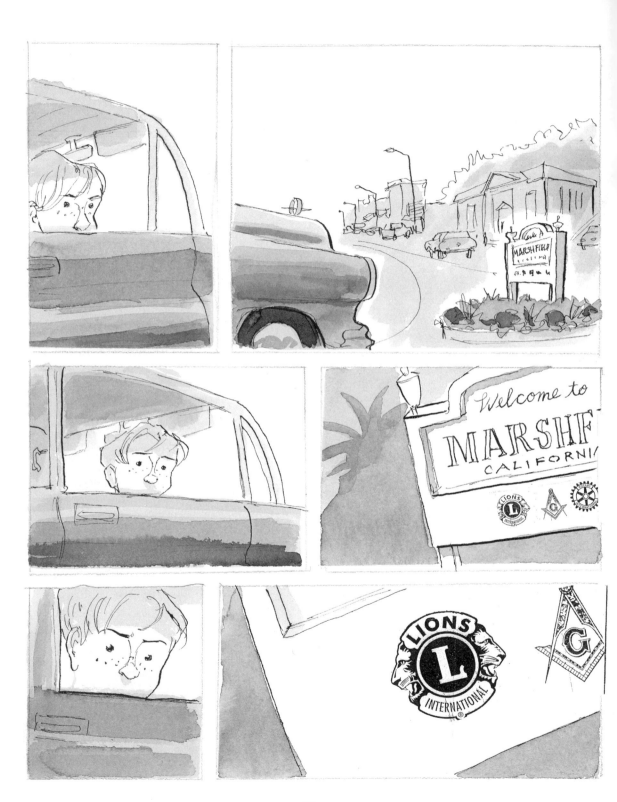

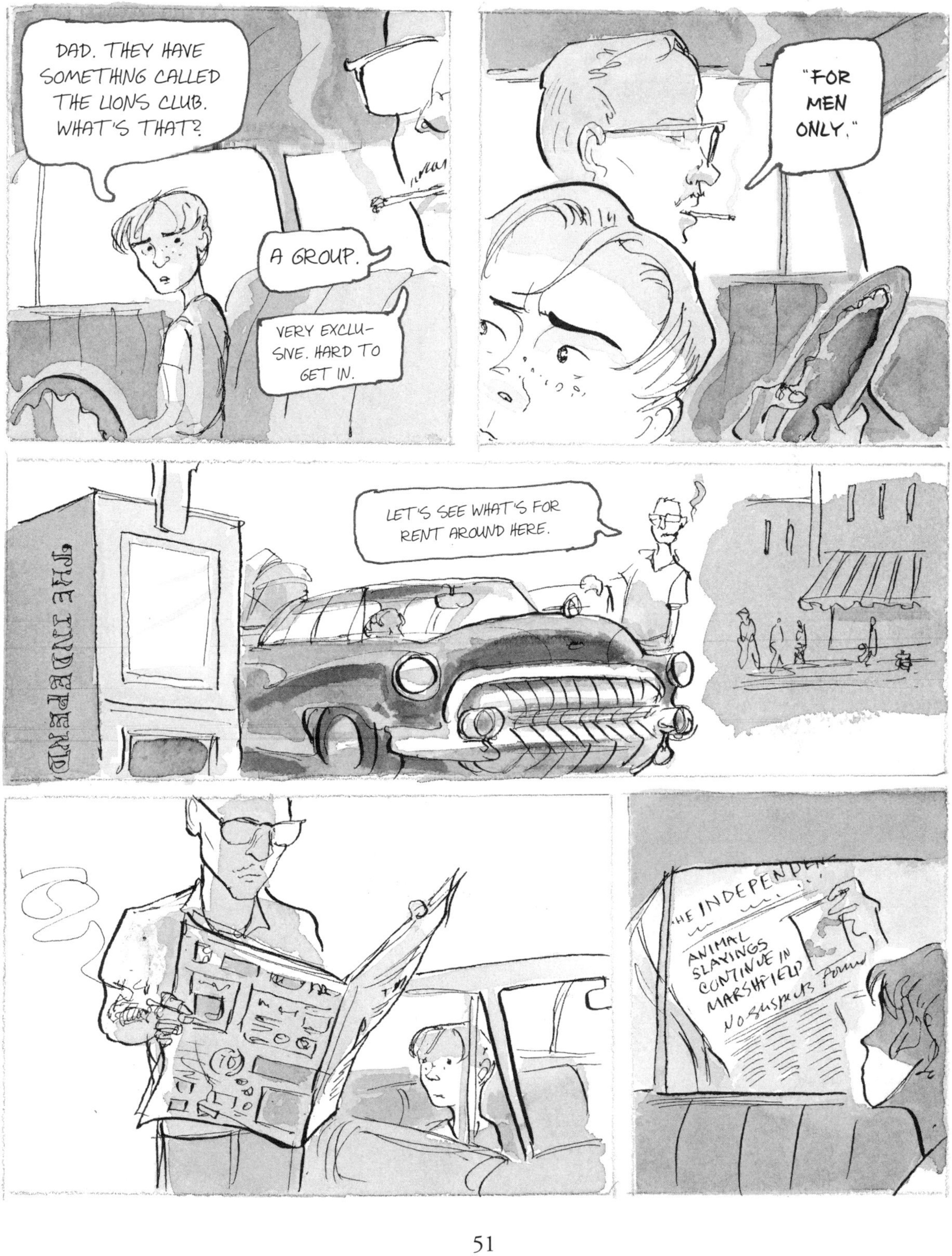
DAD. THEY HAVE SOMETHING CALLED THE LIONS CLUB. WHAT'S THAT?
A GROUP.
VERY EXCLU-SIVE. HARD TO GET IN.
"FOR MEN ONLY."
LET'S SEE WHAT'S FOR RENT AROUND HERE.
ANIMAL SLAYINGS CONTINUE IN MARSHFIELD

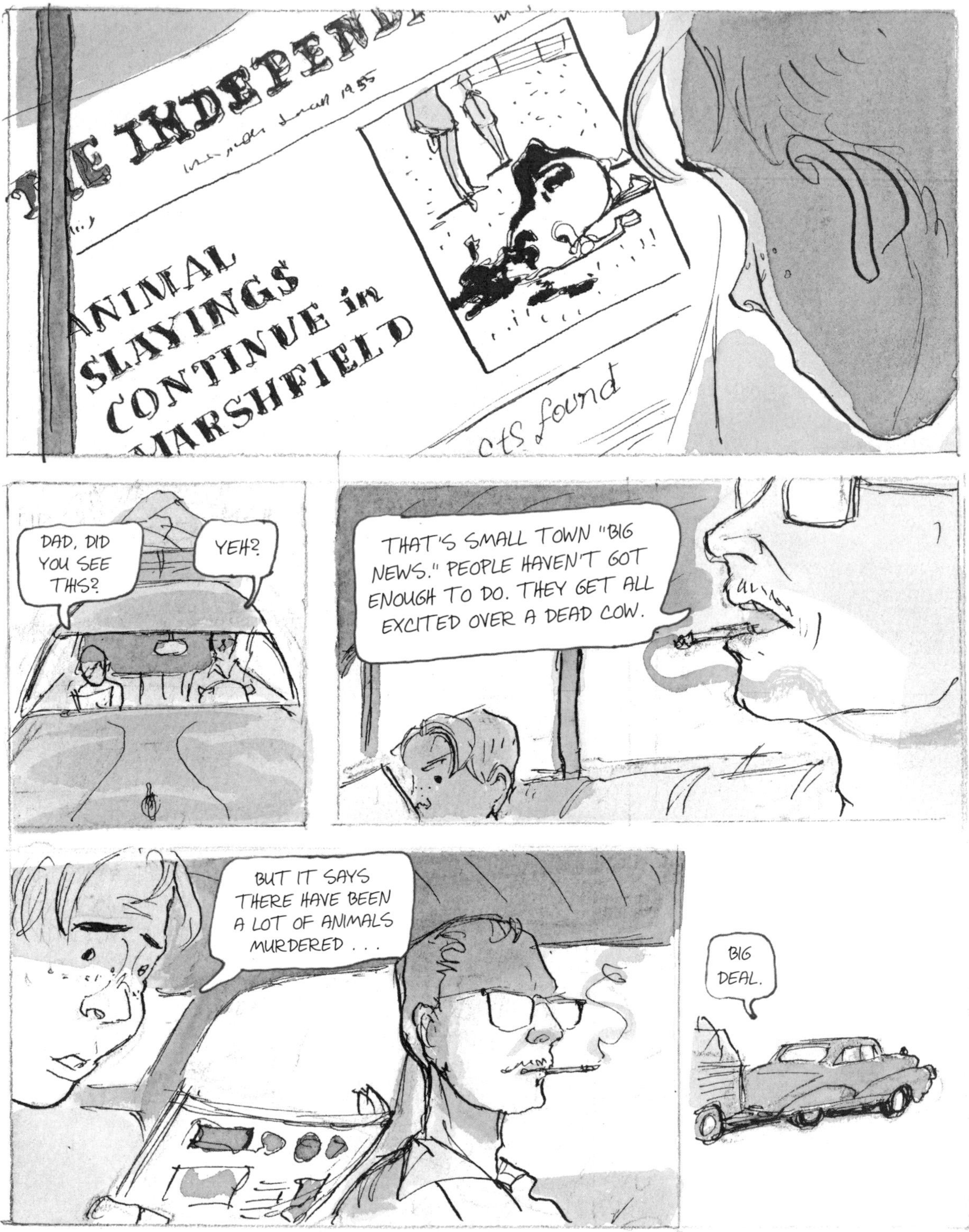
THE INDEPENDE
ANIMAL SLAYINGS CONTINUE in MARSHFIELD
cts found
DAD, DID YOU SEE THIS?
YEH?
THAT'S SMALL TOWN "BIG NEWS." PEOPLE HAVEN'T GOT ENOUGH TO DO. THEY GET ALL EXCITED OVER A DEAD COW.
BUT IT SAYS THERE HAVE BEEN A LOT OF ANIMALS MURDERED . . .
BIG DEAL.

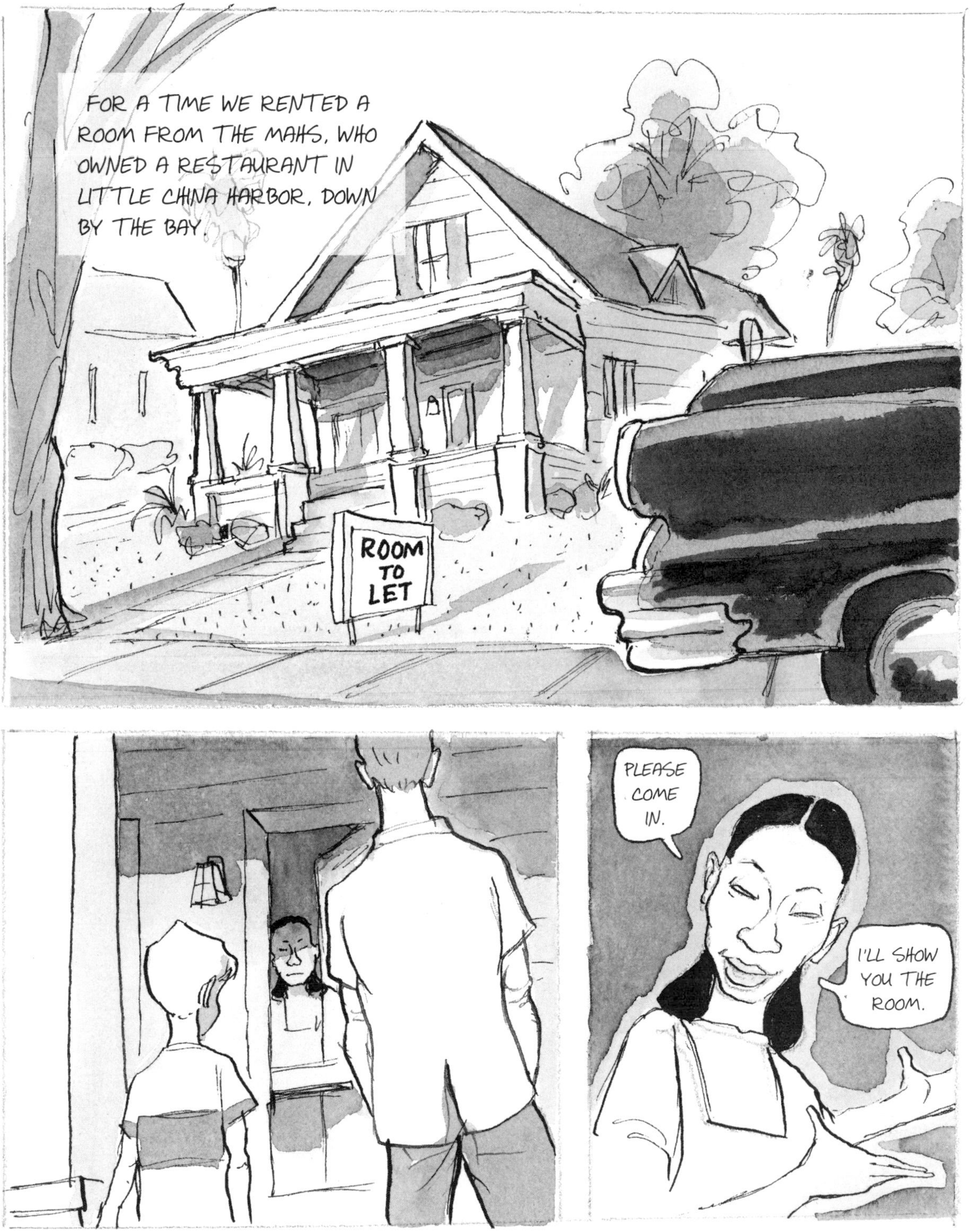
FOR A TIME WE RENTED A ROOM FROM THE MAHS, WHO OWNED A RESTAURANT IN LITTLE CHINA HARBOR, DOWN BY THE BAY.
ROOM TO LET
PLEASE COME IN.
I'LL SHOW YOU THE ROOM.

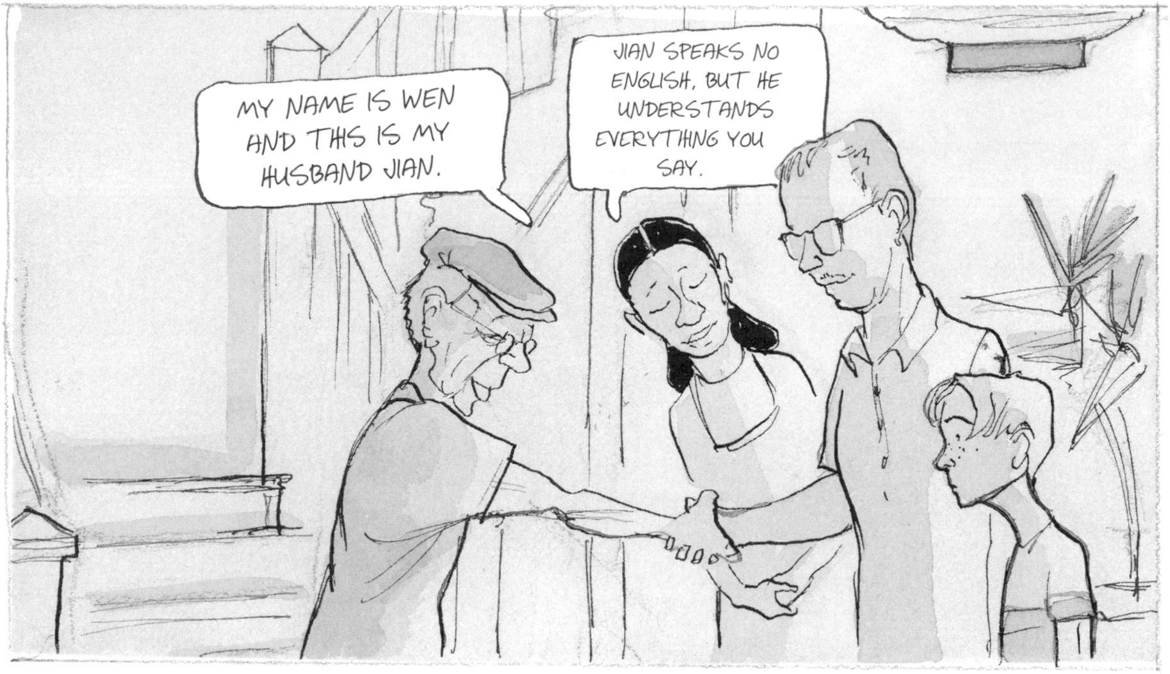
MY NAME IS WEN AND THIS IS MY HUSBAND JIAN.
JIAN SPEAKS NO ENGLISH, BUT HE UNDERSTANDS EVERYTHING YOU SAY.

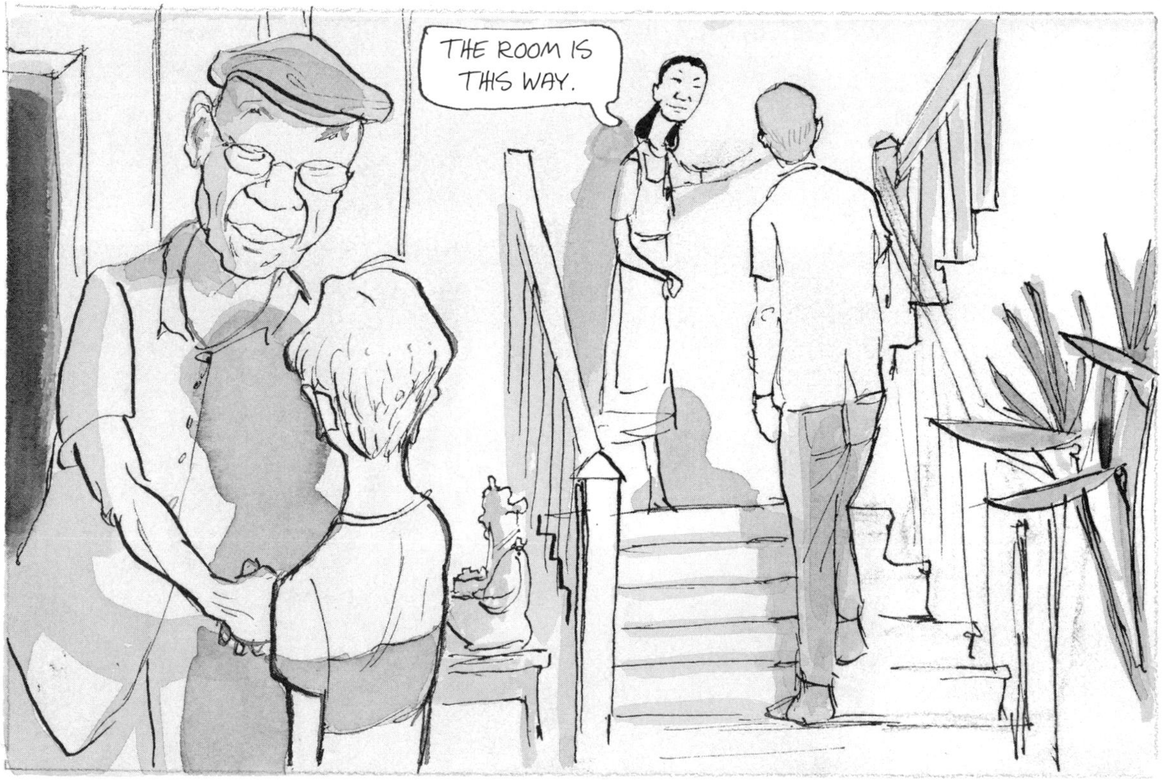
THE ROOM IS THIS WAY.

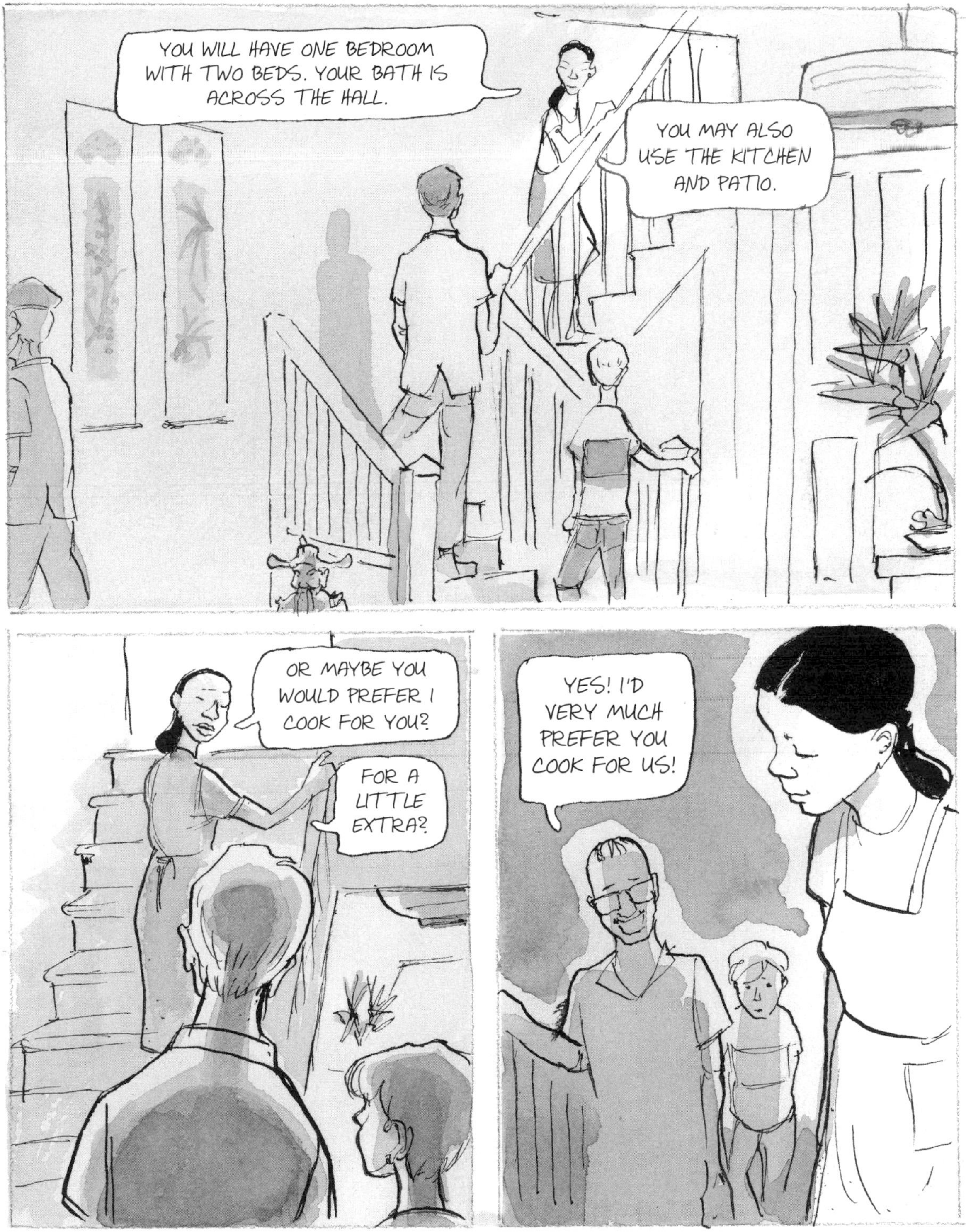
YOU WILL HAVE ONE BEDROOM WITH TWO BEDS. YOUR BATH IS ACROSS THE HALL.
YOU MAY ALSO USE THE KITCHEN AND PATIO.
OR MAYBE YOU WOULD PREFER I COOK FOR YOU?
FOR A LITTLE EXTRA?
YES! I'D VERY MUCH PREFER YOU COOK FOR US!

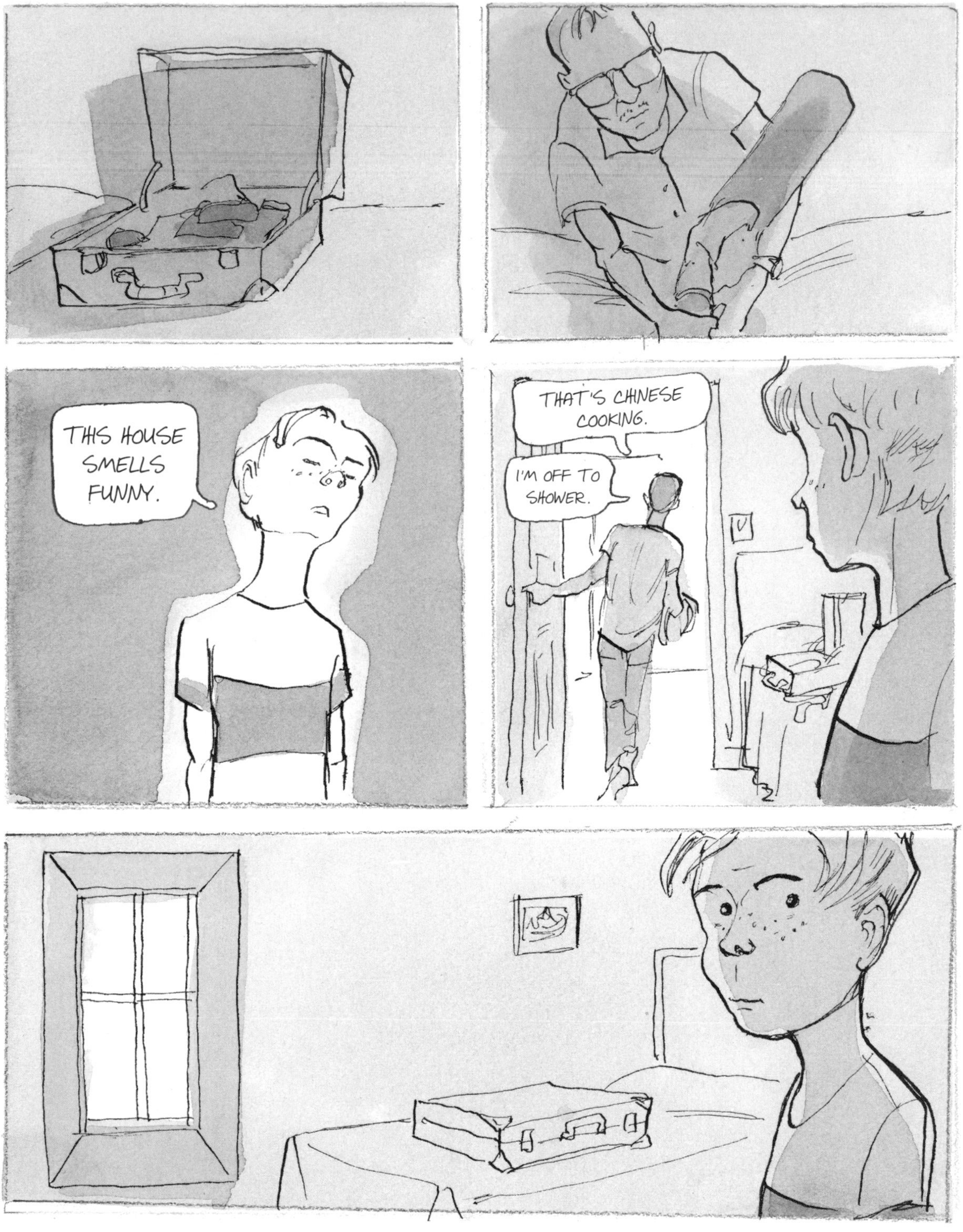
THIS HOUSE SMELLS FUNNY.
THAT'S CHINESE COOKING.
I'M OFF TO SHOWER.

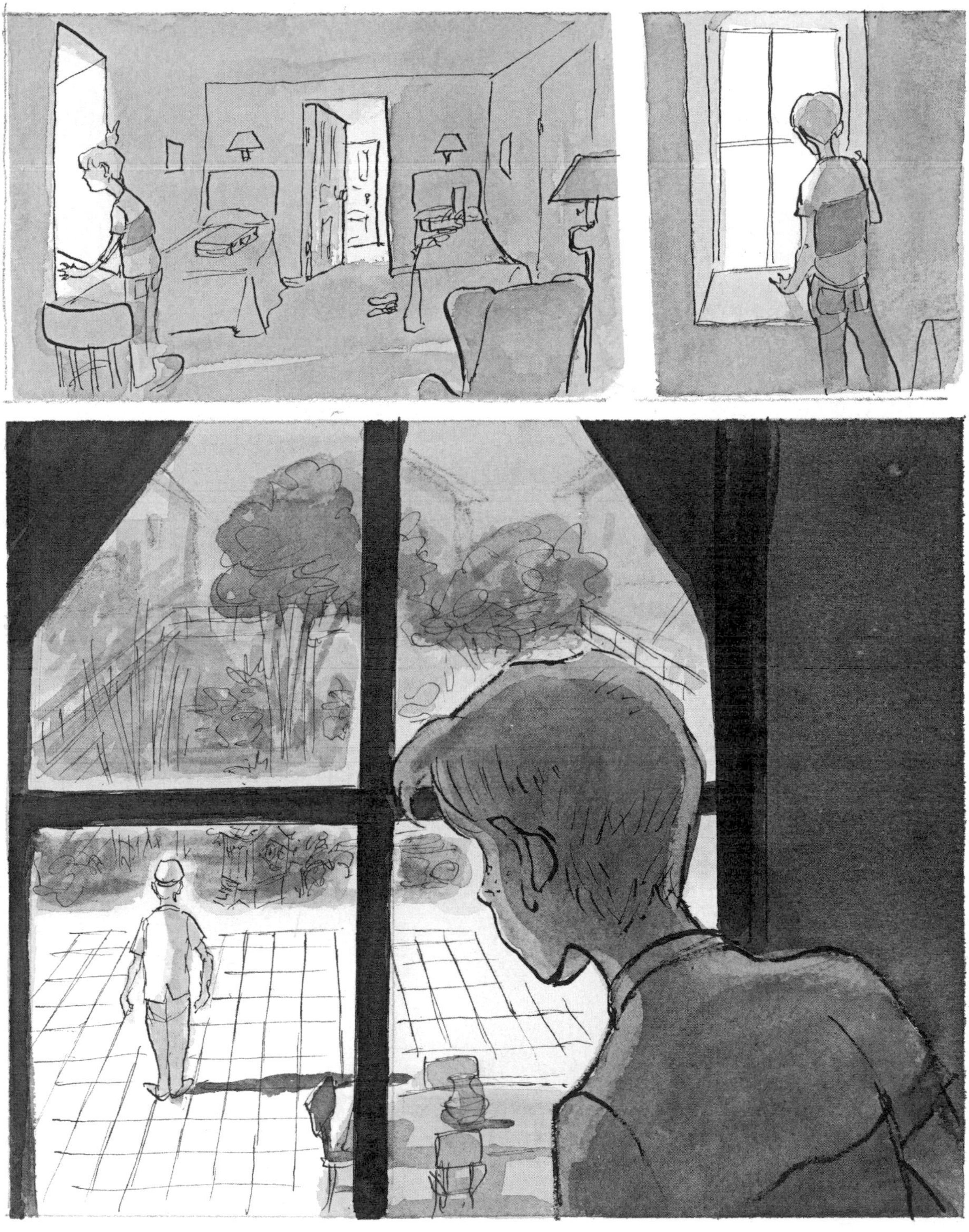

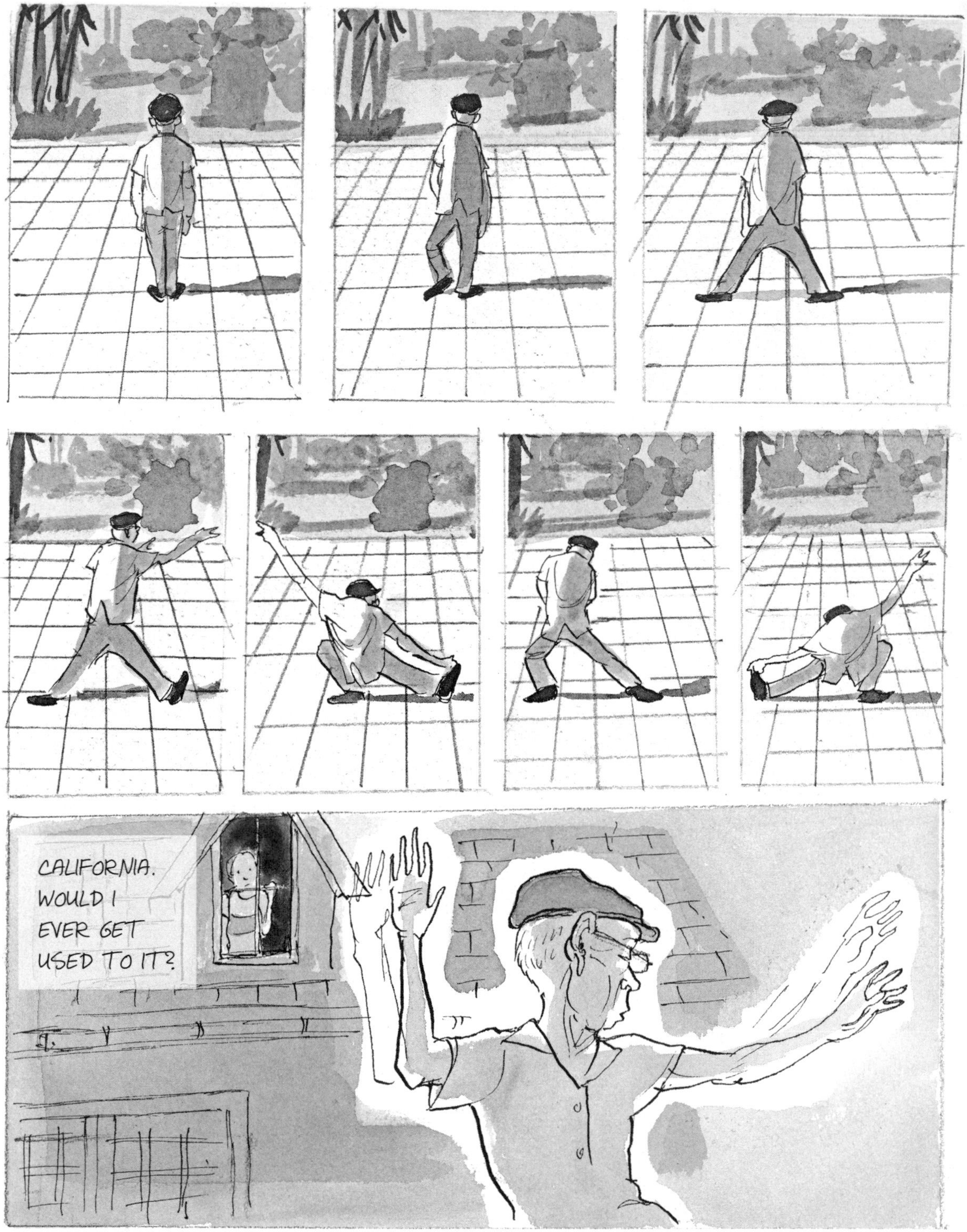
CALIFORNIA. WOULD I EVER GET USED TO IT?

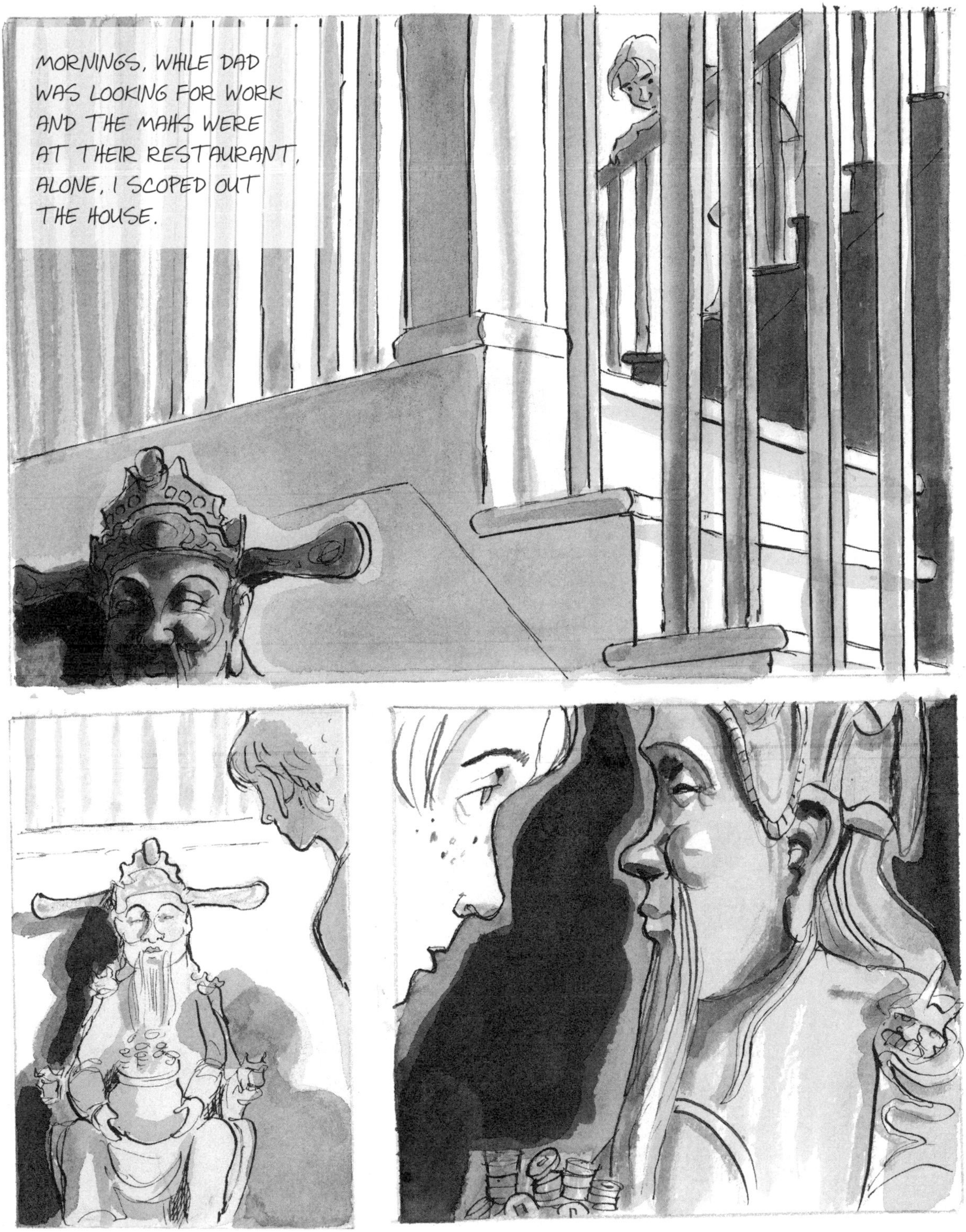
MORNINGS, WHILE DAD WAS LOOKING FOR WORK AND THE MAHS WERE AT THEIR RESTAURANT, ALONE, I SCOPED OUT THE HOUSE.

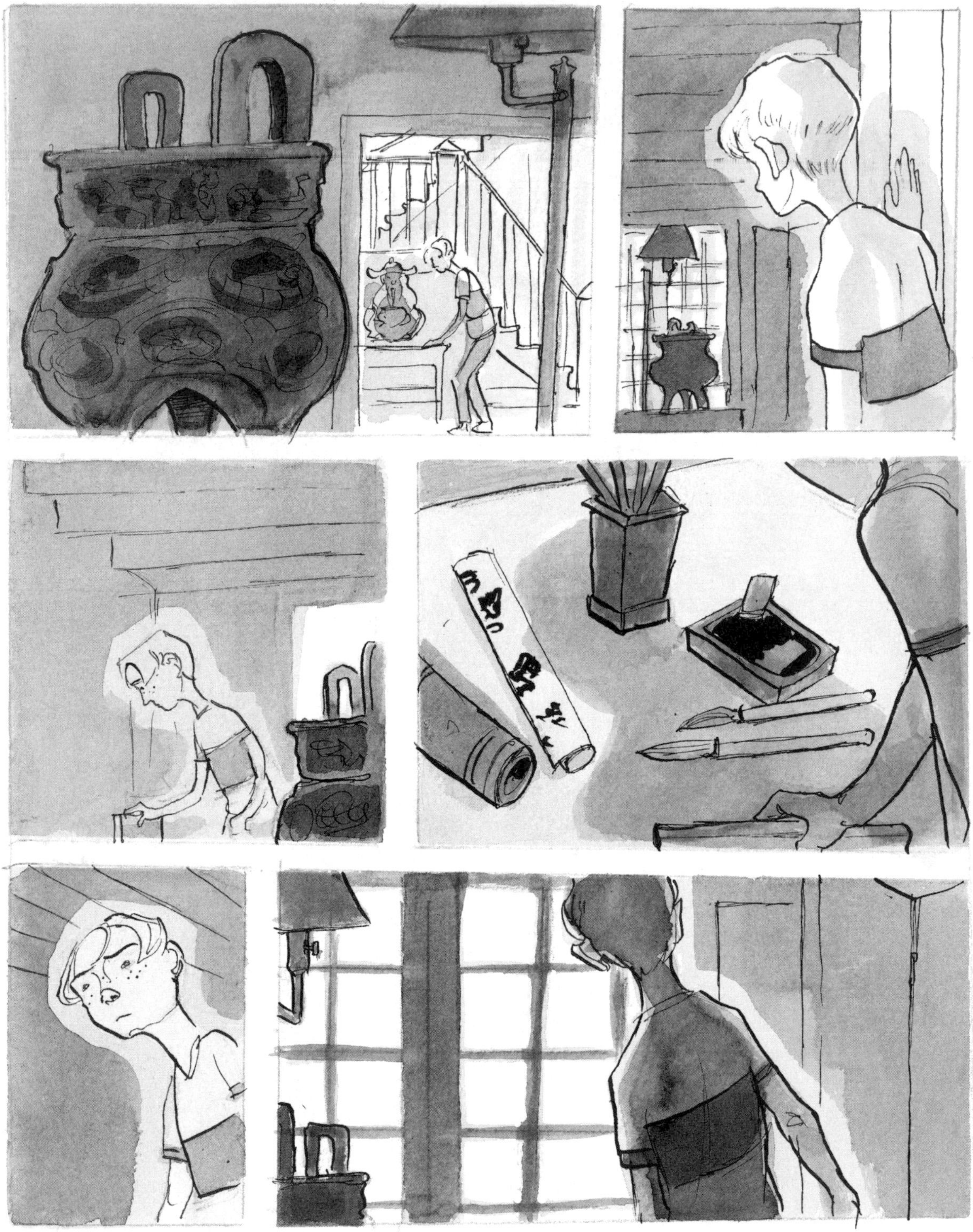

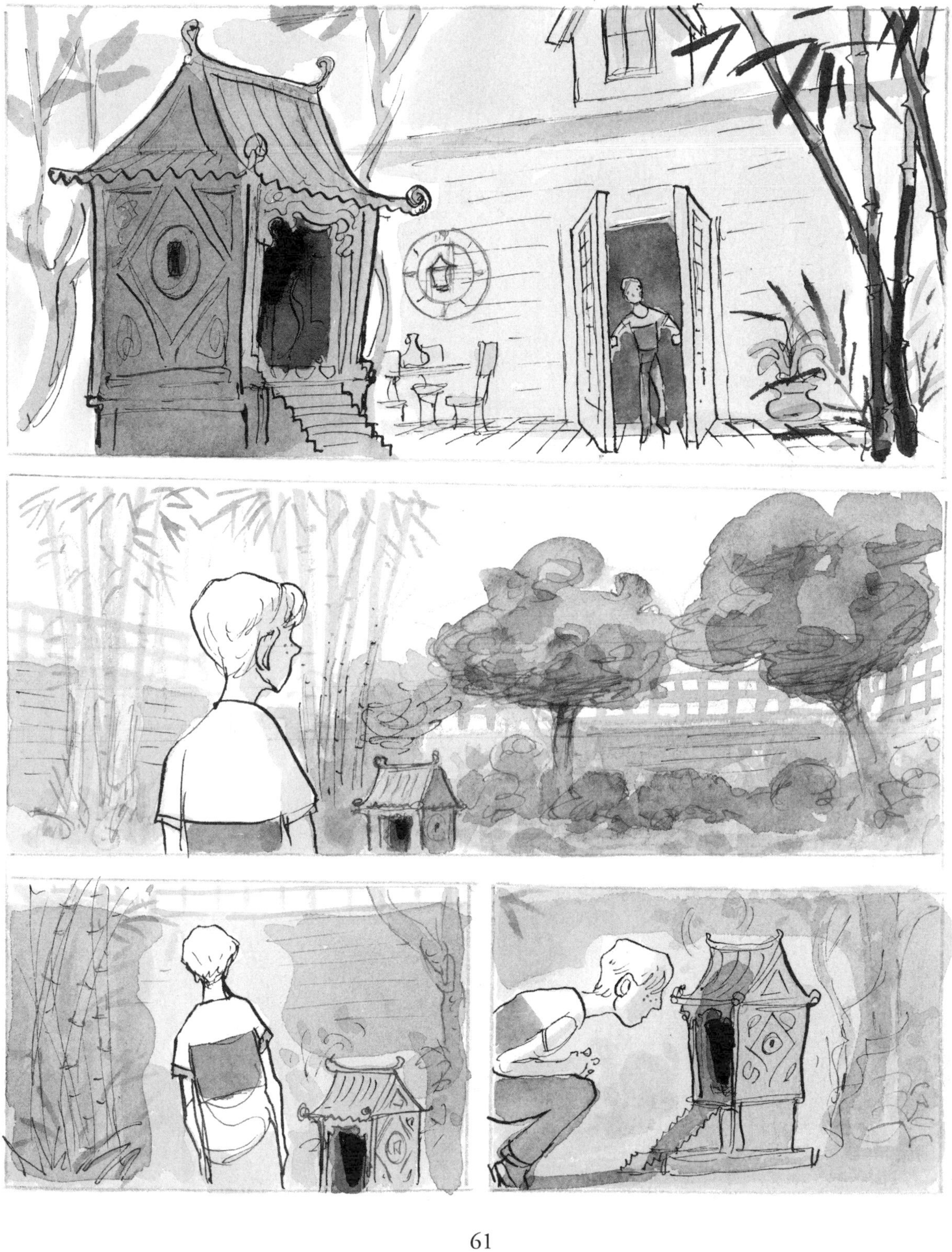

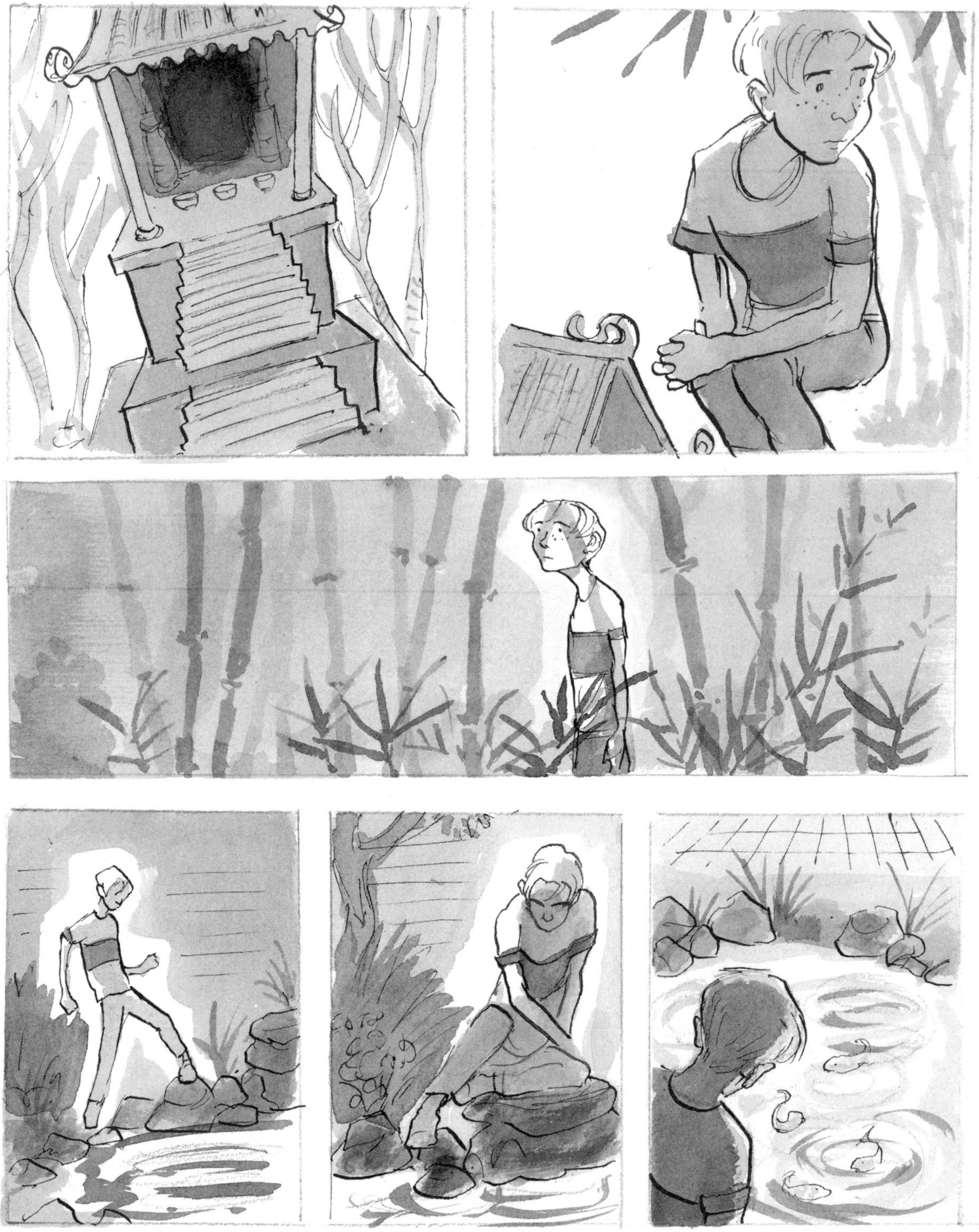

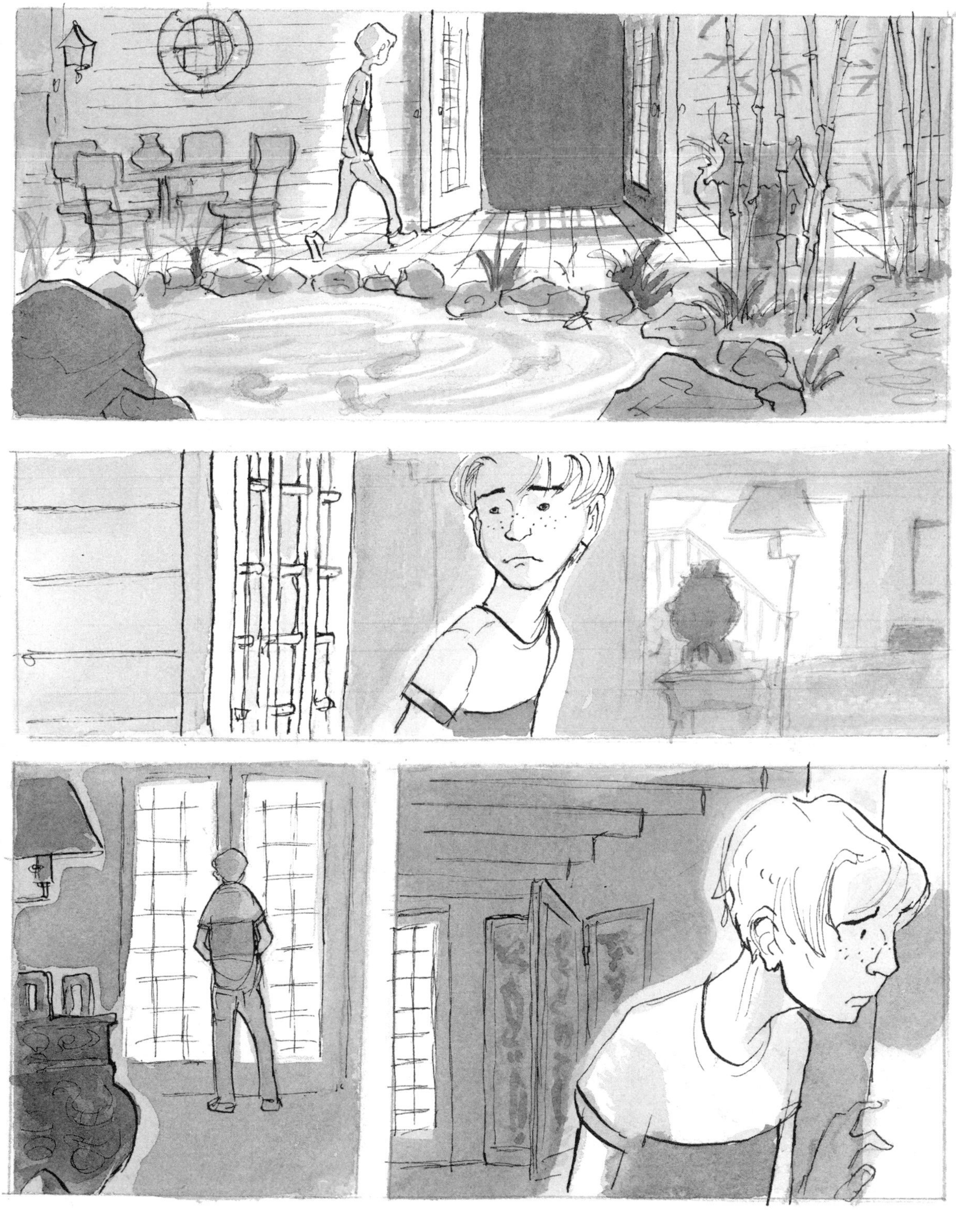

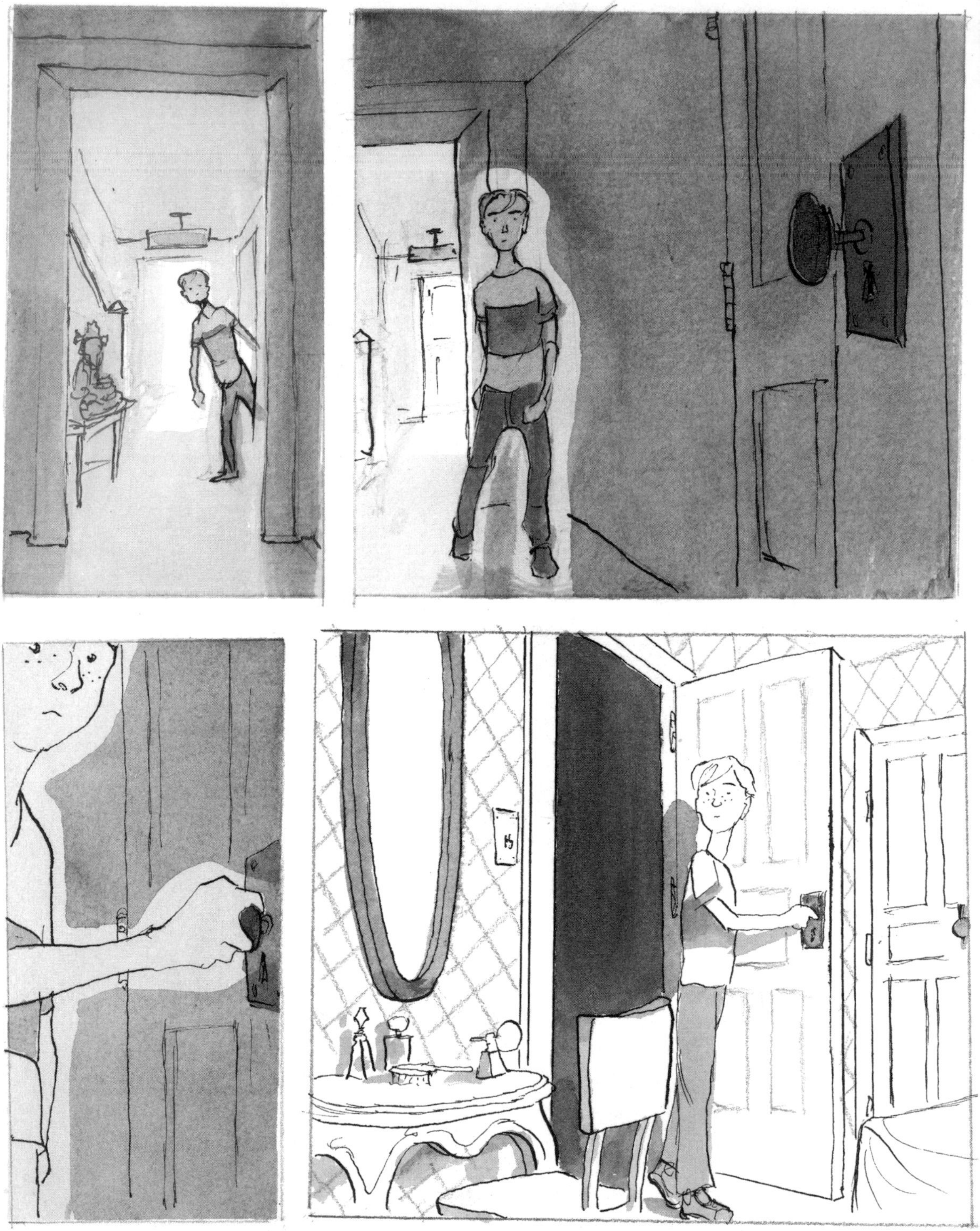

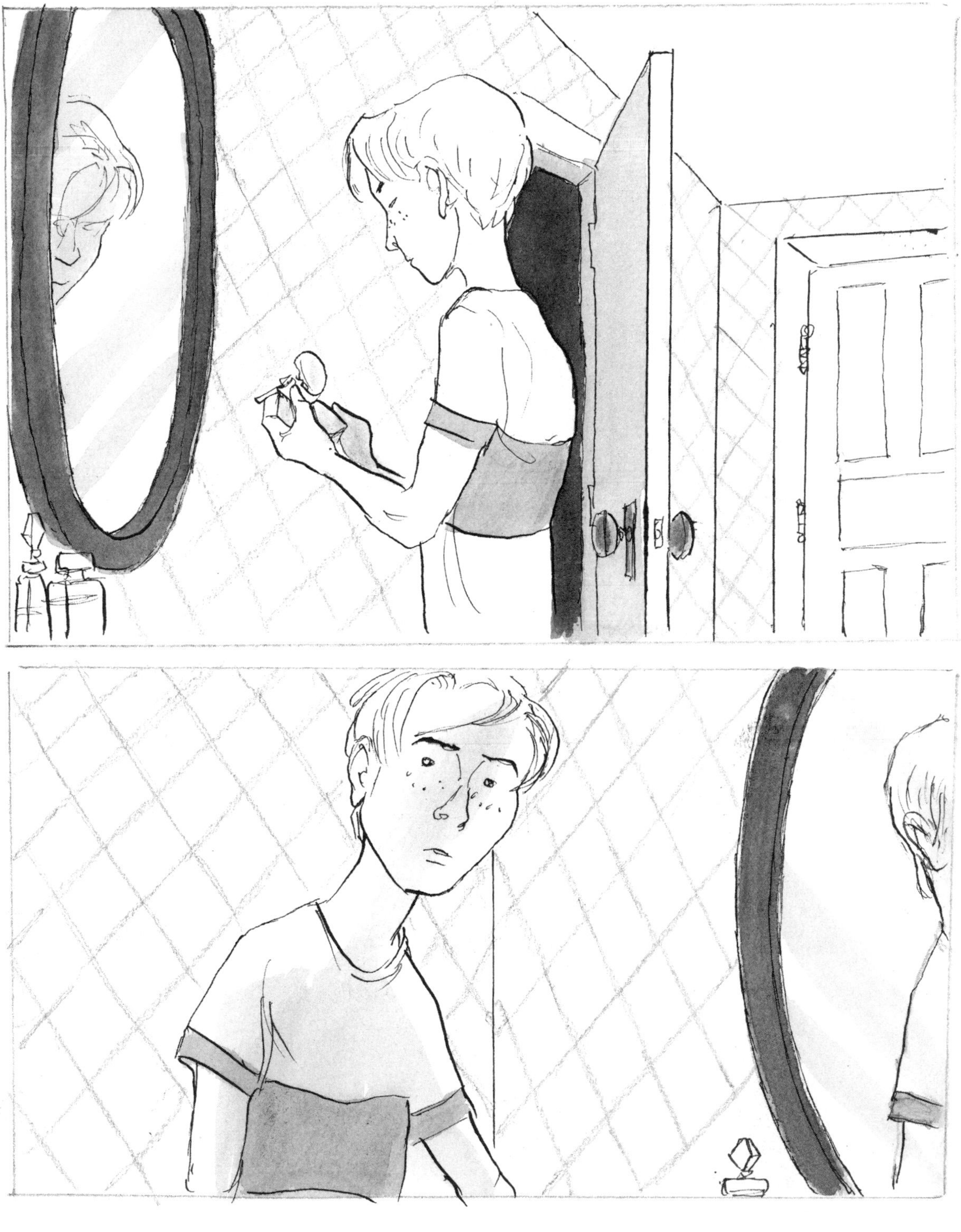

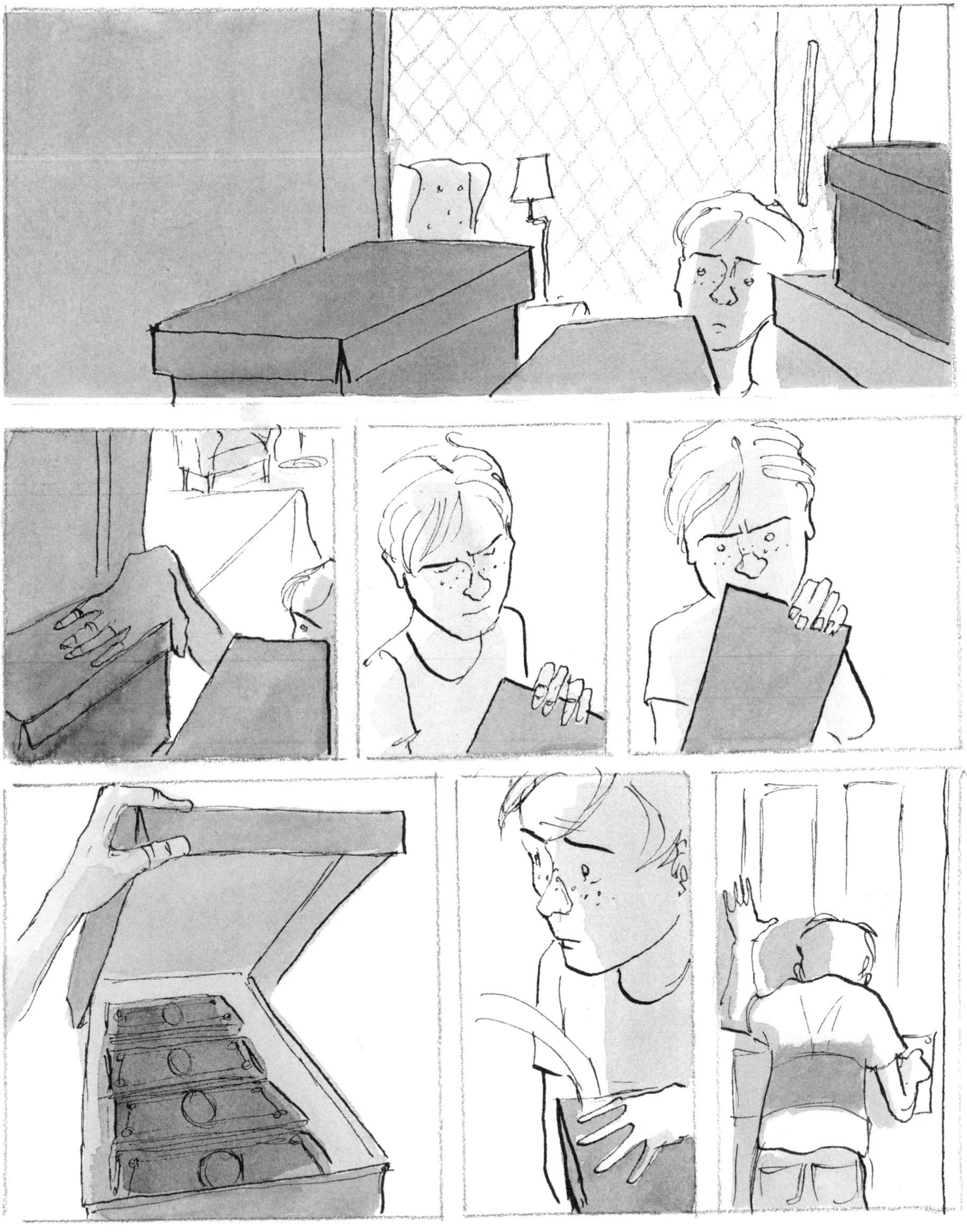

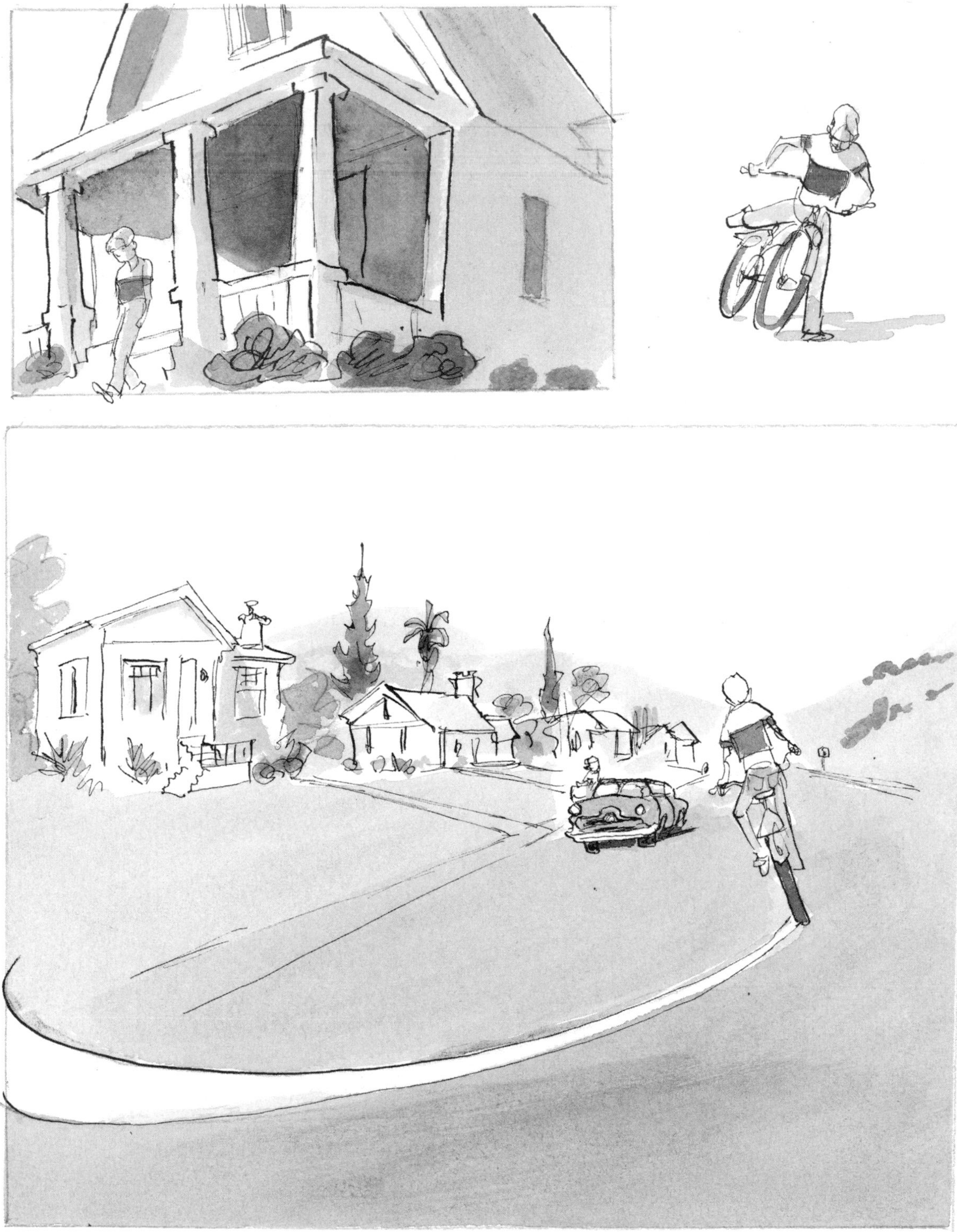

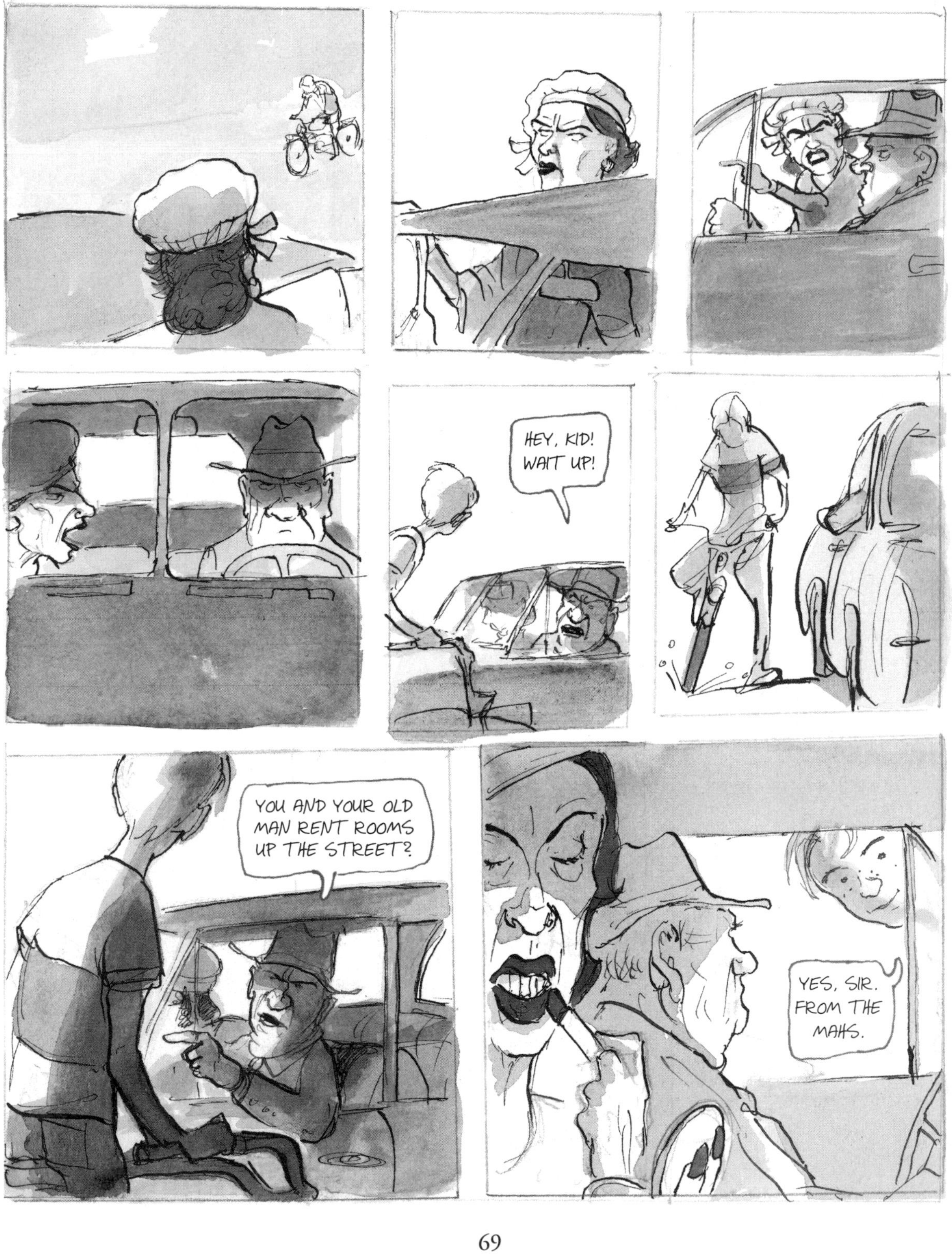
HEY, KID! WAIT UP!
YOU AND YOUR OLD MAN RENT ROOMS UP THE STREET?
YES, SIR. FROM THE MAHS.

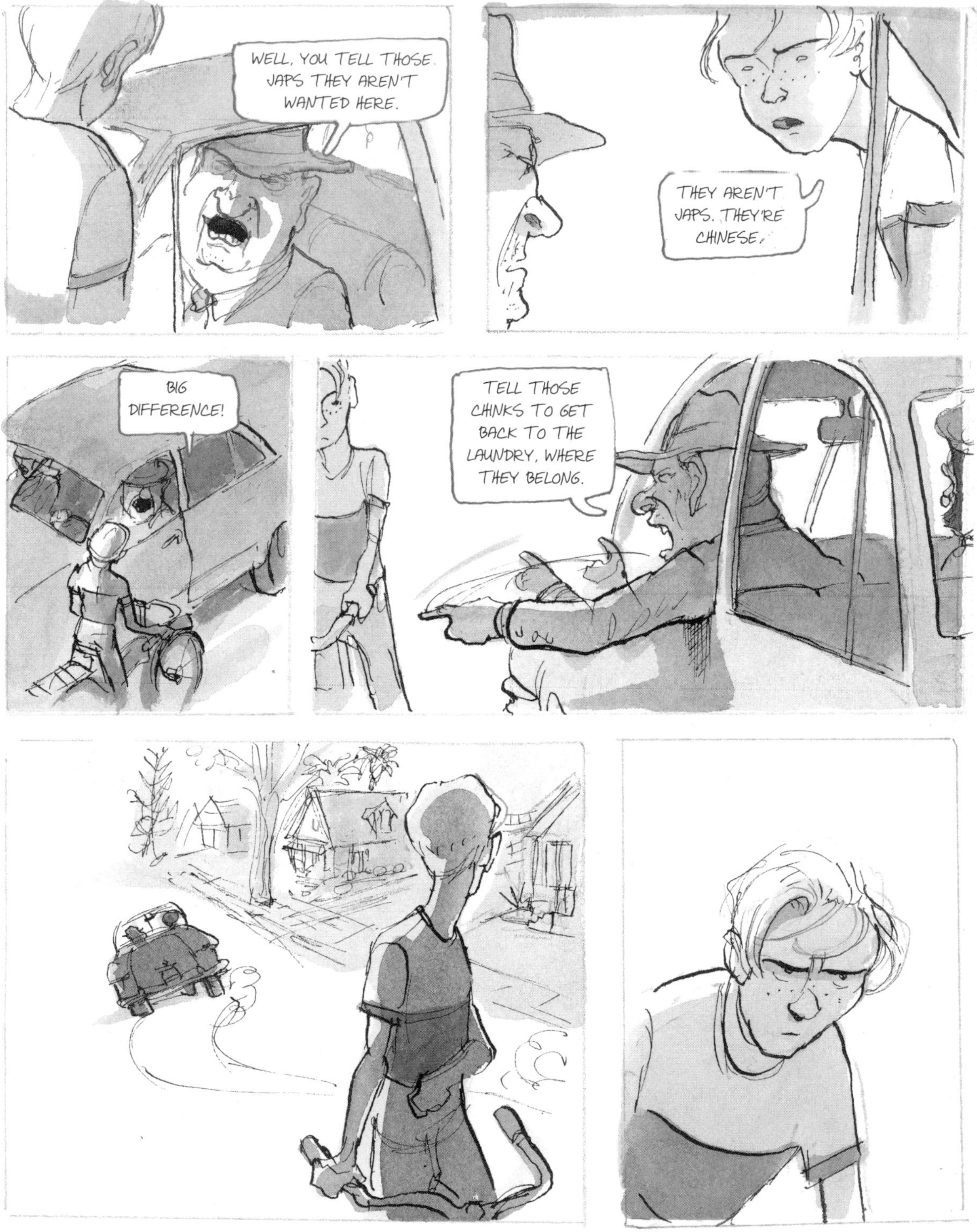
WELL, YOU TELL THOSE JAPS THEY AREN'T WANTED HERE.
THEY AREN'T JAPS. THEY'RE CHINESE.
BIG DIFFERENCE!
TELL THOSE CHINKS TO GET BACK TO THE LAUNDRY, WHERE THEY BELONG.

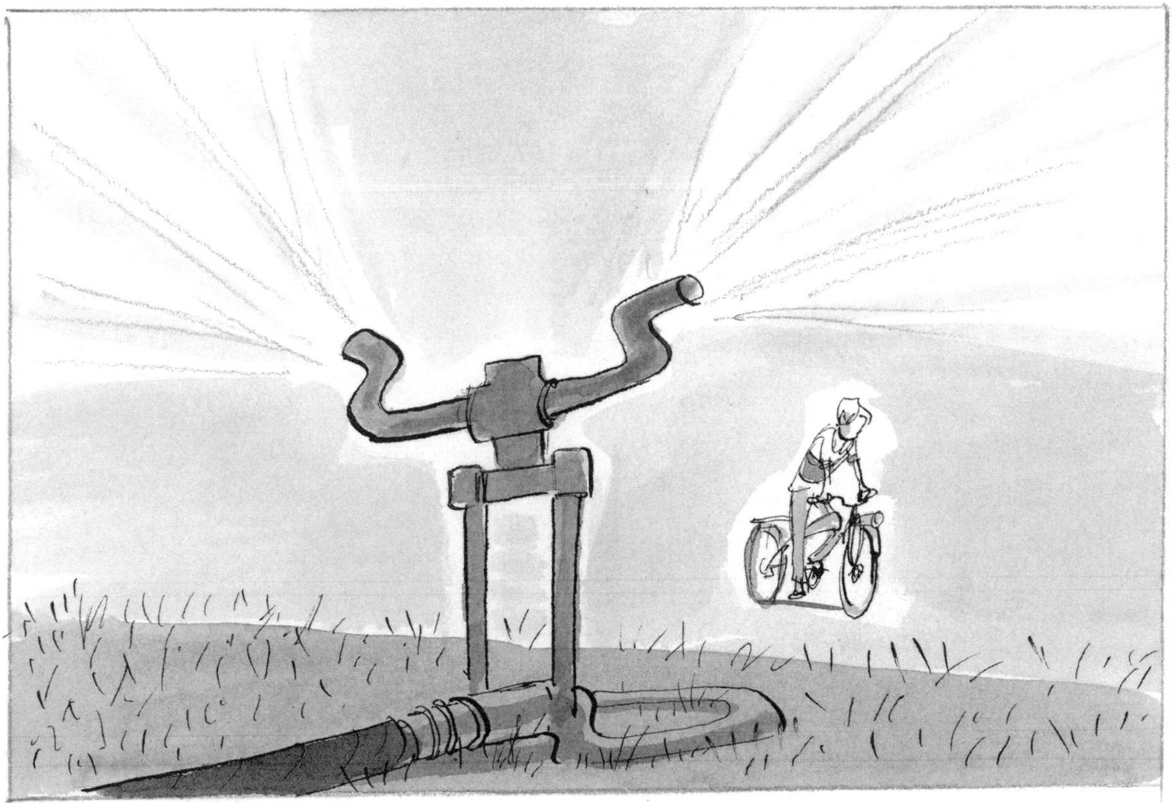

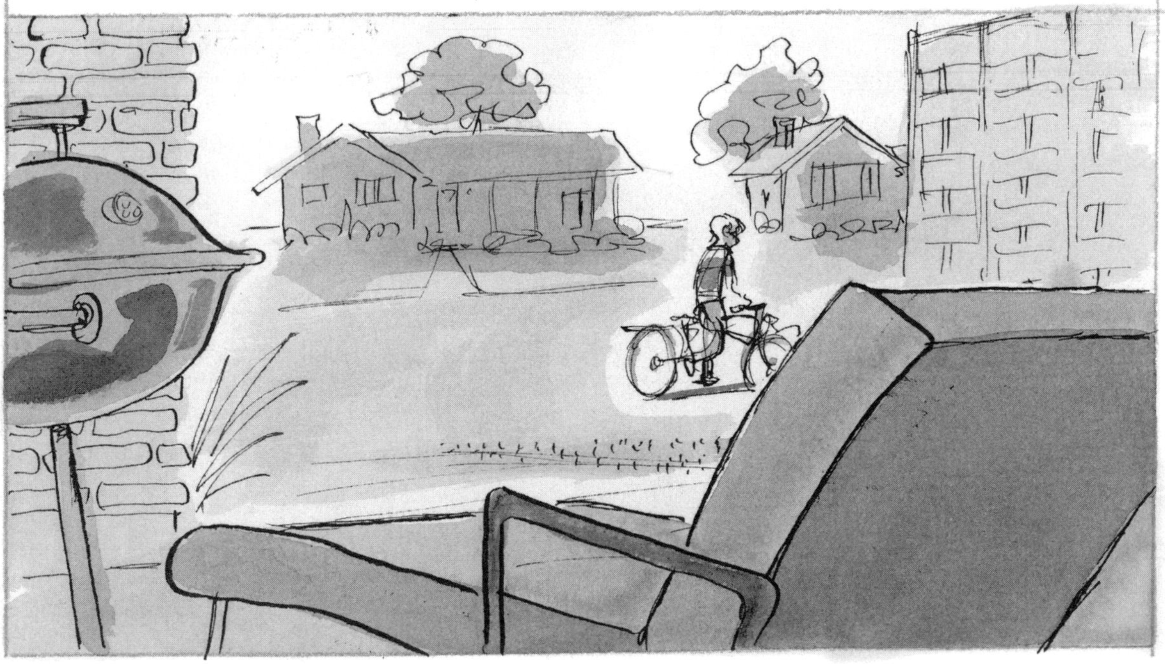

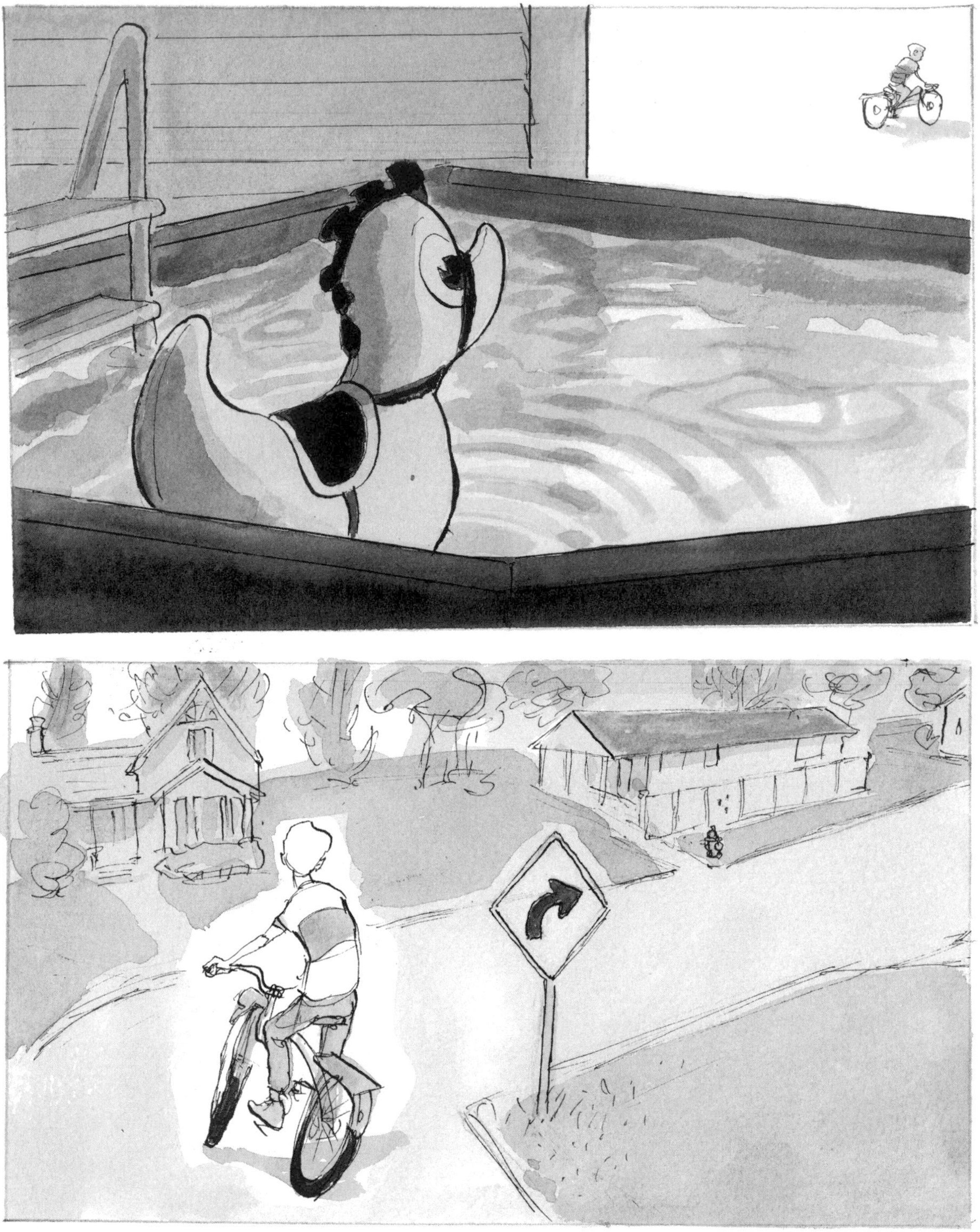

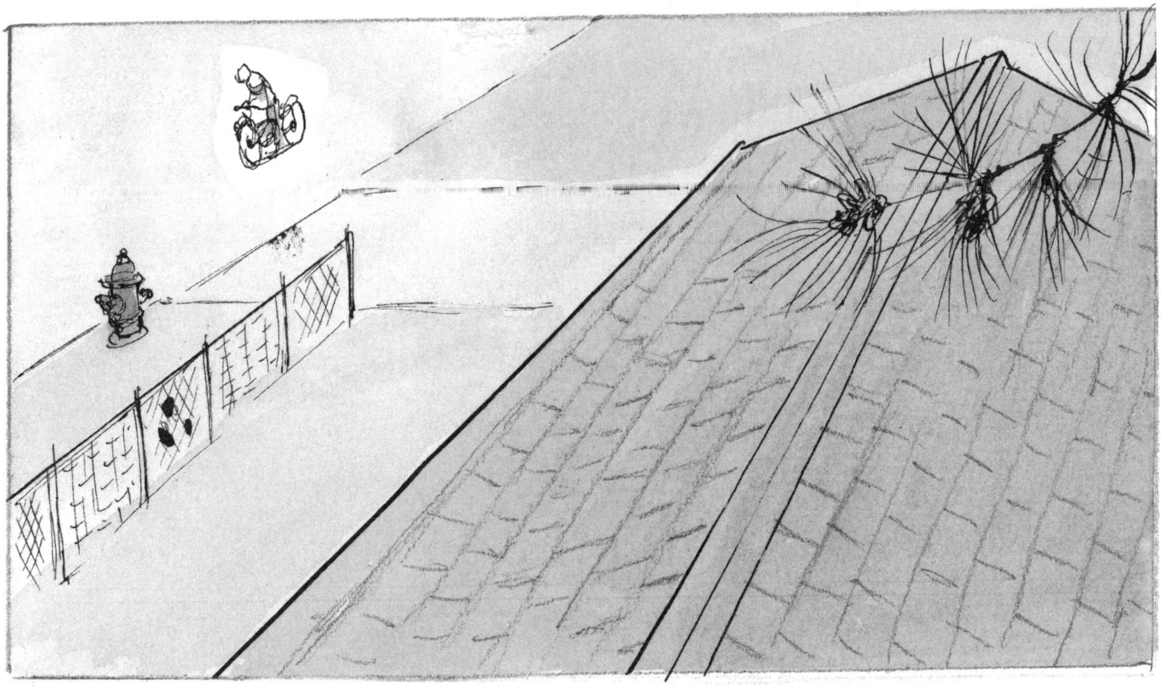
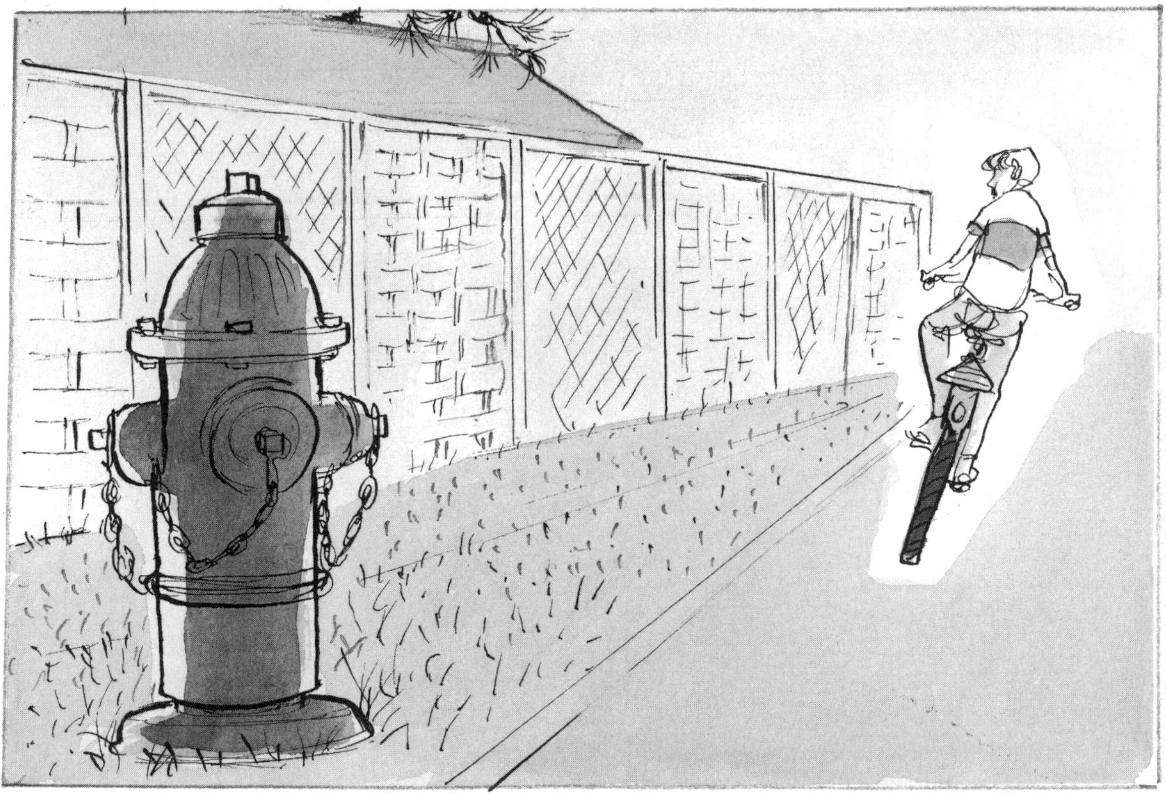

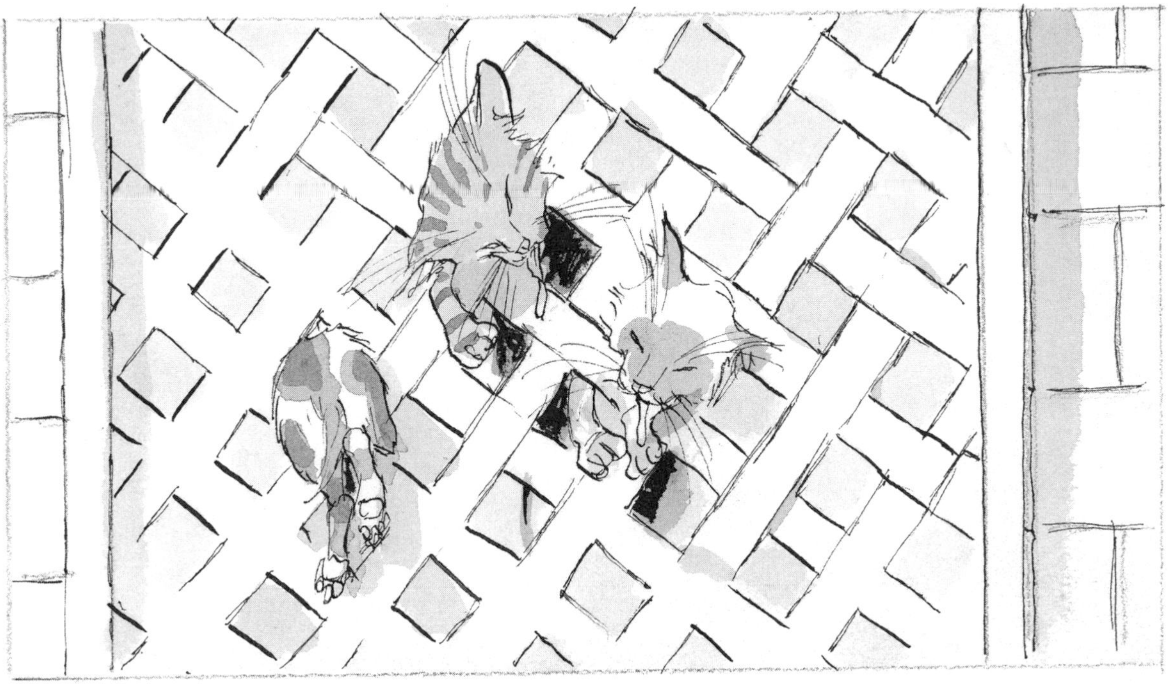

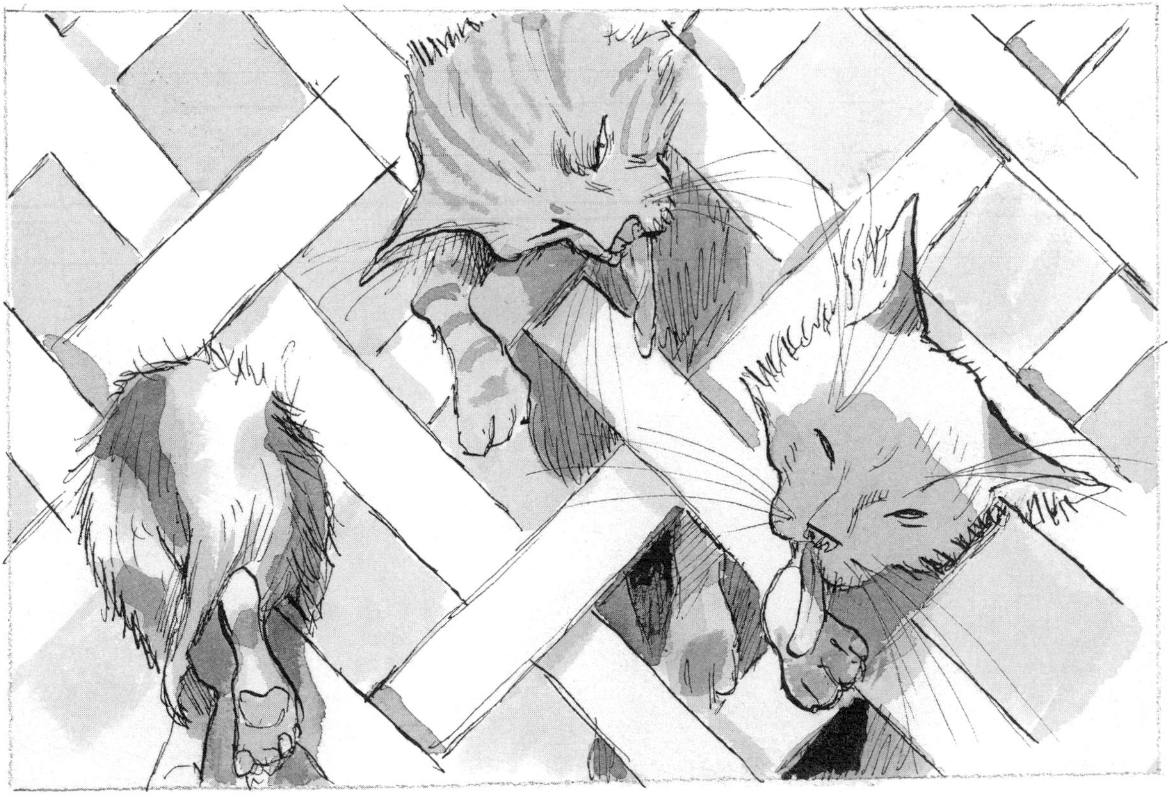

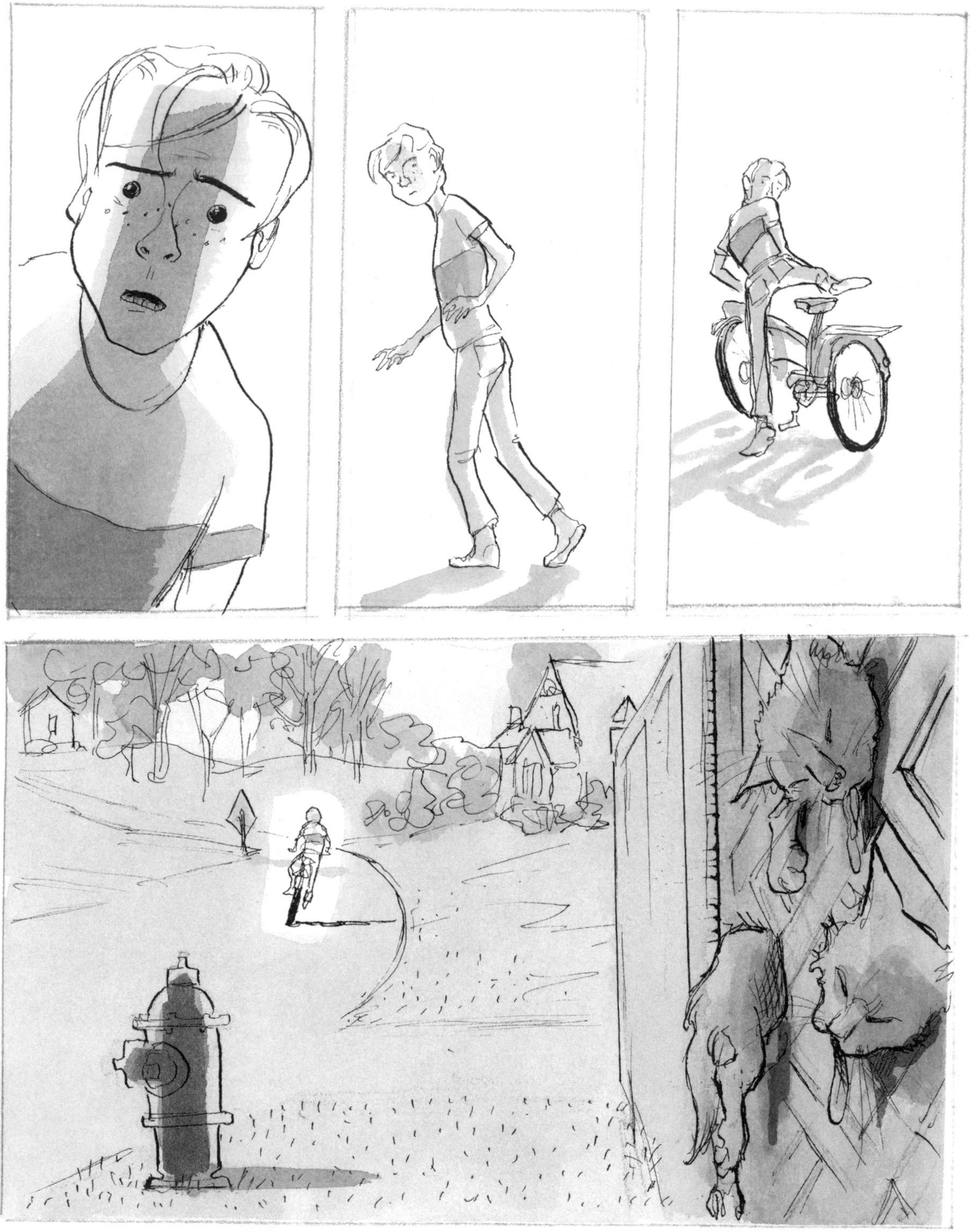

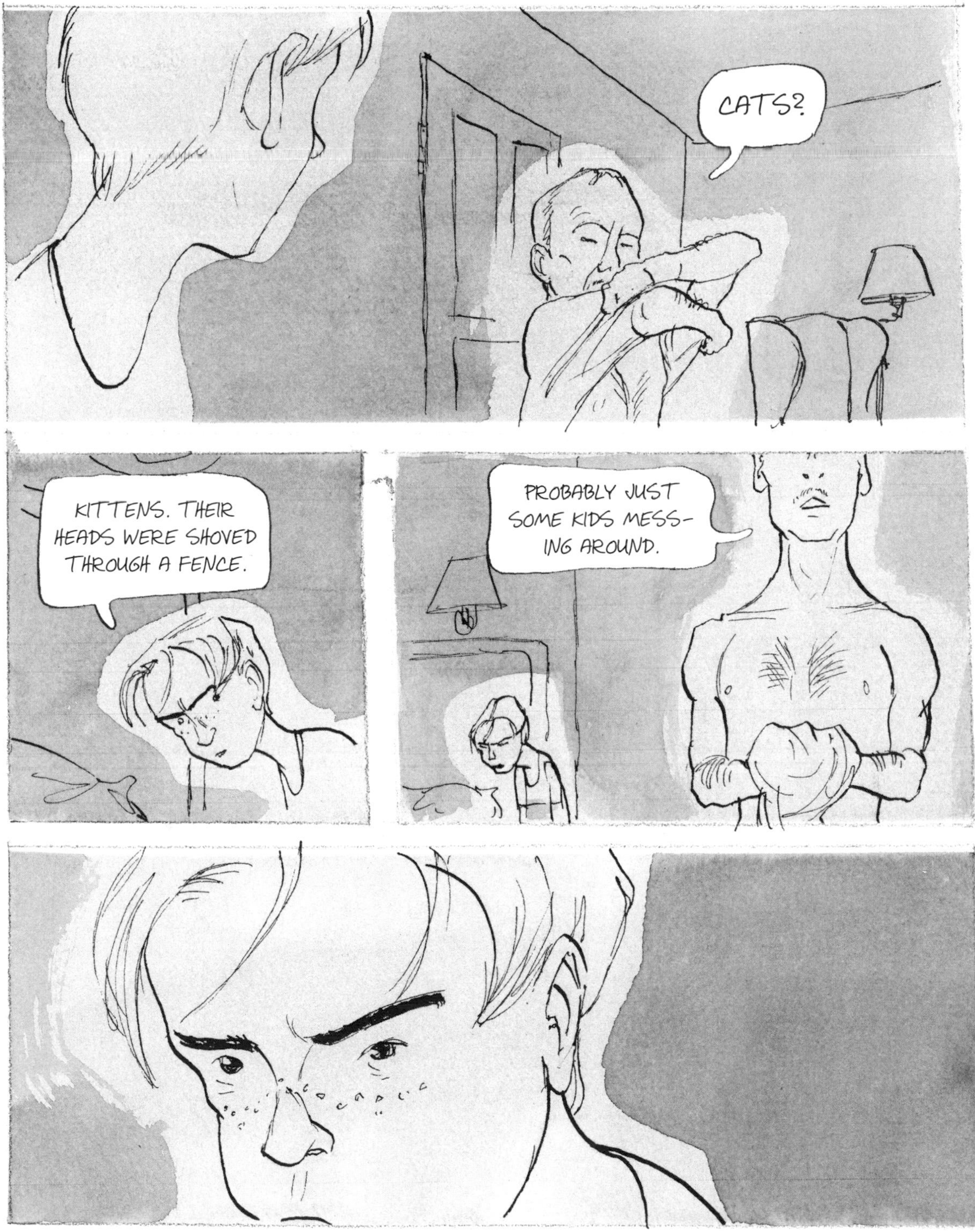
CATS?
KITTENS. THEIR HEADS WERE SHOVED THROUGH A FENCE.
PROBABLY JUST SOME KIDS MESS-ING AROUND.

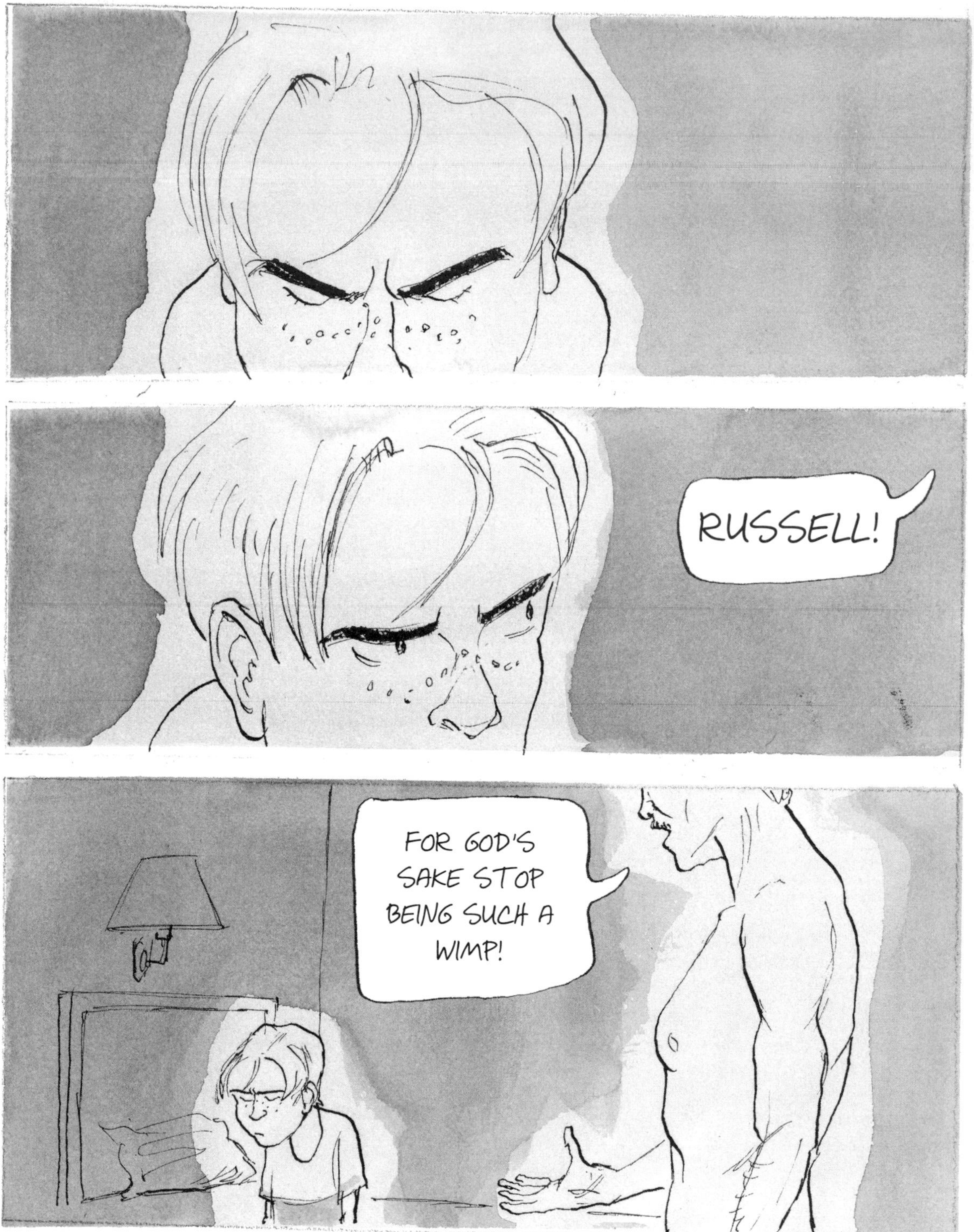
RUSSELL!
FOR GOD'S SAKE STOP BEING SUCH A WIMP!

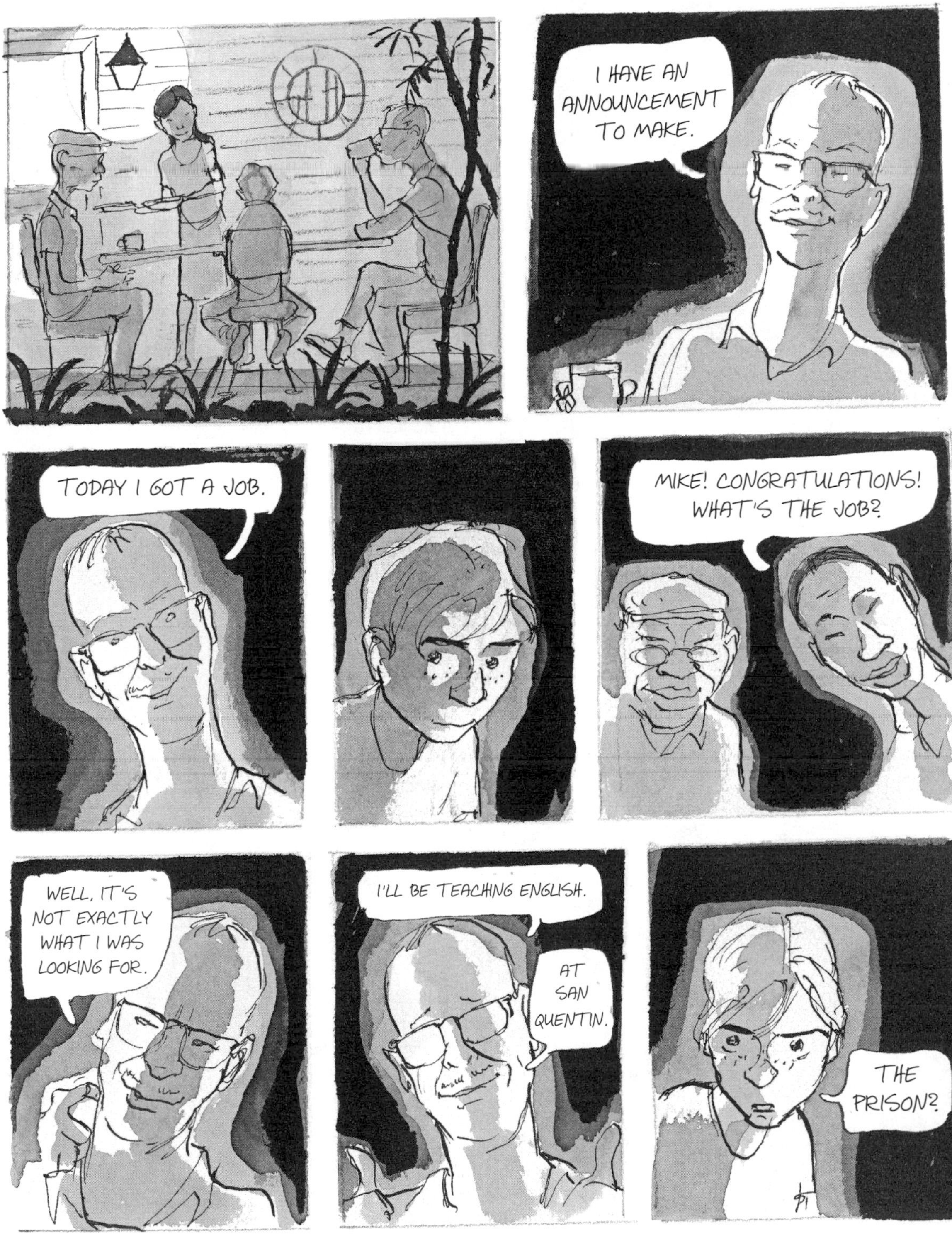
I HAVE AN ANNOUNCEMENT TO MAKE.
TODAY I GOT A JOB.
MIKE! CONGRATULATIONS! WHAT'S THE JOB?
WELL, IT'S NOT EXACTLY WHAT I WAS LOOKING FOR.
I'LL BE TEACHING ENGLISH.
AT SAN QUENTIN.
THE PRISON?

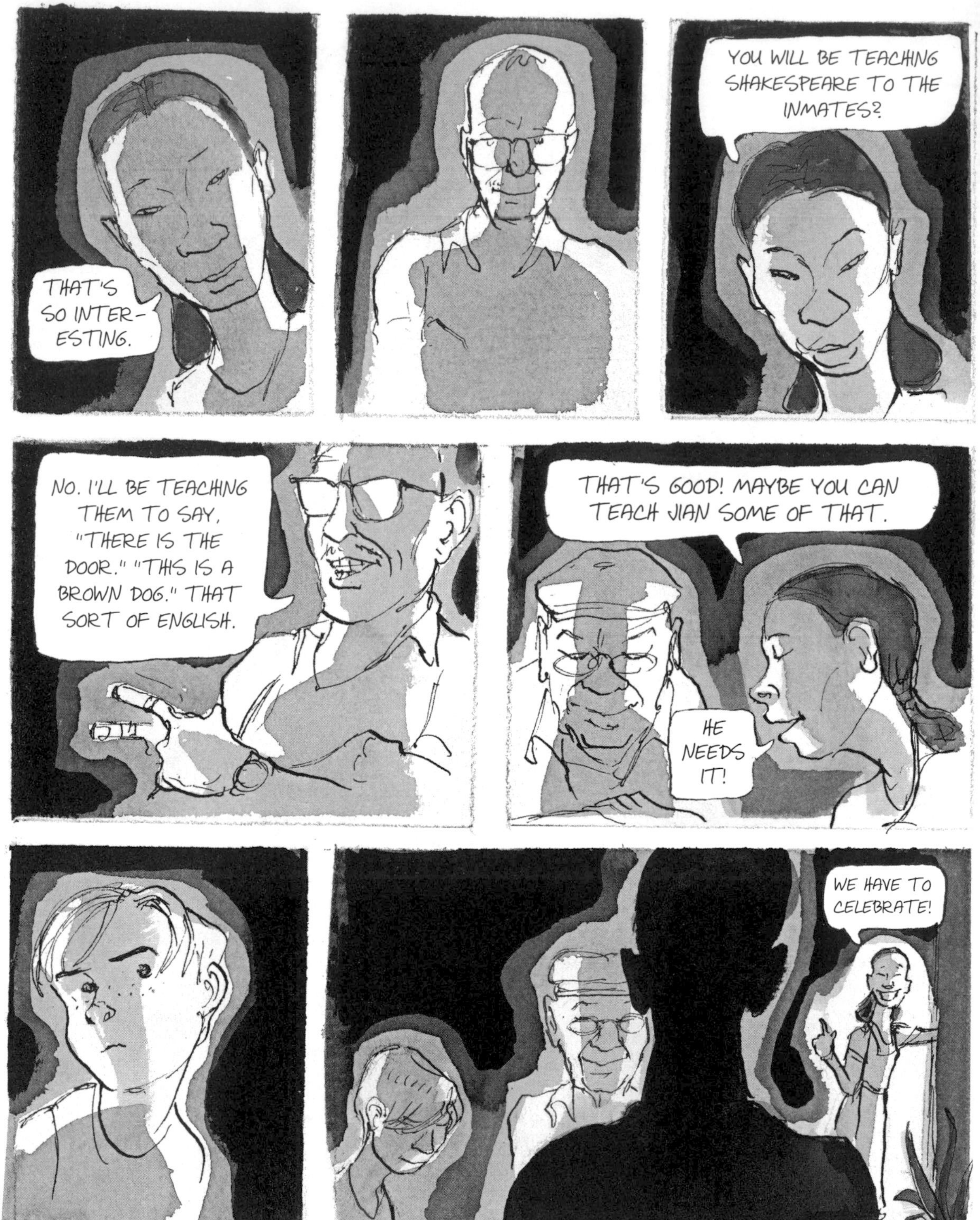
THAT'S SO INTER-ESTING.
YOU WILL BE TEACHING SHAKESPEARE TO THE INMATES?
NO. I'LL BE TEACHING THEM TO SAY, "THERE IS THE DOOR." "THIS IS A BROWN DOG." THAT SORT OF ENGLISH.
THAT'S GOOD! MAYBE YOU CAN TEACH JIAN SOME OF THAT.
HE NEEDS IT!
WE HAVE TO CELEBRATE!

CHAPTER FOUR

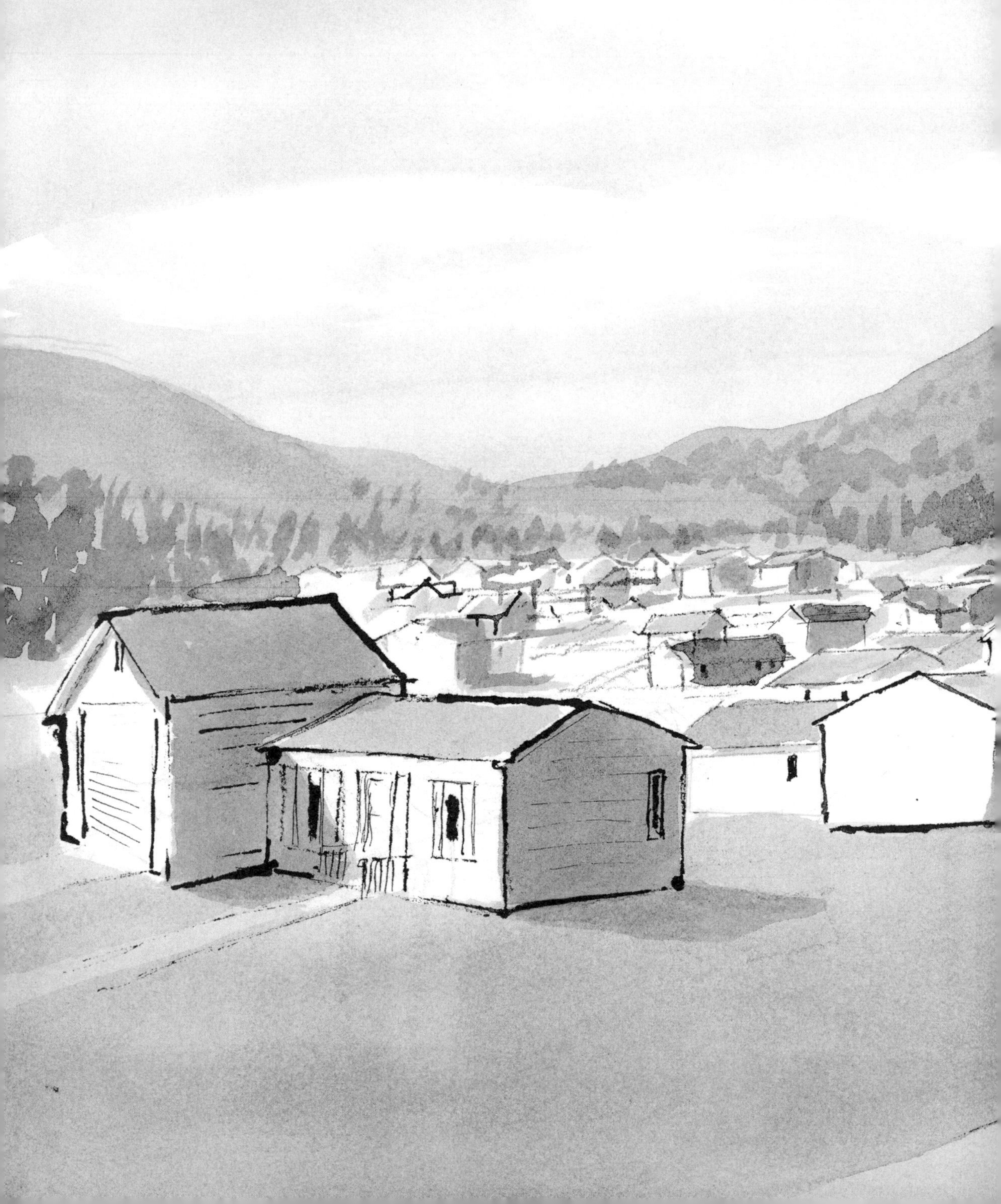

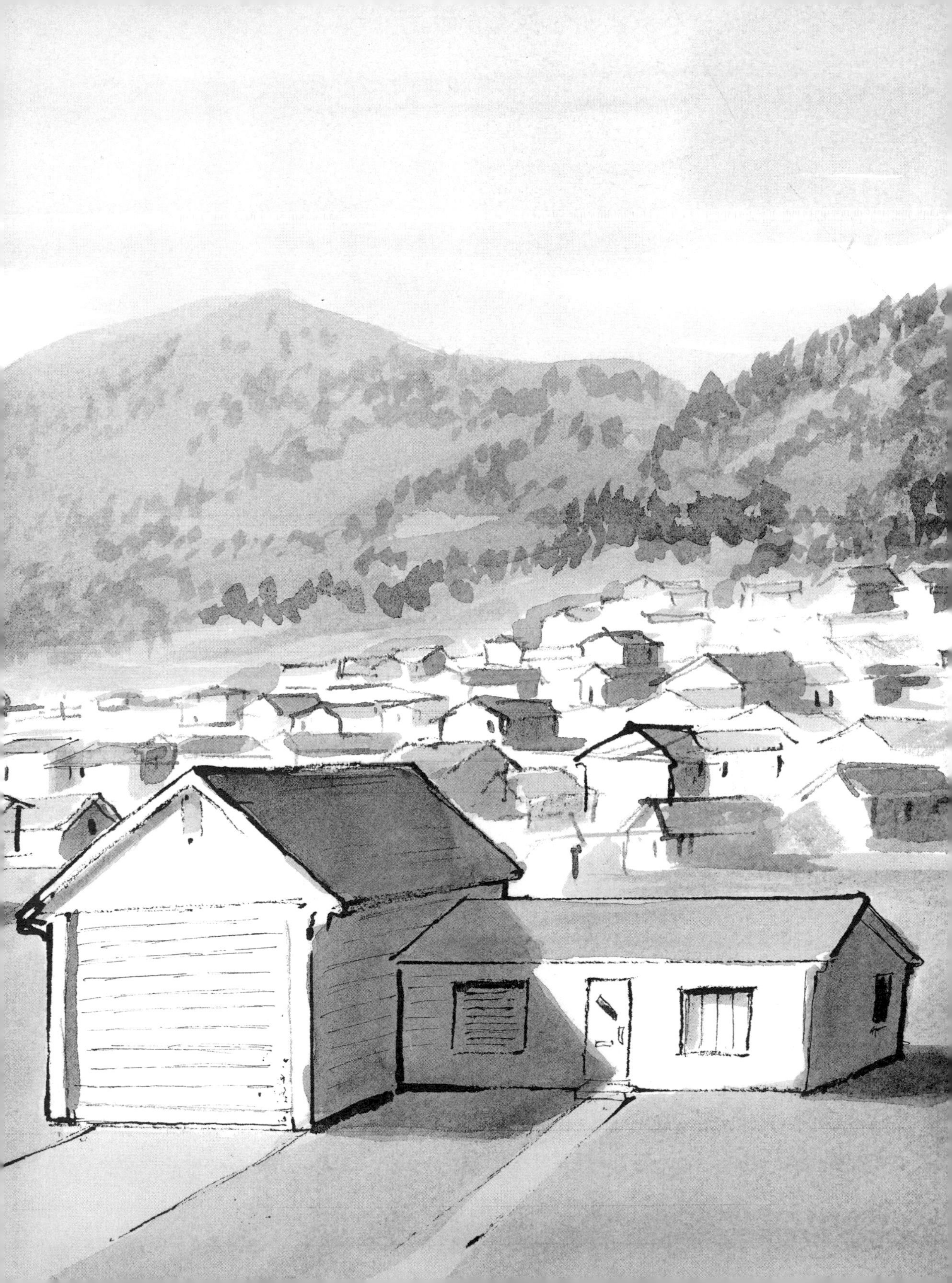

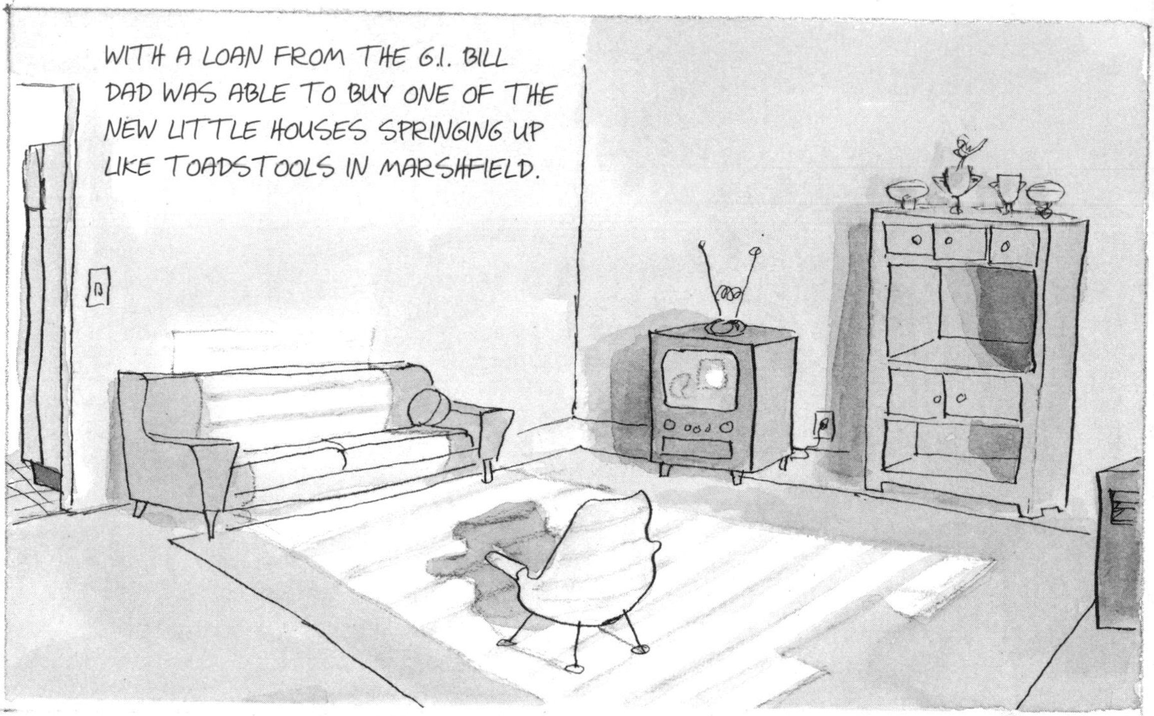
WITH A LOAN FROM THE G.I. BILL DAD WAS ABLE TO BUY ONE OF THE NEW LITTLE HOUSES SPRINGING UP LIKE TOADSTOOLS IN MARSHFIELD.

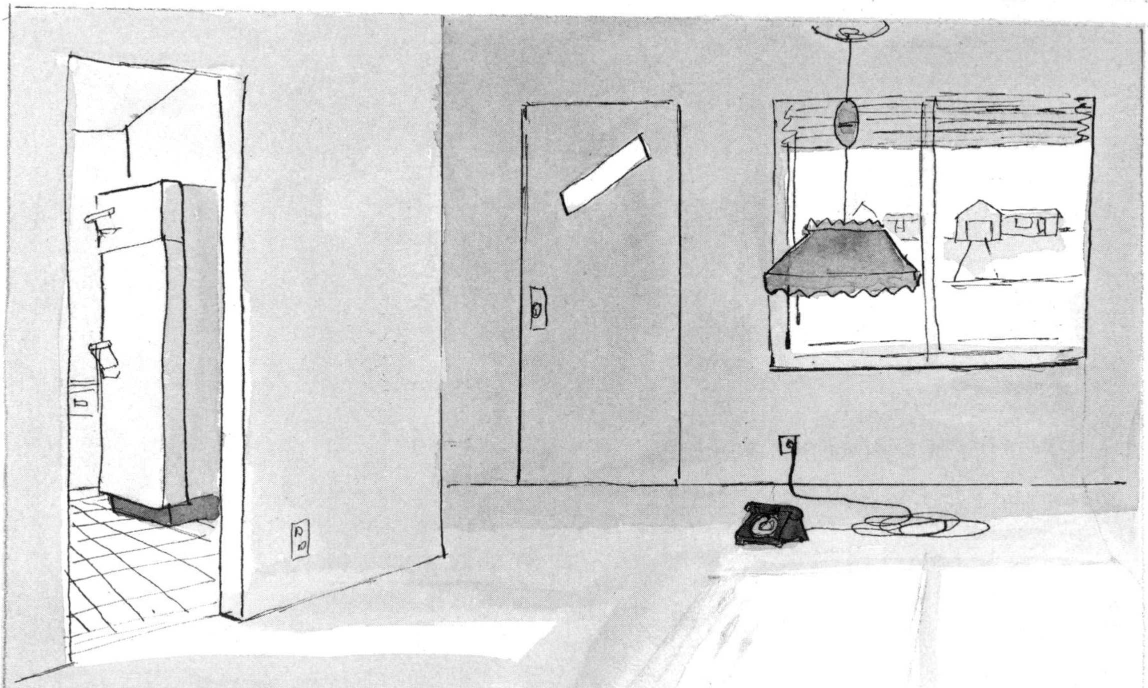

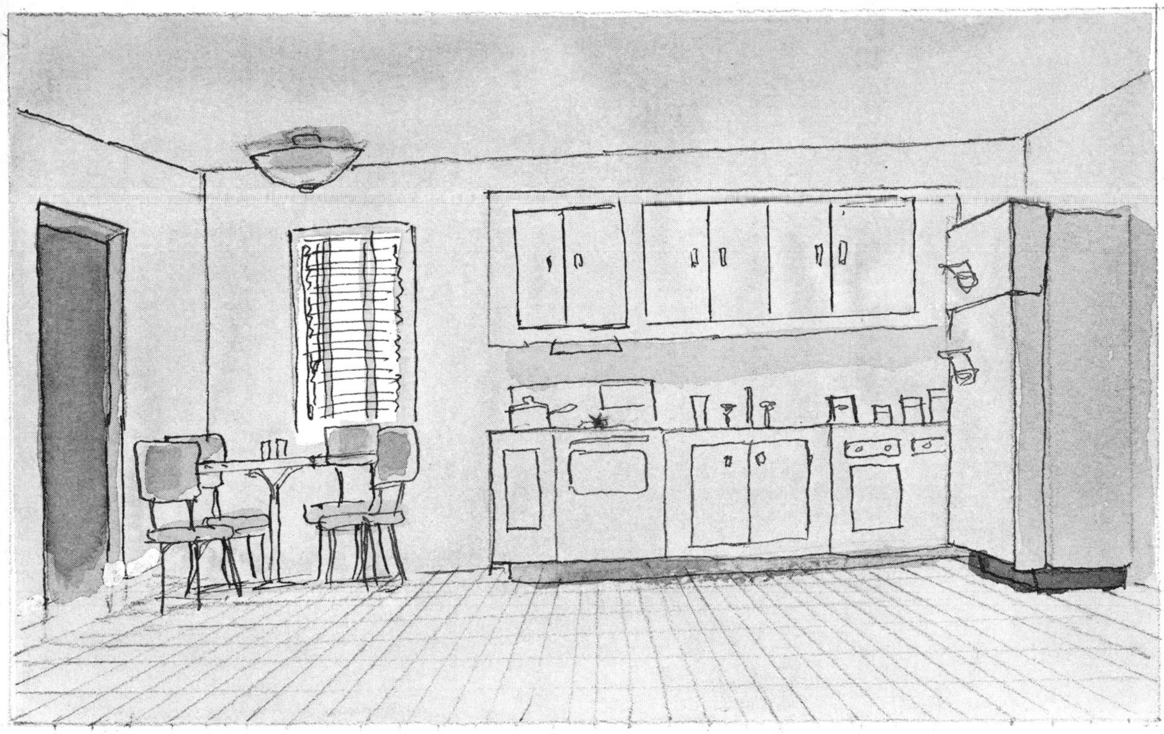

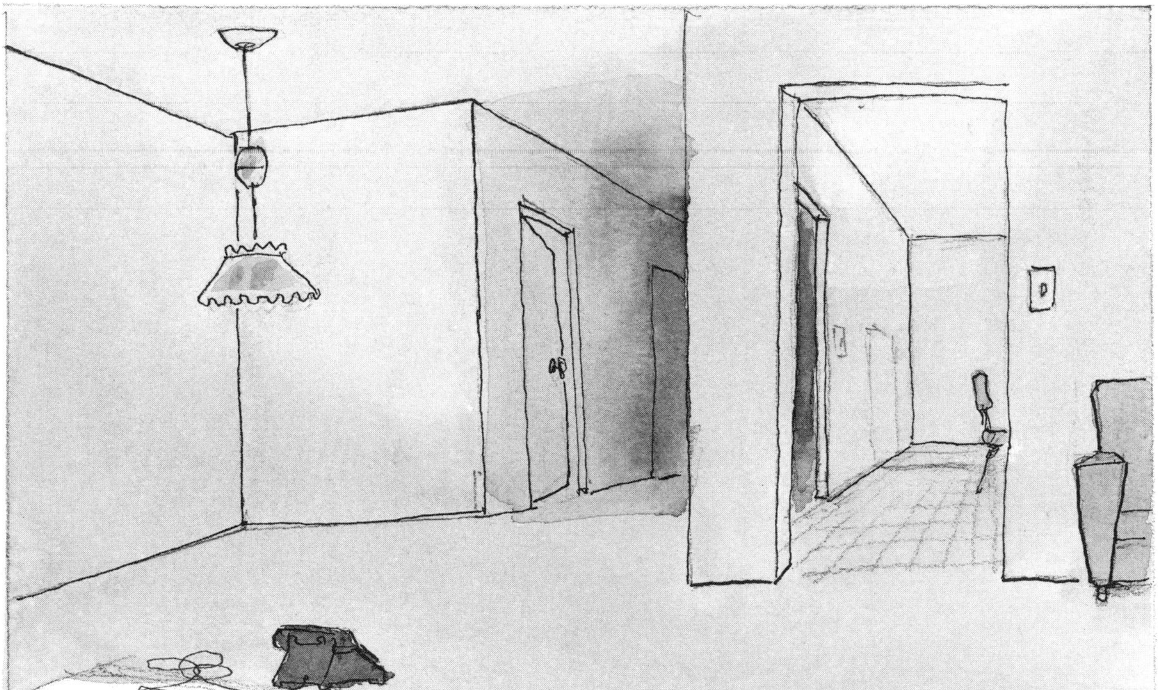

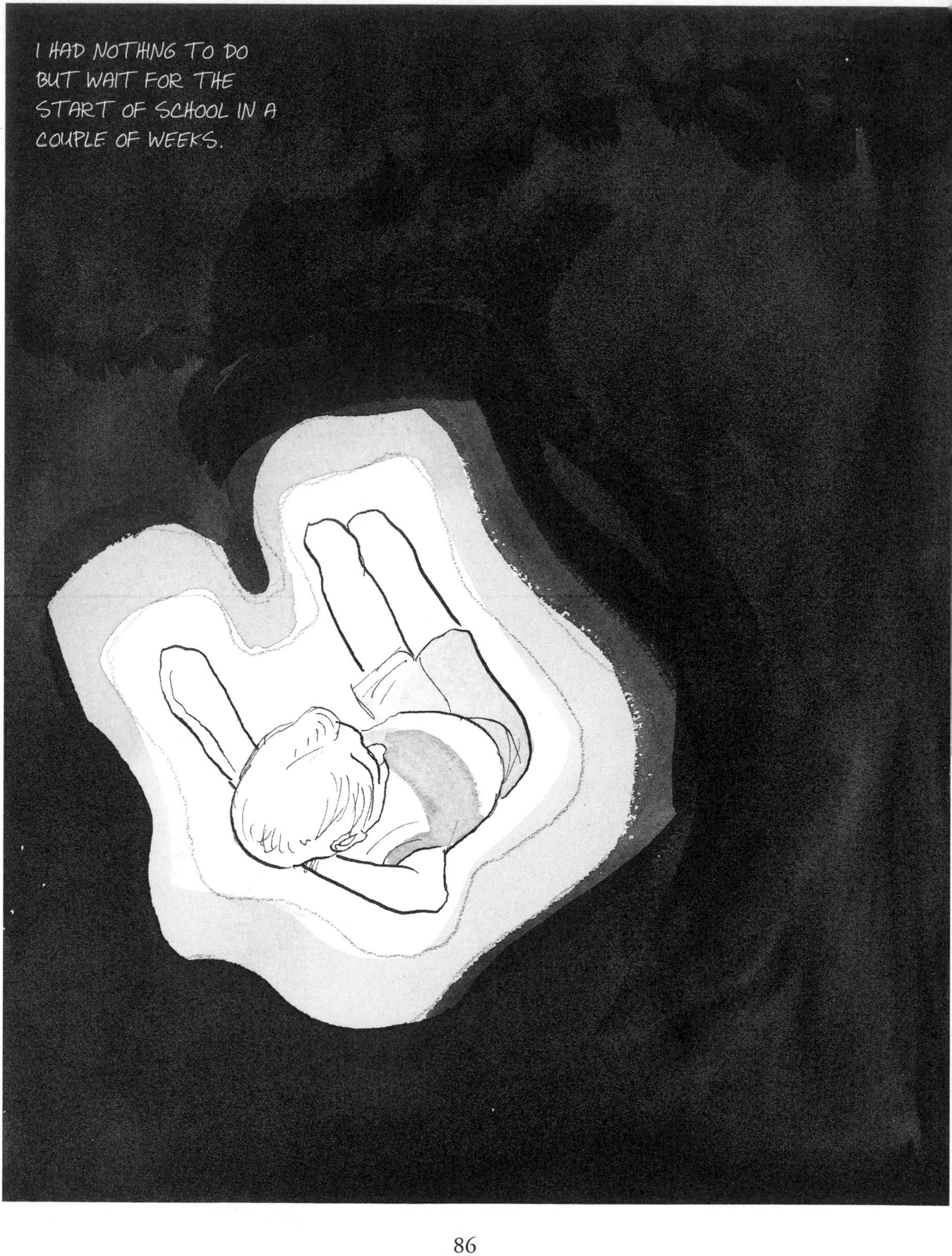
I HAD NOTHING TO DO BUT WAIT FOR THE START OF SCHOOL IN A COUPLE OF WEEKS.

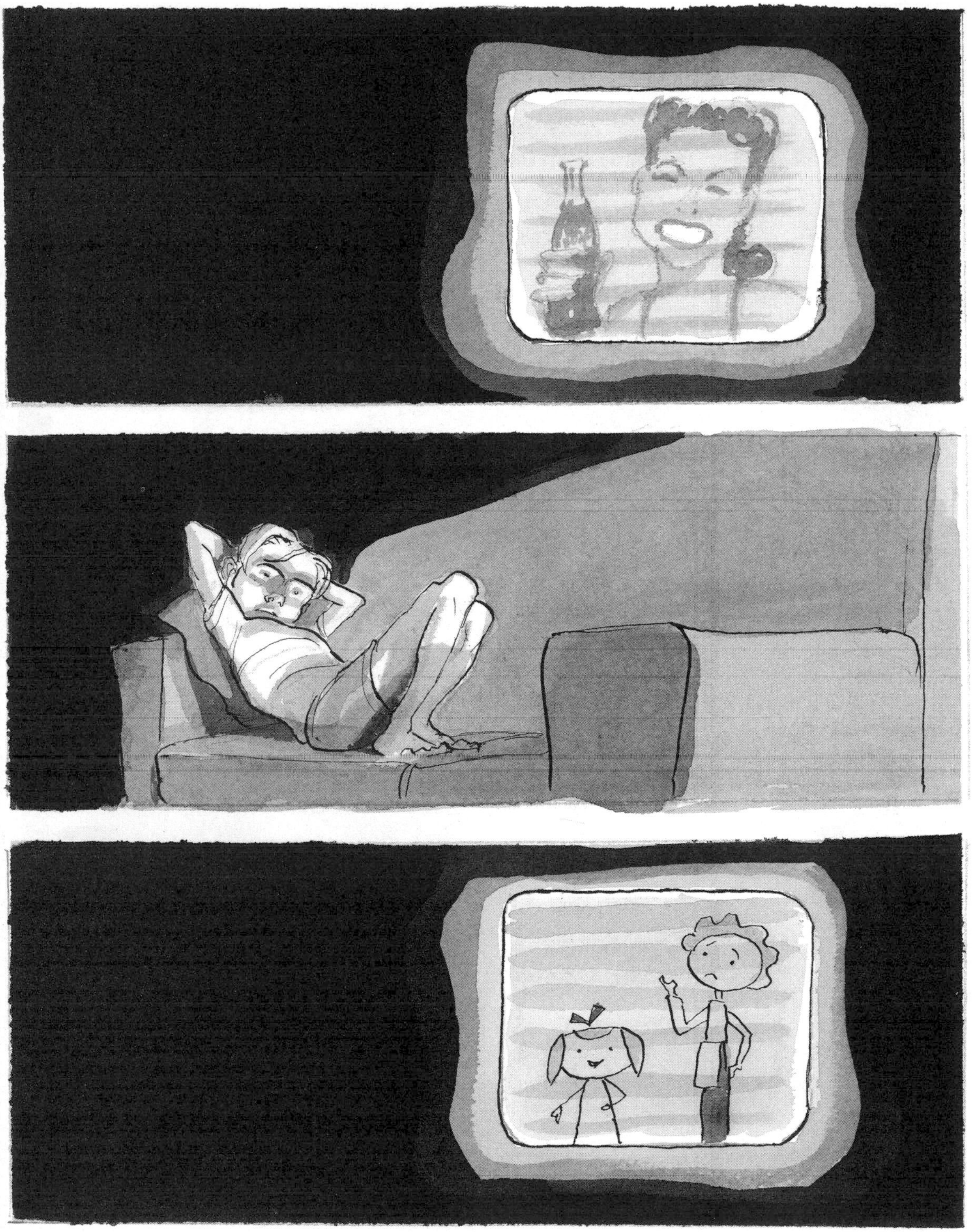

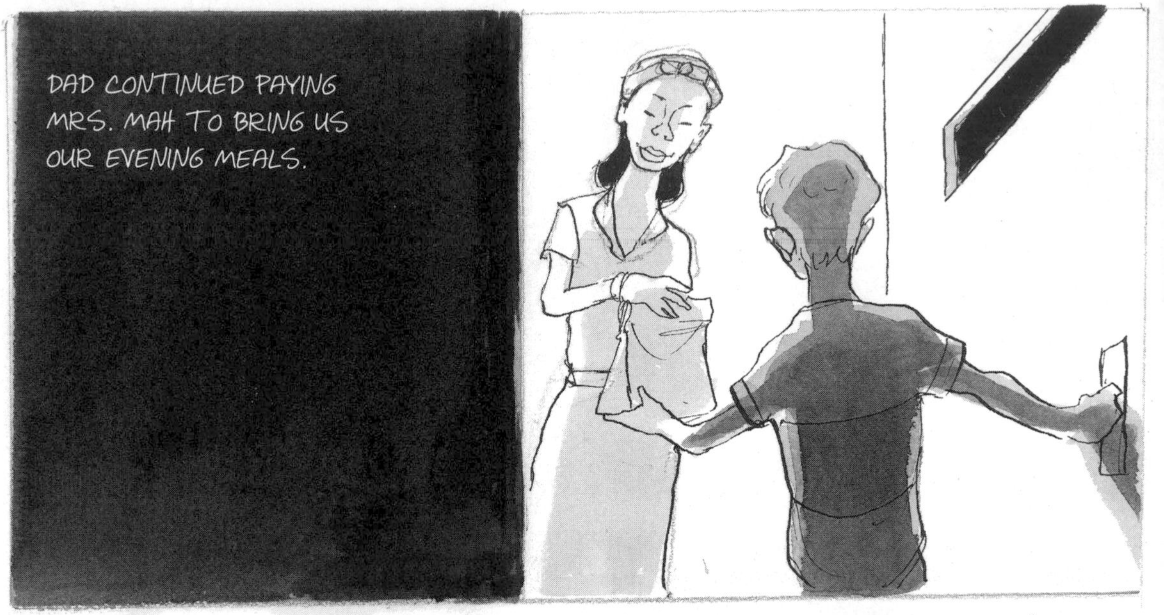
DAD CONTINUED PAYING MRS. MAH TO BRING US OUR EVENING MEALS.

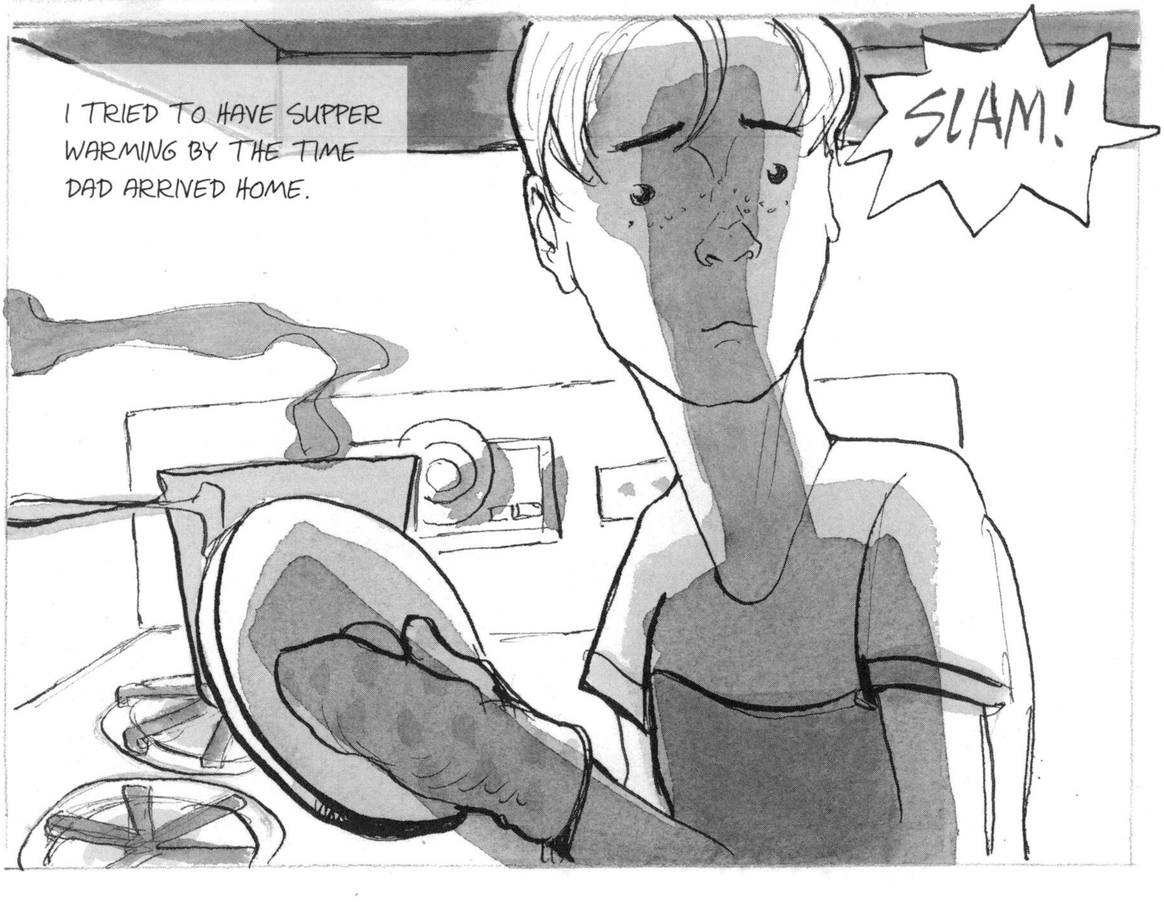
I TRIED TO HAVE SUPPER WARMING BY THE TIME DAD ARRIVED HOME.
SLAM!

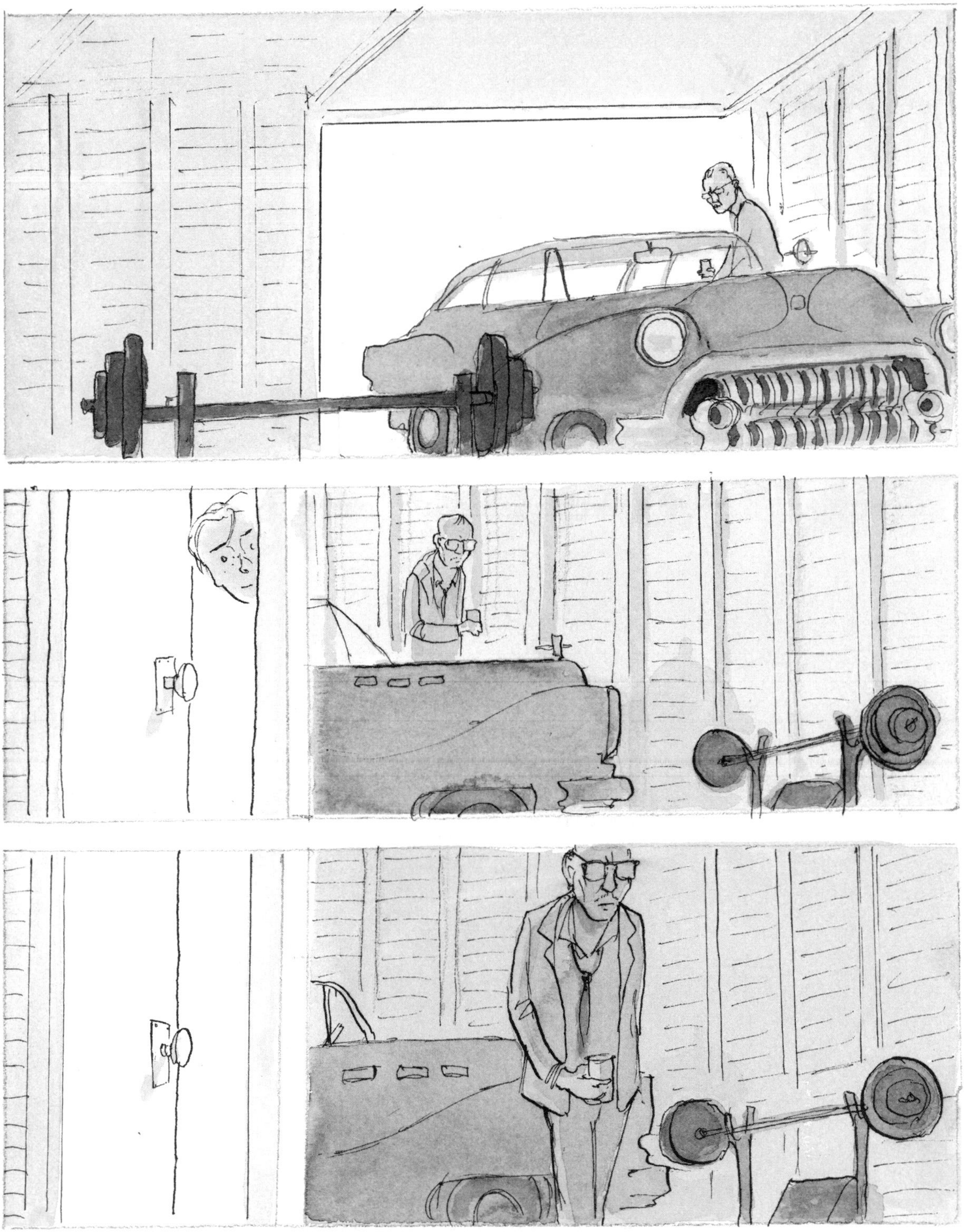

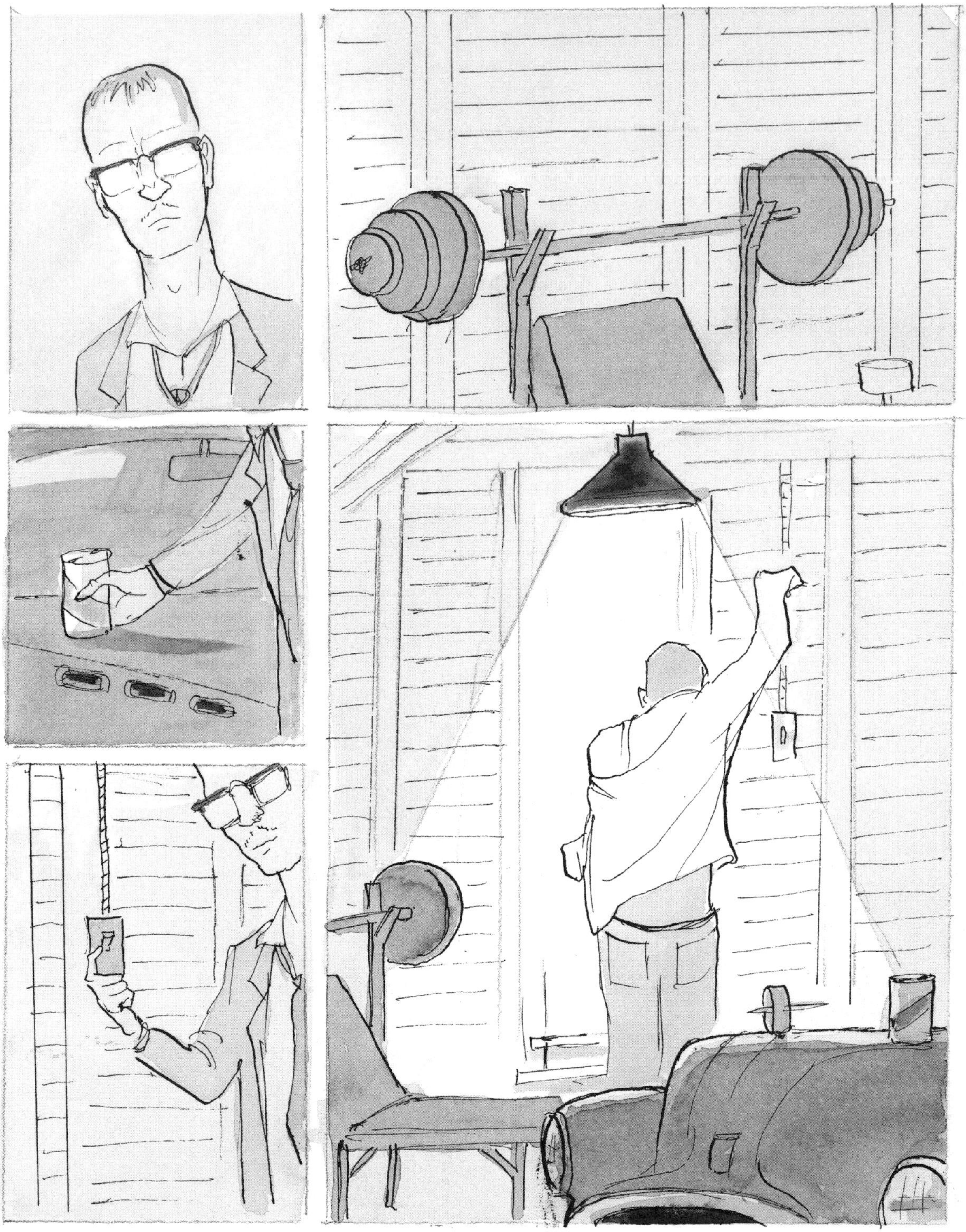

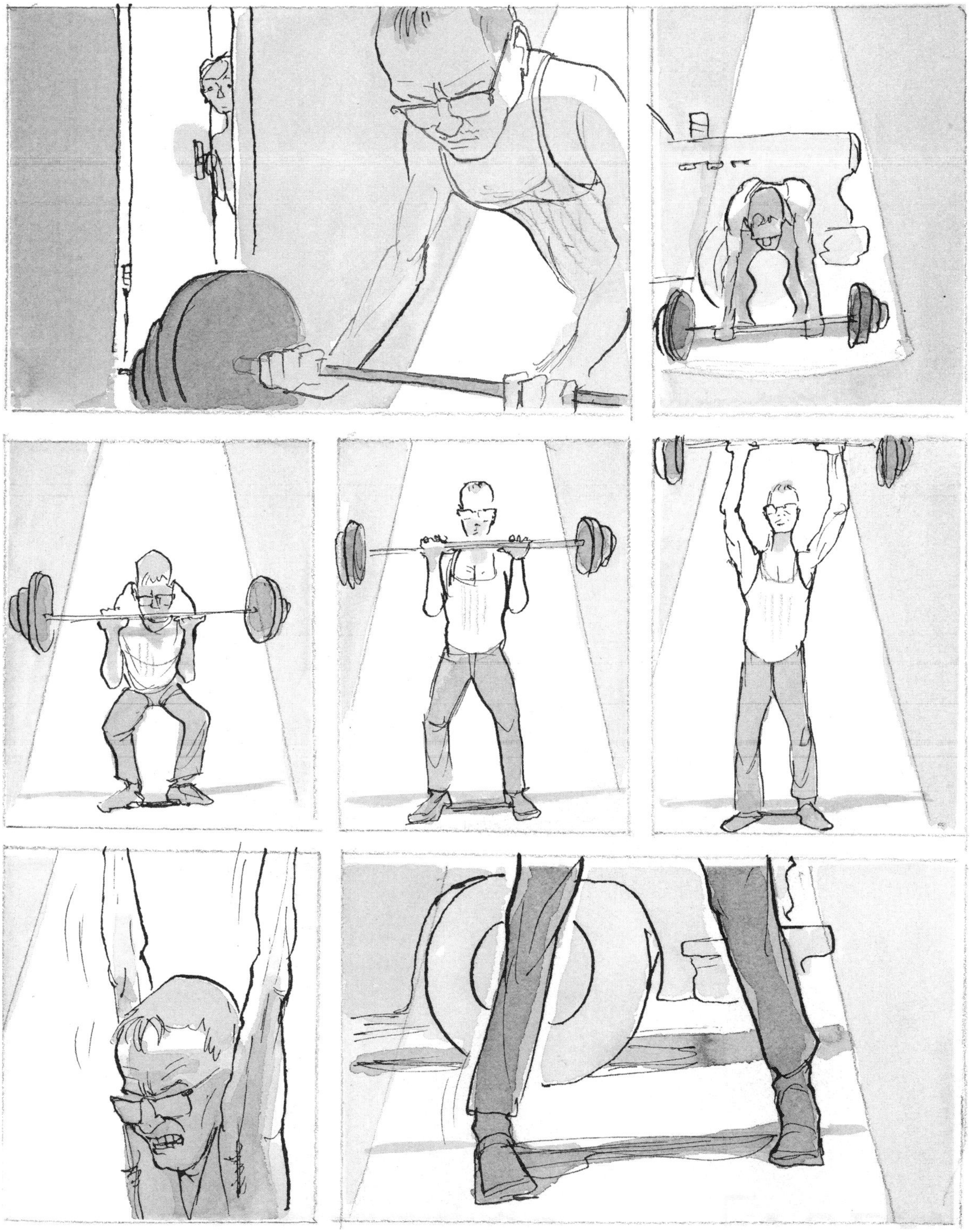

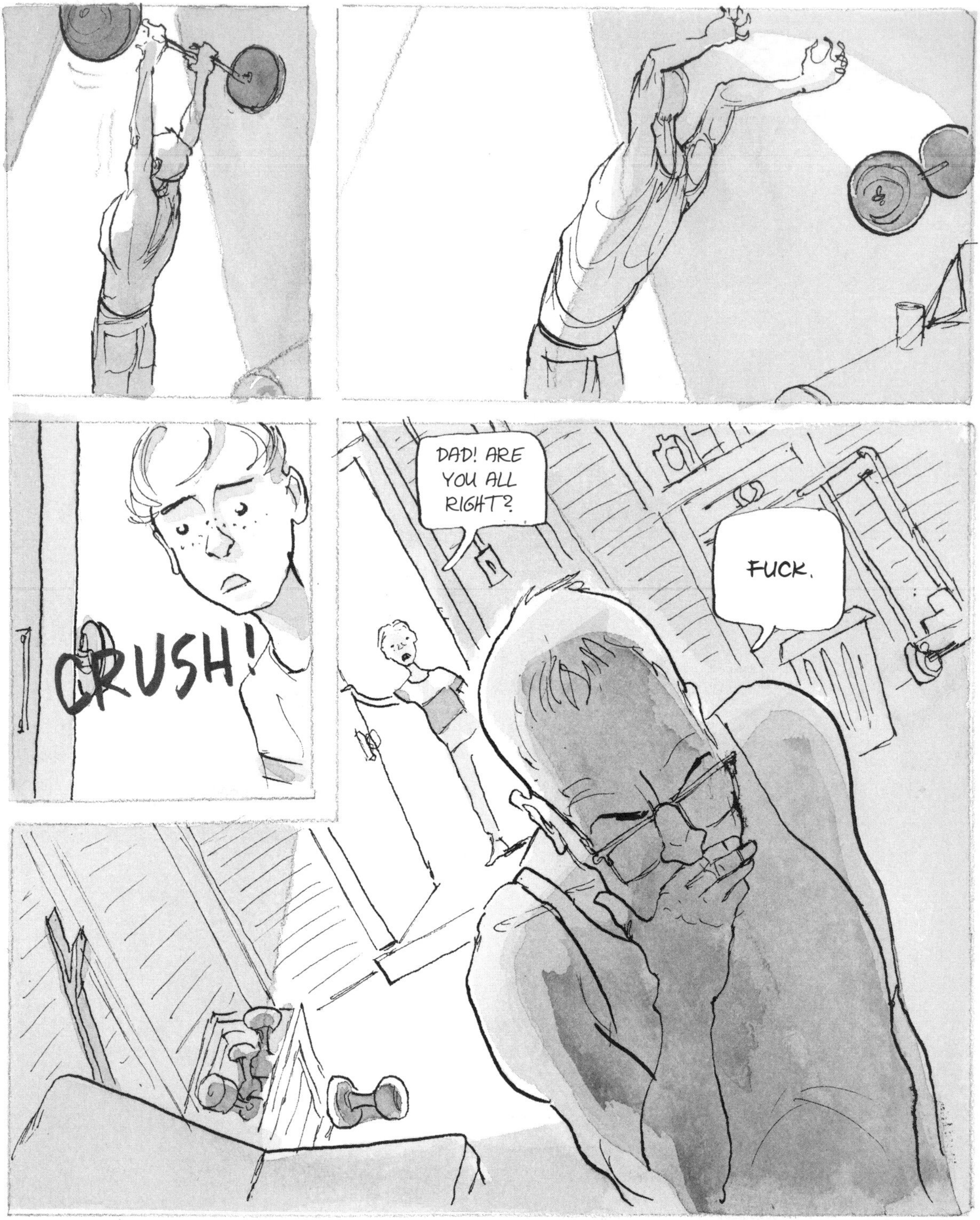
CRUSH!
DAD! ARE YOU ALL RIGHT?
FUCK.

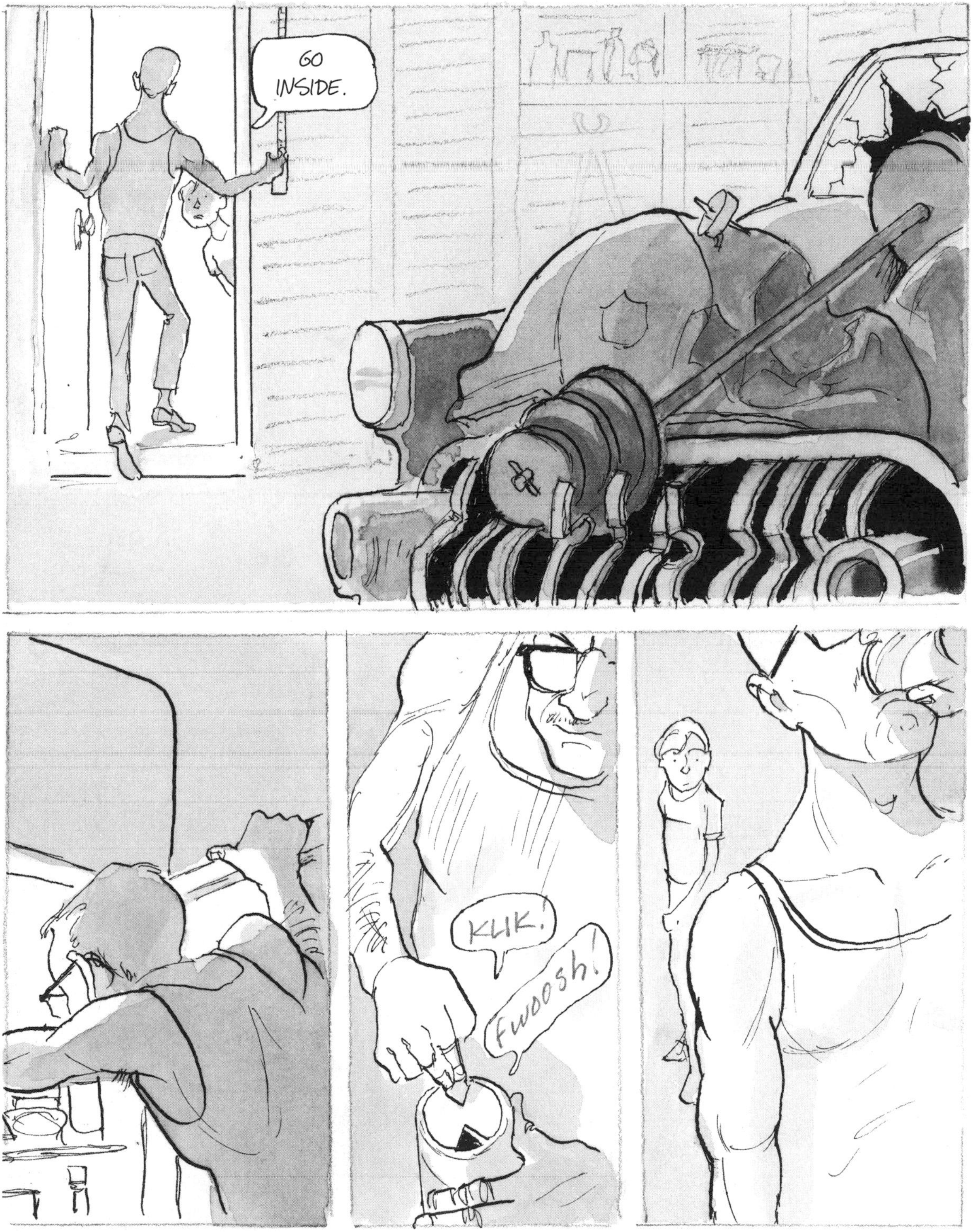
GO INSIDE.
KLIK!
Fwoosh!

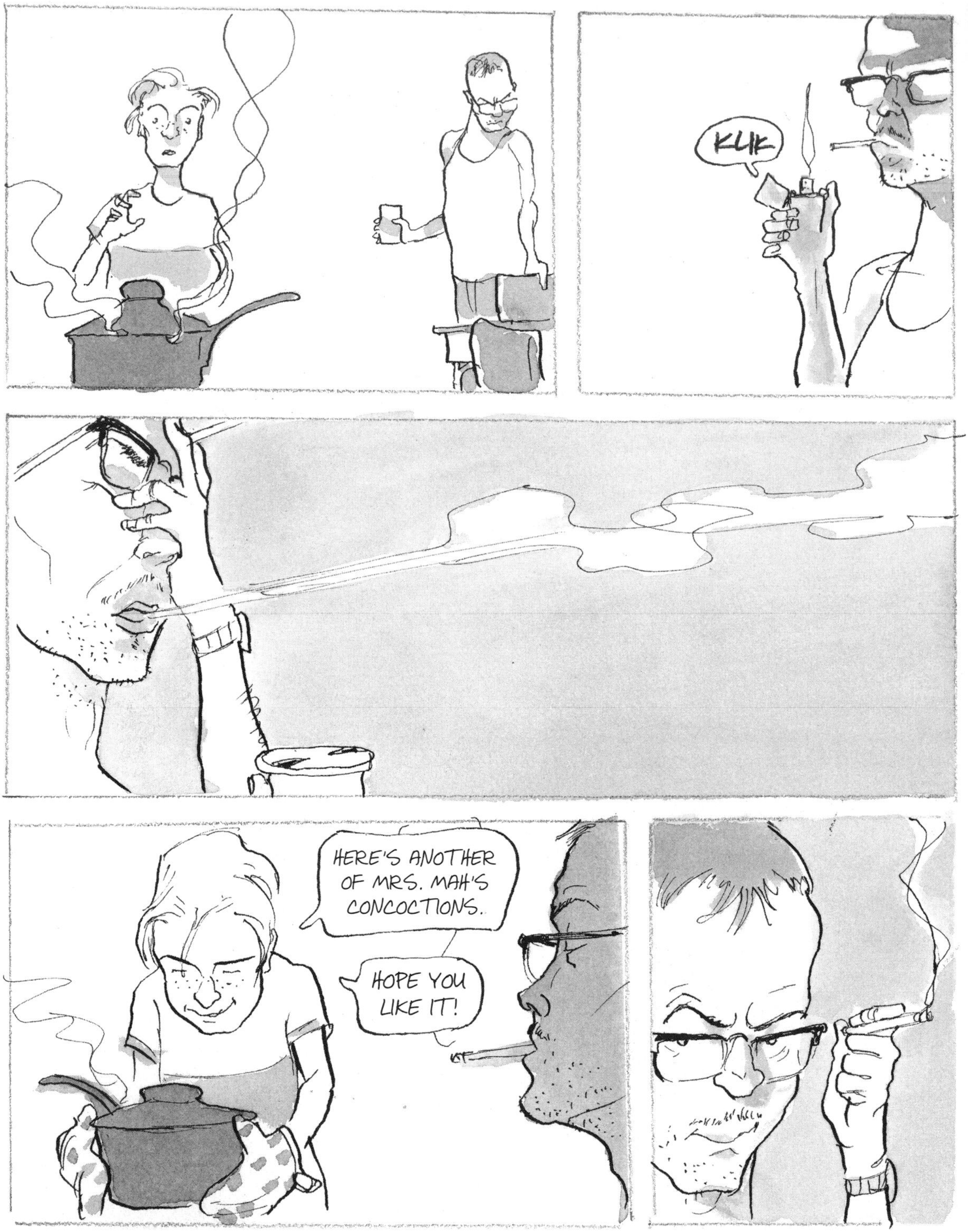
KLIK
HERE'S ANOTHER OF MRS. MAH'S CONCOCTIONS.
HOPE YOU LIKE IT!

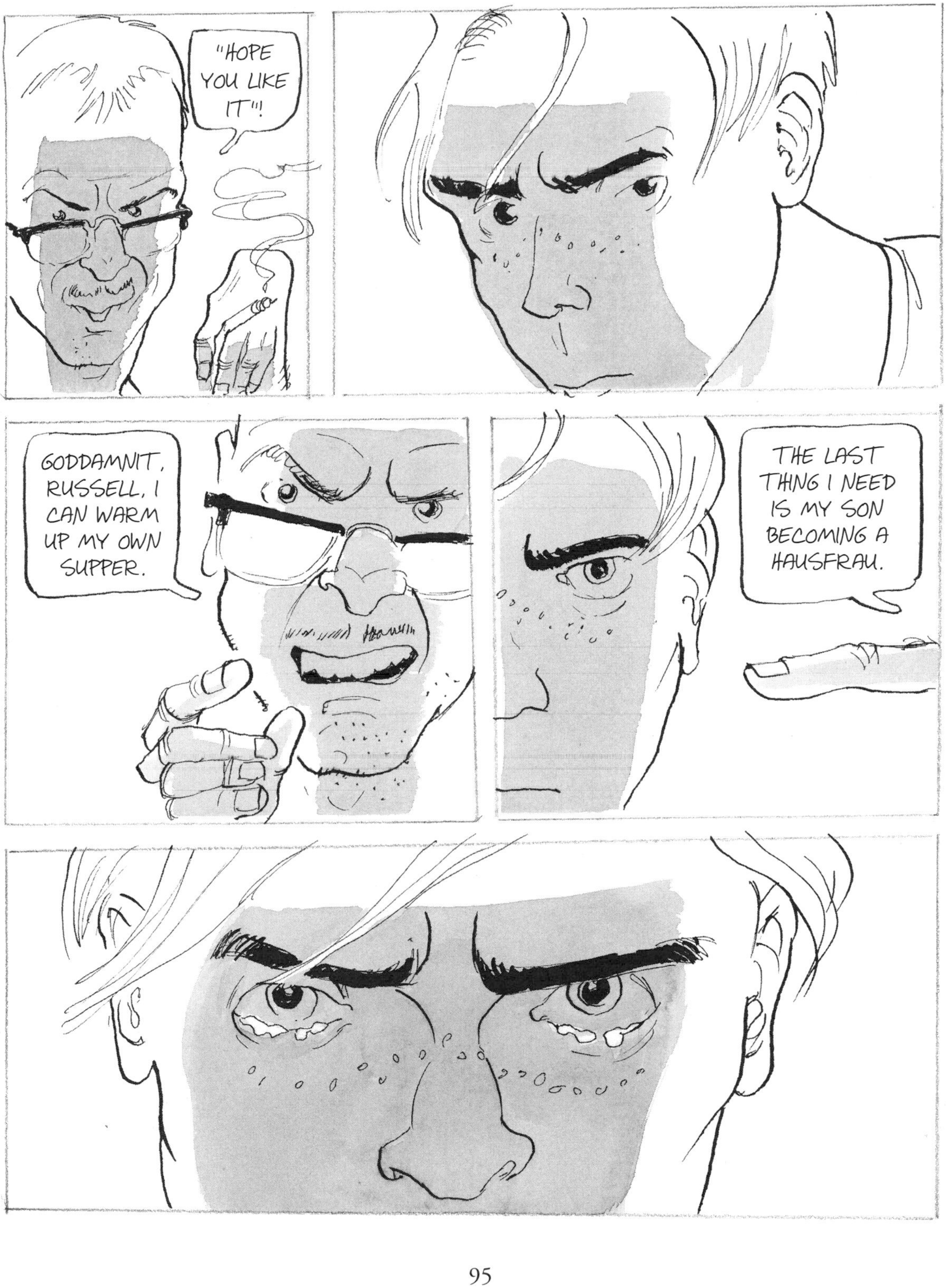
"HOPE YOU LIKE IT"!
GODDAMNIT, RUSSELL, I CAN WARM UP MY OWN SUPPER.
THE LAST THING I NEED IS MY SON BECOMING A HAUSFRAU.

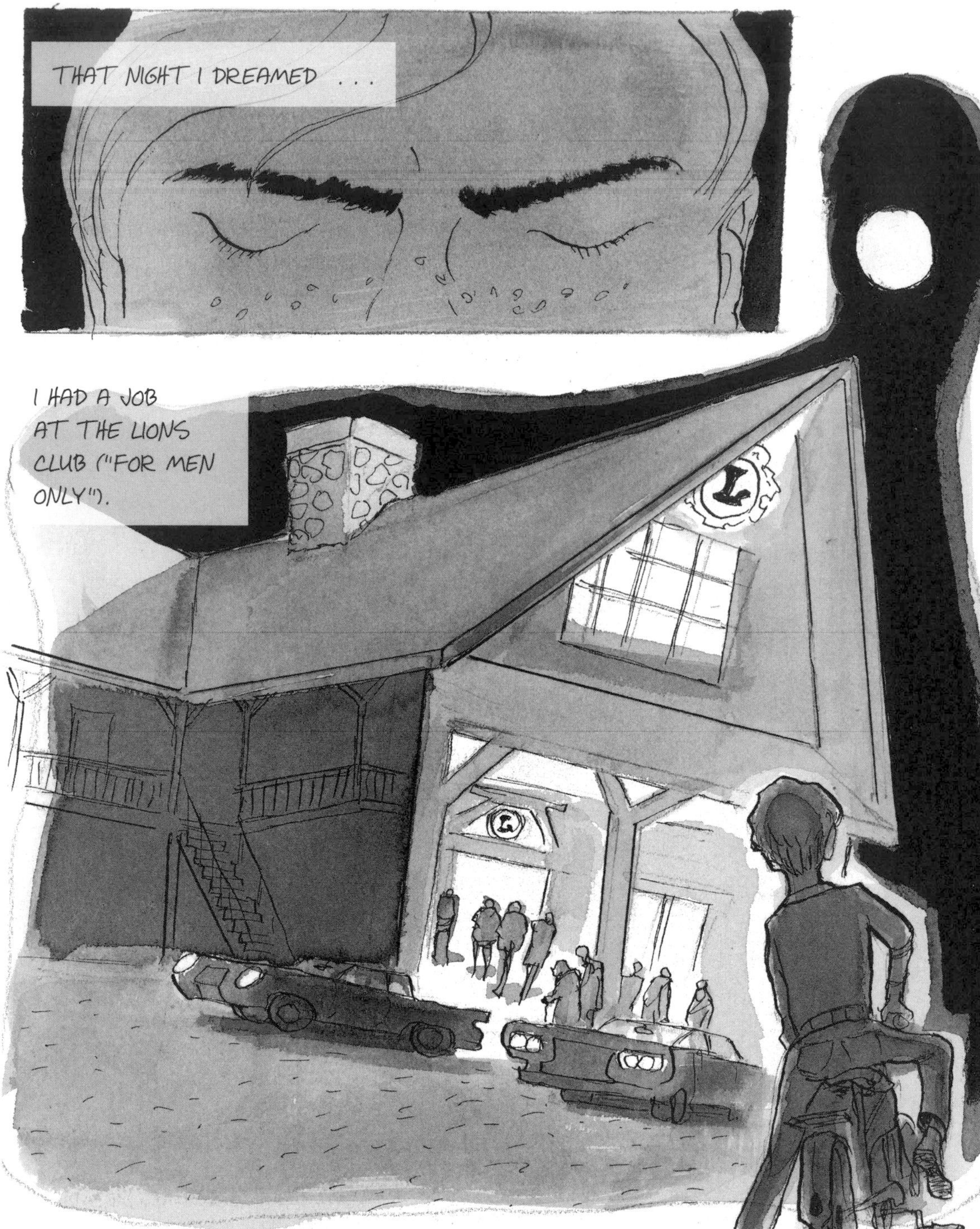
THAT NIGHT I DREAMED . . .
I HAD A JOB AT THE LIONS CLUB ("FOR MEN ONLY").

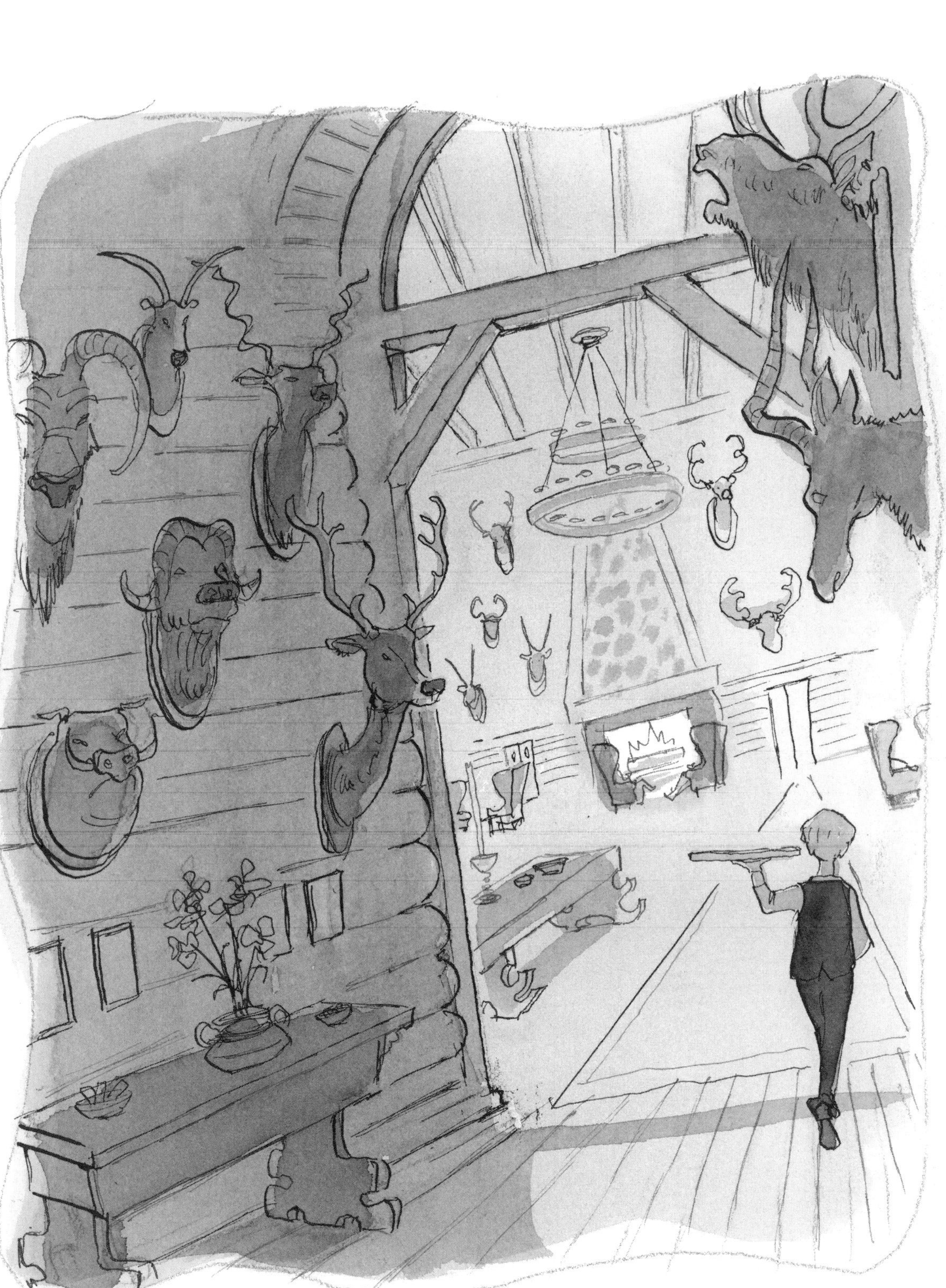

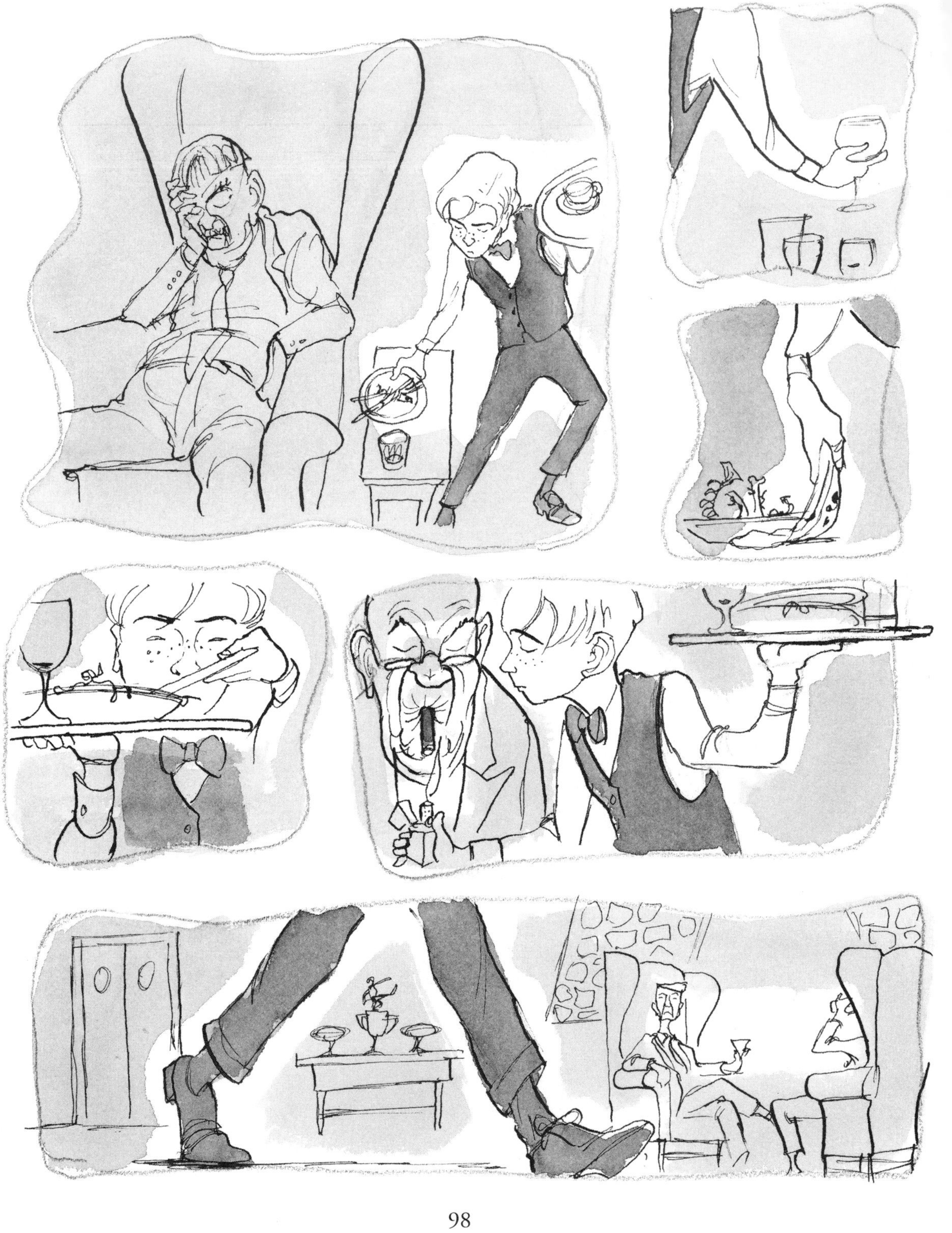

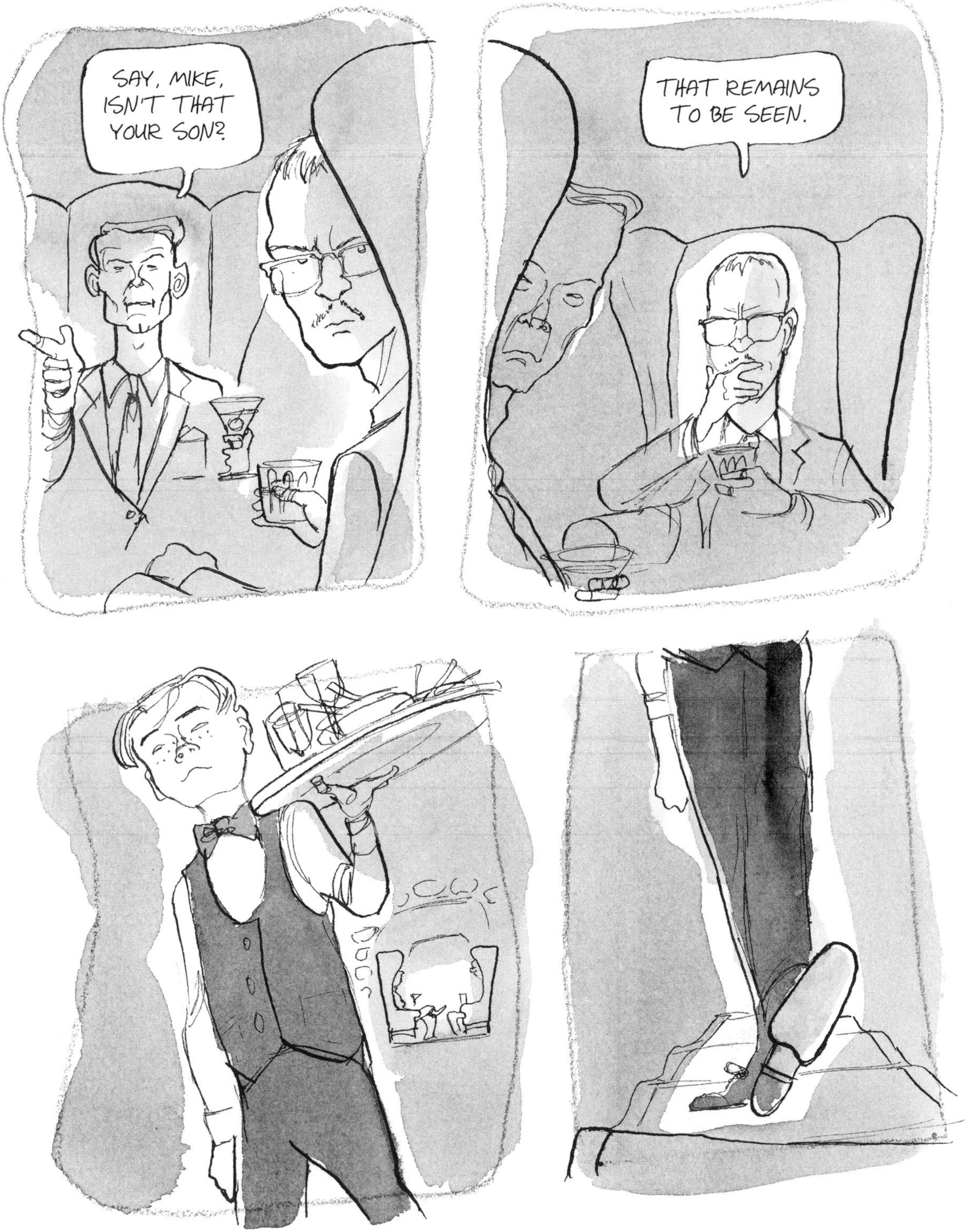
SAY, MIKE, ISN'T THAT YOUR SON?
THAT REMAINS TO BE SEEN.

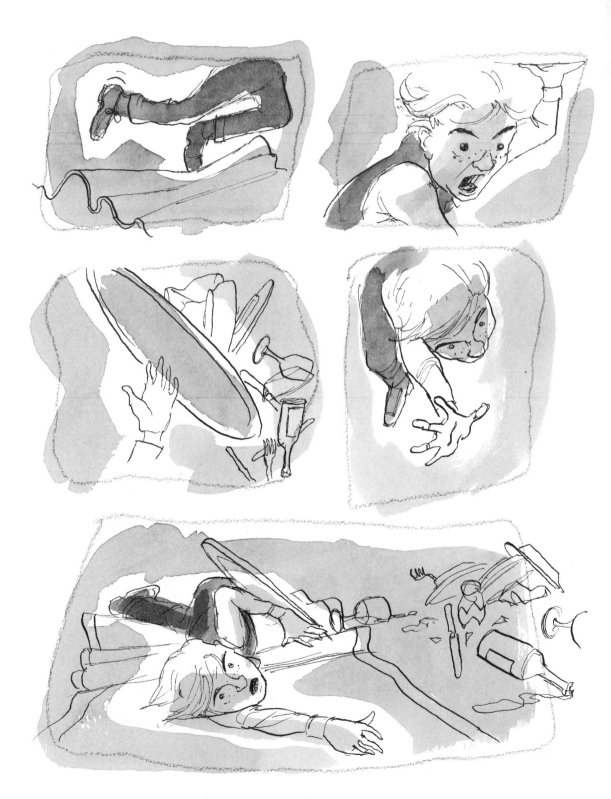

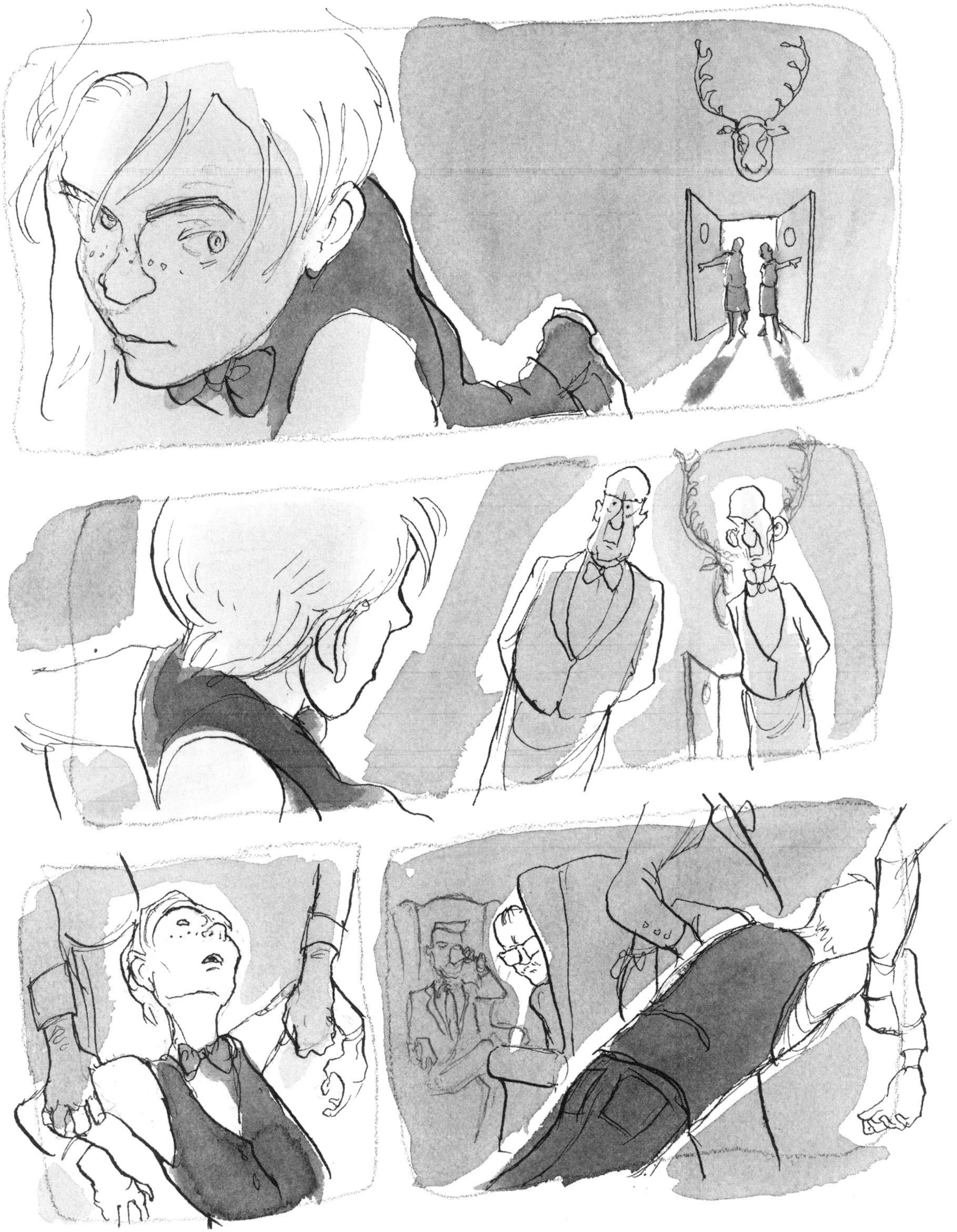

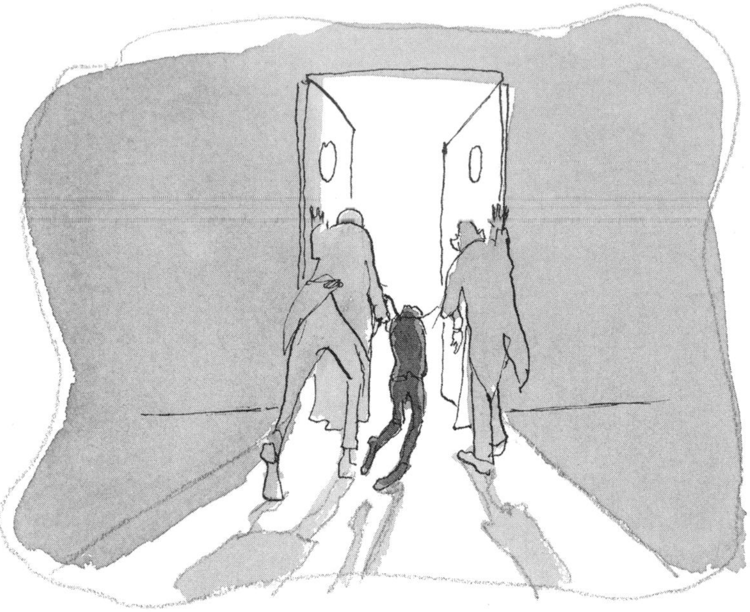

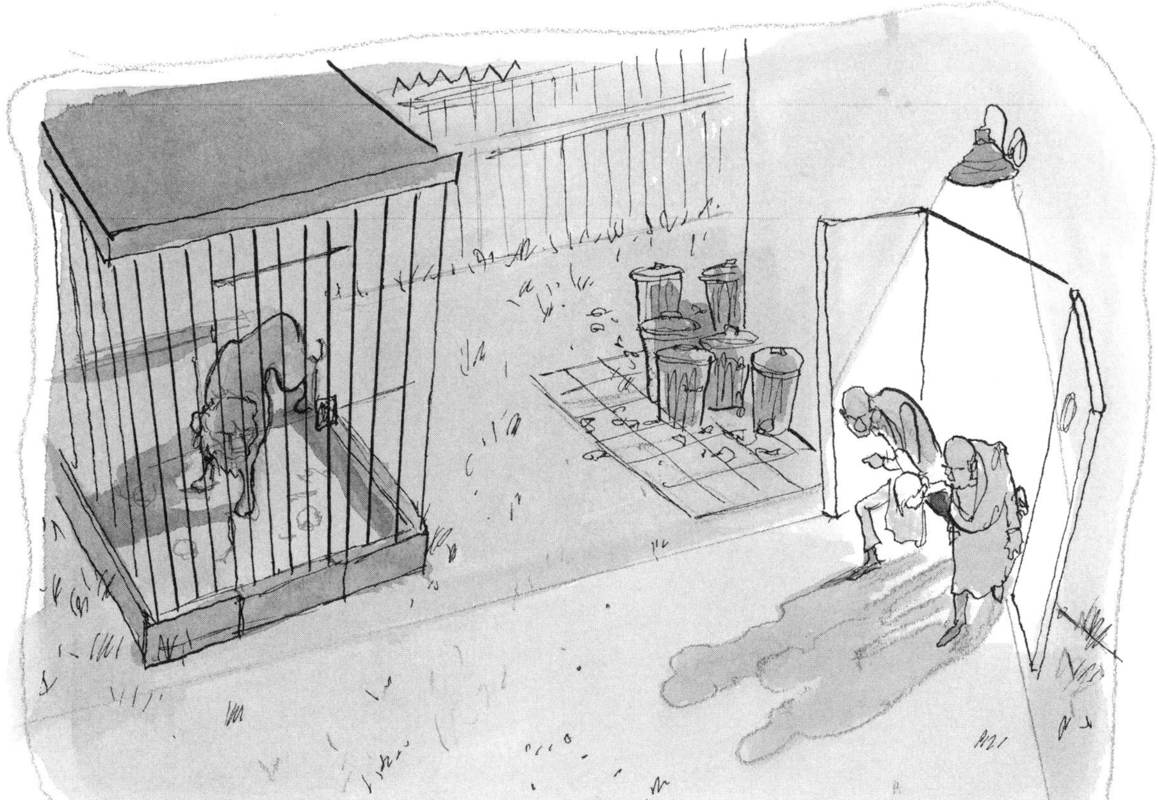

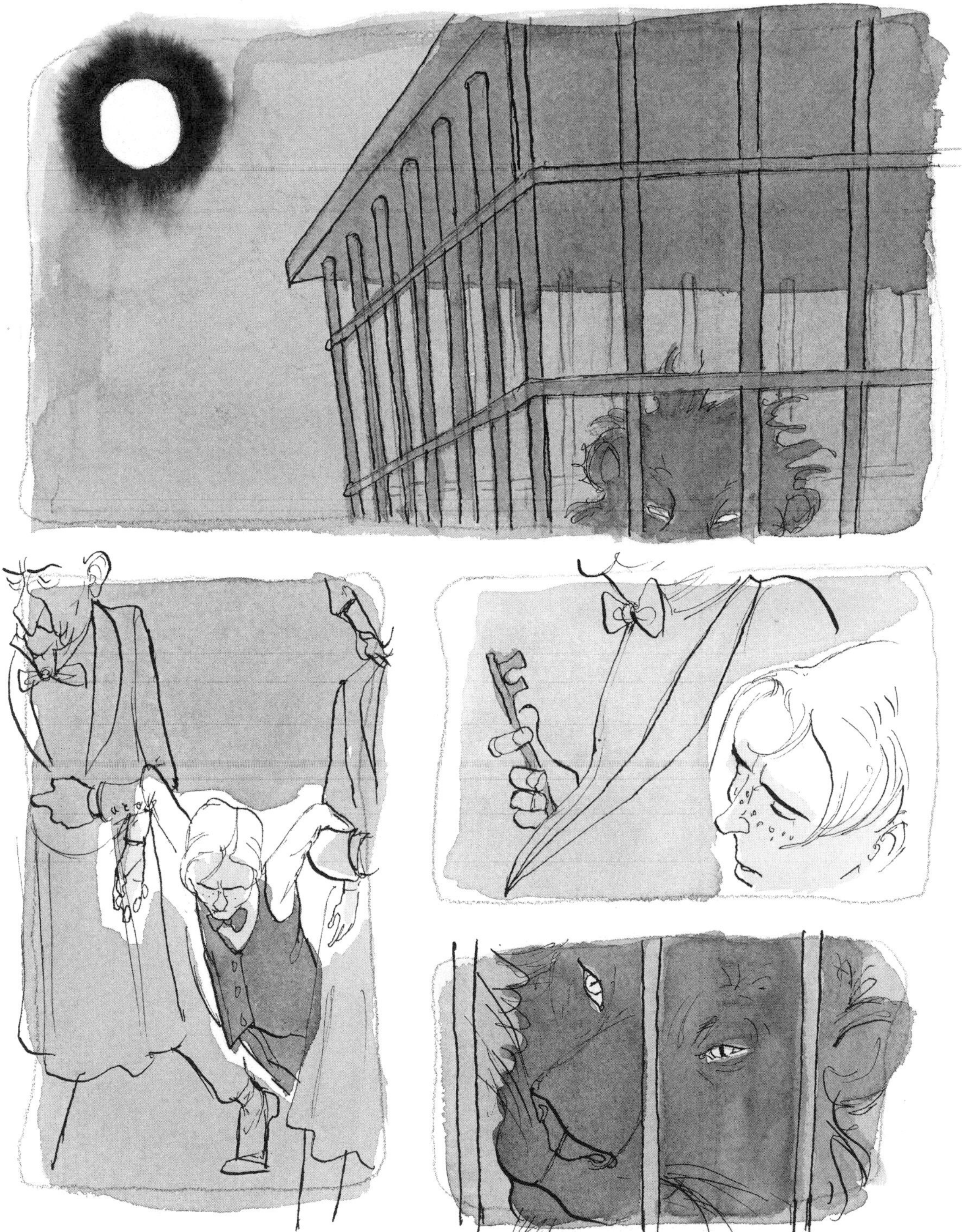

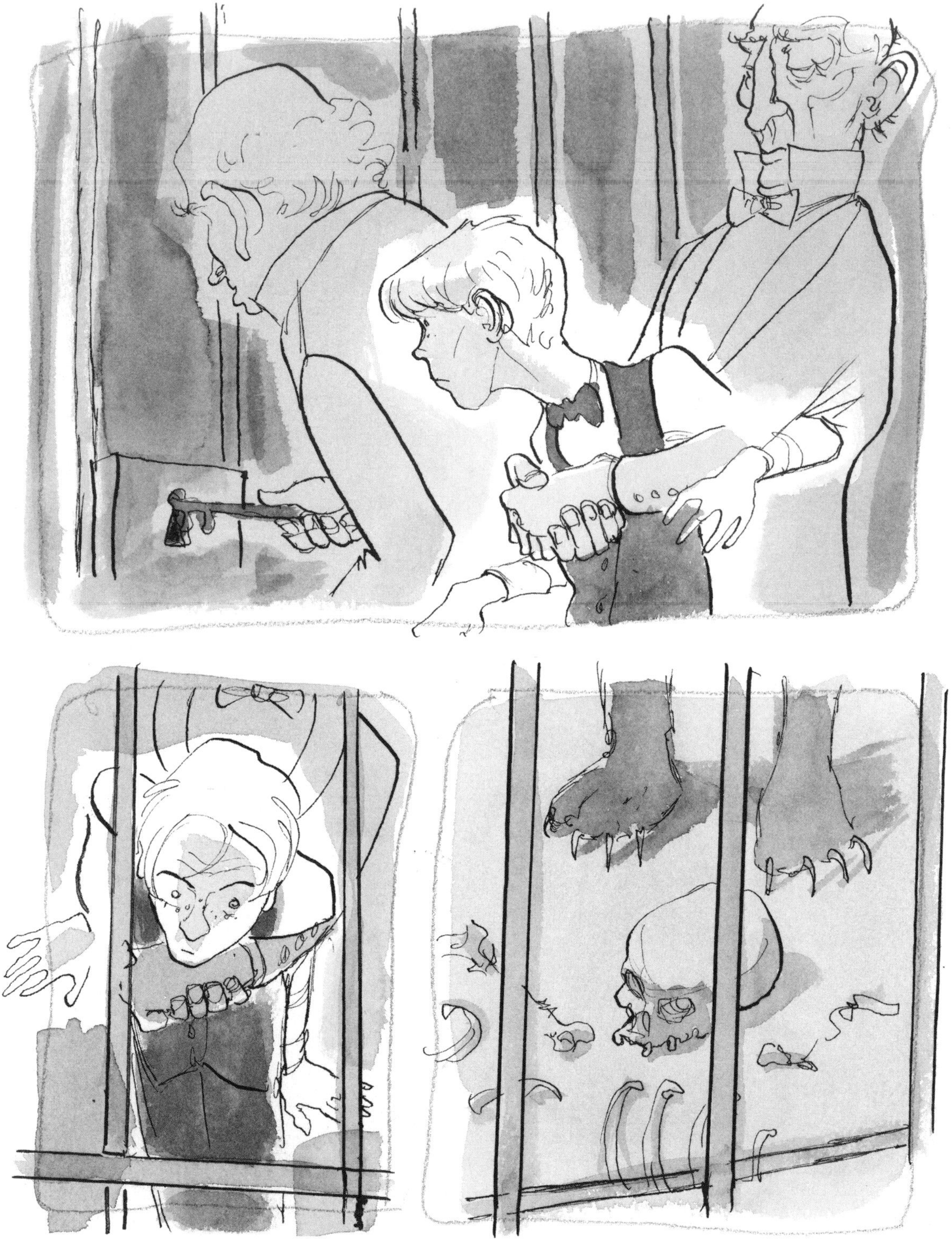

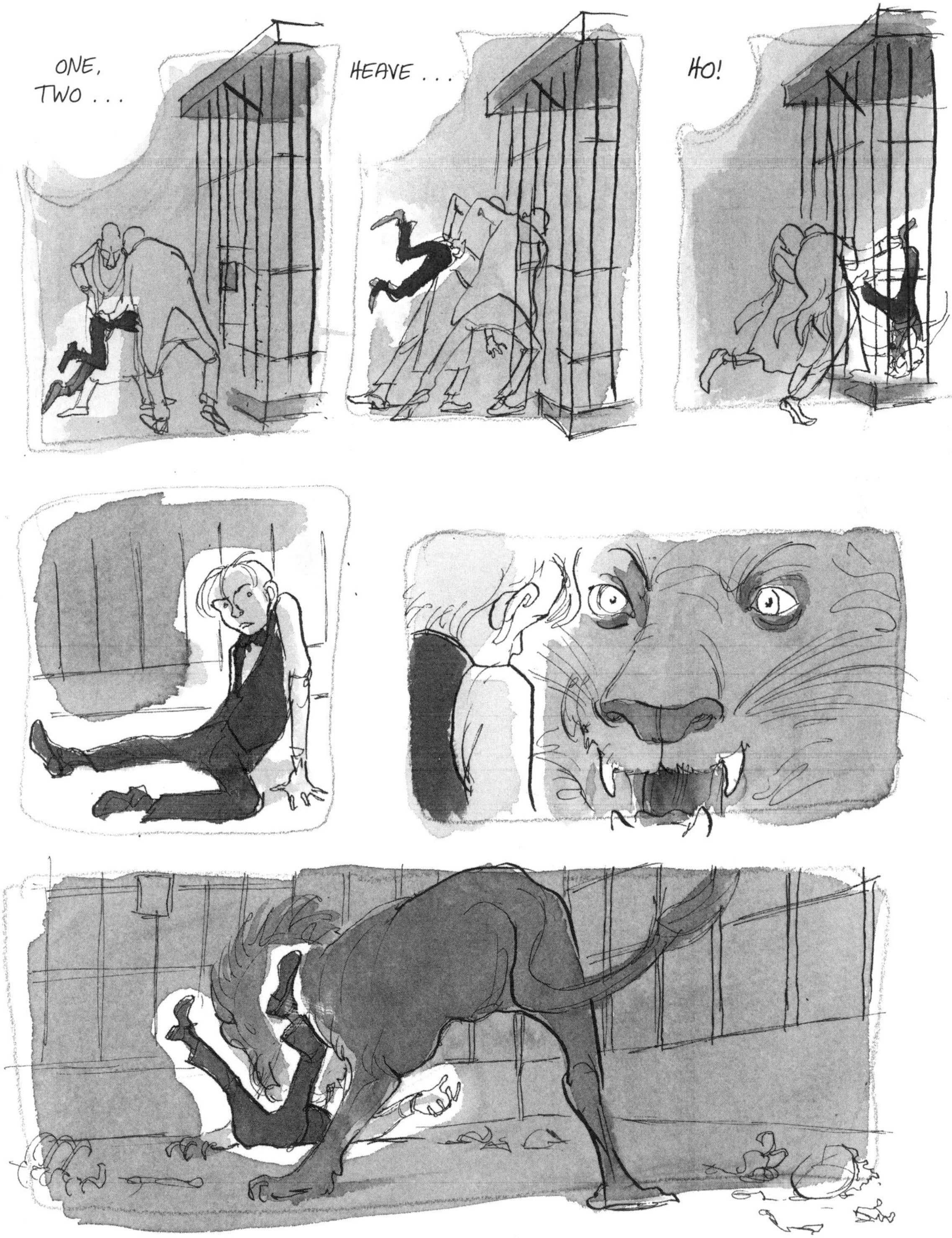
ONE, TWO . . .
HEAVE . . .
HO!

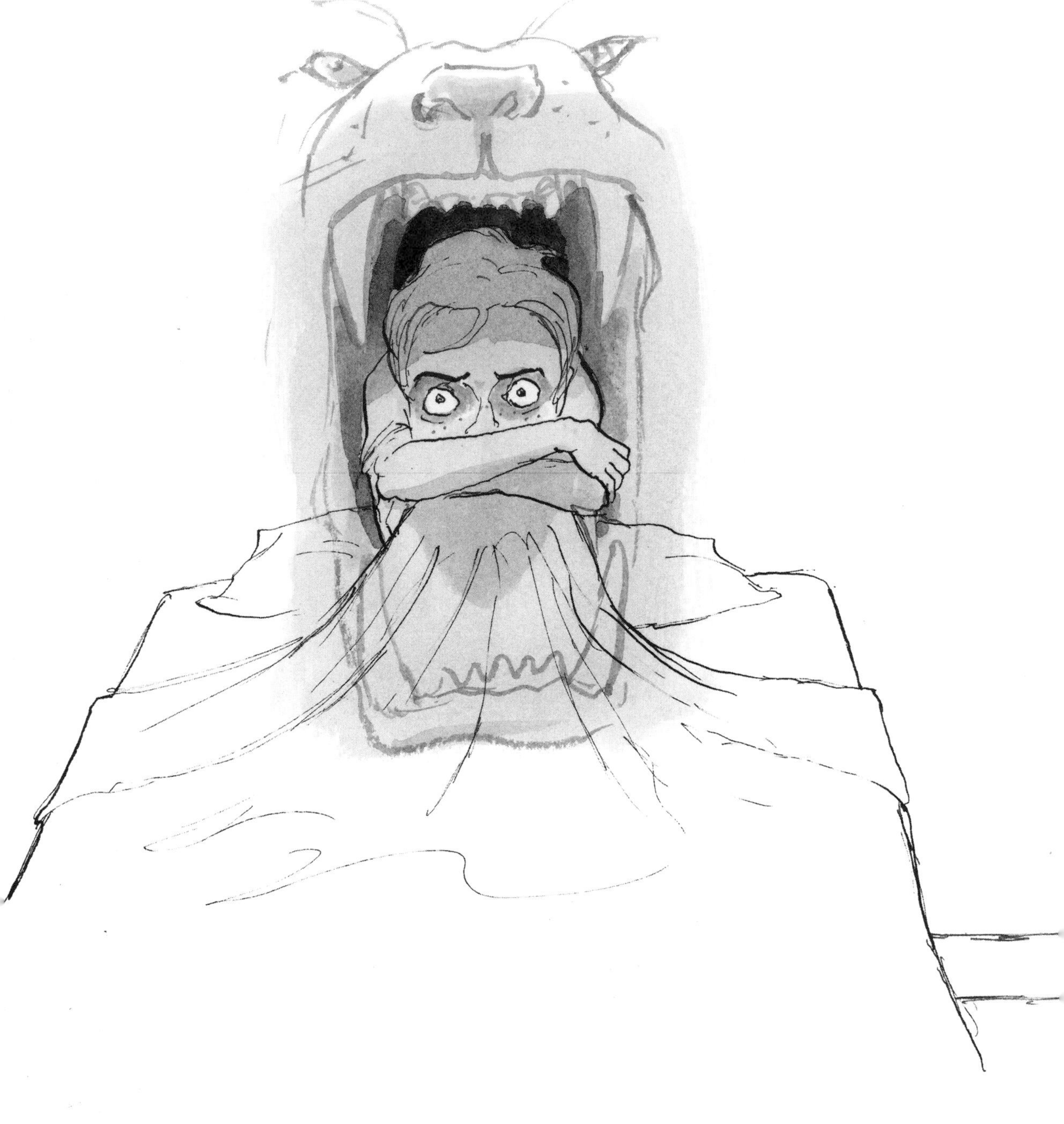

CHAPTER FIVE

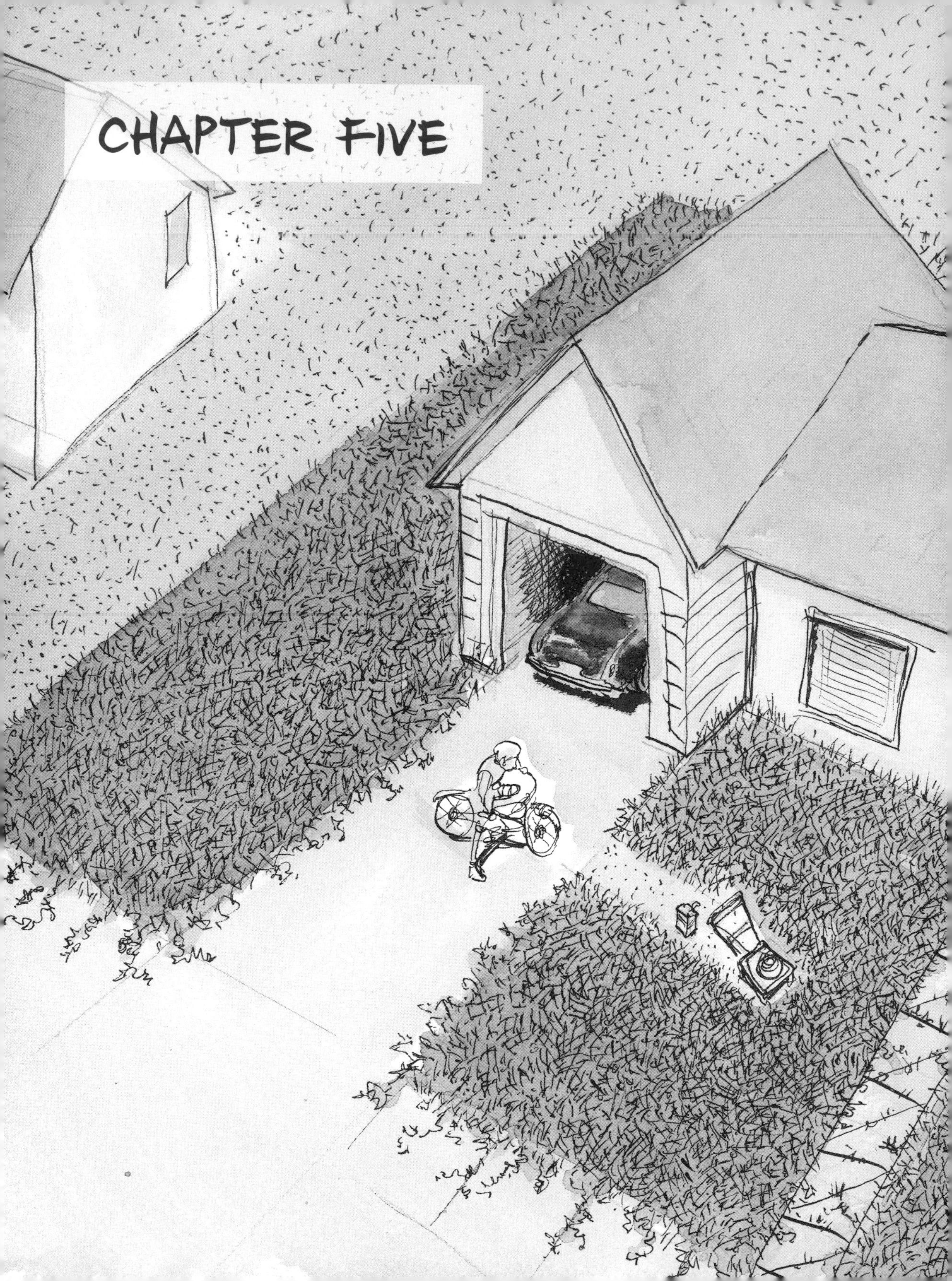

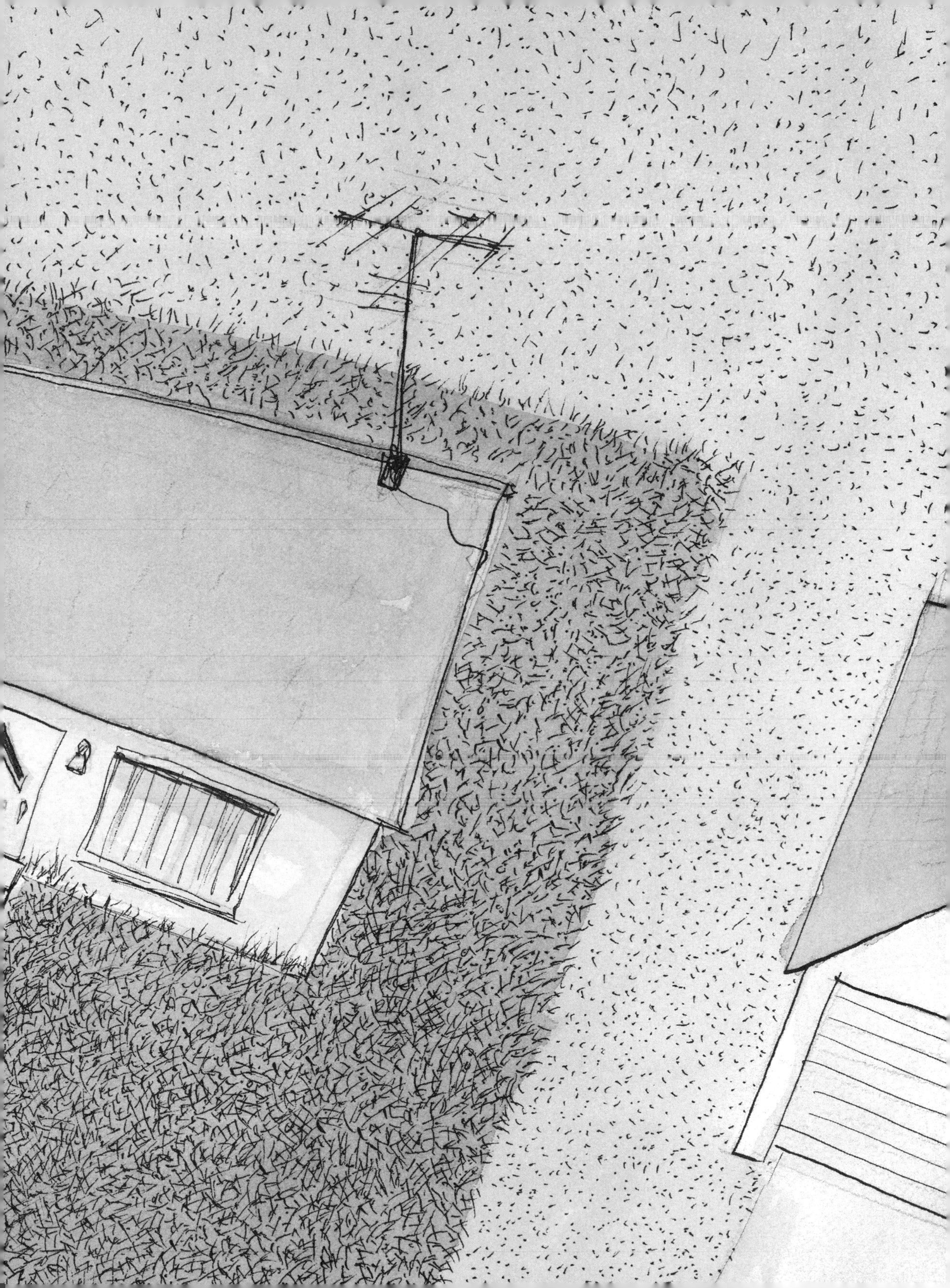

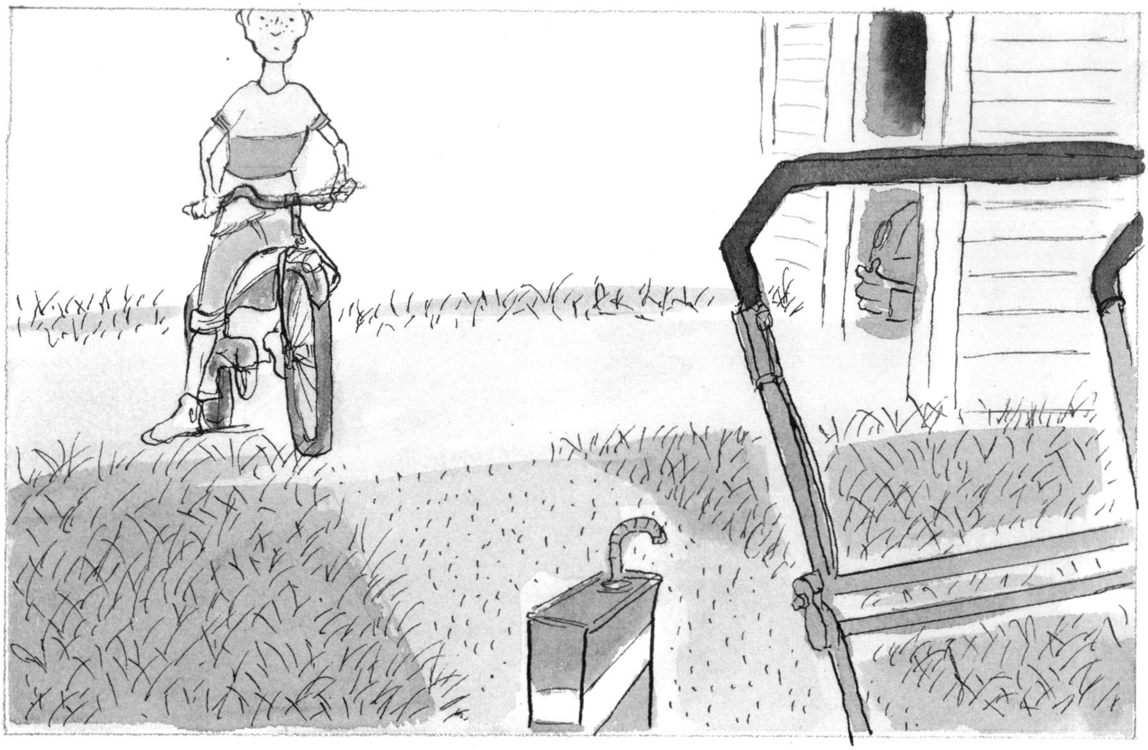

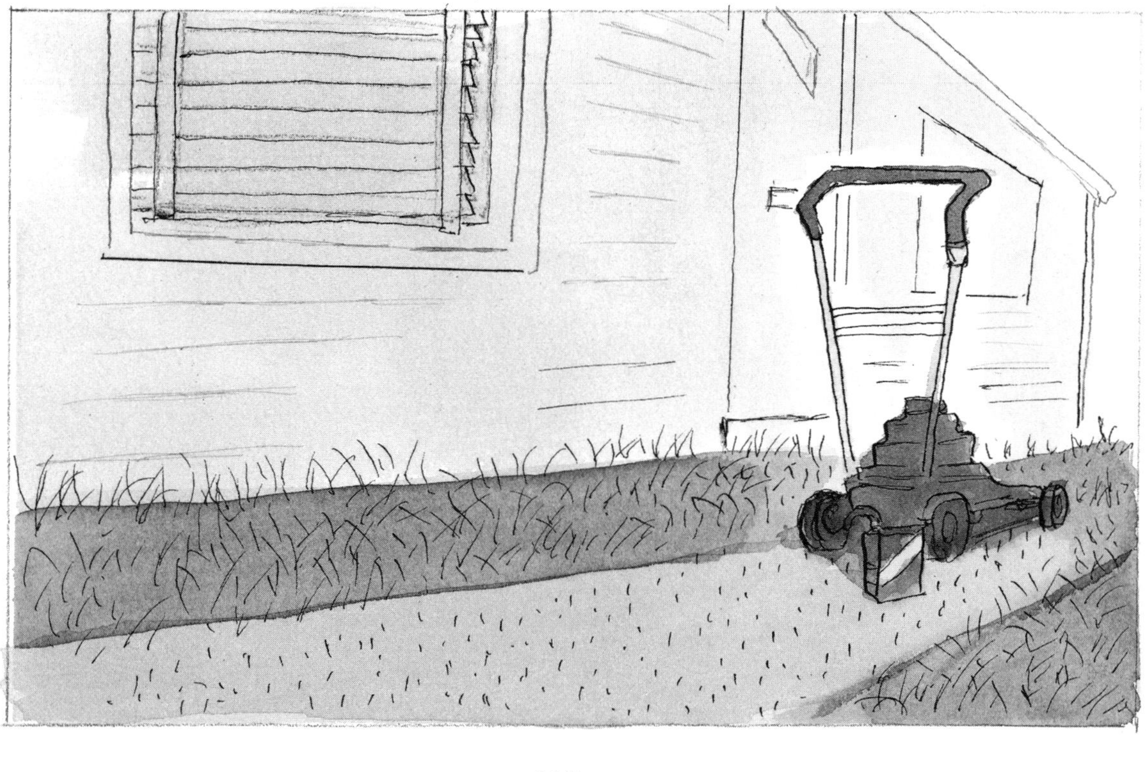

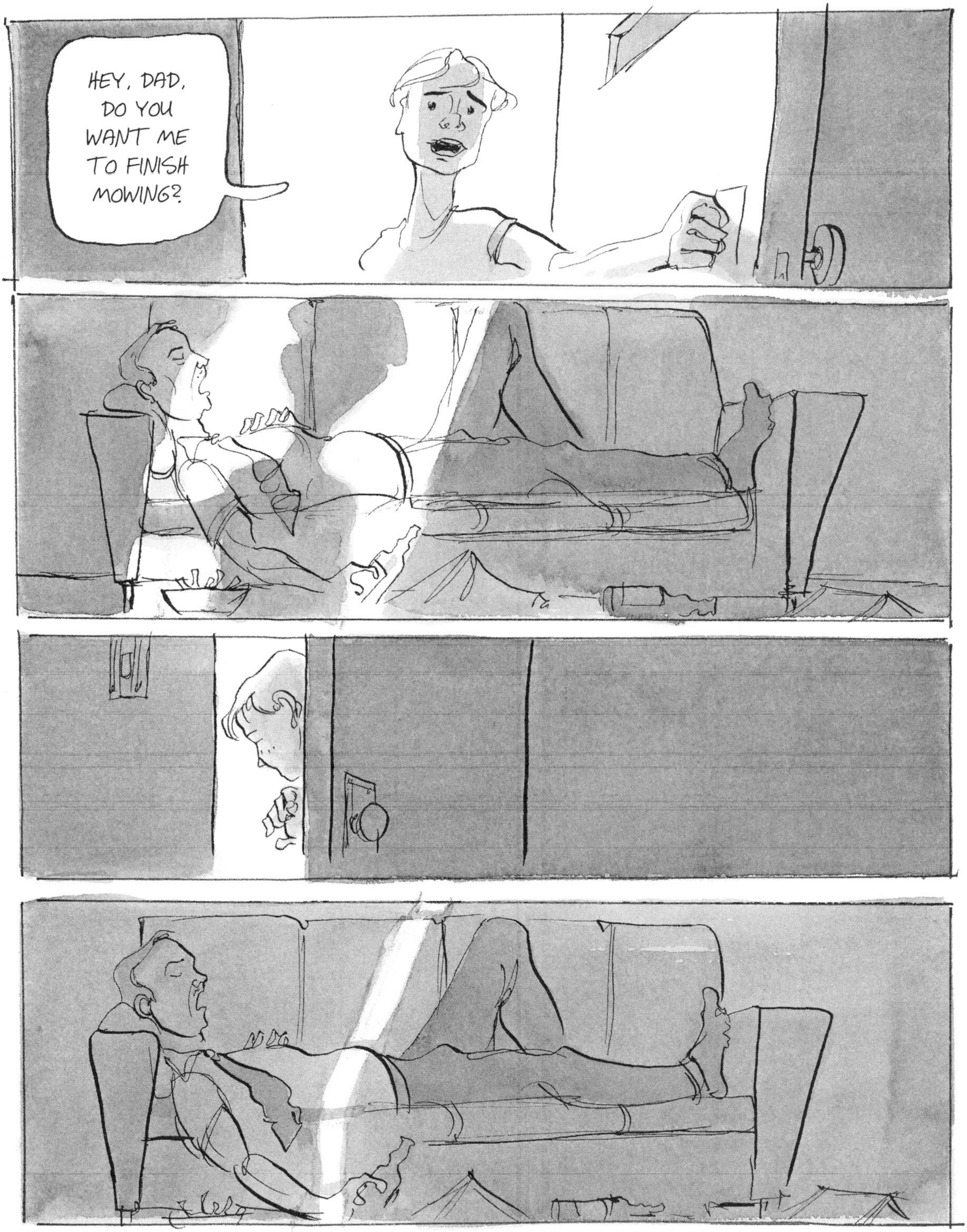
HEY, DAD, DO YOU WANT ME TO FINISH MOWING?

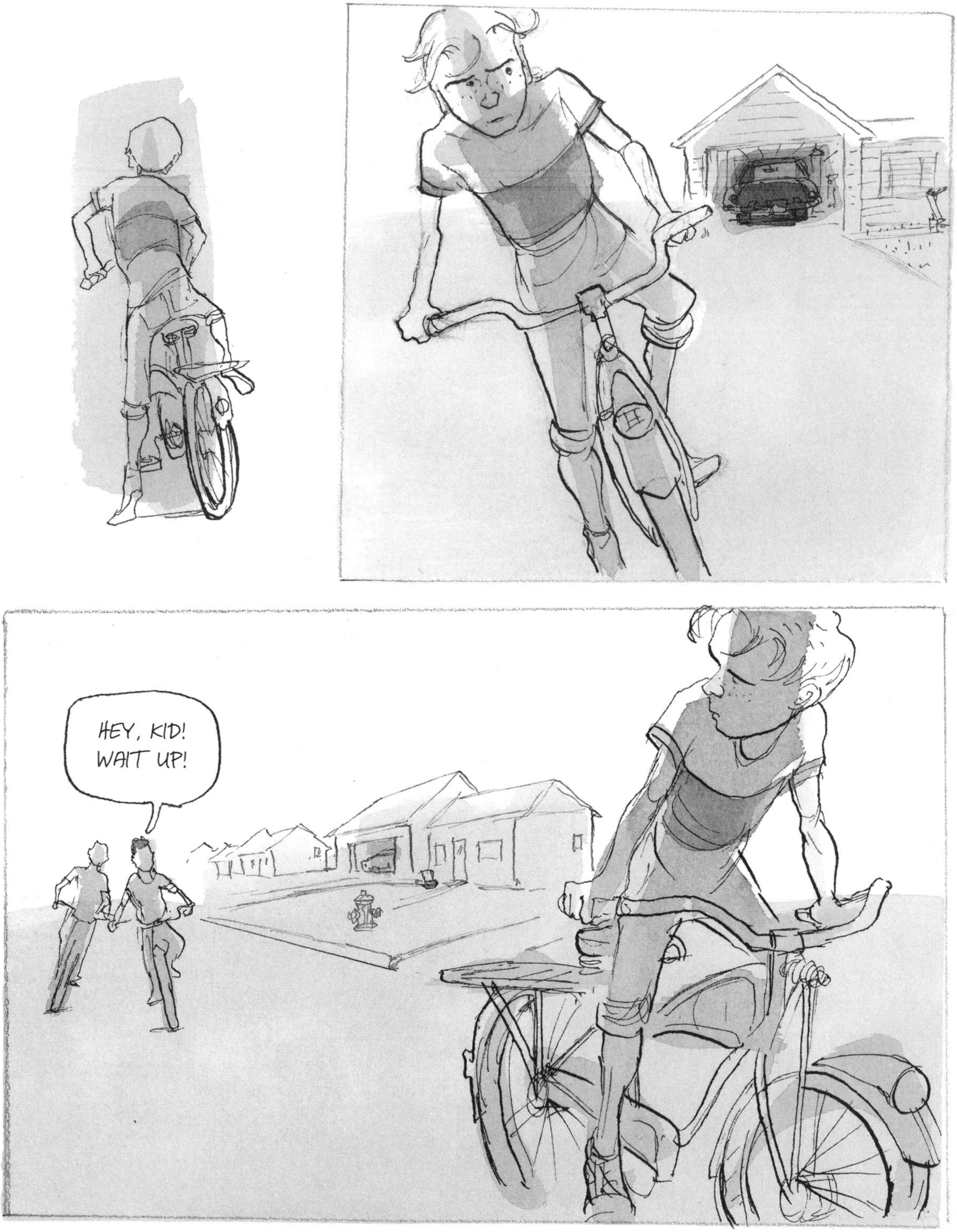
HEY, KID! WAIT UP!

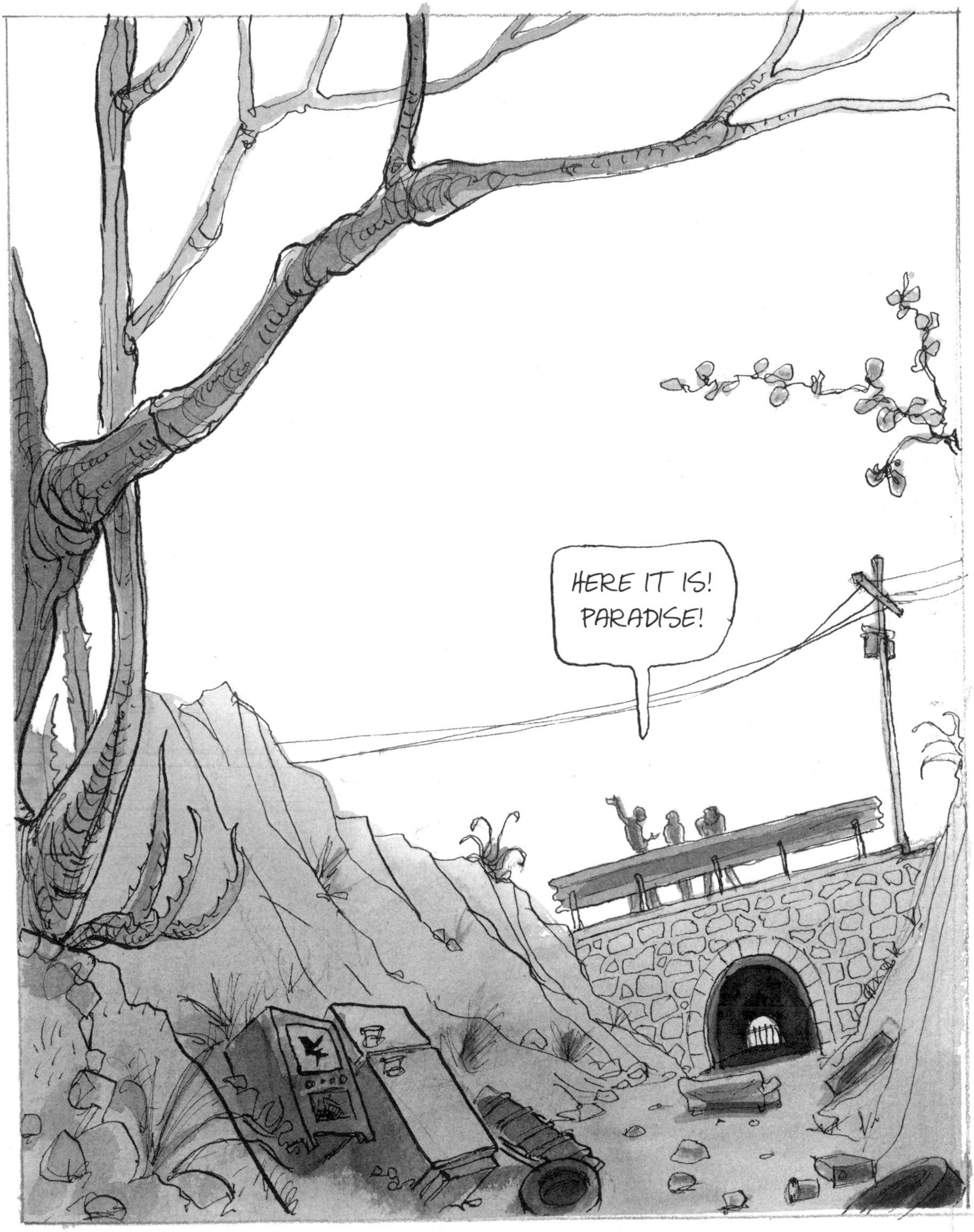
HERE IT IS! PARADISE!

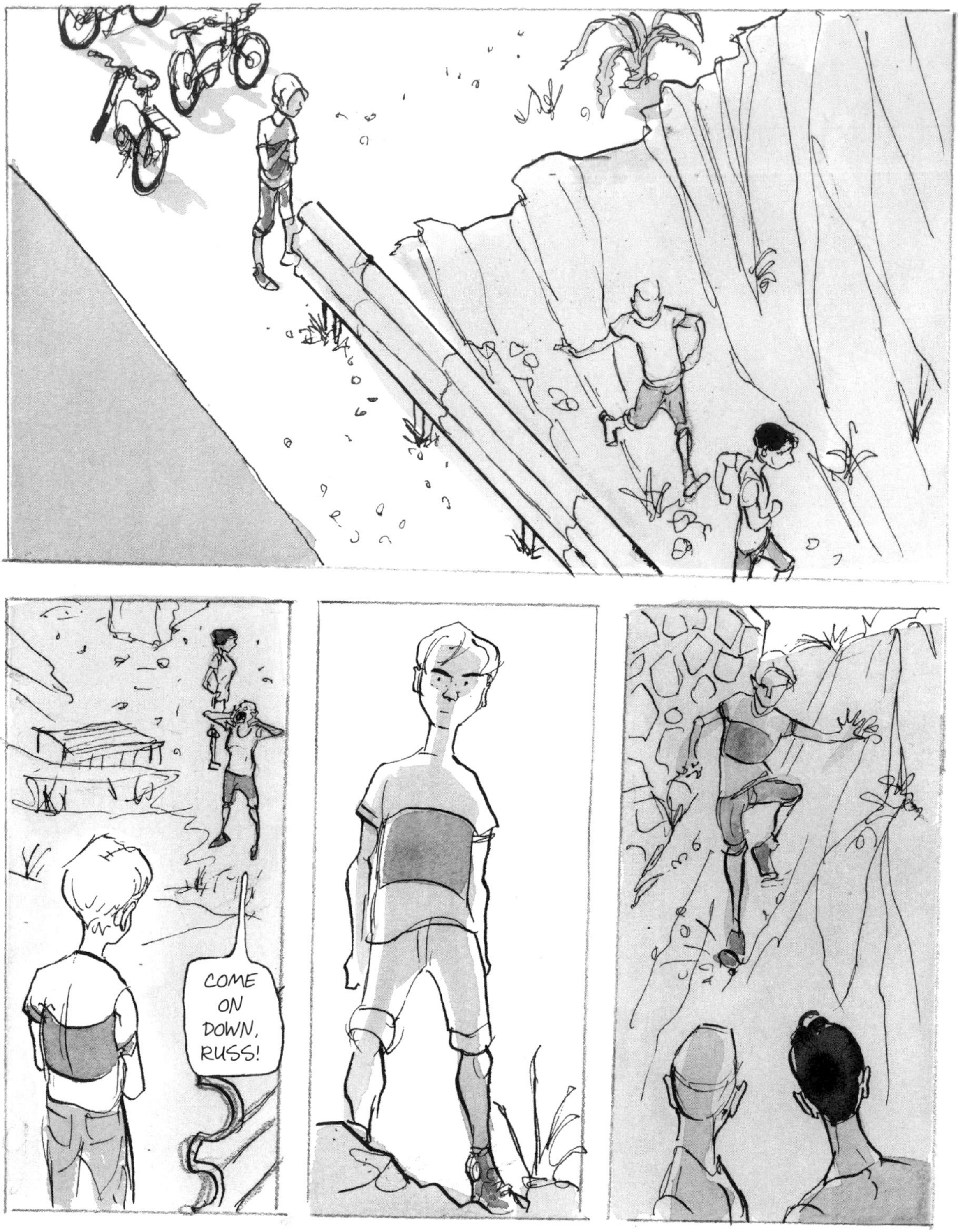
COME ON DOWN, RUSS!

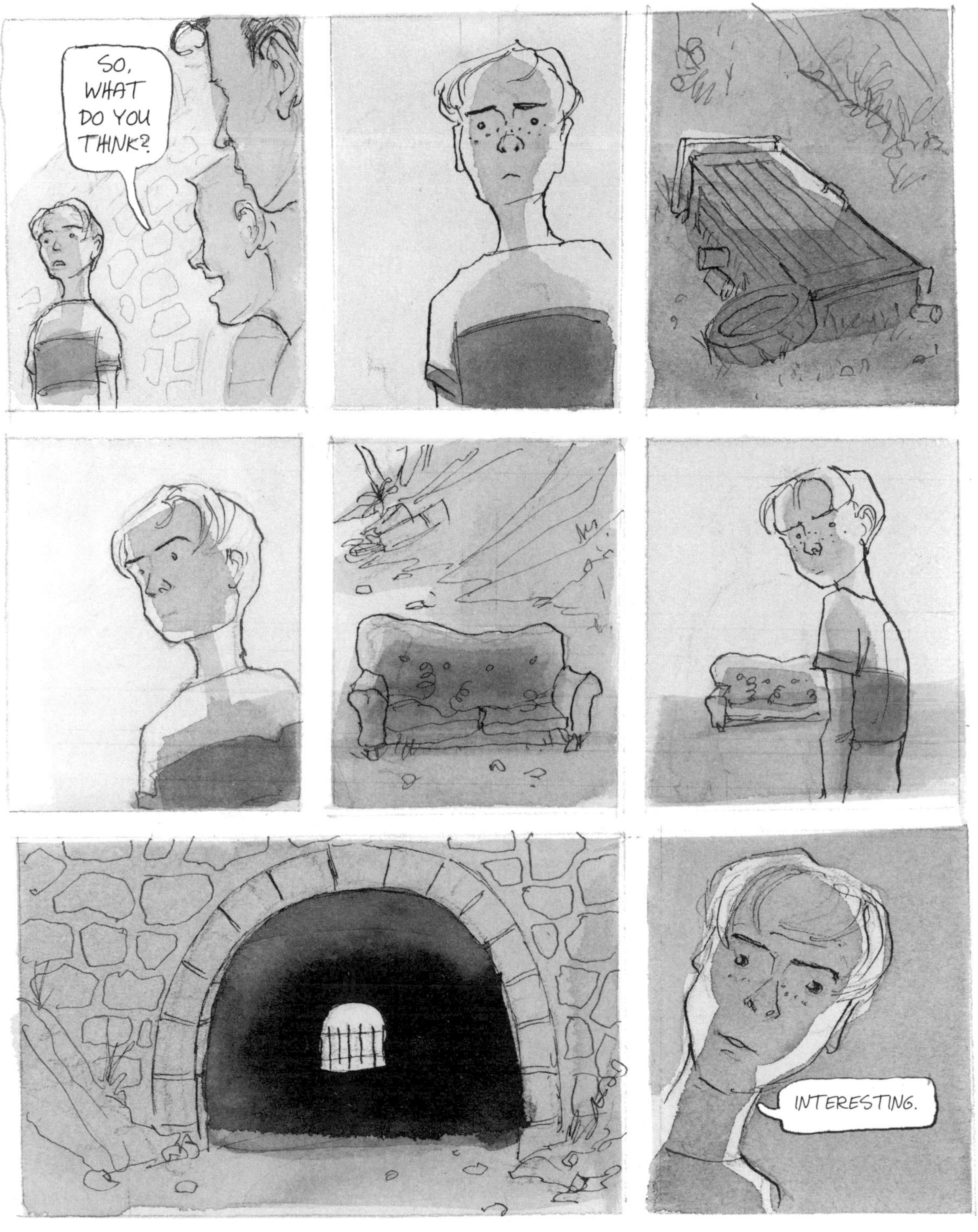
SO, WHAT DO YOU THINK?
INTERESTING.

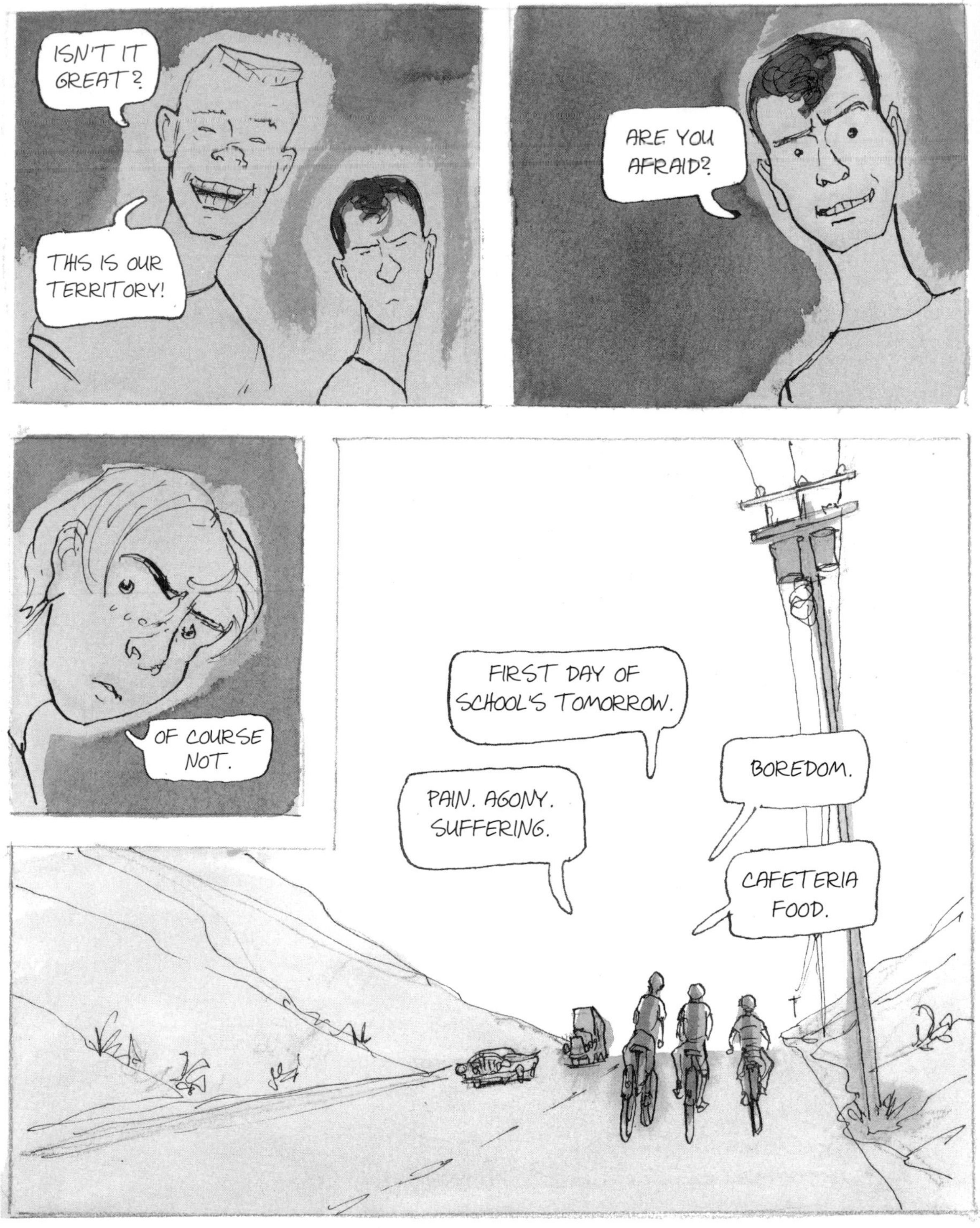
ISN'T IT GREAT?
THIS IS OUR TERRITORY!
ARE YOU AFRAID?
OF COURSE NOT.
FIRST DAY OF SCHOOL'S TOMORROW.
PAIN. AGONY. SUFFERING.
BOREDOM.
CAFETERIA FOOD.

119

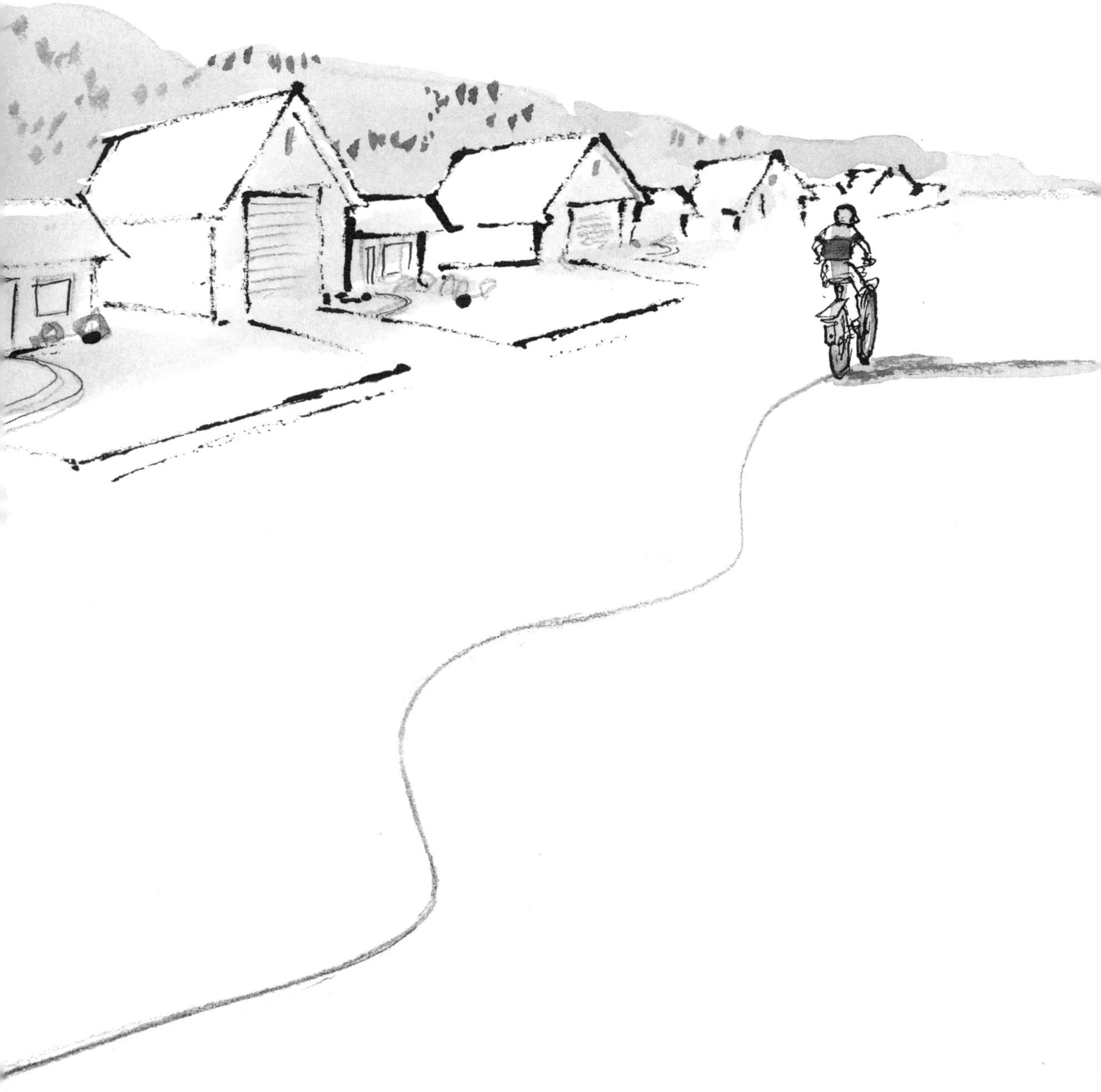

CHAPTER SIX

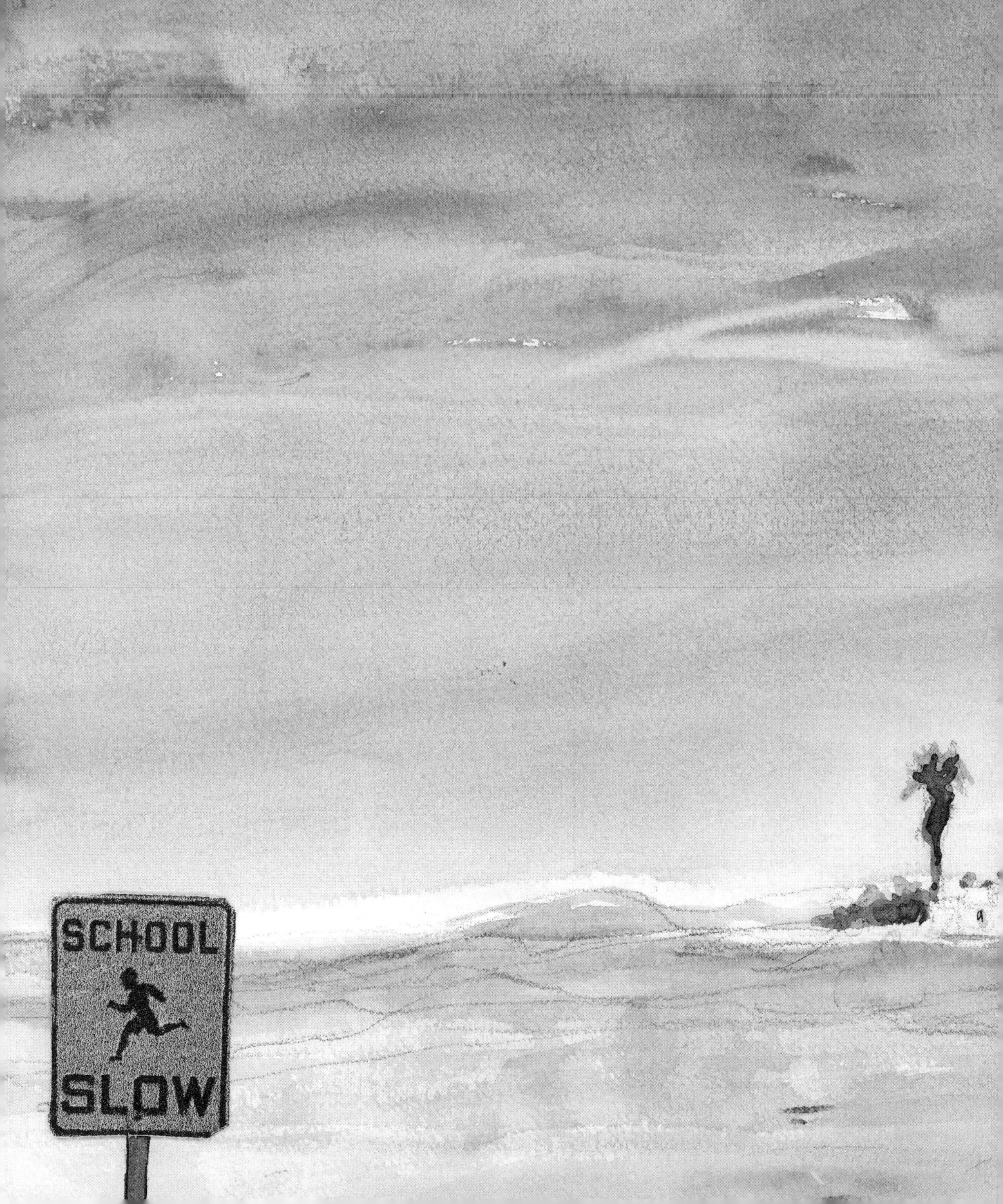
SCHOOL
SLOW

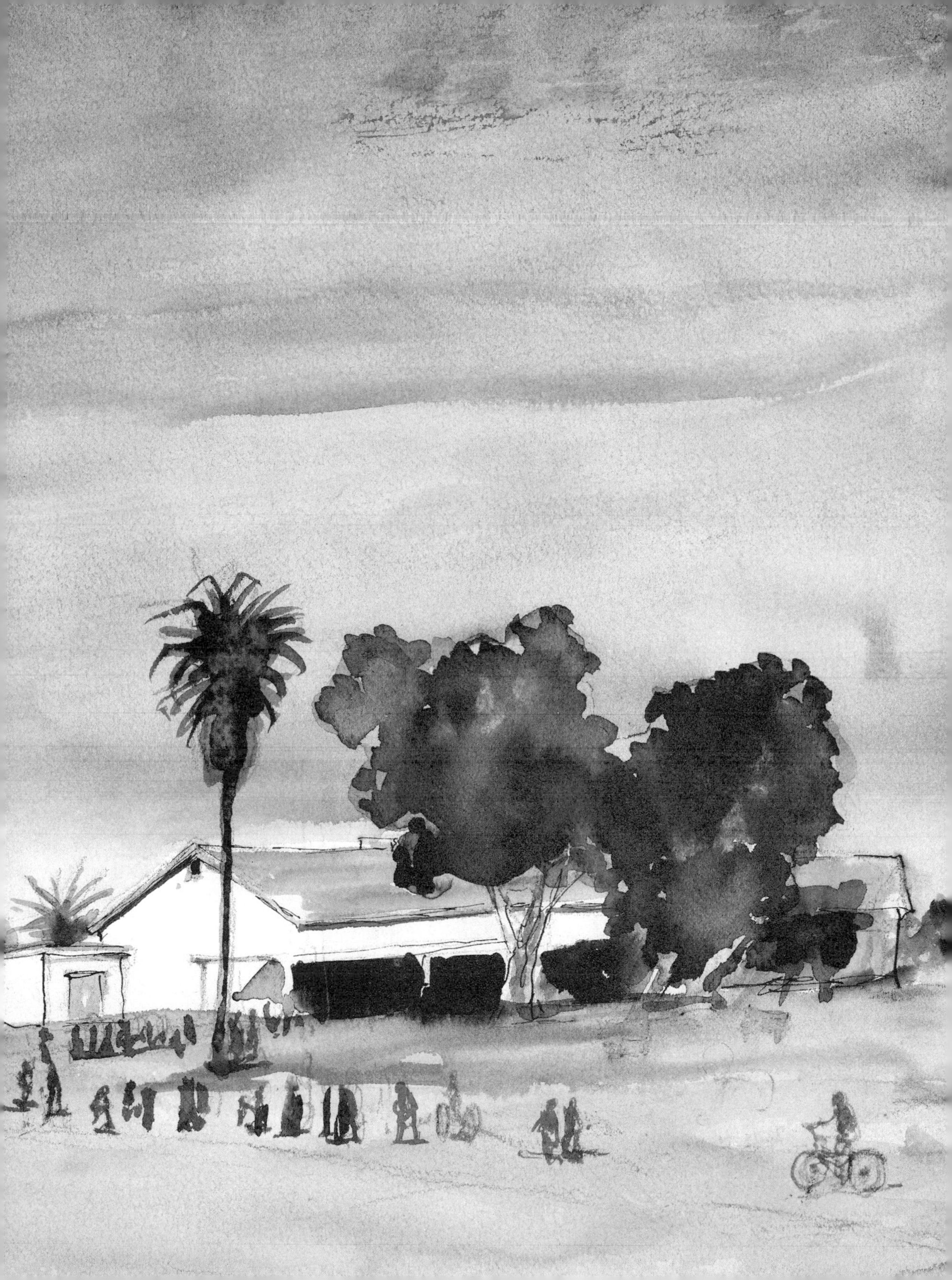

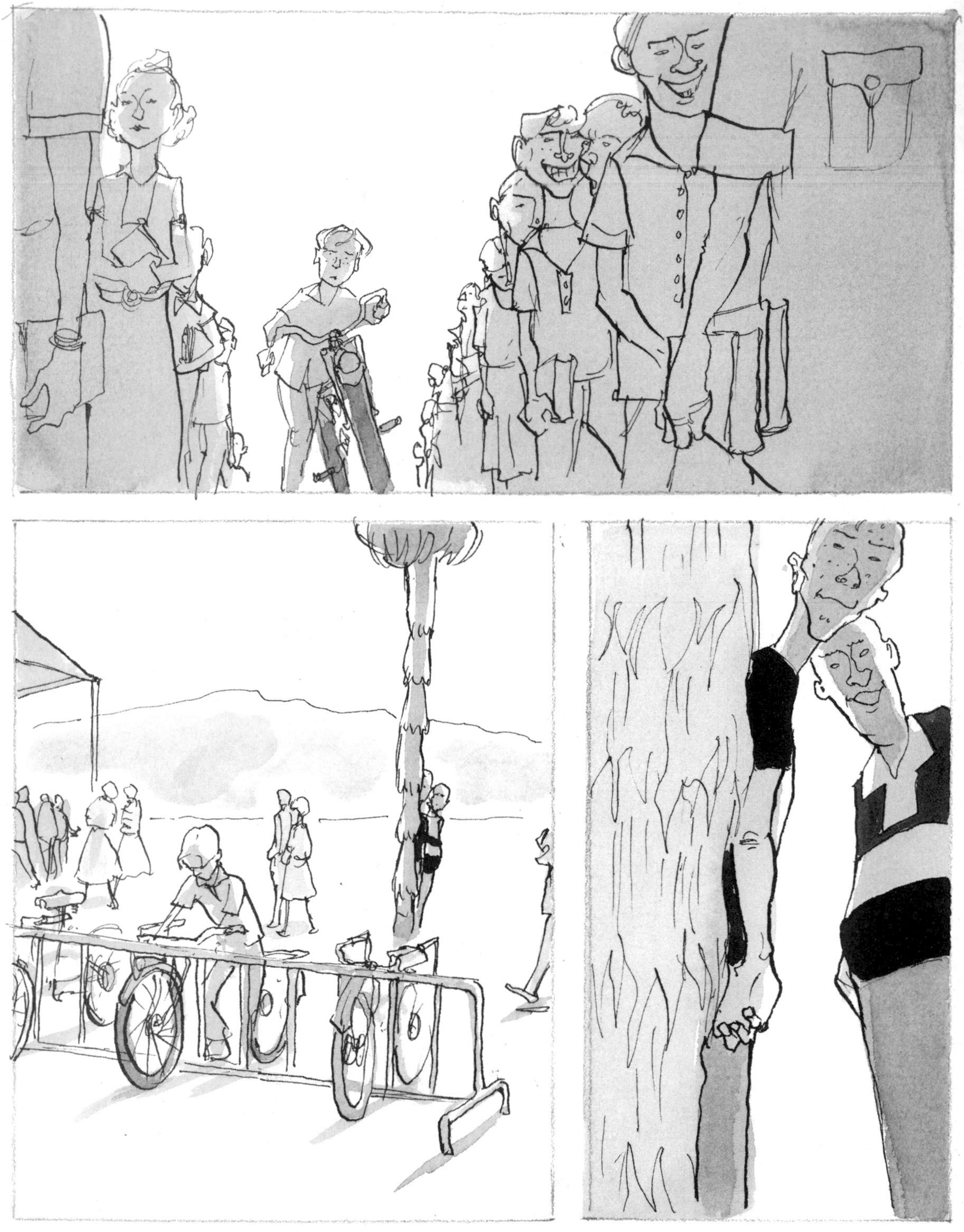

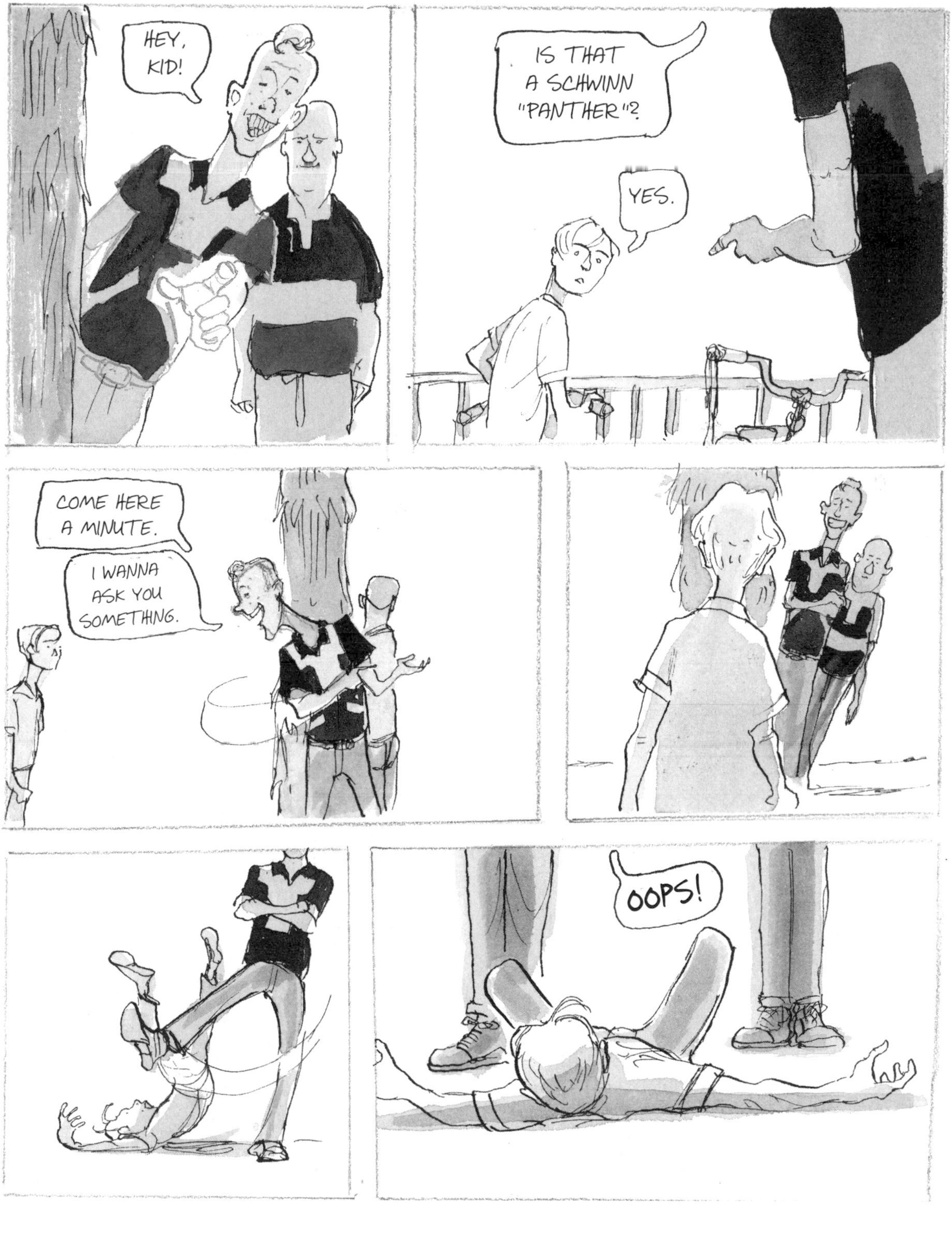
HEY, KID!
IS THAT A SCHWINN "PANTHER"?
YES.
COME HERE A MINUTE.
I WANNA ASK YOU SOMETHING.
OOPS!

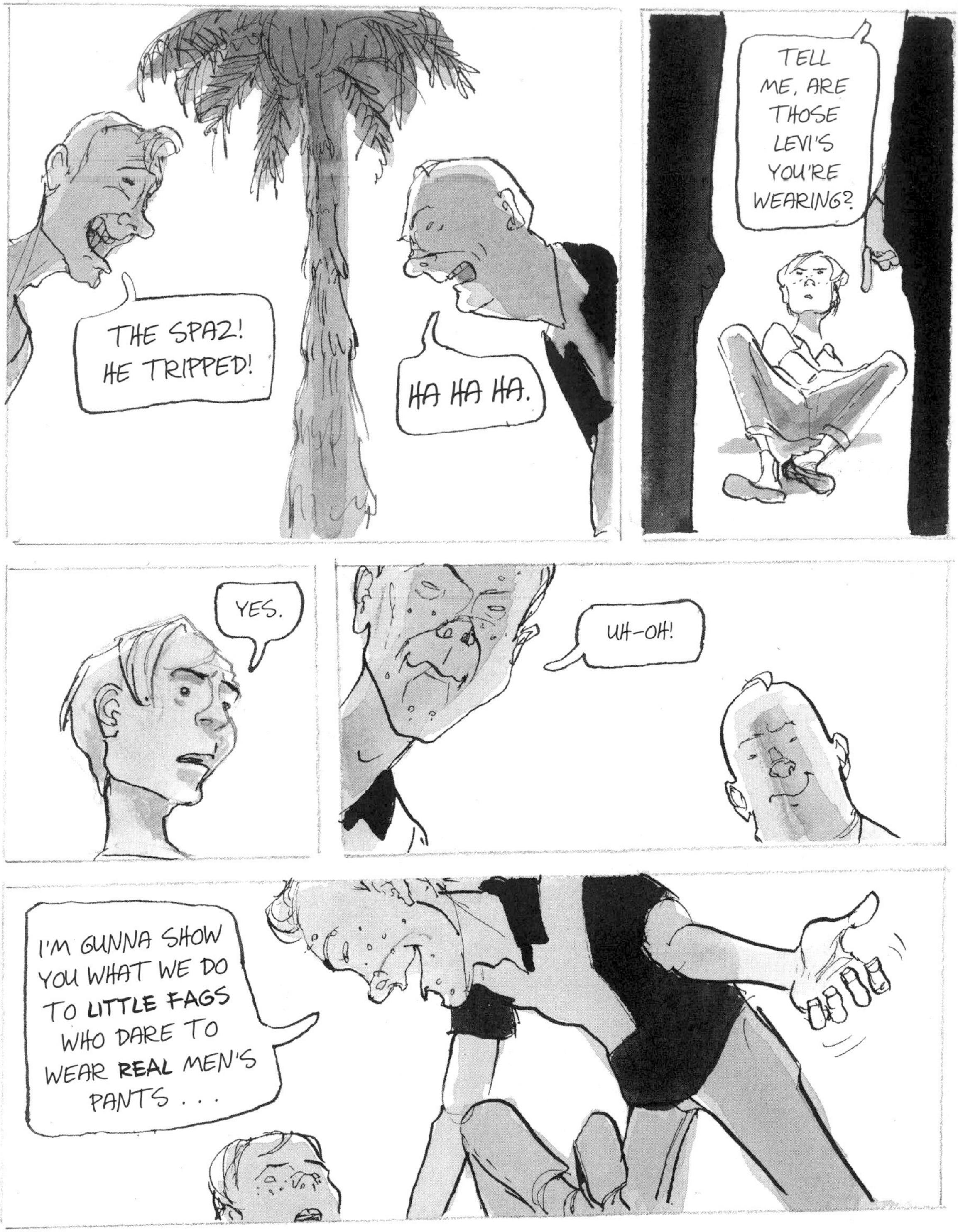
THE SPAZ! HE TRIPPED!
HA HA HA.
TELL ME, ARE THOSE LEVI'S YOU'RE WEARING?
YES.
UH-OH!
I'M GUNNA SHOW YOU WHAT WE DO TO **LITTLE FAGS** WHO DARE TO WEAR **REAL** MEN'S PANTS . . .

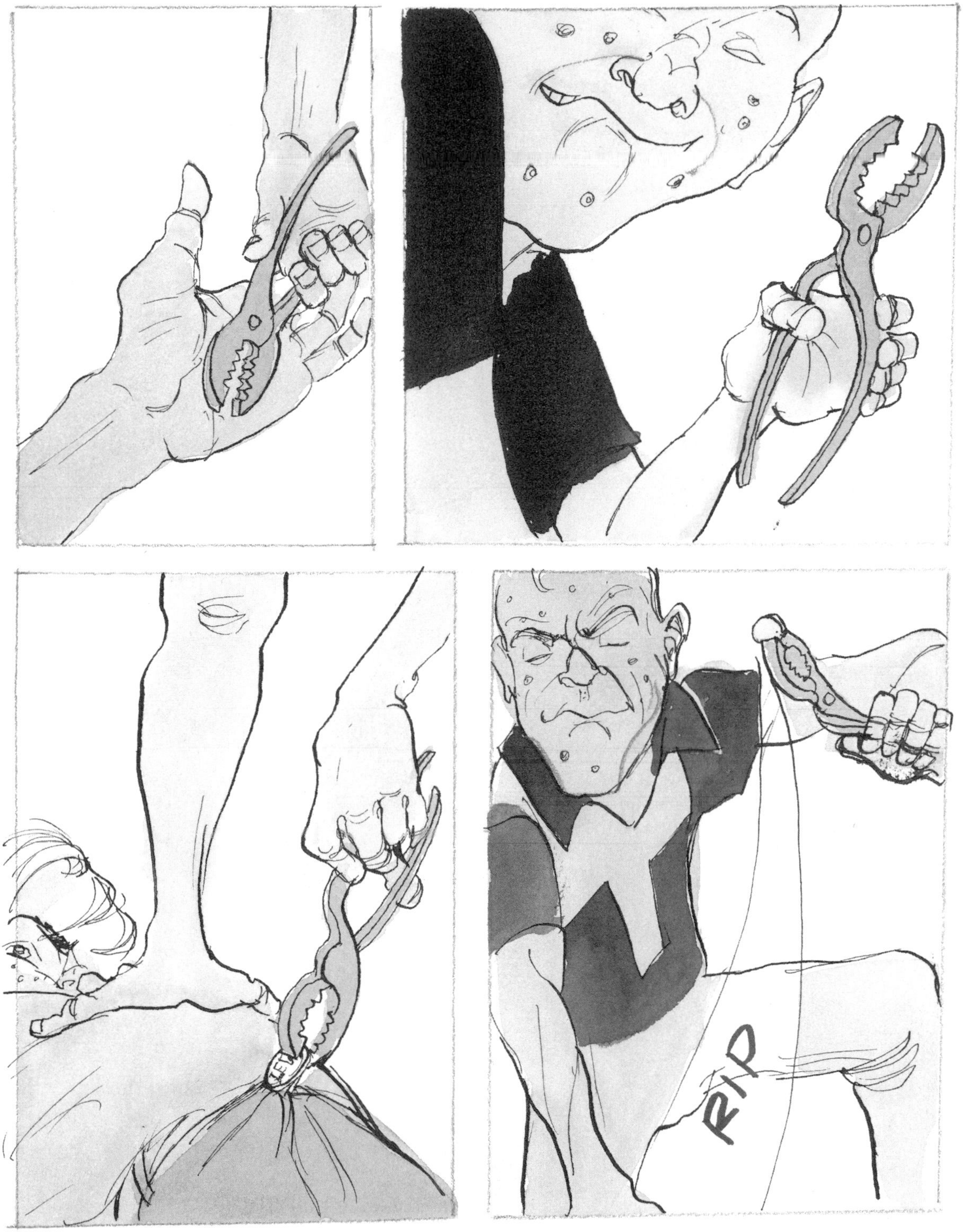
RIP

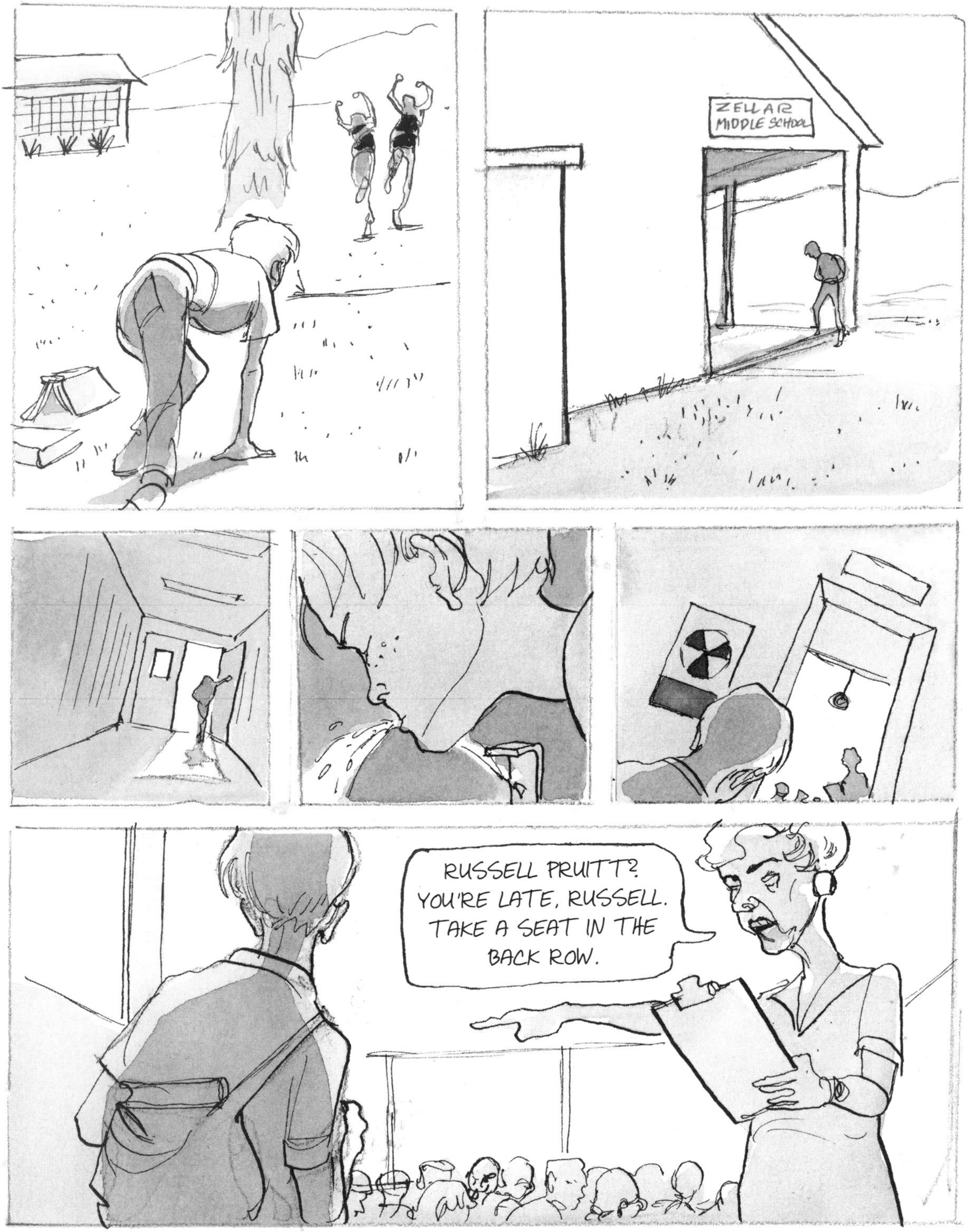
ZELLAR MIDDLE SCHOOL
RUSSELL PRUITT? YOU'RE LATE, RUSSELL. TAKE A SEAT IN THE BACK ROW.

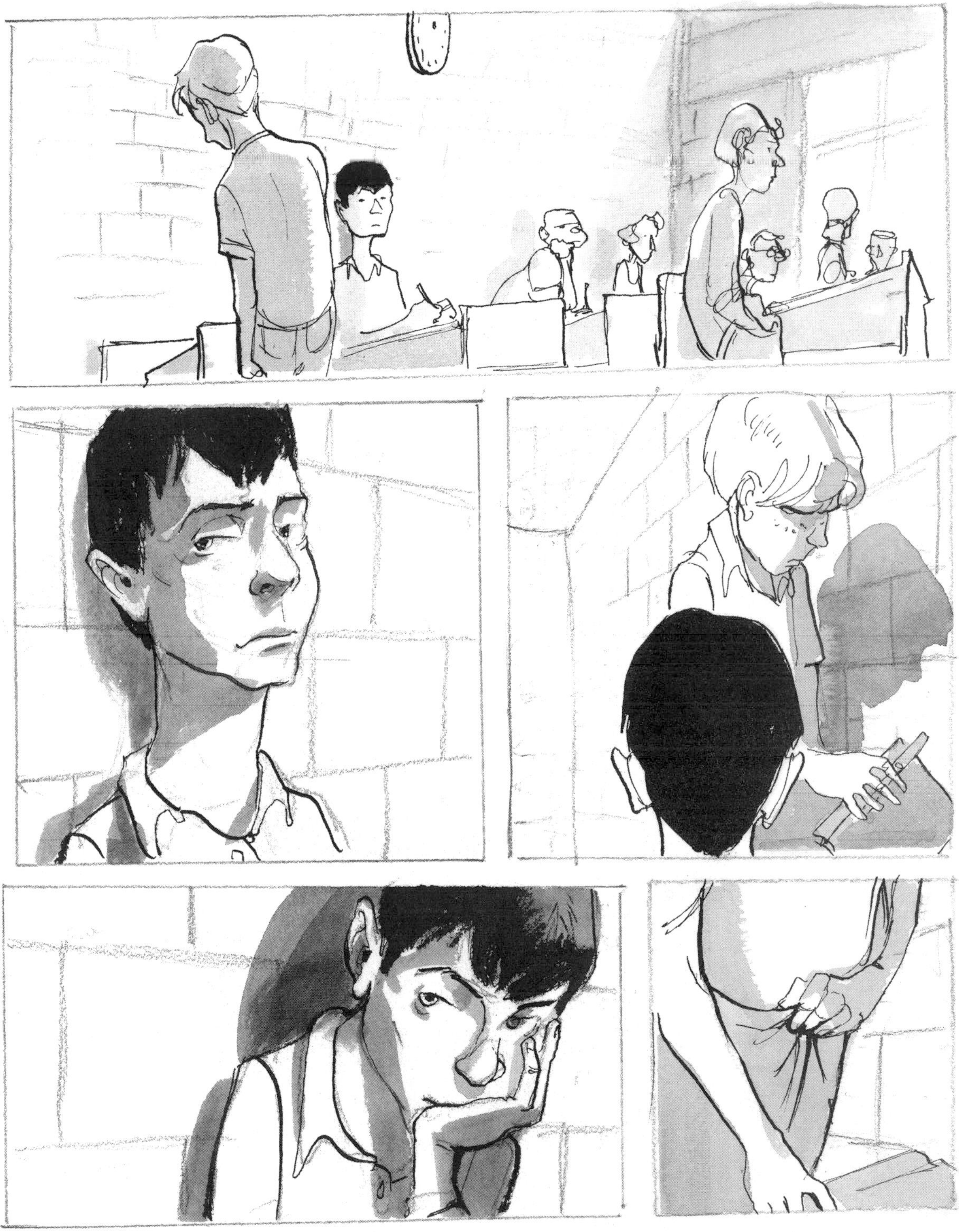

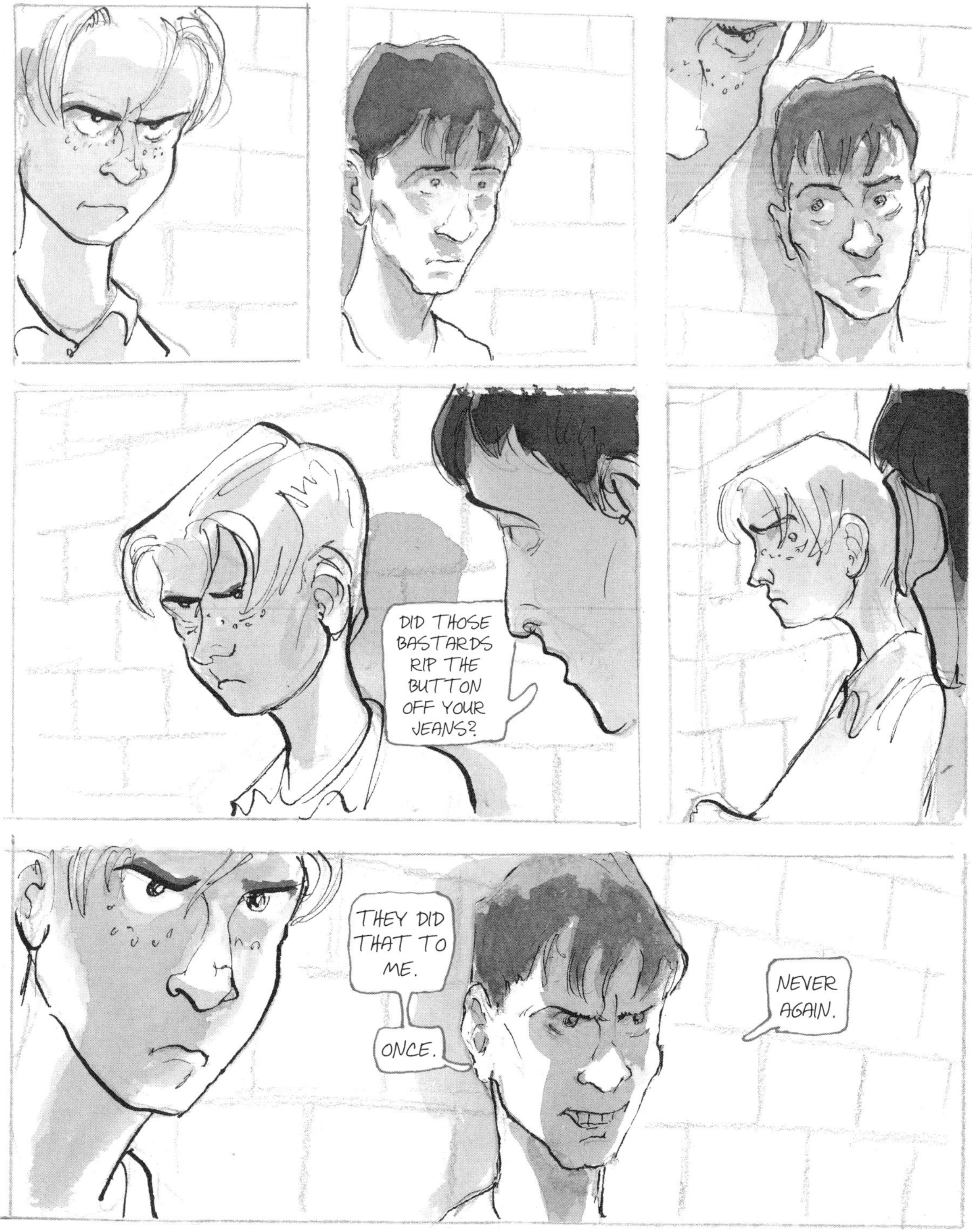
DID THOSE BASTARDS RIP THE BUTTON OFF YOUR JEANS?
THEY DID THAT TO ME.
ONCE.
NEVER AGAIN.

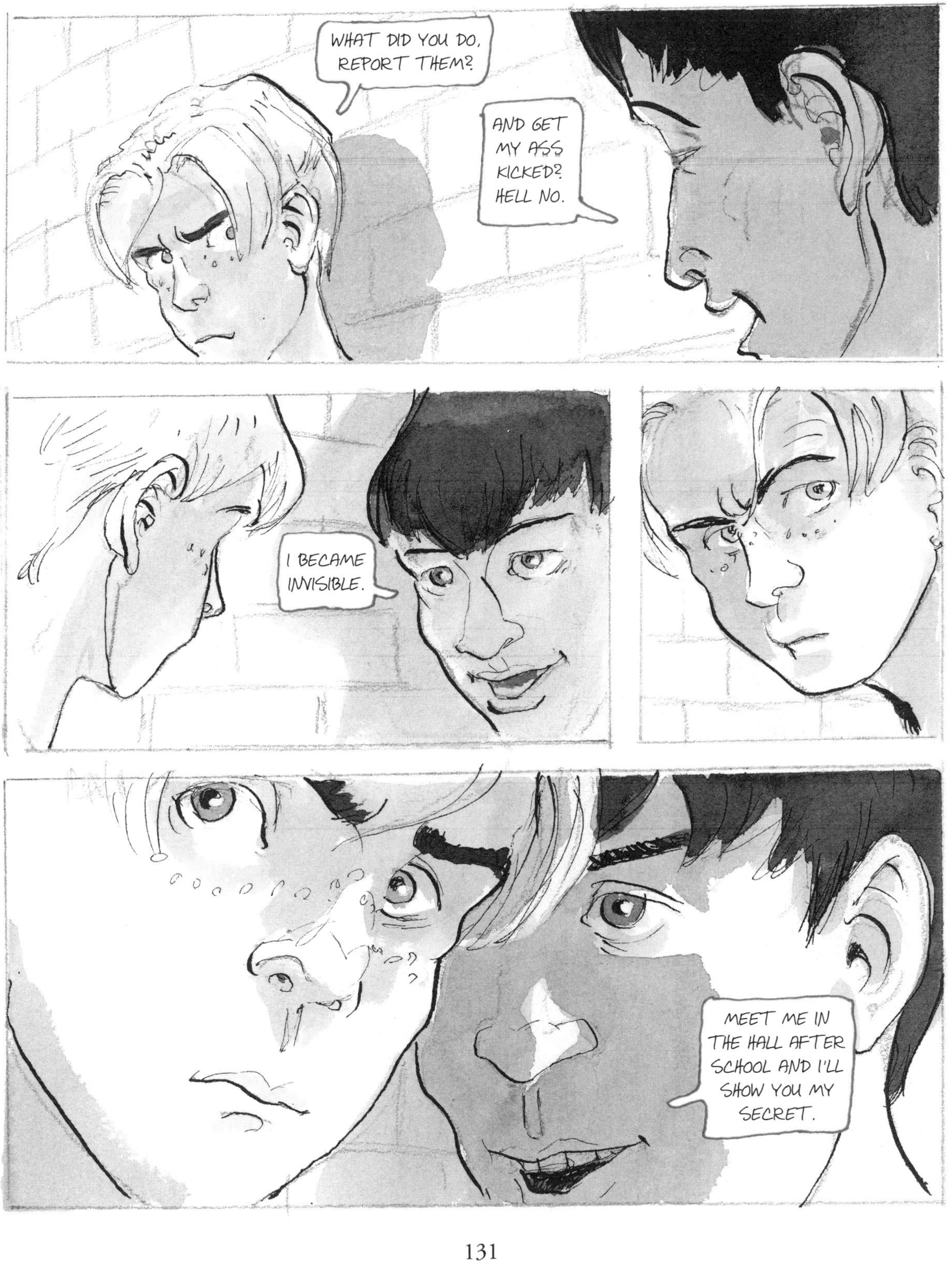
WHAT DID YOU DO, REPORT THEM?
AND GET MY ASS KICKED? HELL NO.
I BECAME INVISIBLE.
MEET ME IN THE HALL AFTER SCHOOL AND I'LL SHOW YOU MY SECRET.

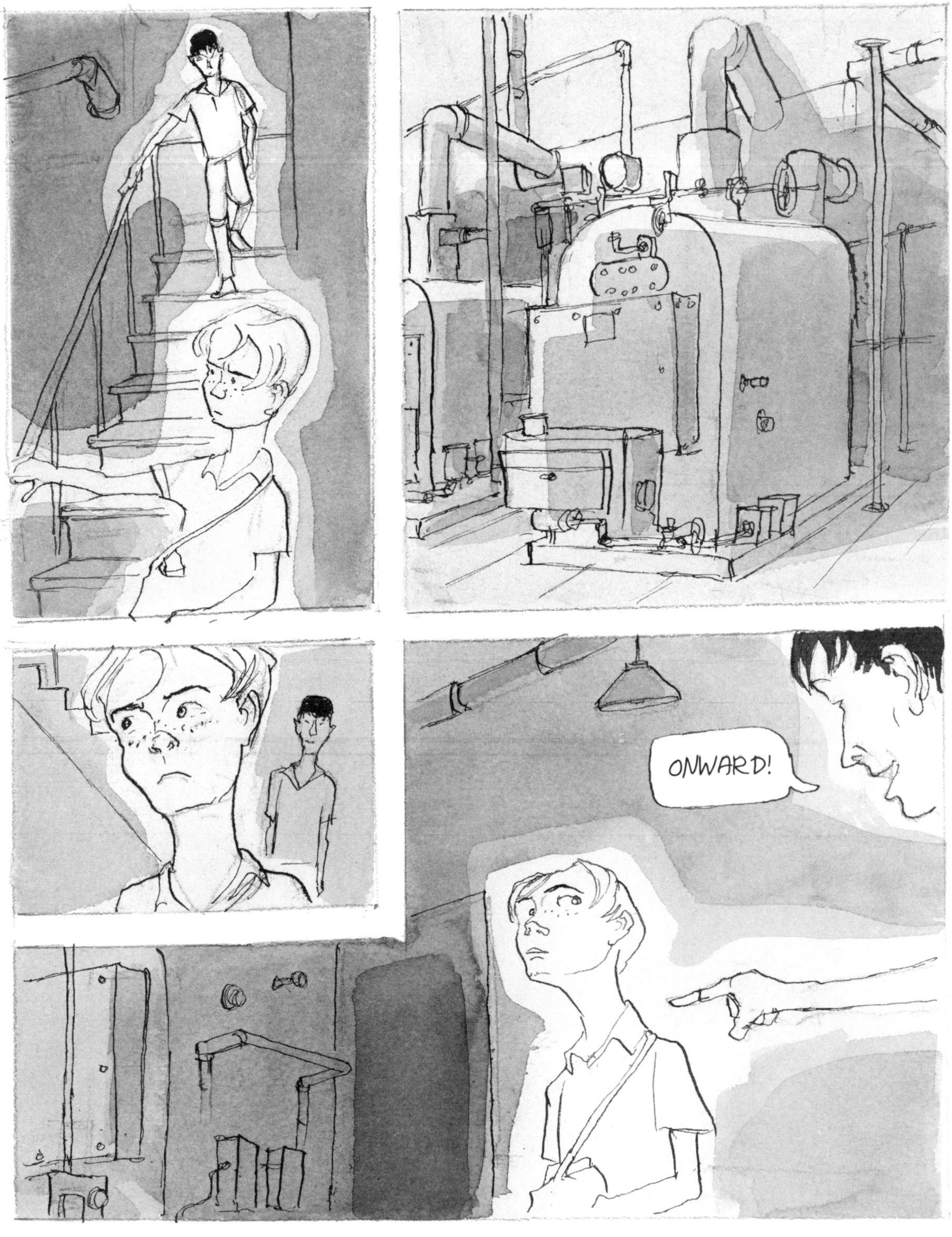
ONWARD!

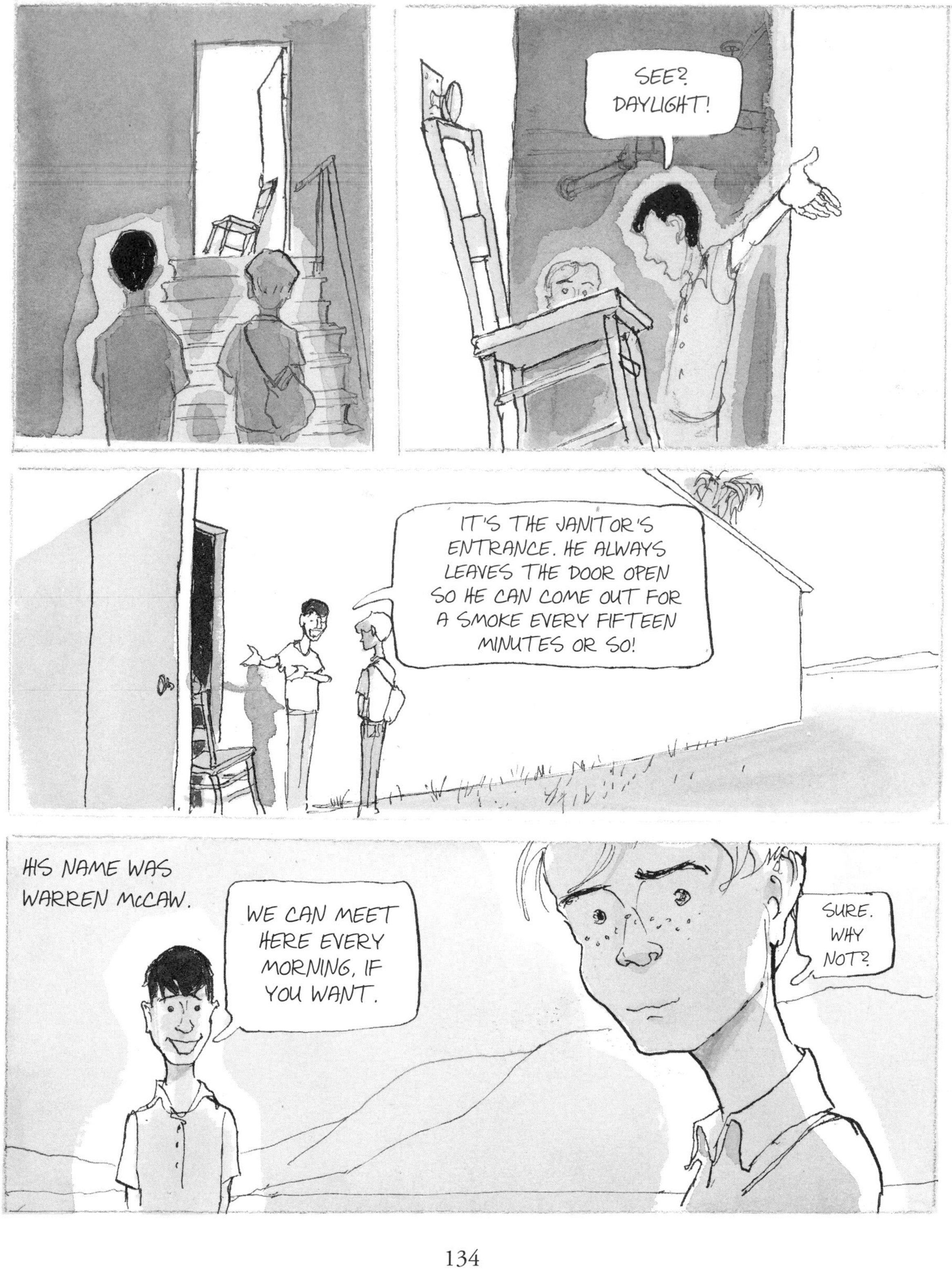
SEE? DAYLIGHT!
IT'S THE JANITOR'S ENTRANCE. HE ALWAYS LEAVES THE DOOR OPEN SO HE CAN COME OUT FOR A SMOKE EVERY FIFTEEN MINUTES OR SO!
HIS NAME WAS WARREN McCAW.
WE CAN MEET HERE EVERY MORNING, IF YOU WANT.
SURE. WHY NOT?

CHAPTER SEVEN

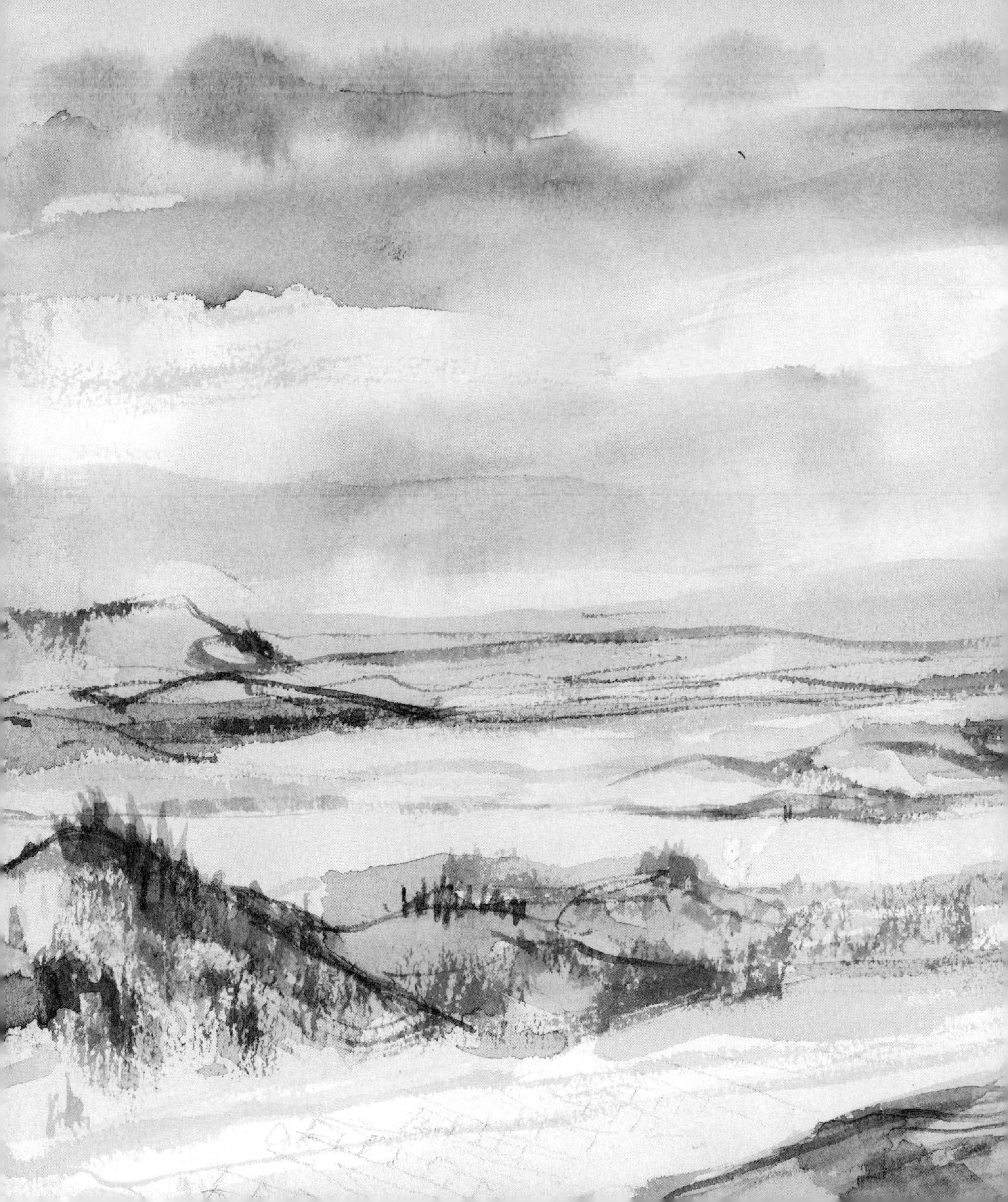

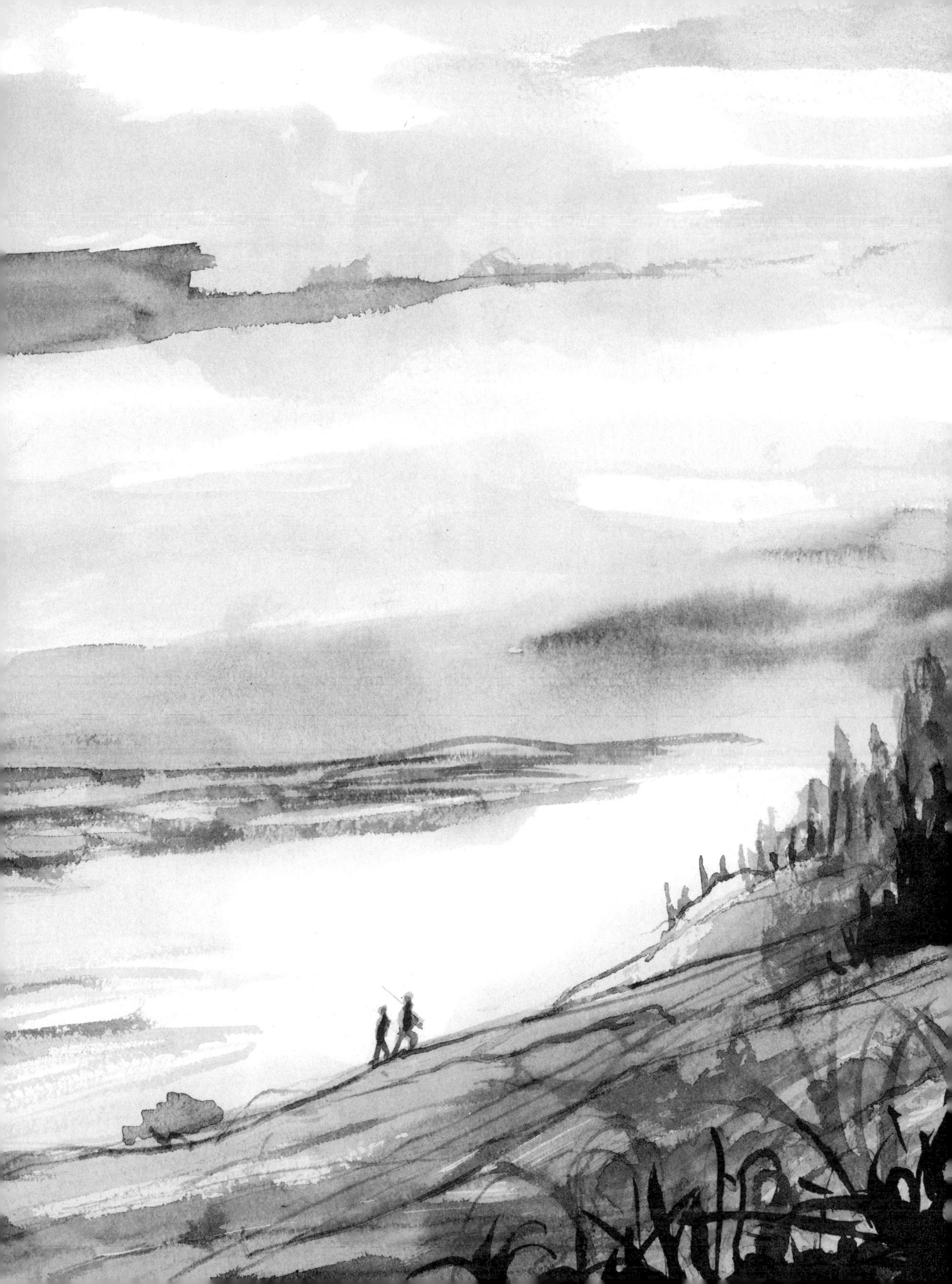

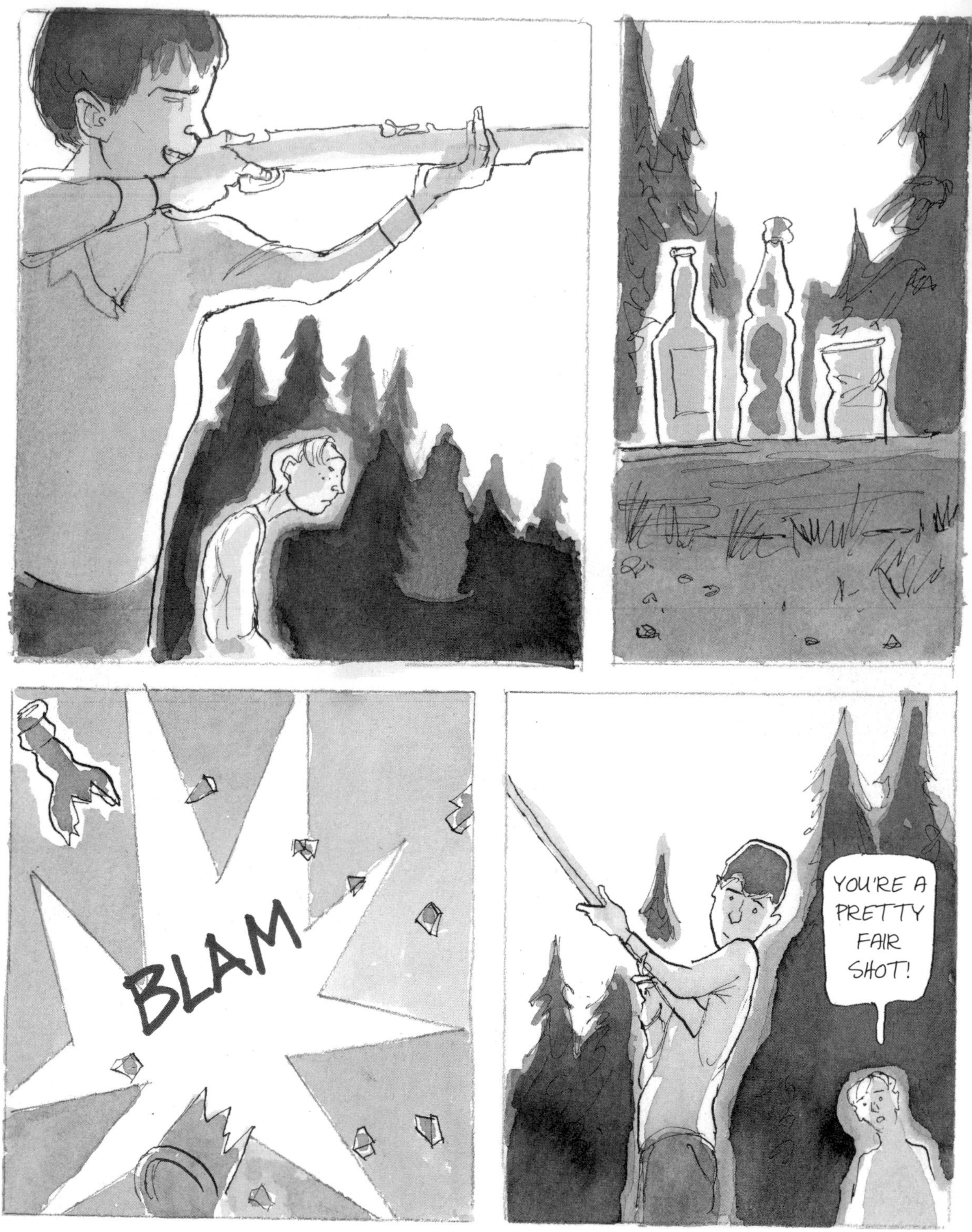
BLAM
YOU'RE A PRETTY FAIR SHOT!

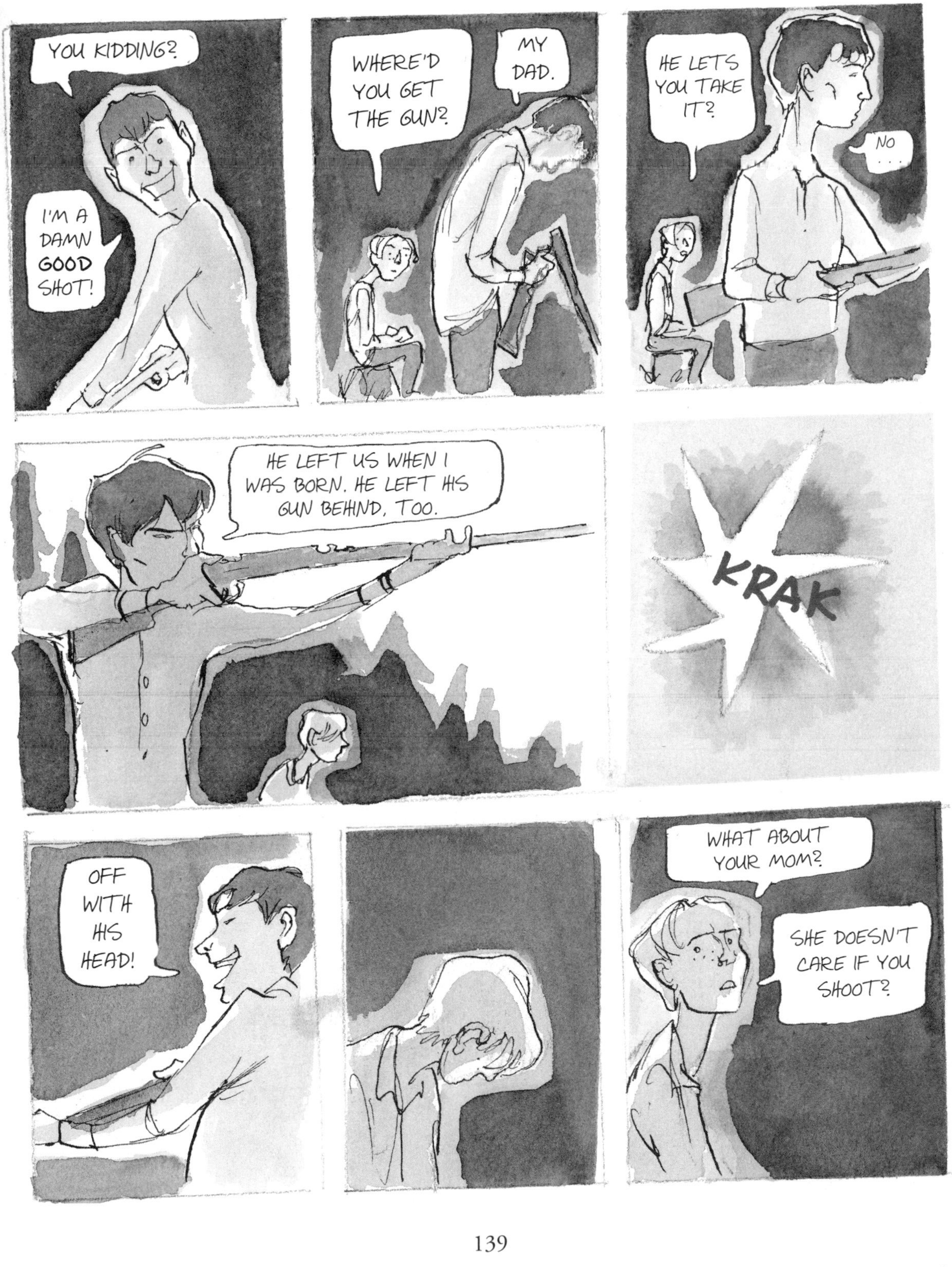
YOU KIDDING?
I'M A DAMN **GOOD** SHOT!
WHERE'D YOU GET THE GUN?
MY DAD.
HE LETS YOU TAKE IT?
NO . . .
HE LEFT US WHEN I WAS BORN. HE LEFT HIS GUN BEHIND, TOO.
KRAK
OFF WITH HIS HEAD!
WHAT ABOUT YOUR MOM?
SHE DOESN'T CARE IF YOU SHOOT?

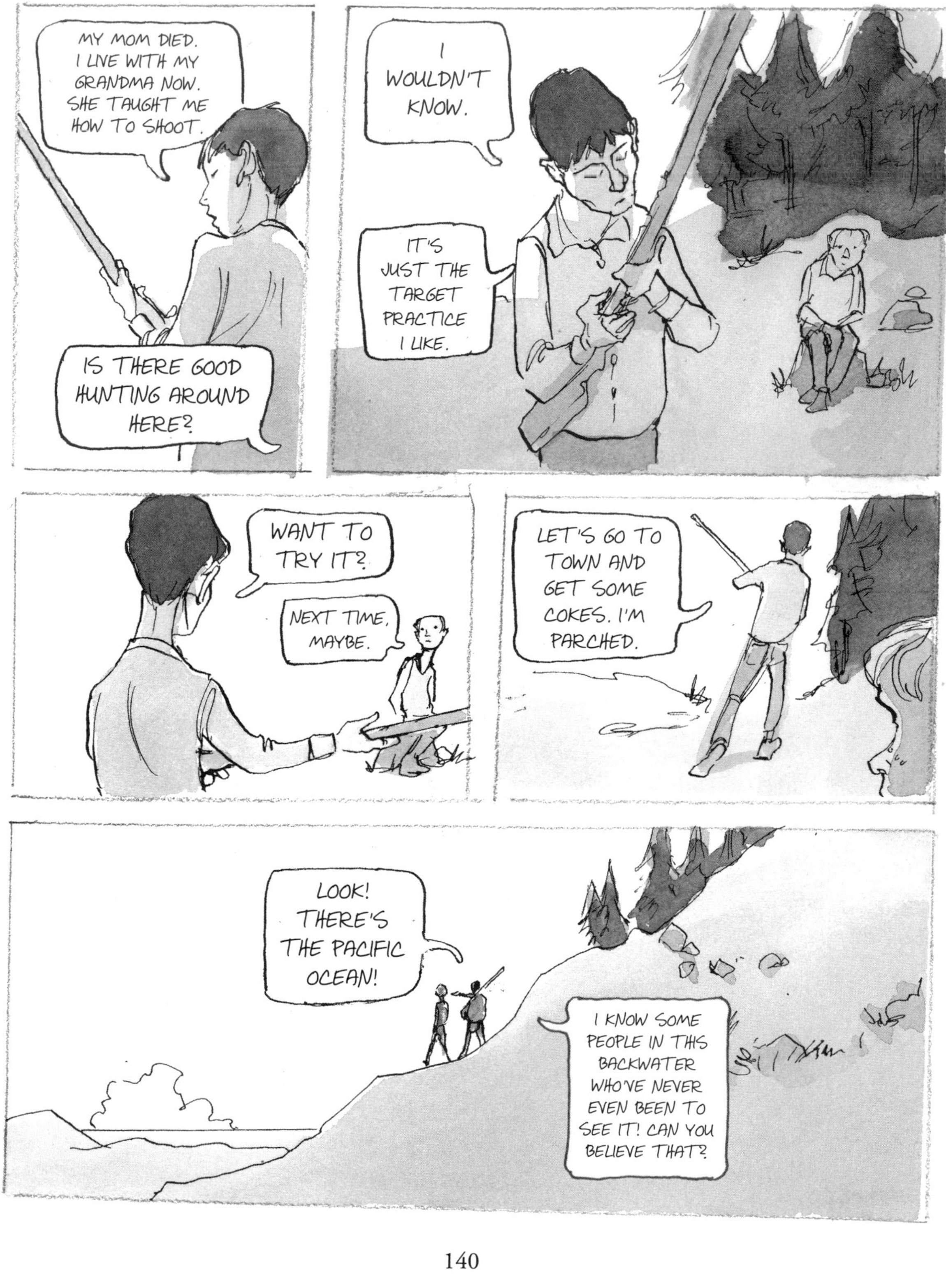
MY MOM DIED. I LIVE WITH MY GRANDMA NOW. SHE TAUGHT ME HOW TO SHOOT.
IS THERE GOOD HUNTING AROUND HERE?
I WOULDN'T KNOW.
IT'S JUST THE TARGET PRACTICE I LIKE.
WANT TO TRY IT?
NEXT TIME, MAYBE.
LET'S GO TO TOWN AND GET SOME COKES. I'M PARCHED.
LOOK! THERE'S THE PACIFIC OCEAN!
I KNOW SOME PEOPLE IN THIS BACKWATER WHO'VE NEVER EVEN BEEN TO SEE IT! CAN YOU BELIEVE THAT?

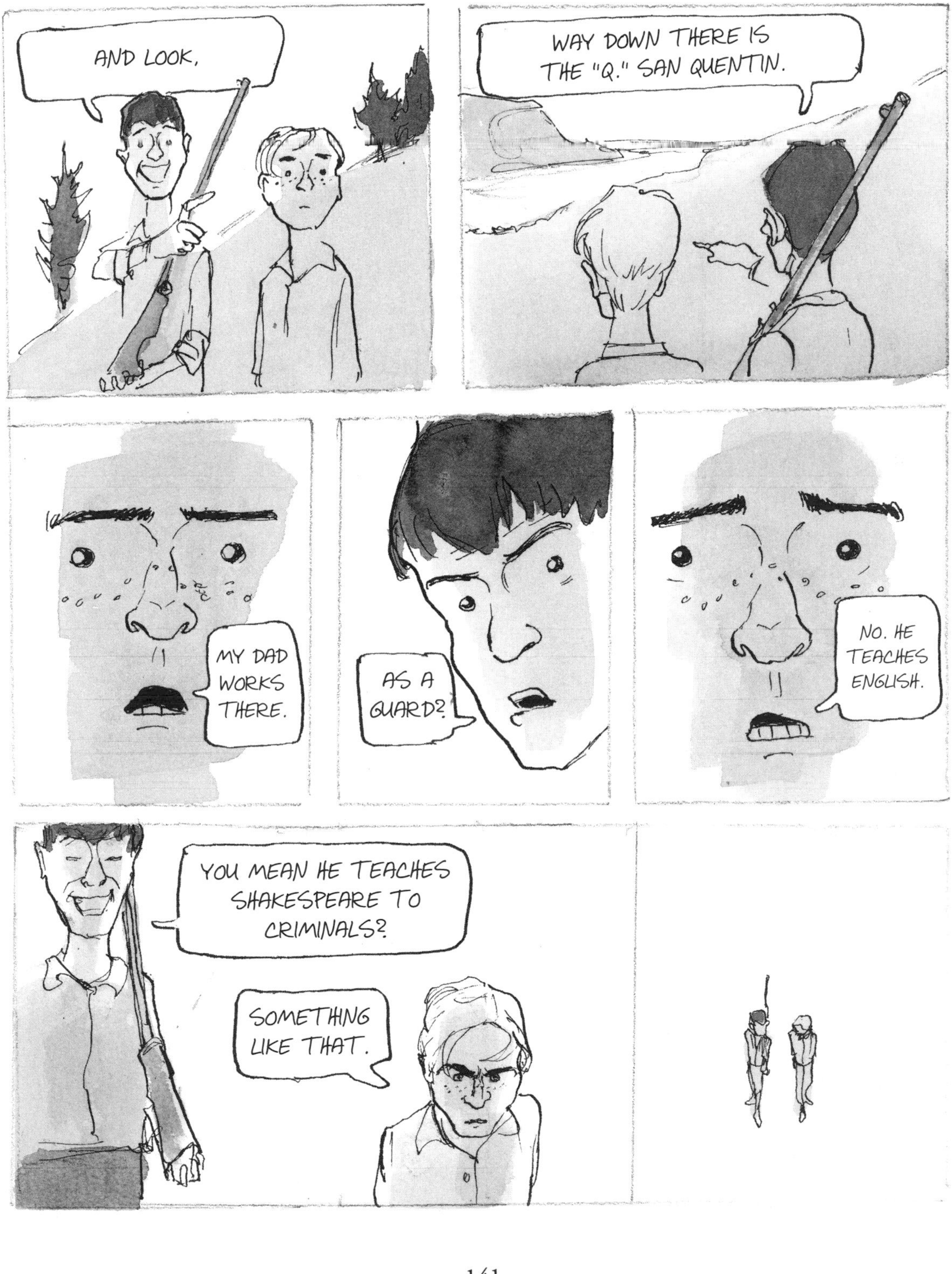
AND LOOK,
WAY DOWN THERE IS THE "Q." SAN QUENTIN.
MY DAD WORKS THERE.
AS A GUARD?
NO. HE TEACHES ENGLISH.
YOU MEAN HE TEACHES SHAKESPEARE TO CRIMINALS?
SOMETHING LIKE THAT.

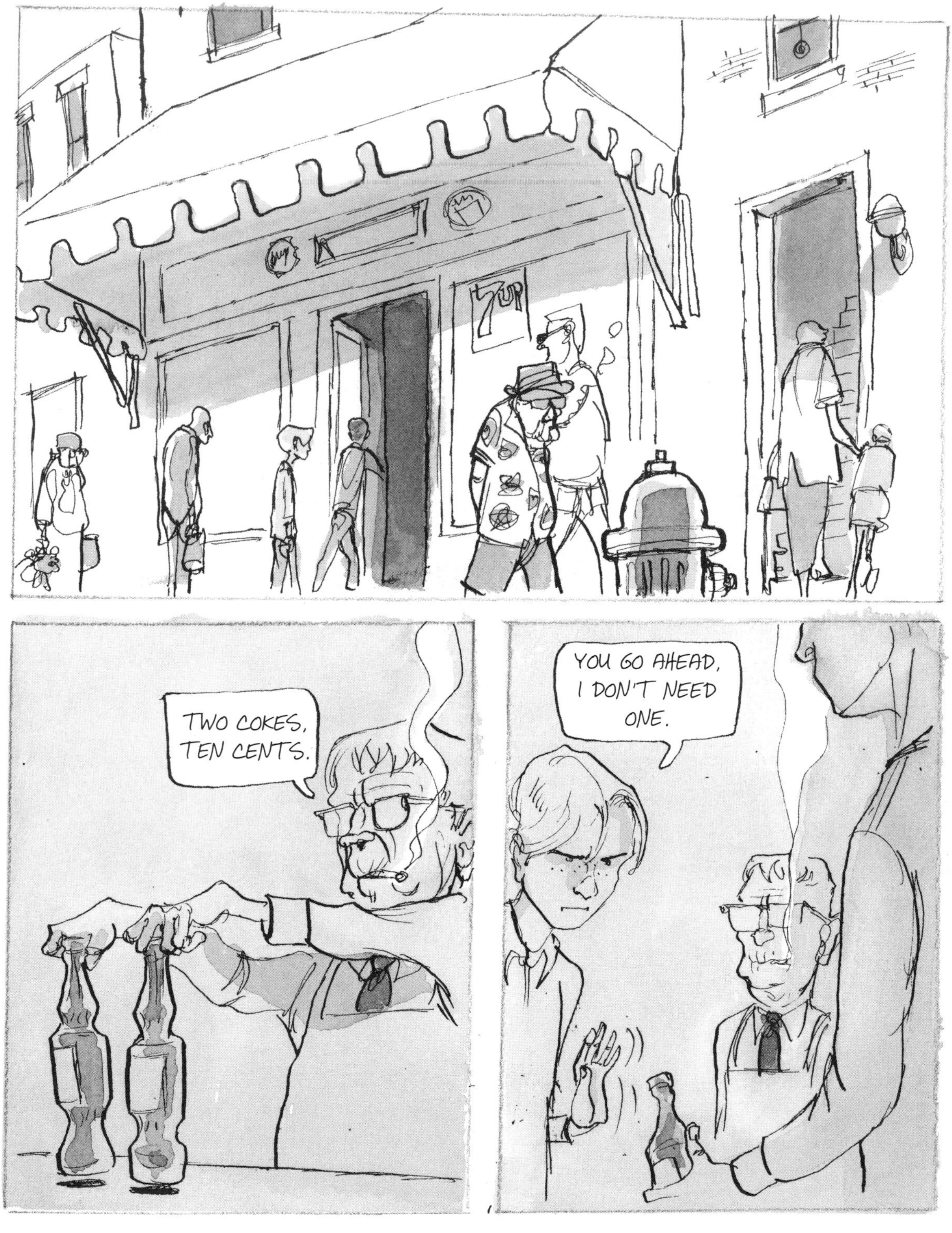
7UP
TWO COKES, TEN CENTS.
YOU GO AHEAD, I DON'T NEED ONE.

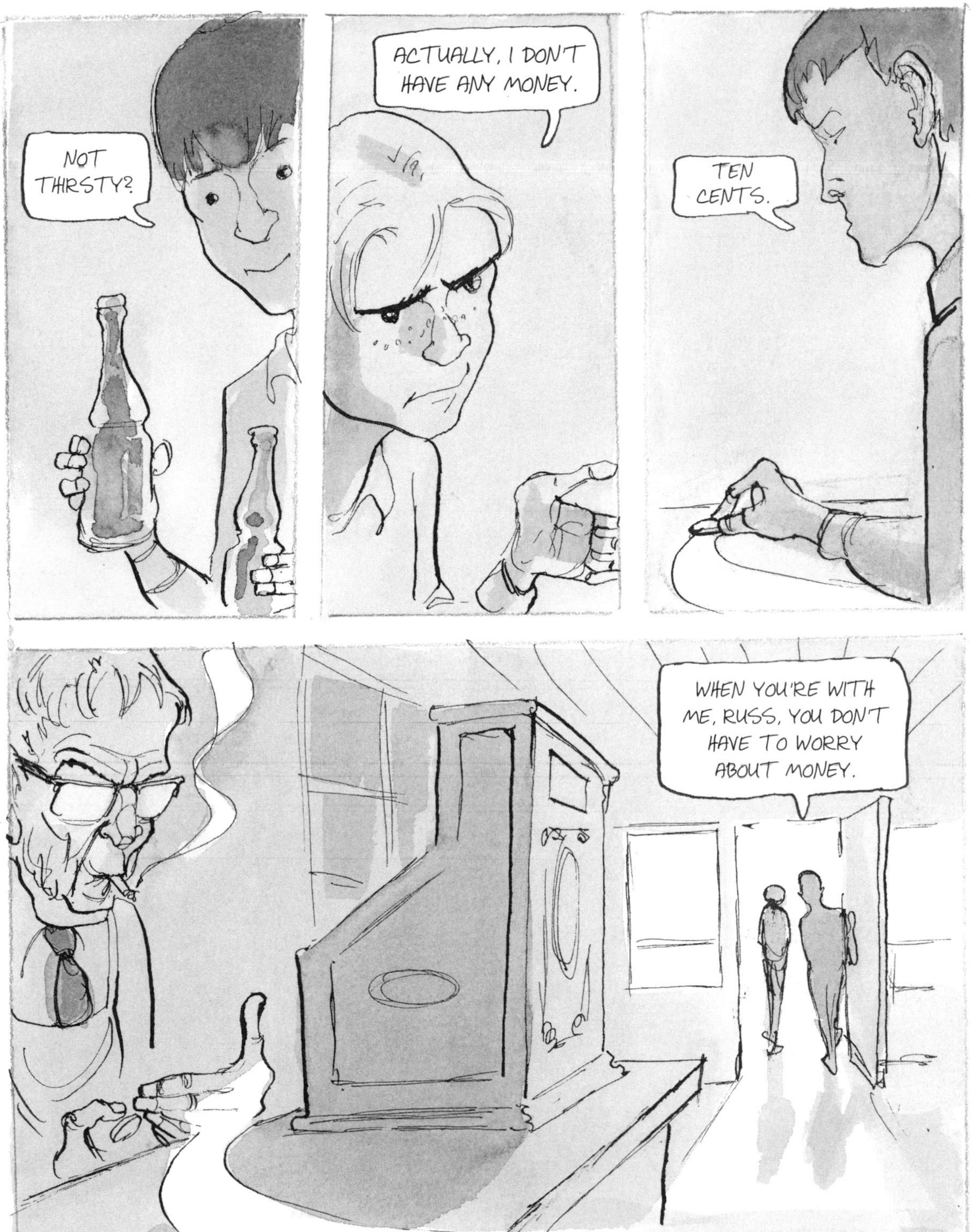
NOT THIRSTY?
ACTUALLY, I DON'T HAVE ANY MONEY.
TEN CENTS.
WHEN YOU'RE WITH ME, RUSS, YOU DON'T HAVE TO WORRY ABOUT MONEY.

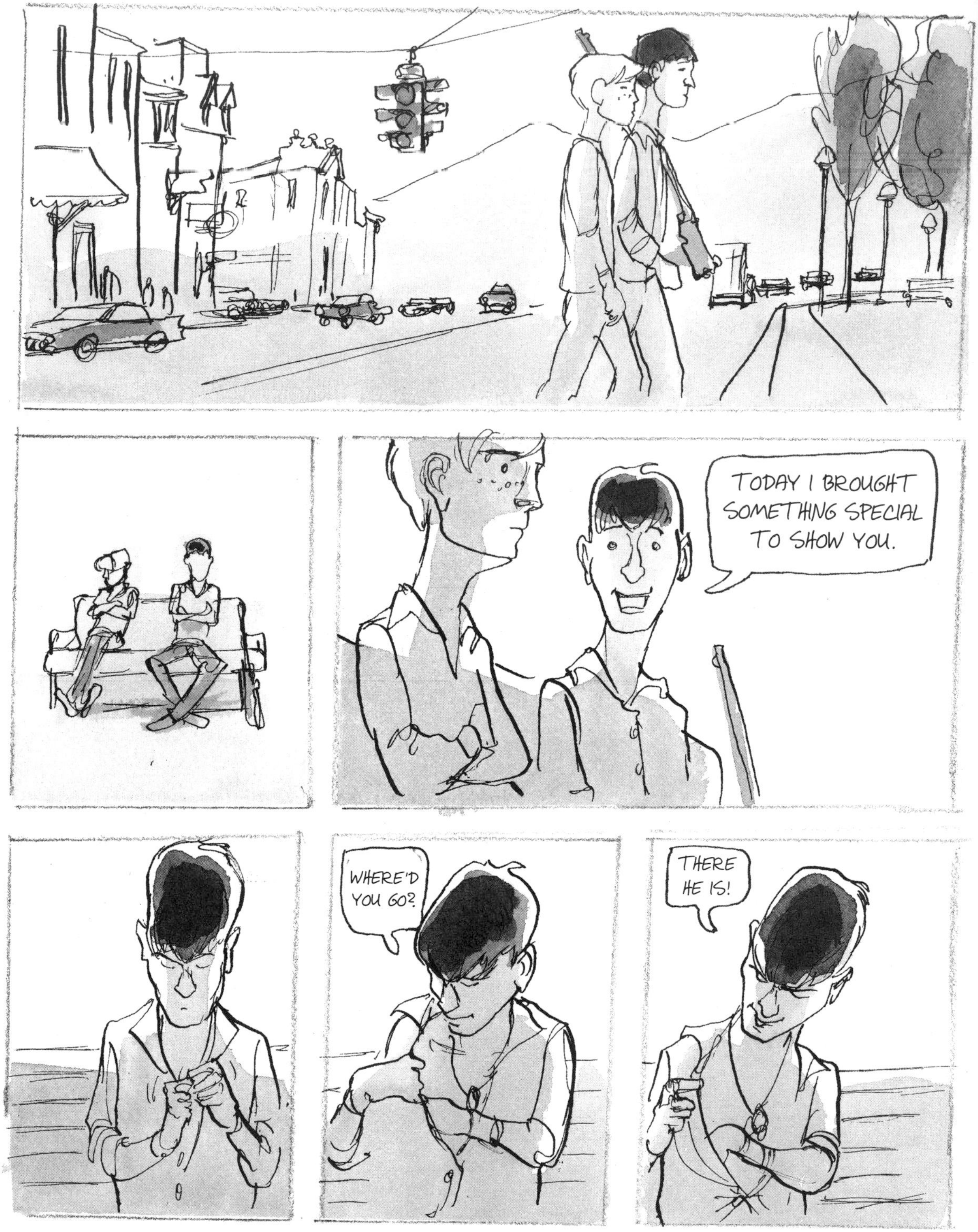
TODAY I BROUGHT SOMETHING SPECIAL TO SHOW YOU.
WHERE'D YOU GO?
THERE HE IS!

145

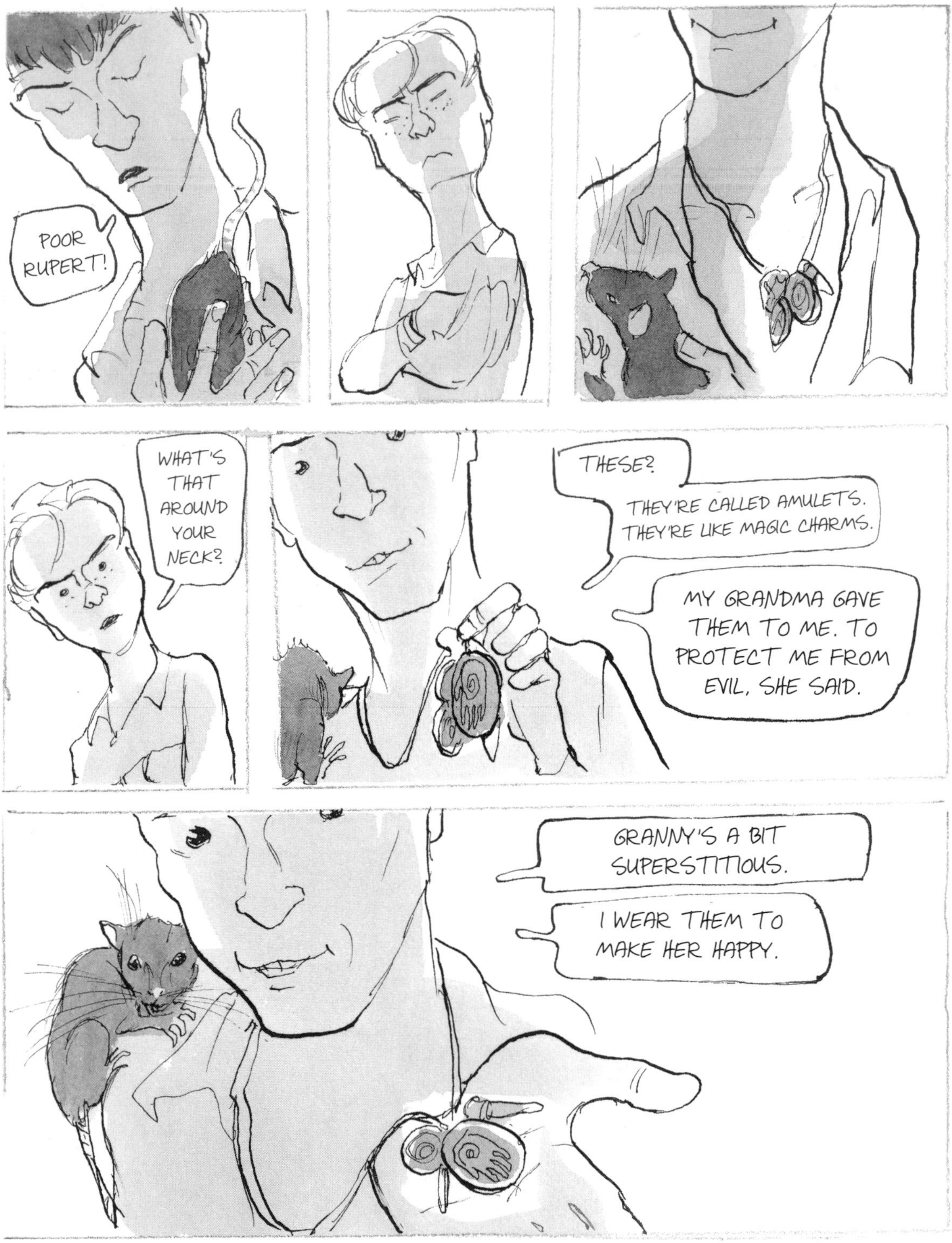
POOR RUPERT!
WHAT'S THAT AROUND YOUR NECK?
THESE?
THEY'RE CALLED AMULETS. THEY'RE LIKE MAGIC CHARMS.
MY GRANDMA GAVE THEM TO ME. TO PROTECT ME FROM EVIL, SHE SAID.
GRANNY'S A BIT SUPERSTITIOUS.
I WEAR THEM TO MAKE HER HAPPY.

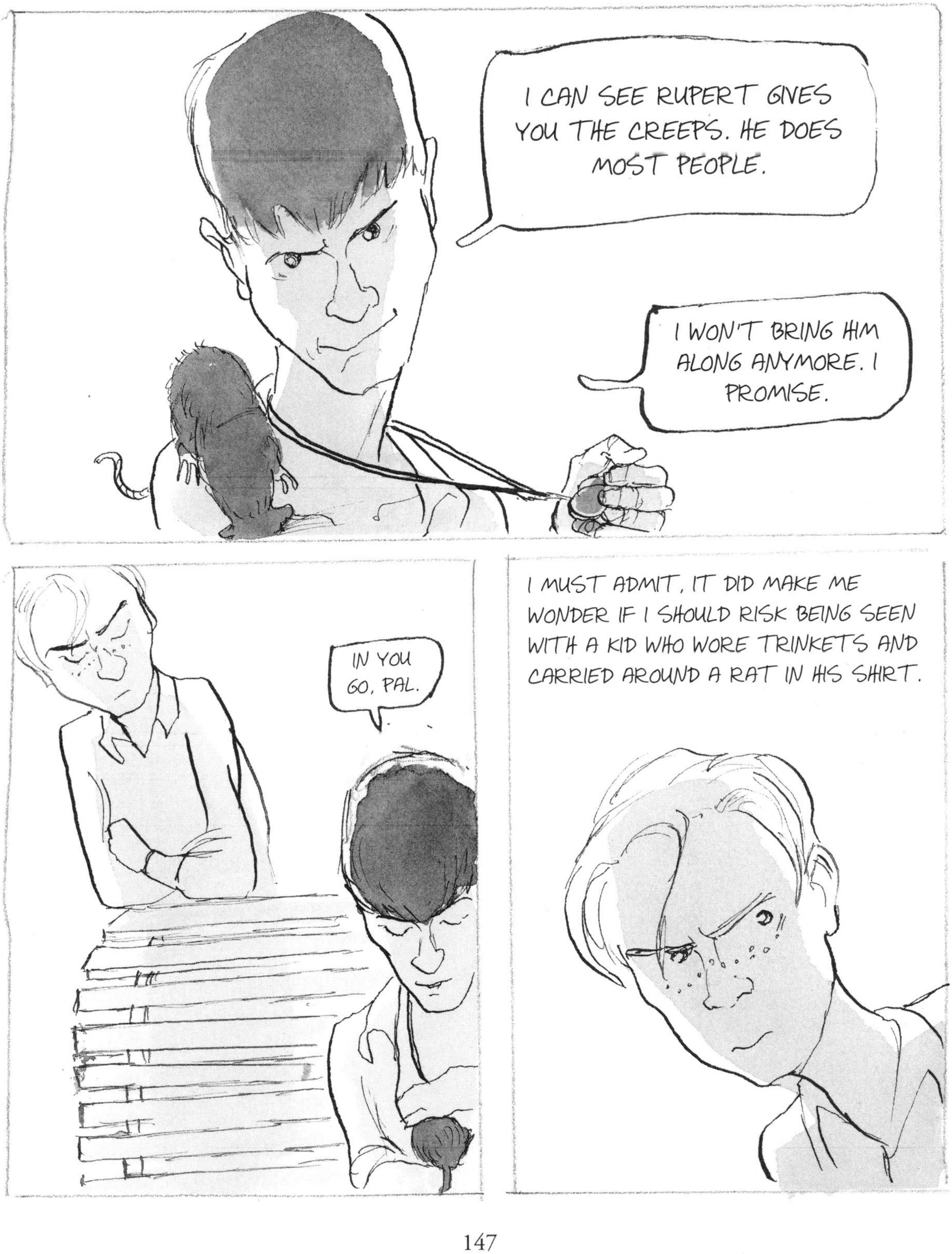
I CAN SEE RUPERT GIVES YOU THE CREEPS. HE DOES MOST PEOPLE.
I WON'T BRING HIM ALONG ANYMORE. I PROMISE.
IN YOU GO, PAL.
I MUST ADMIT, IT DID MAKE ME WONDER IF I SHOULD RISK BEING SEEN WITH A KID WHO WORE TRINKETS AND CARRIED AROUND A RAT IN HIS SHIRT.

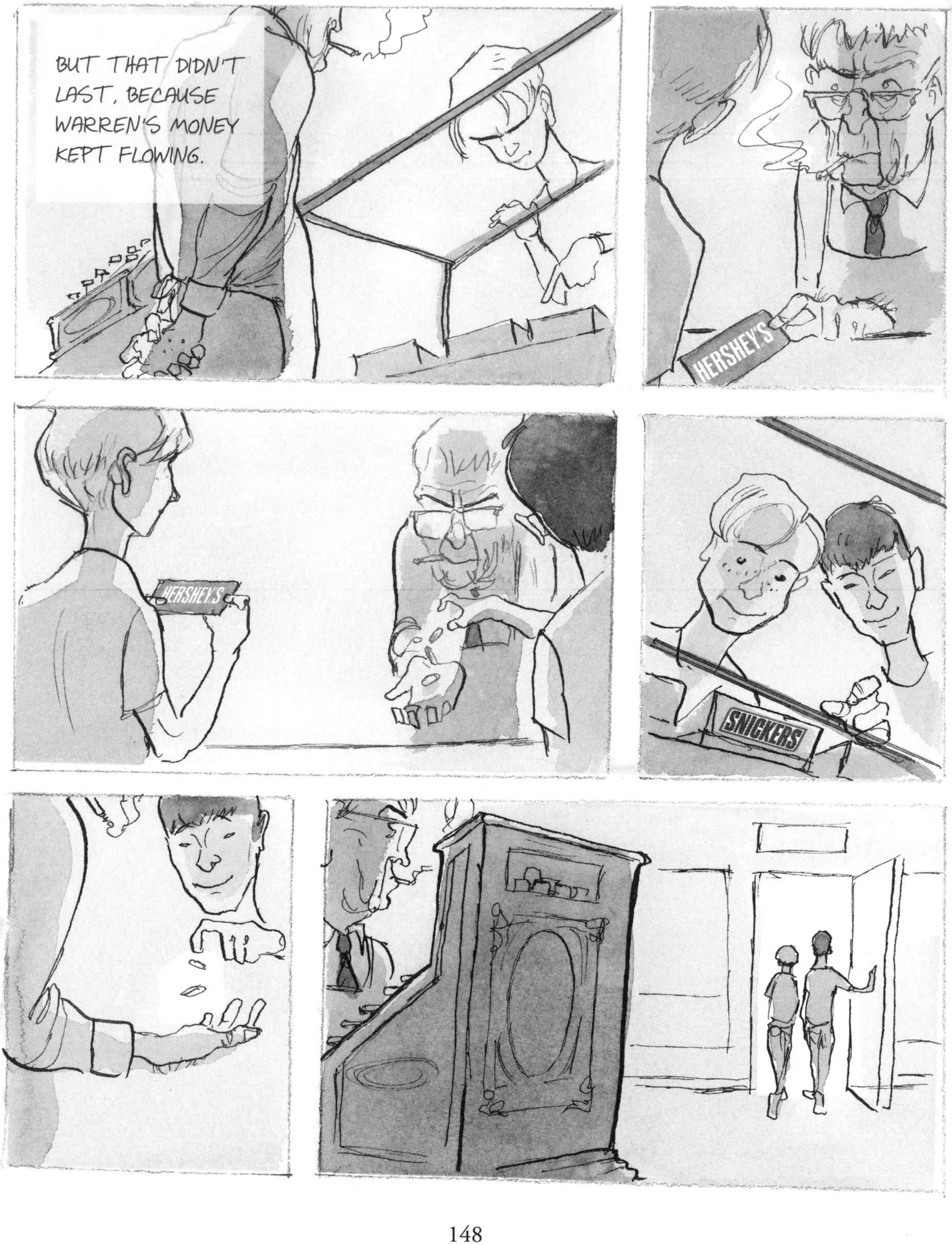
BUT THAT DIDN'T LAST, BECAUSE WARREN'S MONEY KEPT FLOWING.
HERSHEY'S
HERSHEY'S
SNICKERS

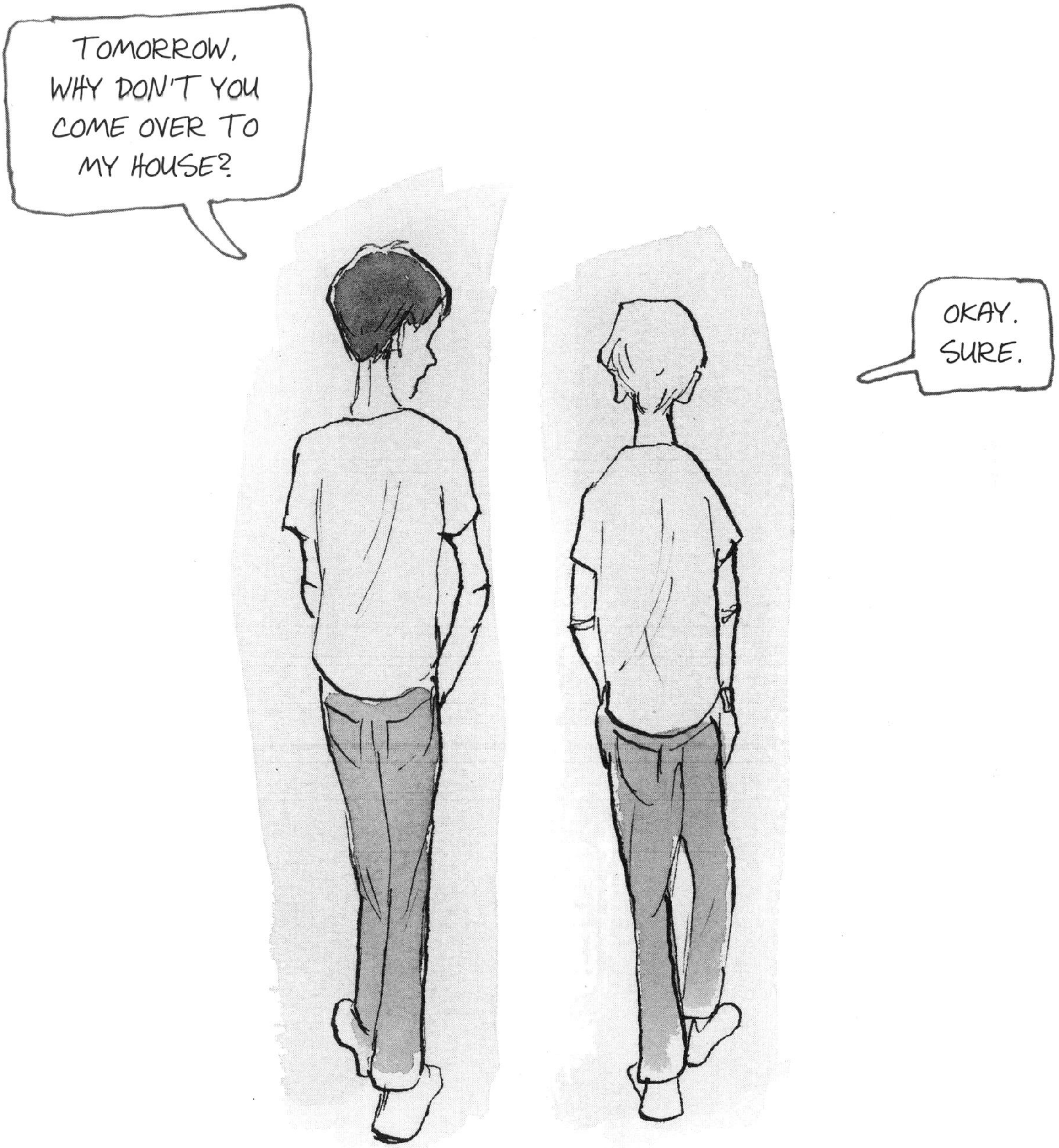
TOMORROW, WHY DON'T YOU COME OVER TO MY HOUSE?
OKAY. SURE.

CHAPTER EIGHT

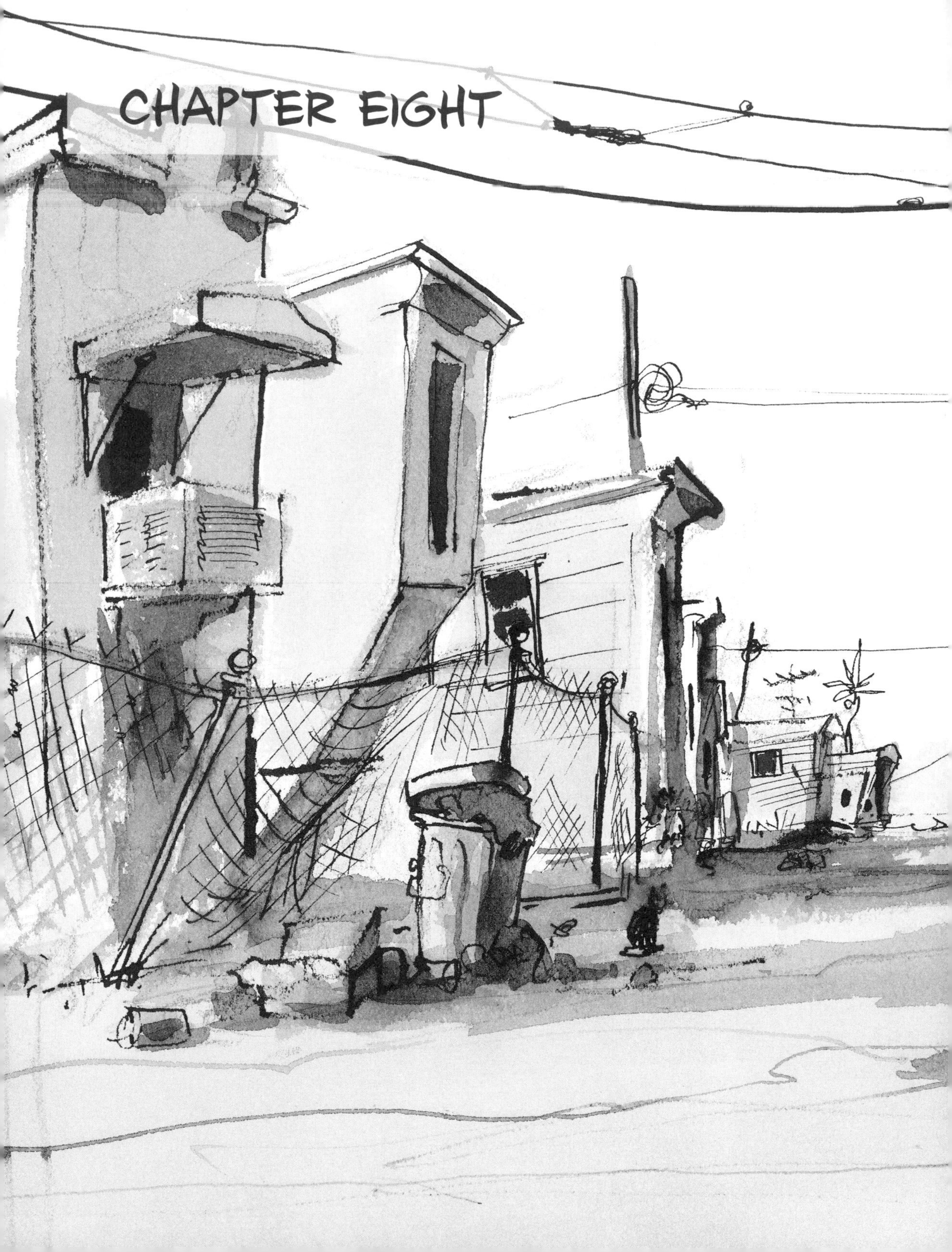

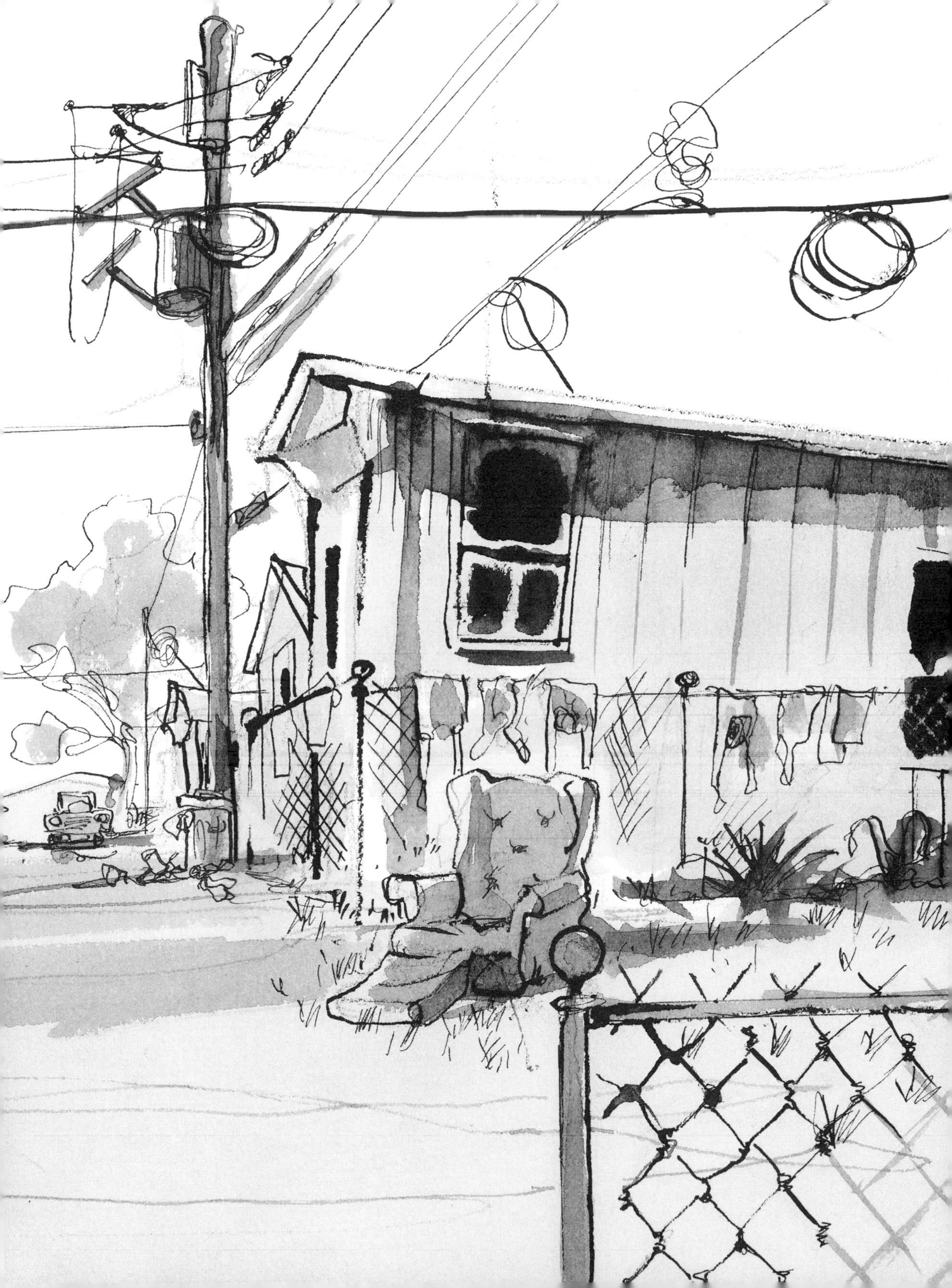

154

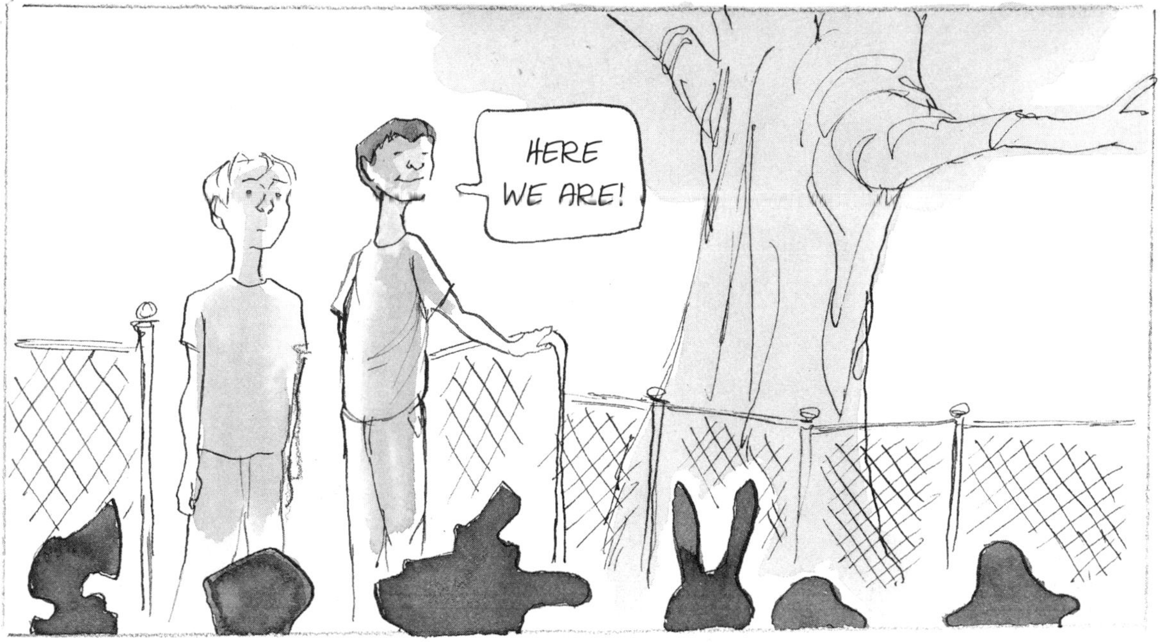
HERE WE ARE!

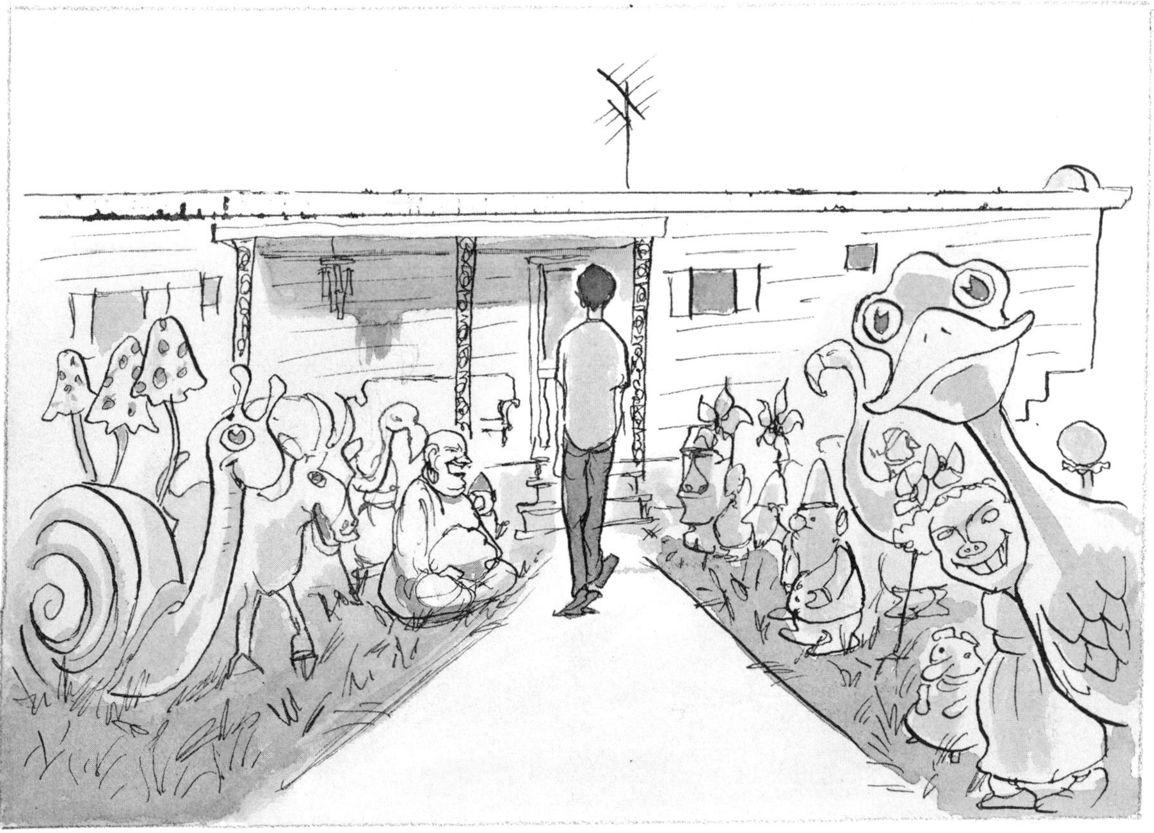

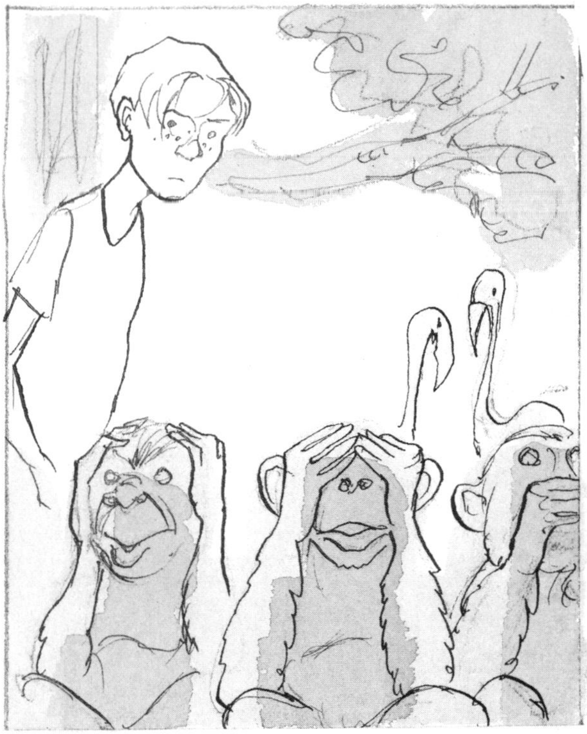

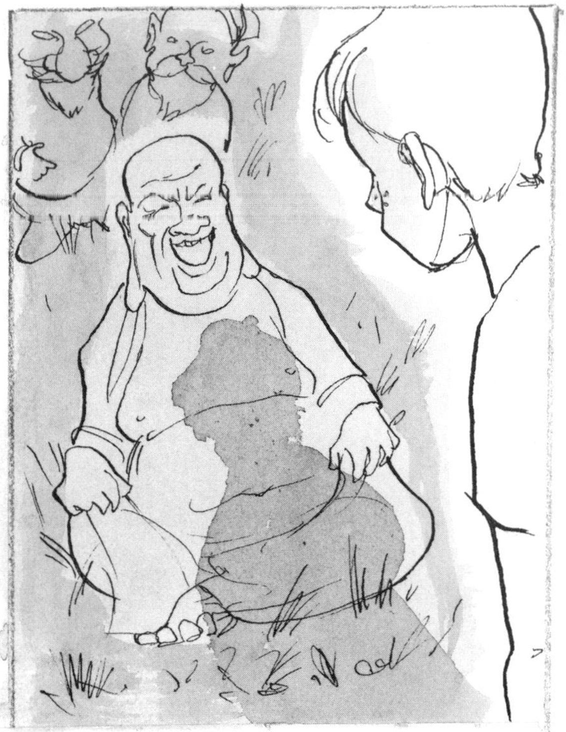

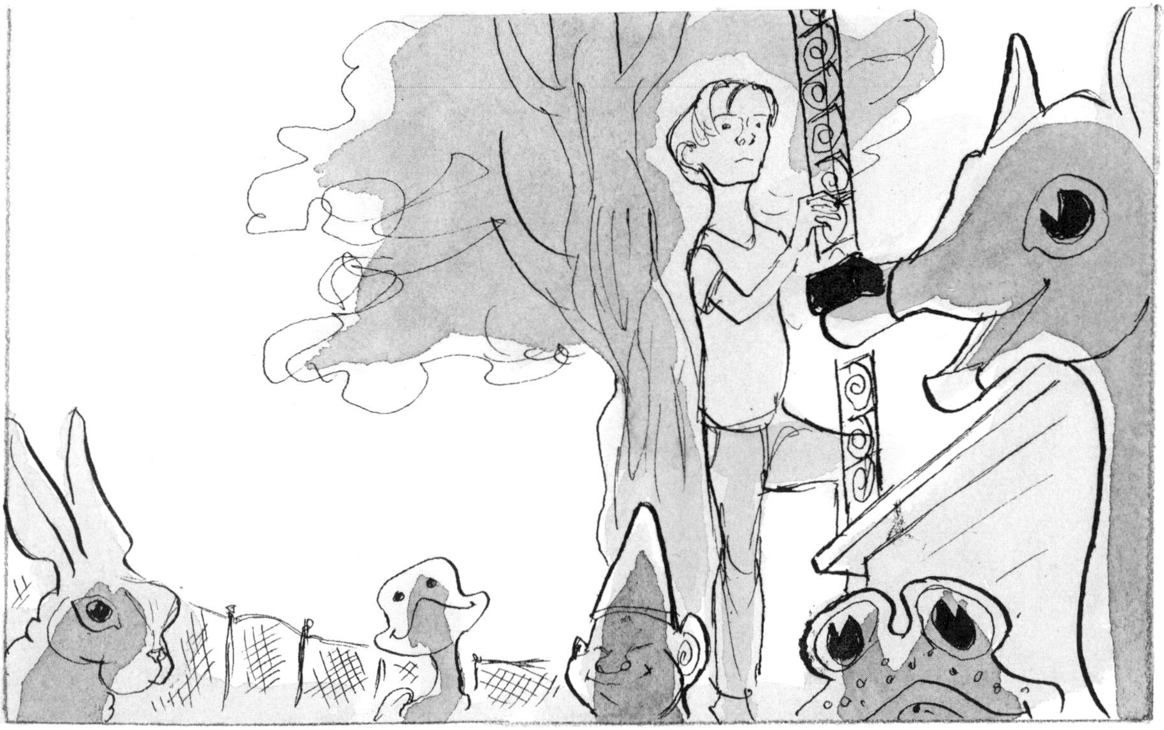

159

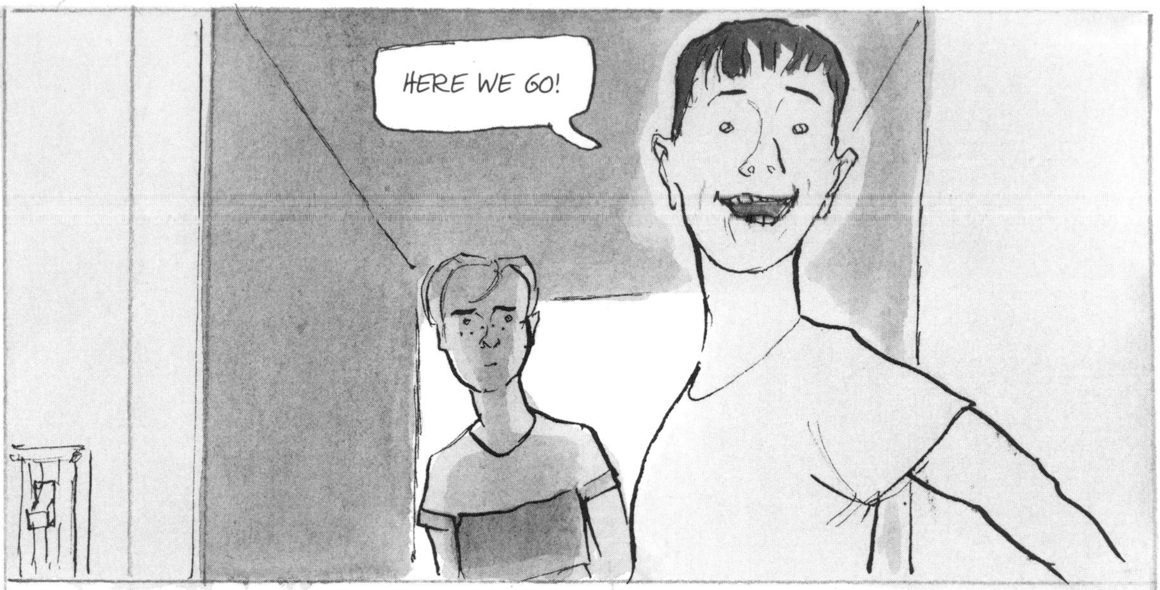
HERE WE GO!

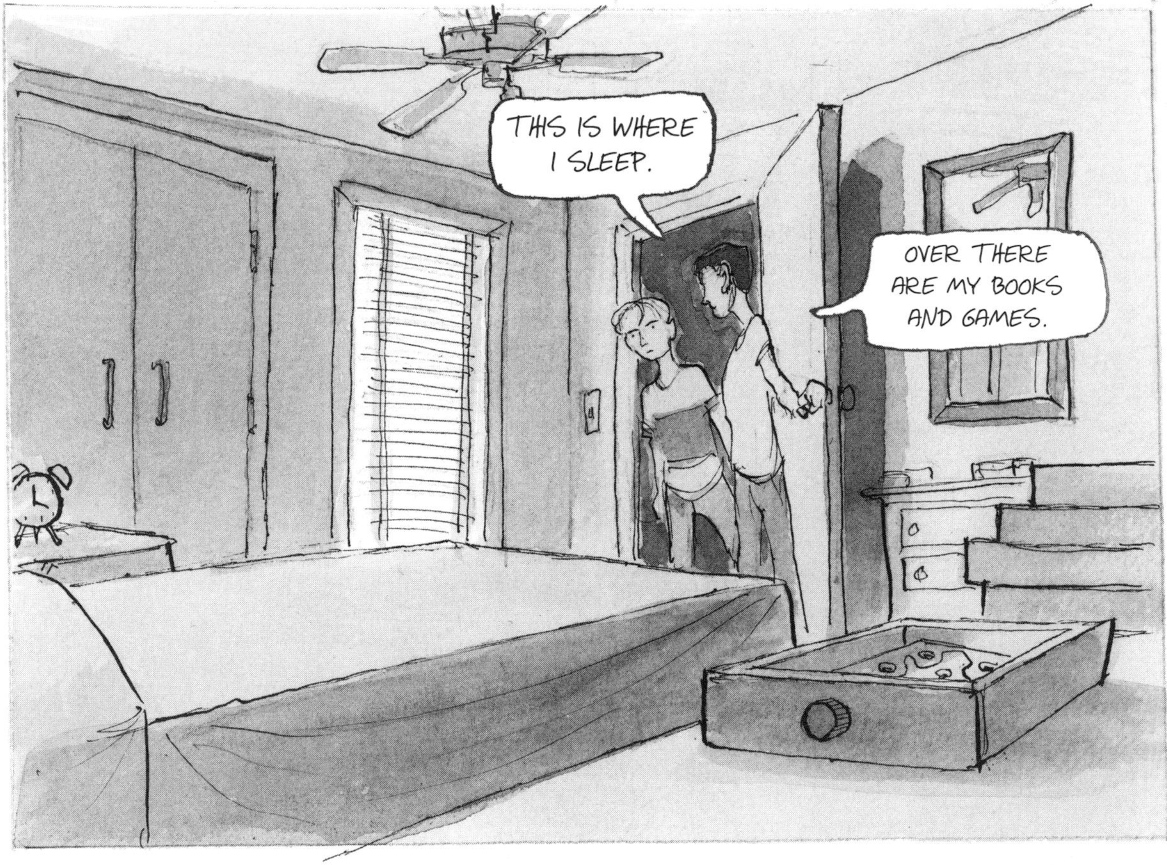
THIS IS WHERE I SLEEP.
OVER THERE ARE MY BOOKS AND GAMES.

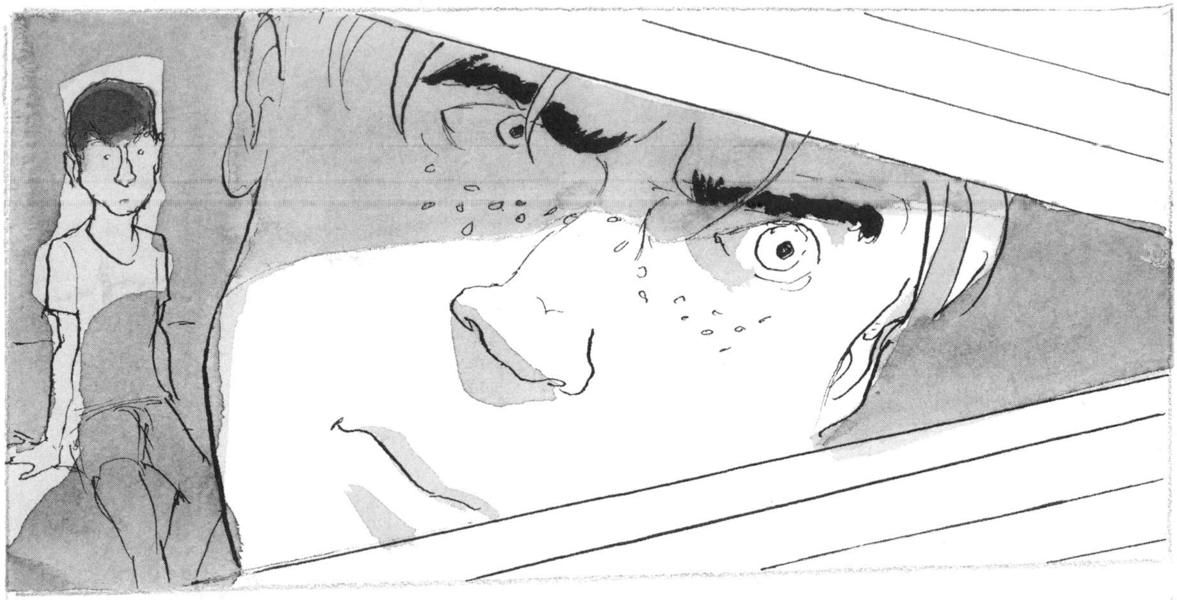

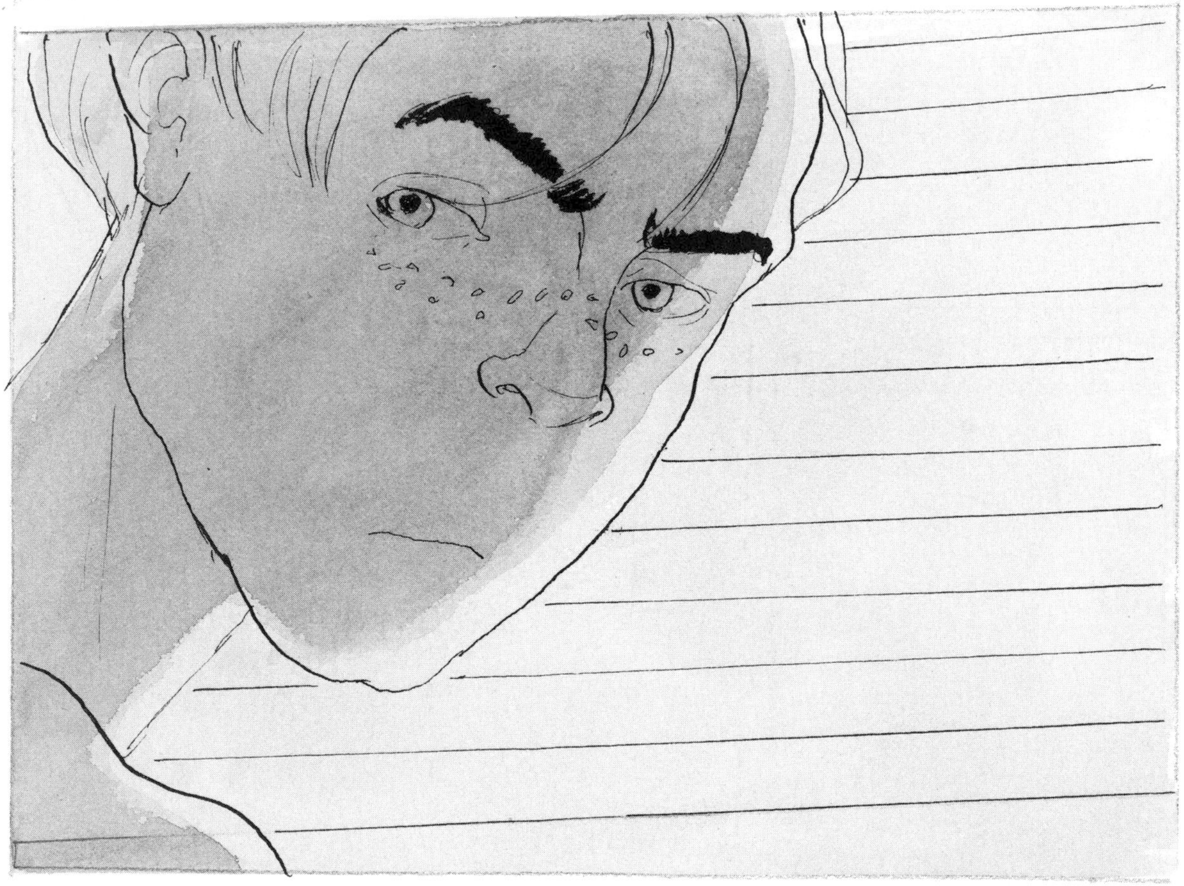

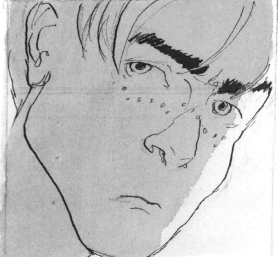
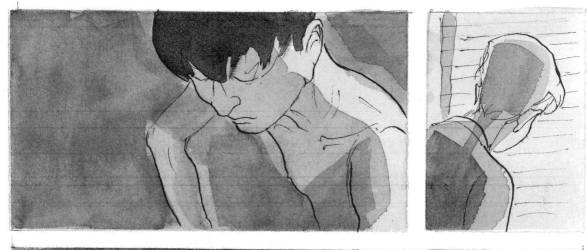
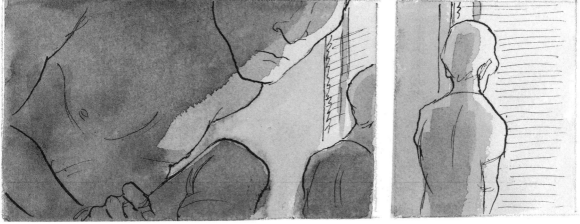

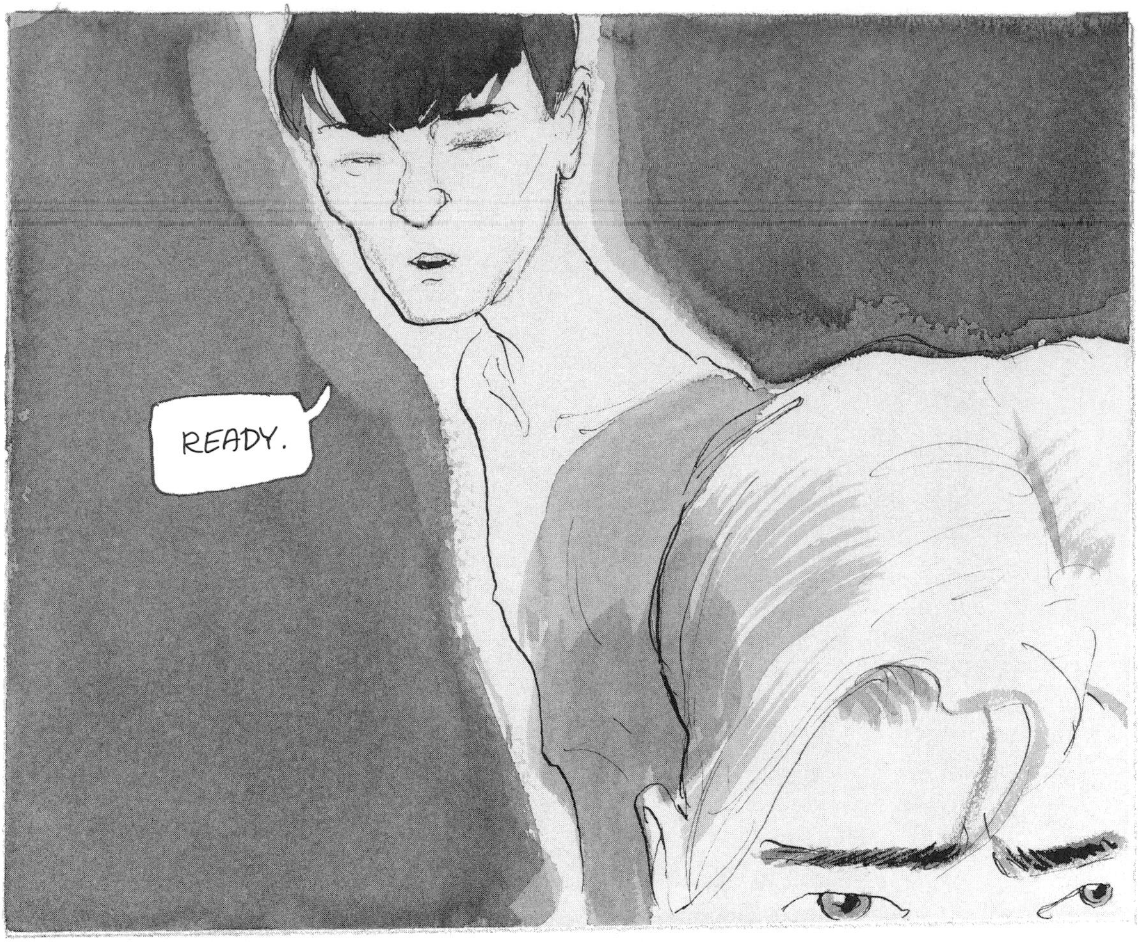
READY.

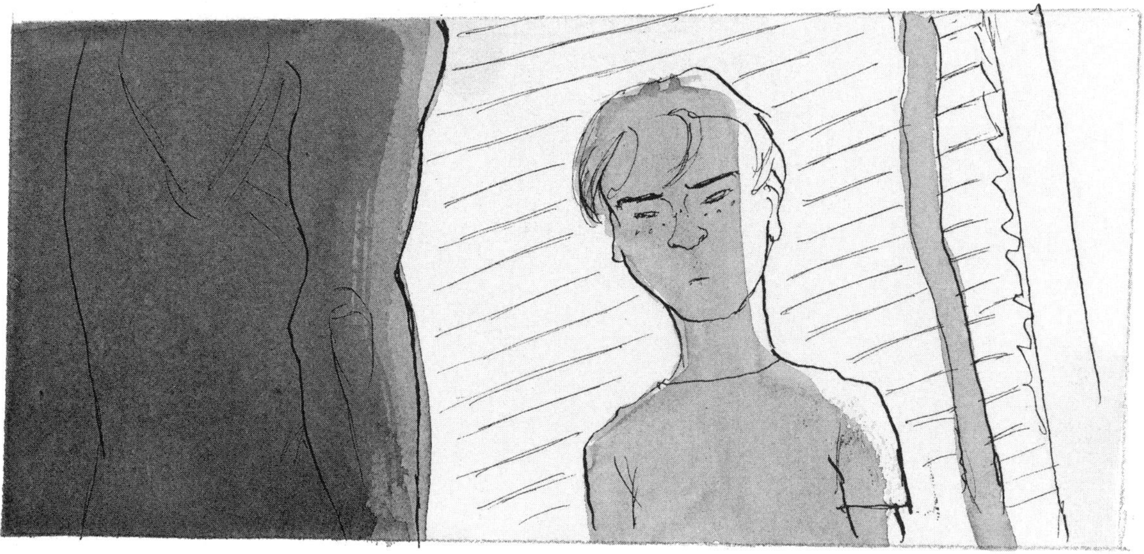

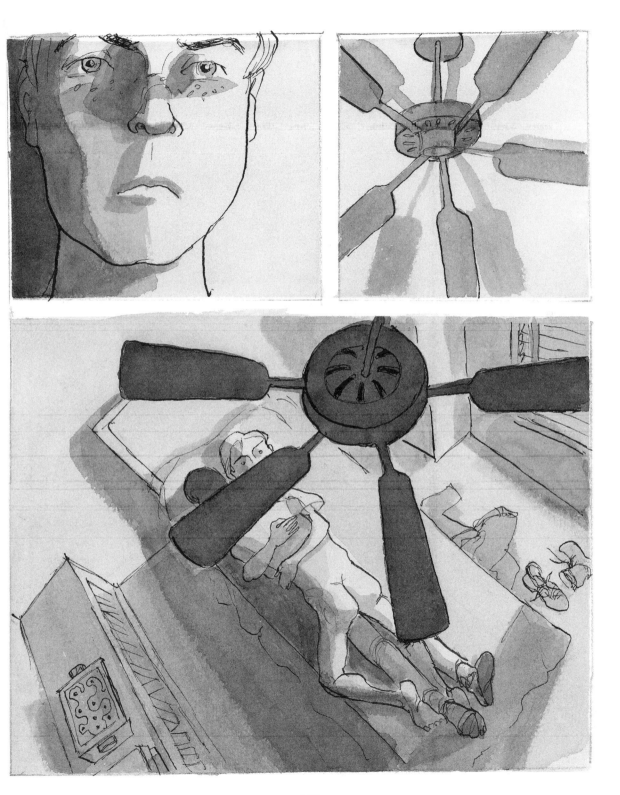

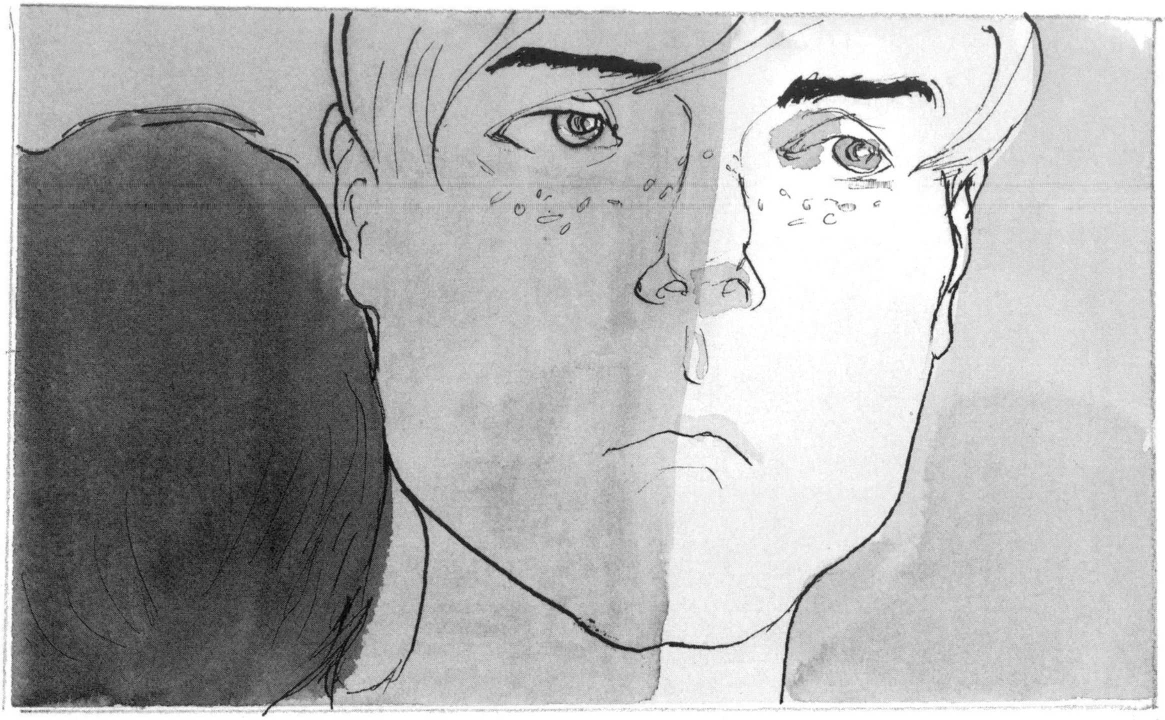

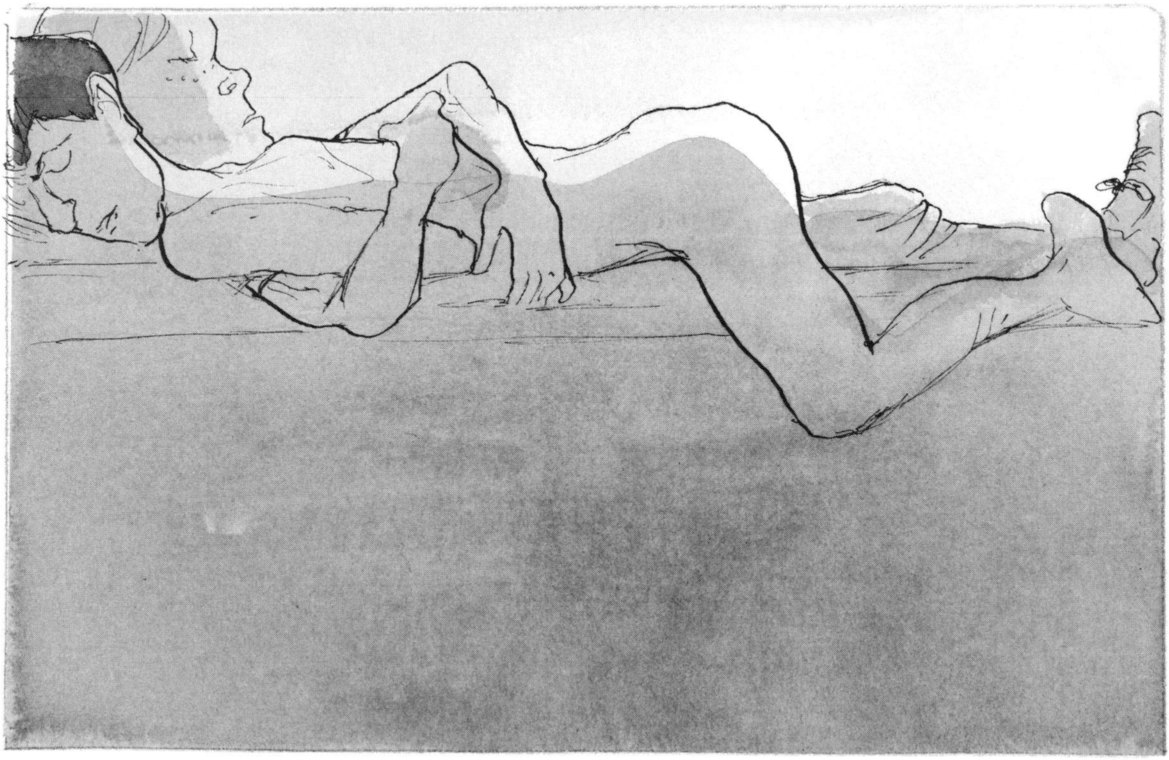

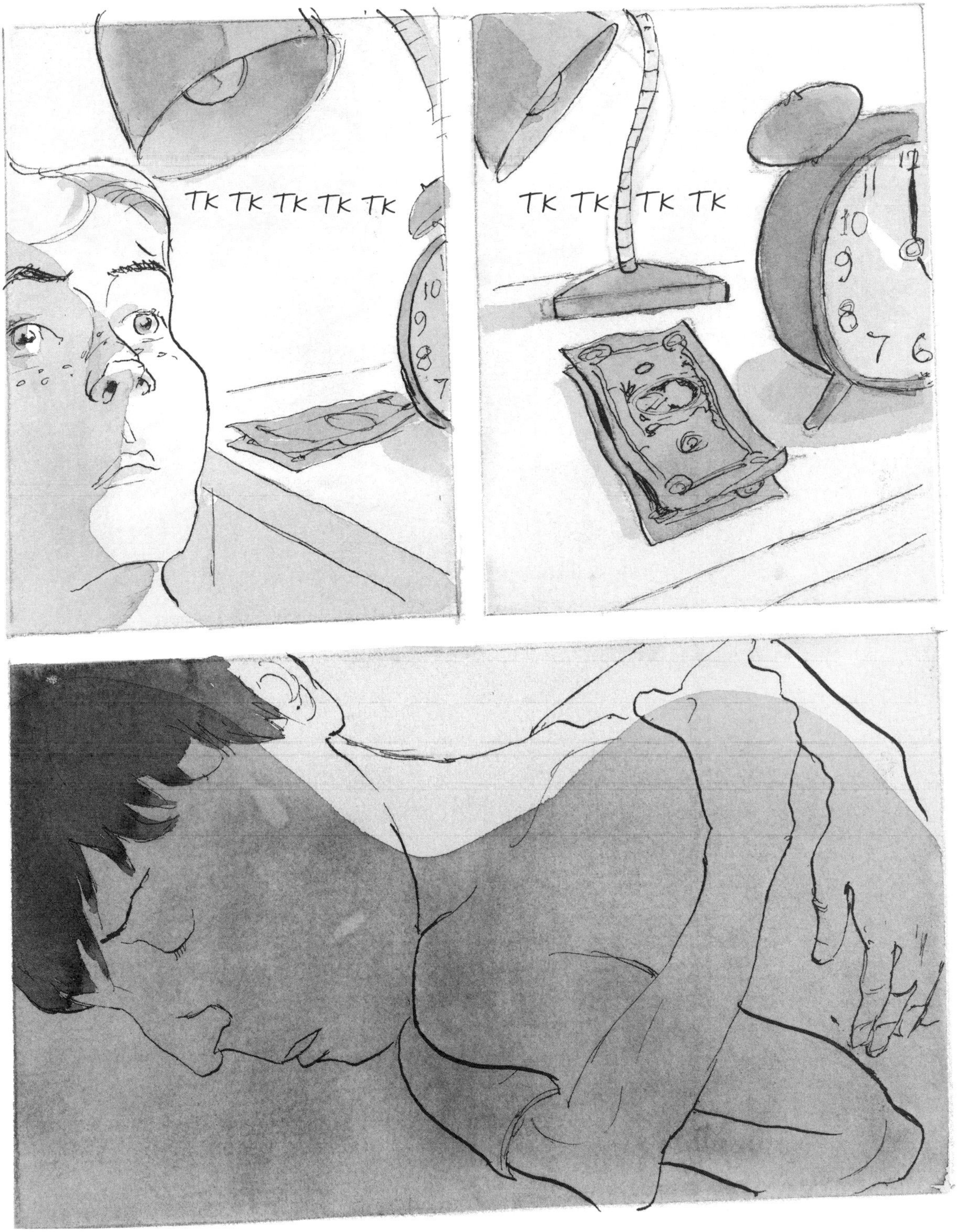
TK TK TK TK TK
TK TK TK TK

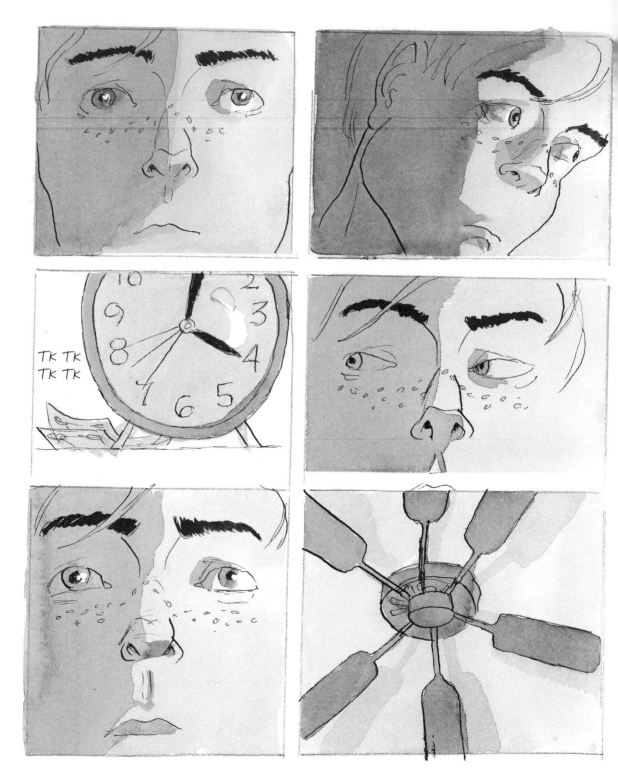

Tk Tk
Tk Tk

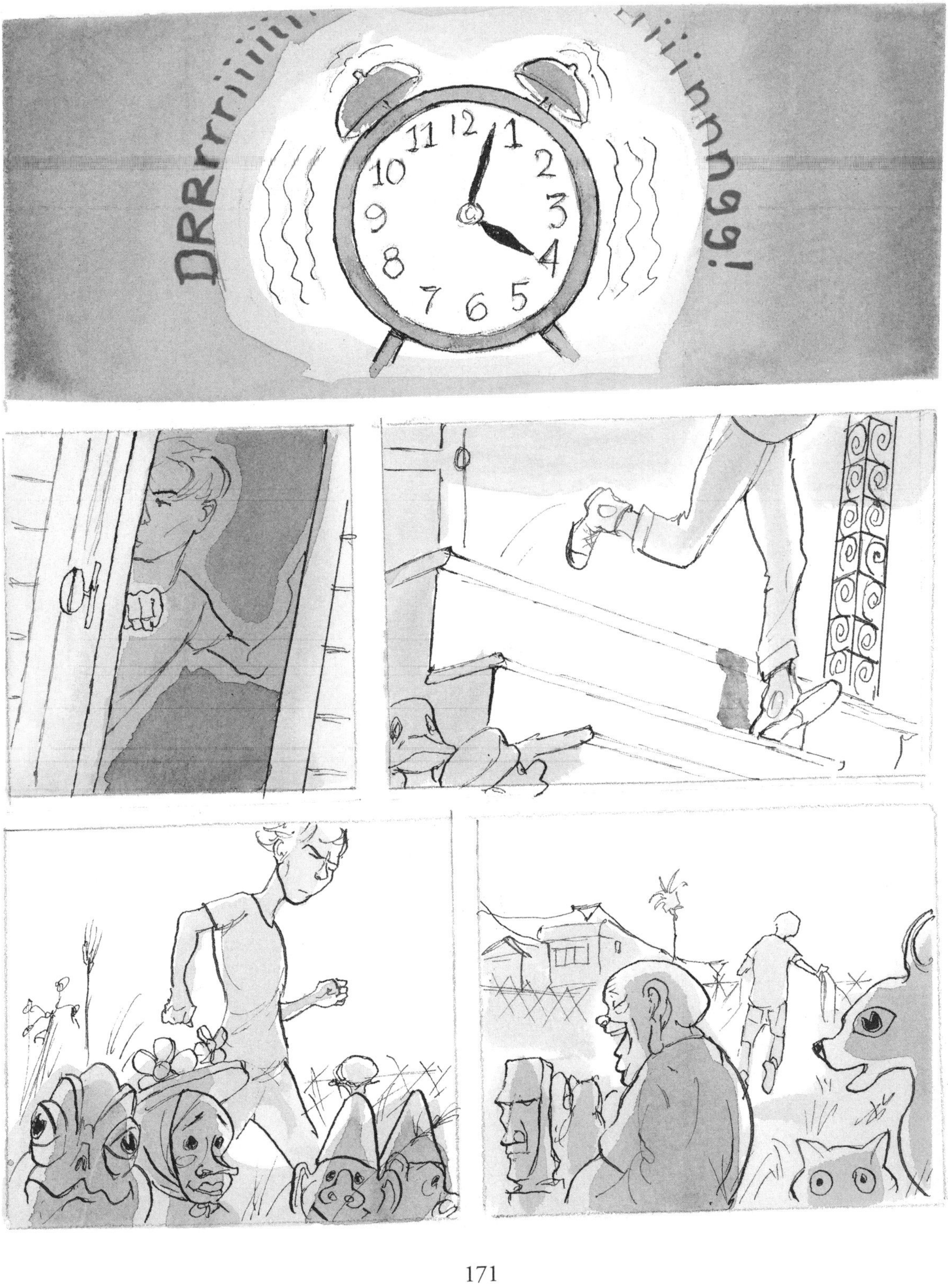
DRRrrriiii
iiiinnngg!

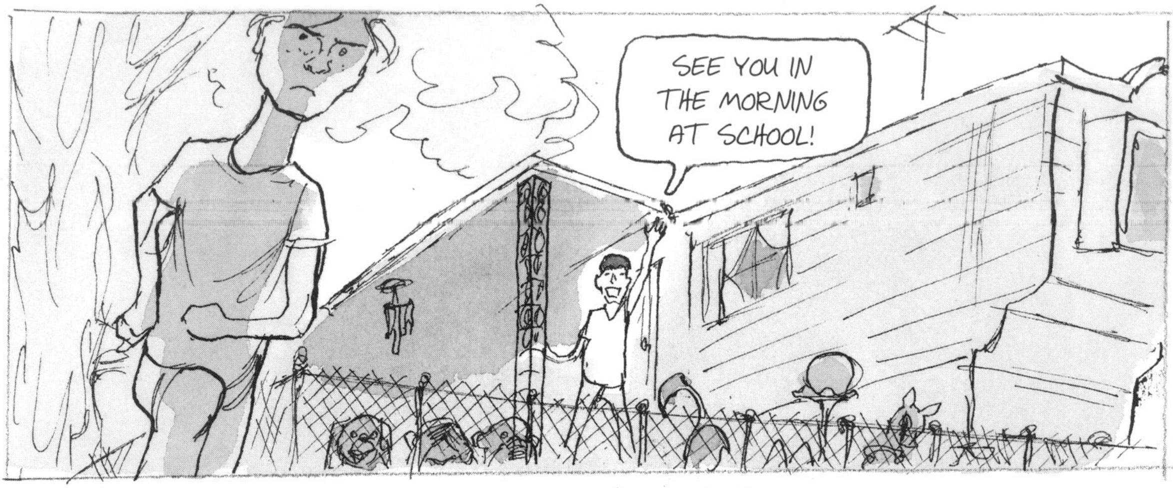
SEE YOU IN THE MORNING AT SCHOOL!

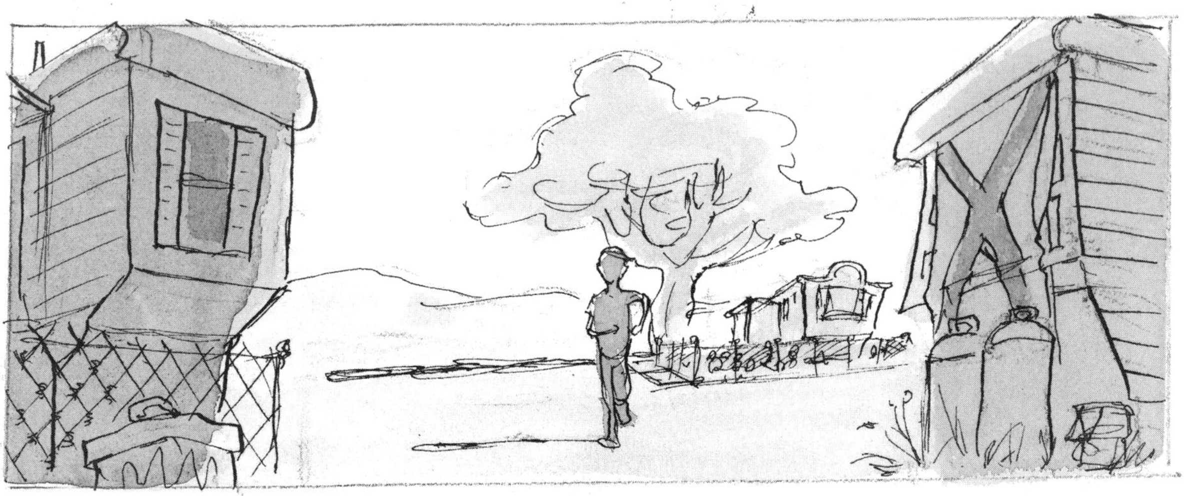

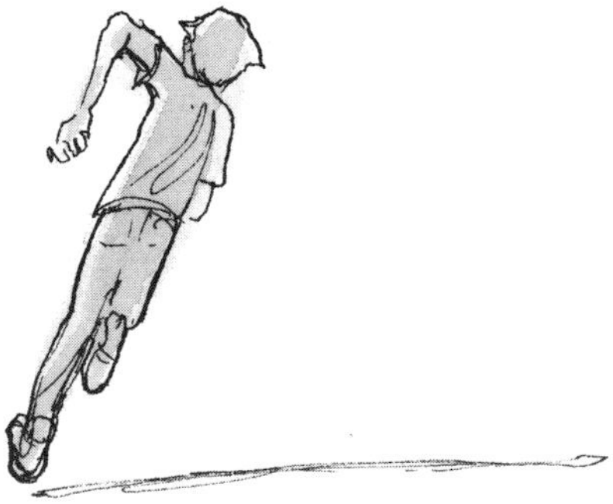

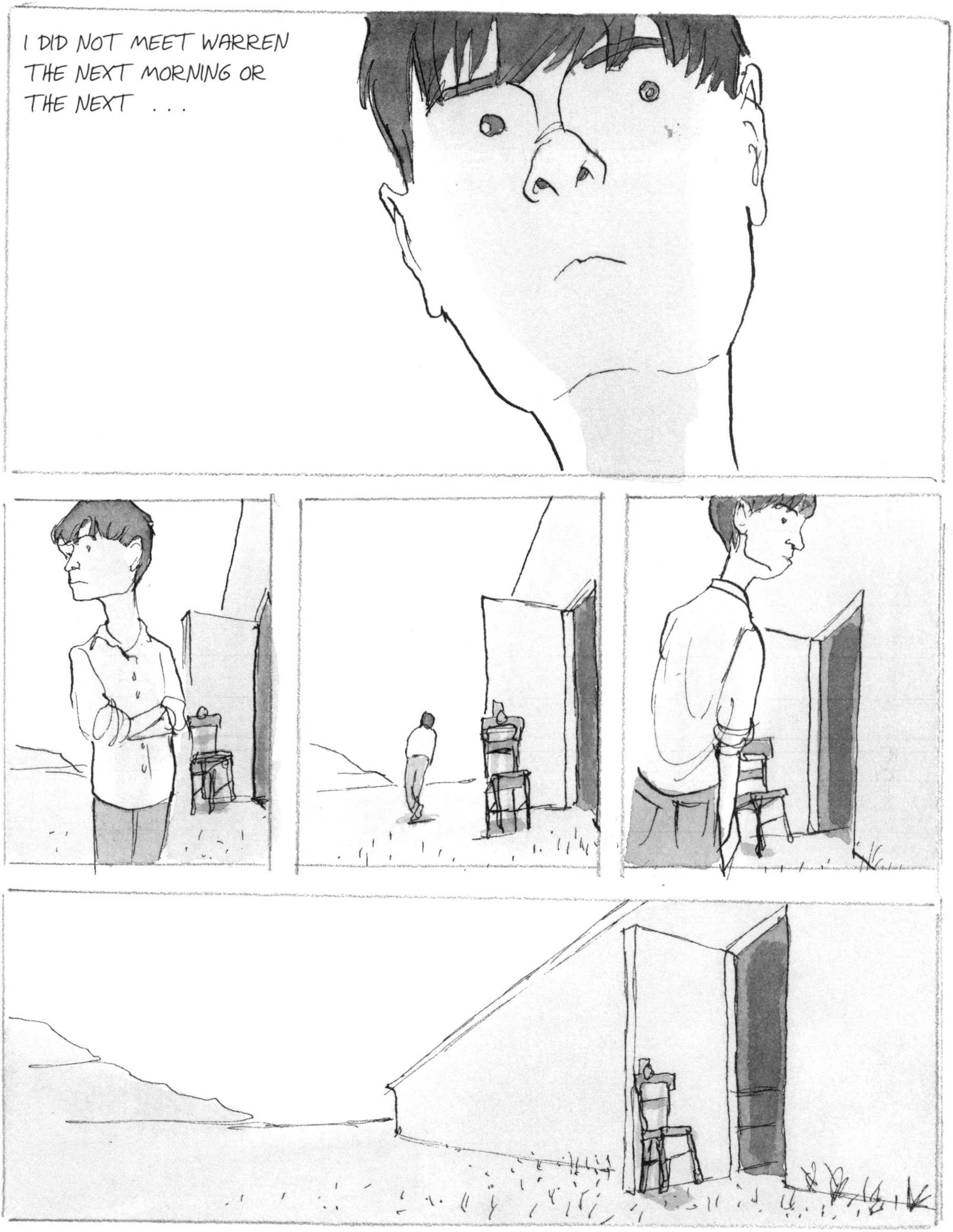
I DID NOT MEET WARREN THE NEXT MORNING OR THE NEXT . . .

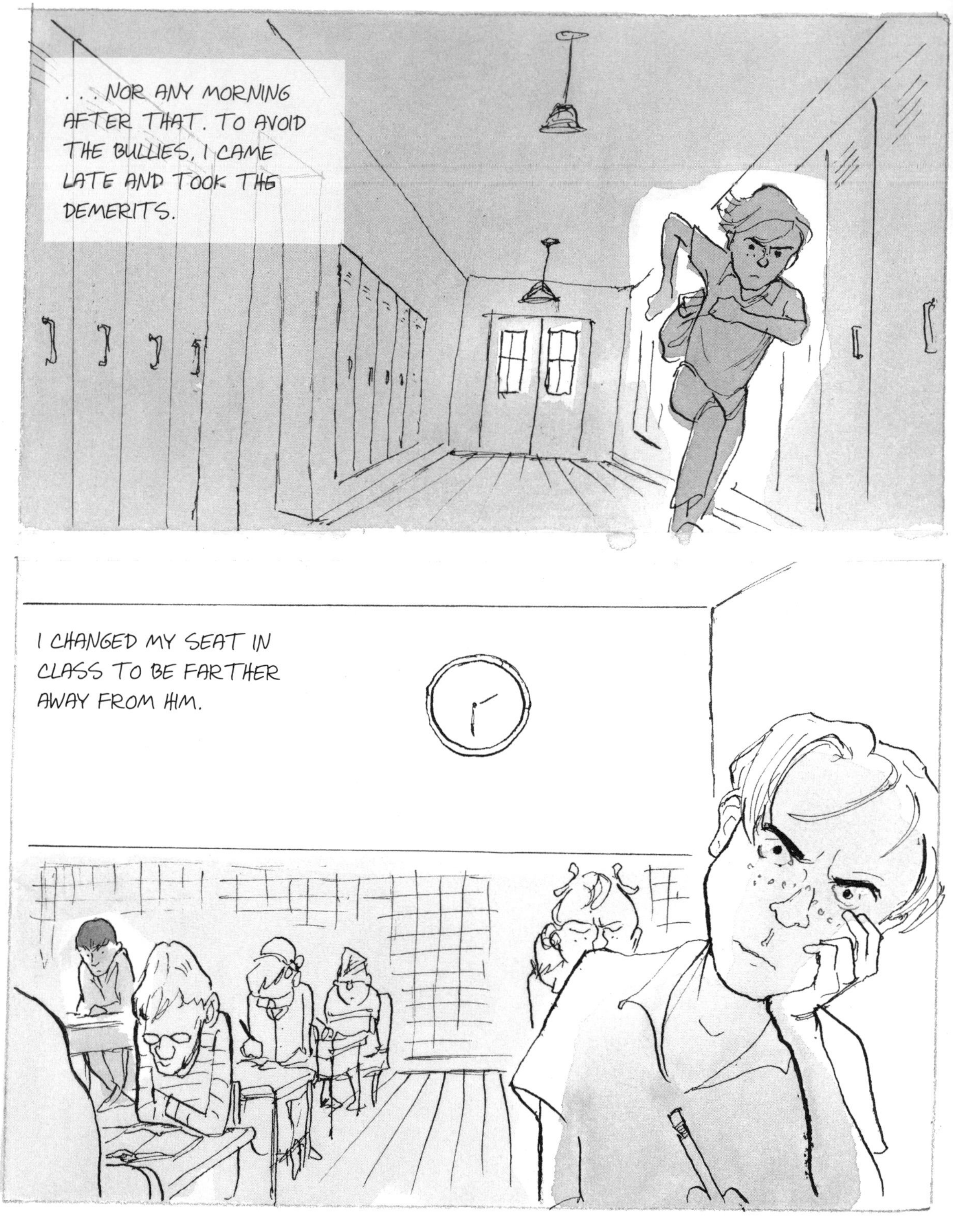
. . . NOR ANY MORNING AFTER THAT. TO AVOID THE BULLIES, I CAME LATE AND TOOK THE DEMERITS.
I CHANGED MY SEAT IN CLASS TO BE FARTHER AWAY FROM HIM.

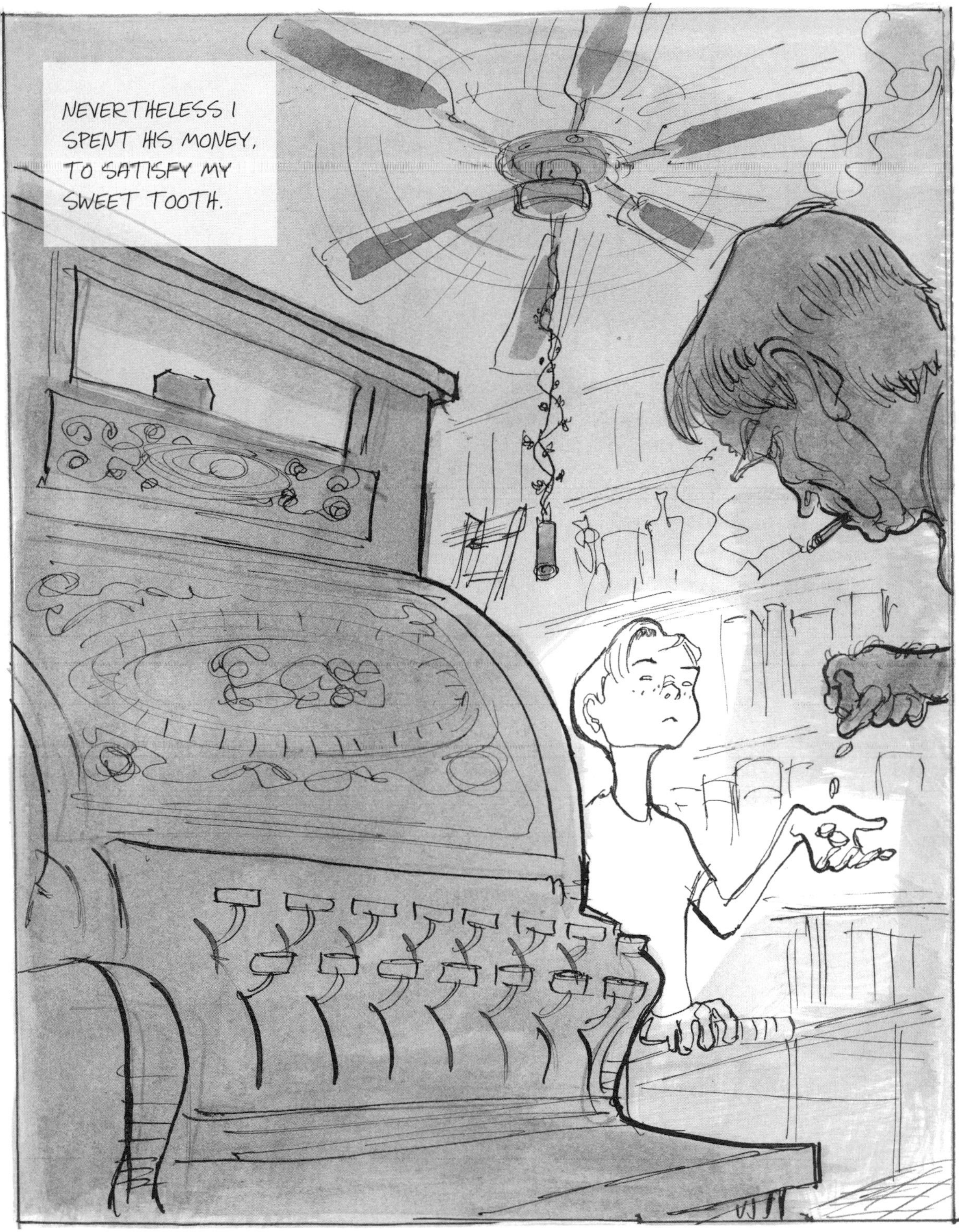
NEVERTHELESS I SPENT HIS MONEY, TO SATISFY MY SWEET TOOTH.

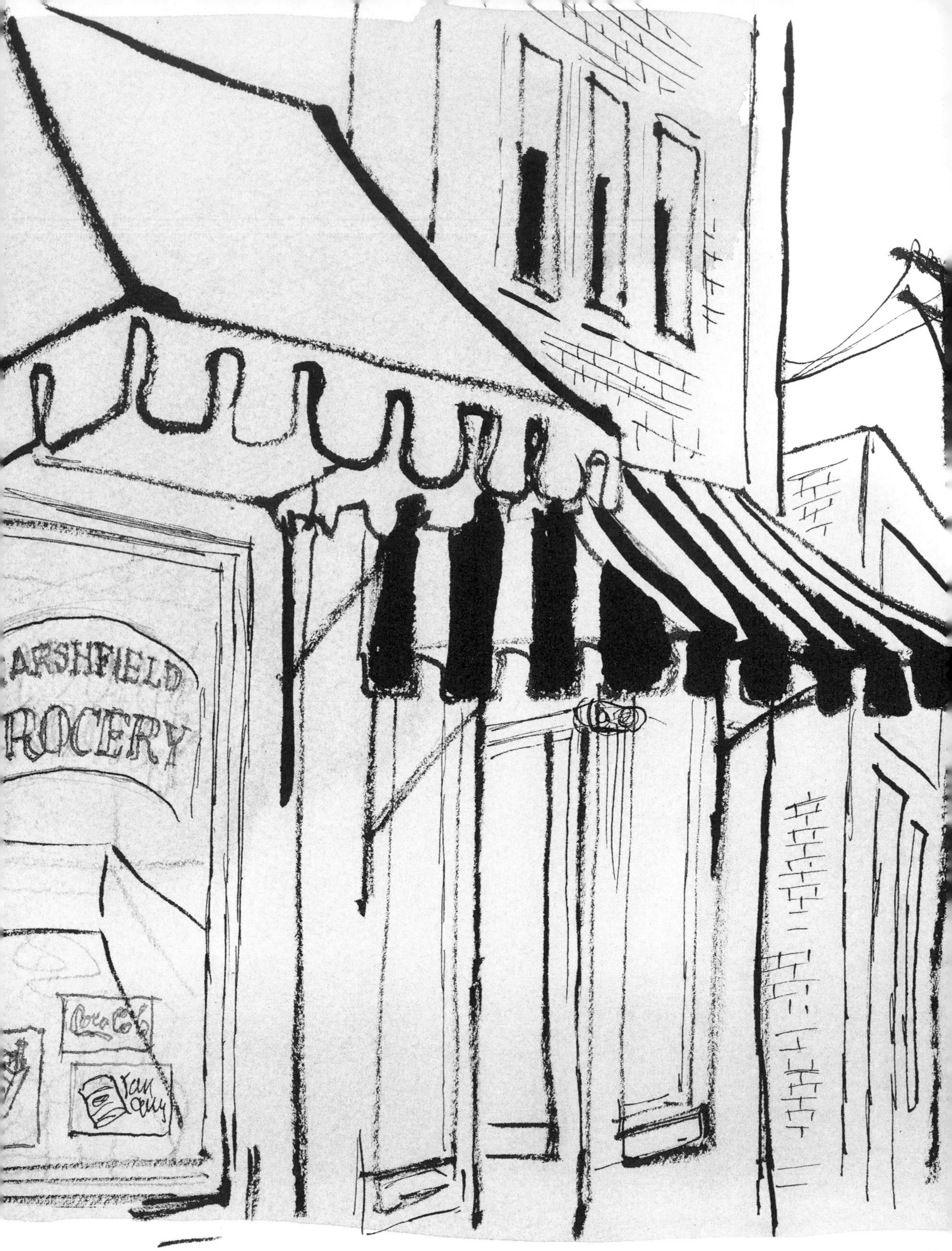
ARSHFIELD
ROCERY

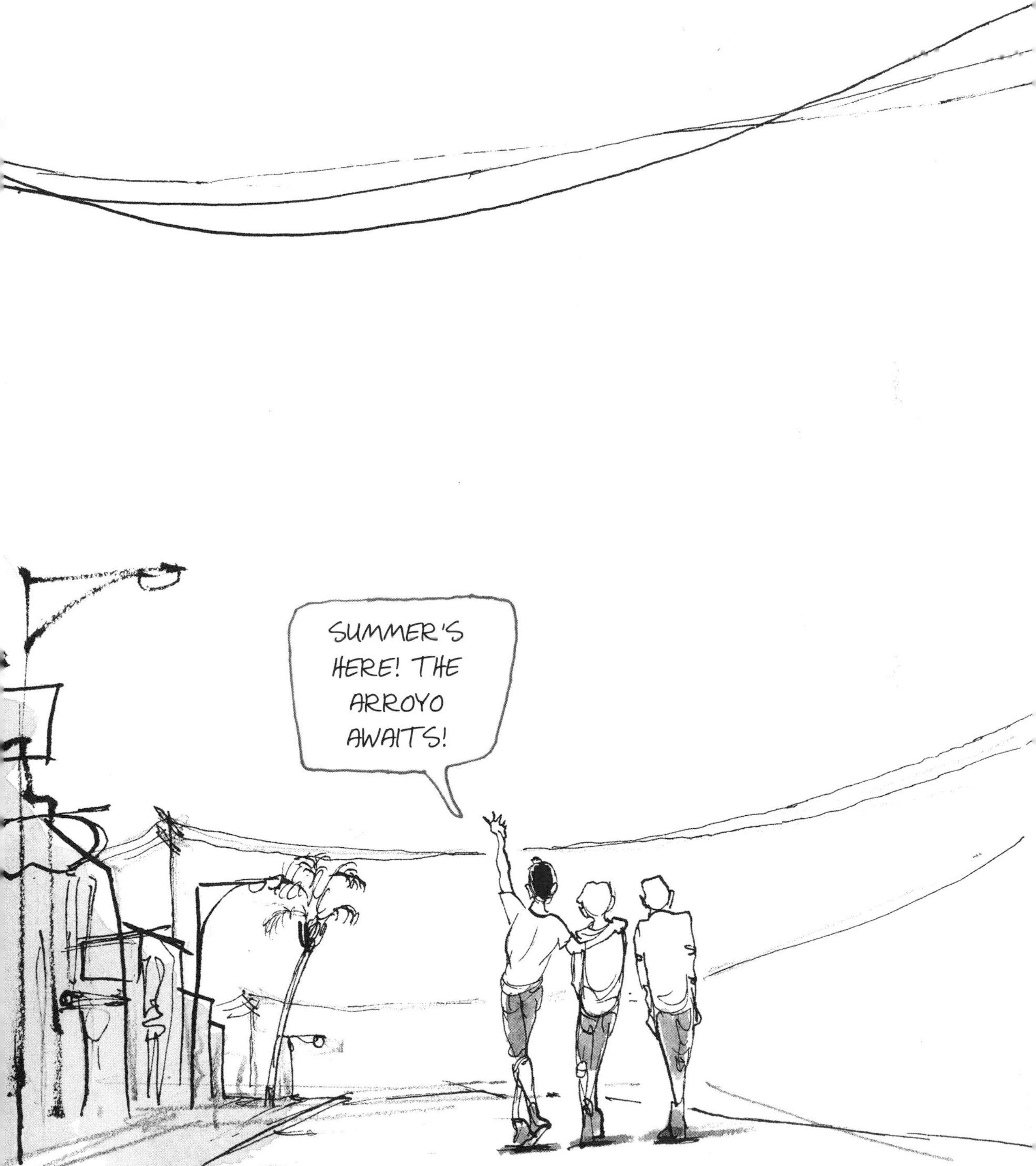
SUMMER'S HERE! THE ARROYO AWAITS!

CHAPTER NINE

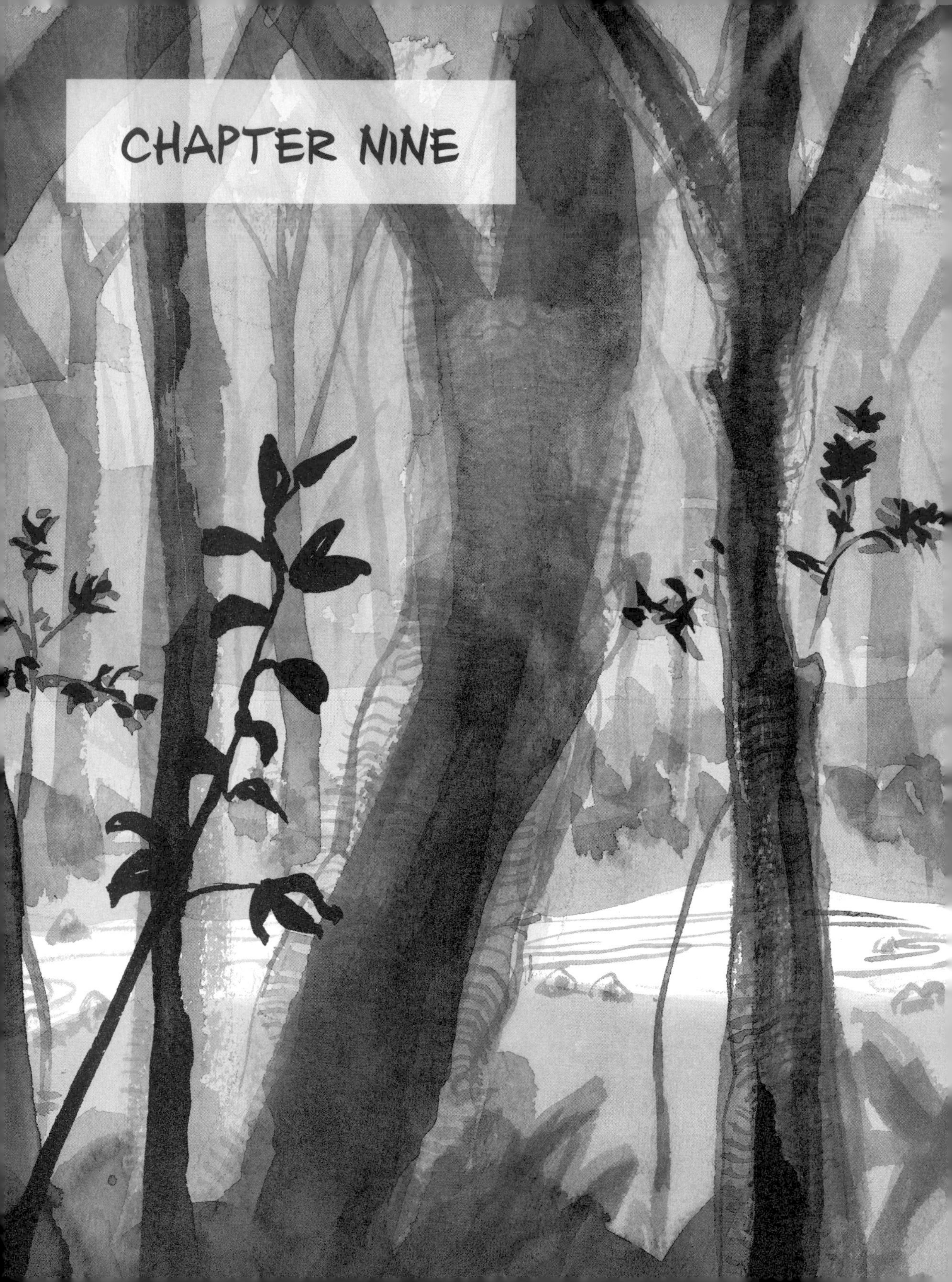

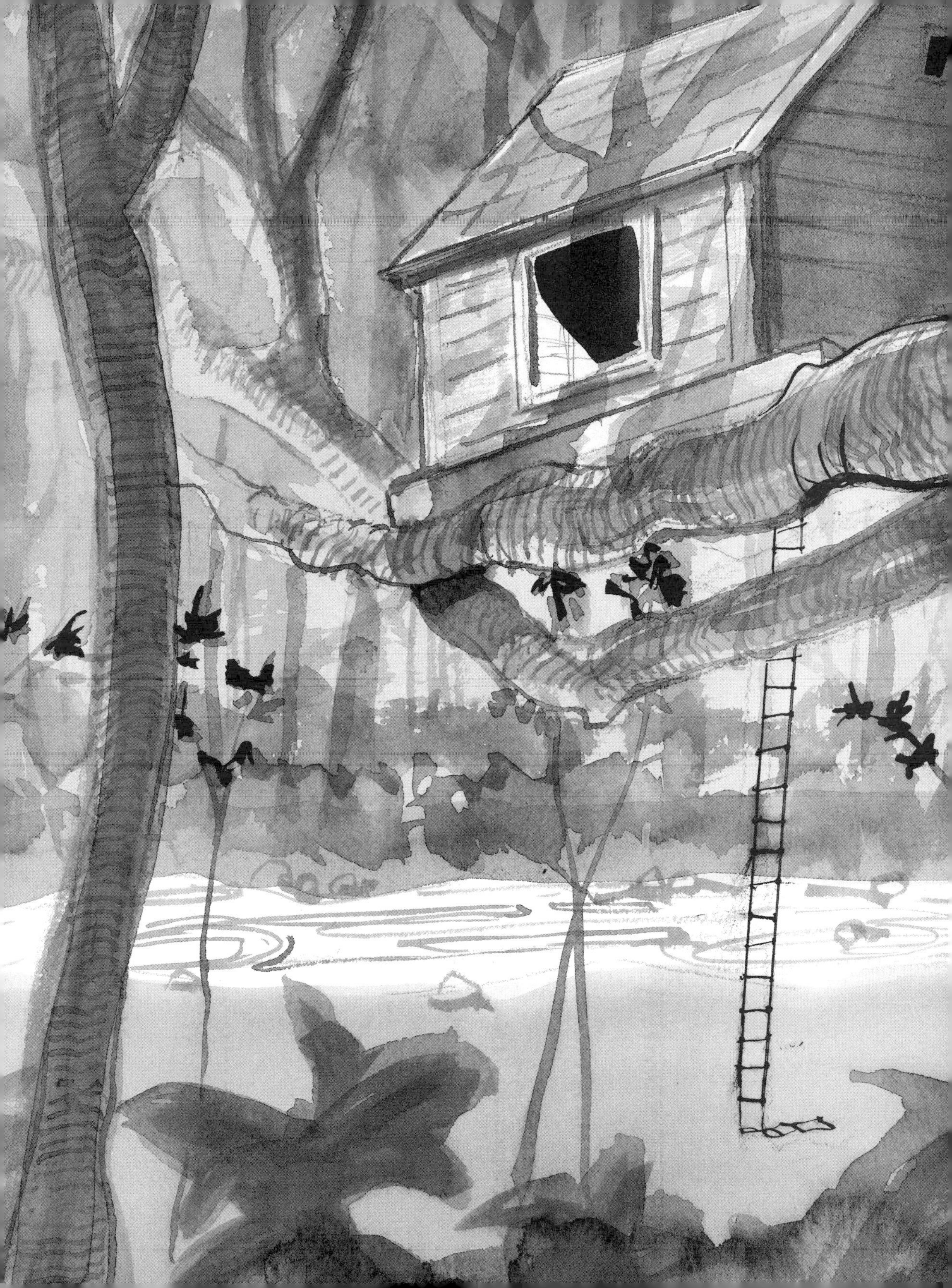

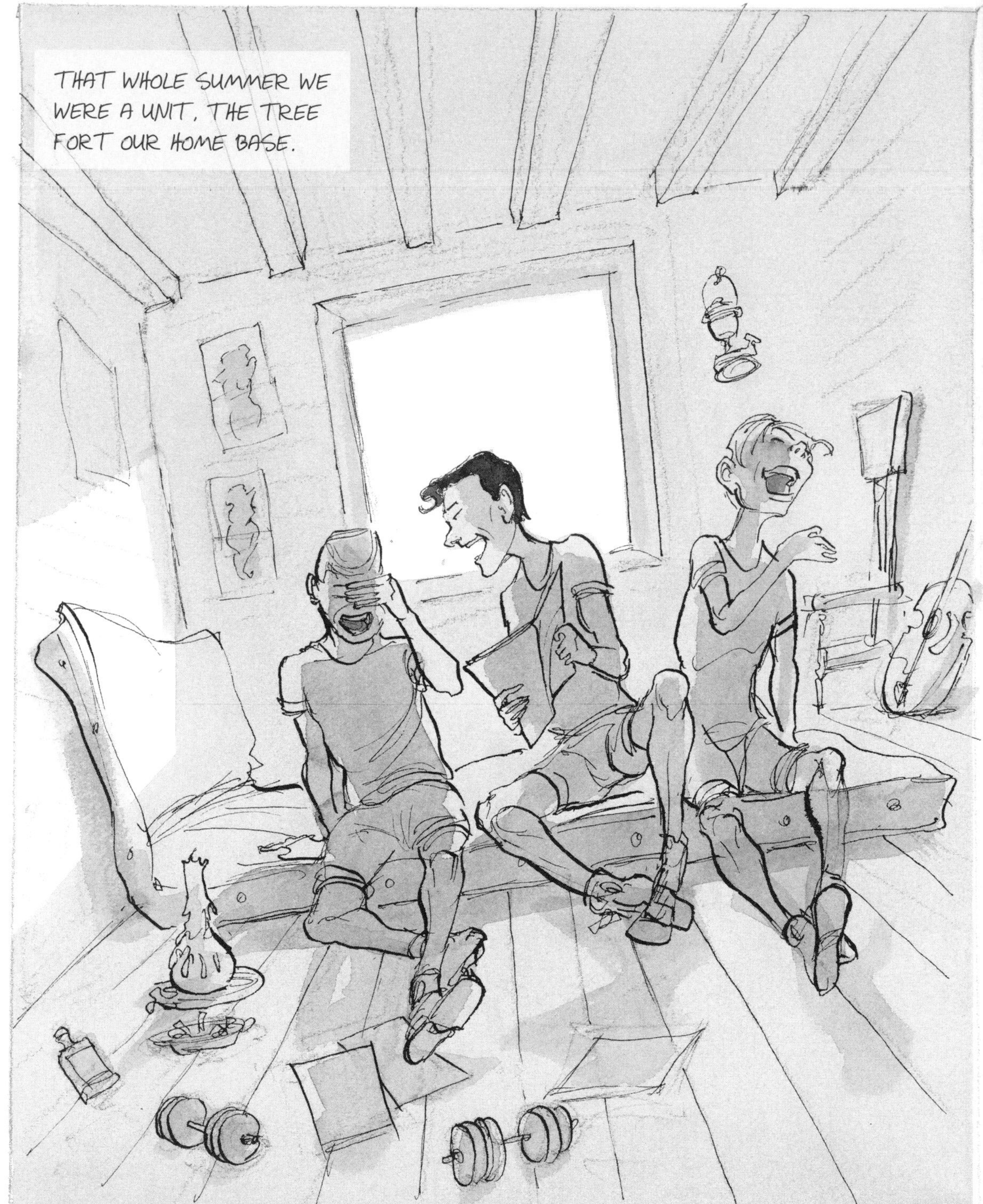
THAT WHOLE SUMMER WE WERE A UNIT, THE TREE FORT OUR HOME BASE.

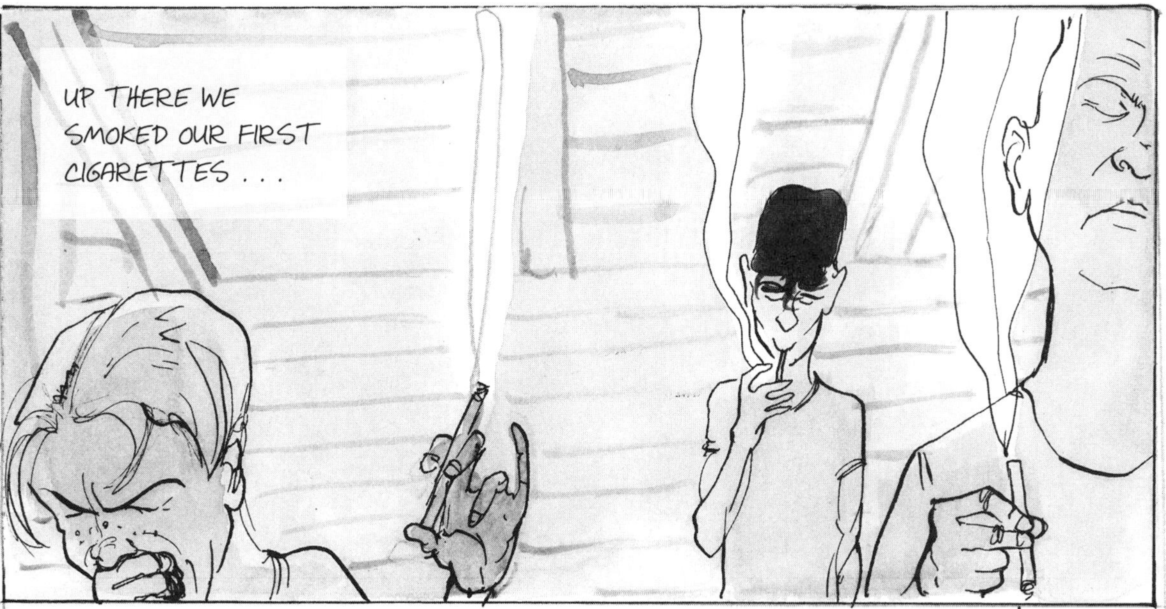
UP THERE WE SMOKED OUR FIRST CIGARETTES . . .

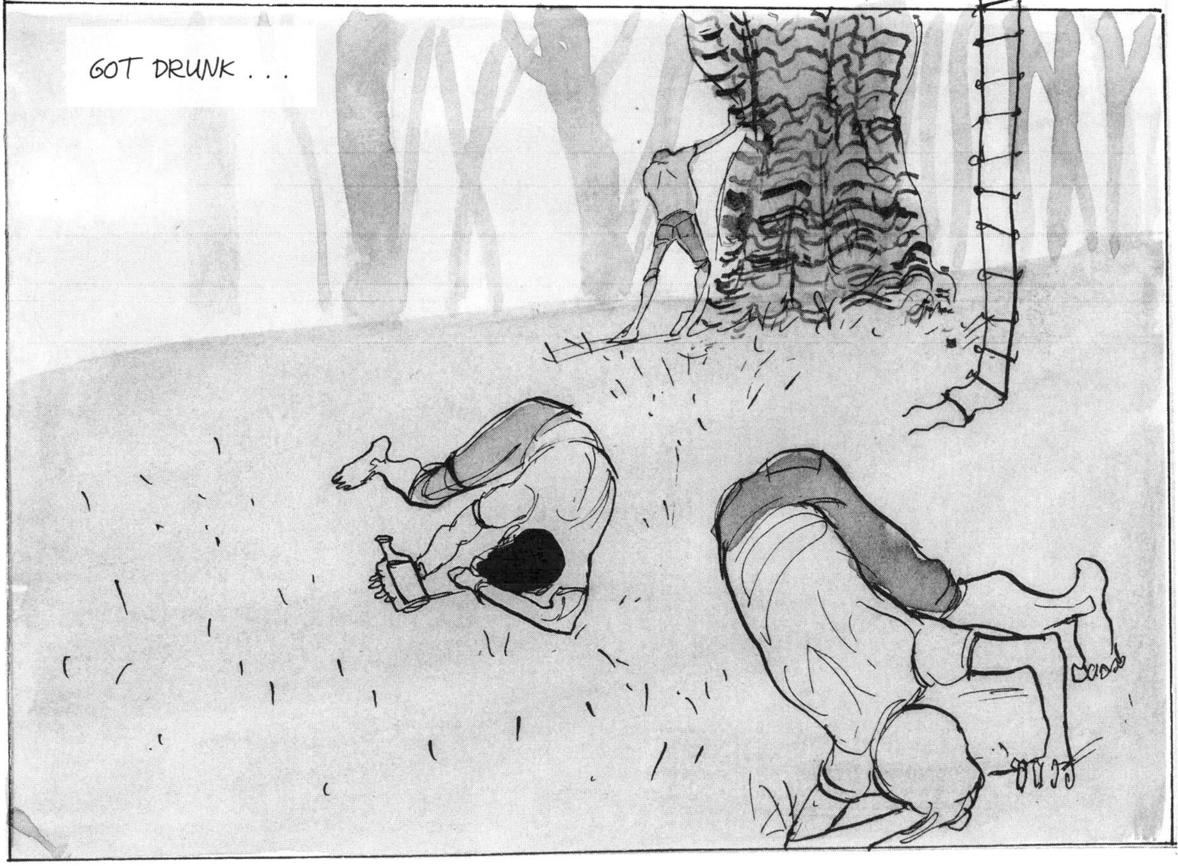
GOT DRUNK . . .

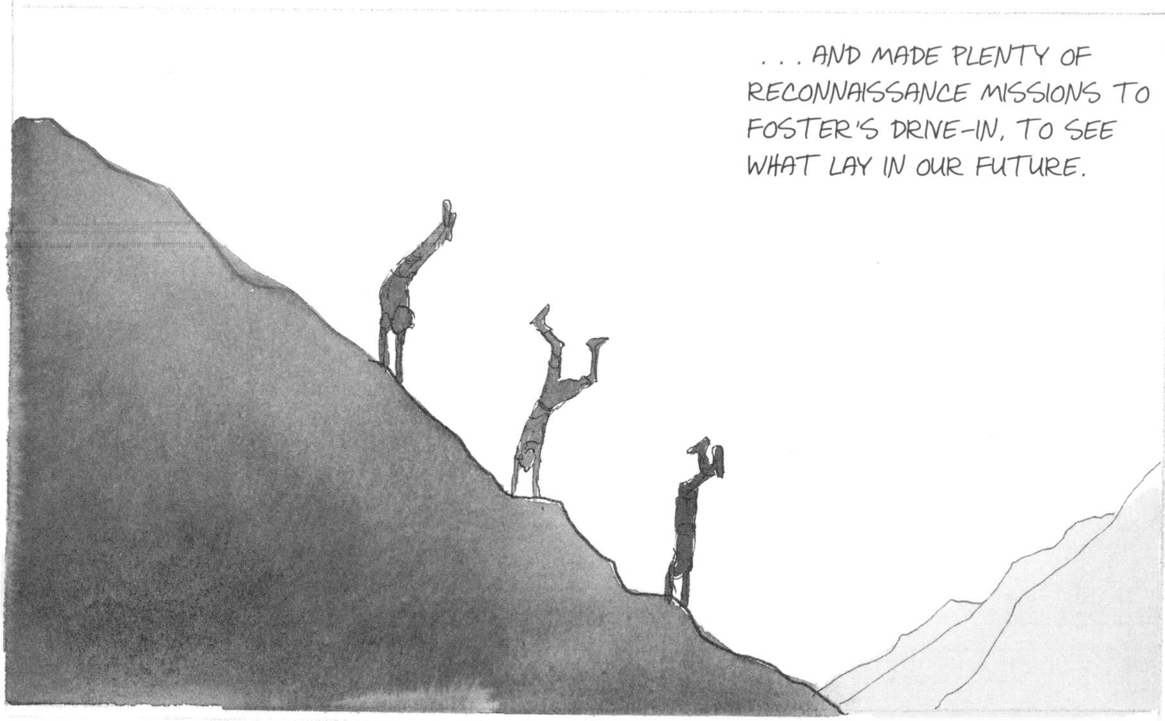
. . . AND MADE PLENTY OF RECONNAISSANCE MISSIONS TO FOSTER'S DRIVE-IN, TO SEE WHAT LAY IN OUR FUTURE.

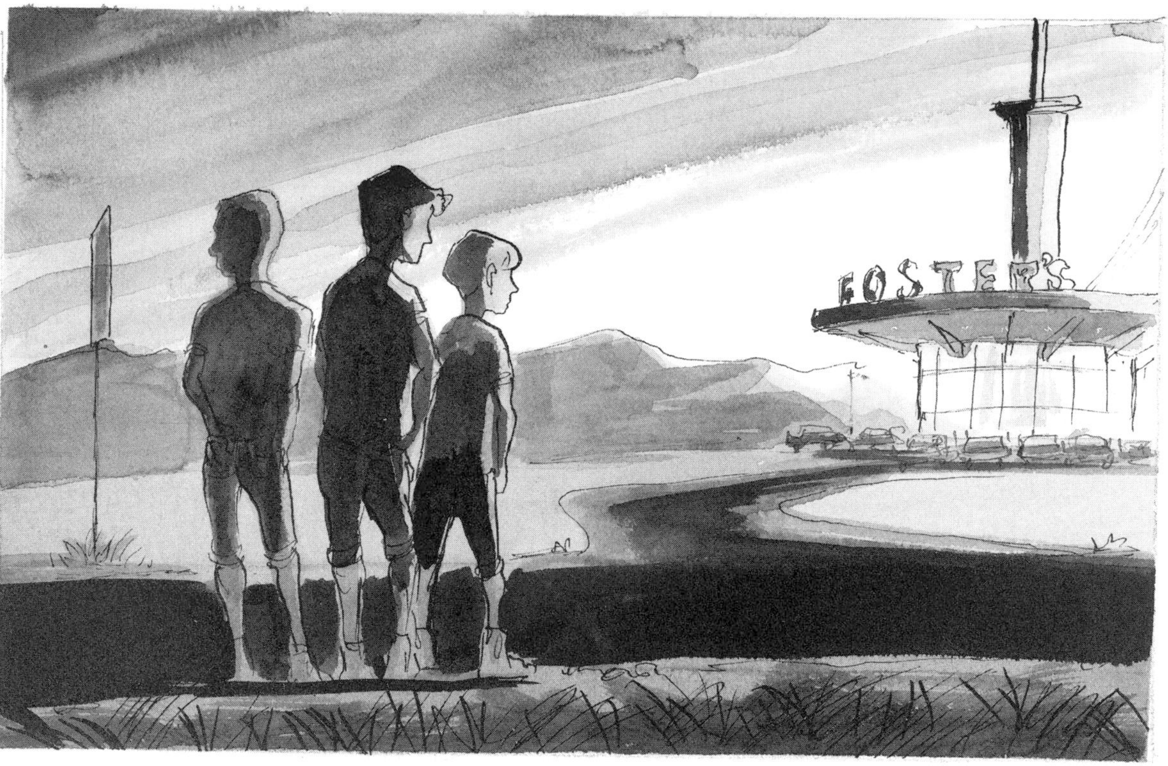
FOSTER'S

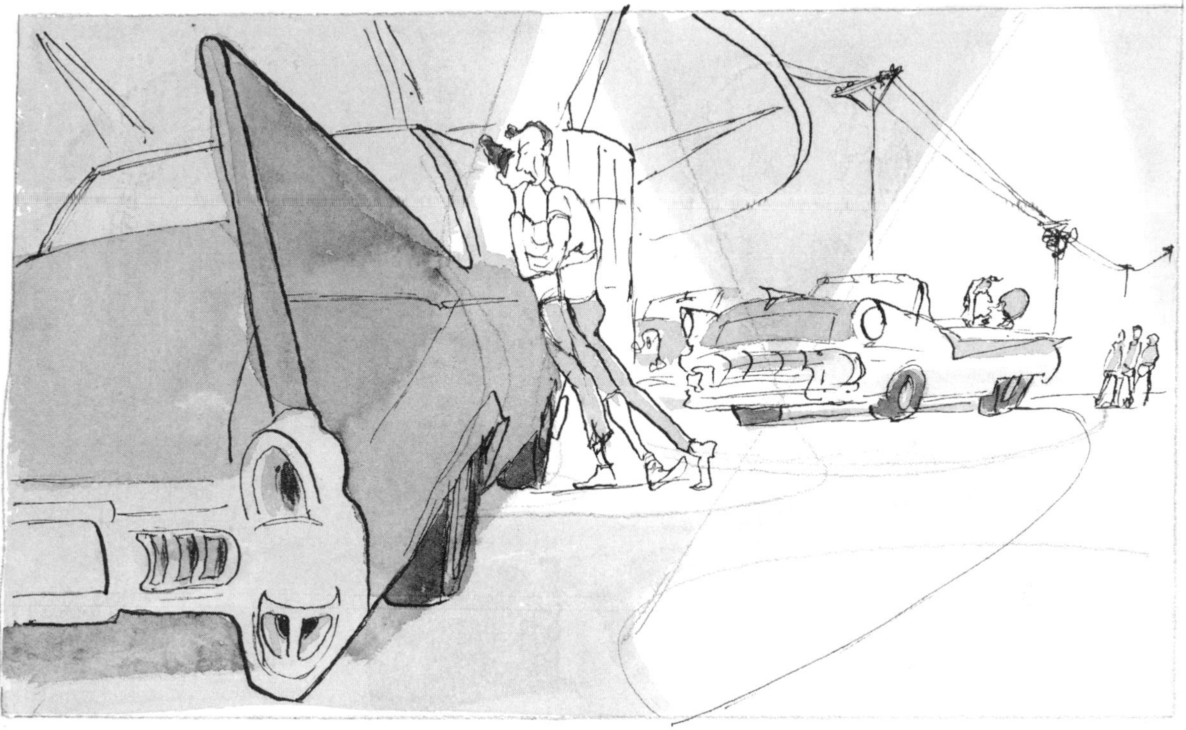

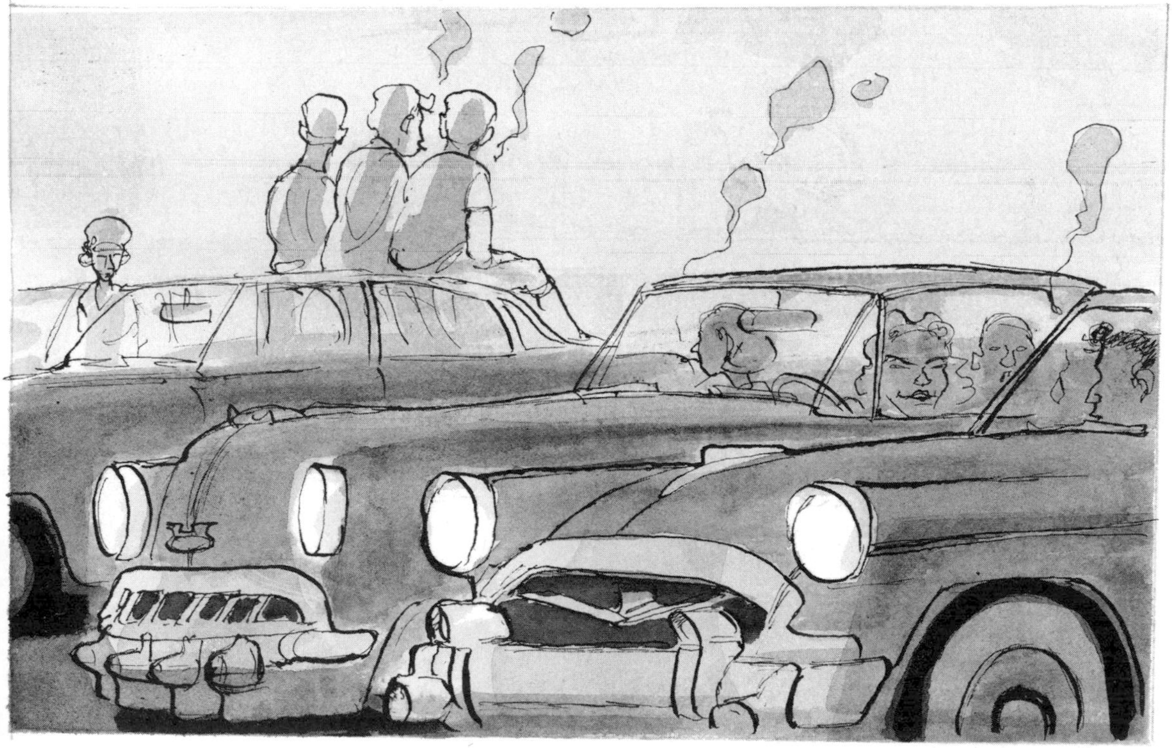

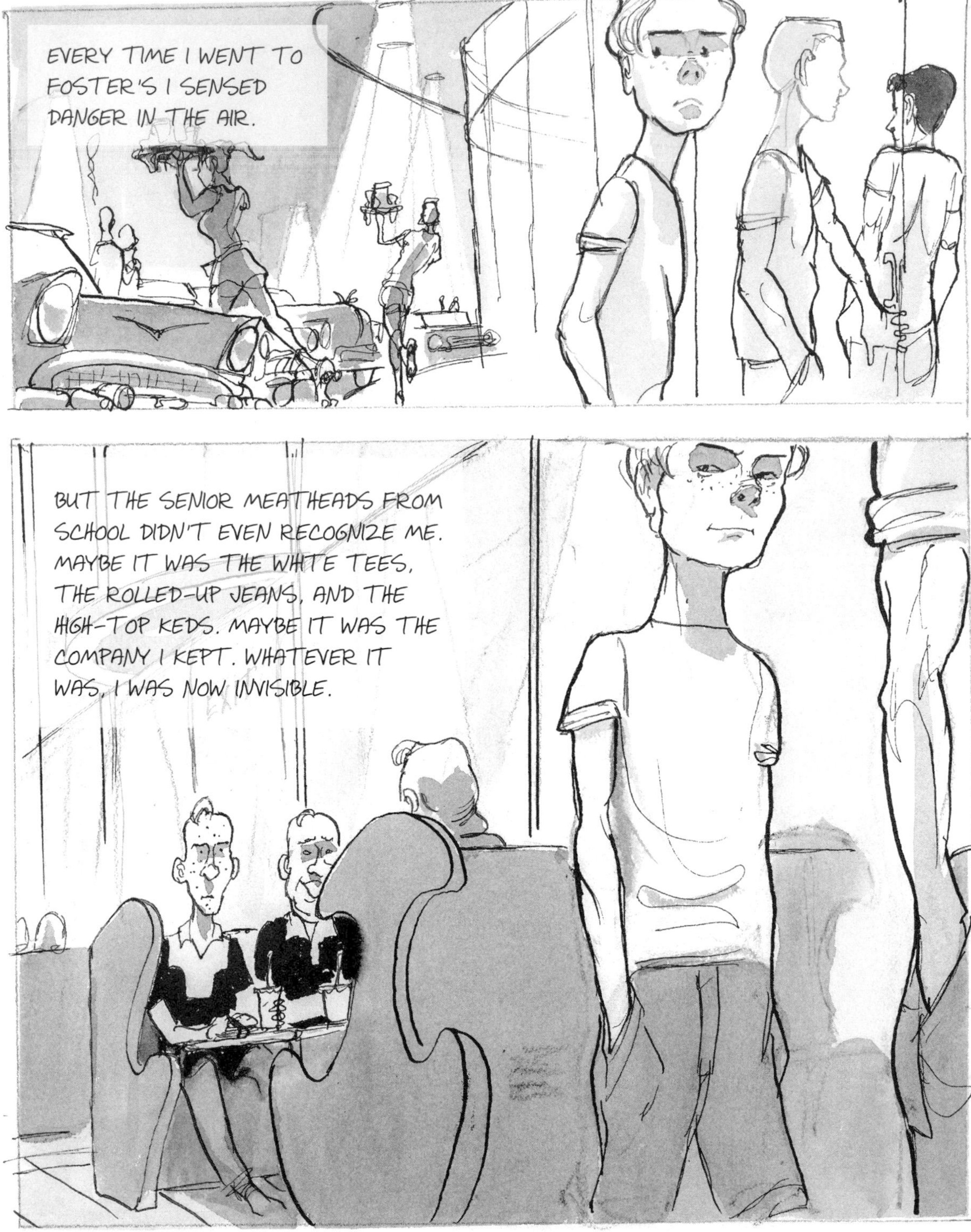
EVERY TIME I WENT TO FOSTER'S I SENSED DANGER IN THE AIR.
BUT THE SENIOR MEATHEADS FROM SCHOOL DIDN'T EVEN RECOGNIZE ME. MAYBE IT WAS THE WHITE TEES, THE ROLLED-UP JEANS, AND THE HIGH-TOP KEDS. MAYBE IT WAS THE COMPANY I KEPT. WHATEVER IT WAS, I WAS NOW INVISIBLE.

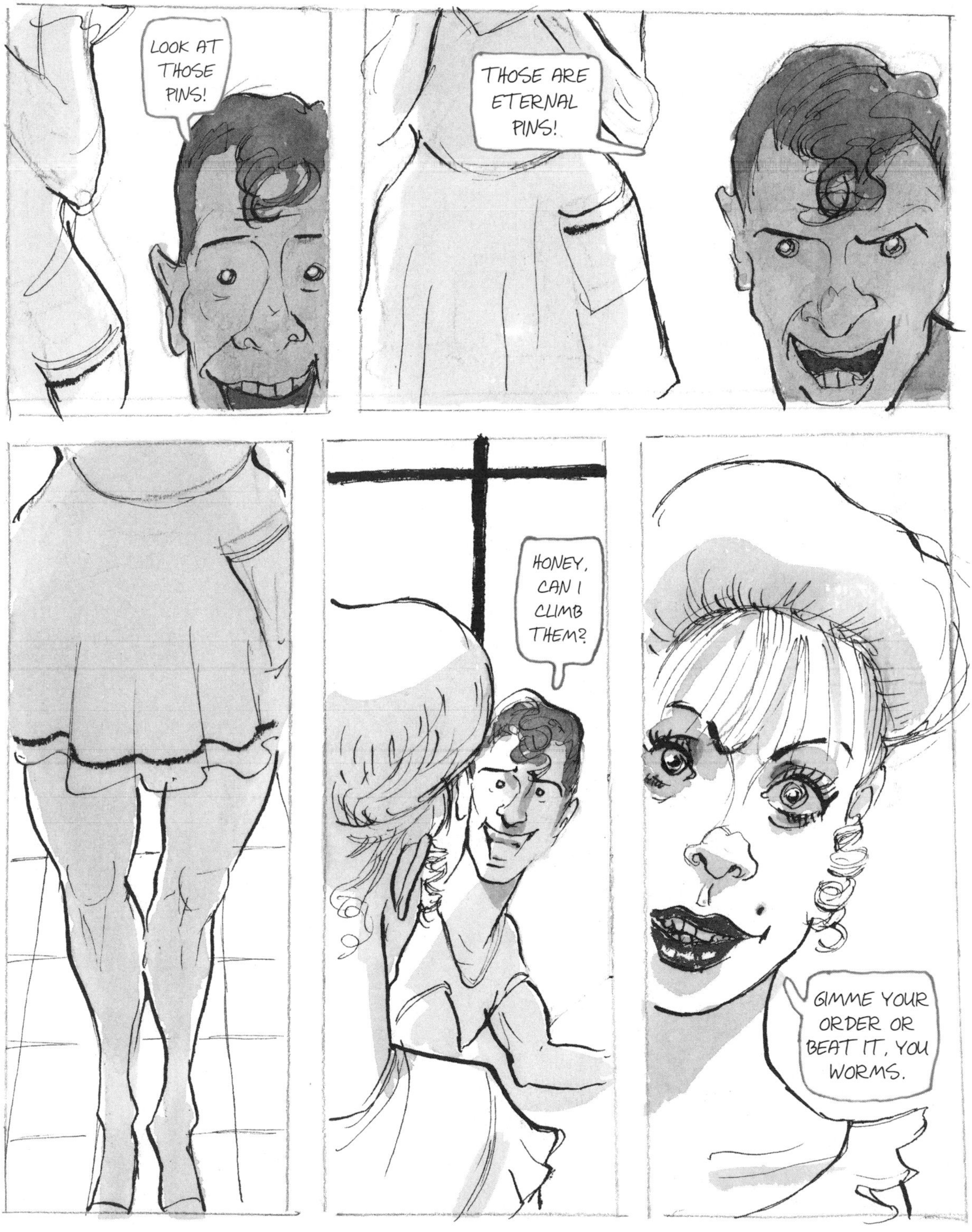
LOOK AT THOSE PINS!
THOSE ARE ETERNAL PINS!
HONEY, CAN I CLIMB THEM?
GIMME YOUR ORDER OR BEAT IT, YOU WORMS.

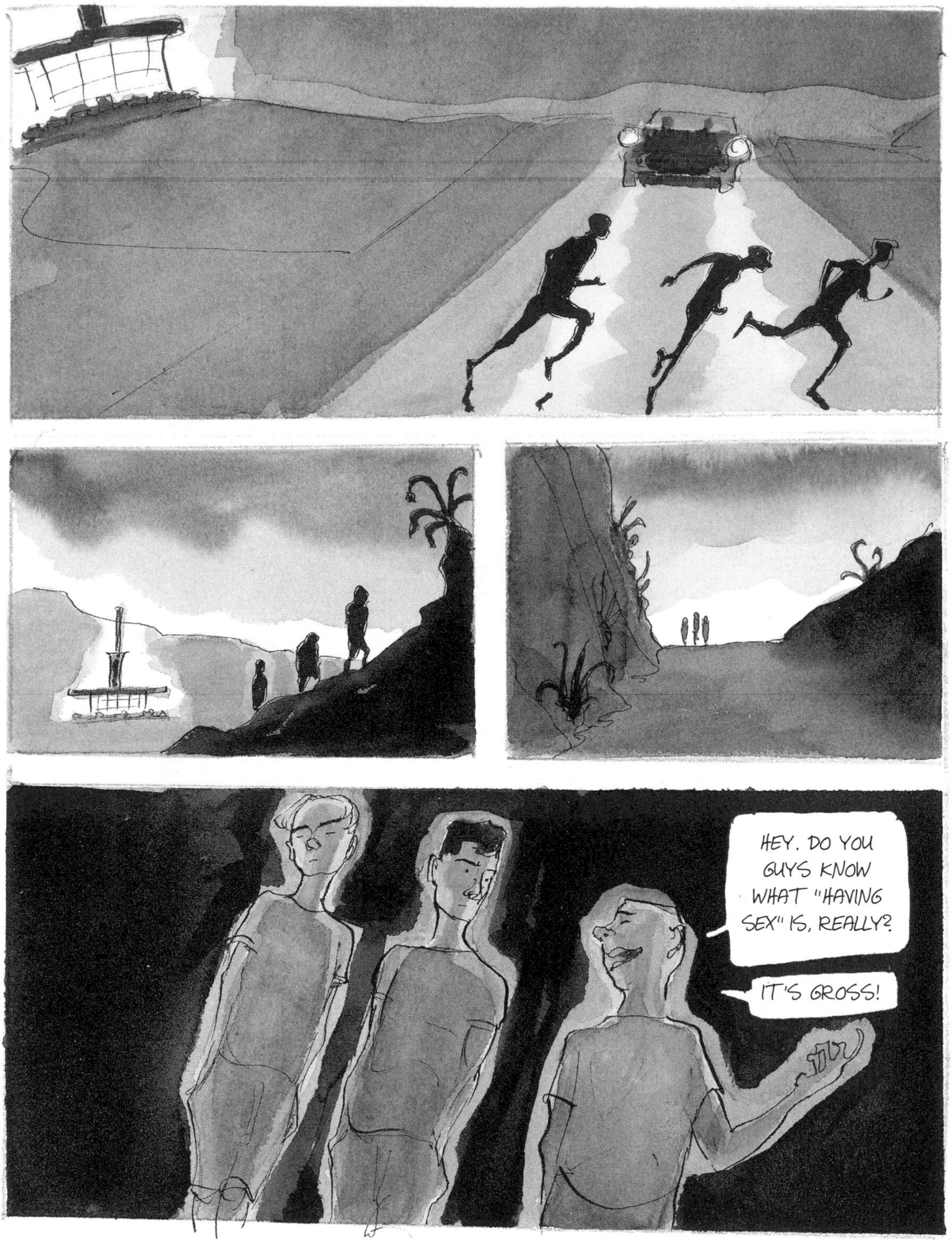
HEY. DO YOU GUYS KNOW WHAT "HAVING SEX" IS, REALLY?
IT'S GROSS!

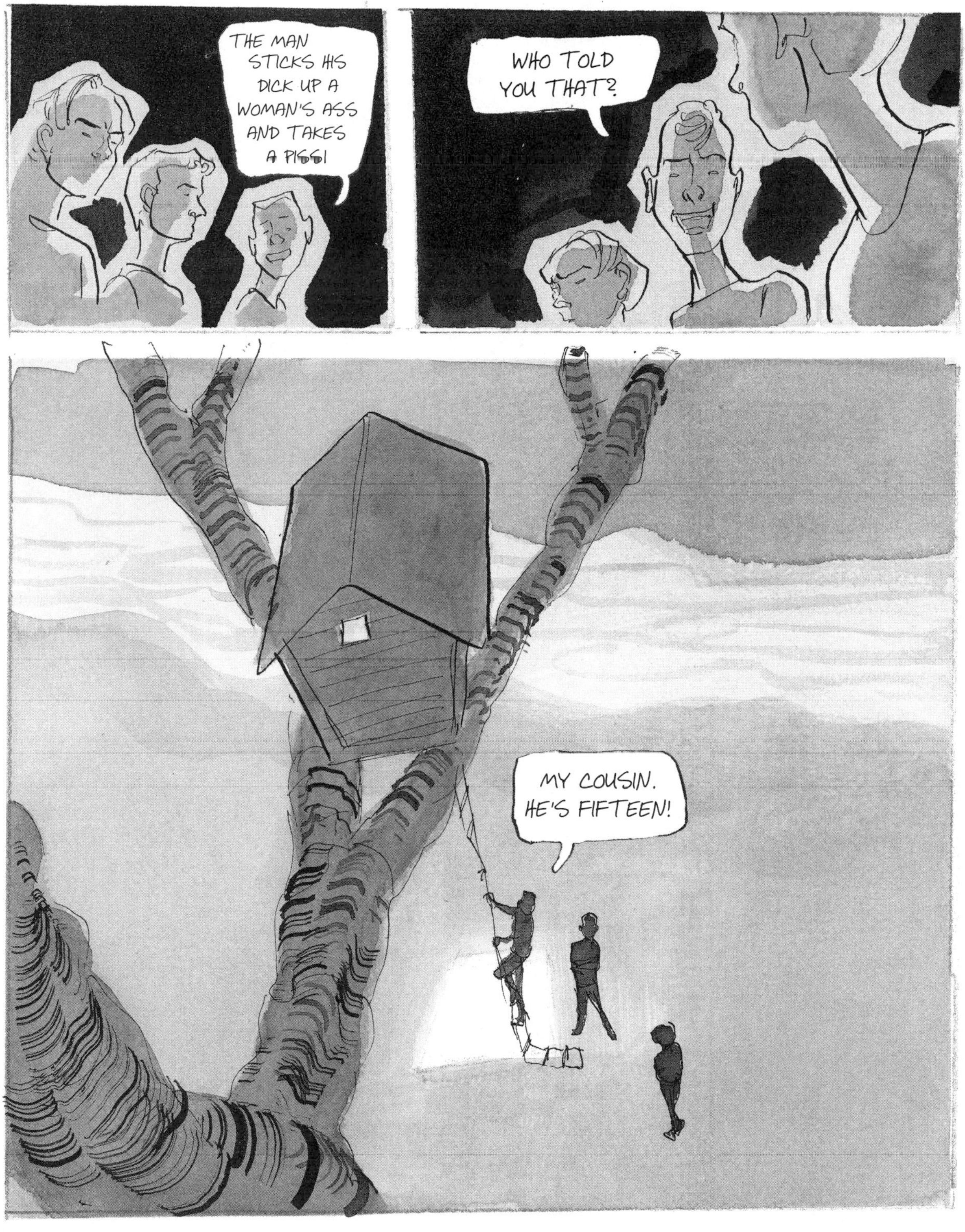
THE MAN STICKS HIS DICK UP A WOMAN'S ASS AND TAKES A PISS!
WHO TOLD YOU THAT?
MY COUSIN. HE'S FIFTEEN!

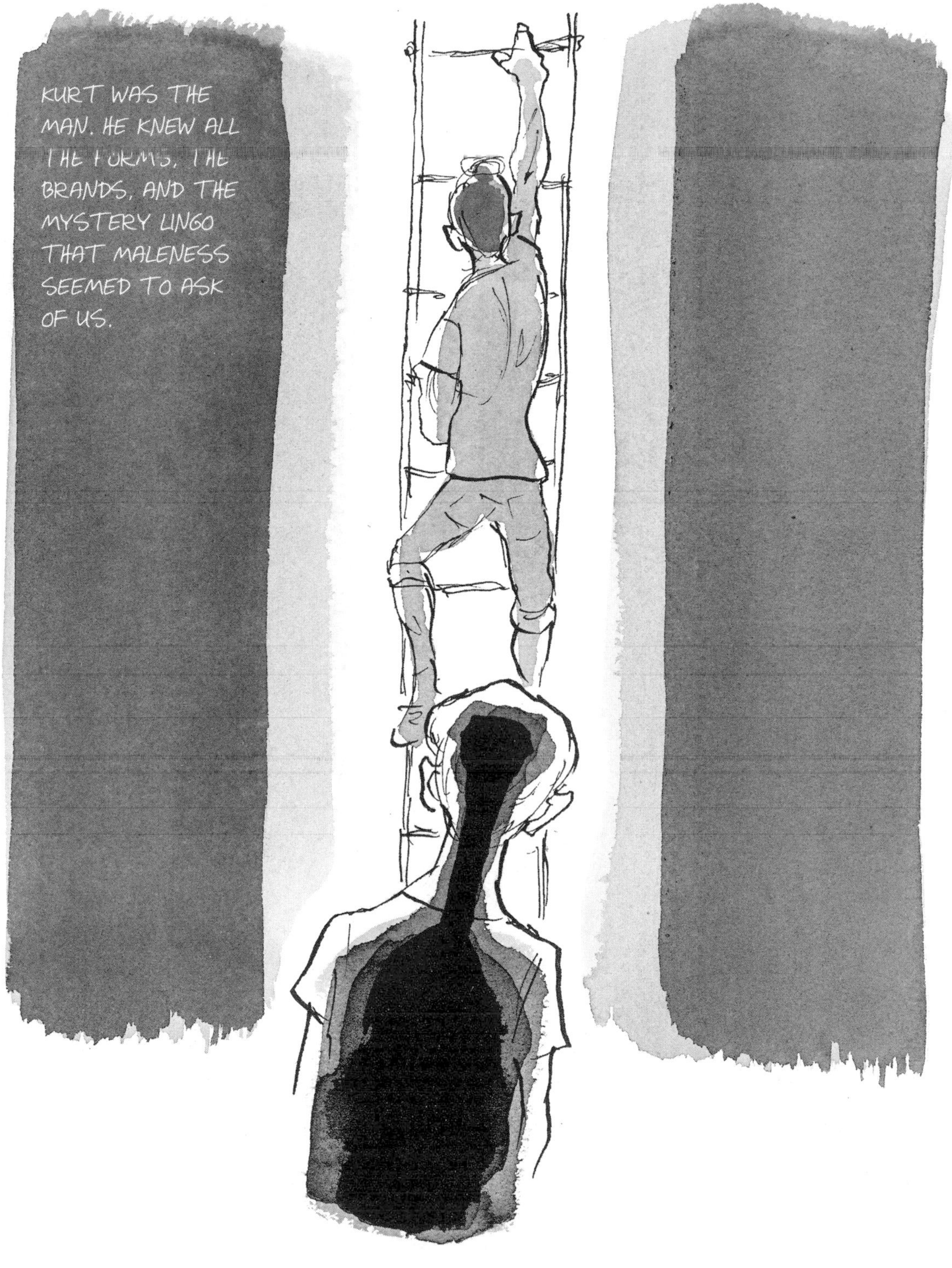
KURT WAS THE MAN. HE KNEW ALL THE FORMS, THE BRANDS, AND THE MYSTERY LINGO THAT MALENESS SEEMED TO ASK OF US.

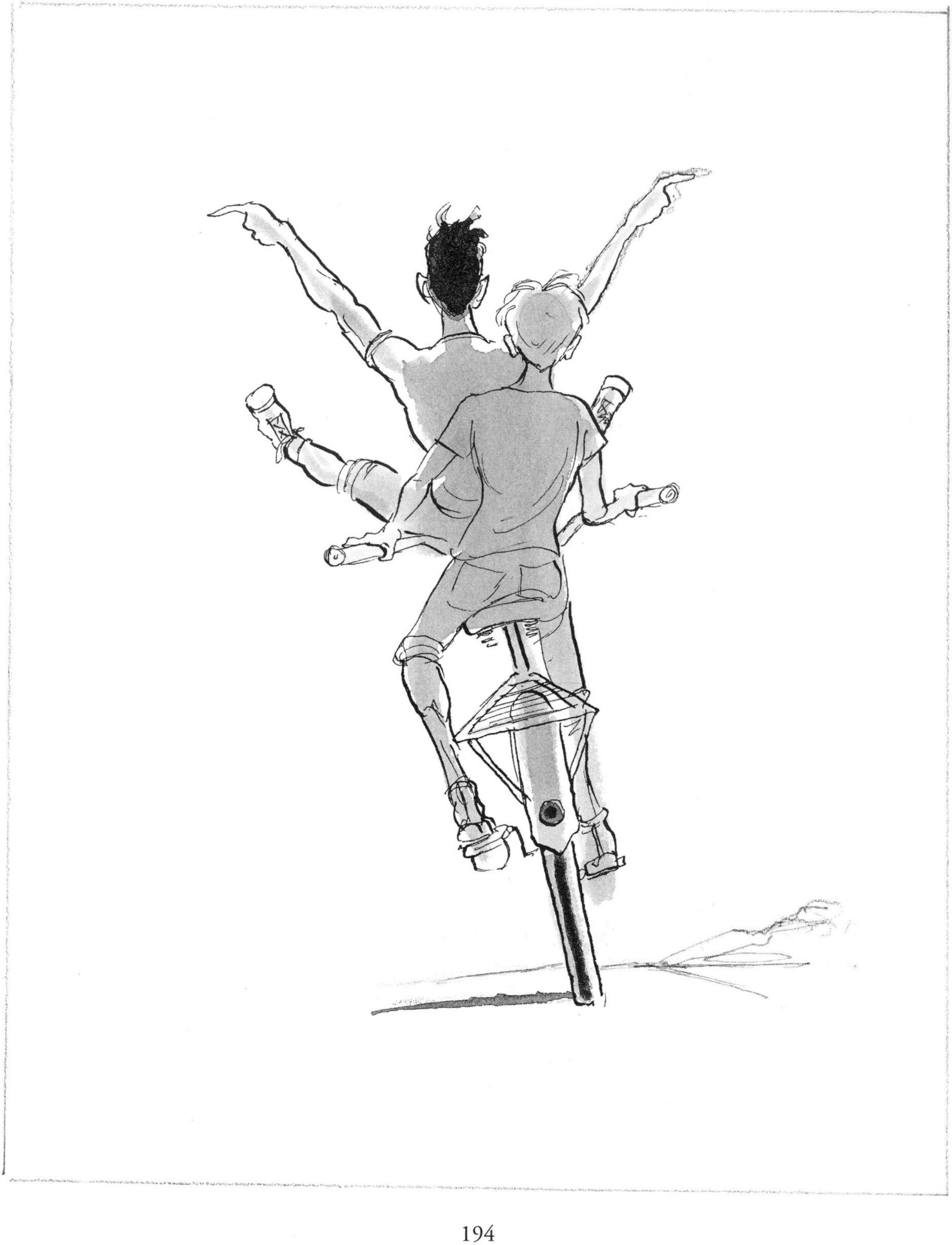

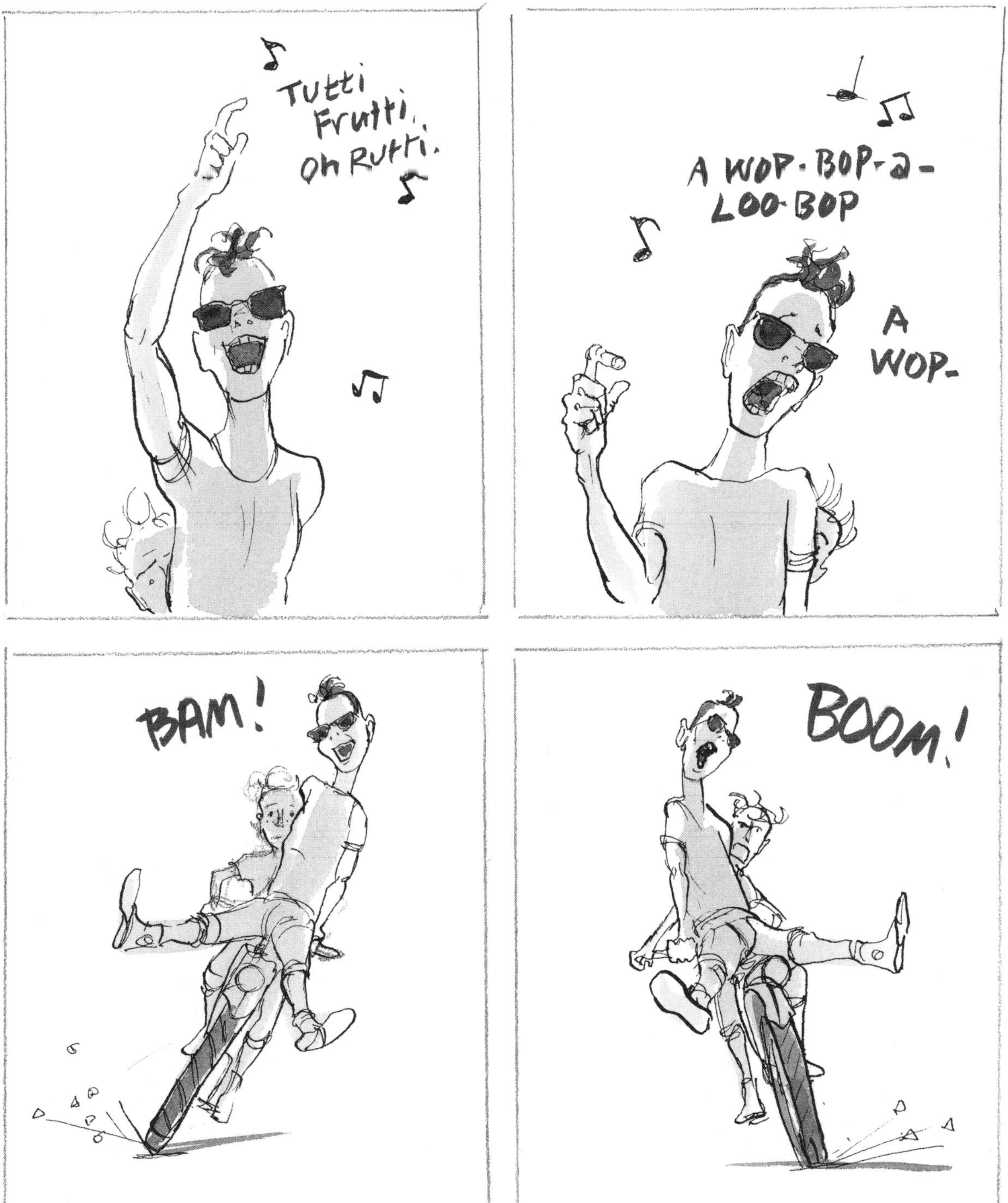
Tutti Frutti, Oh Rutti.
A WOP-BOP-a-LOO-BOP
A WOP-
BAM!
BOOM!

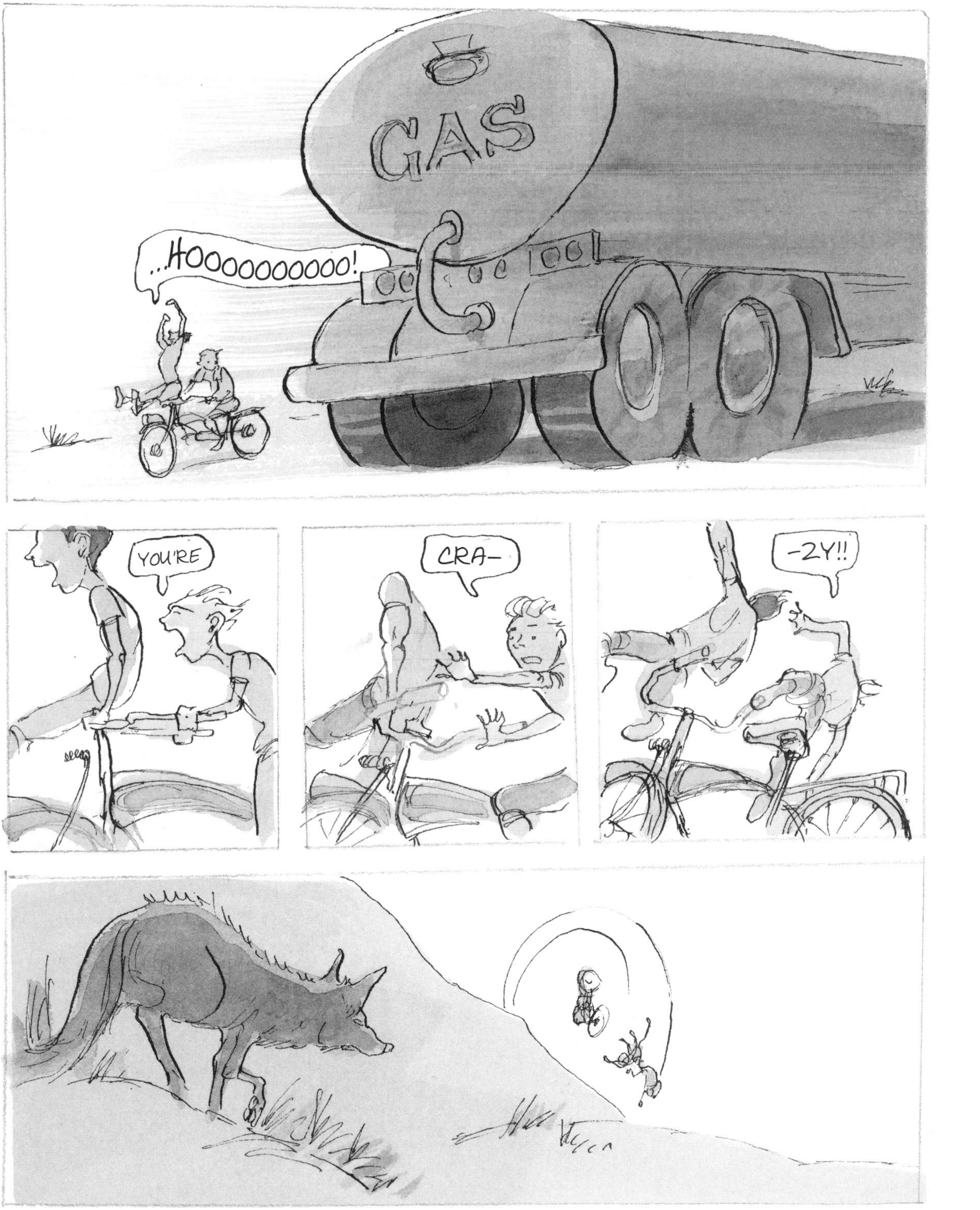
...HOOOOOOOOOO!
GAS
YOU'RE
CRA-
-ZY!!

198

199

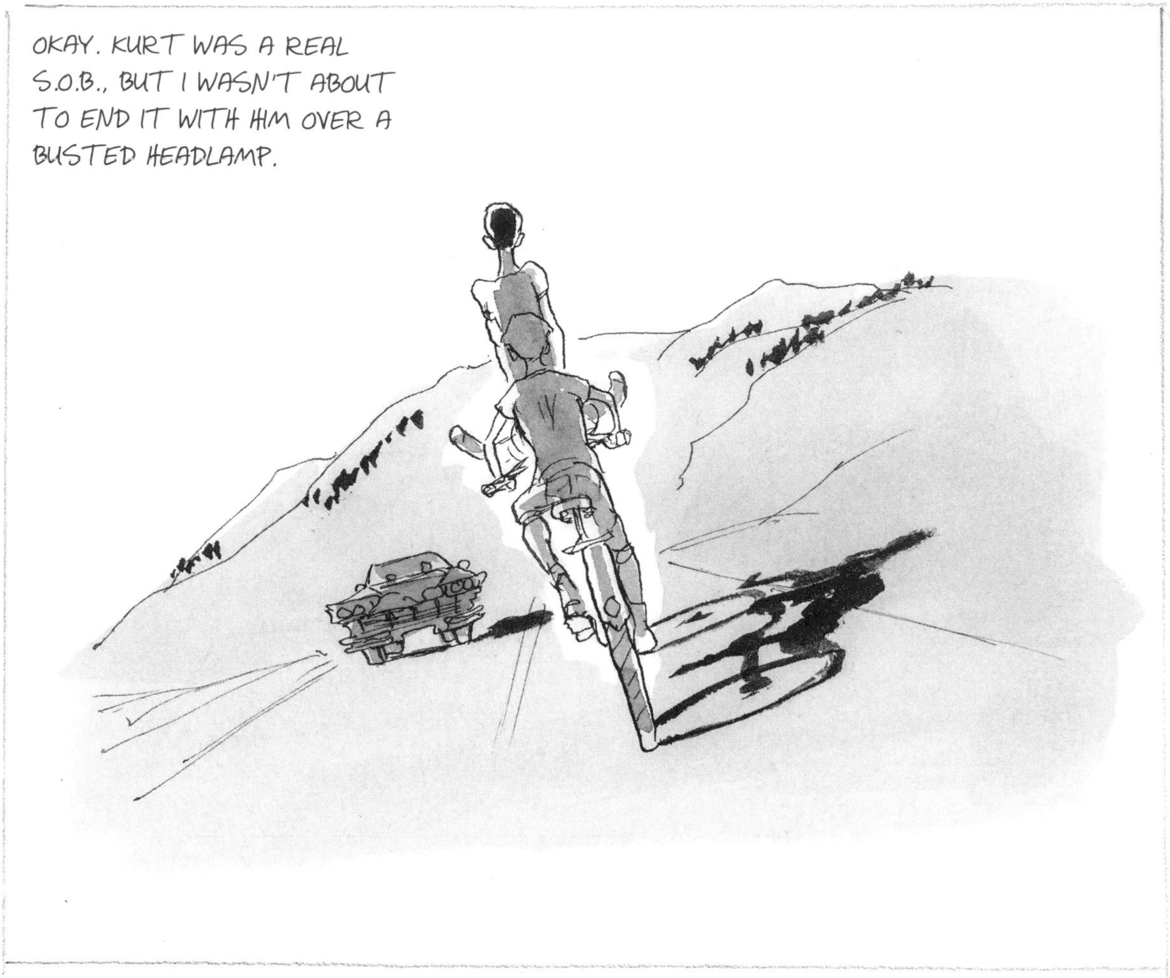
OKAY. KURT WAS A REAL S.O.B., BUT I WASN'T ABOUT TO END IT WITH HIM OVER A BUSTED HEADLAMP.

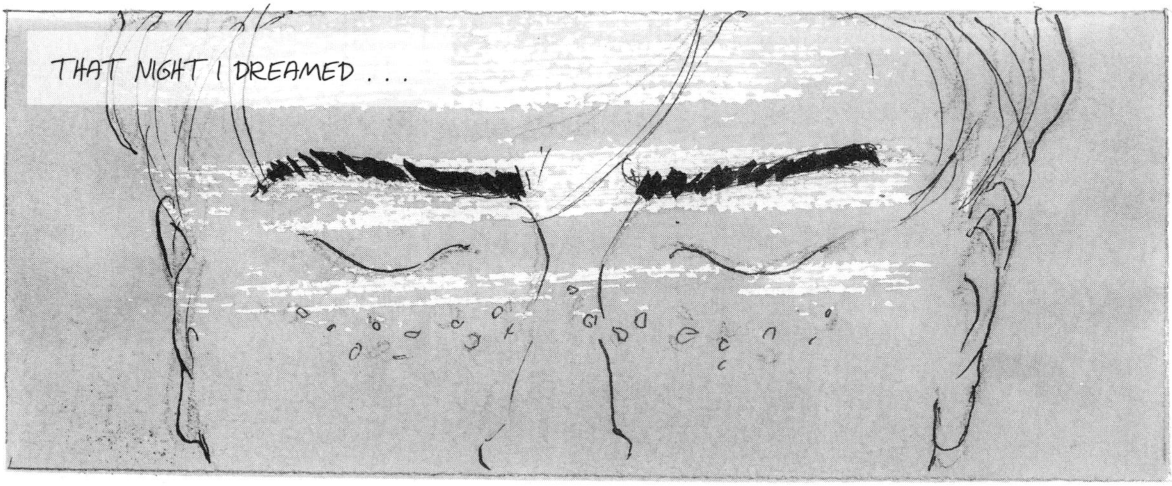
THAT NIGHT I DREAMED . . .

MY TWISTED BEDCLOTHES BECAME A TUNNEL.

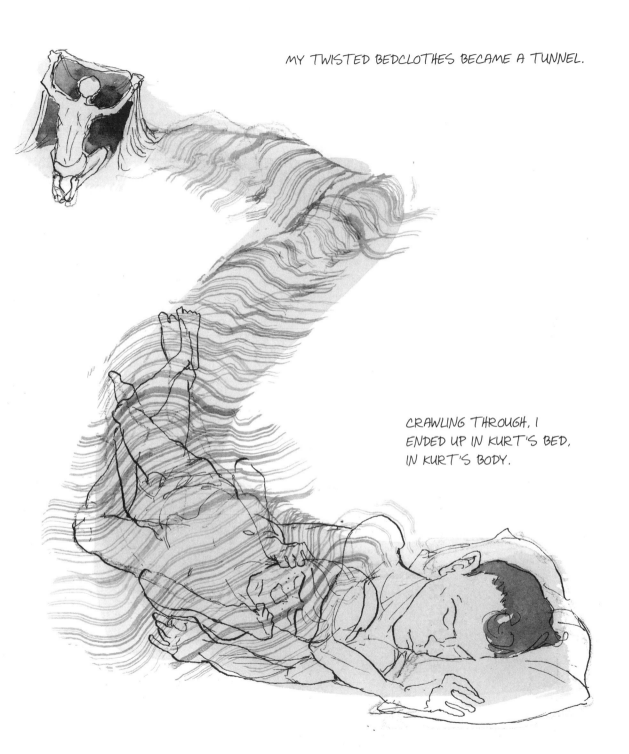

CRAWLING THROUGH, I
ENDED UP IN KURT'S BED,
IN KURT'S BODY.

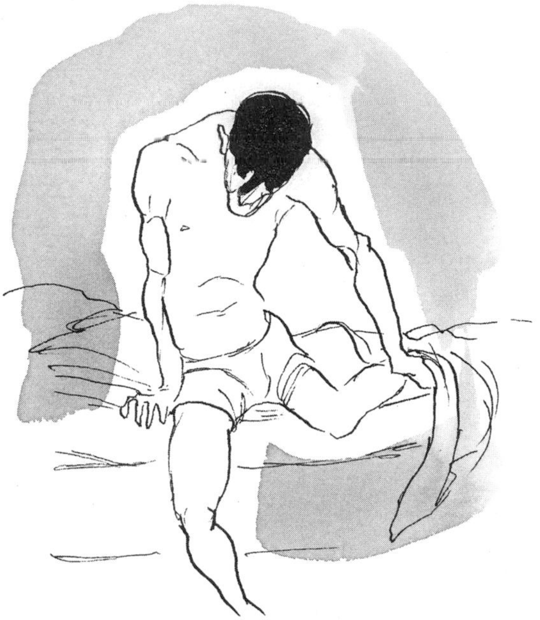
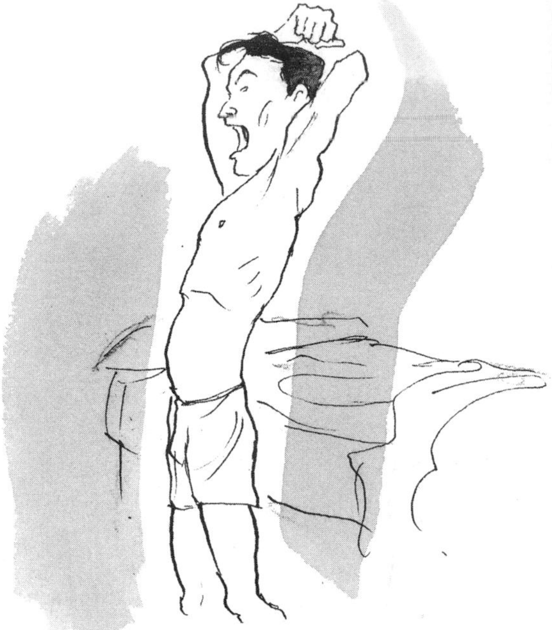
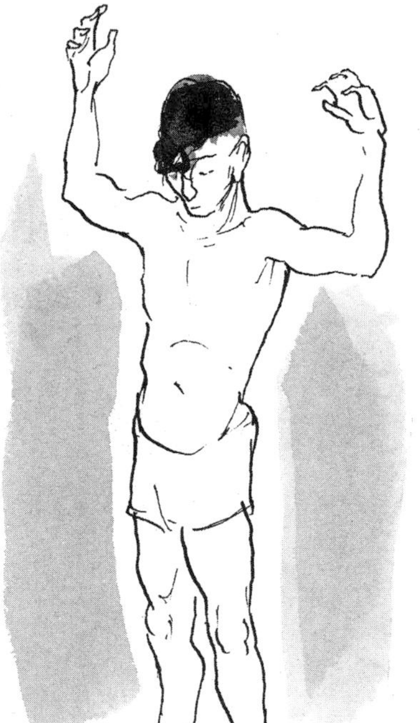
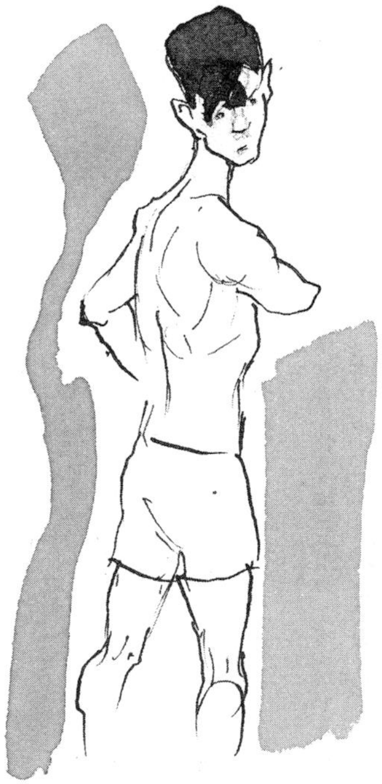
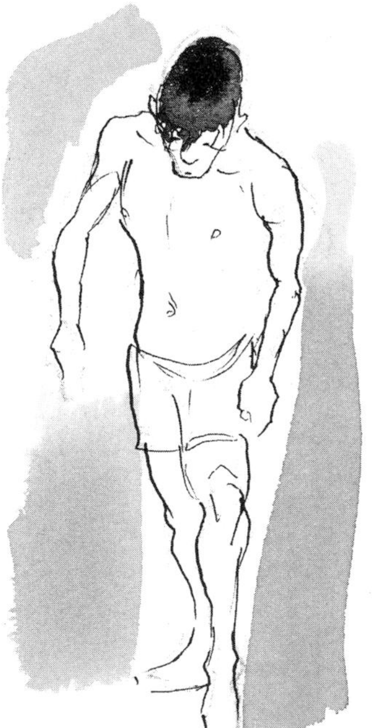

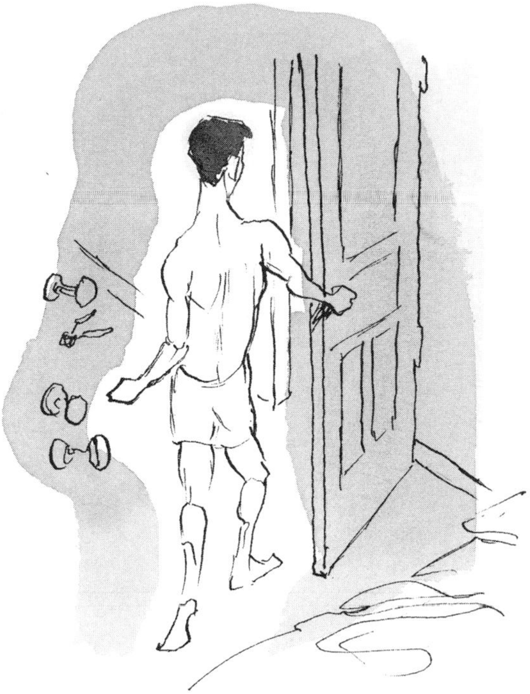

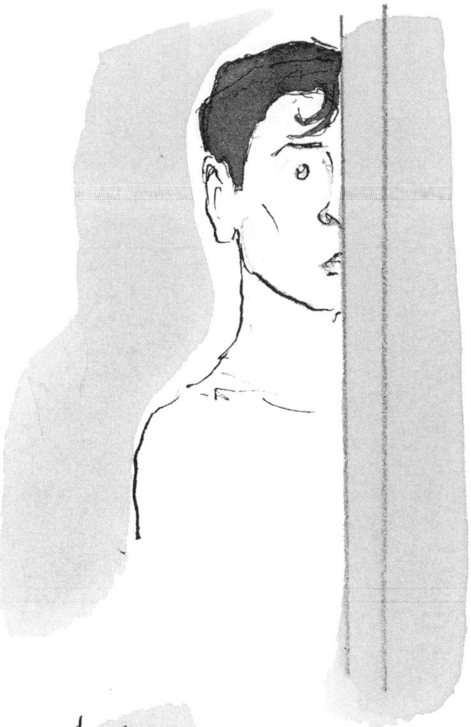

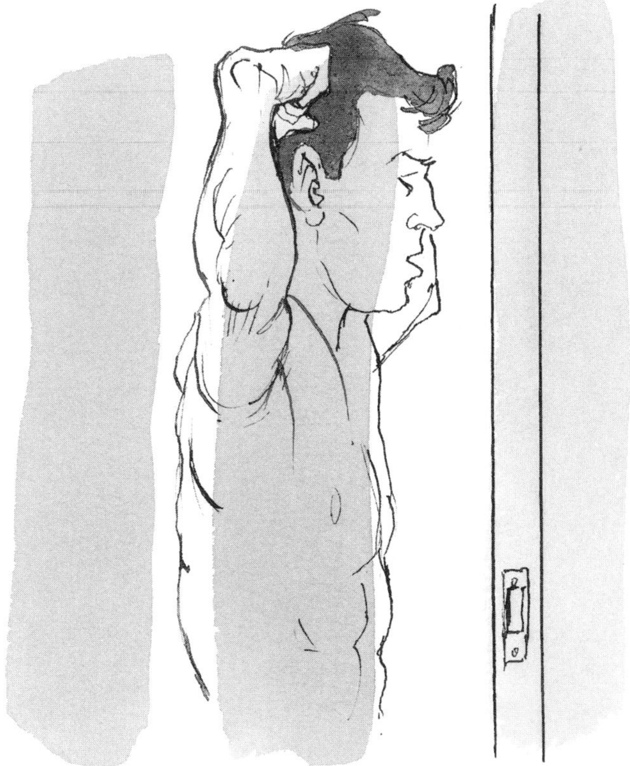

IF KURT KNEW
OF THIS SICK
DREAM . . .

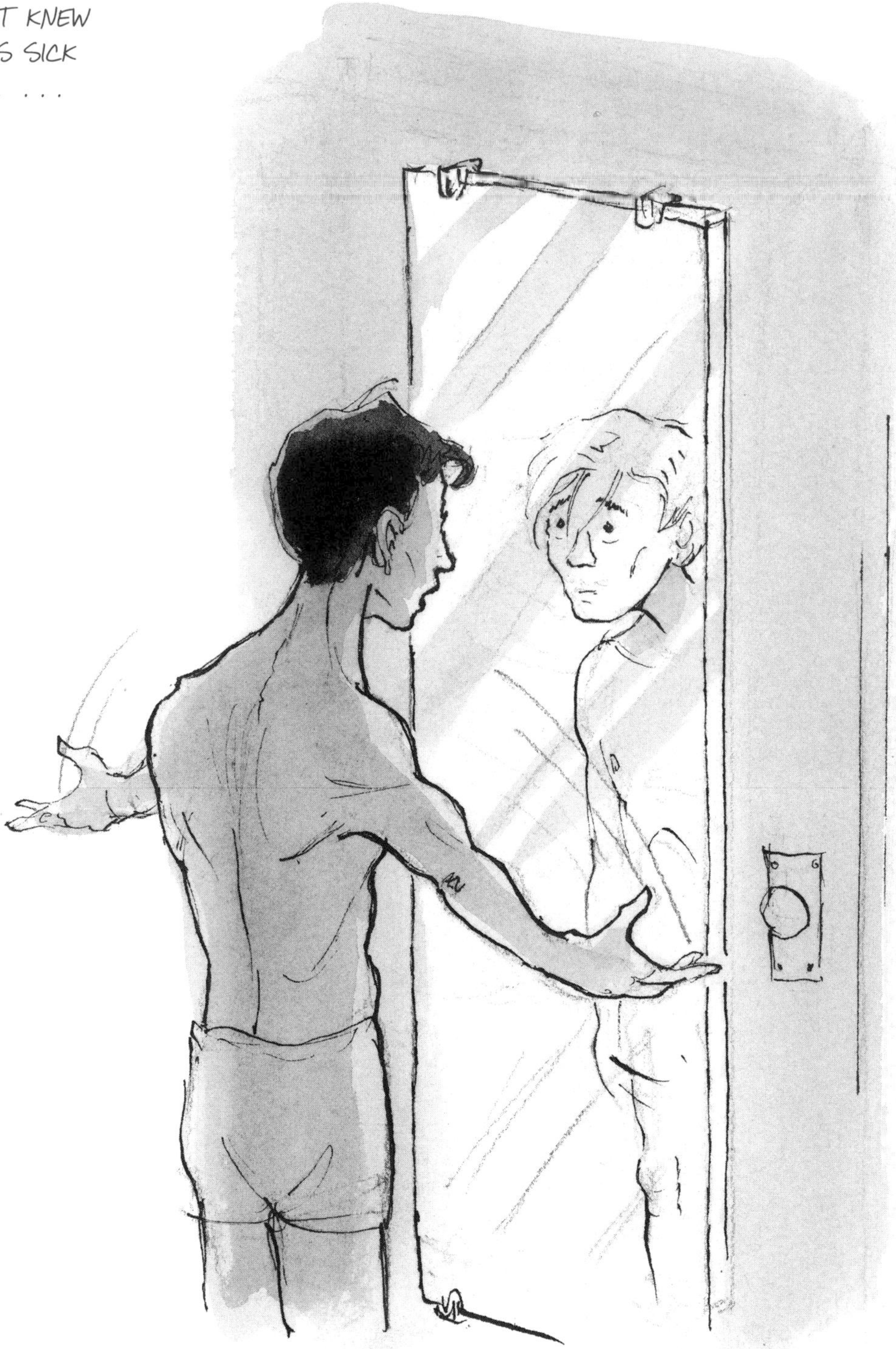

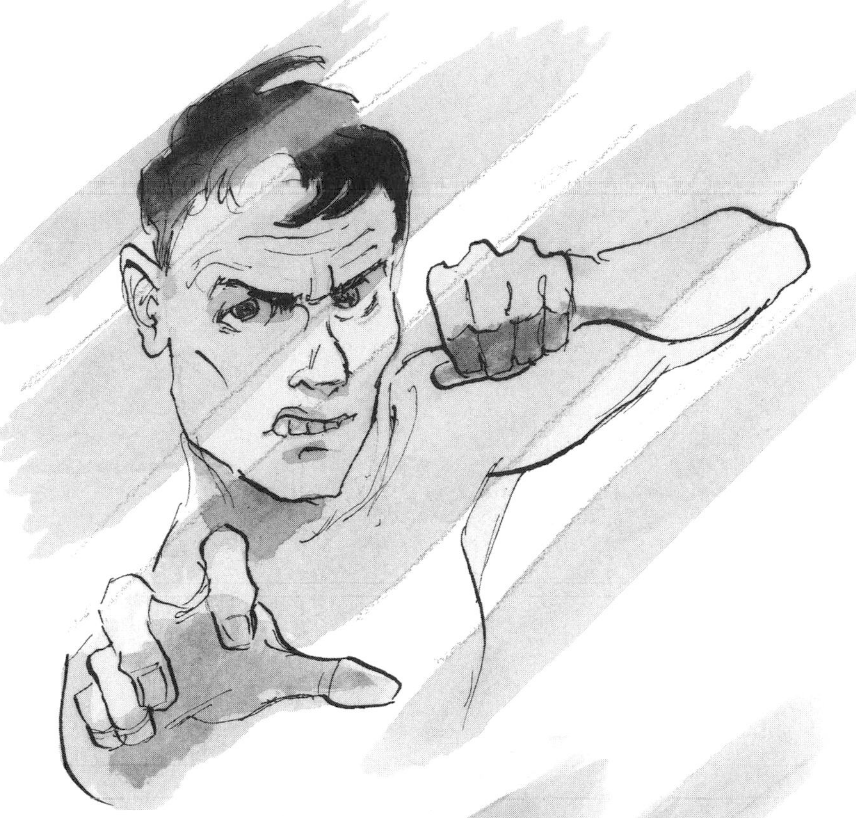

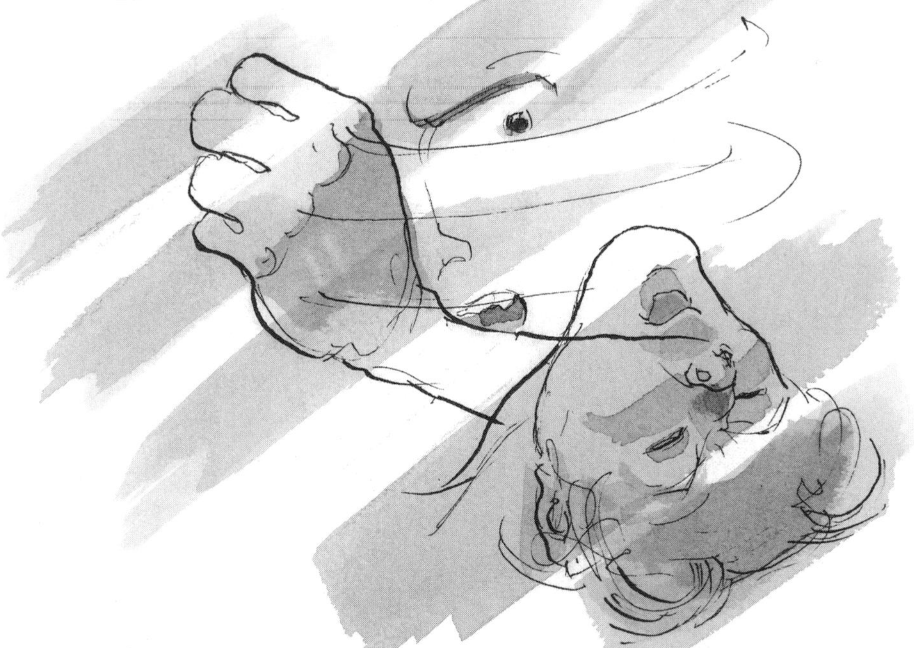

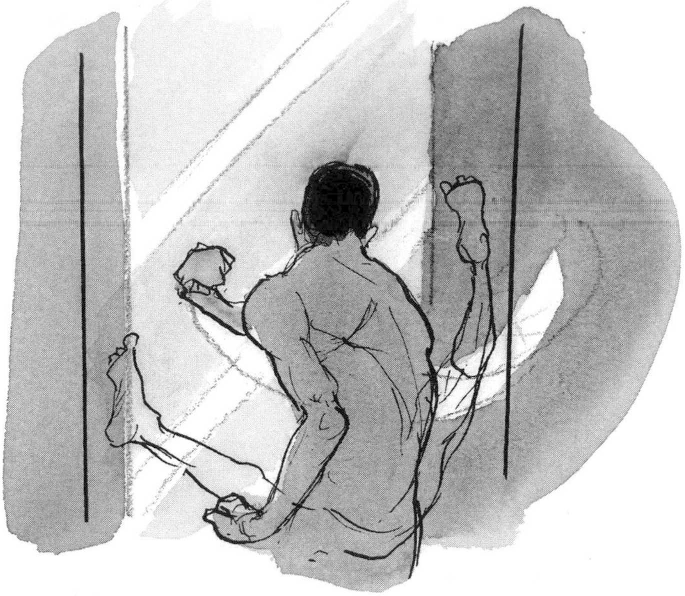

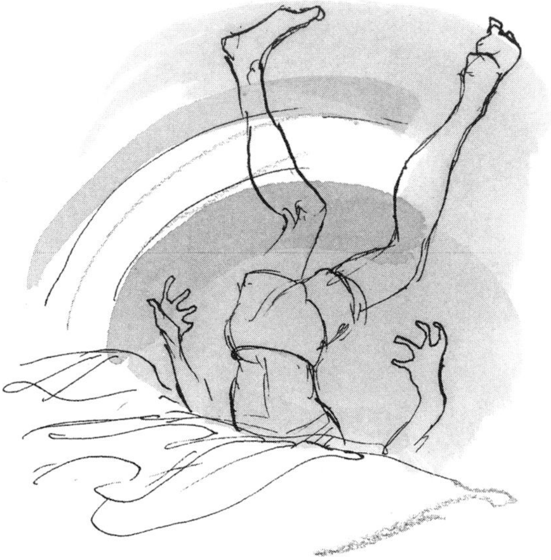

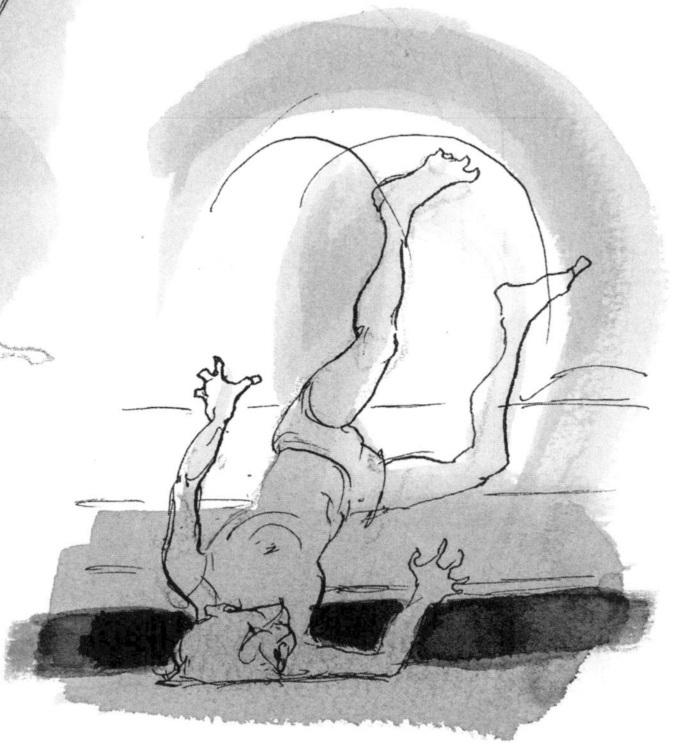

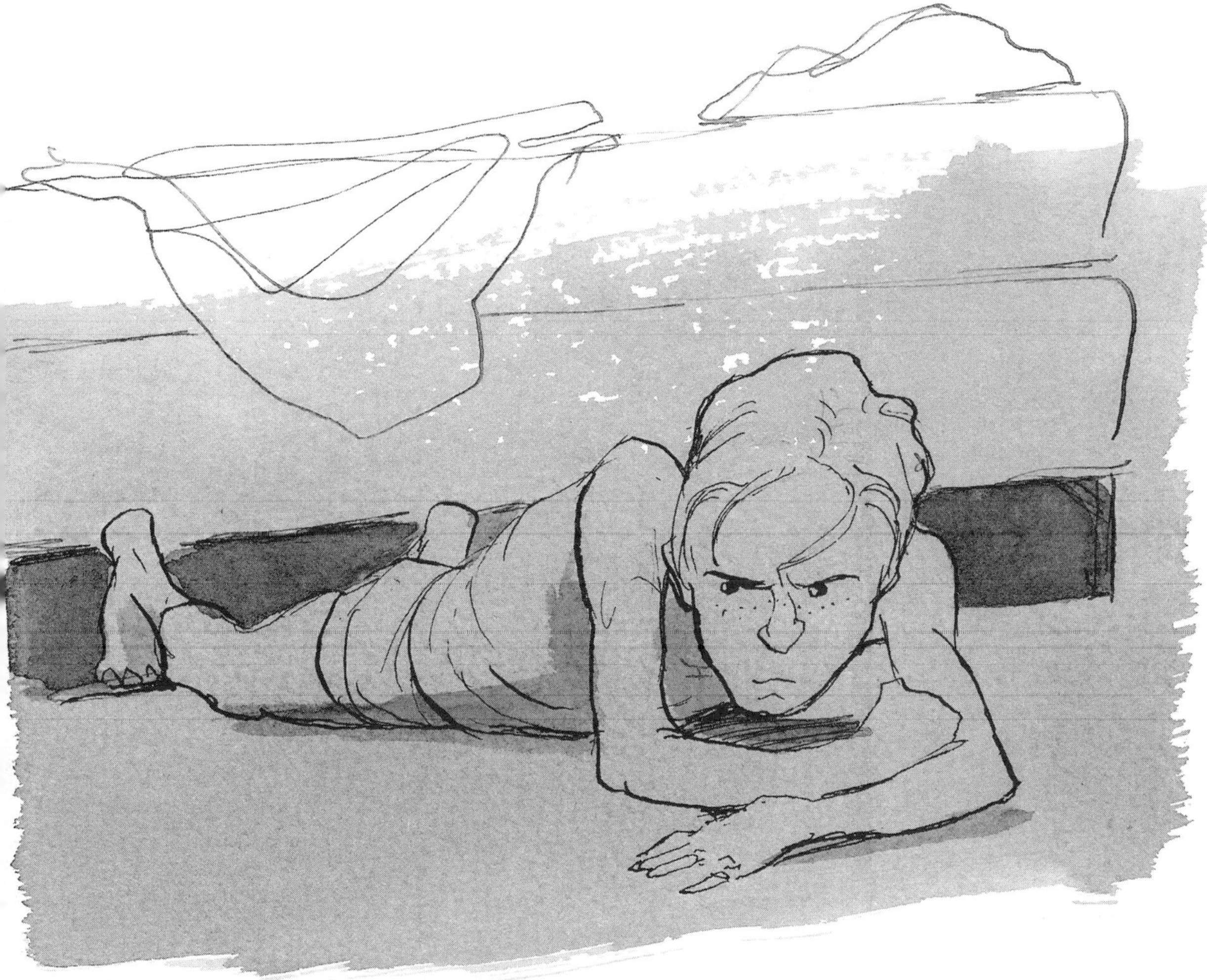

CHAPTER TEN

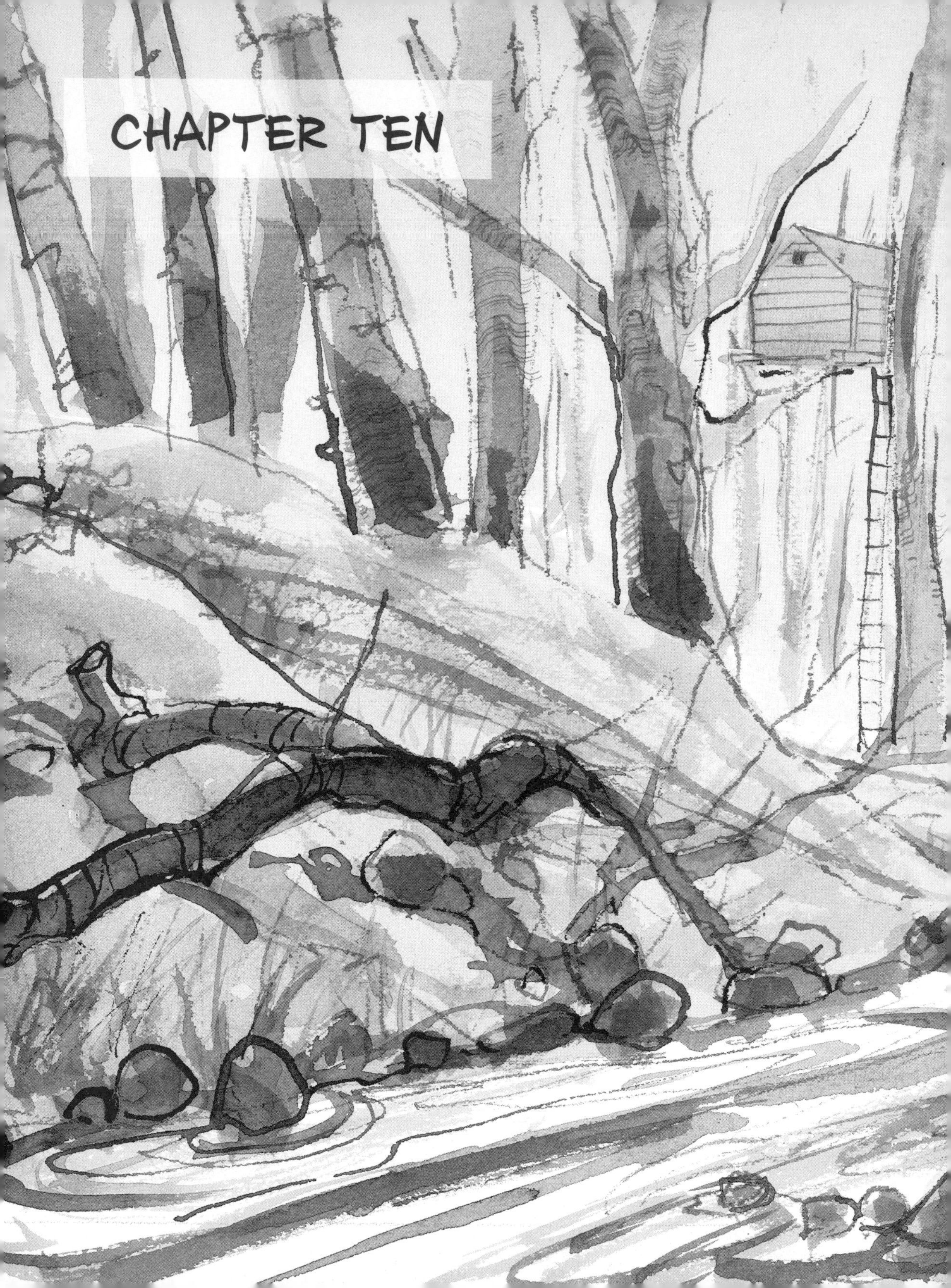

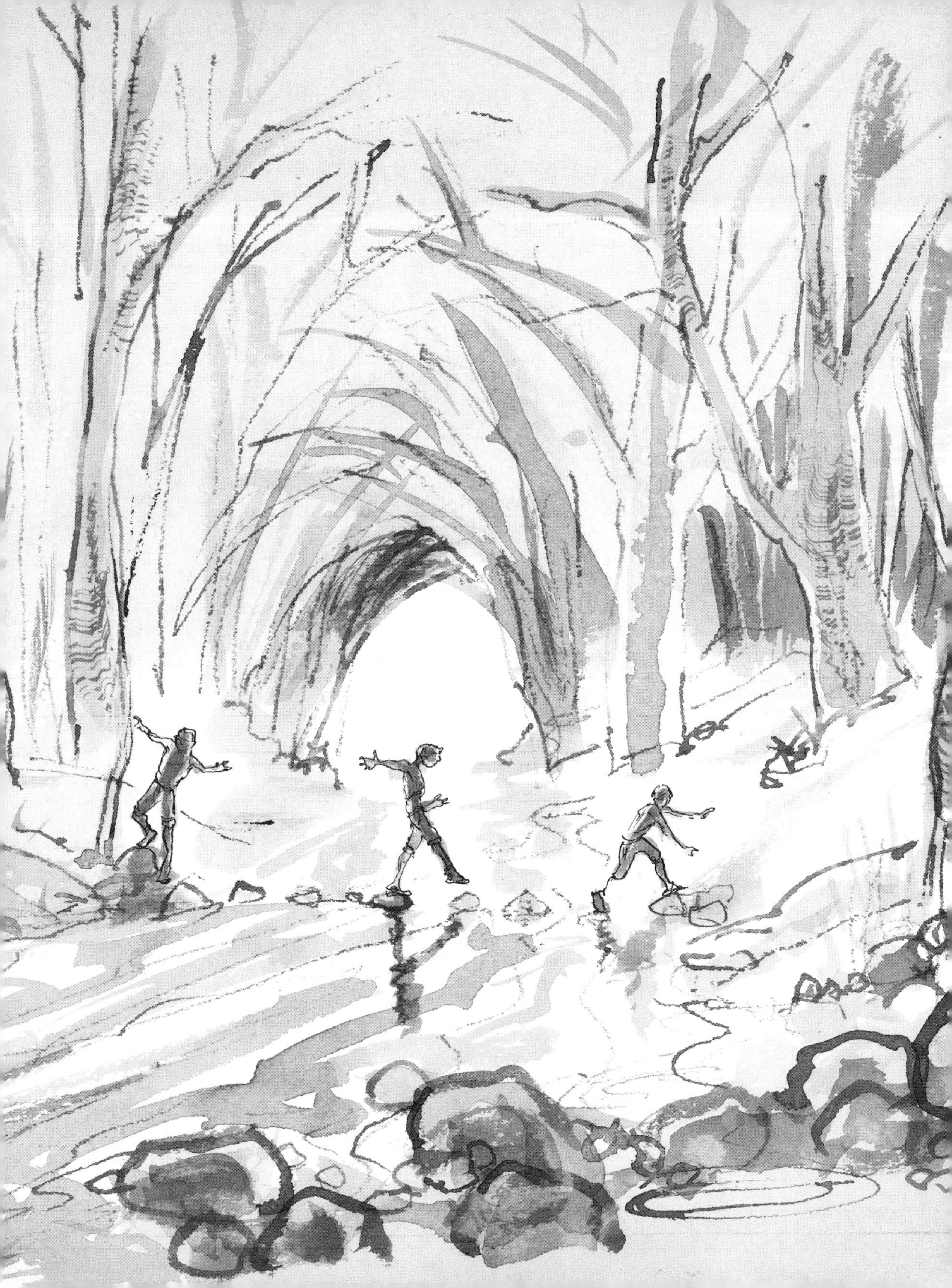

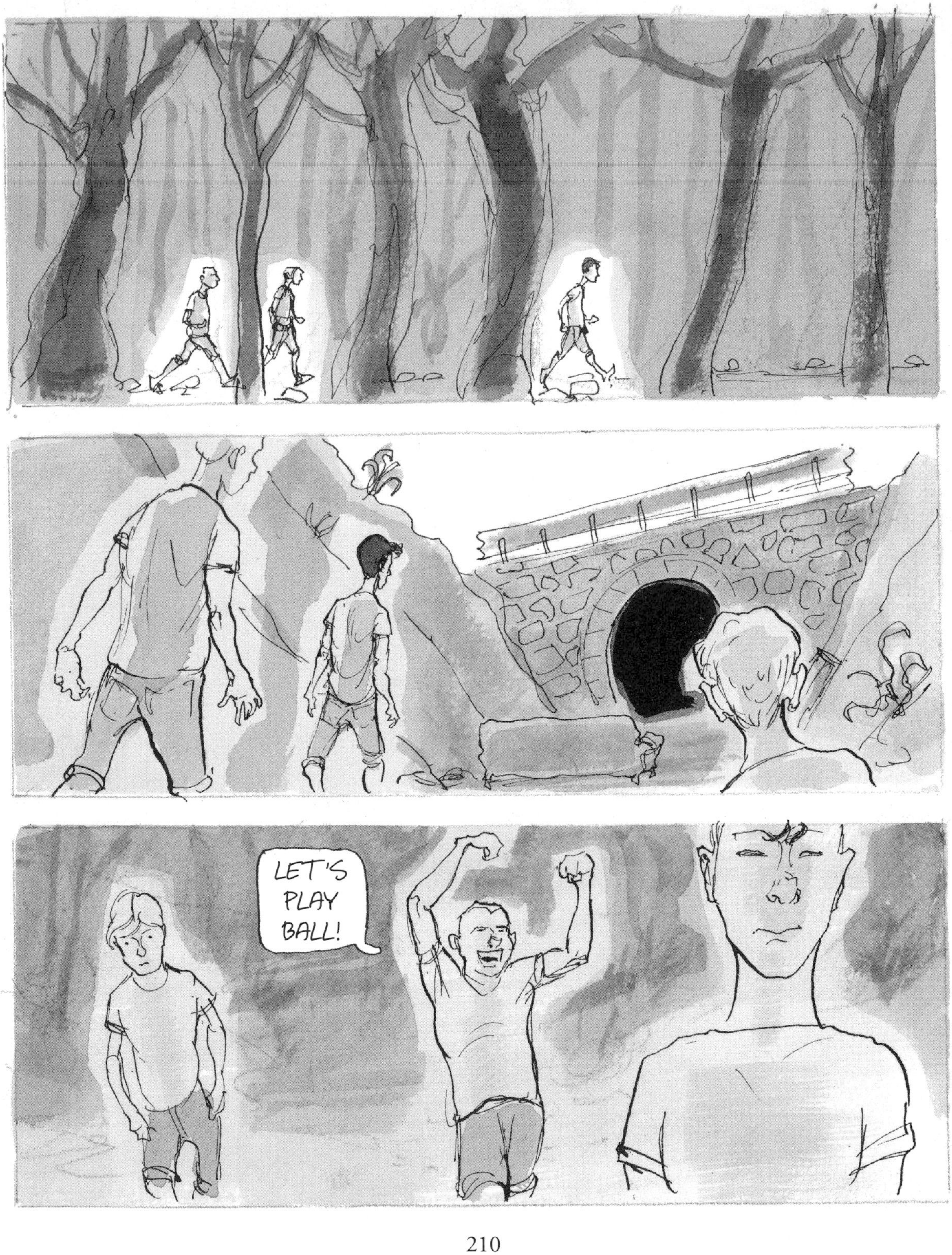
LET'S PLAY BALL!

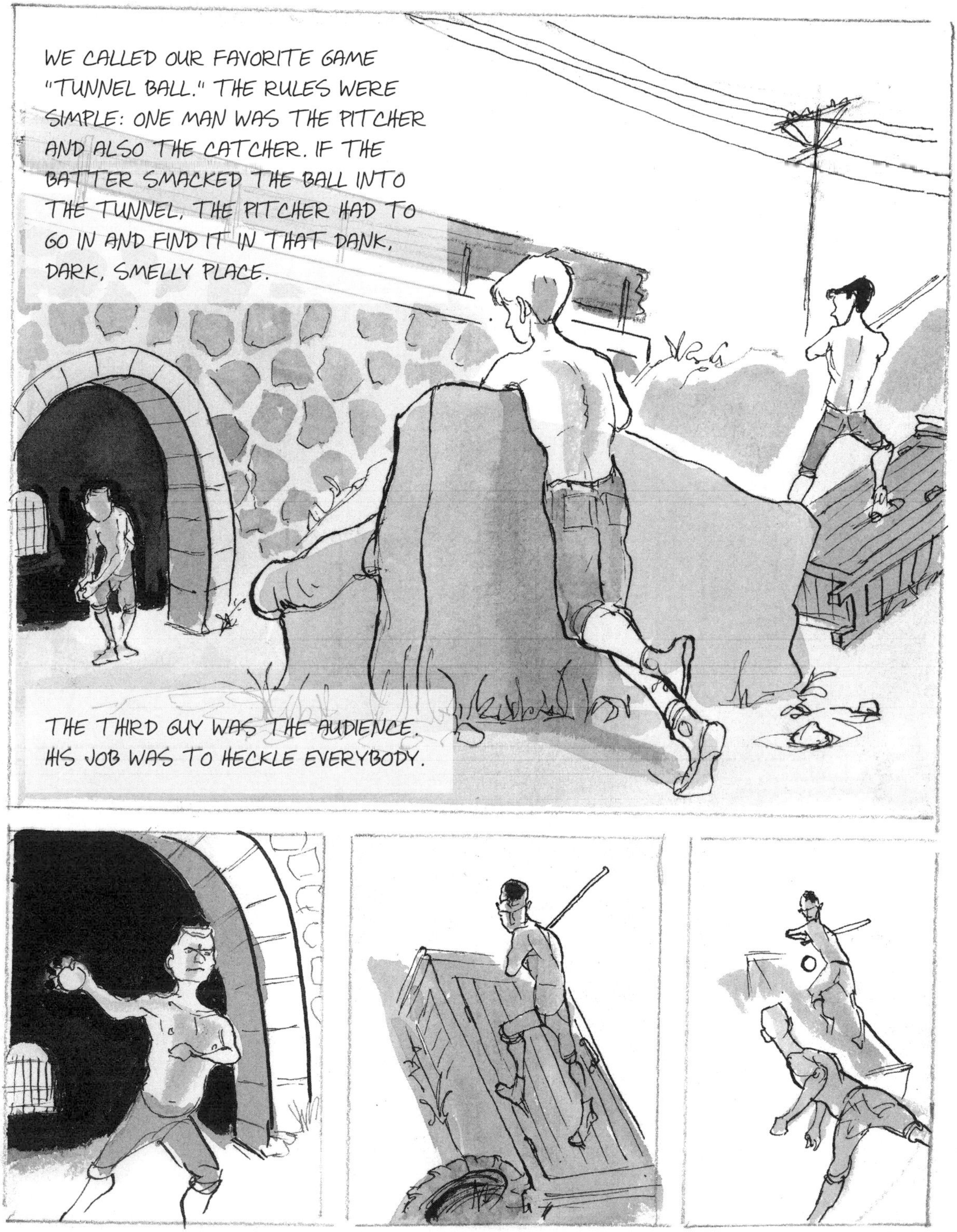
WE CALLED OUR FAVORITE GAME "TUNNEL BALL." THE RULES WERE SIMPLE: ONE MAN WAS THE PITCHER AND ALSO THE CATCHER. IF THE BATTER SMACKED THE BALL INTO THE TUNNEL, THE PITCHER HAD TO GO IN AND FIND IT IN THAT DANK, DARK, SMELLY PLACE.
THE THIRD GUY WAS THE AUDIENCE. HIS JOB WAS TO HECKLE EVERYBODY.

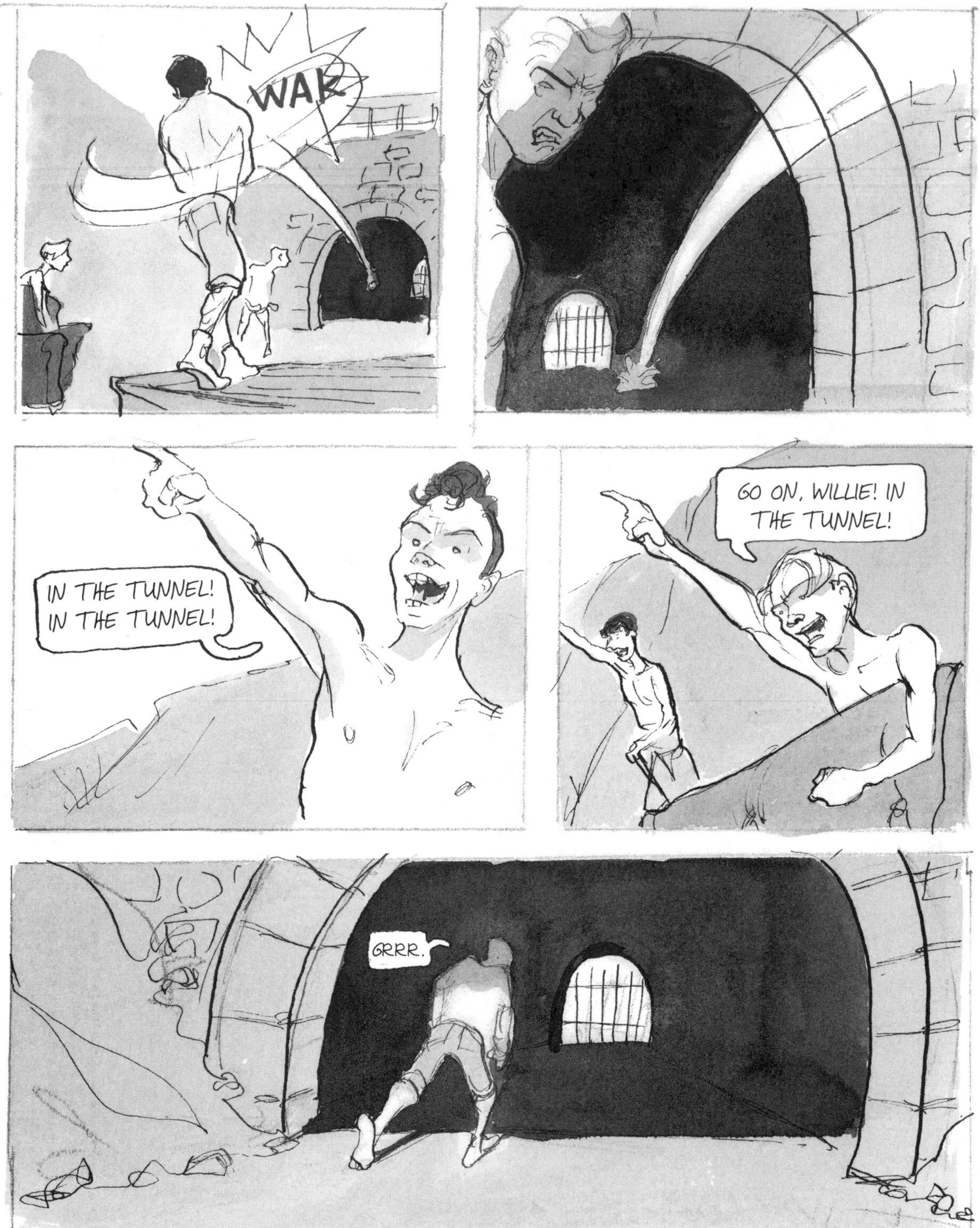
WAK
IN THE TUNNEL! IN THE TUNNEL!
GO ON, WILLIE! IN THE TUNNEL!
GRRR.

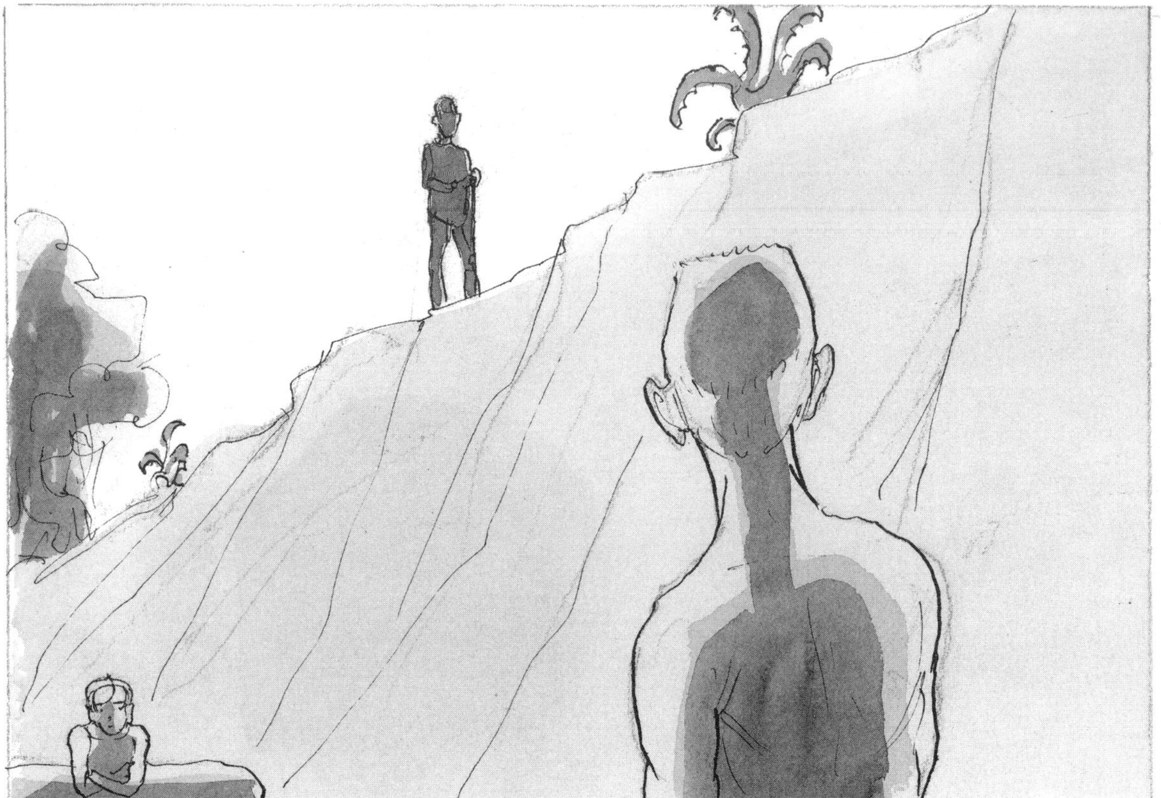
WHO IS THAT?

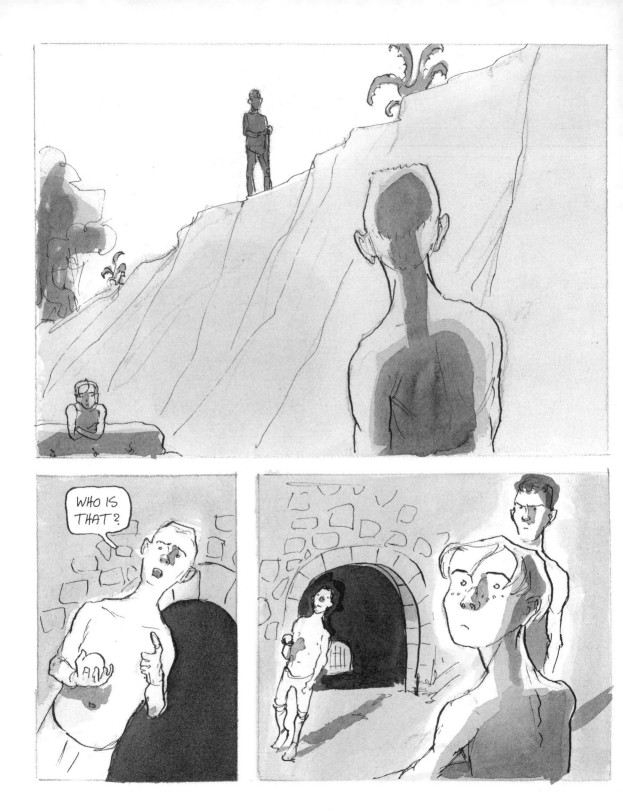

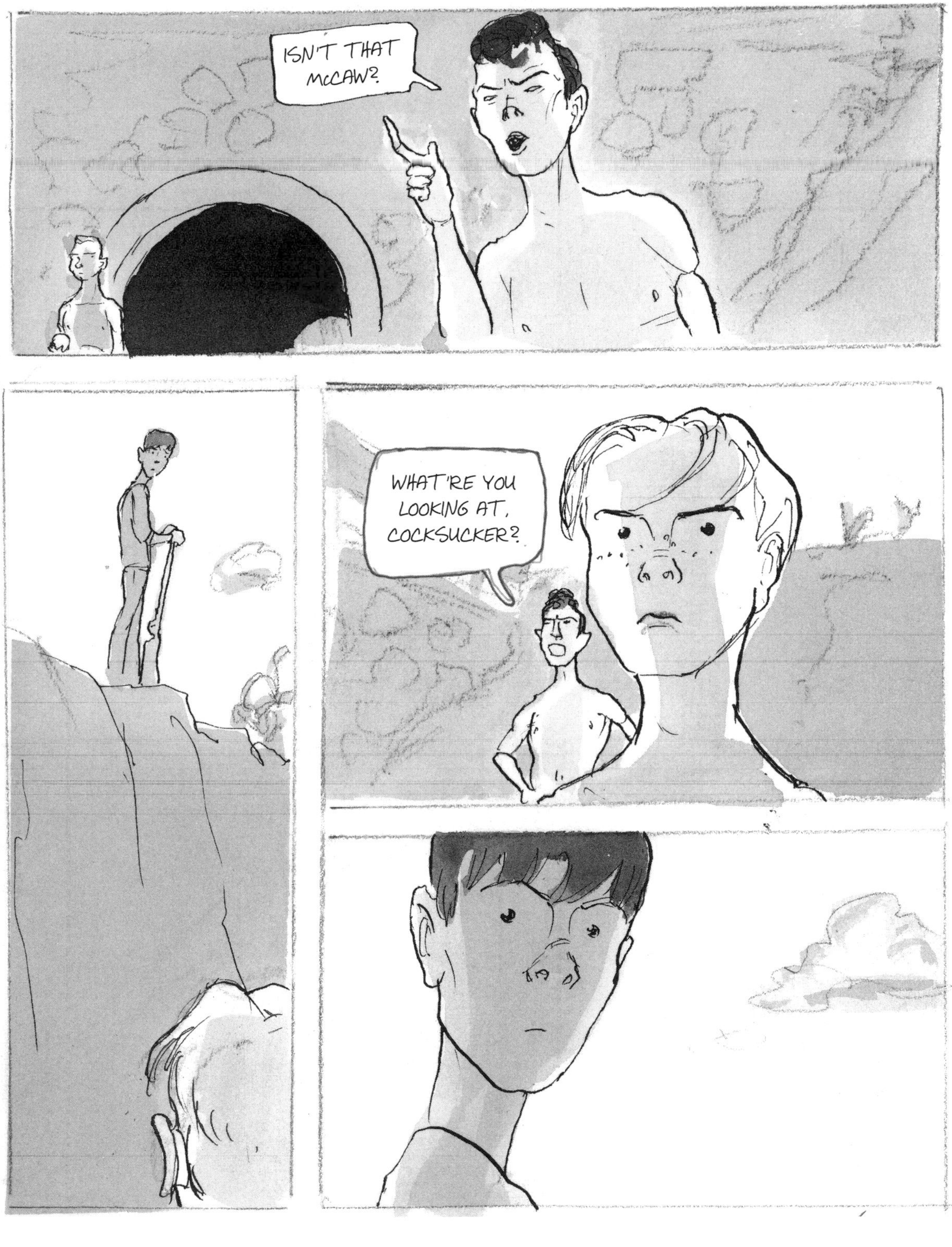
ISN'T THAT McCAW?
WHAT'RE YOU LOOKING AT, COCKSUCKER?

216

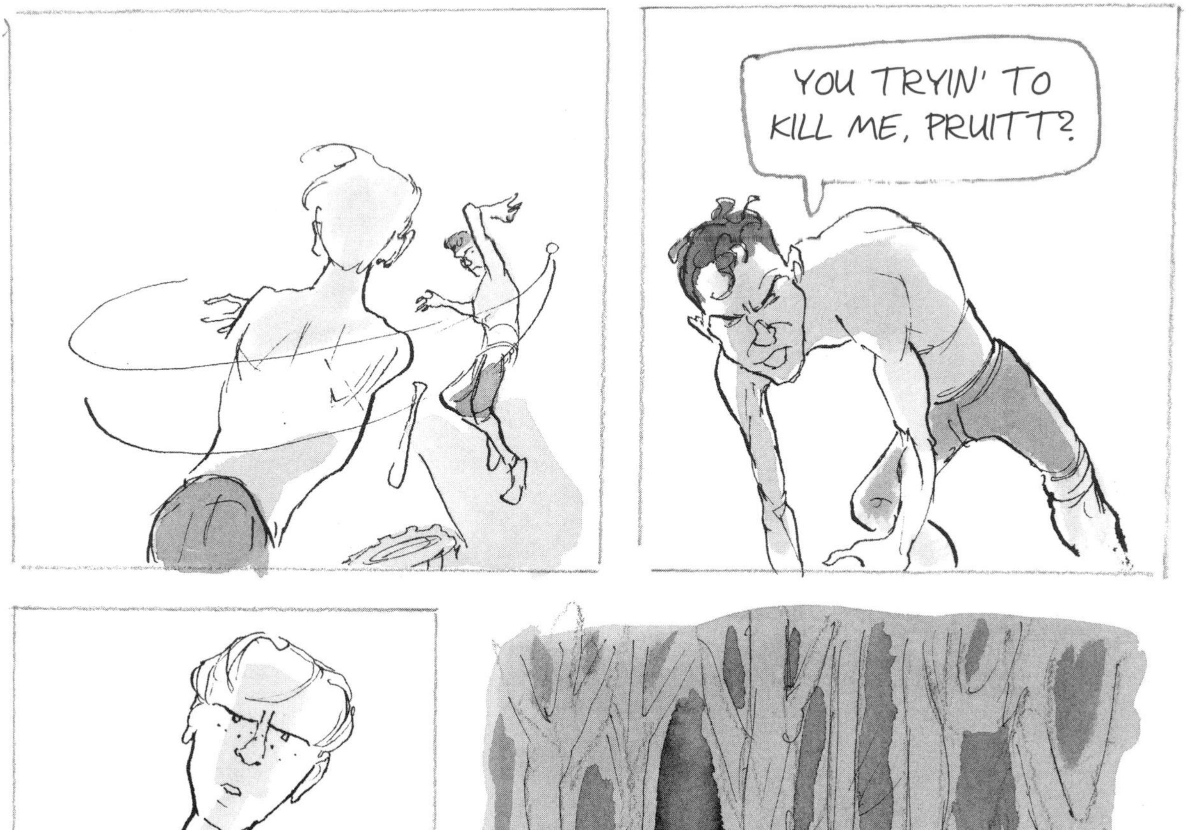
YOU TRYIN' TO KILL ME, PRUITT?
SORRY.

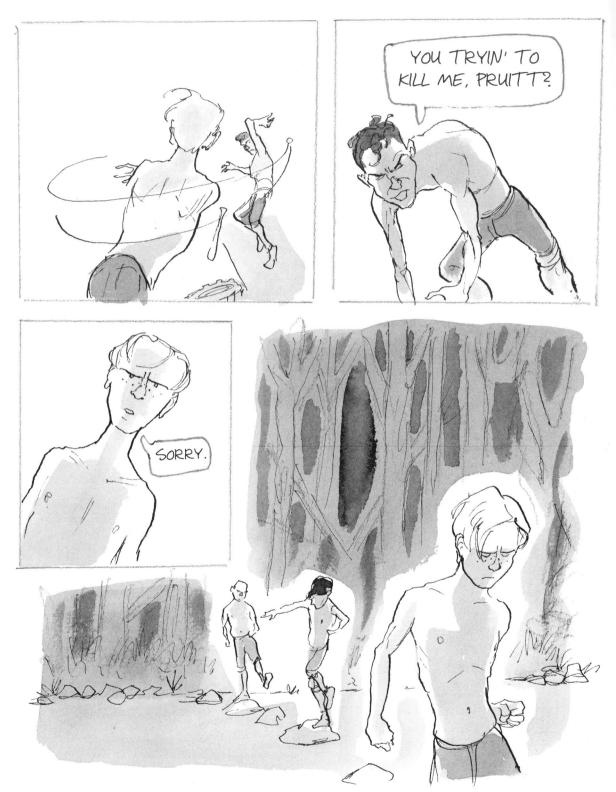

WHY I DID IT, I CAN'T REALLY SAY, BUT ONE NIGHT, IN A MOMENT OF DRUNKEN EARNESTNESS, I HAD TOLD KURT AND WILLIE ABOUT WARREN AND THE HUGGING THING.

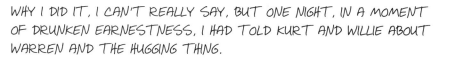

220

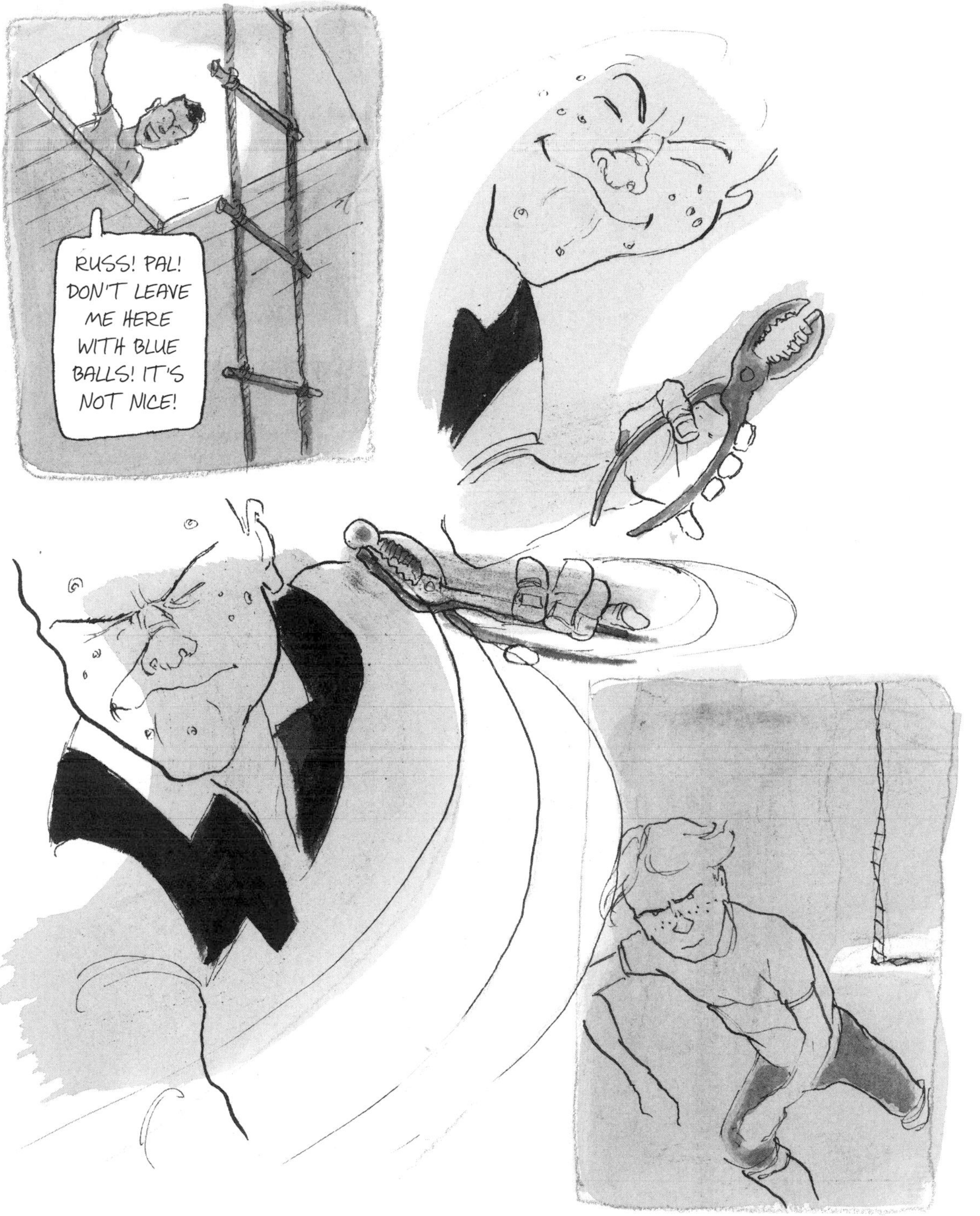
RUSS! PAL! DON'T LEAVE ME HERE WITH BLUE BALLS! IT'S NOT NICE!

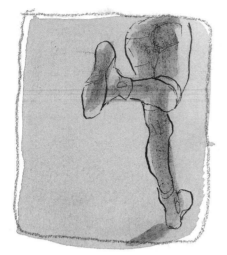

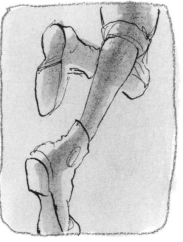

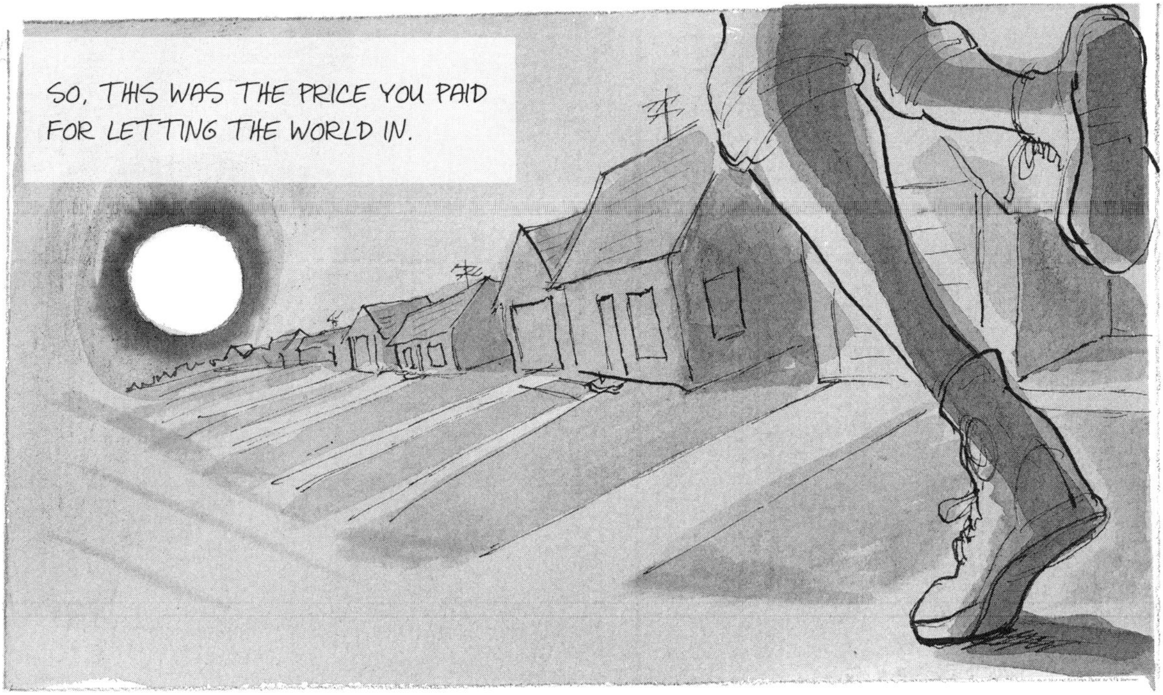
SO, THIS WAS THE PRICE YOU PAID FOR LETTING THE WORLD IN.

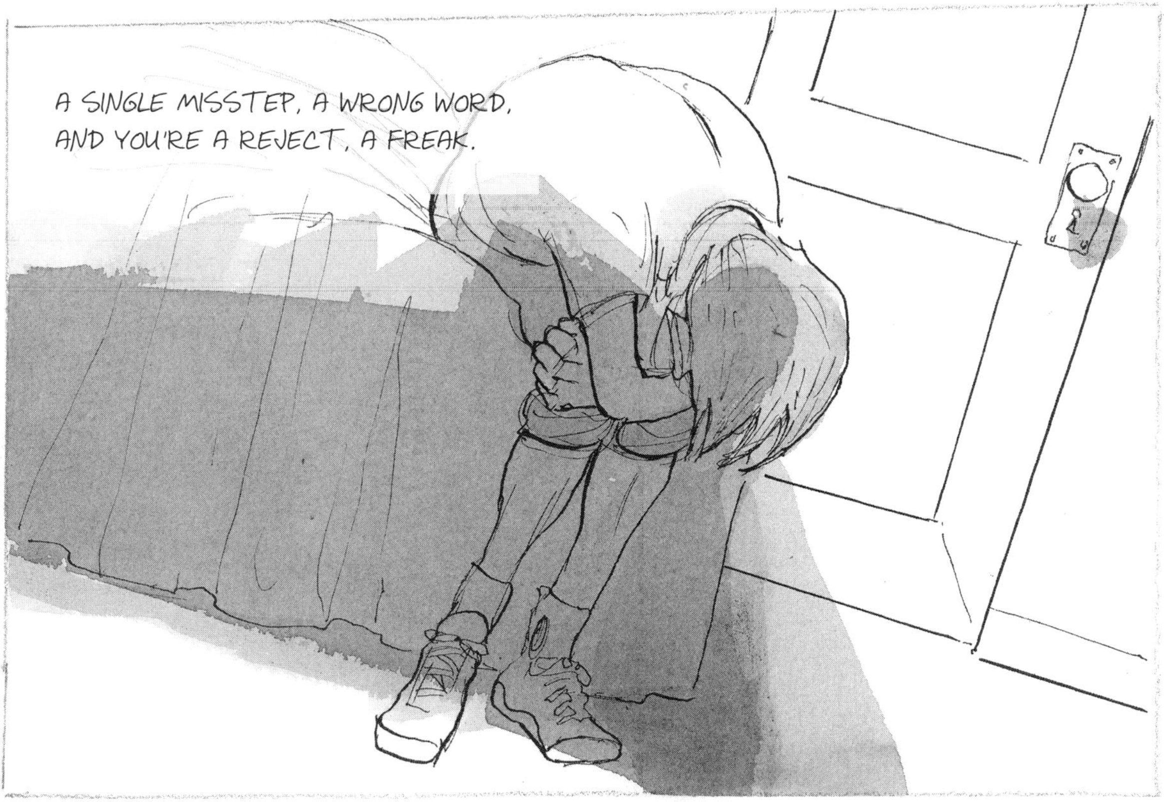
A SINGLE MISSTEP, A WRONG WORD, AND YOU'RE A REJECT, A FREAK.

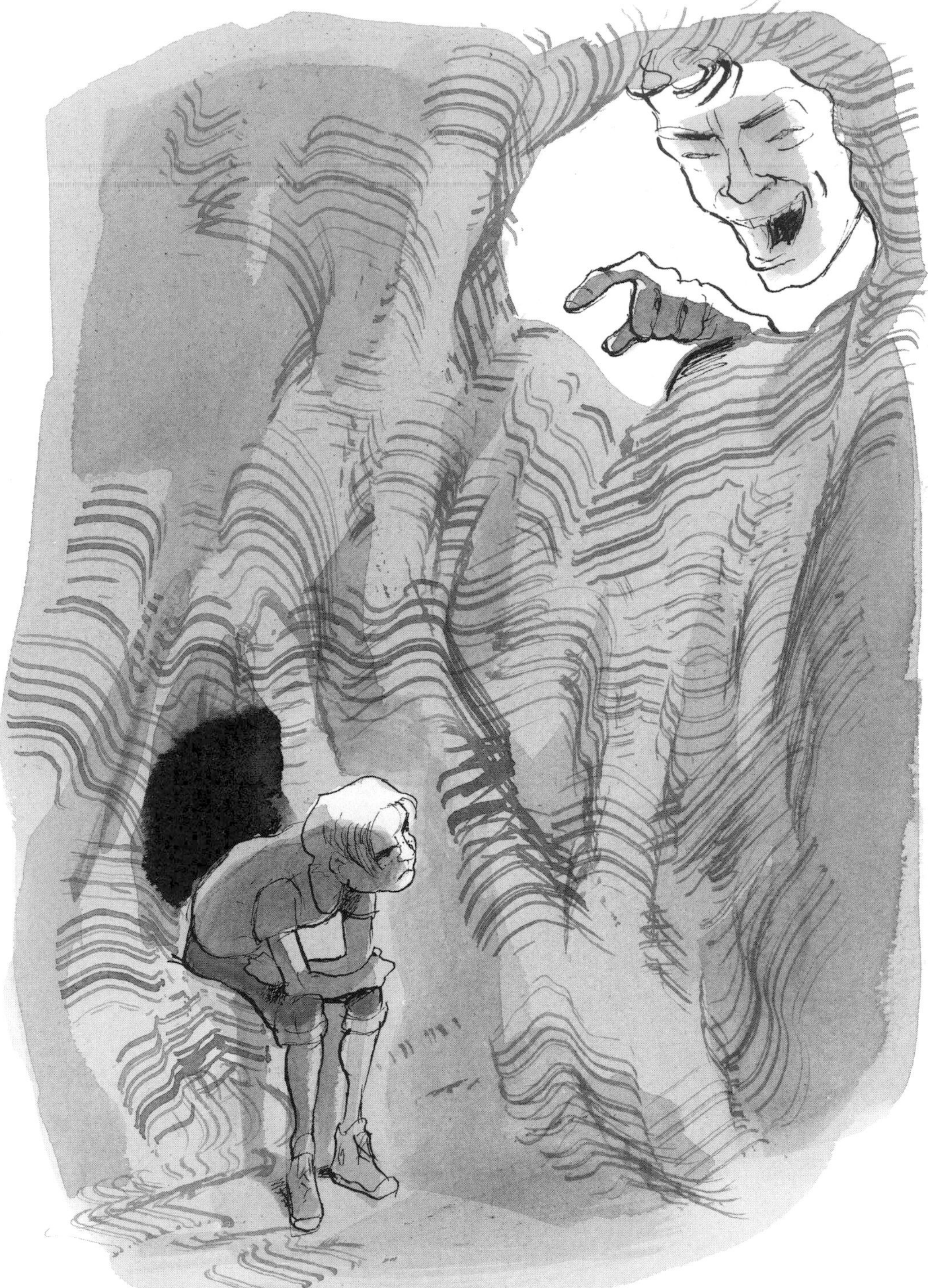

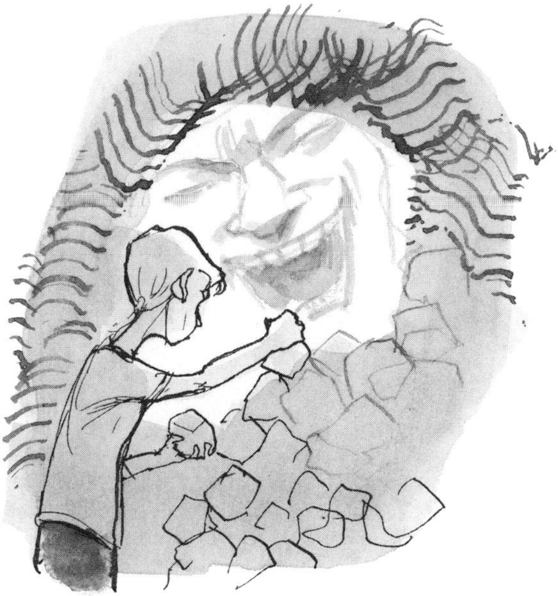

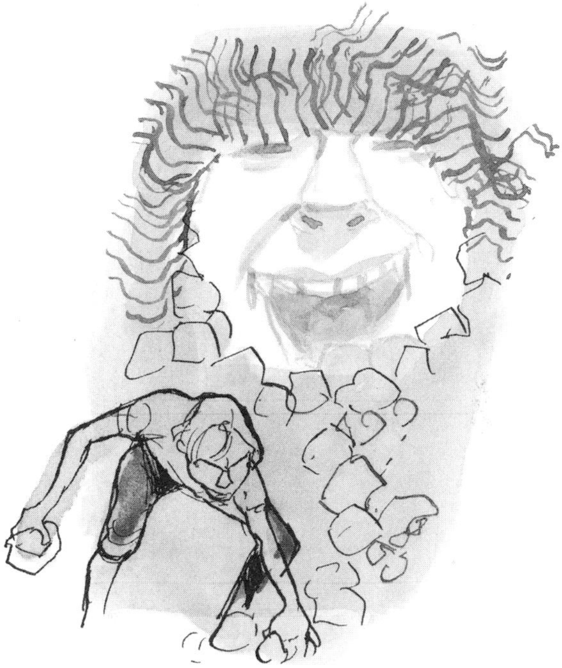

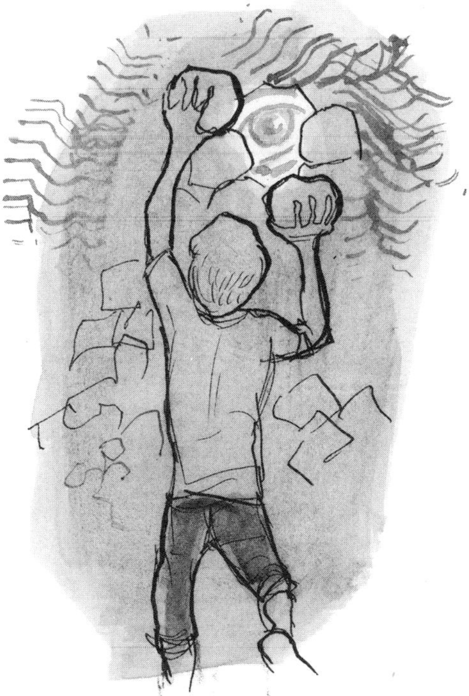

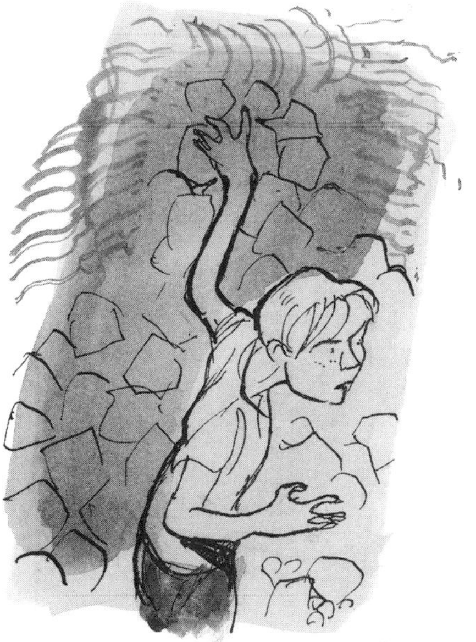

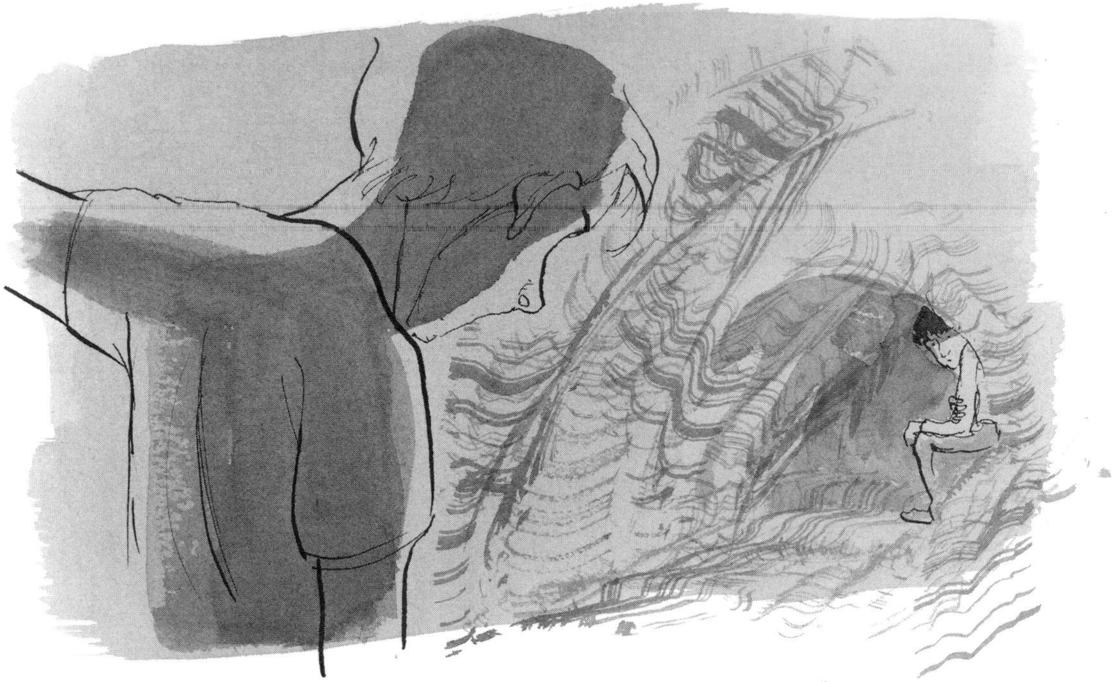

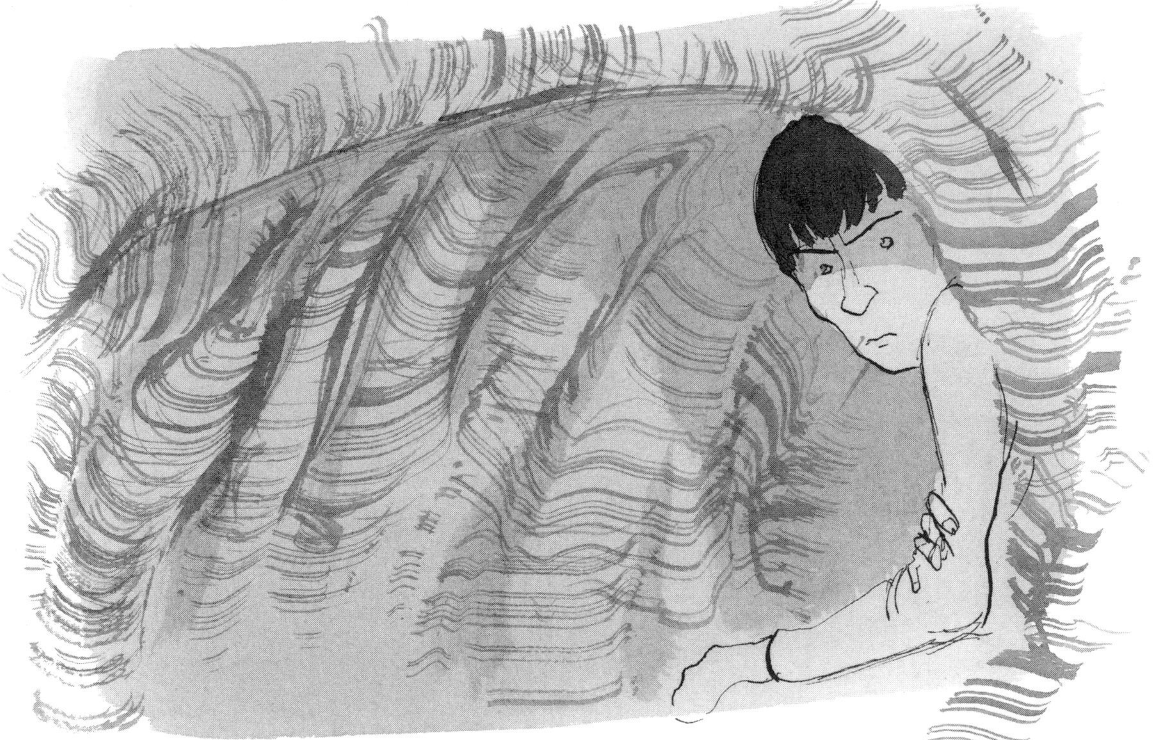

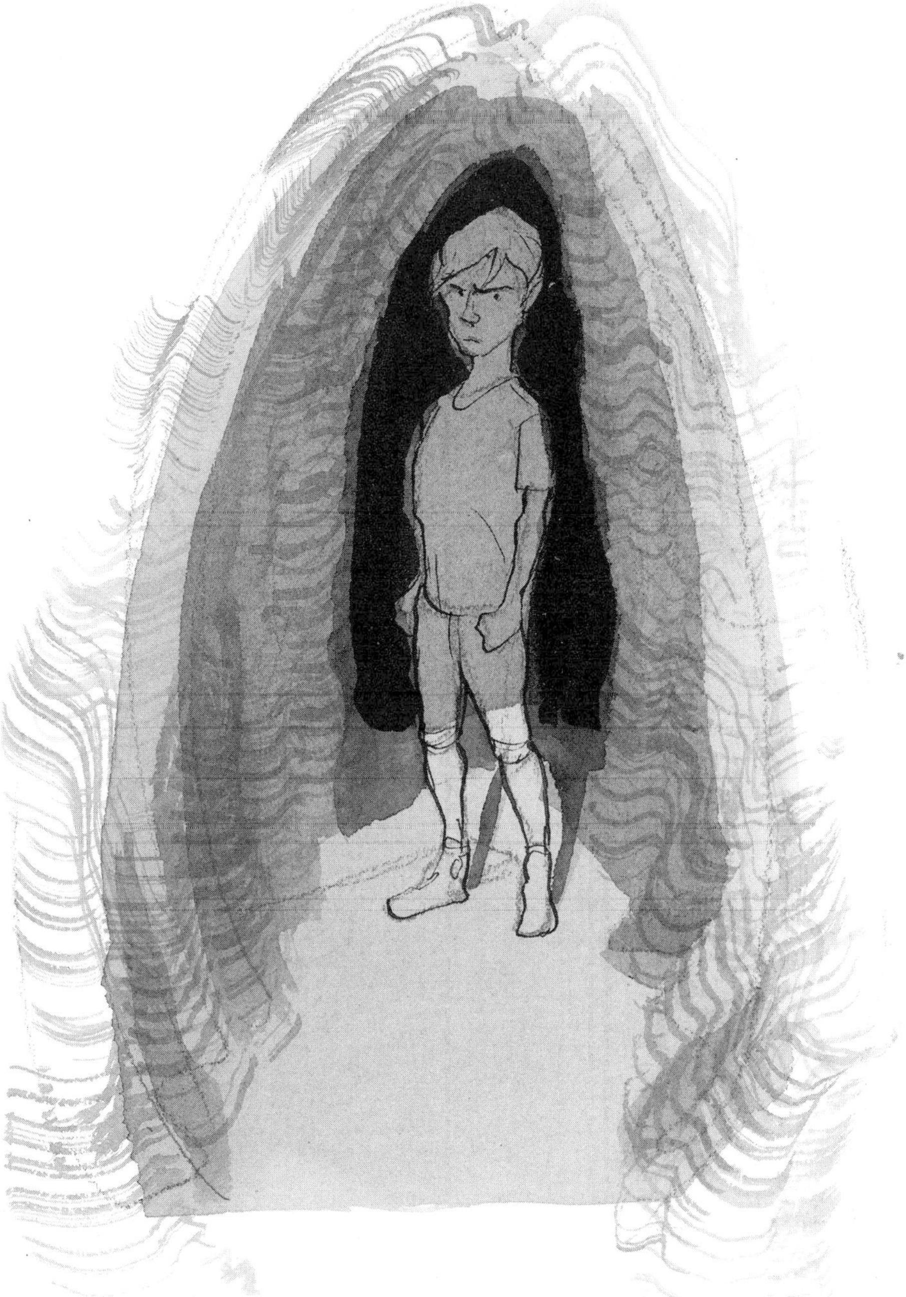

CHAPTER ELEVEN

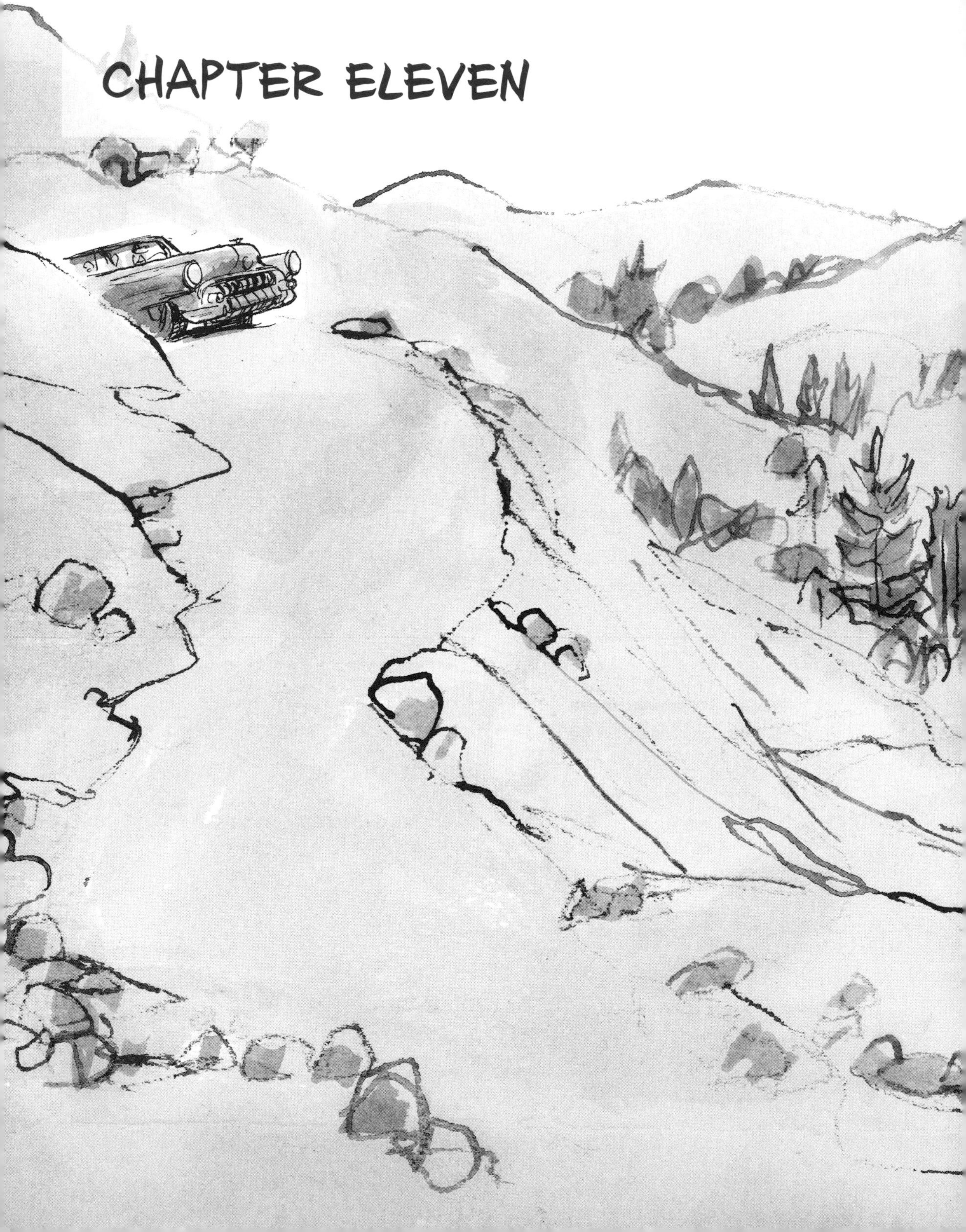

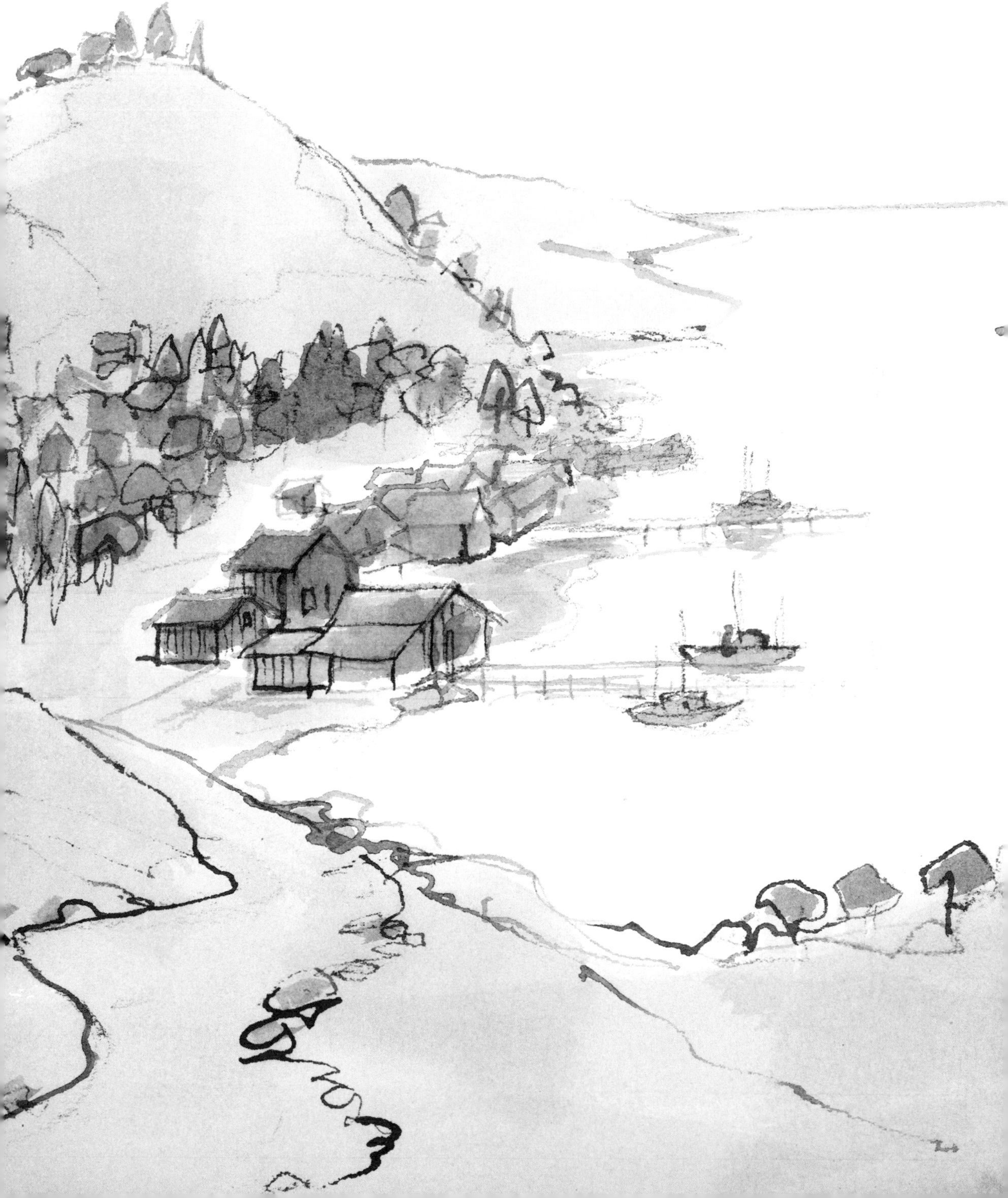

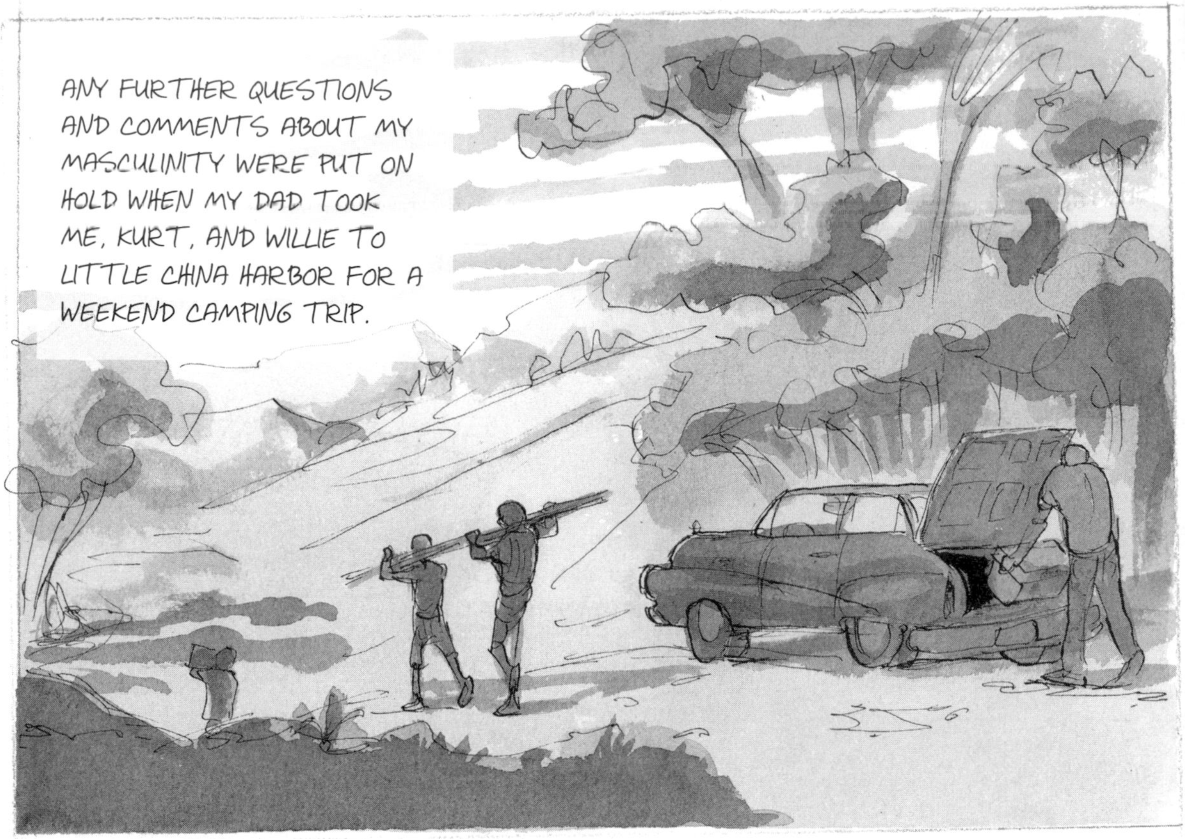
ANY FURTHER QUESTIONS AND COMMENTS ABOUT MY MASCULINITY WERE PUT ON HOLD WHEN MY DAD TOOK ME, KURT, AND WILLIE TO LITTLE CHINA HARBOR FOR A WEEKEND CAMPING TRIP.

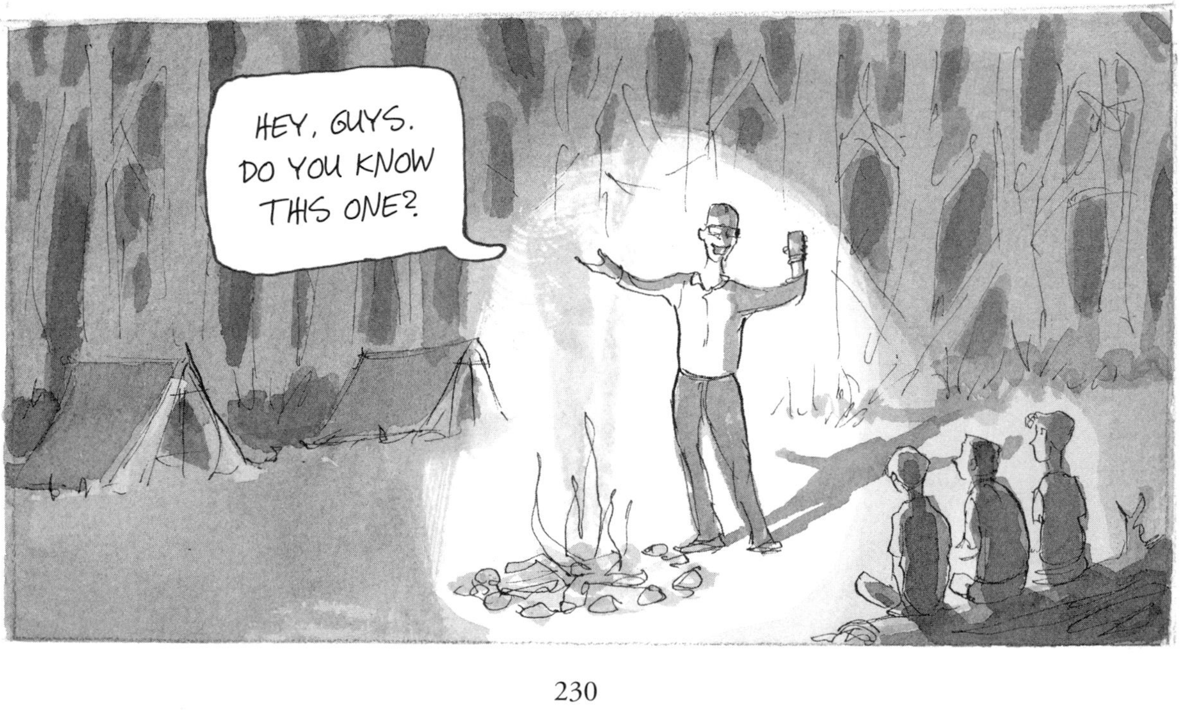
HEY, GUYS. DO YOU KNOW THIS ONE?

232

233

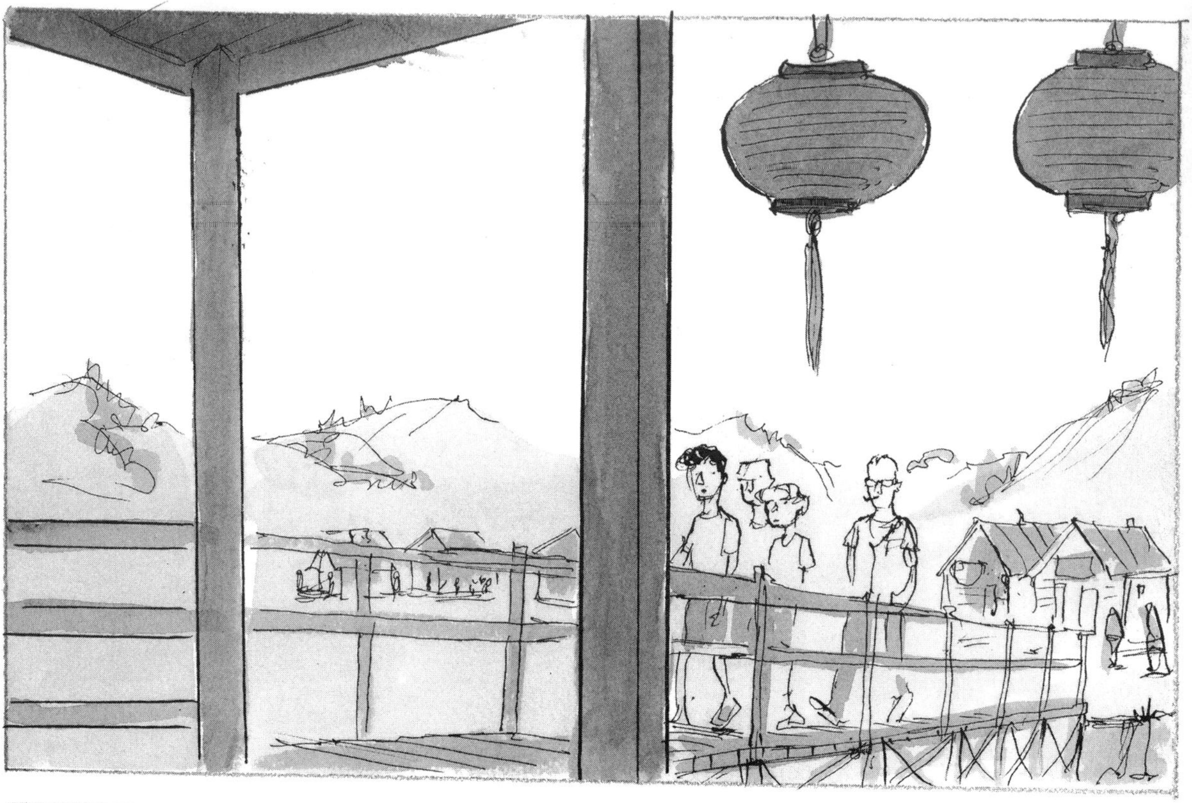

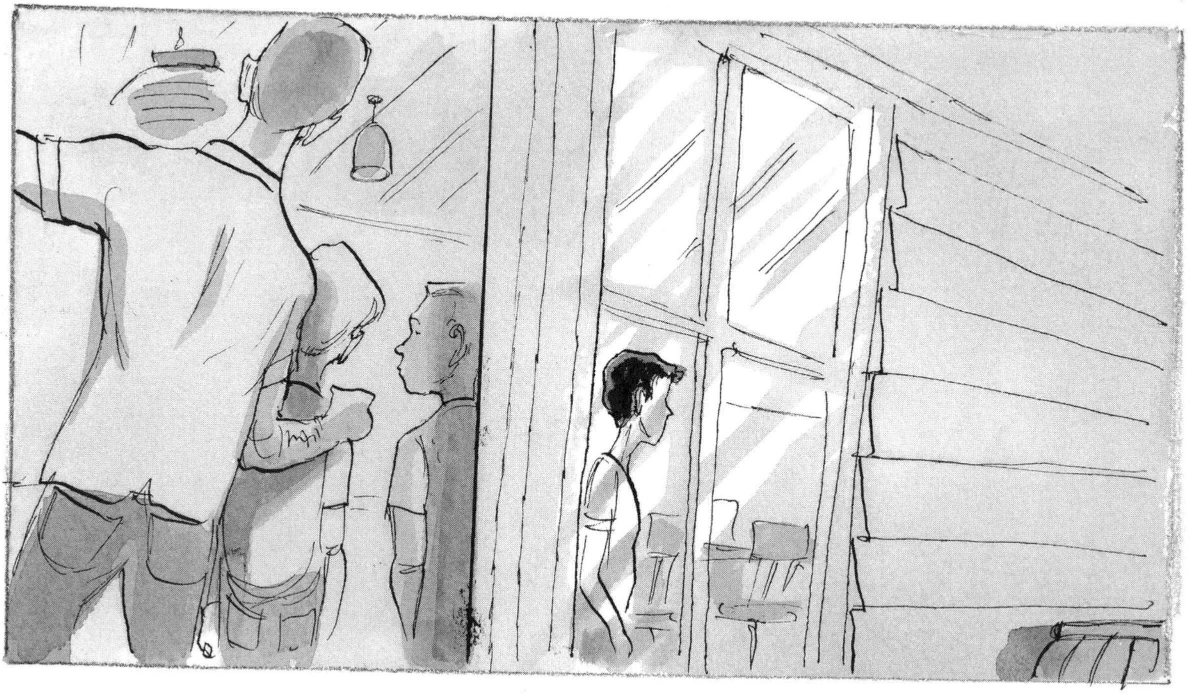

235

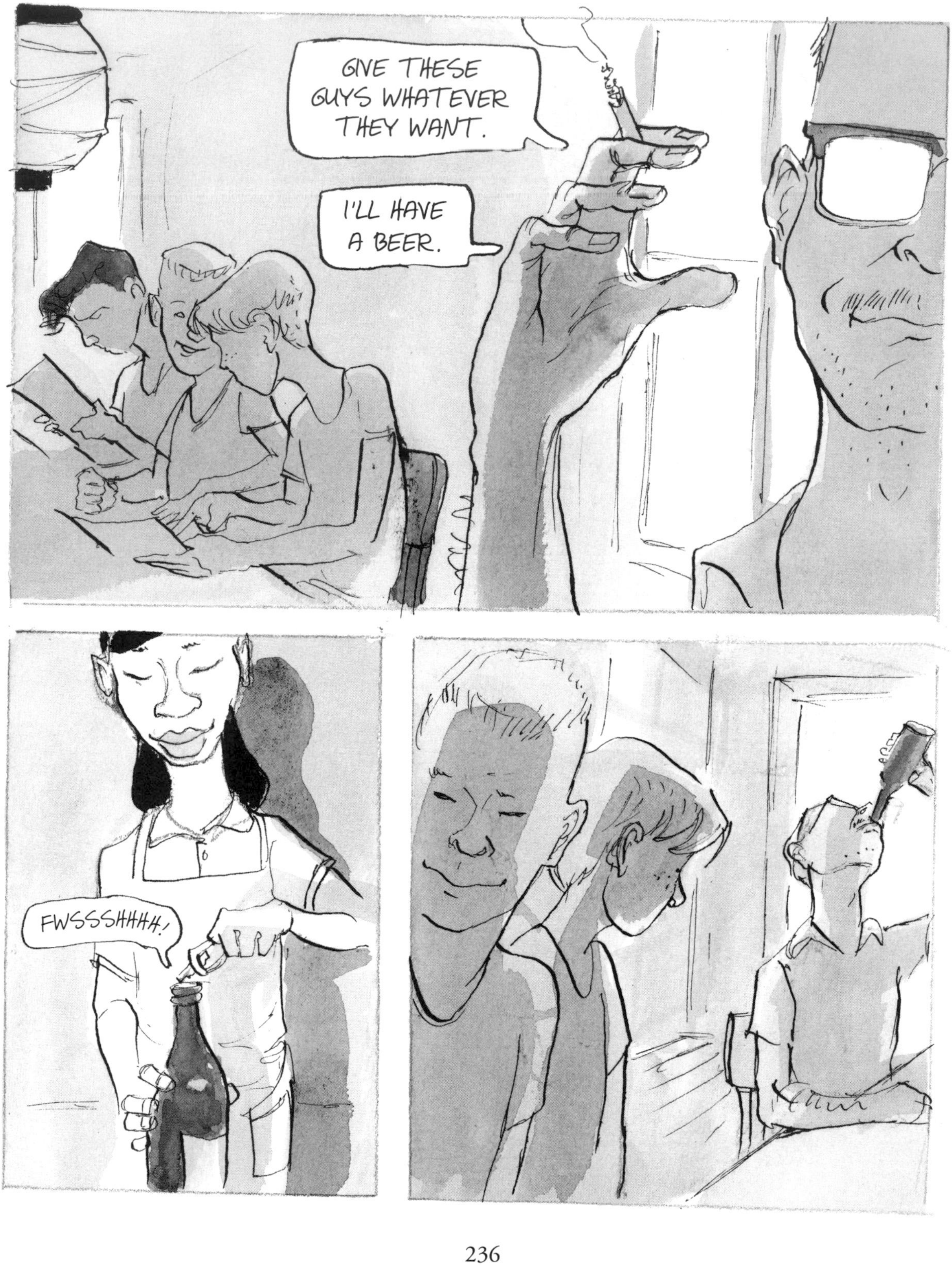
GIVE THESE GUYS WHATEVER THEY WANT.
I'LL HAVE A BEER.
FWSSSHHHH!

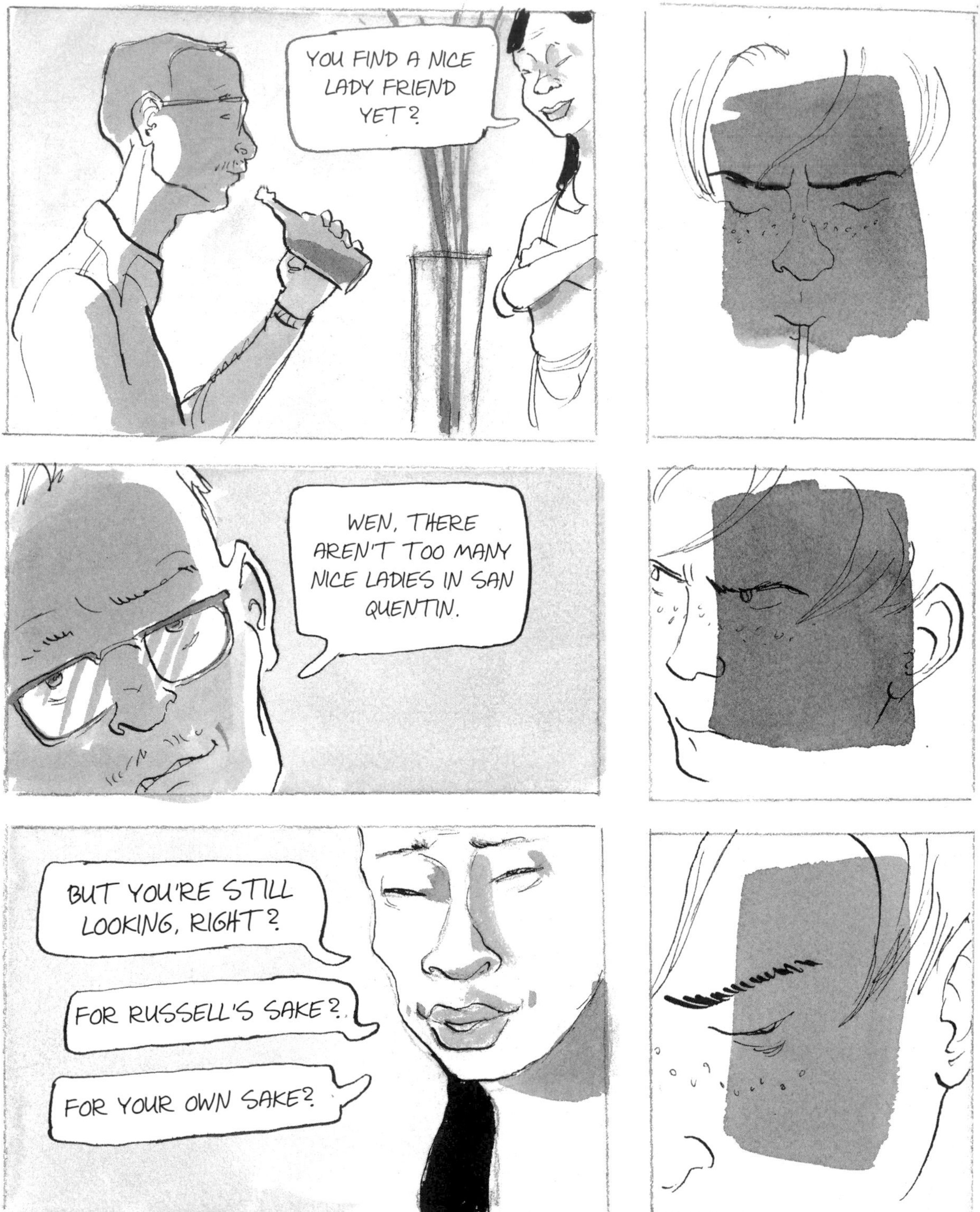
YOU FIND A NICE LADY FRIEND YET?
WEN, THERE AREN'T TOO MANY NICE LADIES IN SAN QUENTIN.
BUT YOU'RE STILL LOOKING, RIGHT?
FOR RUSSELL'S SAKE?
FOR YOUR OWN SAKE?

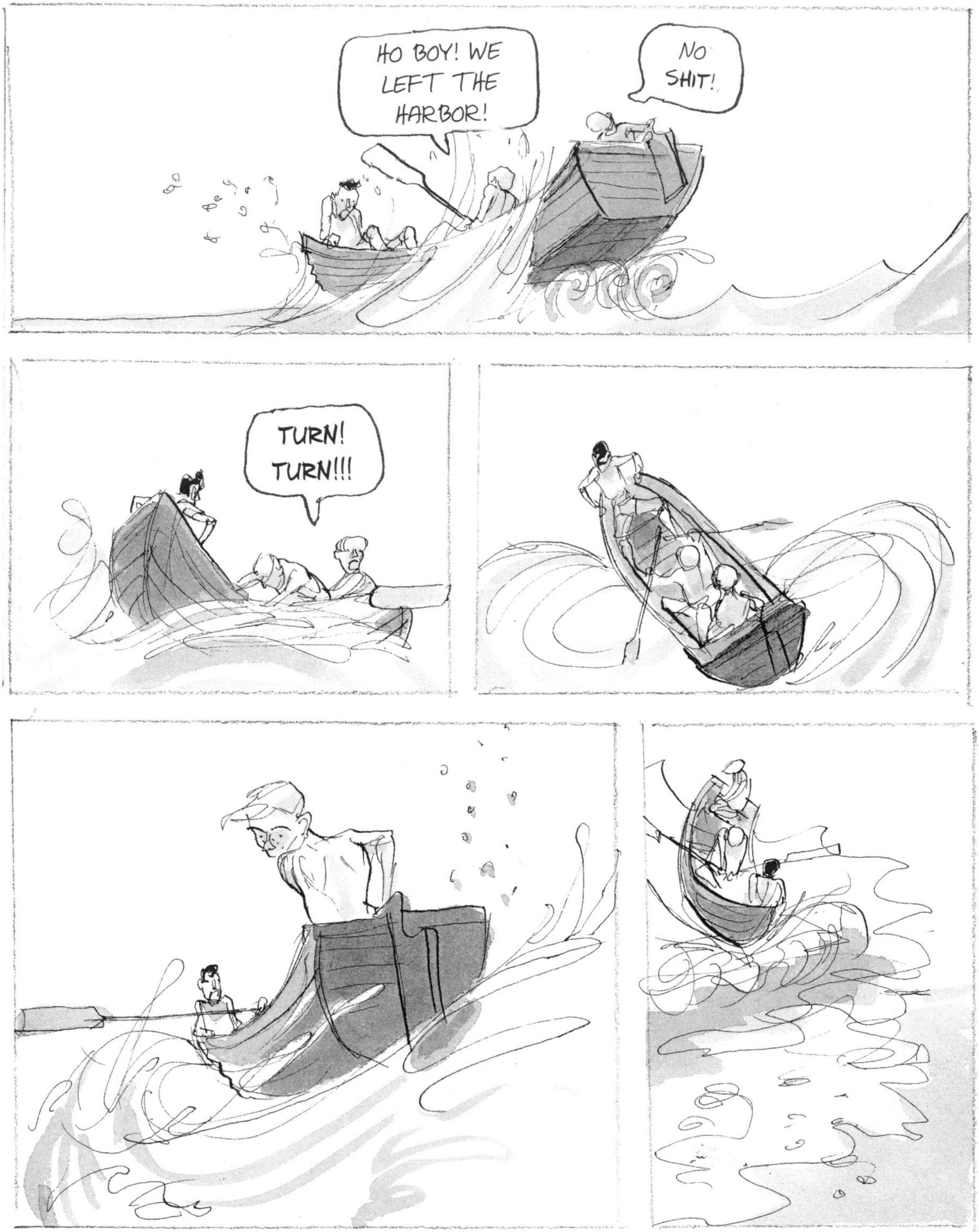
HO BOY! WE LEFT THE HARBOR!
NO SHIT!
TURN! TURN!!!

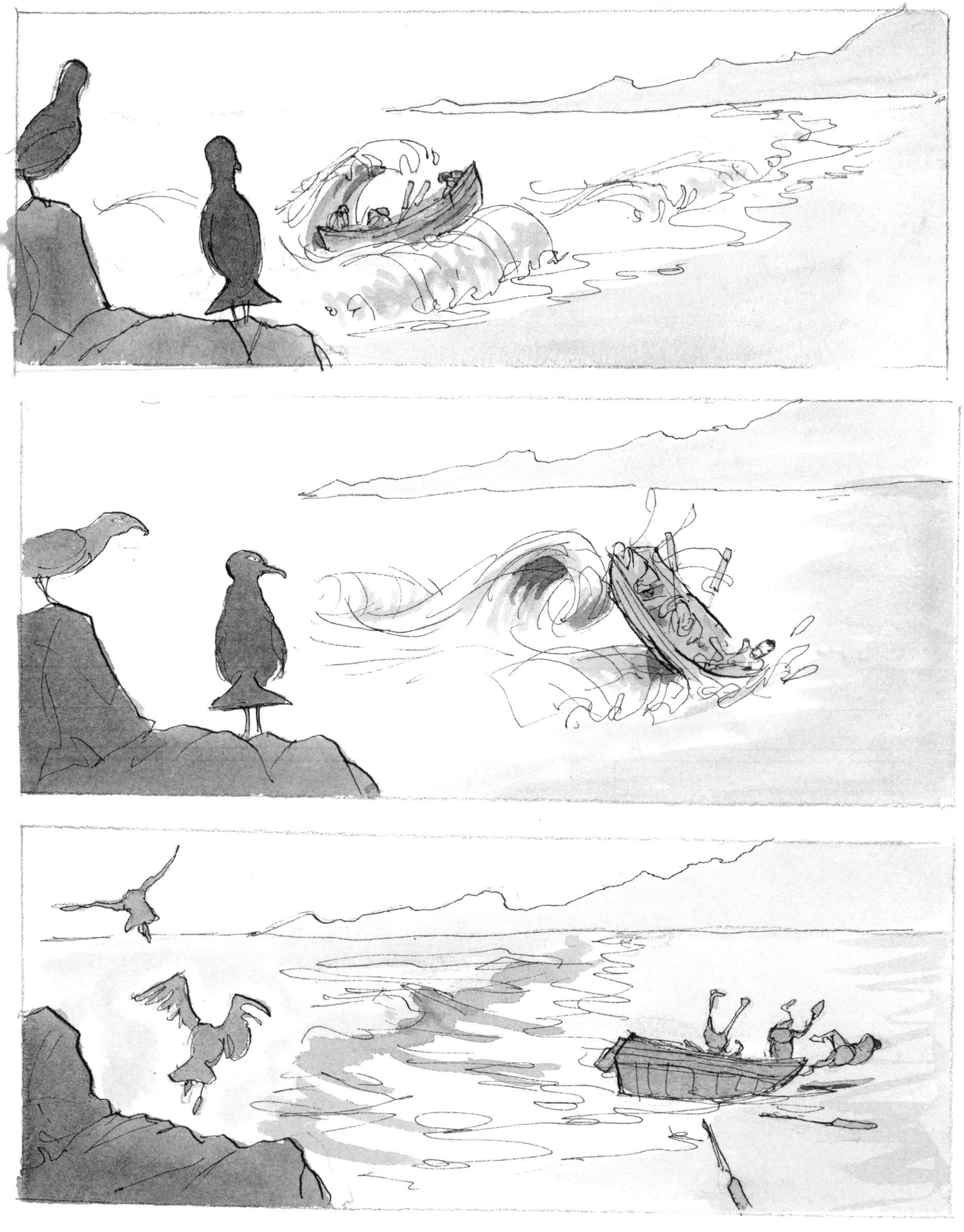

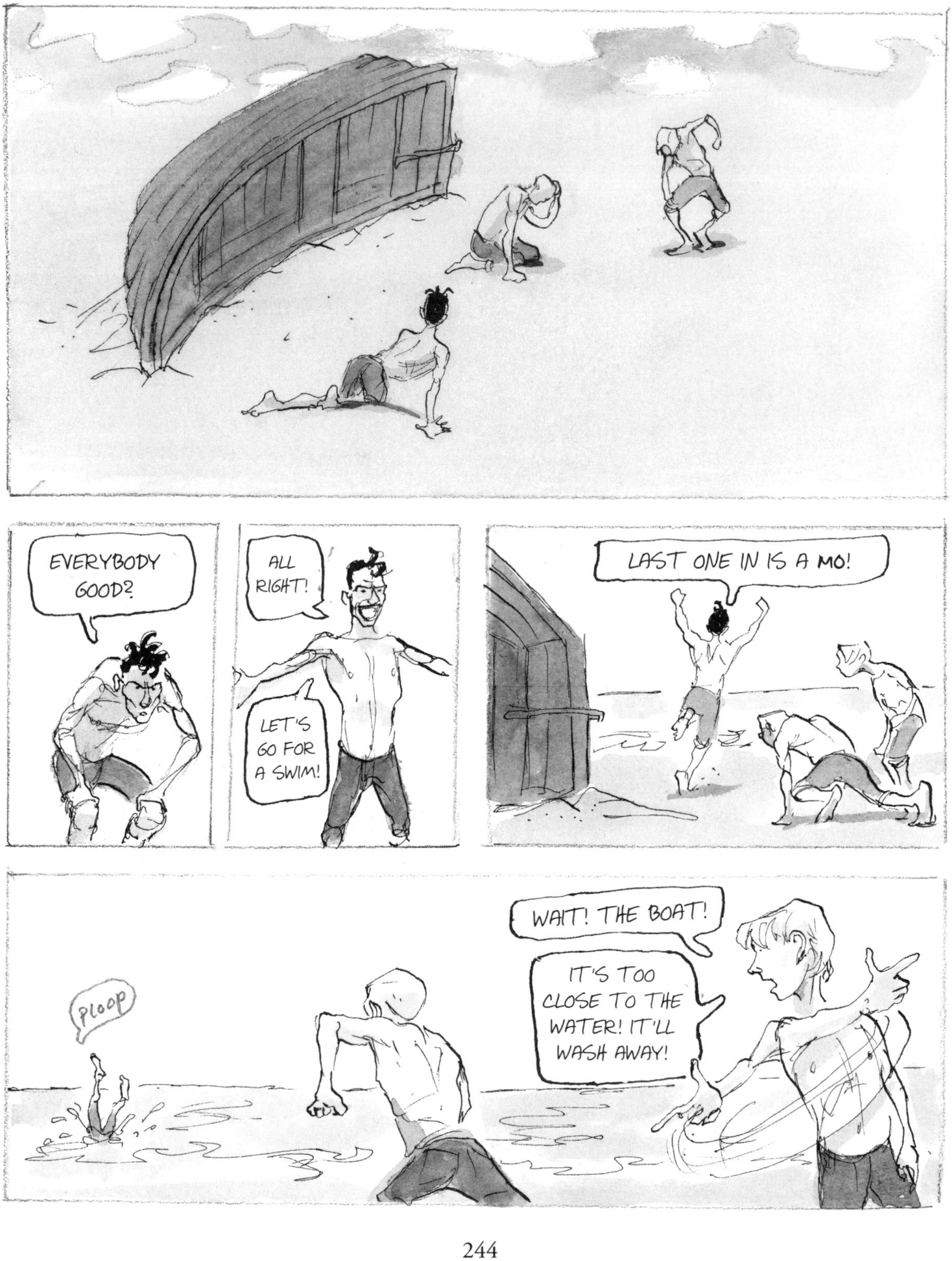
EVERYBODY GOOD?
ALL RIGHT!
LET'S GO FOR A SWIM!
LAST ONE IN IS A MO!
WAIT! THE BOAT!
IT'S TOO CLOSE TO THE WATER! IT'LL WASH AWAY!
PLOOP

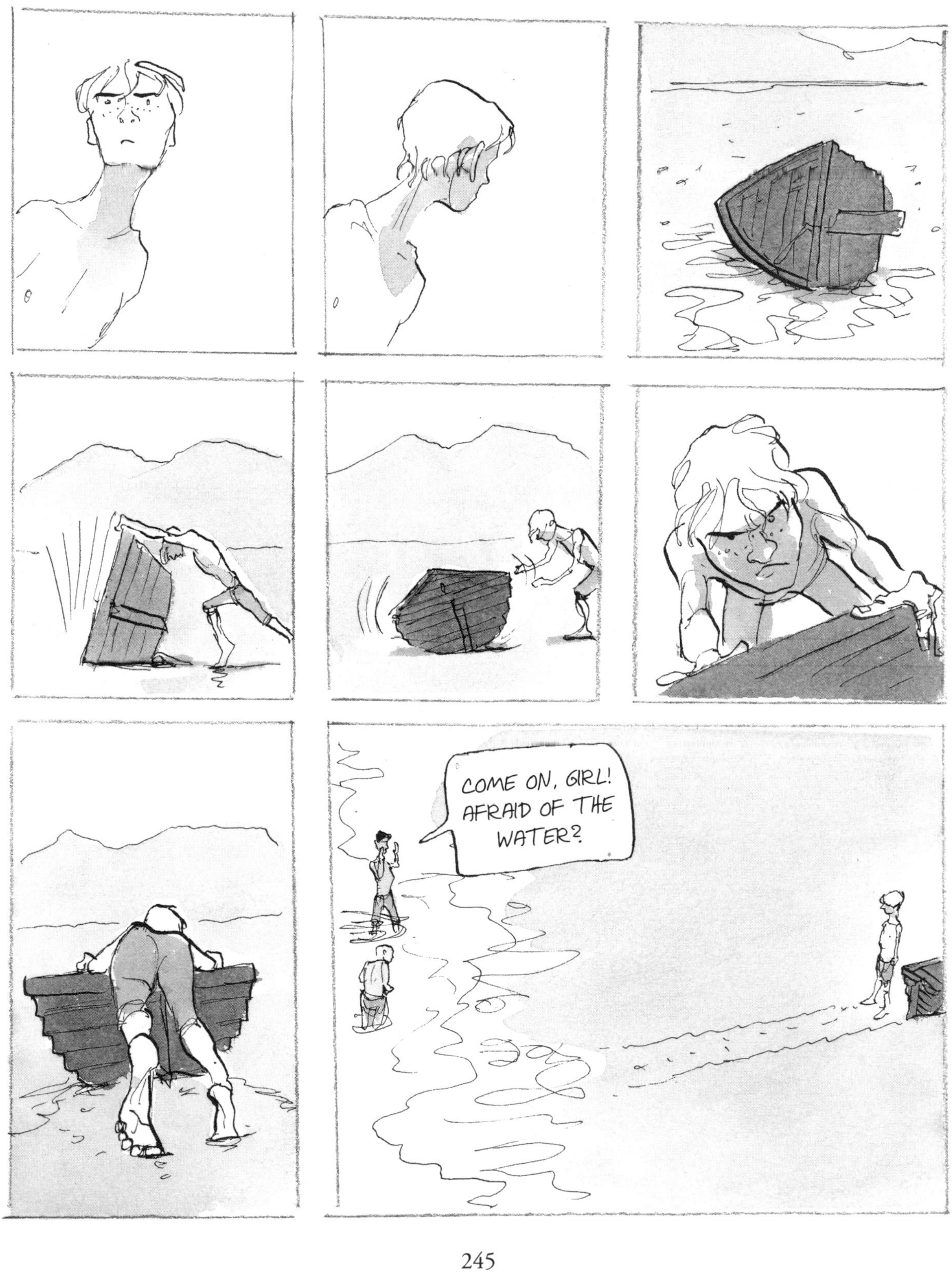
COME ON, GIRL! AFRAID OF THE WATER?

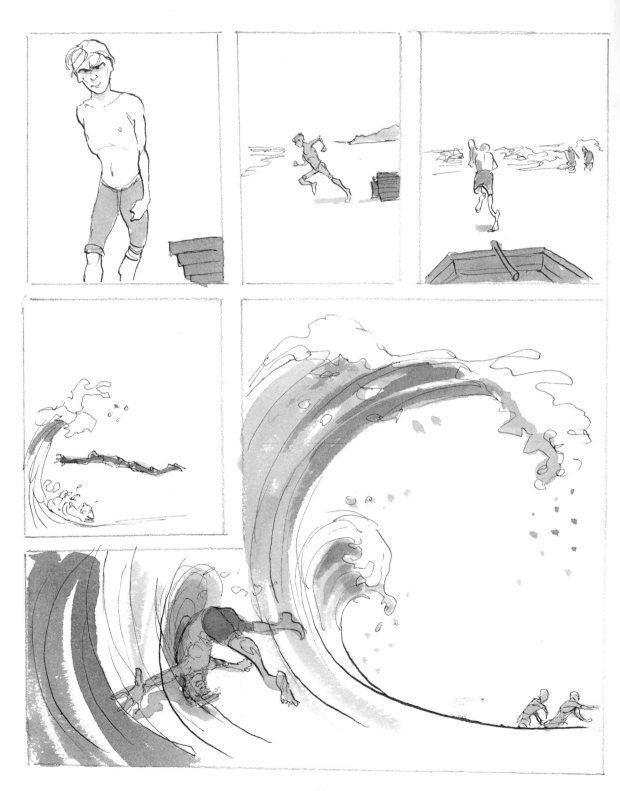

247

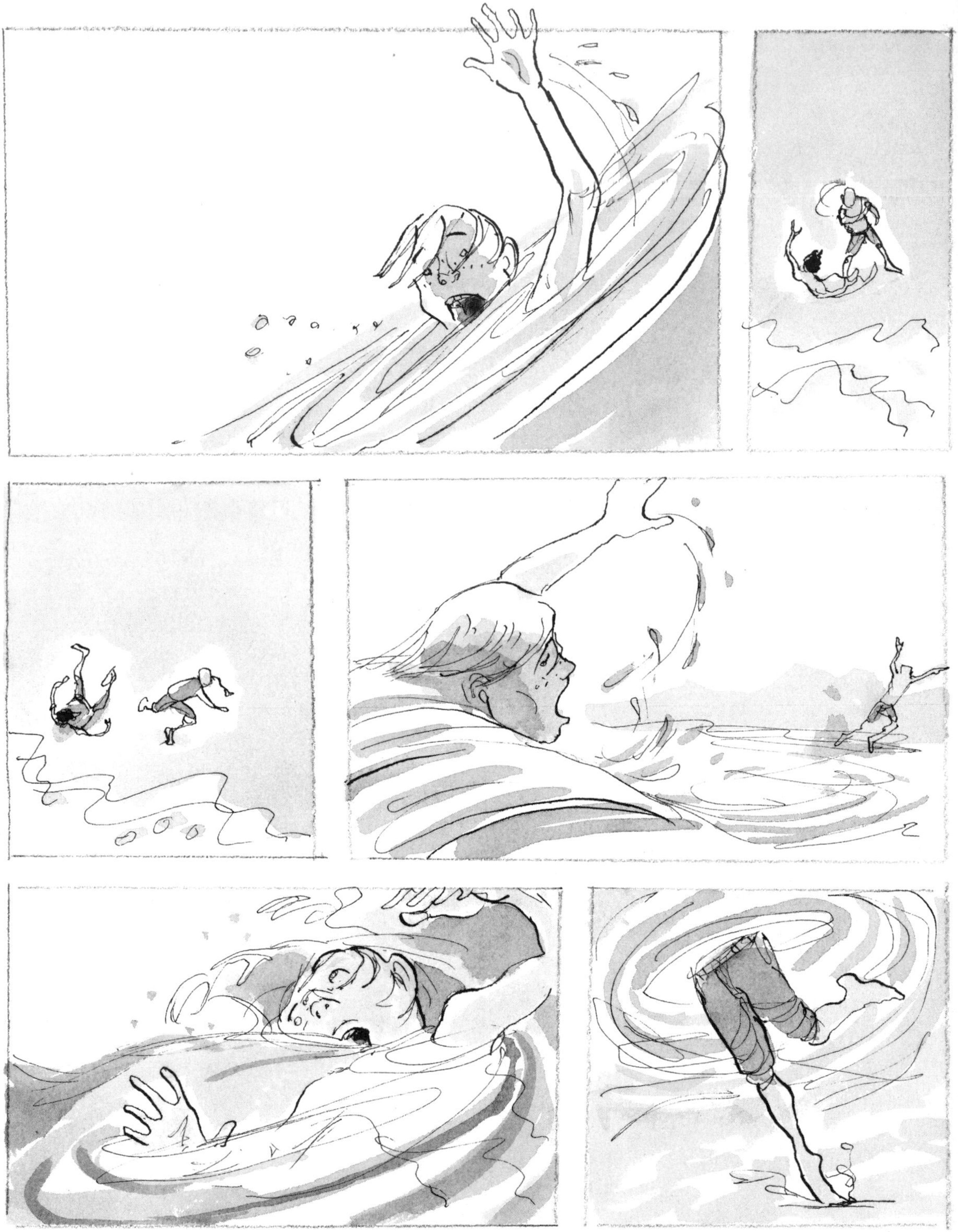

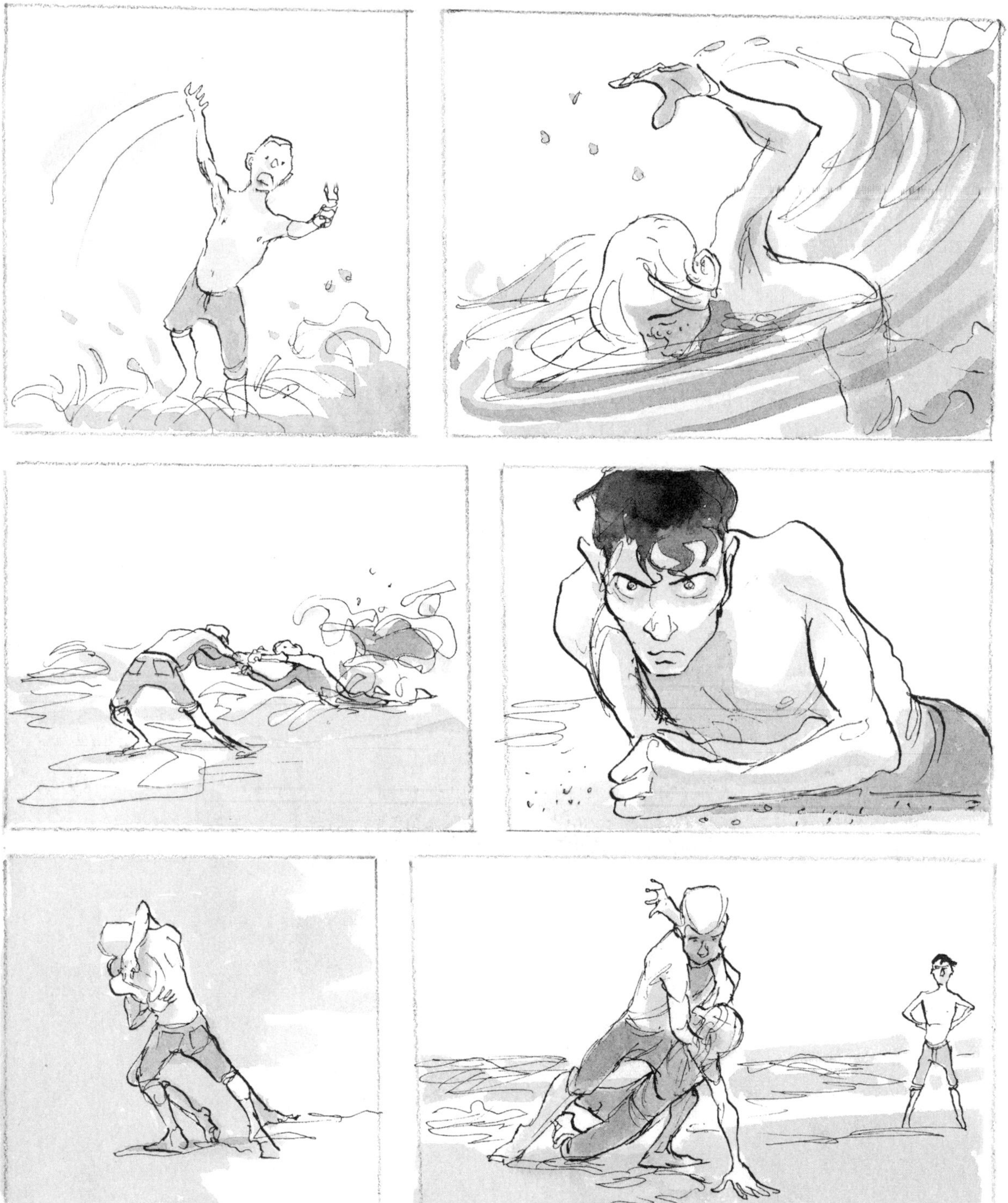

250

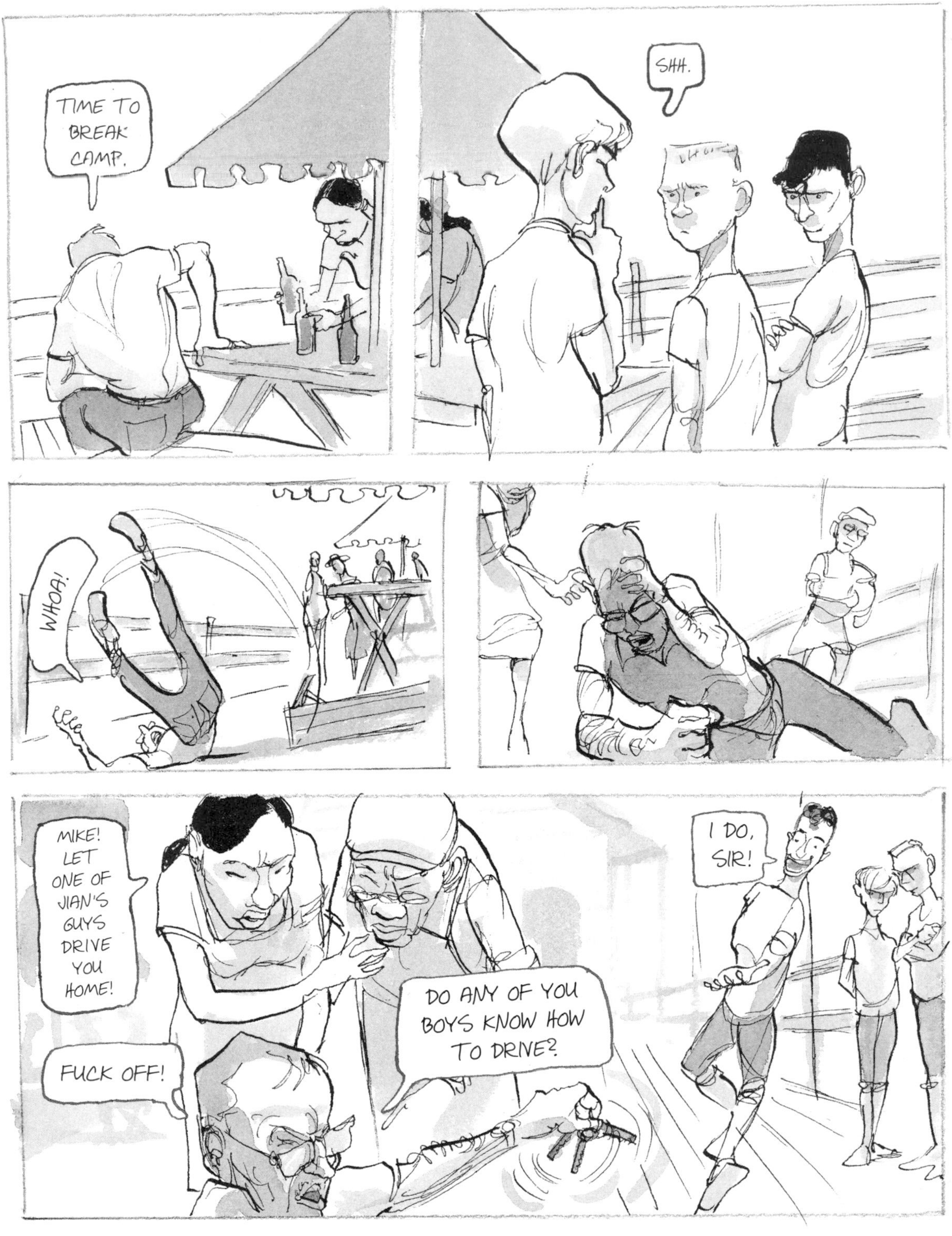
TIME TO BREAK CAMP.
SHH.
WHOA!
MIKE! LET ONE OF JIAN'S GUYS DRIVE YOU HOME!
FUCK OFF!
DO ANY OF YOU BOYS KNOW HOW TO DRIVE?
I DO, SIR!

255

THAT WAS THE LAST TIME
I EVER SAW MY FATHER.

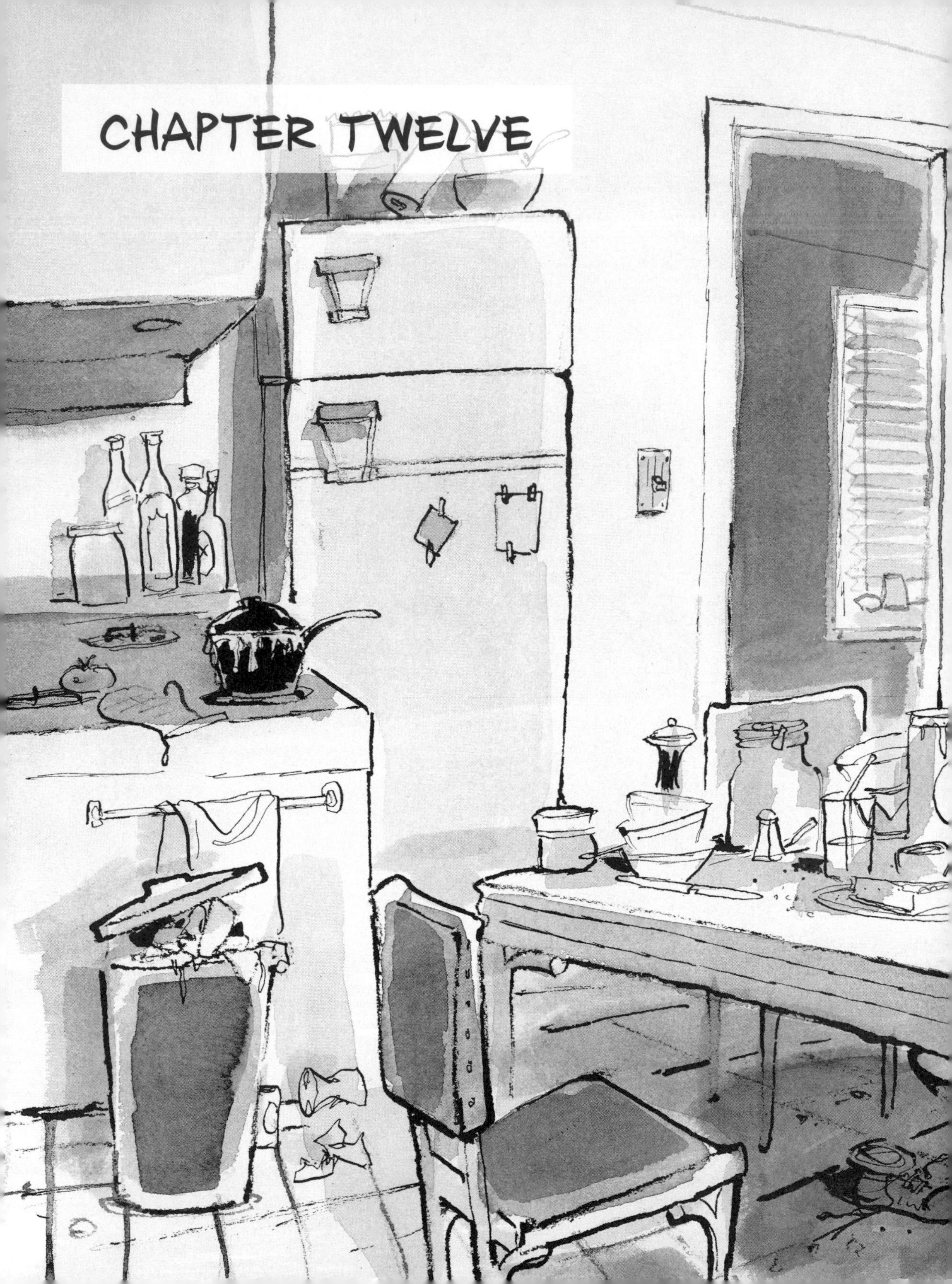
CHAPTER TWELVE

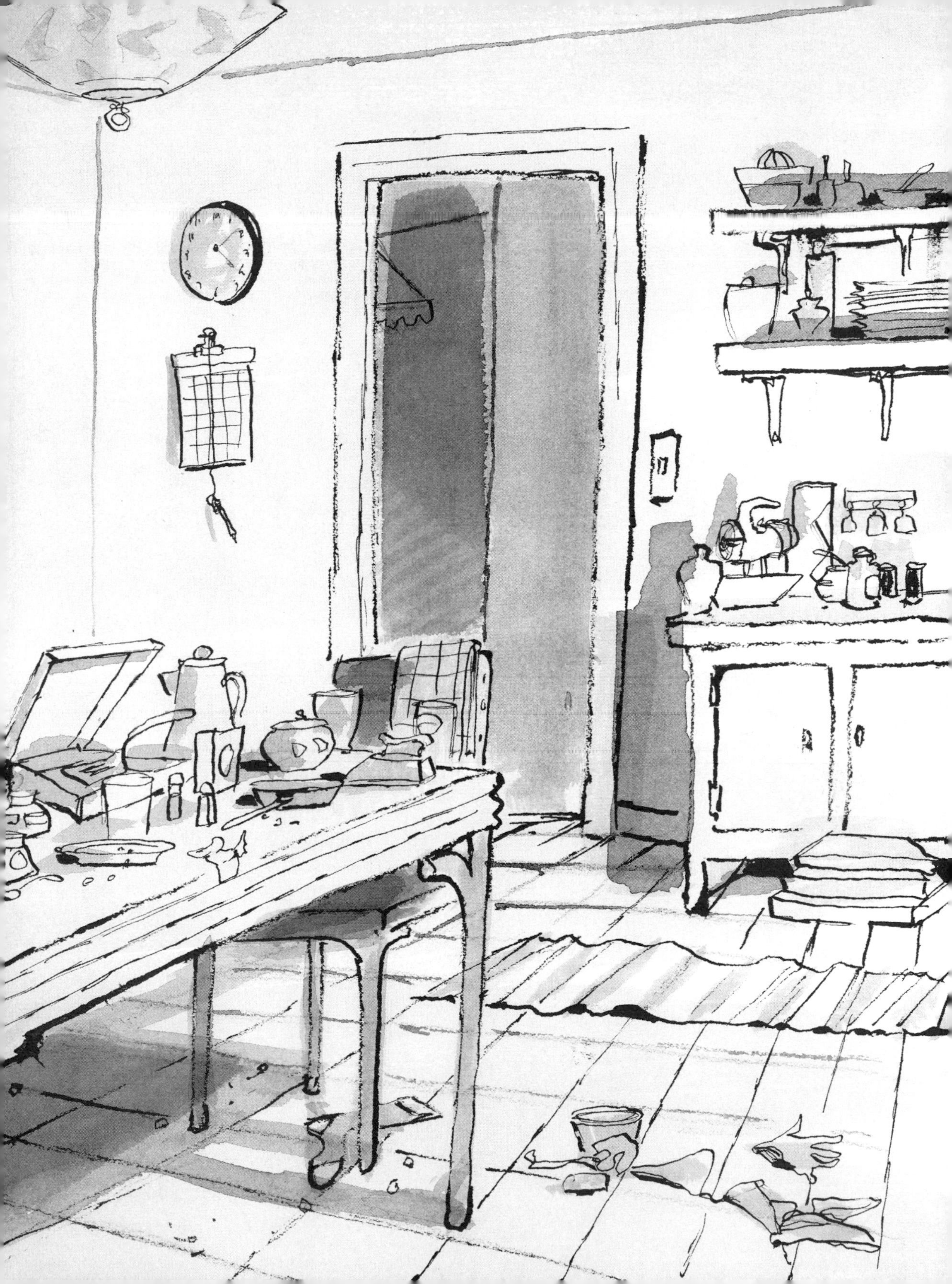

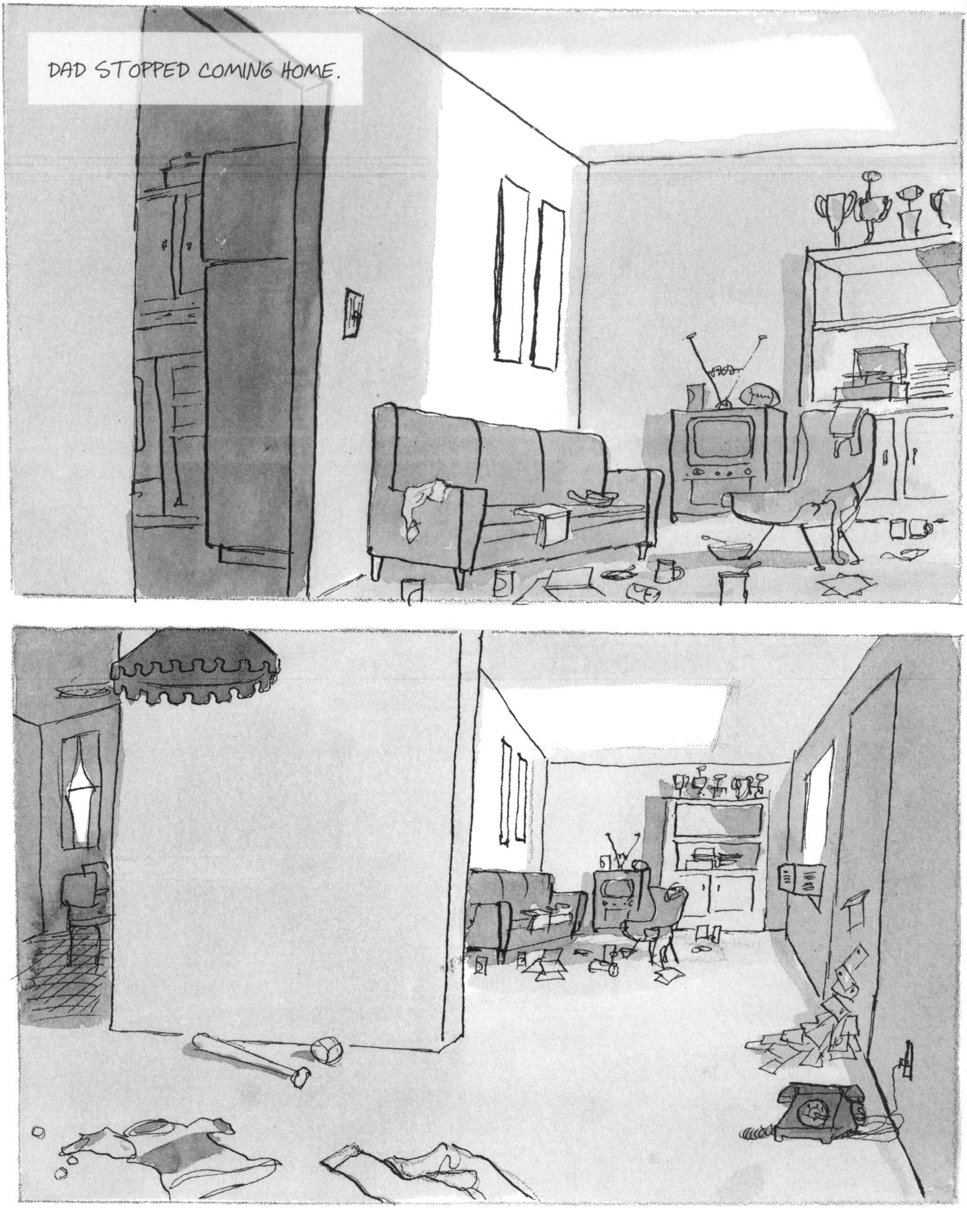
DAD STOPPED COMING HOME.

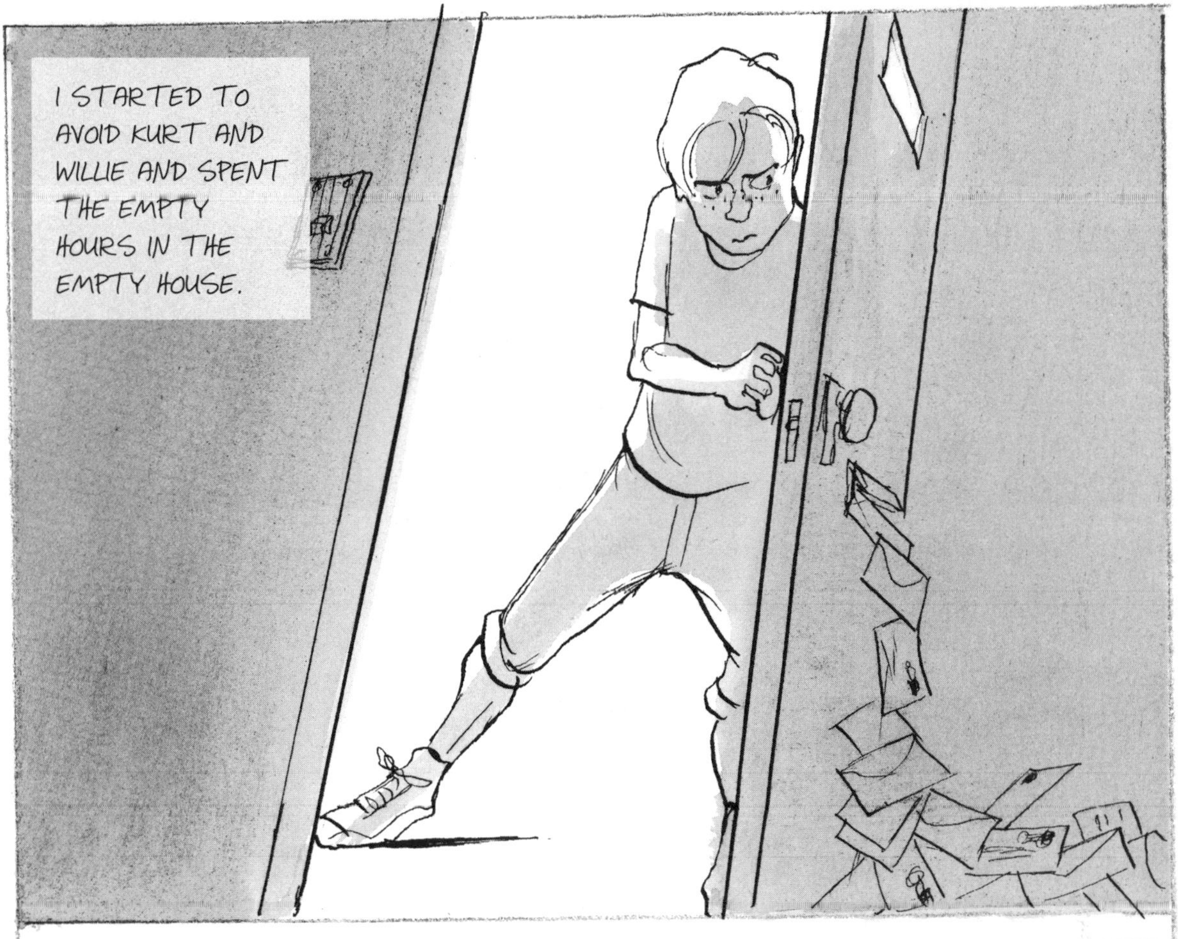
I STARTED TO AVOID KURT AND WILLIE AND SPENT THE EMPTY HOURS IN THE EMPTY HOUSE.

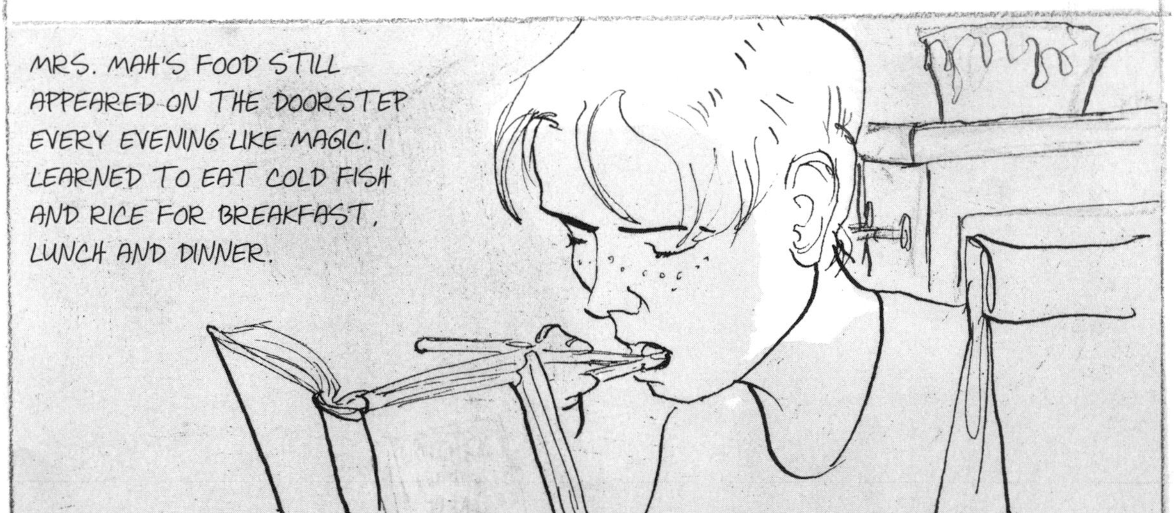
MRS. MAH'S FOOD STILL APPEARED ON THE DOORSTEP EVERY EVENING LIKE MAGIC. I LEARNED TO EAT COLD FISH AND RICE FOR BREAKFAST, LUNCH AND DINNER.

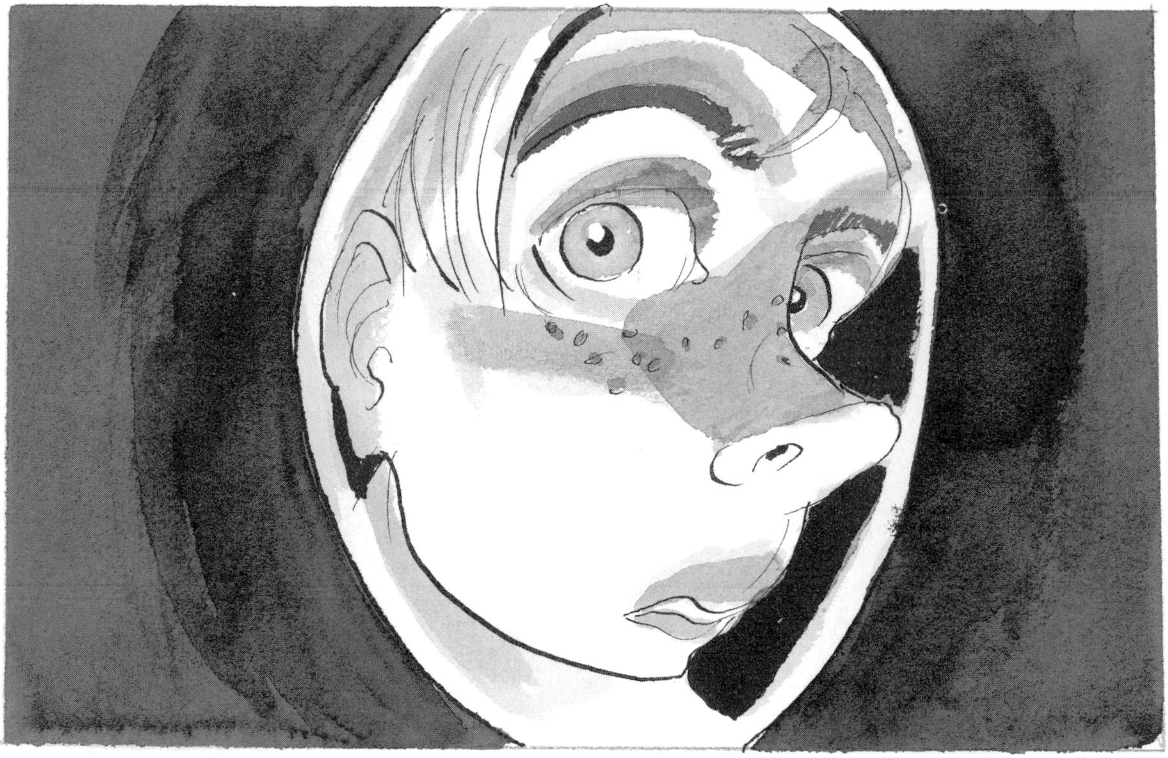

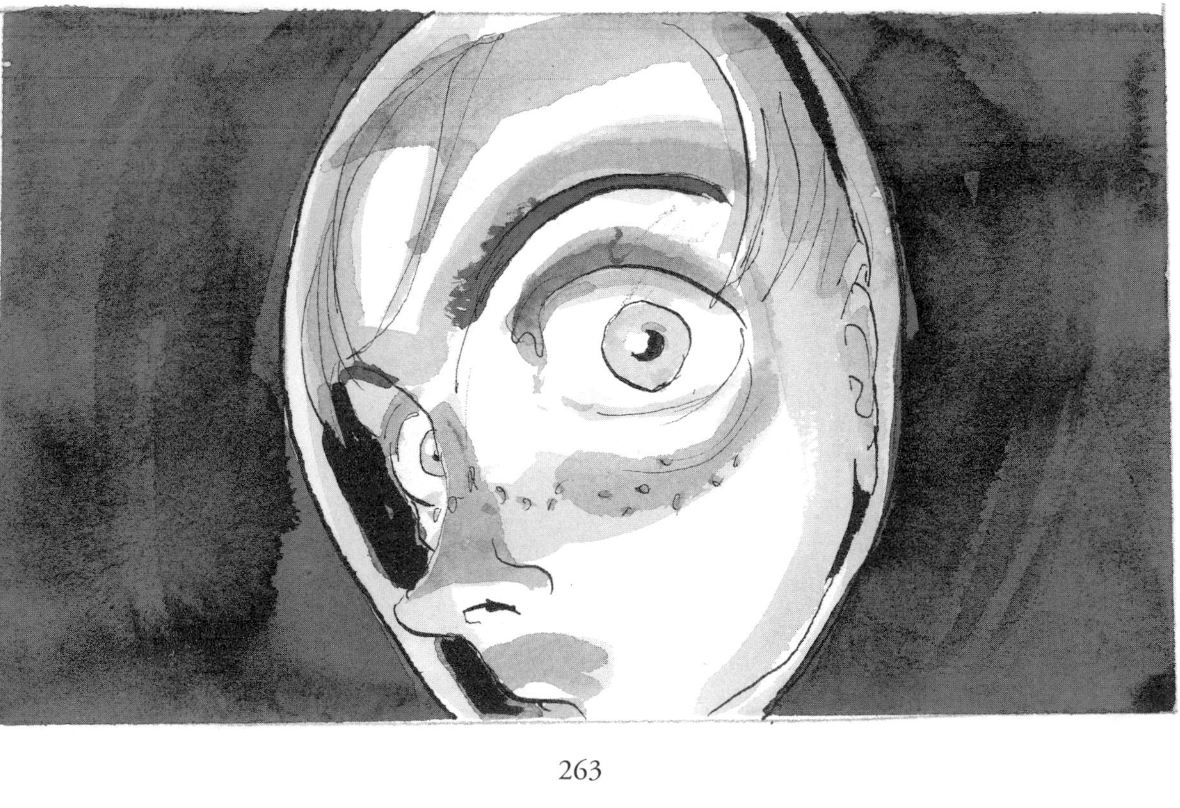

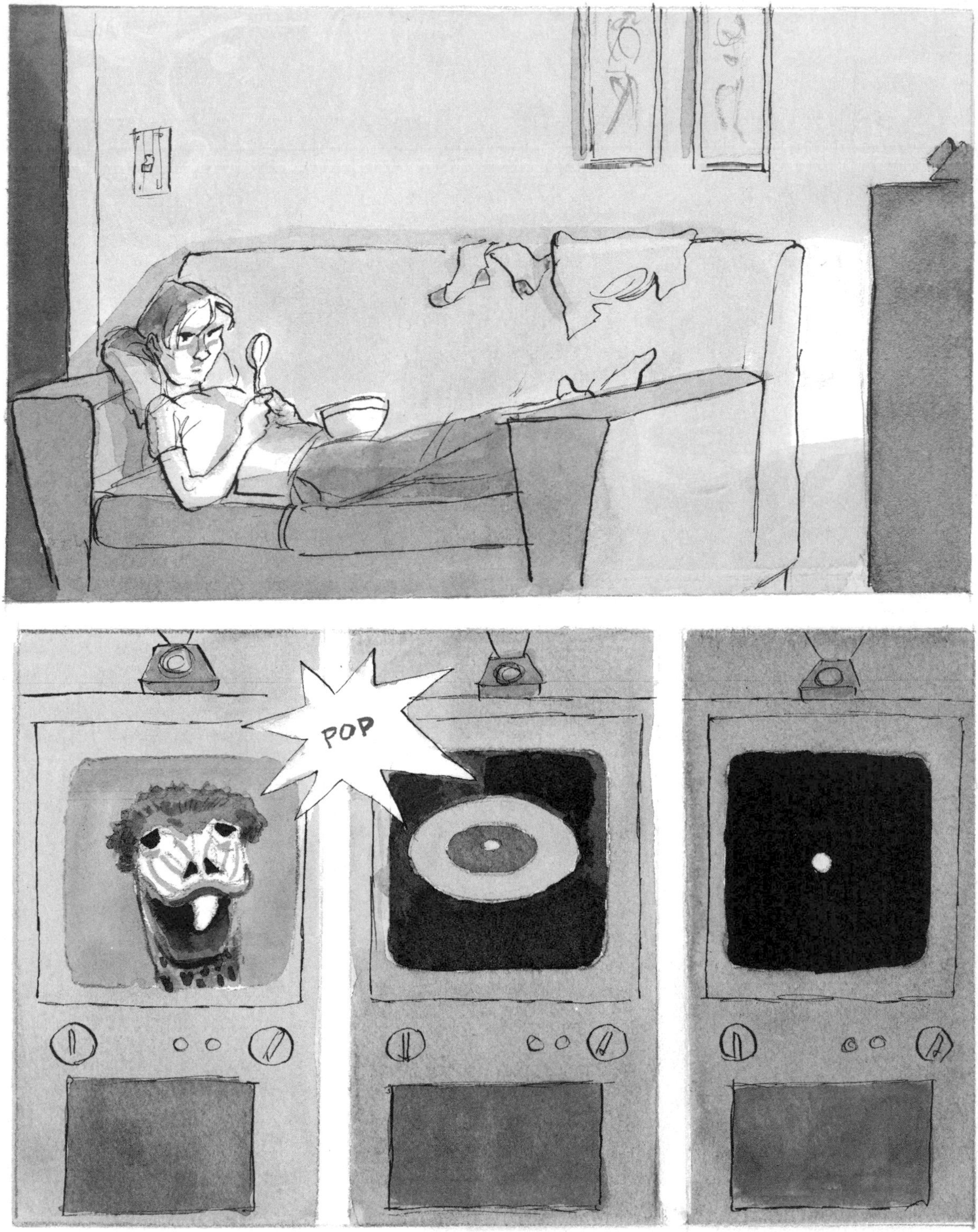
POP

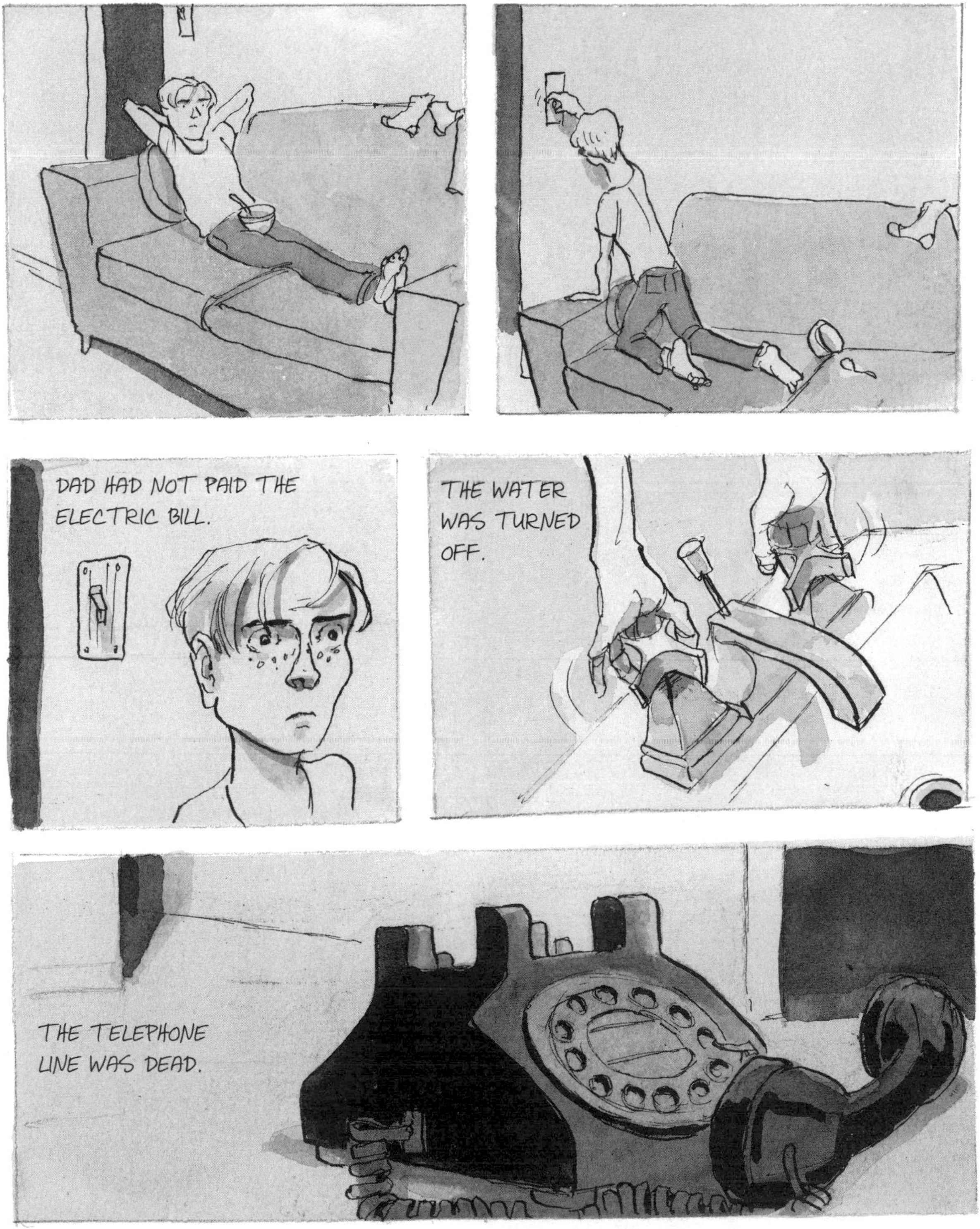
DAD HAD NOT PAID THE ELECTRIC BILL.
THE WATER WAS TURNED OFF.
THE TELEPHONE LINE WAS DEAD.

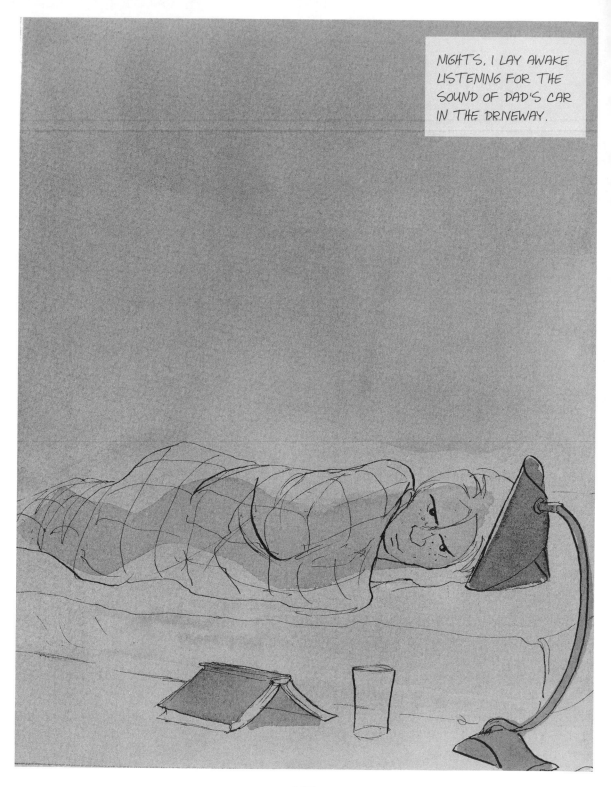

NIGHTS, I LAY AWAKE LISTENING FOR THE SOUND OF DAD'S CAR IN THE DRIVEWAY.

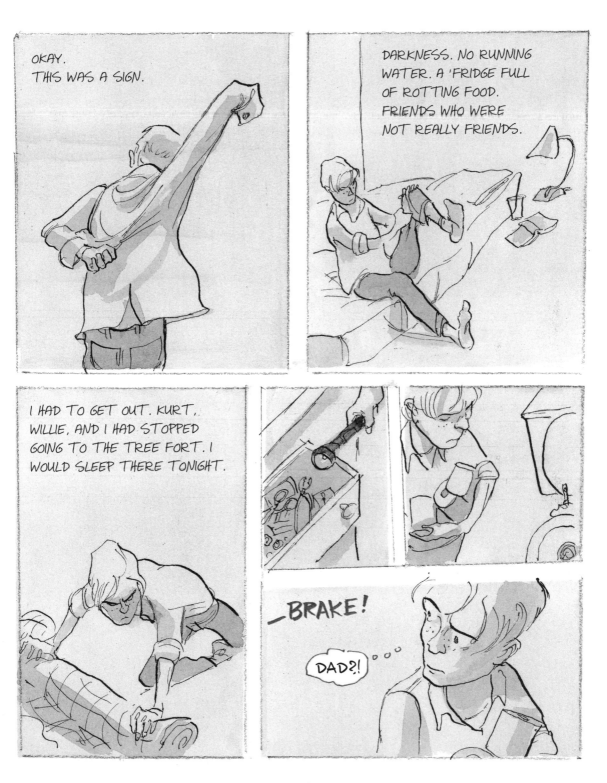

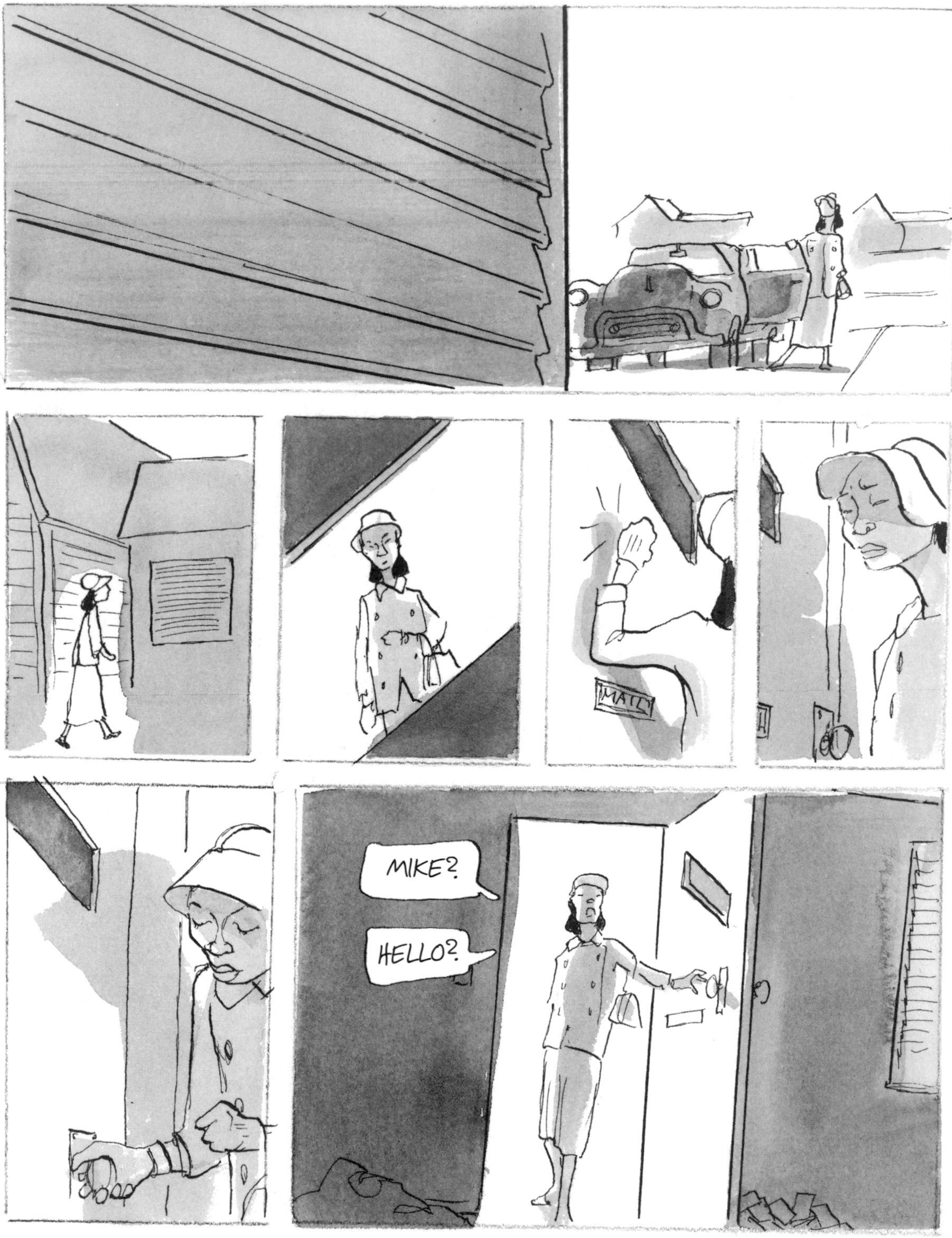
MIKE?
HELLO?

270

272

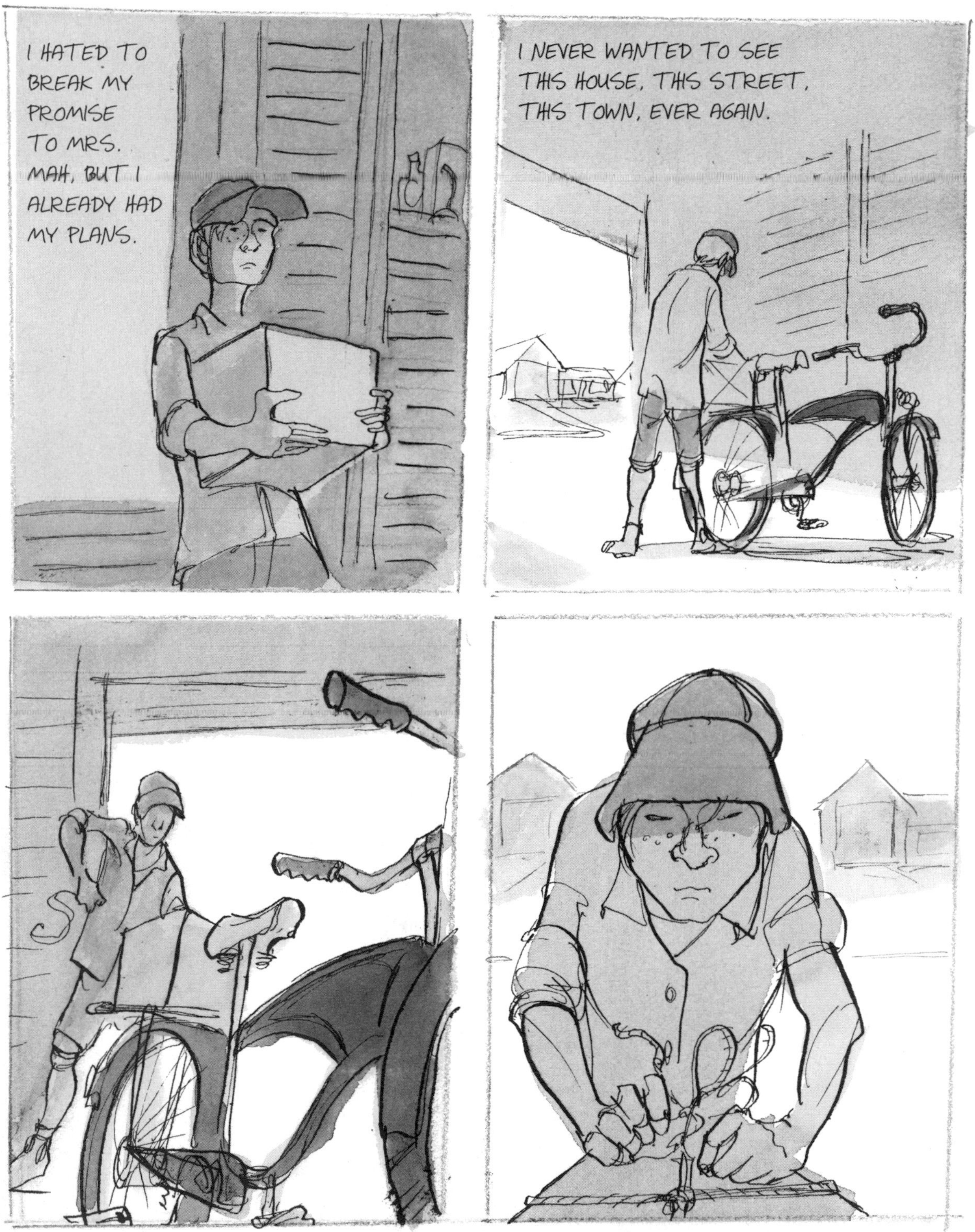
I HATED TO BREAK MY PROMISE TO MRS. MAH, BUT I ALREADY HAD MY PLANS.
I NEVER WANTED TO SEE THIS HOUSE, THIS STREET, THIS TOWN, EVER AGAIN.

I WOULD SLEEP THAT NIGHT IN THE
TREE FORT. THEN, TOMORROW,
I WOULD BIKE TO ALASKA. I WOULD
LIVE AMONG THE ESKIMOS.
NO ONE WOULD KNOW ME.
NO ONE COULD SPEAK TO ME.
I WOULD START ALL OVER.
EVERYTHNG THERE WOULD BE
FRESH, OPEN, CLEAN AND FREE.

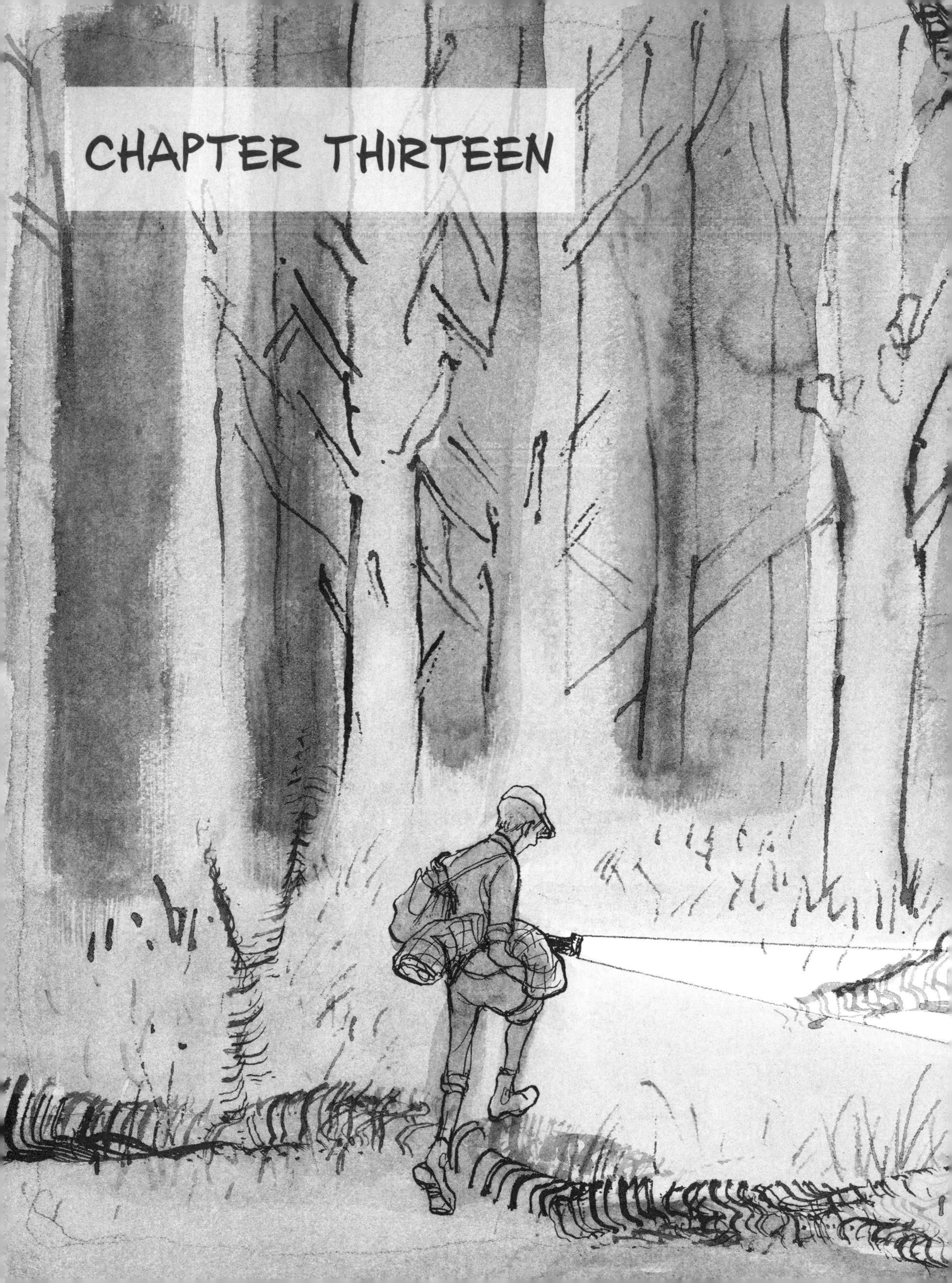
CHAPTER THIRTEEN

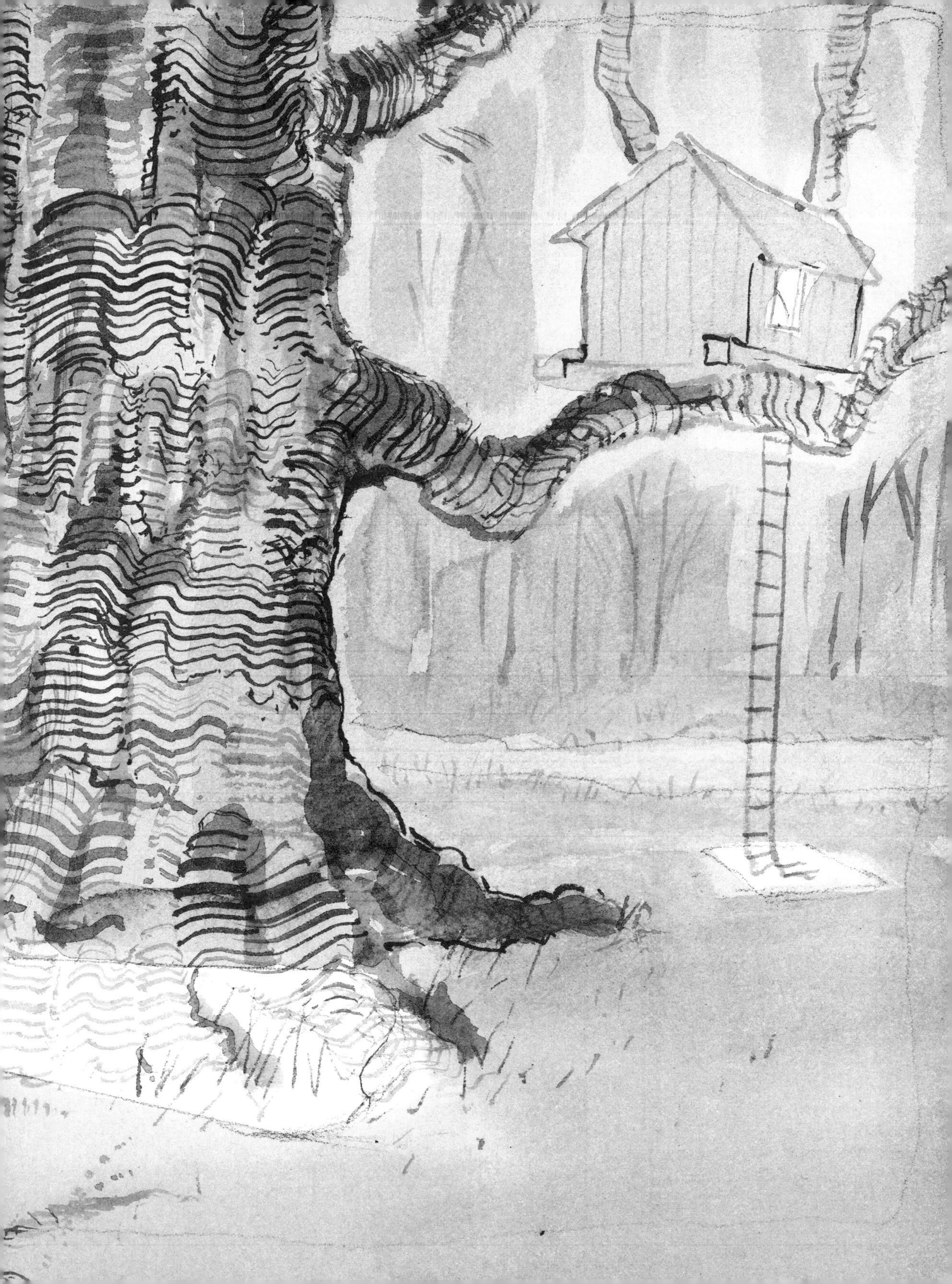

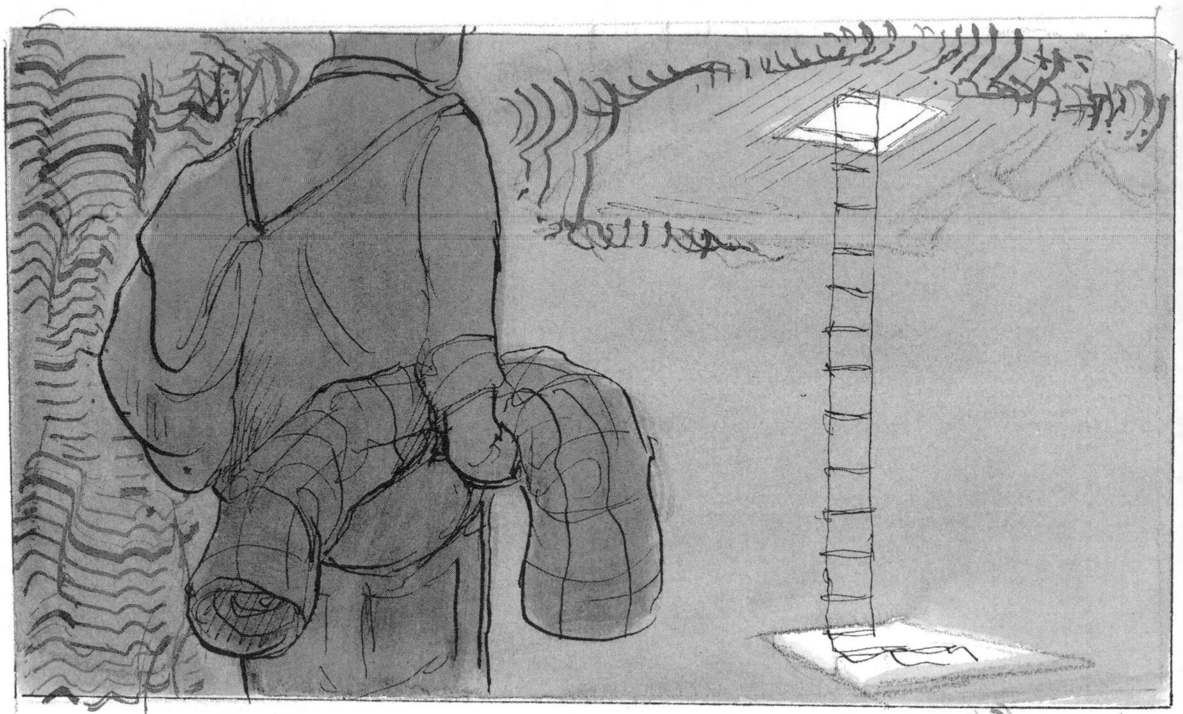

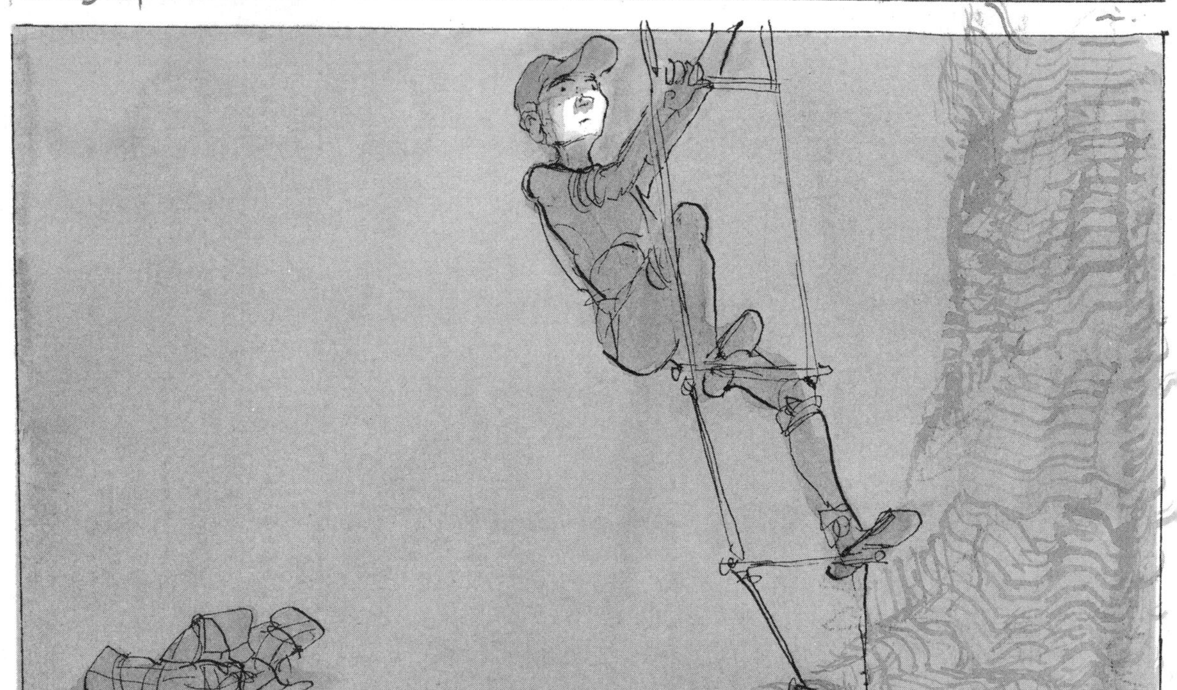

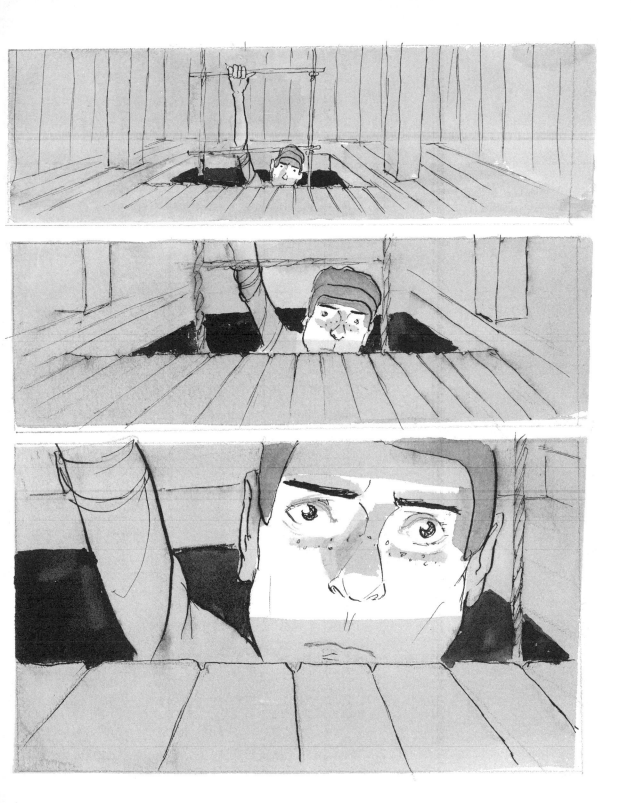

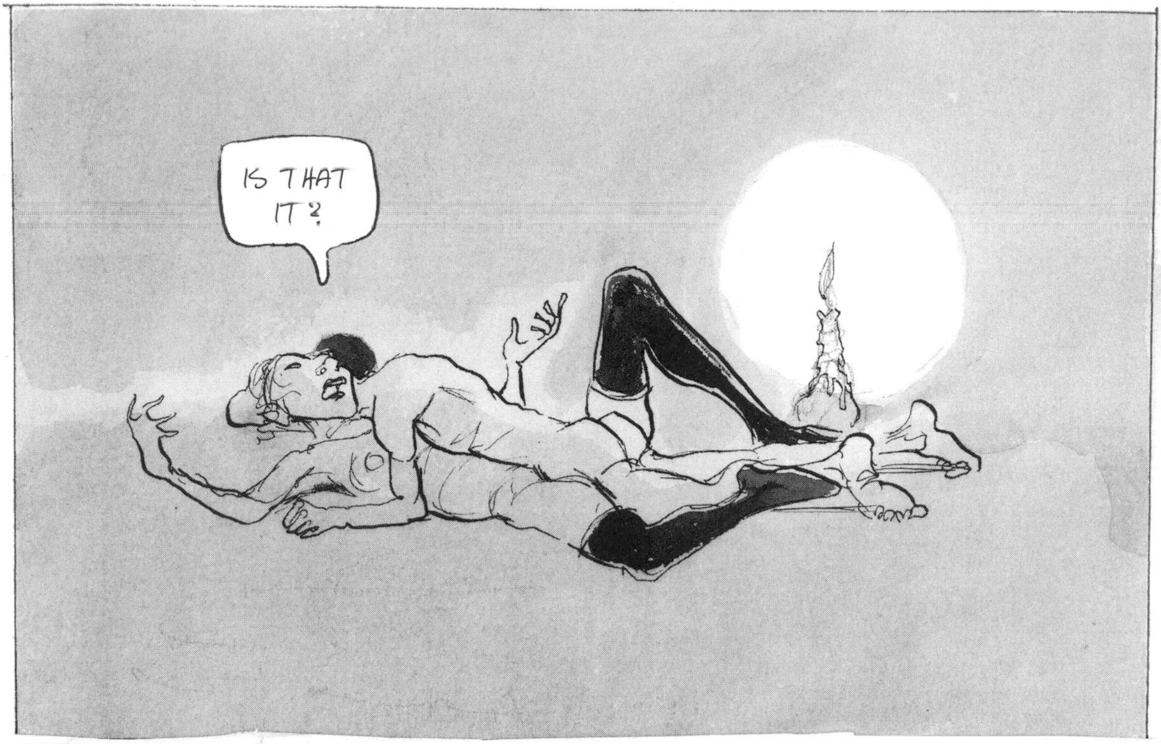
IS THAT IT?

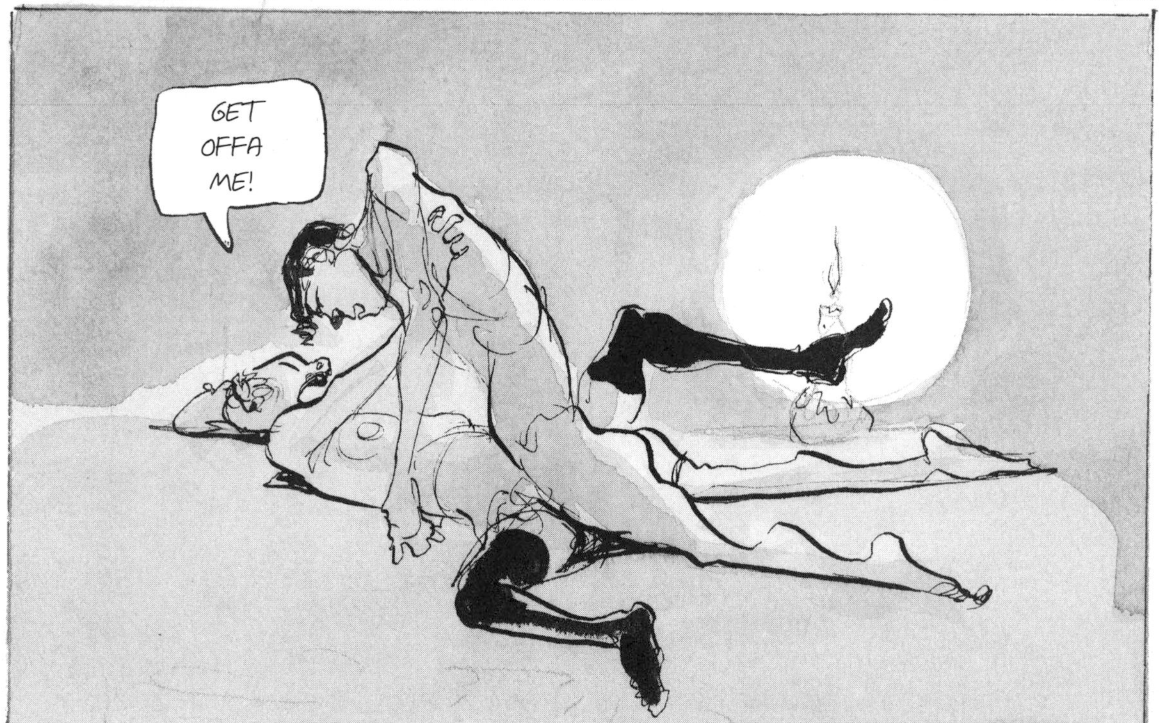
GET OFFA ME!

281

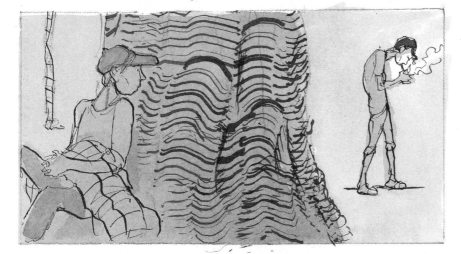

I WAITED UNTIL I WAS
CERTAIN KURT WAS
NOT COMING BACK.

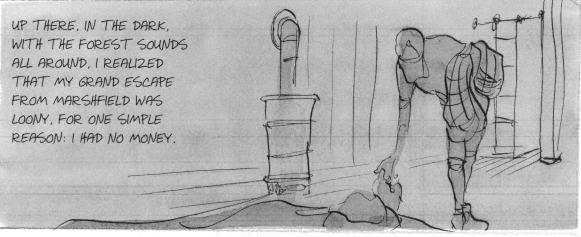

UP THERE, IN THE DARK,
WITH THE FOREST SOUNDS
ALL AROUND, I REALIZED
THAT MY GRAND ESCAPE
FROM MARSHFIELD WAS
LOONY, FOR ONE SIMPLE
REASON: I HAD NO MONEY.

I FELT AN ACHE OF LONELINESS
AND HELPLESS CONFUSION THAT
KEPT ME AWAKE UNTIL SUNUP.
THEN I FEEL INTO A DEEP,
EXHAUSTED SLEEP.

284

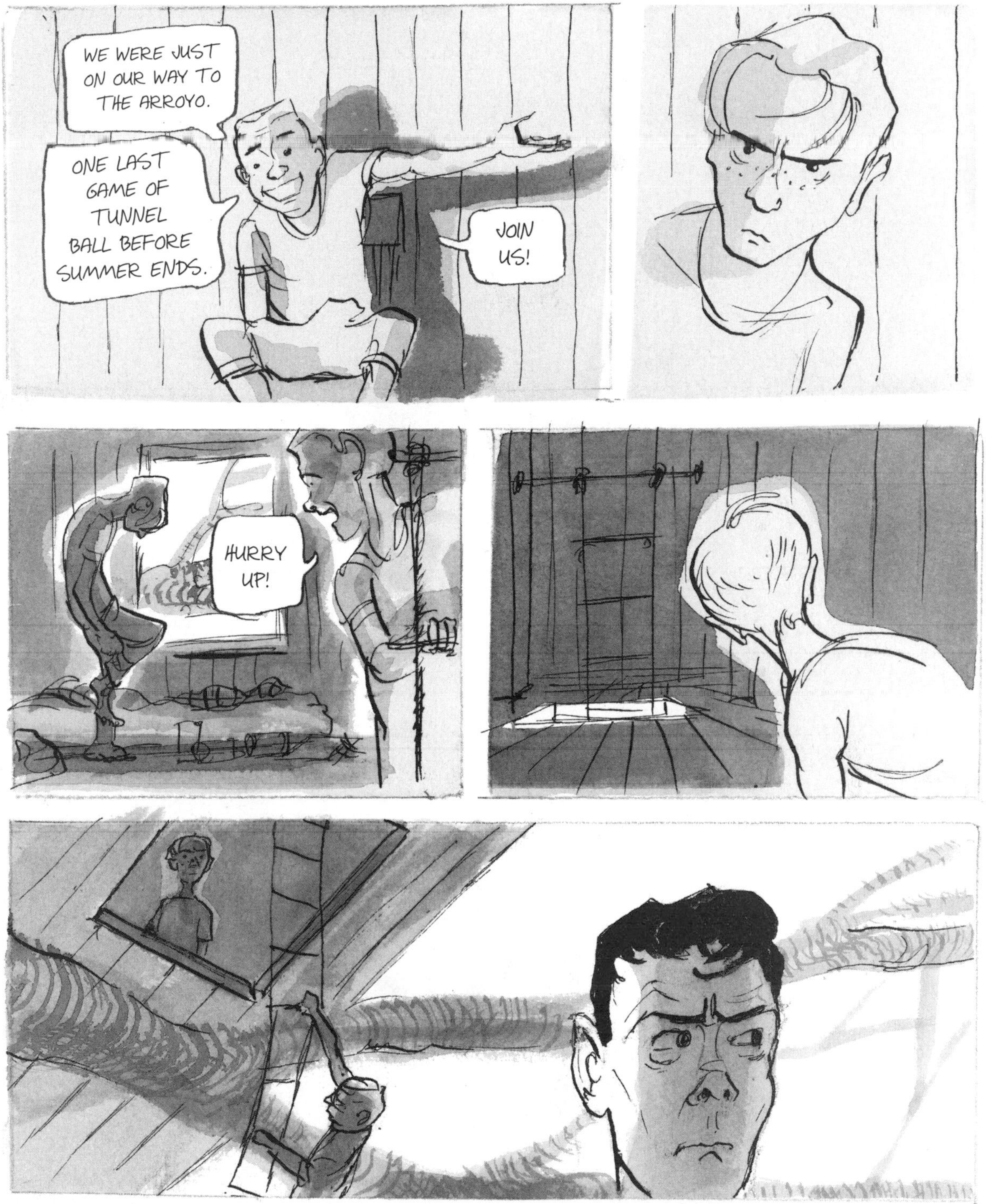
WE WERE JUST ON OUR WAY TO THE ARROYO.
ONE LAST GAME OF TUNNEL BALL BEFORE SUMMER ENDS.
JOIN US!
HURRY UP!

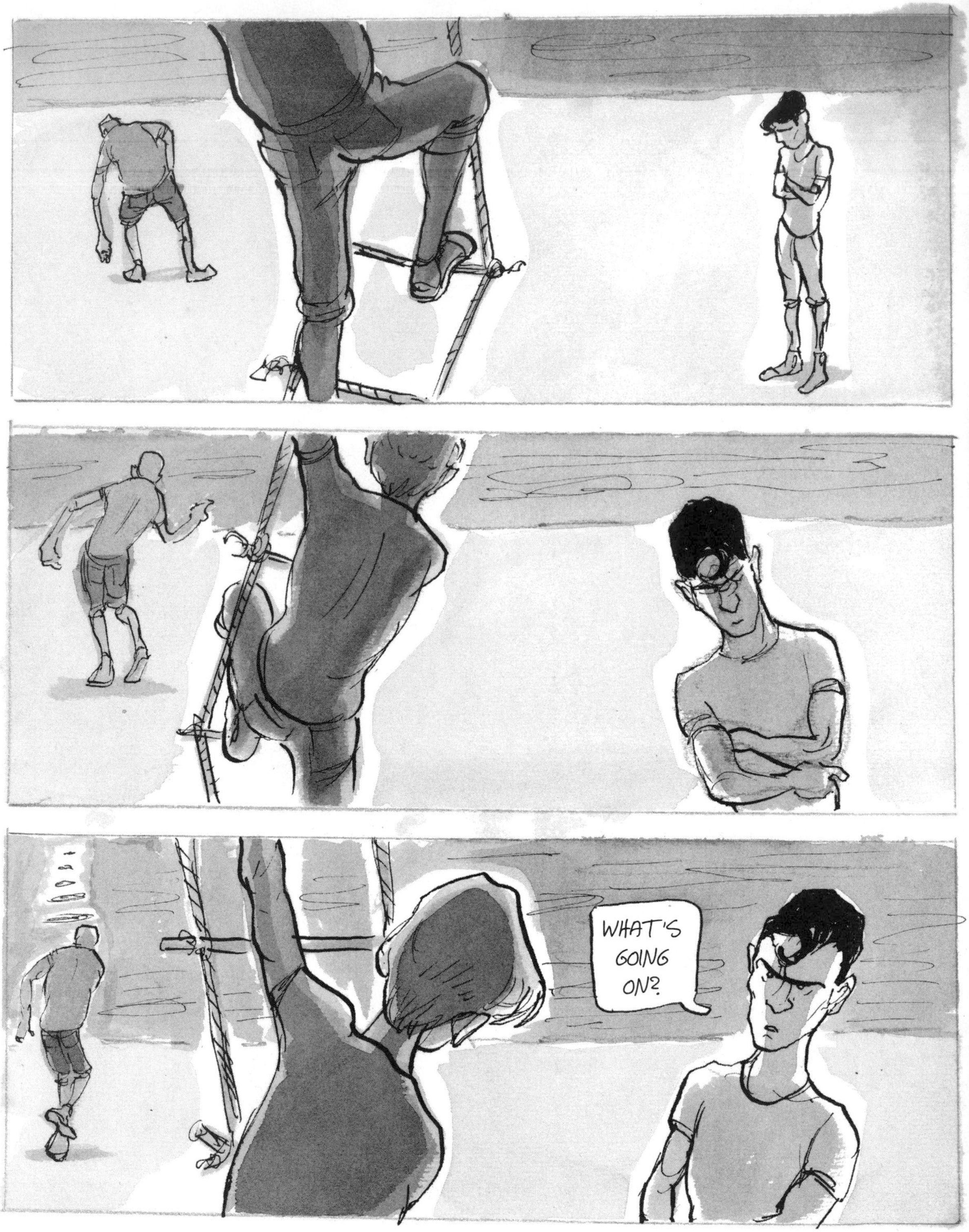
WHAT'S GOING ON?

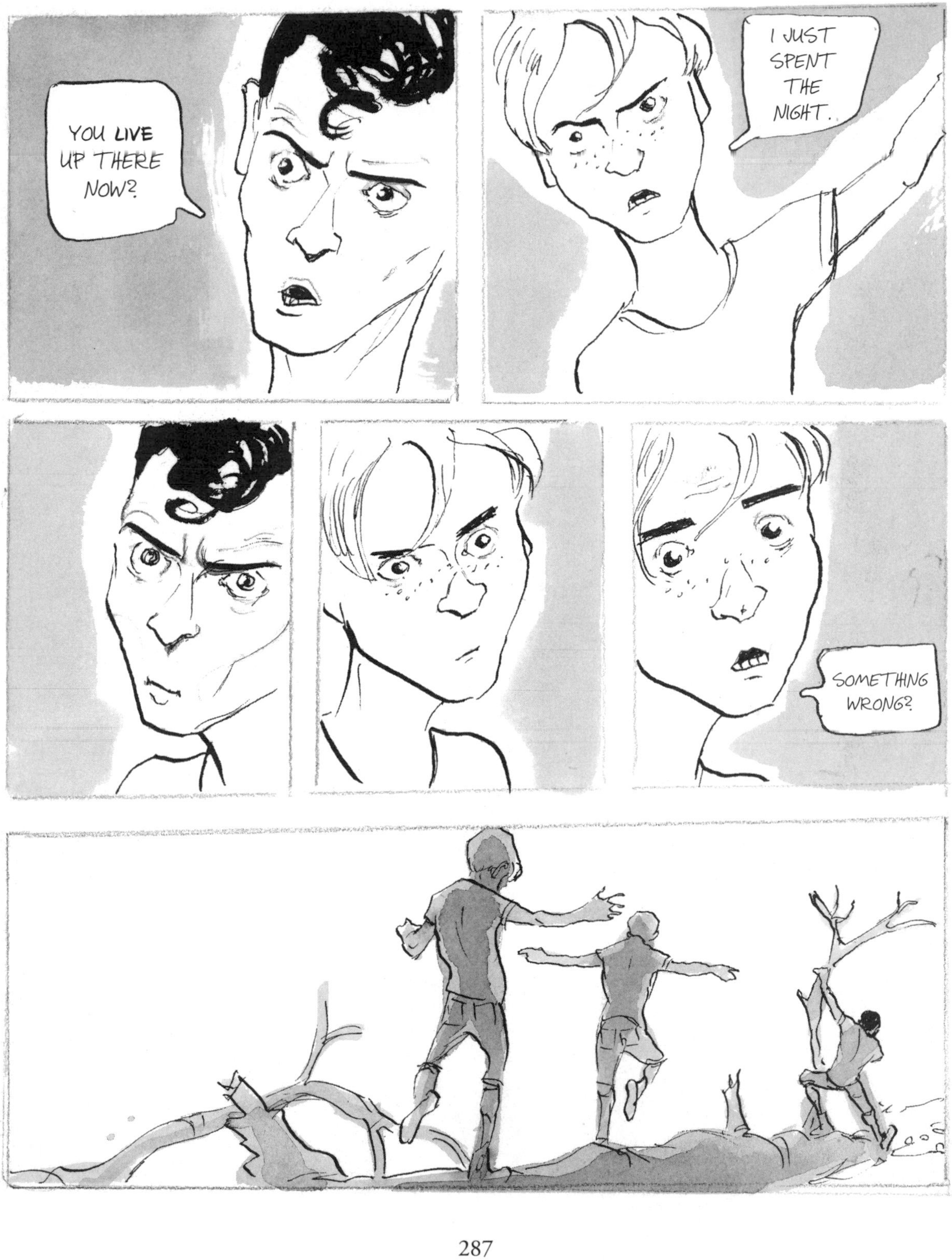
YOU LIVE UP THERE NOW?
I JUST SPENT THE NIGHT.
SOMETHING WRONG?

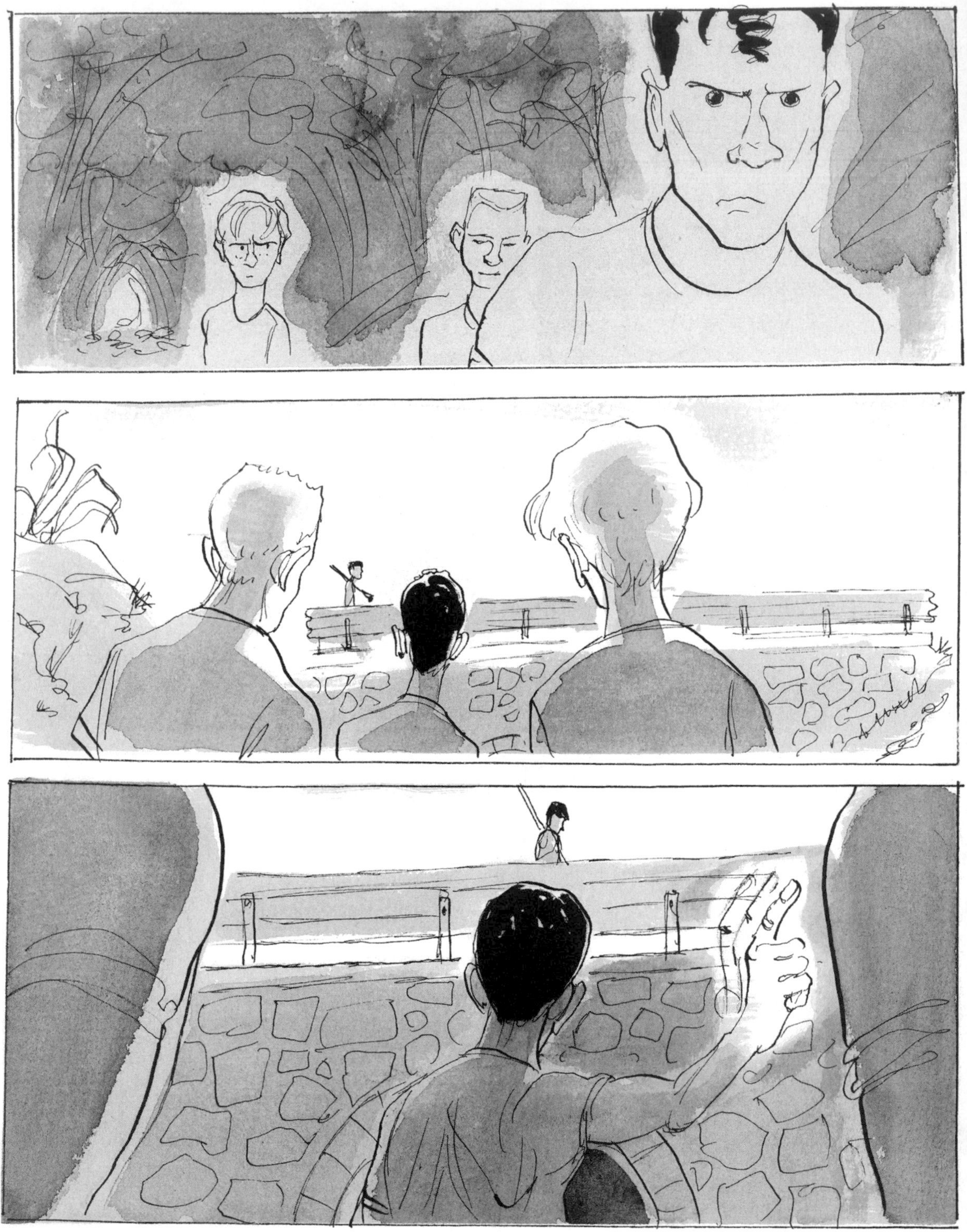

289

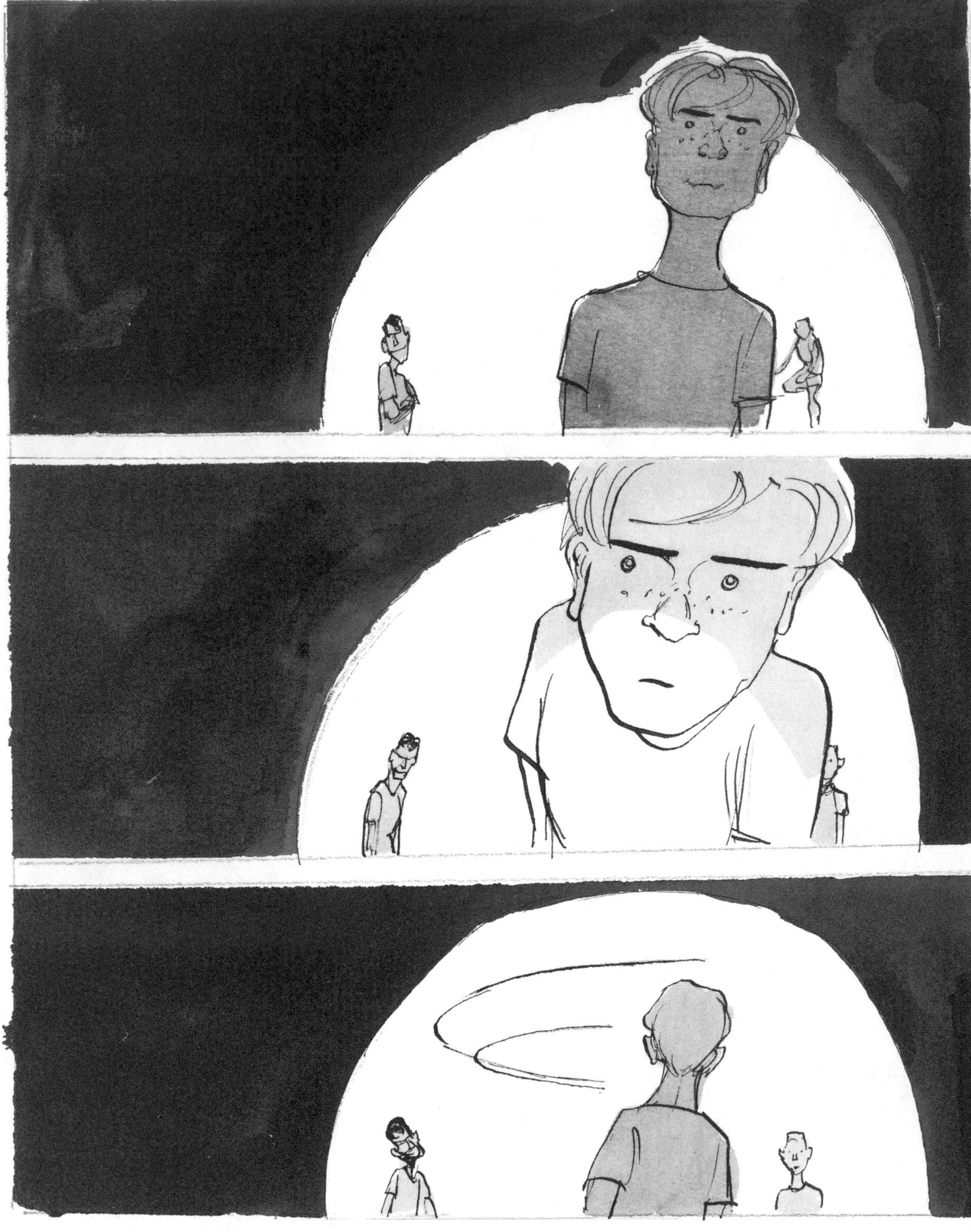

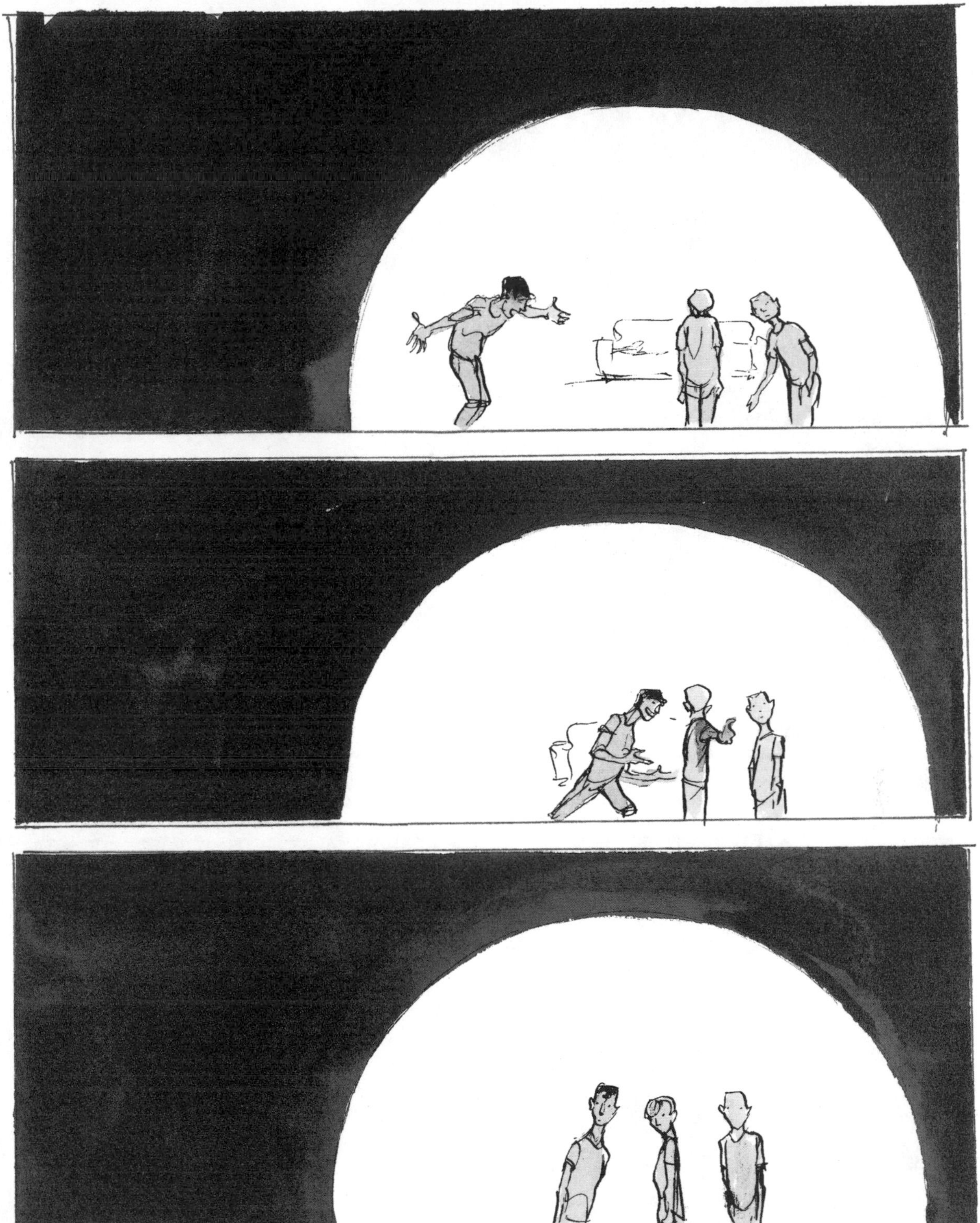

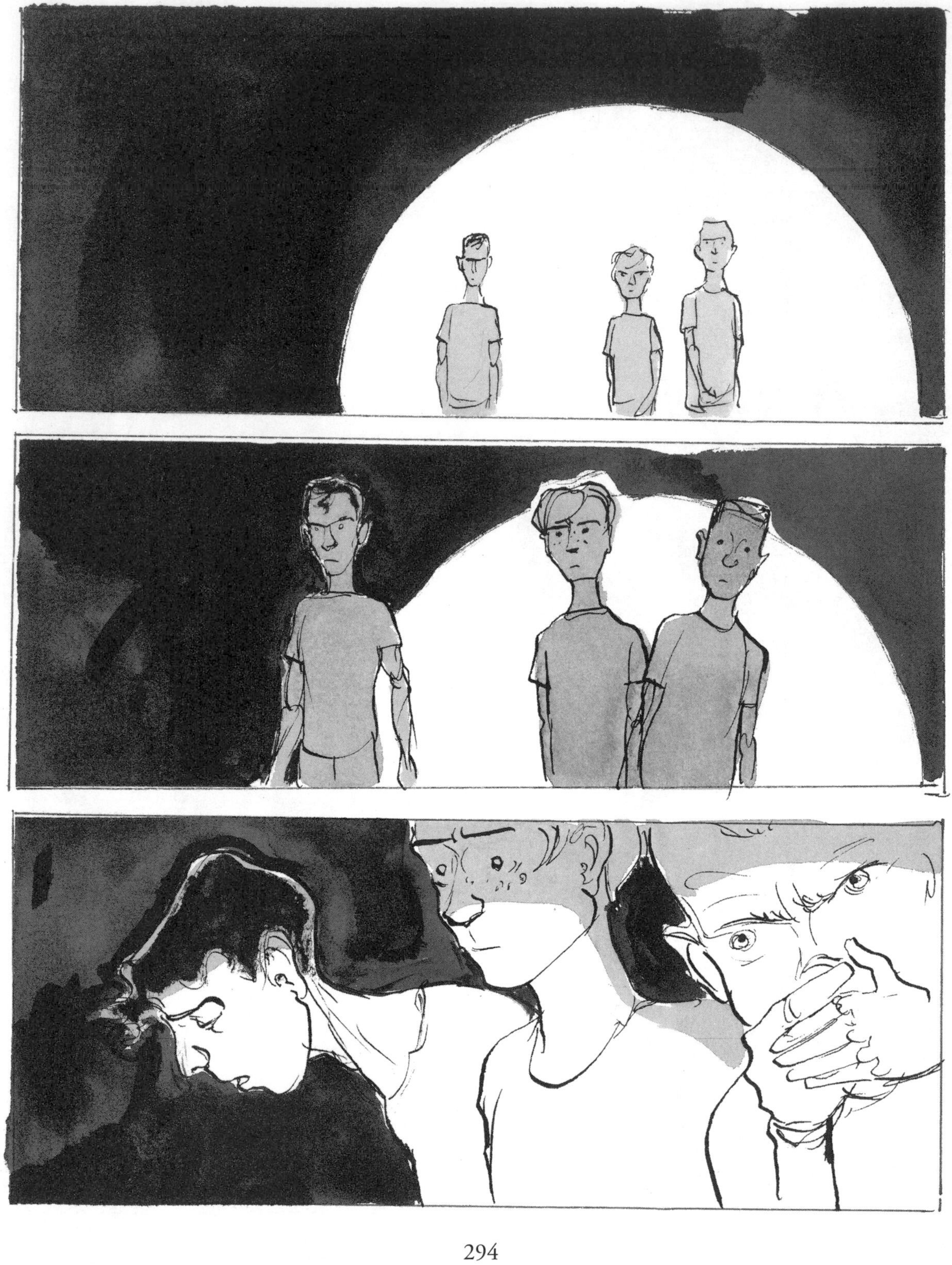

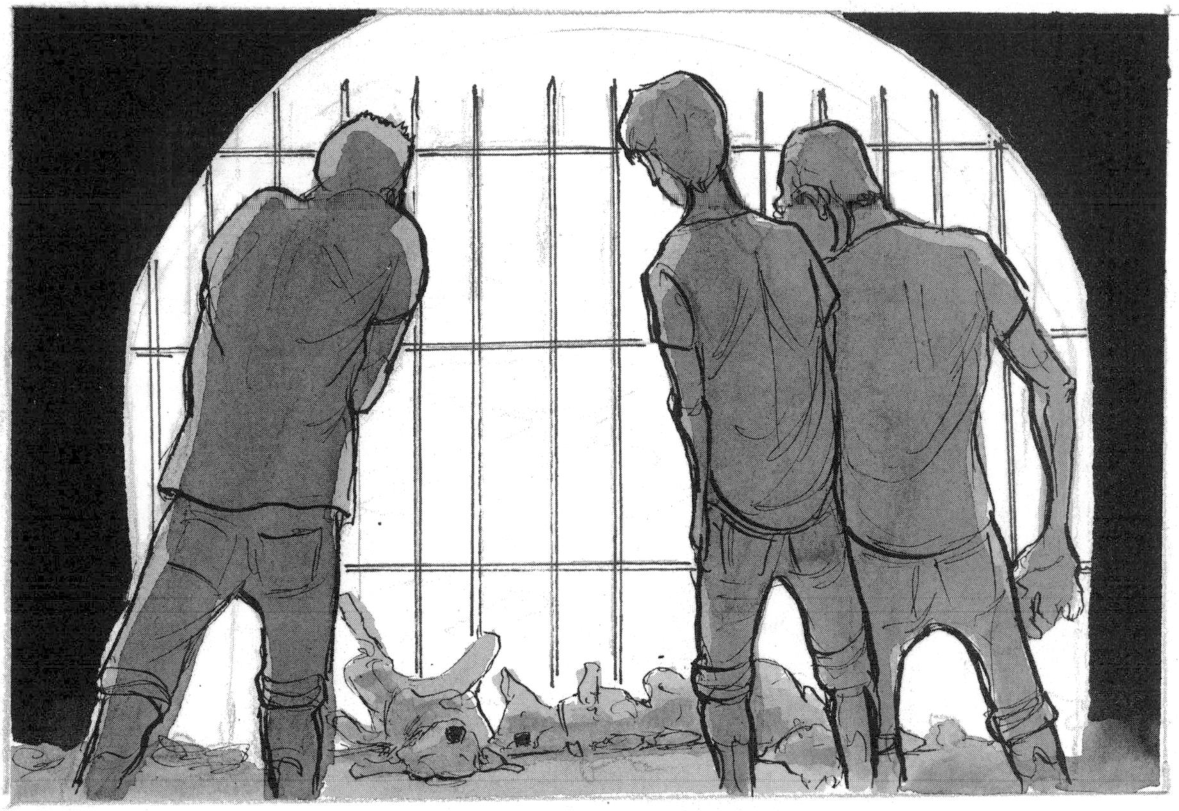

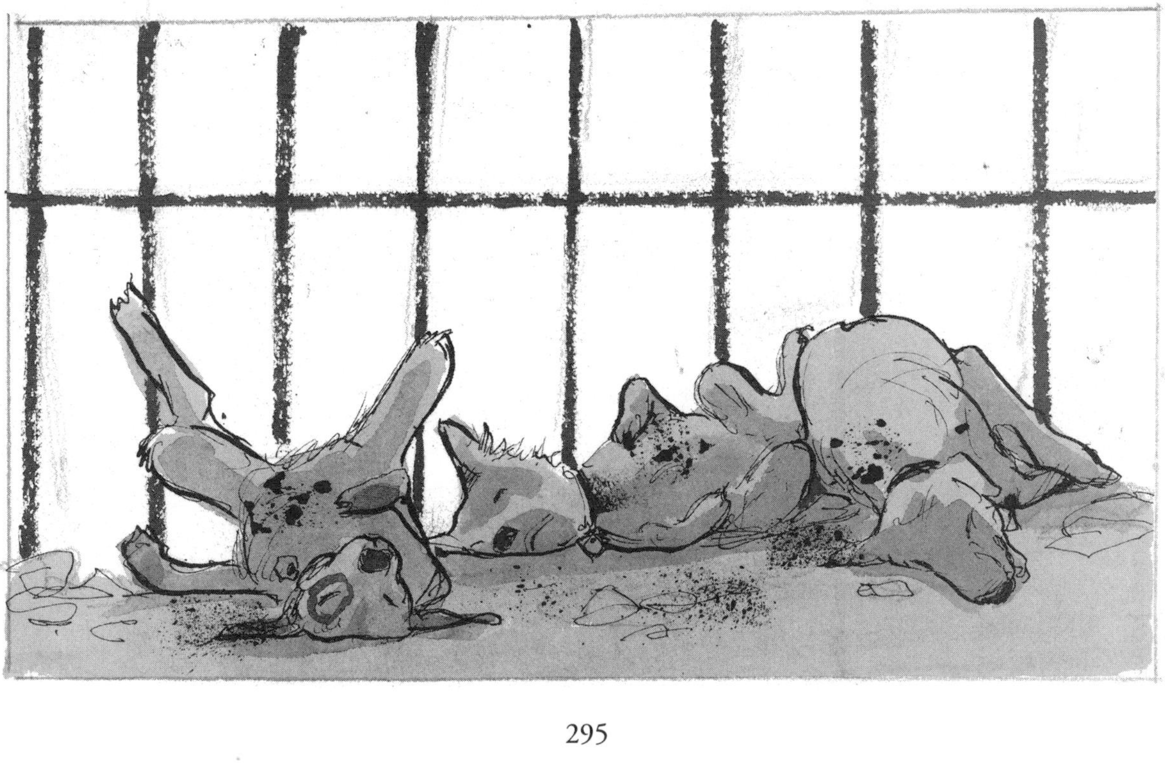

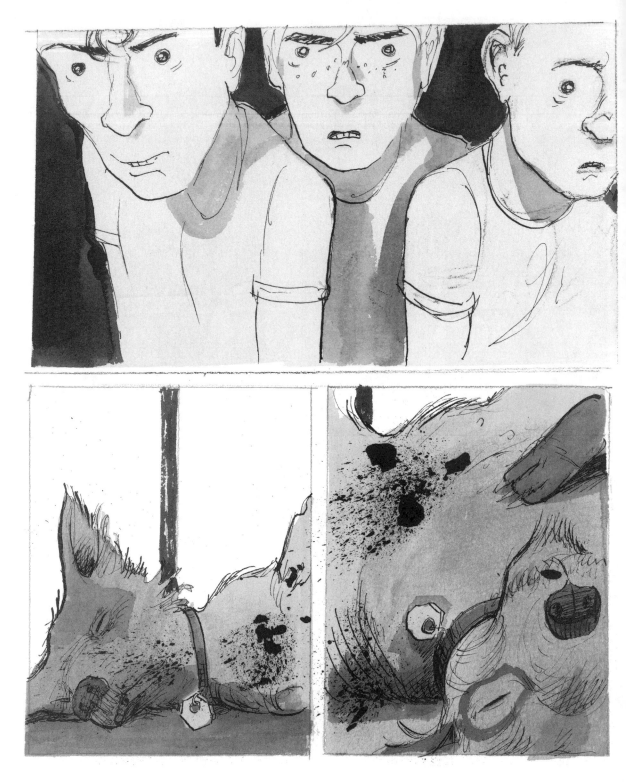

THE COPS. KURT WOULD TELL THEM WARREN DID IT. I'D HAVE TO GO AGAINST HIM.

I KNEW WARREN WOULDN'T HURT ANYTHING.

WHY WERE THESE STRANGERS
BEING SO KIND TO ME? THEY HAD
NO IDEA WHAT A WORTHLESS
SHIT I REALLY WAS.

CHAPTER FOURTEEN

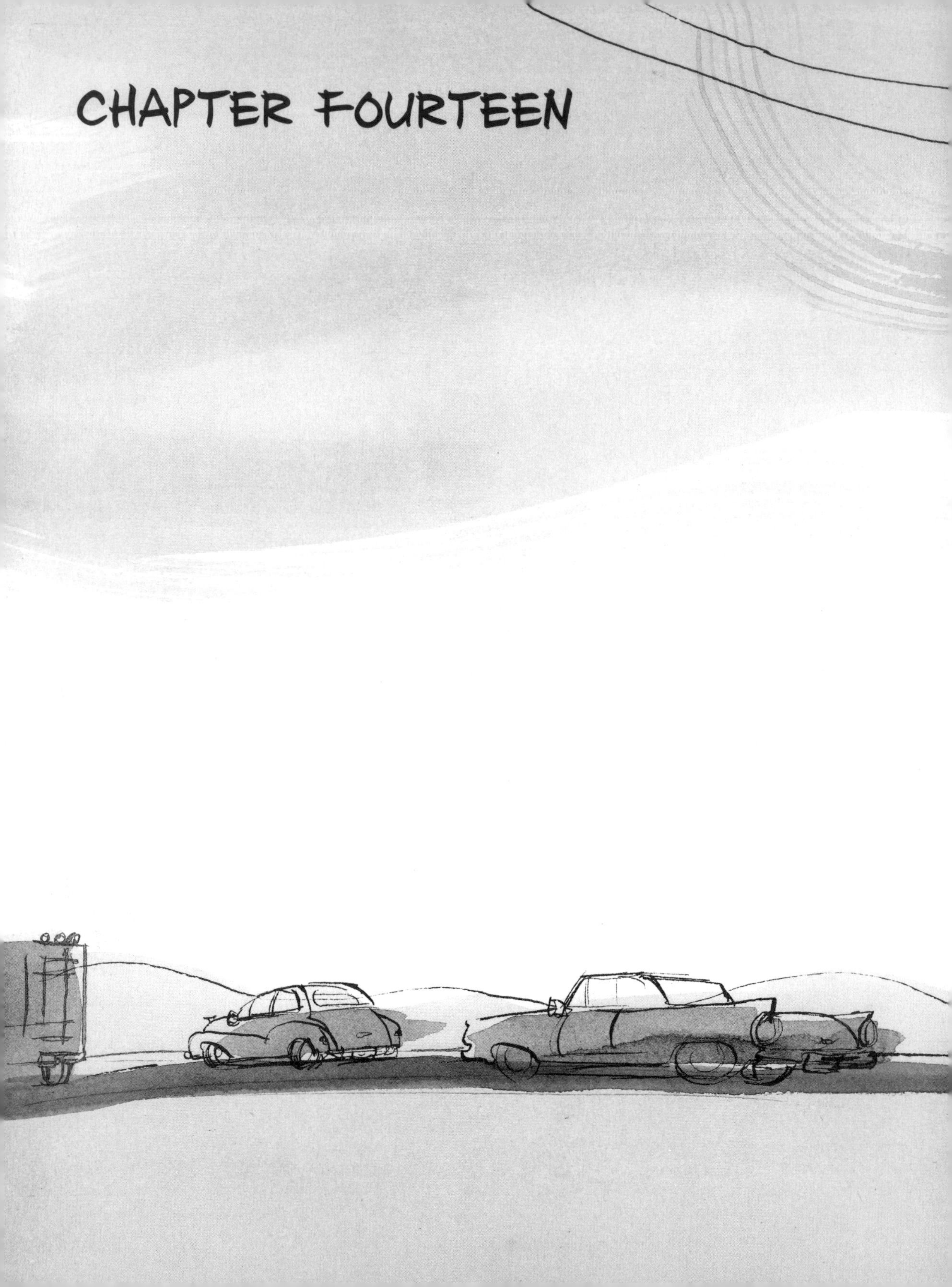

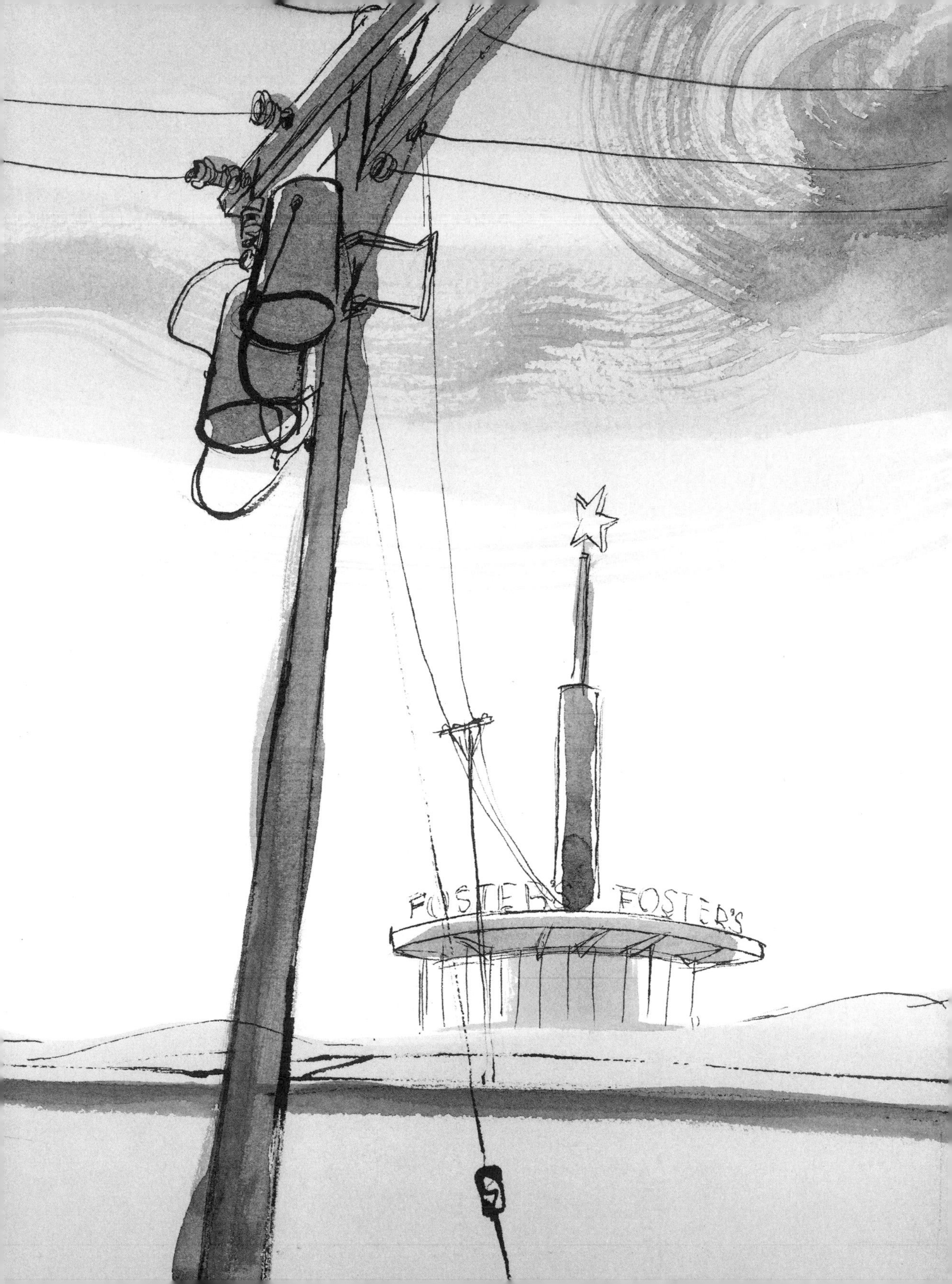
FOSTER'S
FOSTER'S

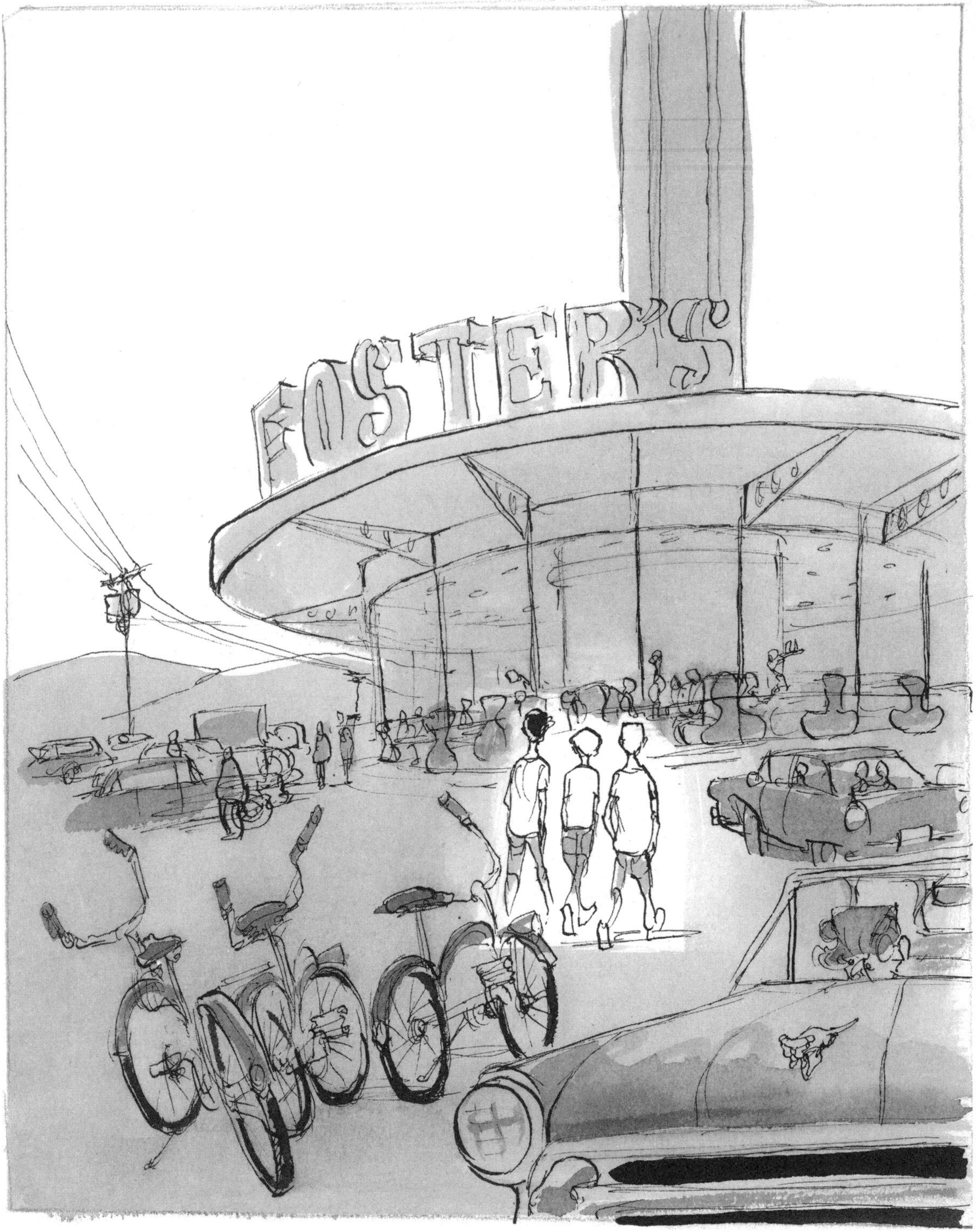
FOSTER'S

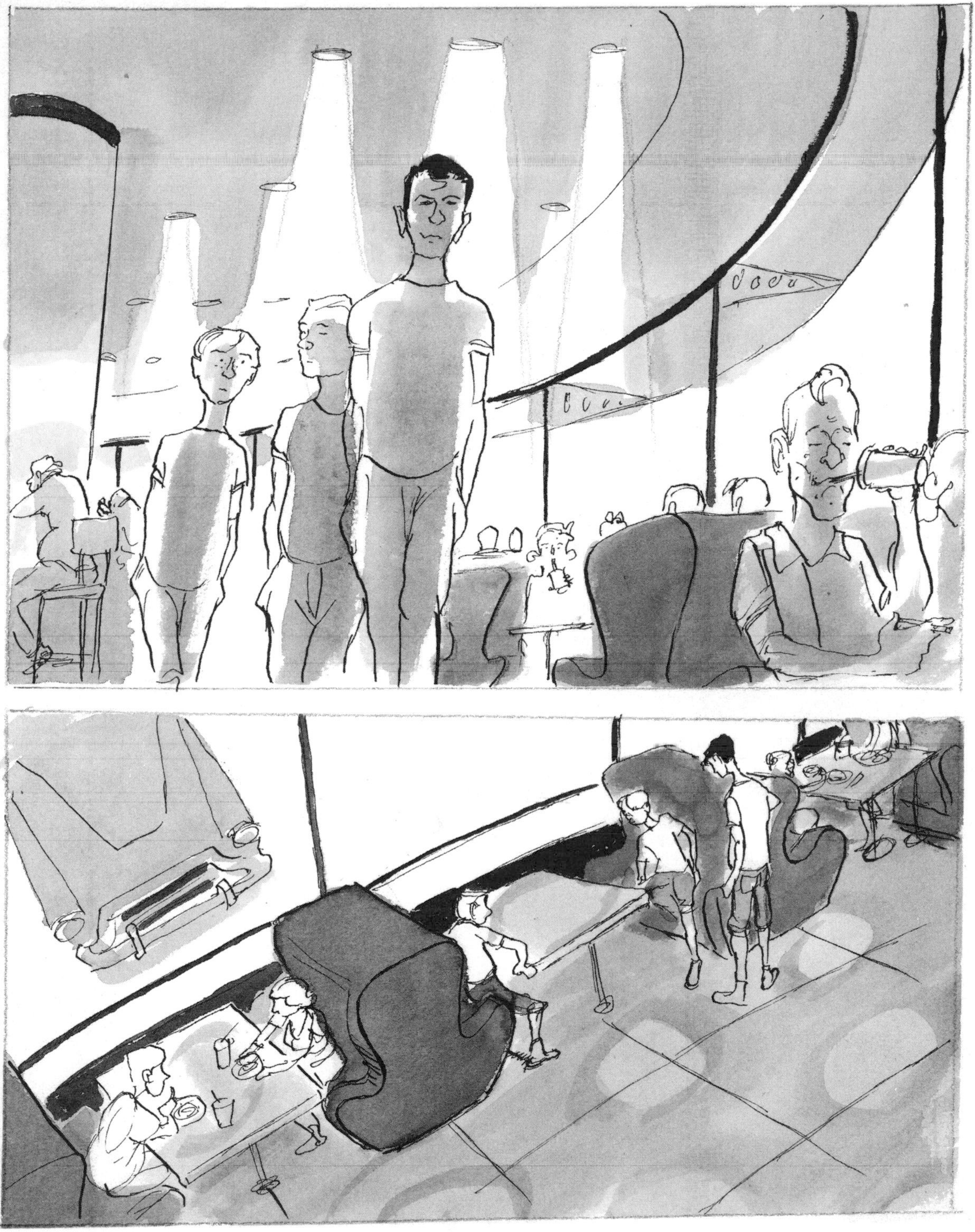

310

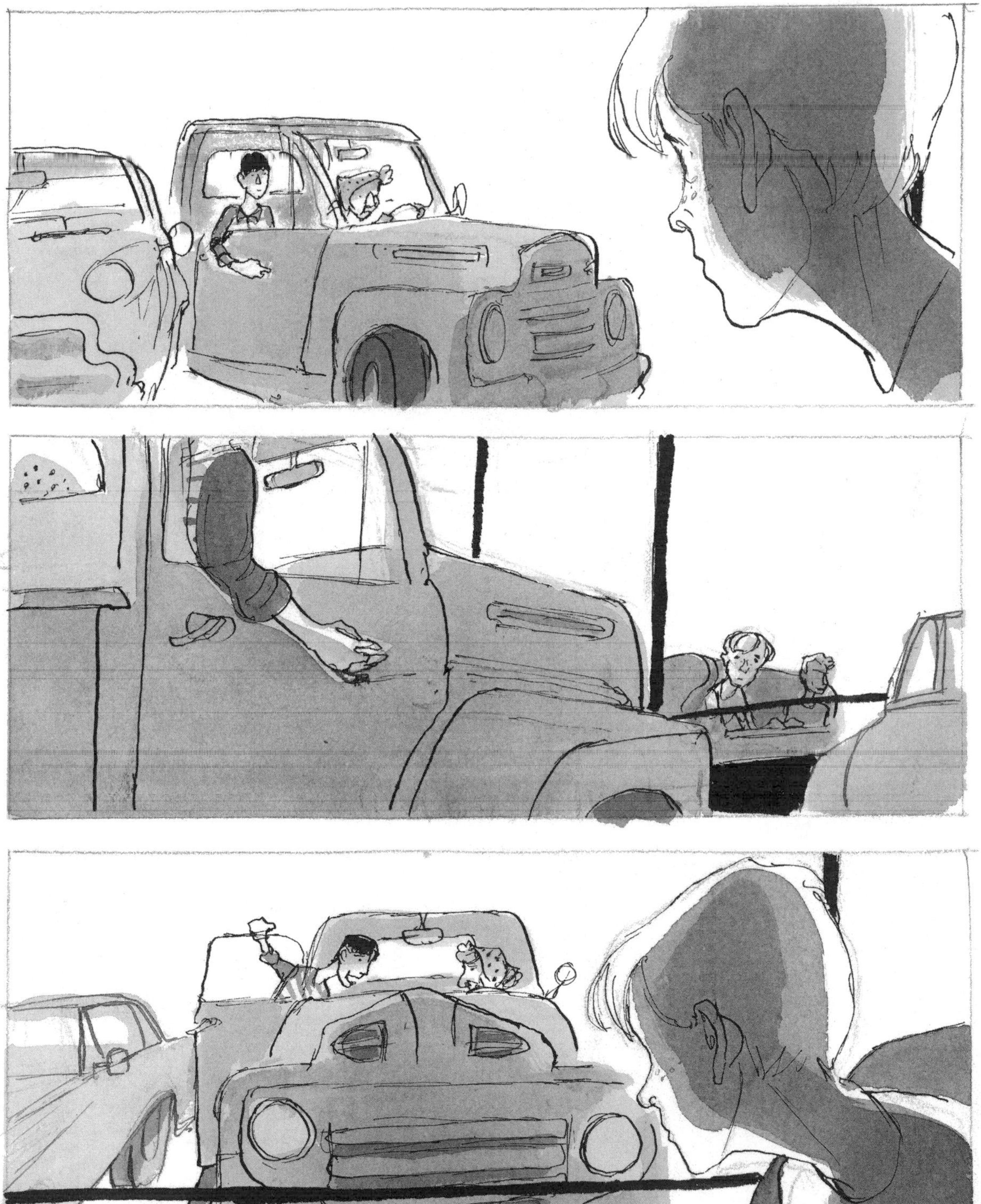

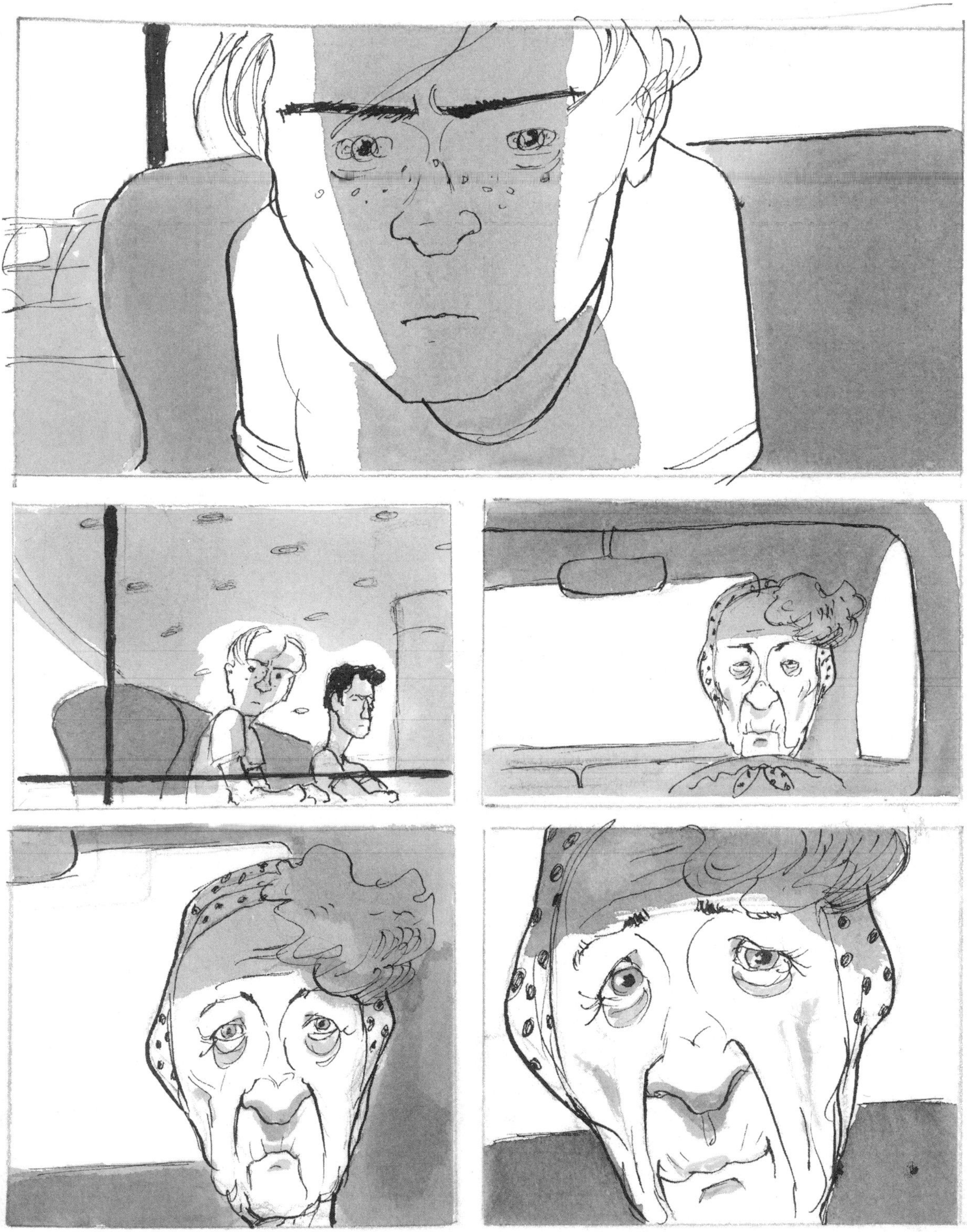

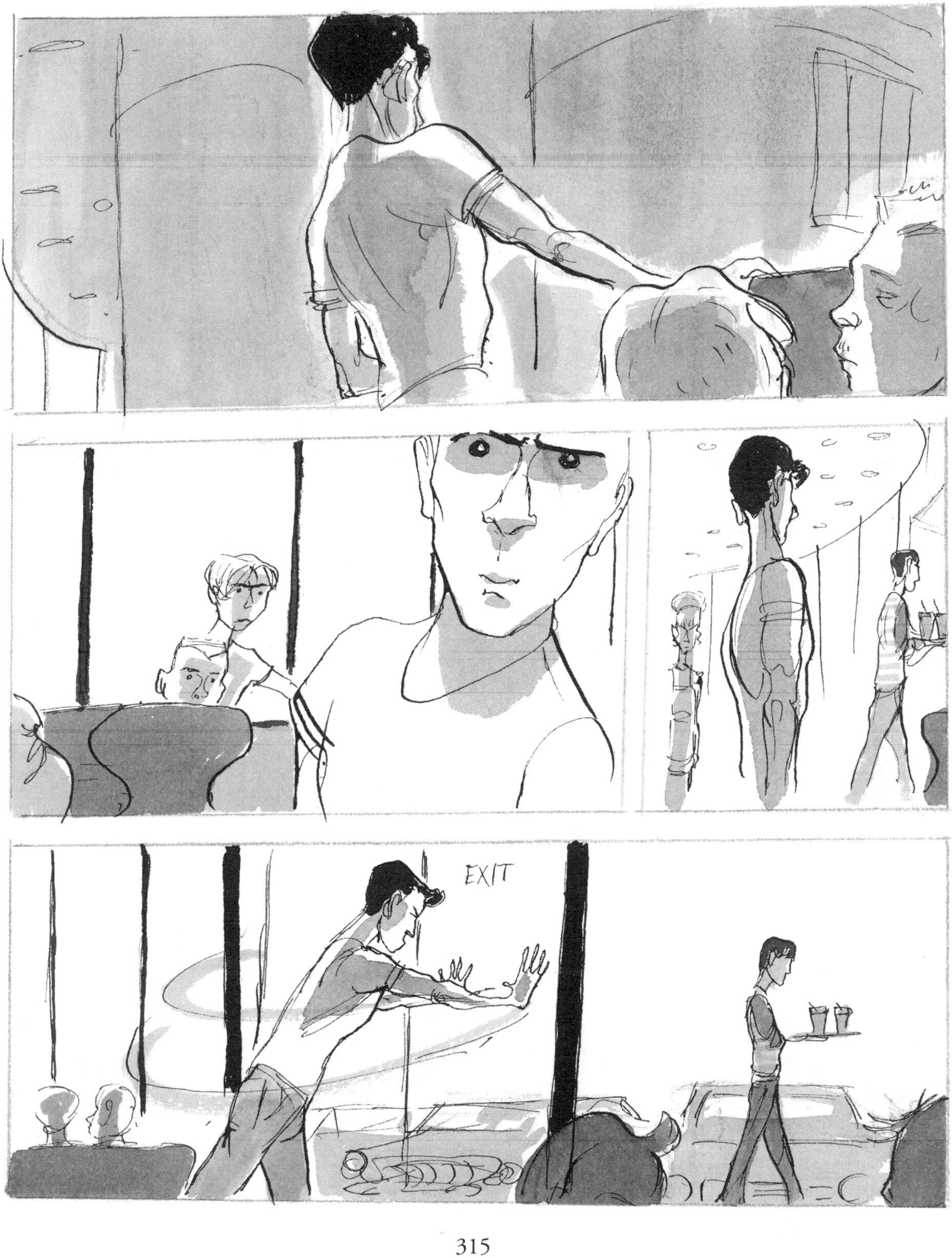
EXIT

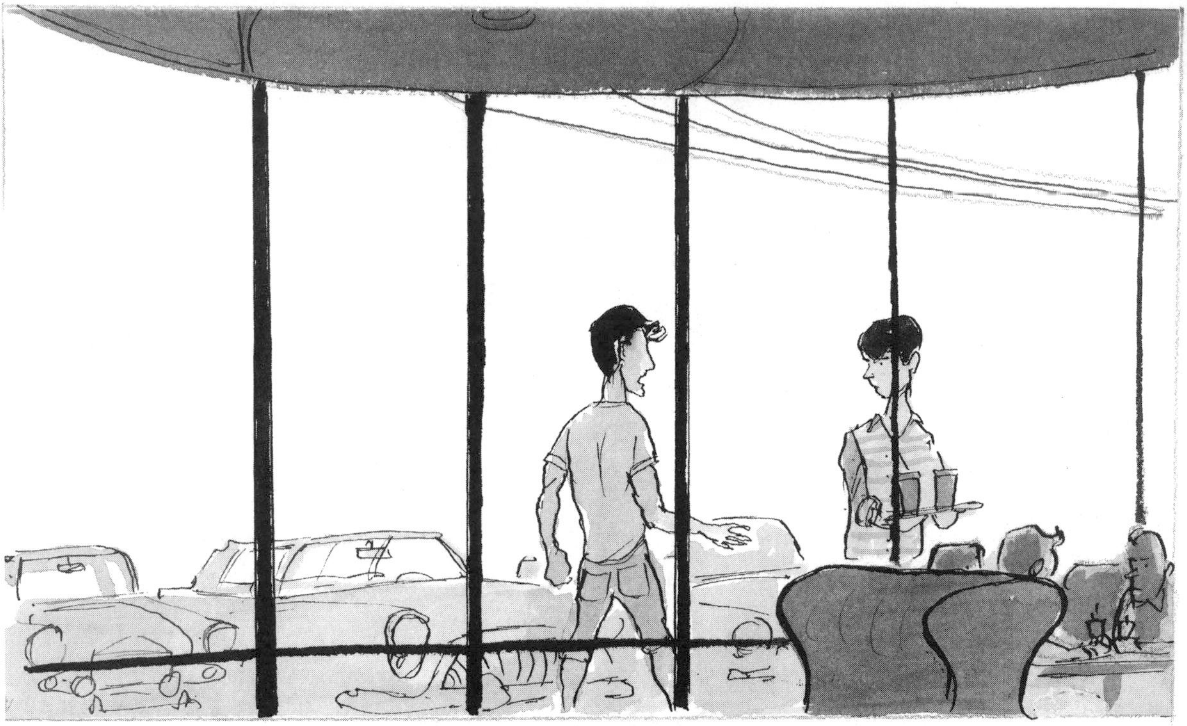

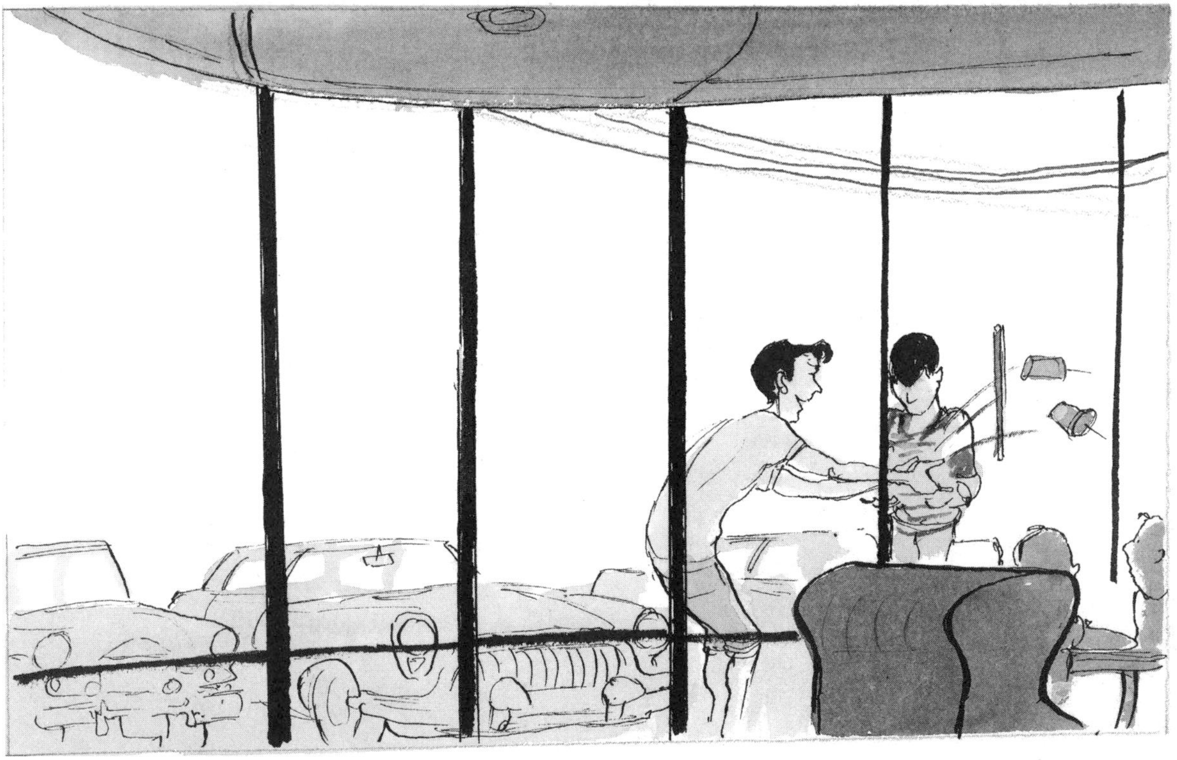

317

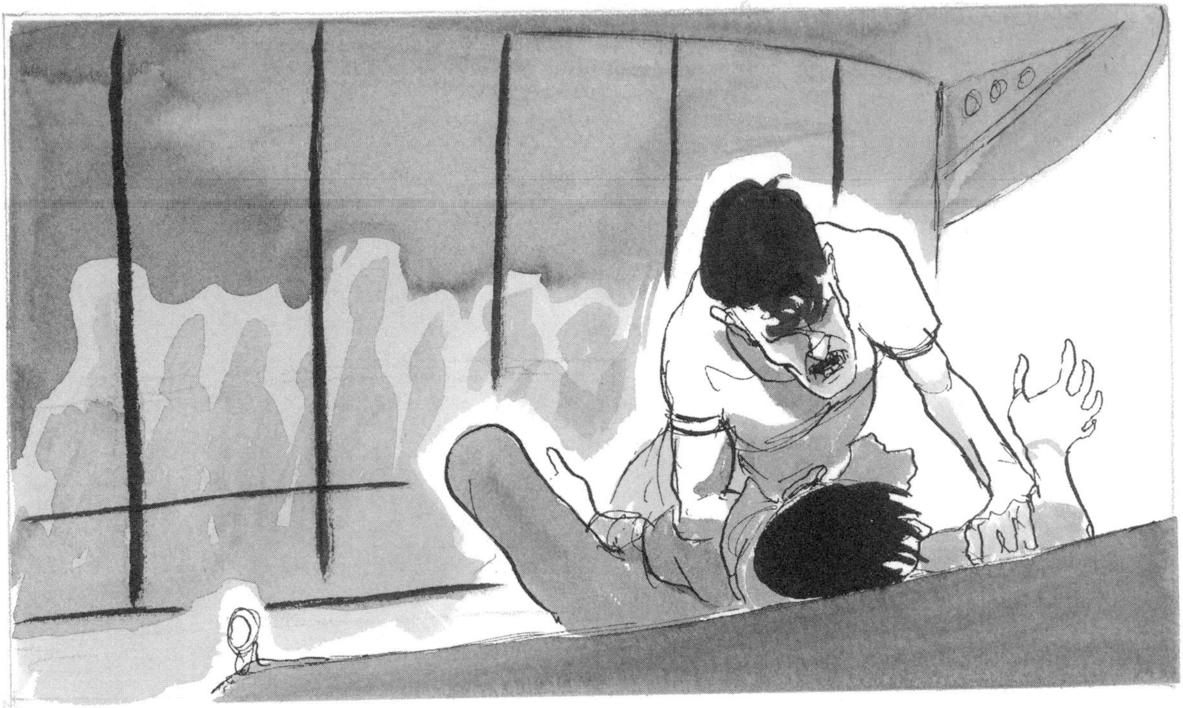

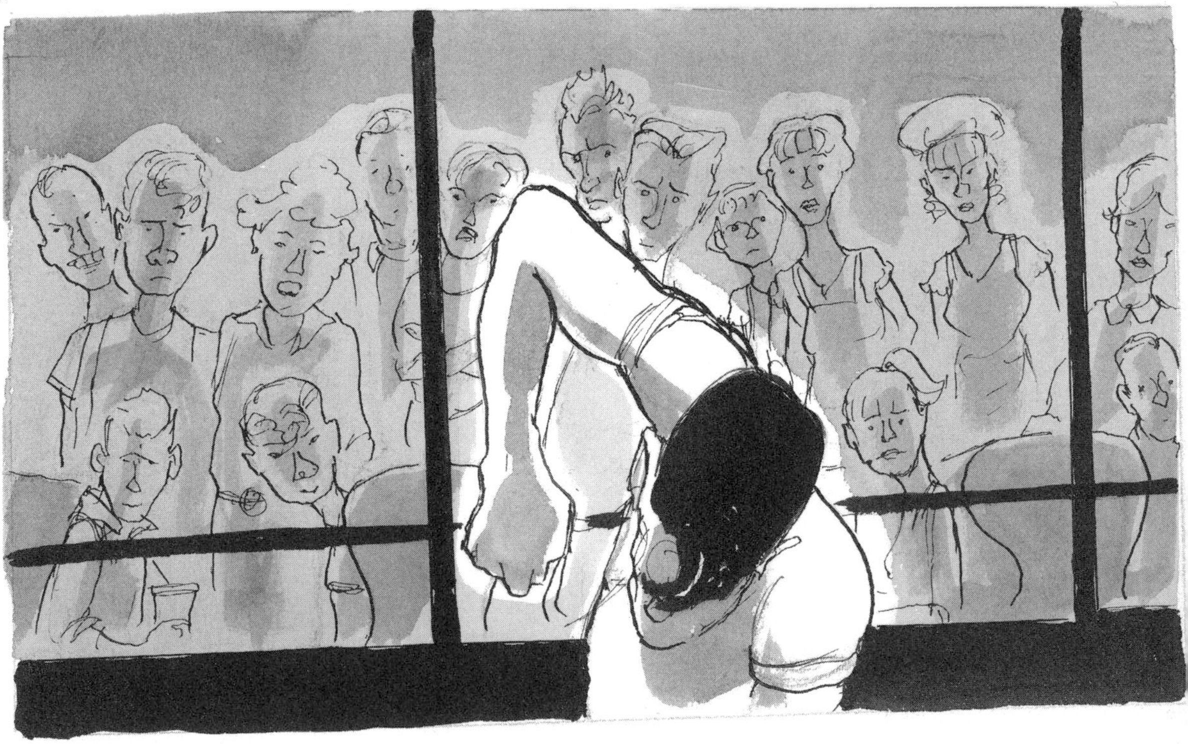

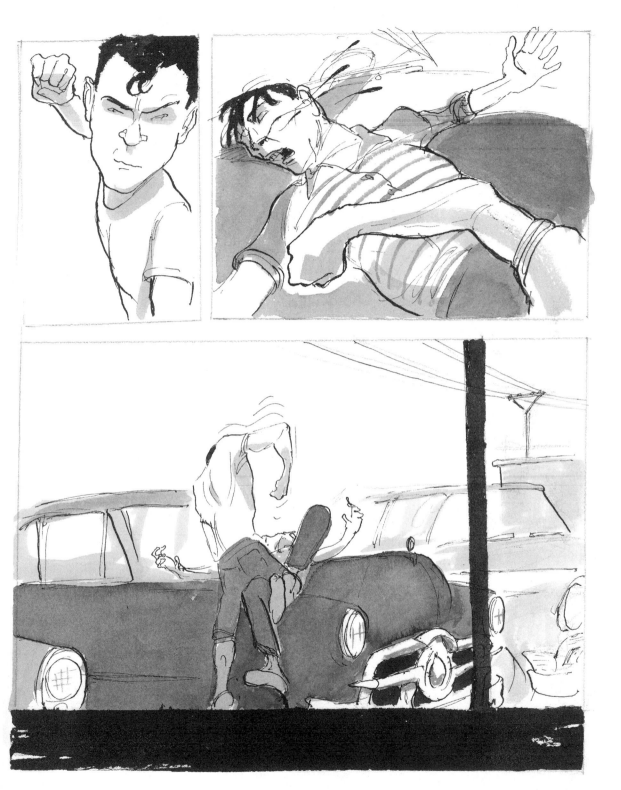

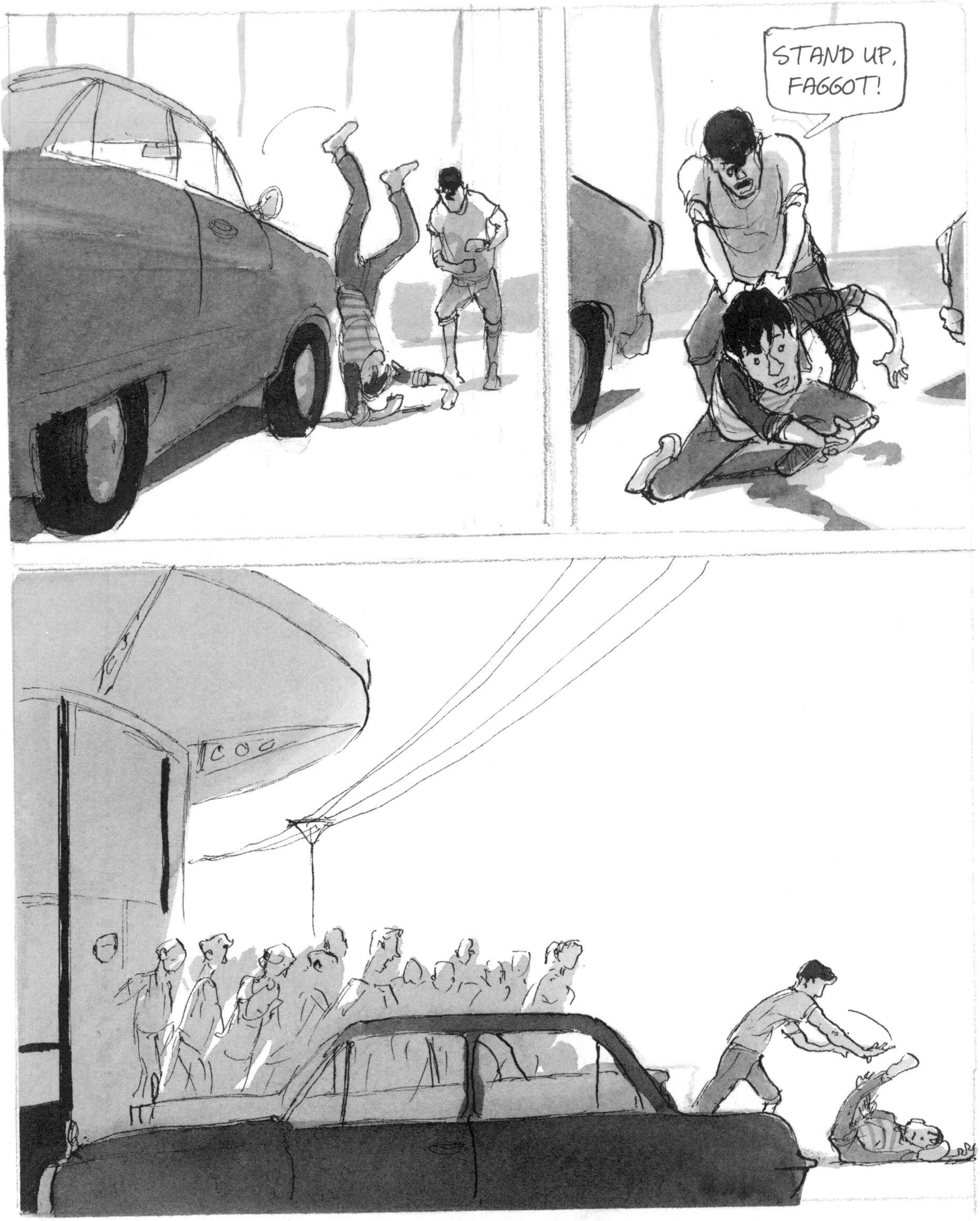
STAND UP, FAGGOT!

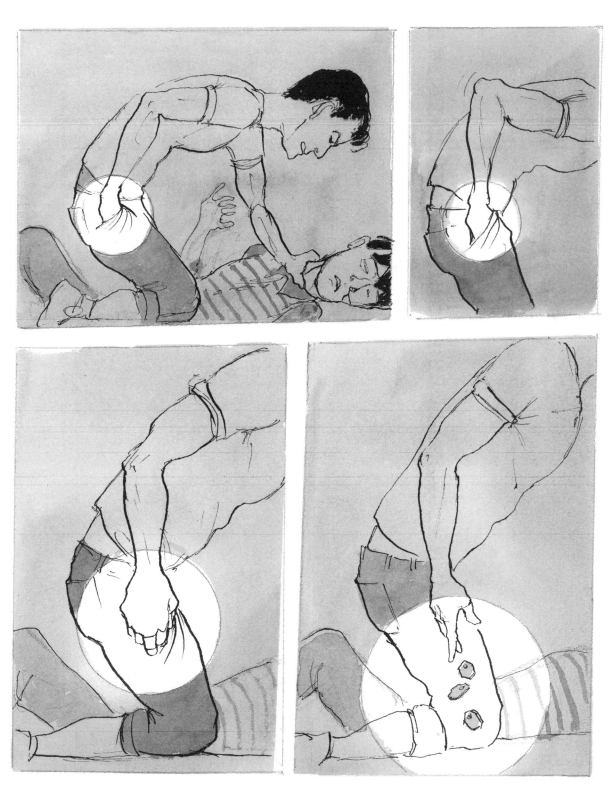

322

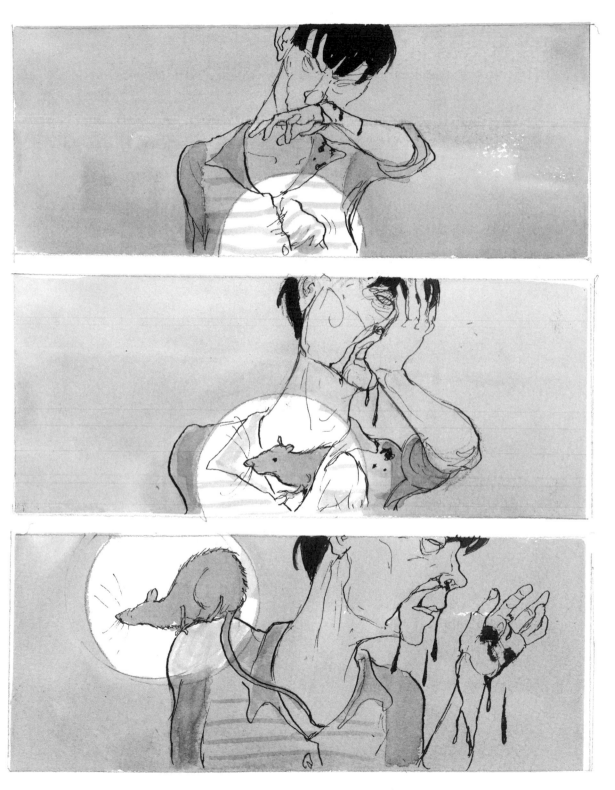

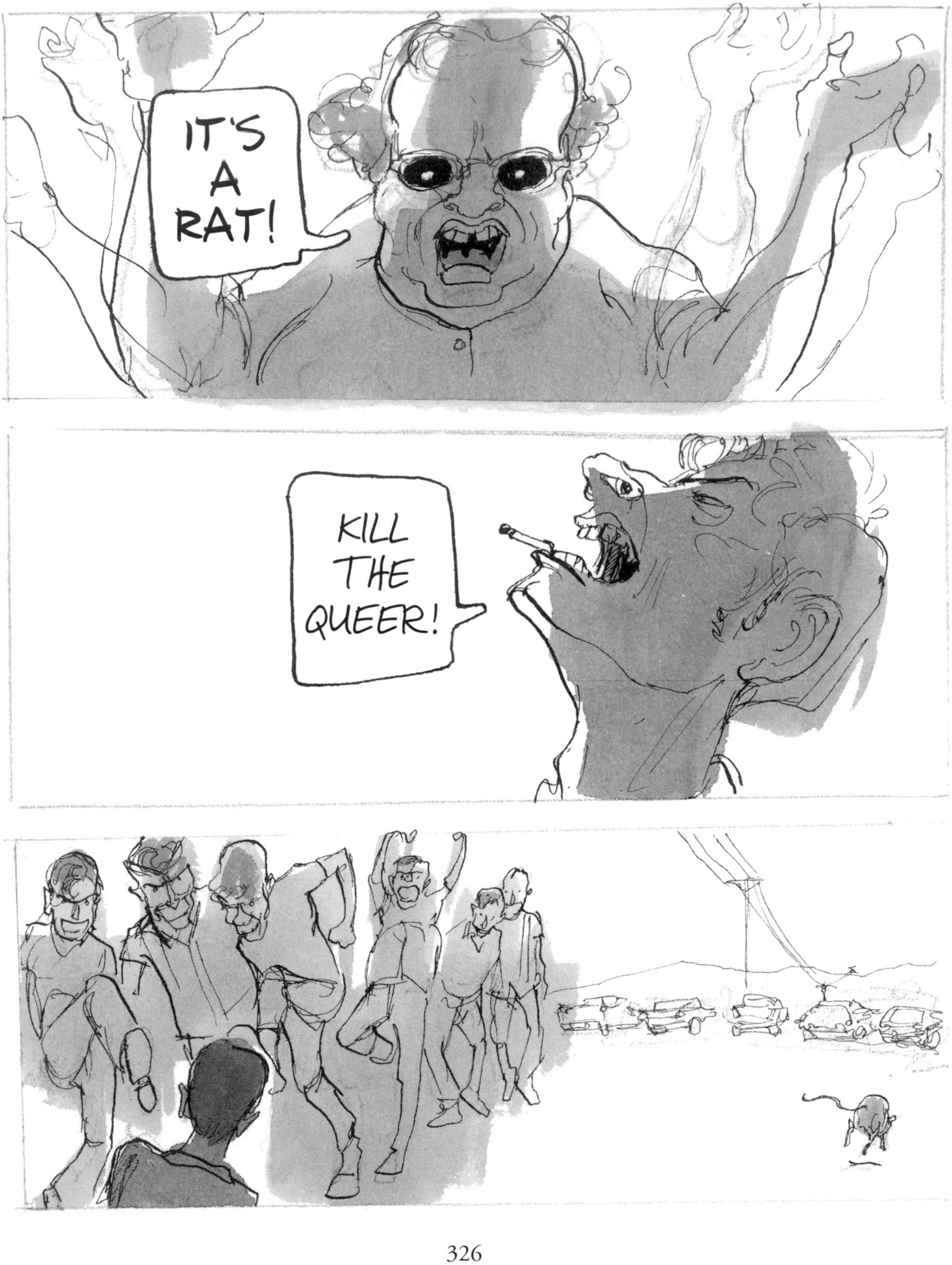
IT'S A RAT!
KILL THE QUEER!

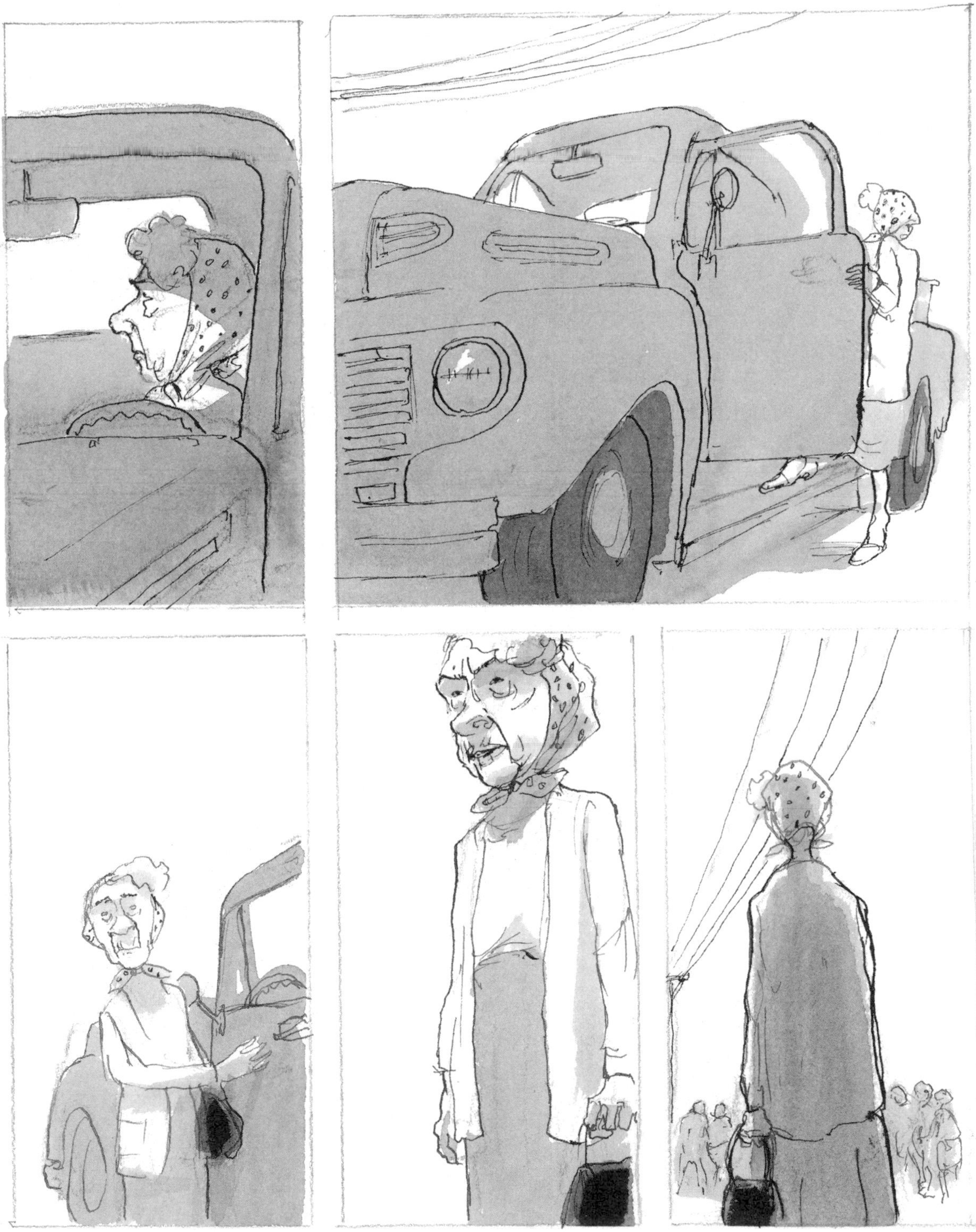

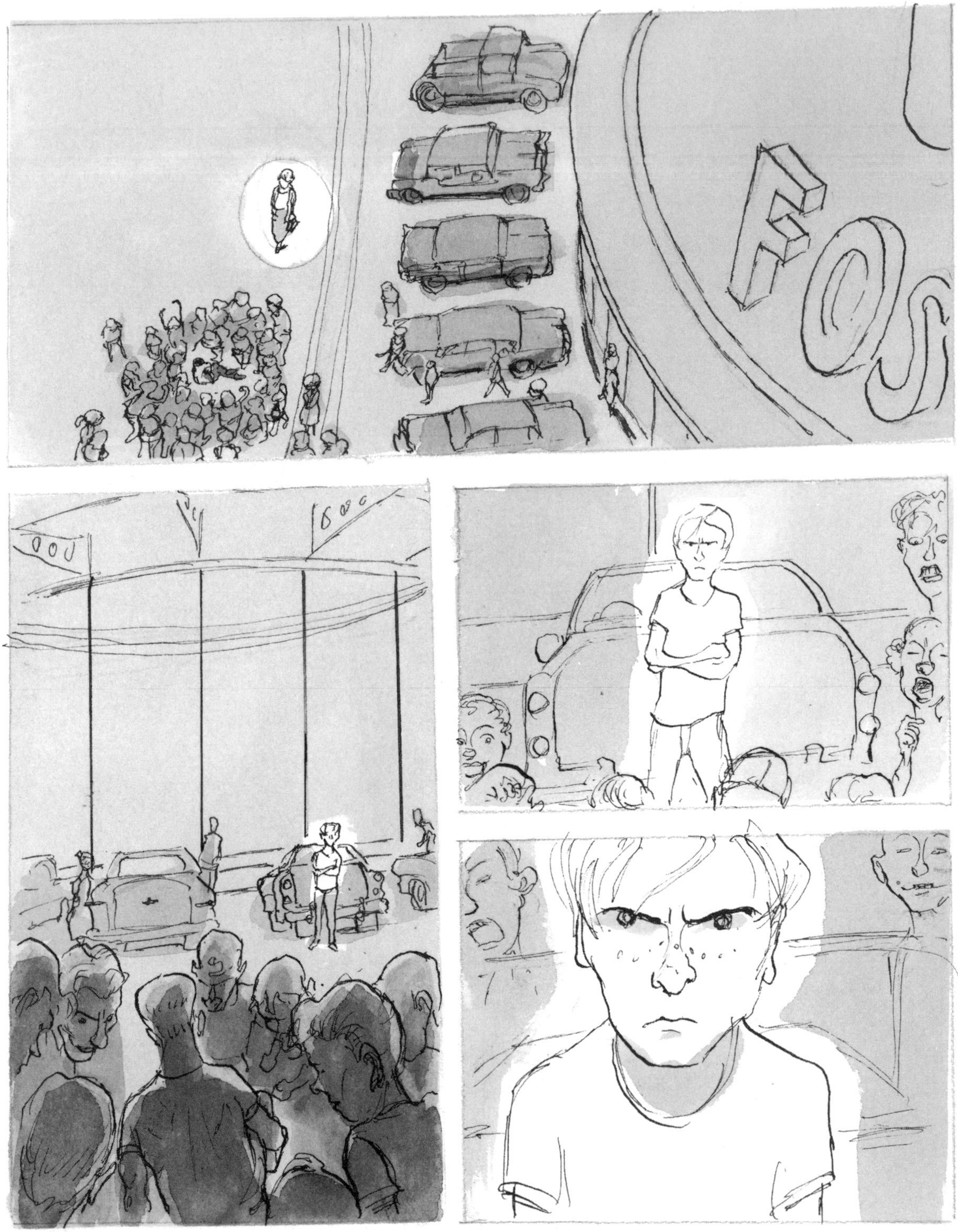
FOS

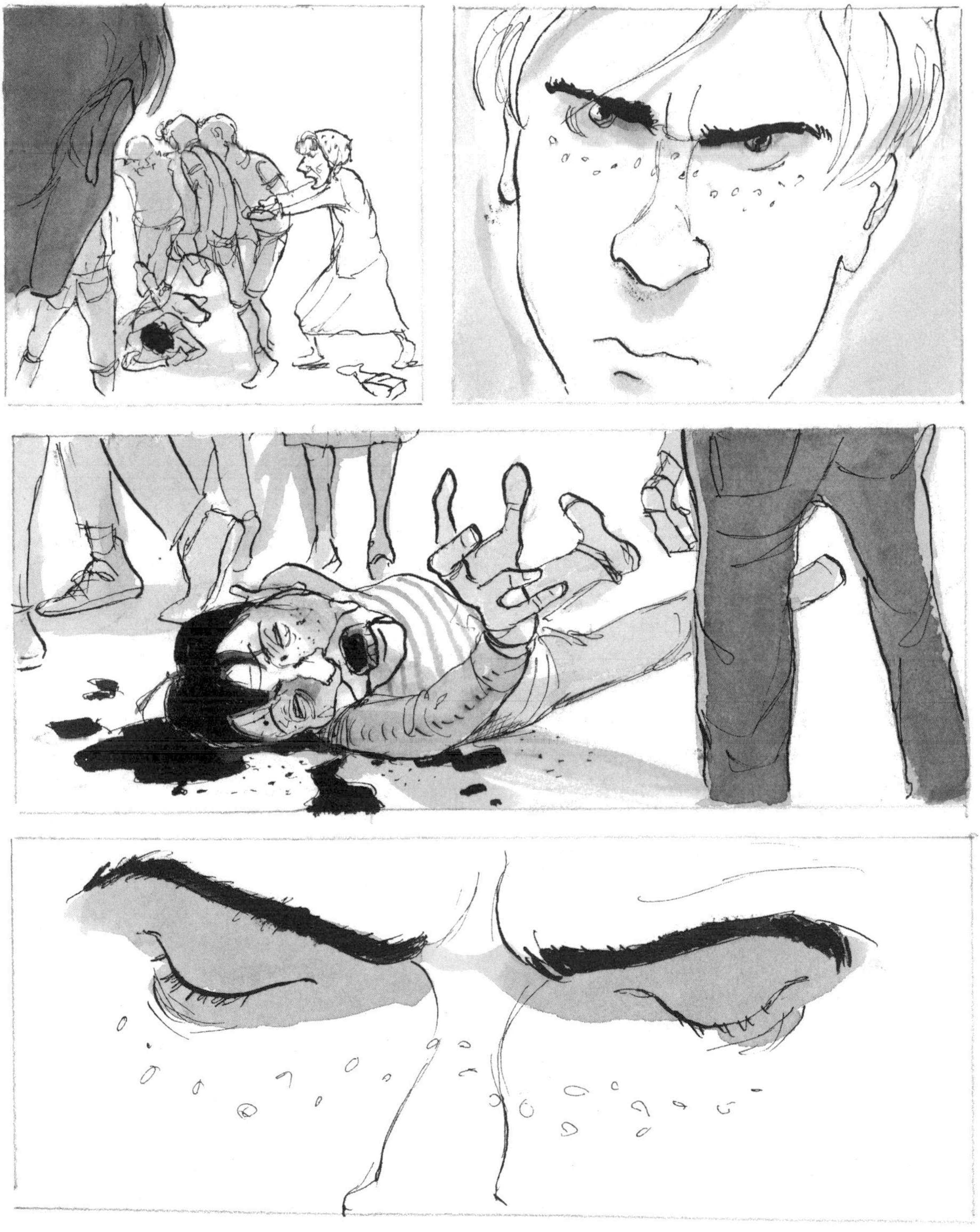

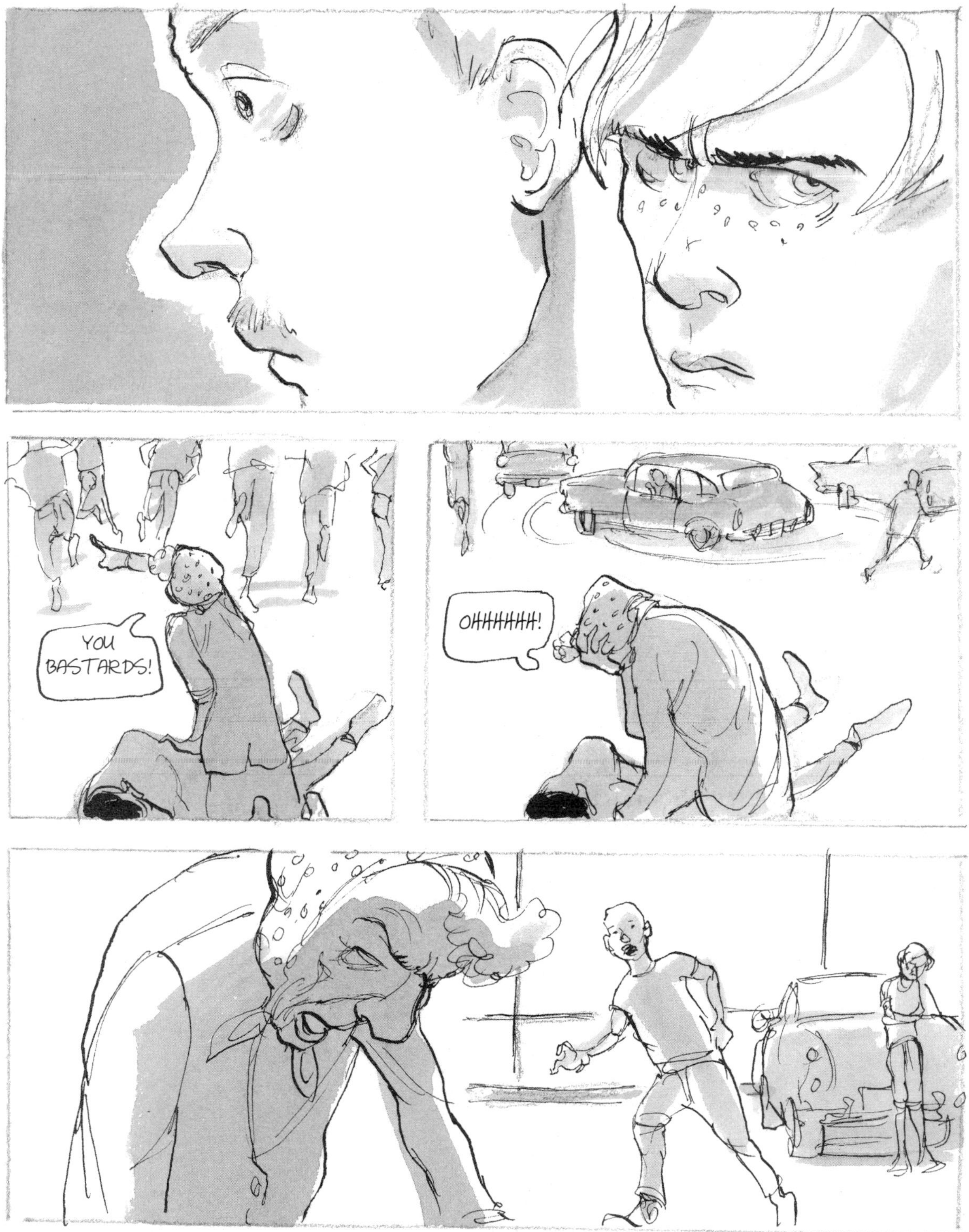
YOU BASTARDS!
OHHHHHH!

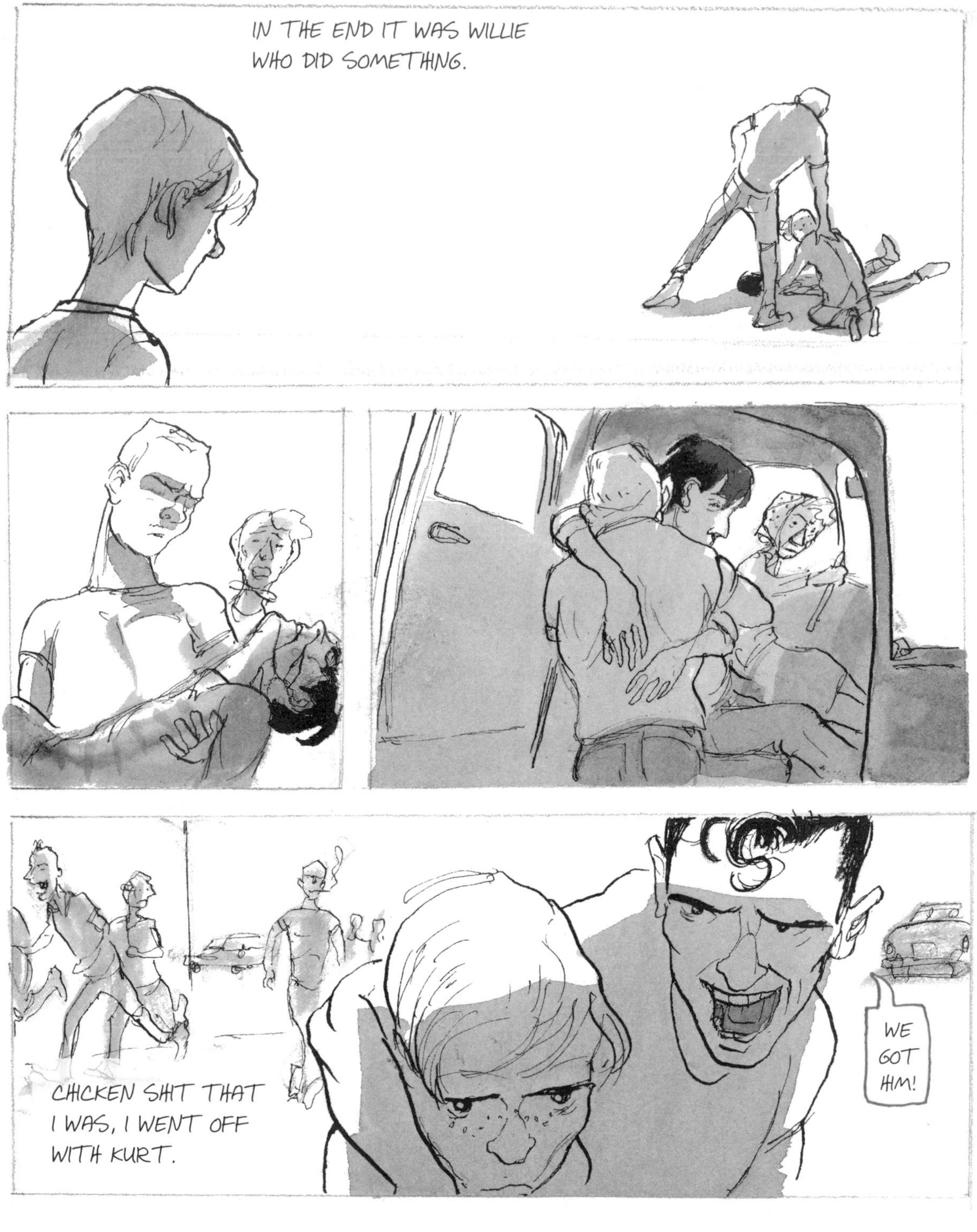
IN THE END IT WAS WILLIE WHO DID SOMETHING.
CHICKEN SHIT THAT I WAS, I WENT OFF WITH KURT.
WE GOT HIM!

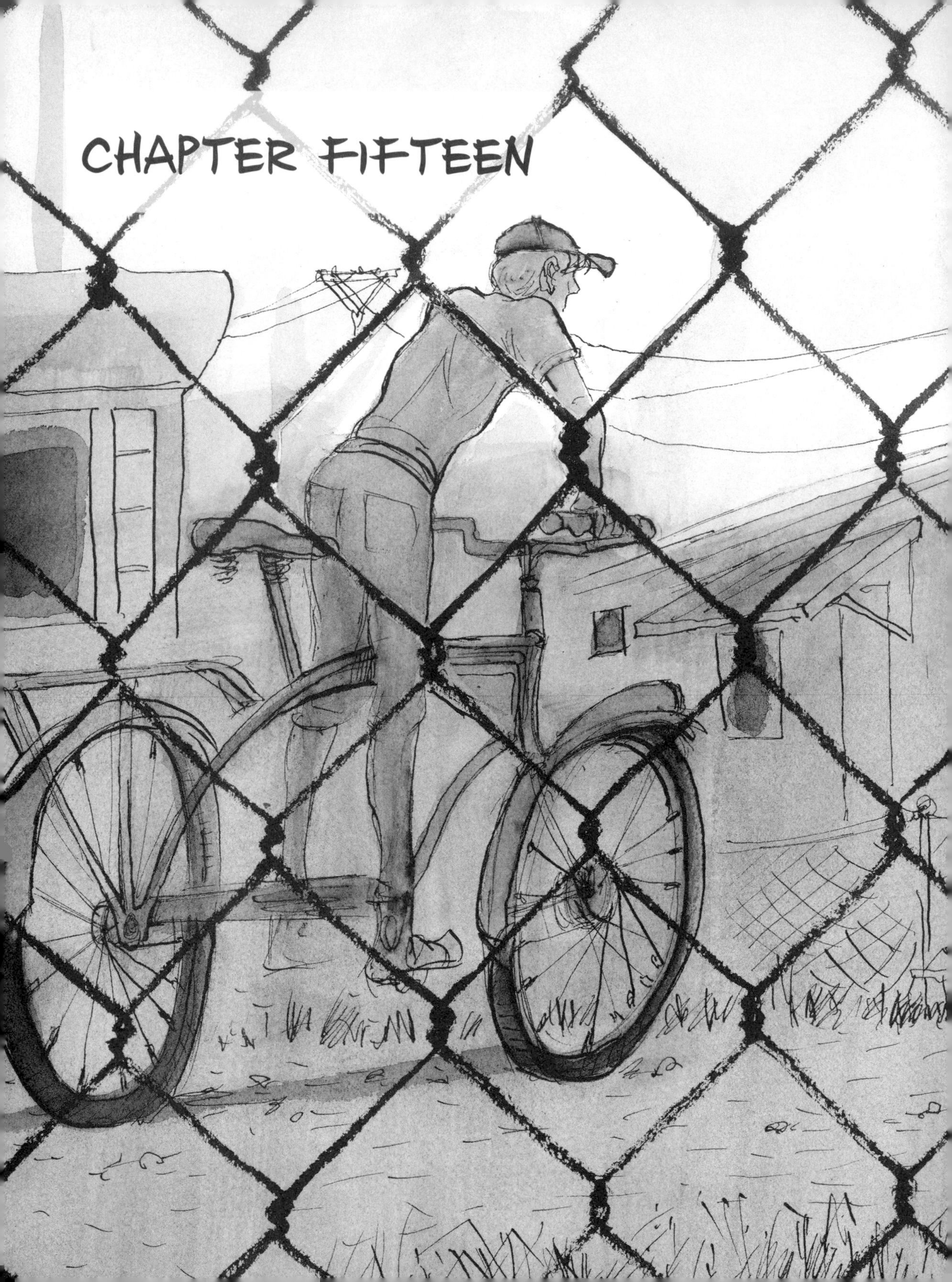
CHAPTER FIFTEEN

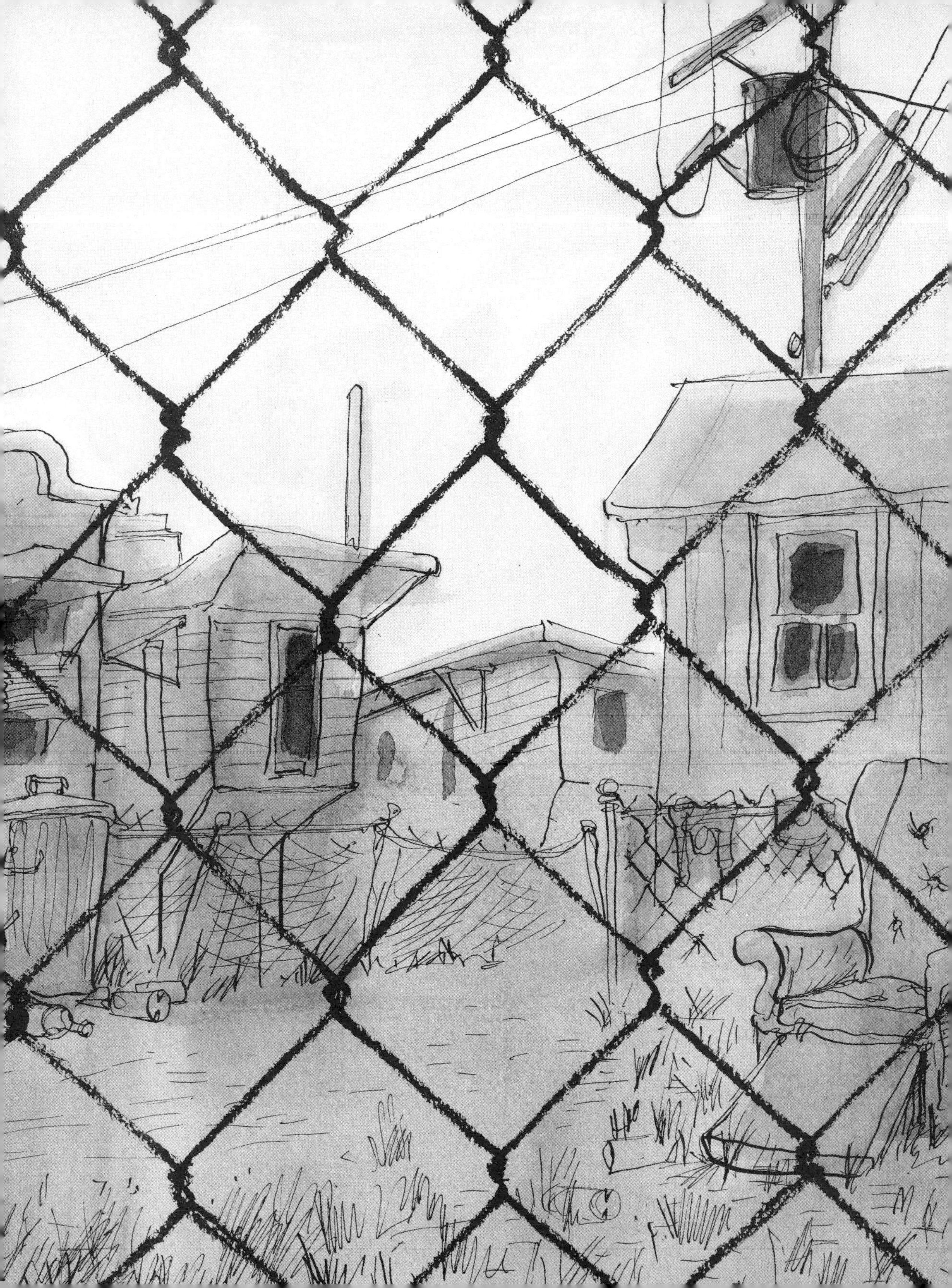

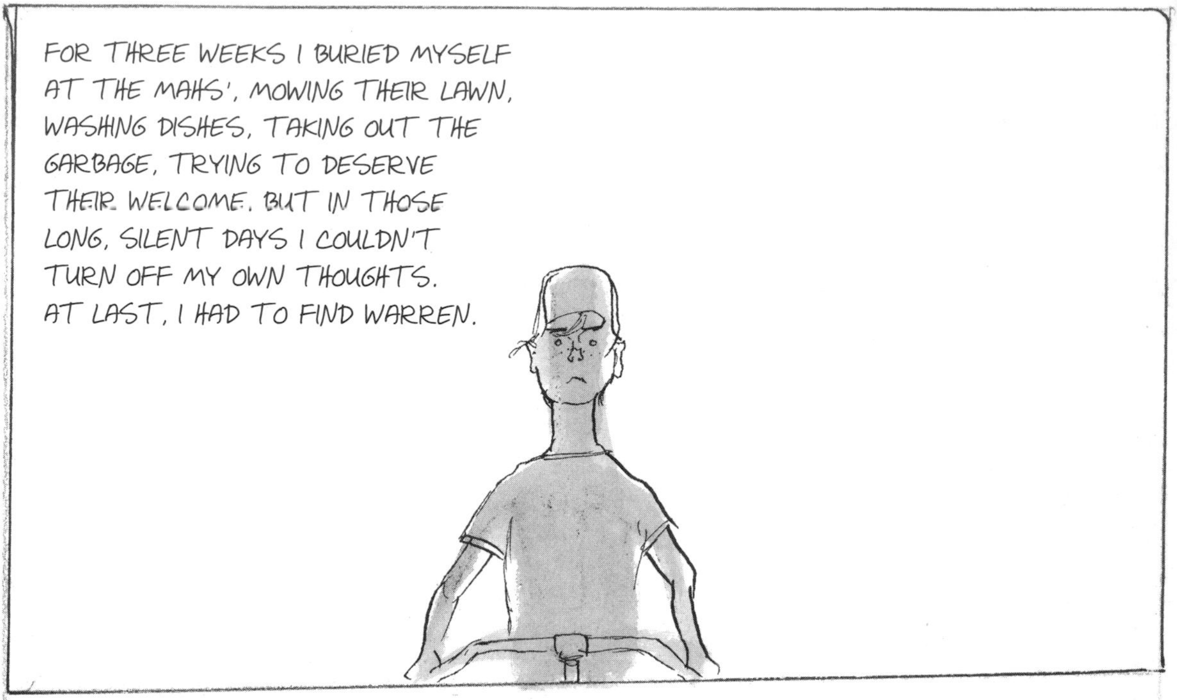
FOR THREE WEEKS I BURIED MYSELF AT THE MAHS', MOWING THEIR LAWN, WASHING DISHES, TAKING OUT THE GARBAGE, TRYING TO DESERVE THEIR WELCOME. BUT IN THOSE LONG, SILENT DAYS I COULDN'T TURN OFF MY OWN THOUGHTS. AT LAST, I HAD TO FIND WARREN.

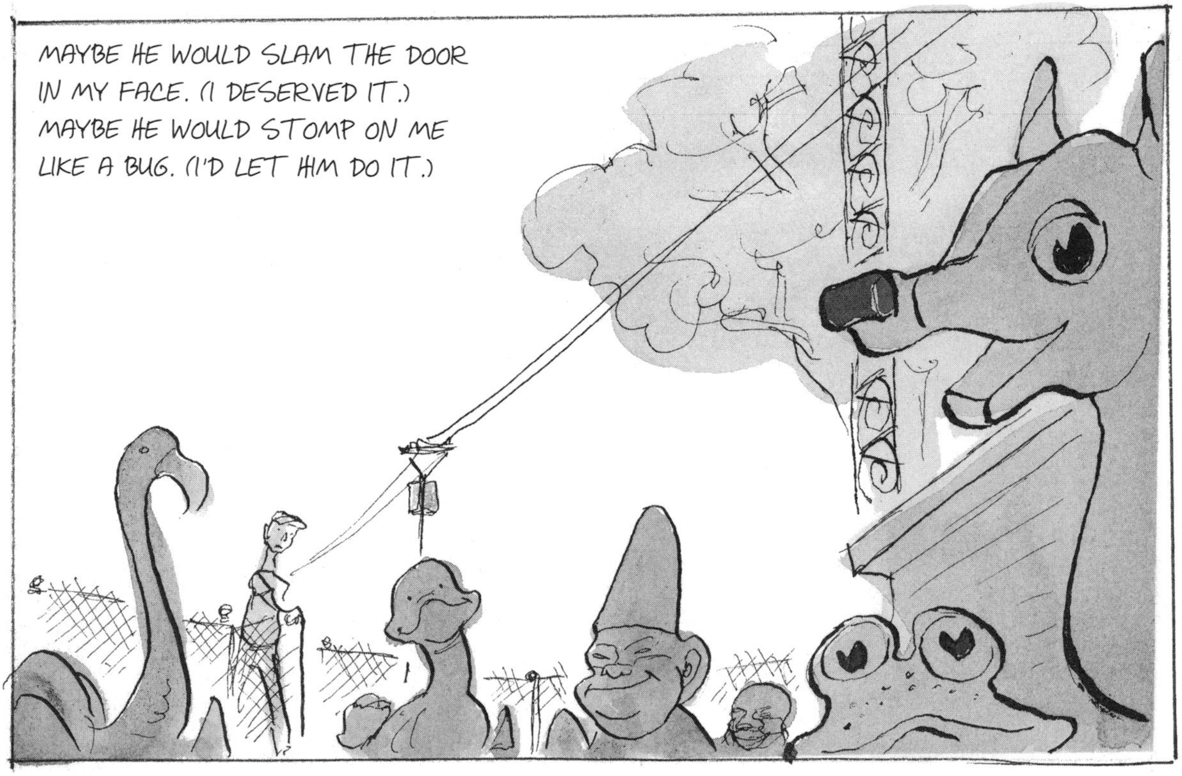
MAYBE HE WOULD SLAM THE DOOR IN MY FACE. (I DESERVED IT.) MAYBE HE WOULD STOMP ON ME LIKE A BUG. (I'D LET HIM DO IT.)

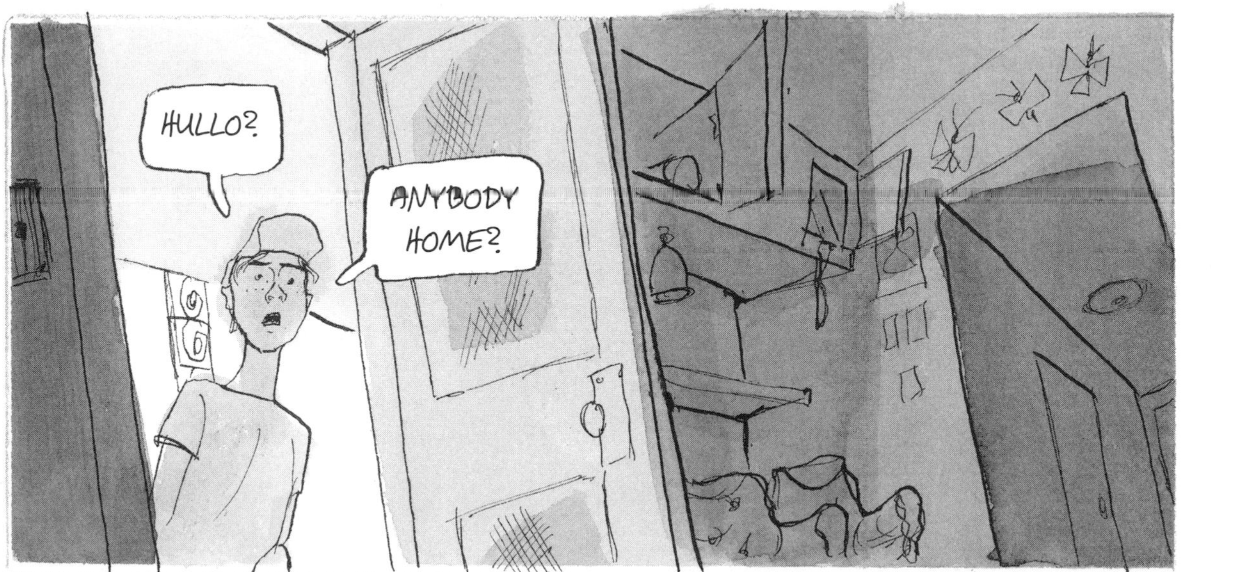
HULLO?
ANYBODY HOME?

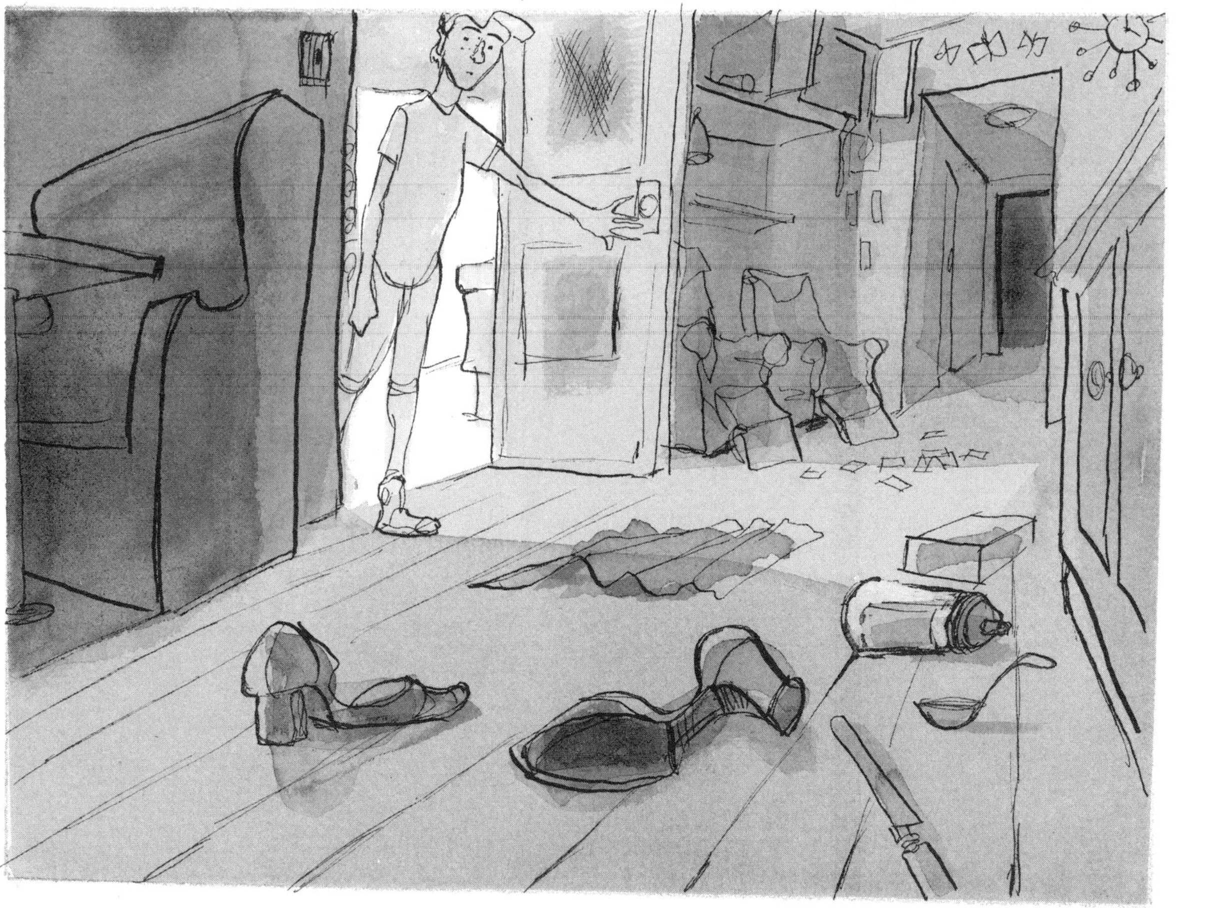

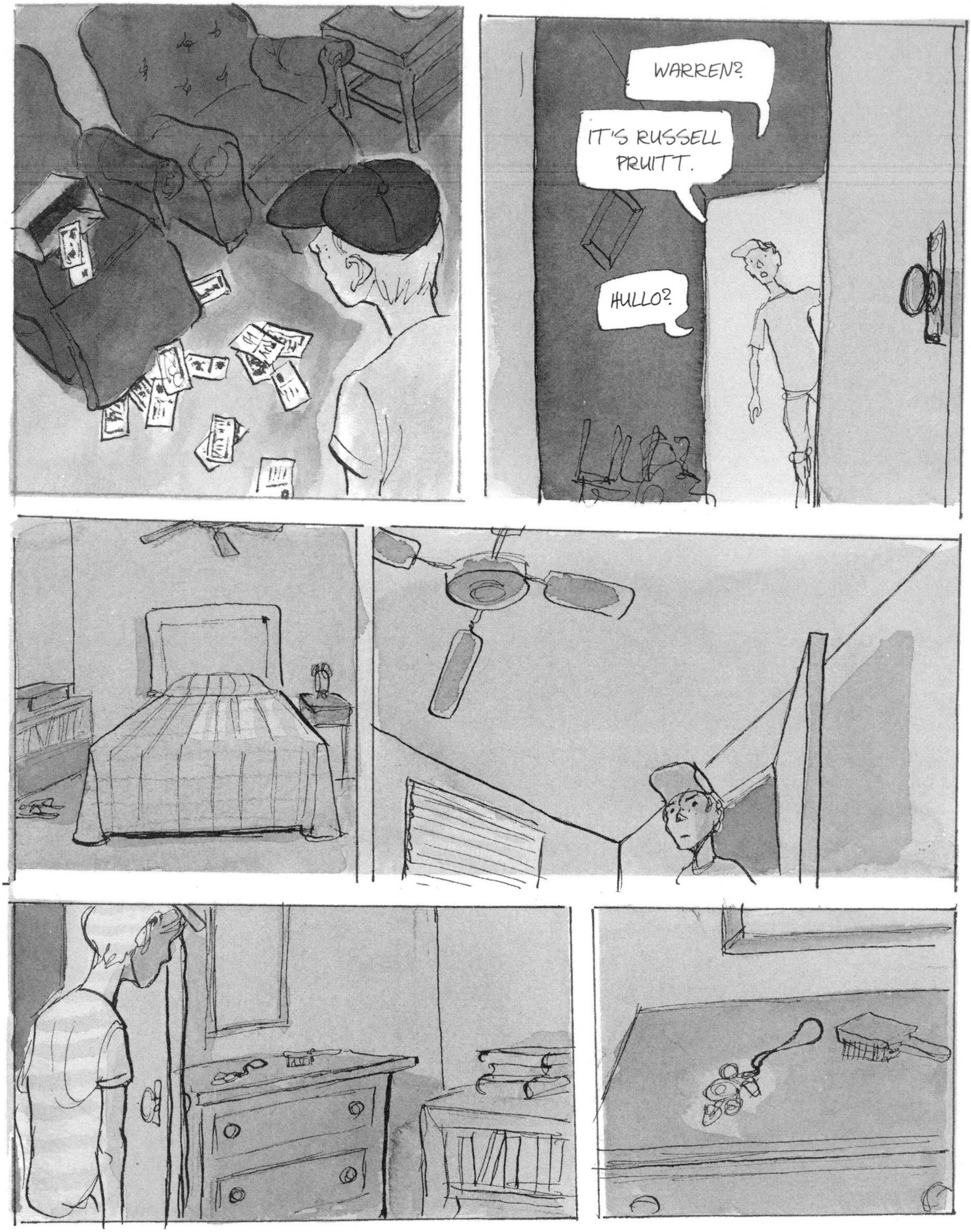
WARREN?
IT'S RUSSELL PRUITT.
HULLO?

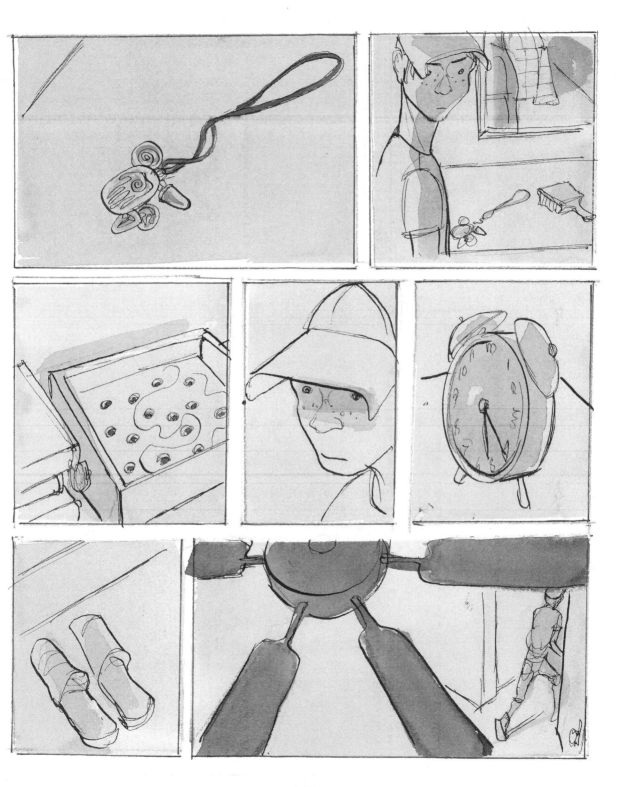

339

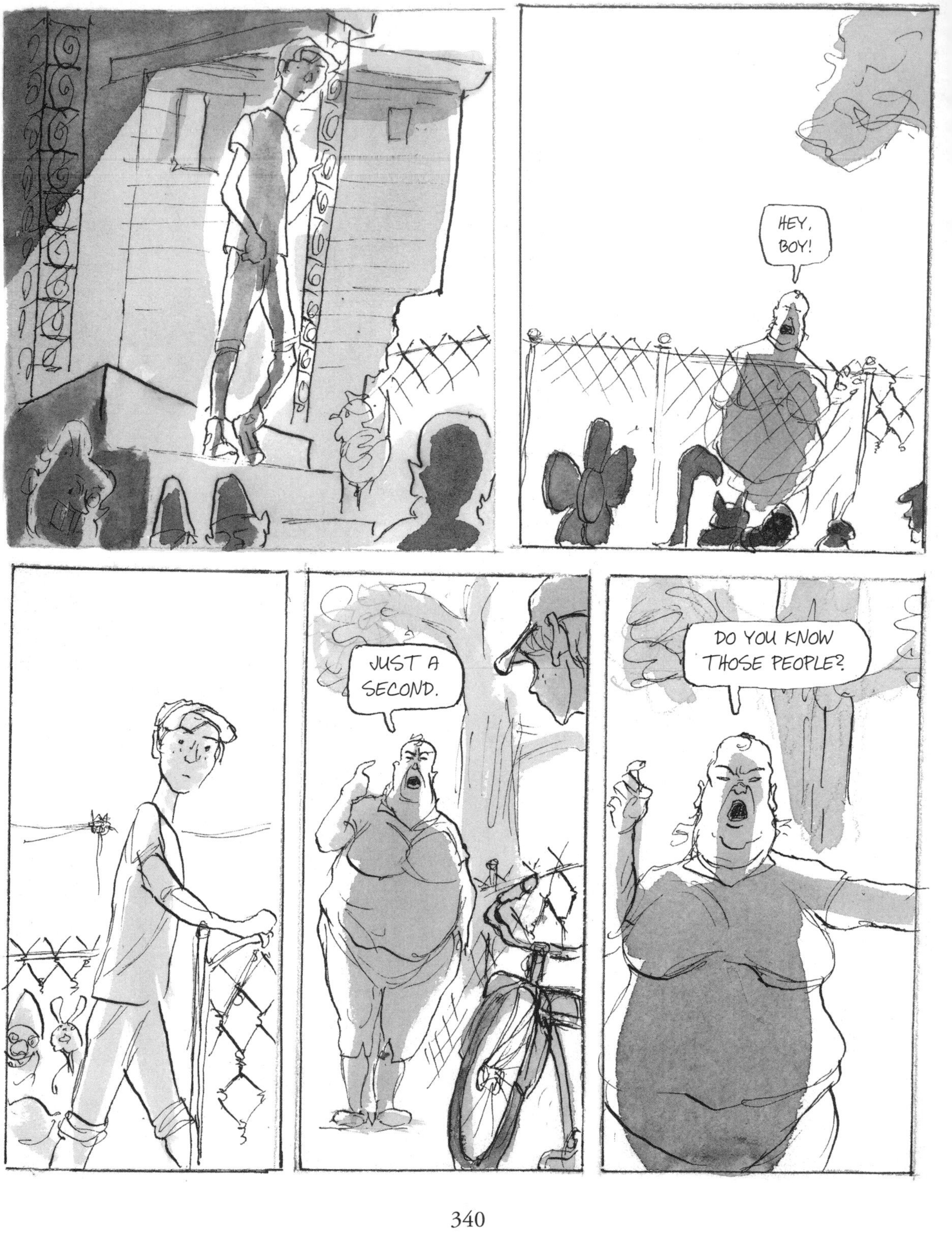
HEY, BOY!
JUST A SECOND.
DO YOU KNOW THOSE PEOPLE?

341

343

344

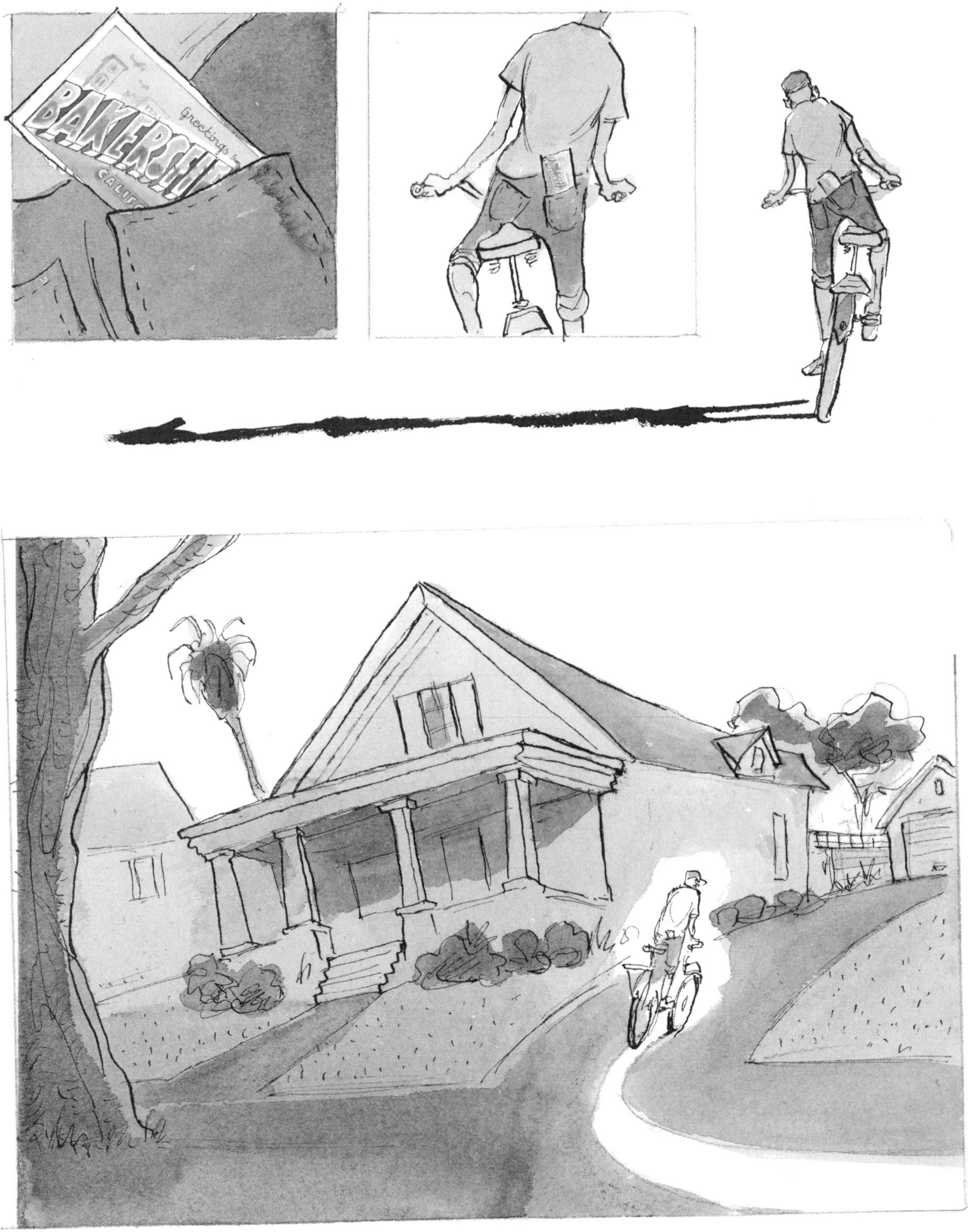
Greetings

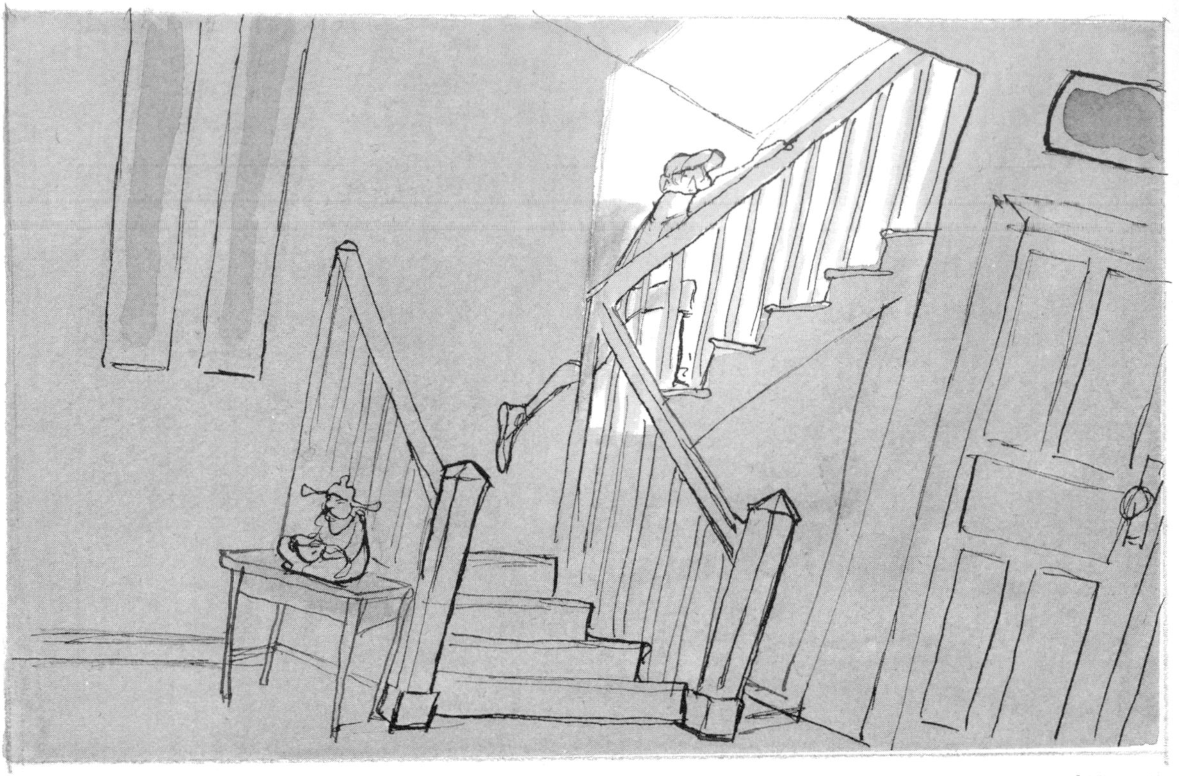

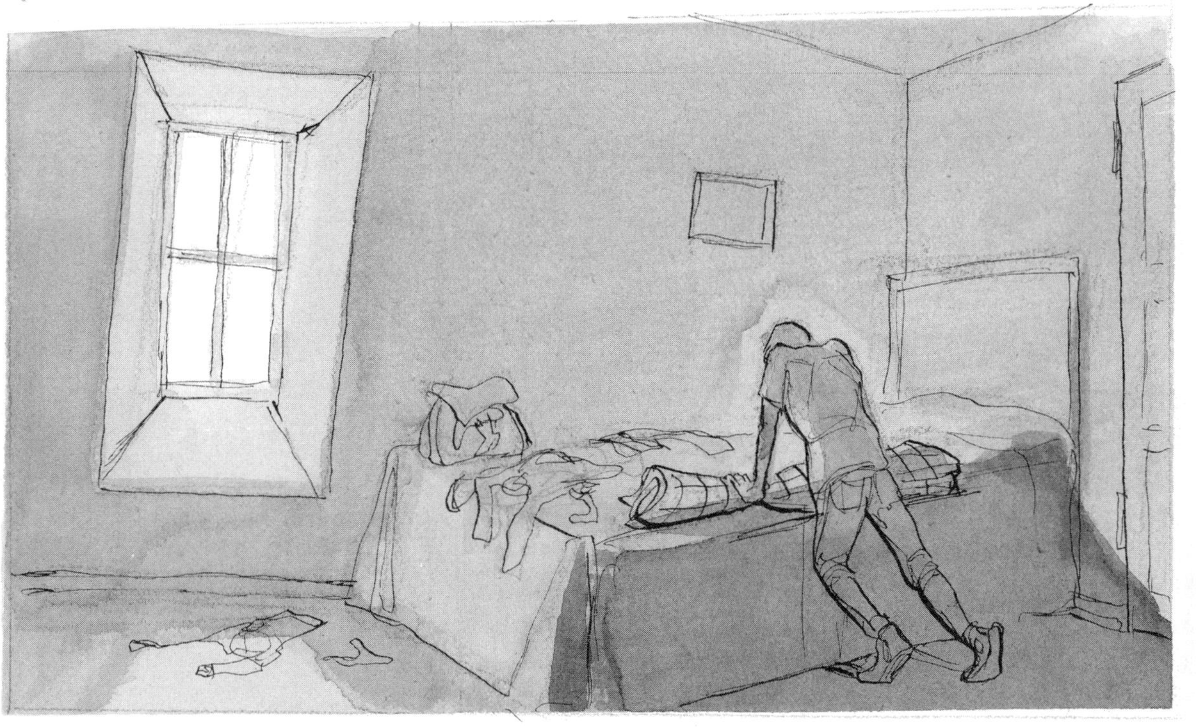

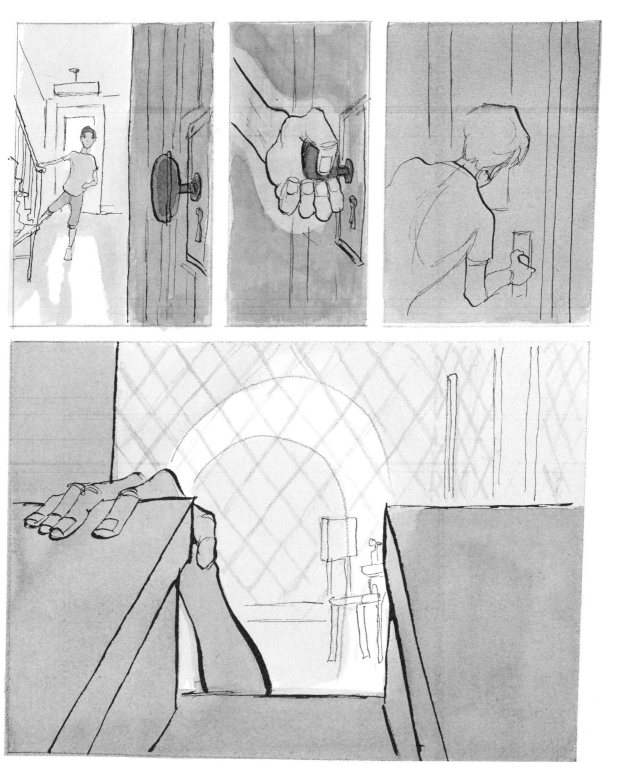

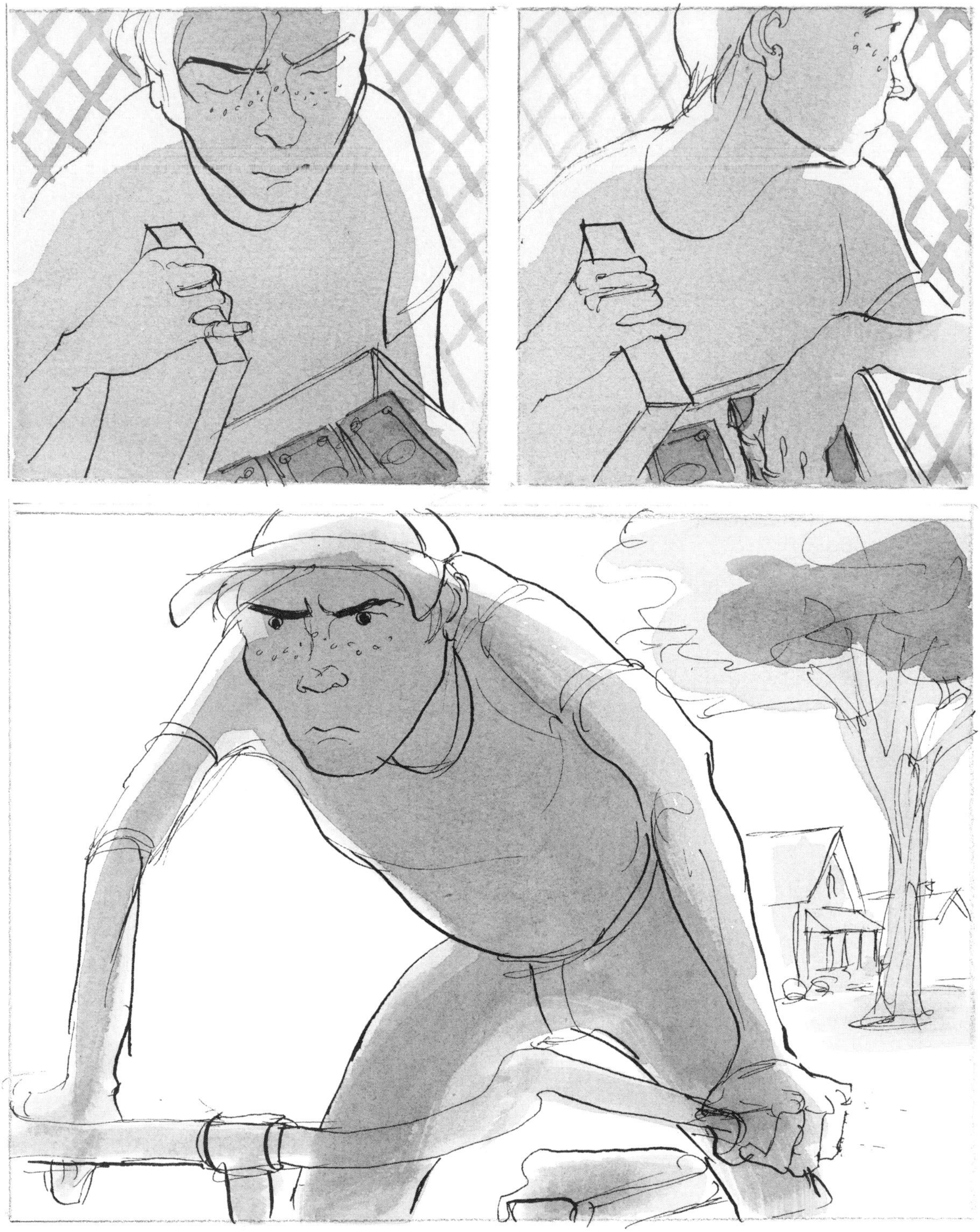

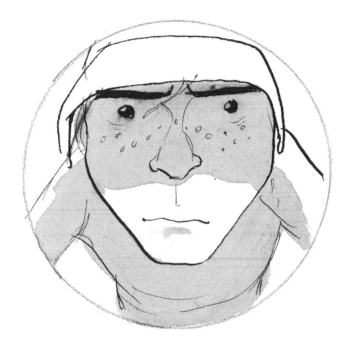

CHAPTER SIXTEEN

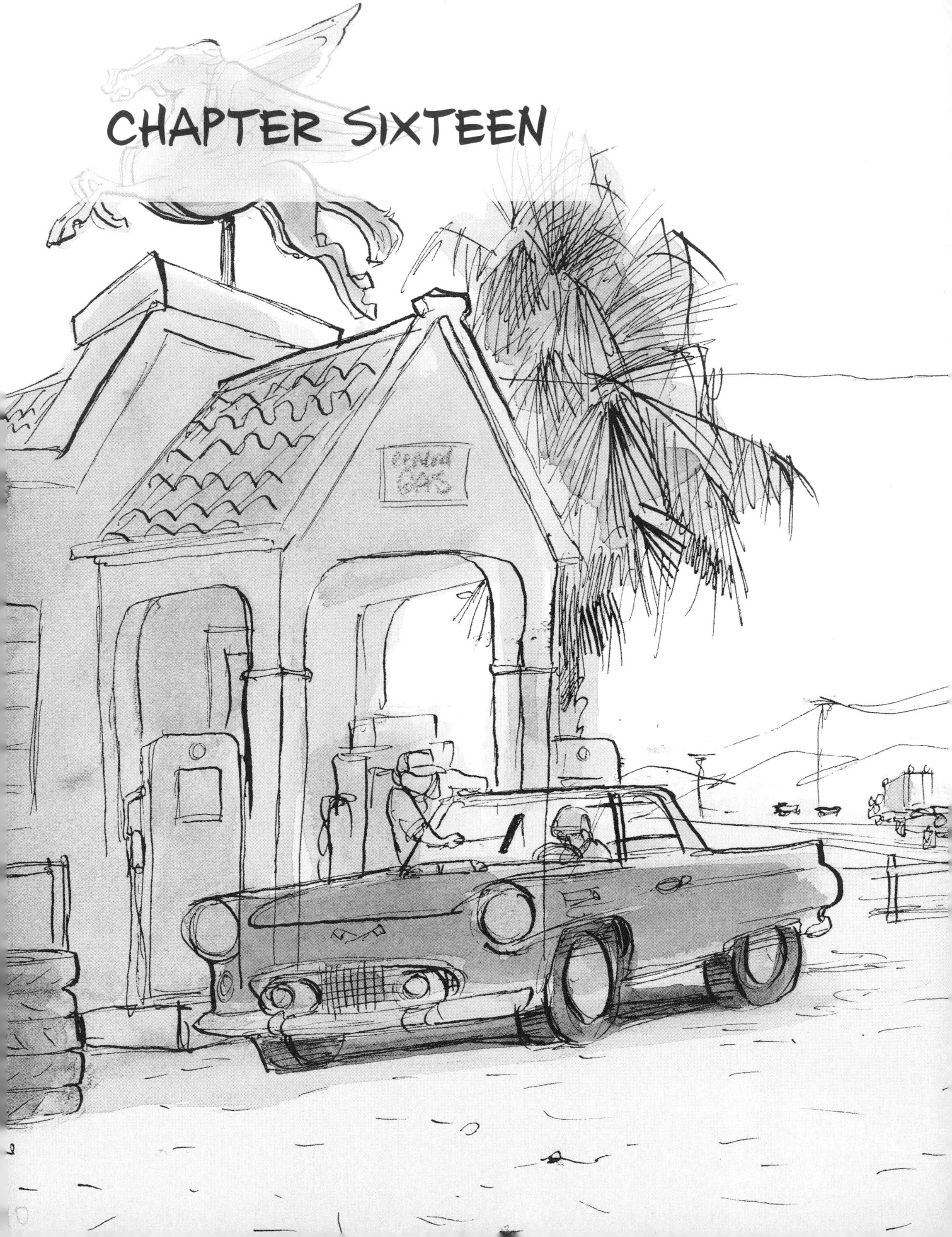

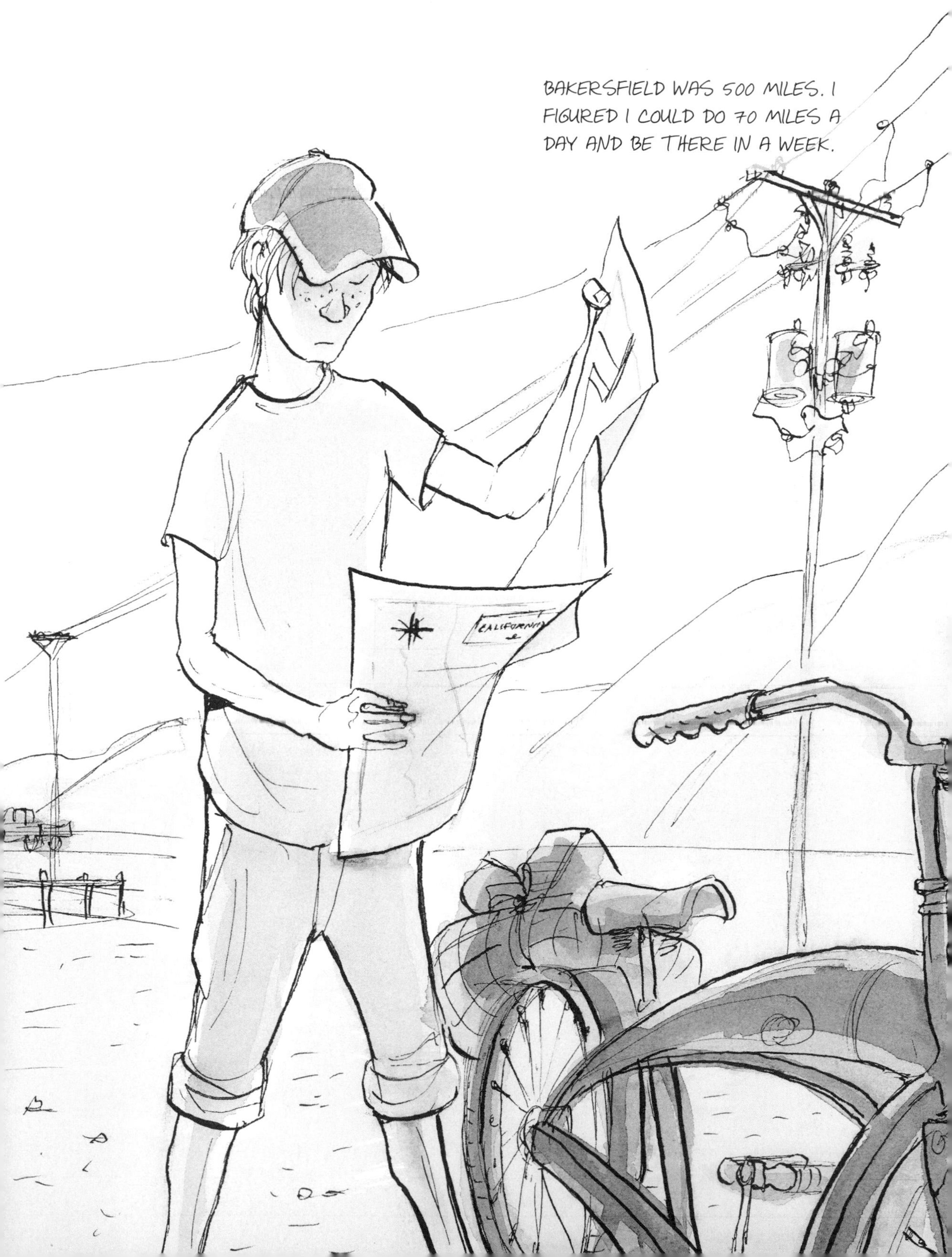
BAKERSFIELD WAS 500 MILES. I FIGURED I COULD DO 70 MILES A DAY AND BE THERE IN A WEEK.
CALIFORNIA

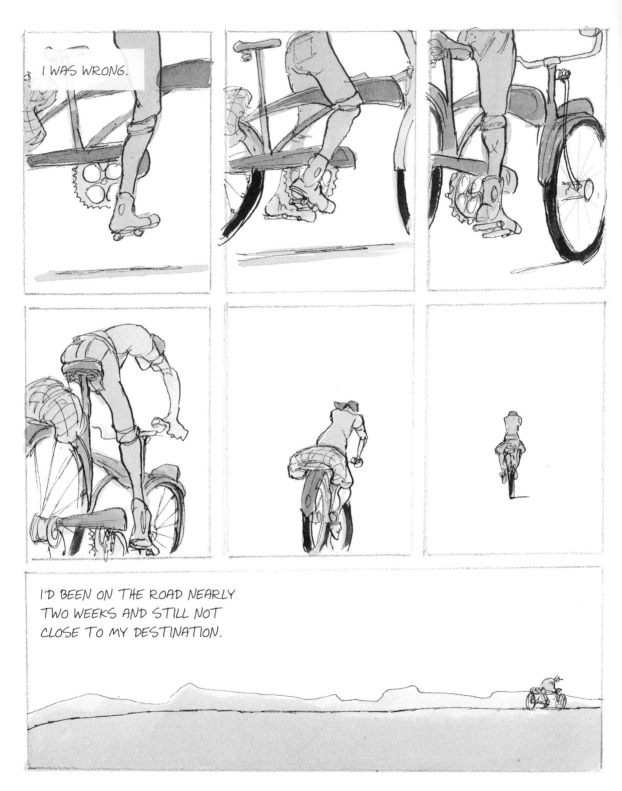

I WAS WRONG.

I'D BEEN ON THE ROAD NEARLY
TWO WEEKS AND STILL NOT
CLOSE TO MY DESTINATION.

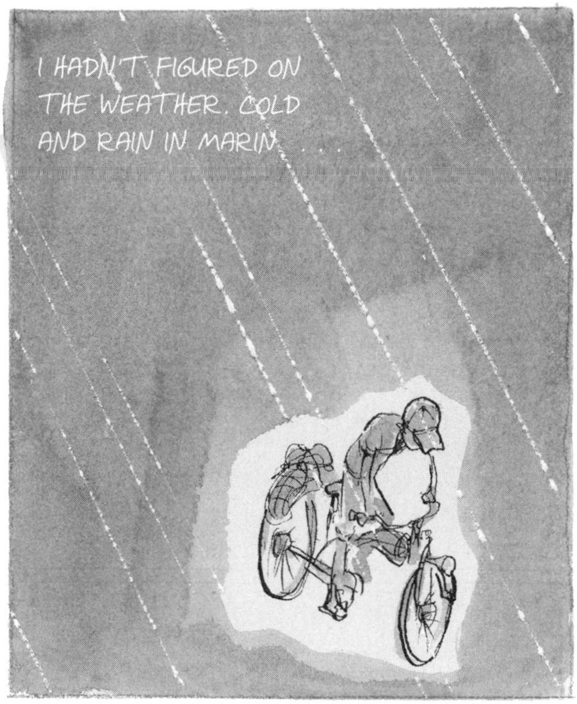
I HADN'T FIGURED ON THE WEATHER. COLD AND RAIN IN MARIN . . .

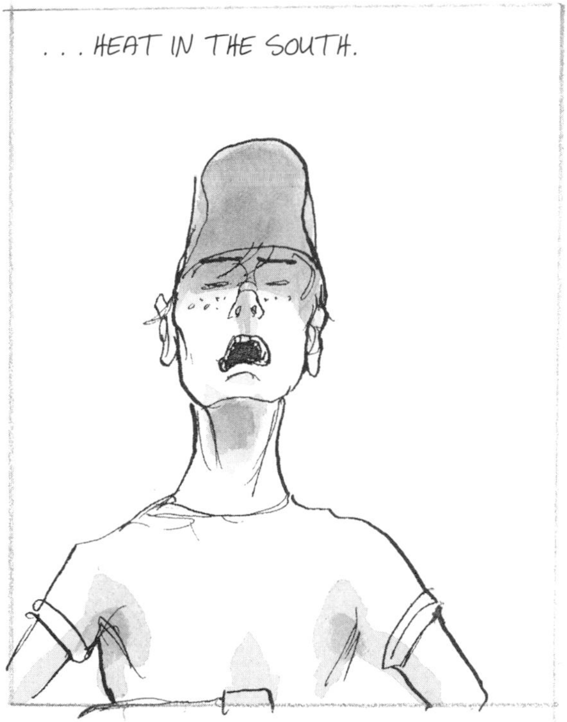
. . . HEAT IN THE SOUTH.

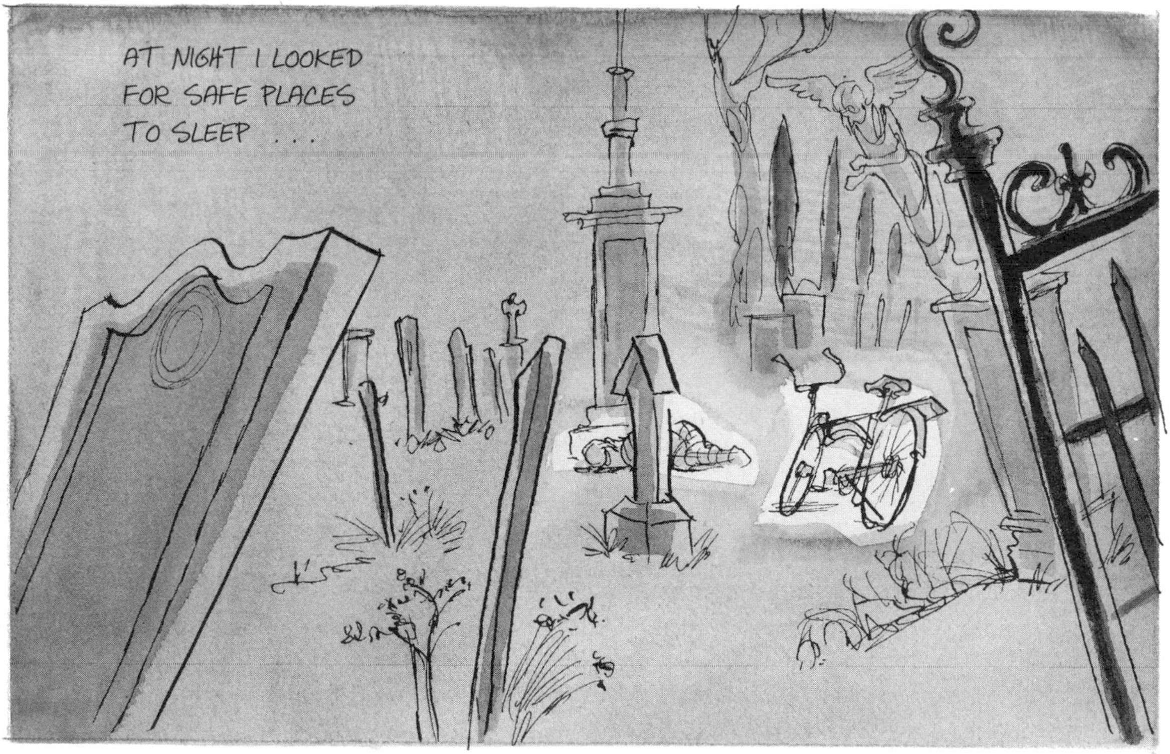
AT NIGHT I LOOKED FOR SAFE PLACES TO SLEEP . . .

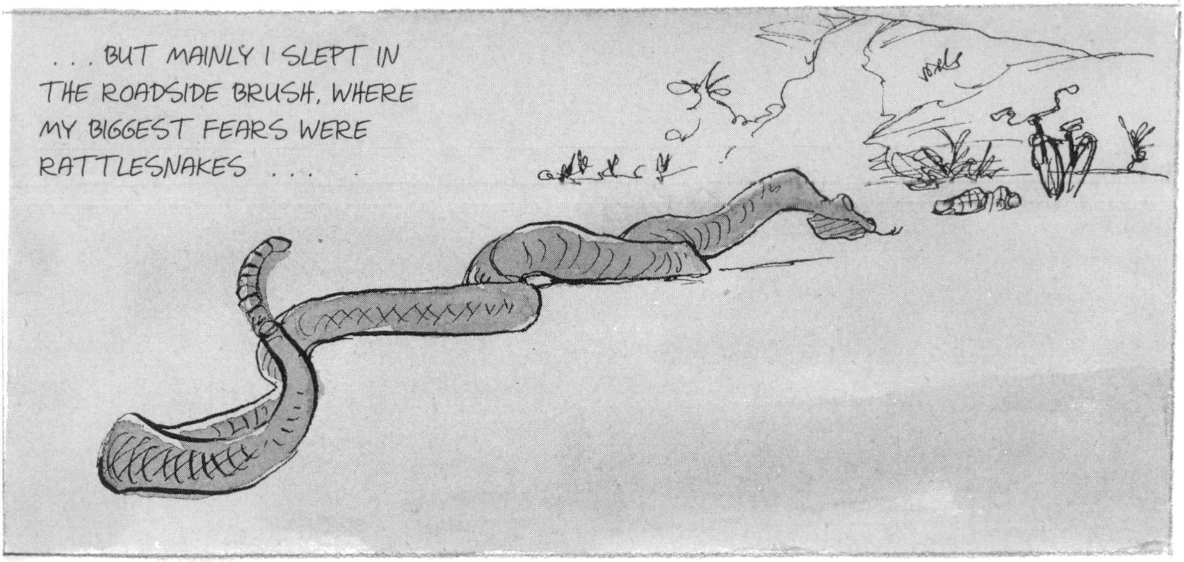
. . . BUT MAINLY I SLEPT IN THE ROADSIDE BRUSH, WHERE MY BIGGEST FEARS WERE RATTLESNAKES . . .

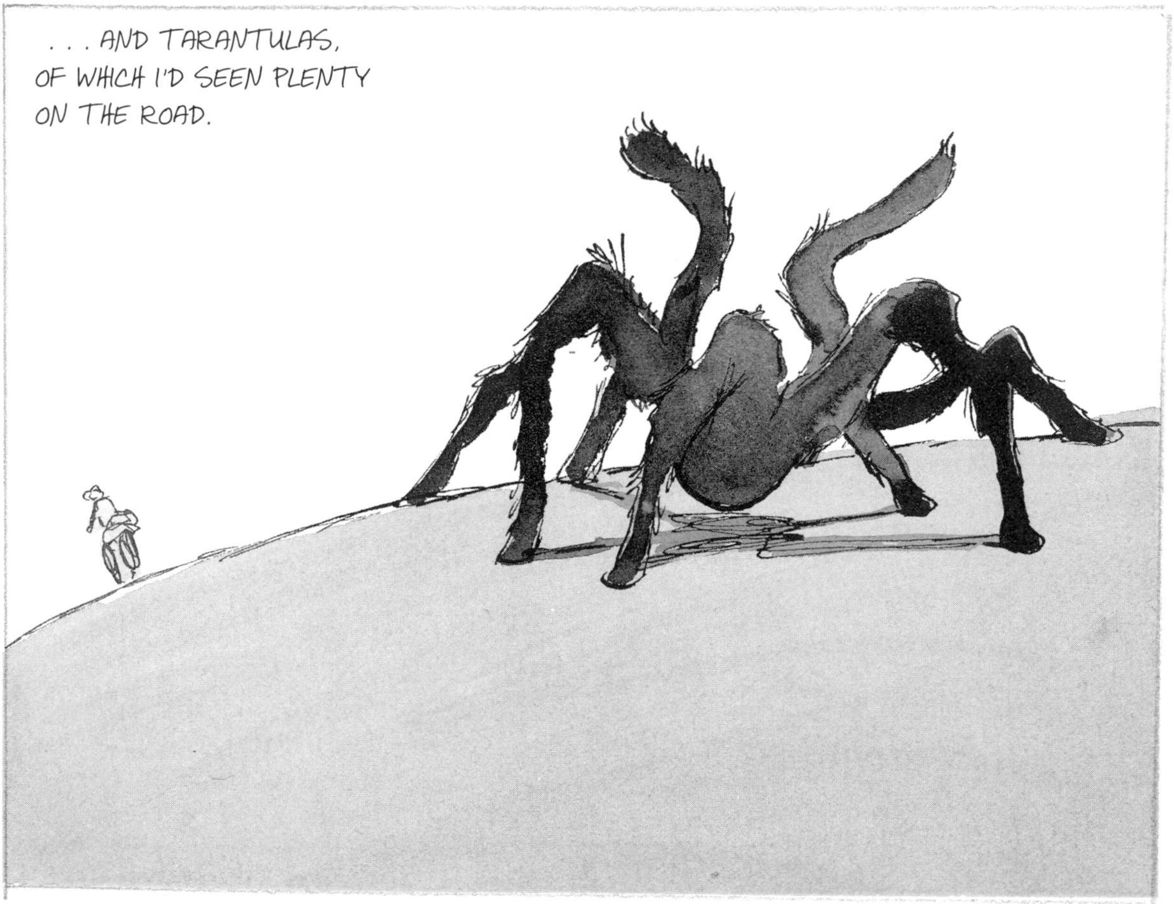
. . . AND TARANTULAS, OF WHICH I'D SEEN PLENTY ON THE ROAD.

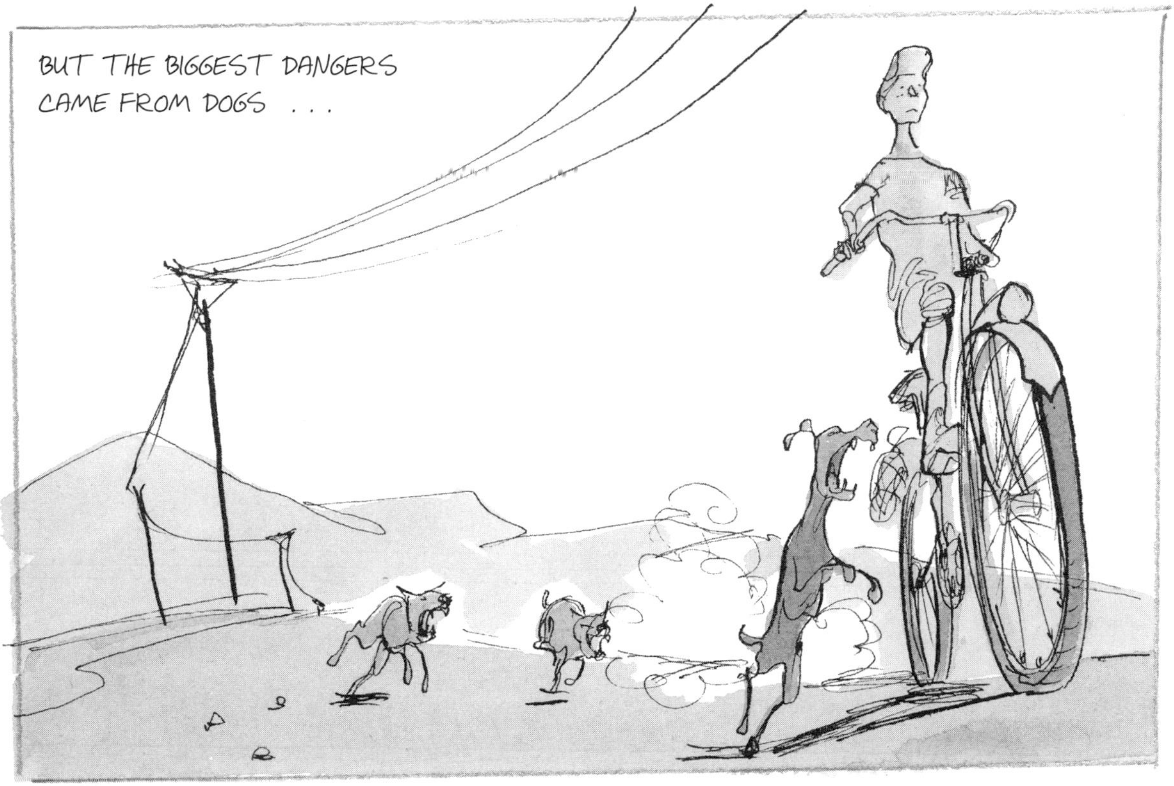
BUT THE BIGGEST DANGERS CAME FROM DOGS . . .

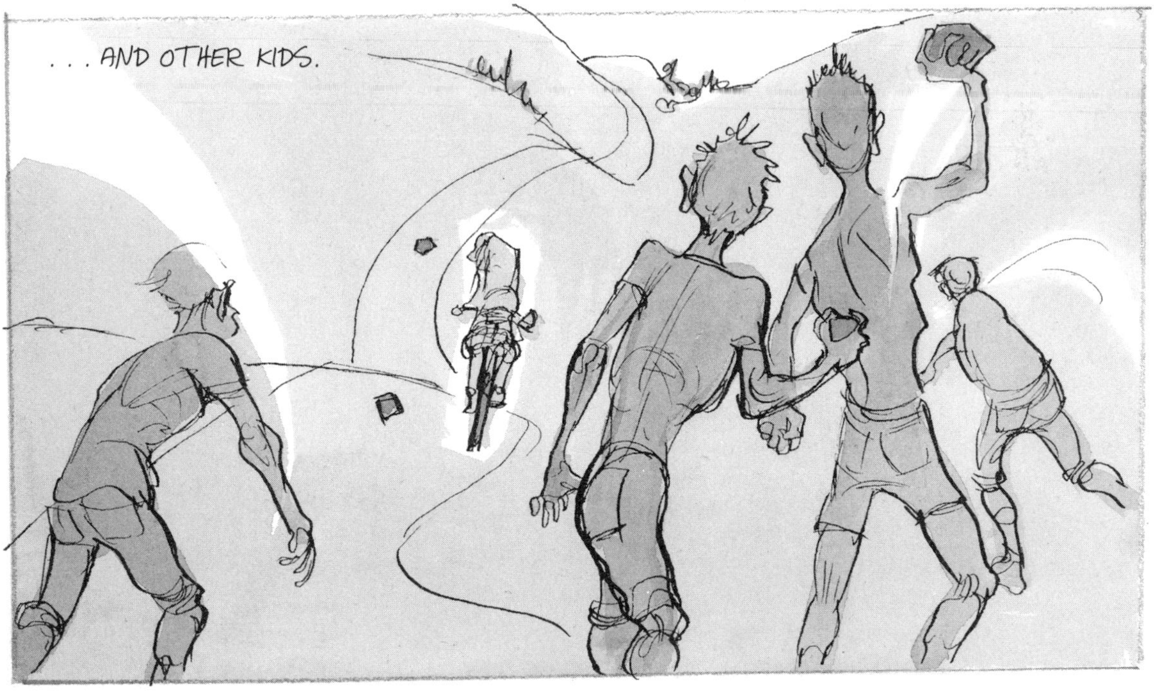
. . . AND OTHER KIDS.

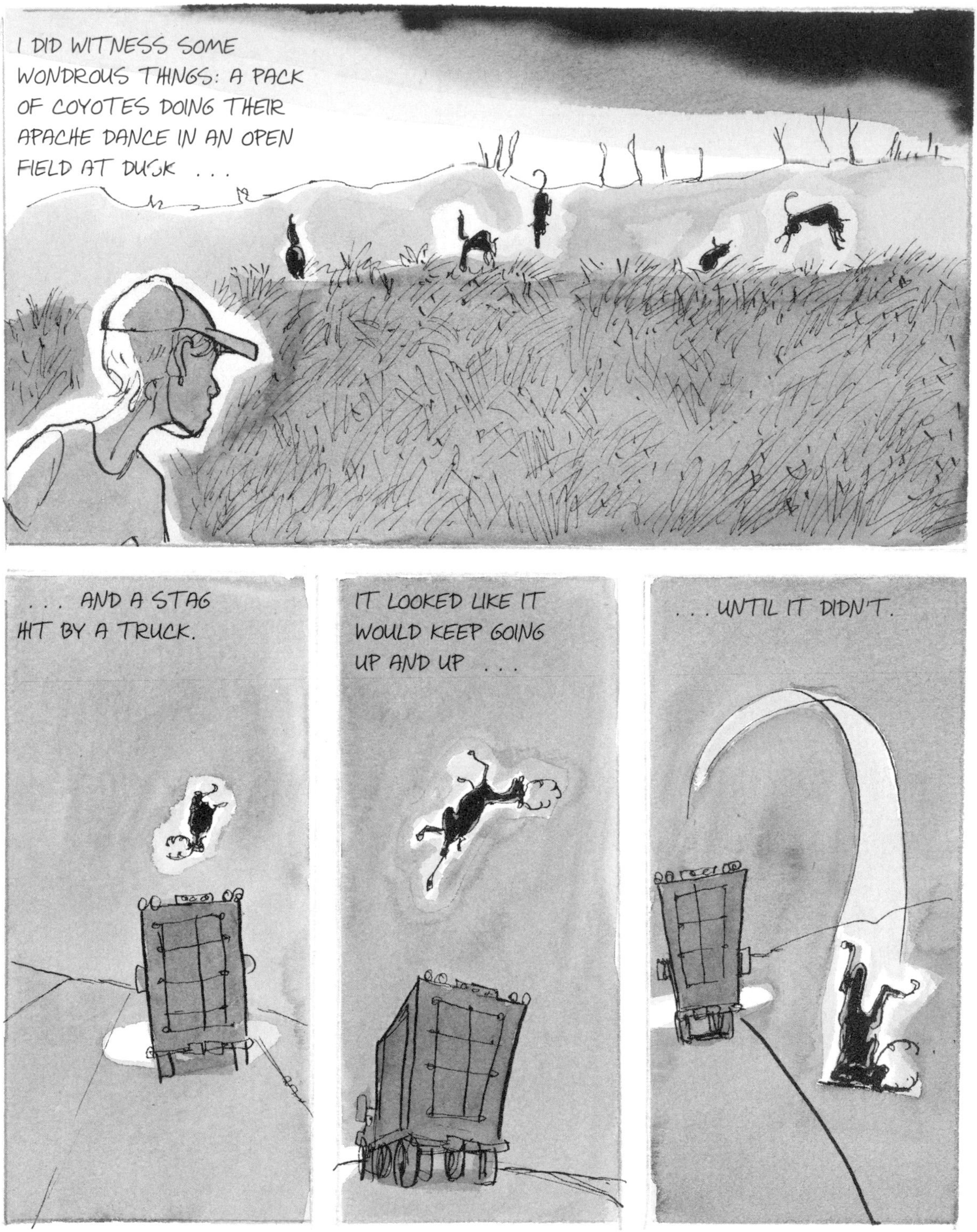
I DID WITNESS SOME WONDROUS THINGS: A PACK OF COYOTES DOING THEIR APACHE DANCE IN AN OPEN FIELD AT DUSK . . .
. . . AND A STAG HIT BY A TRUCK.
IT LOOKED LIKE IT WOULD KEEP GOING UP AND UP . . .
. . . UNTIL IT DIDN'T.

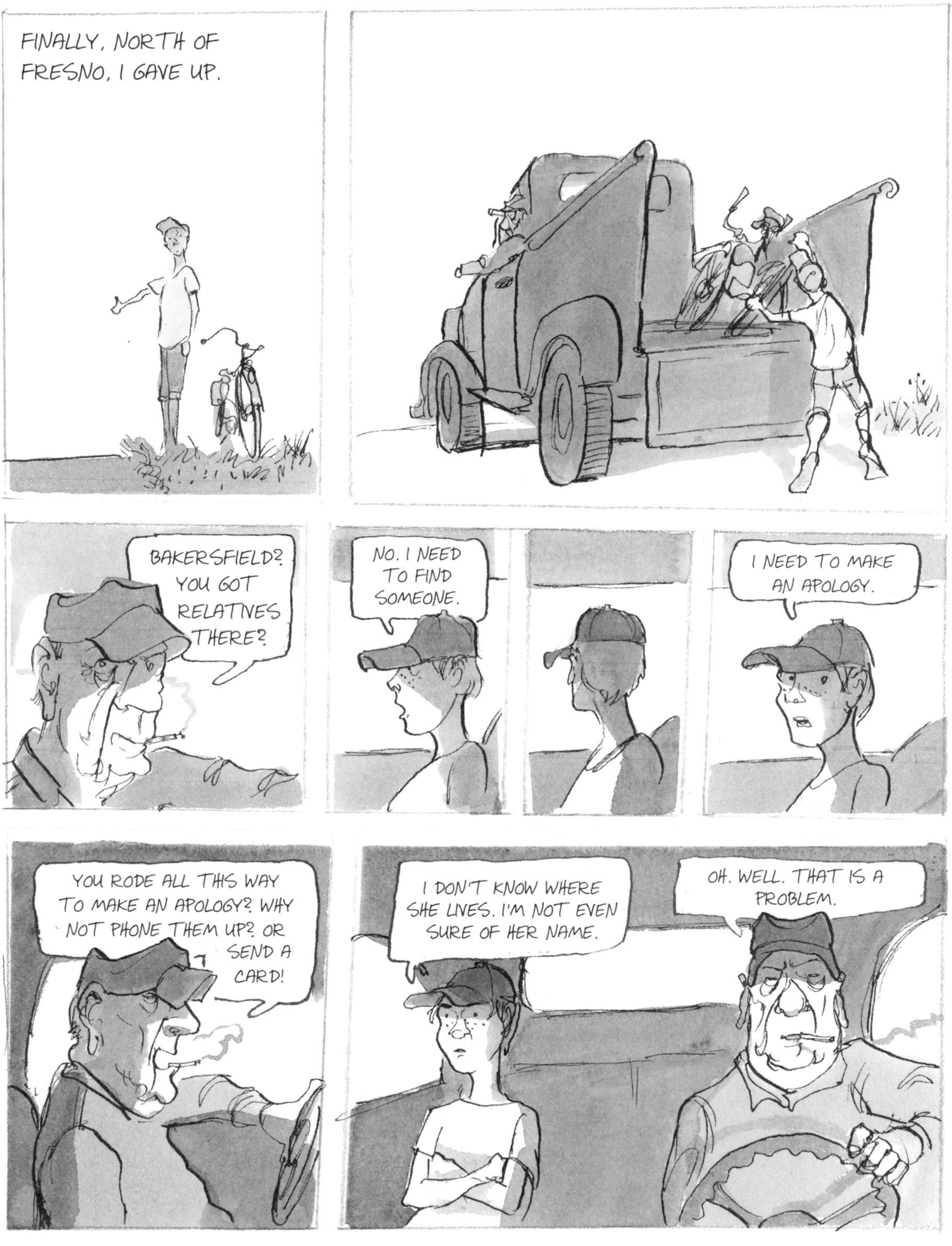
FINALLY, NORTH OF FRESNO, I GAVE UP.
BAKERSFIELD? YOU GOT RELATIVES THERE?
NO. I NEED TO FIND SOMEONE.
I NEED TO MAKE AN APOLOGY.
YOU RODE ALL THIS WAY TO MAKE AN APOLOGY? WHY NOT PHONE THEM UP? OR SEND A CARD!
I DON'T KNOW WHERE SHE LIVES. I'M NOT EVEN SURE OF HER NAME.
OH. WELL. THAT IS A PROBLEM.

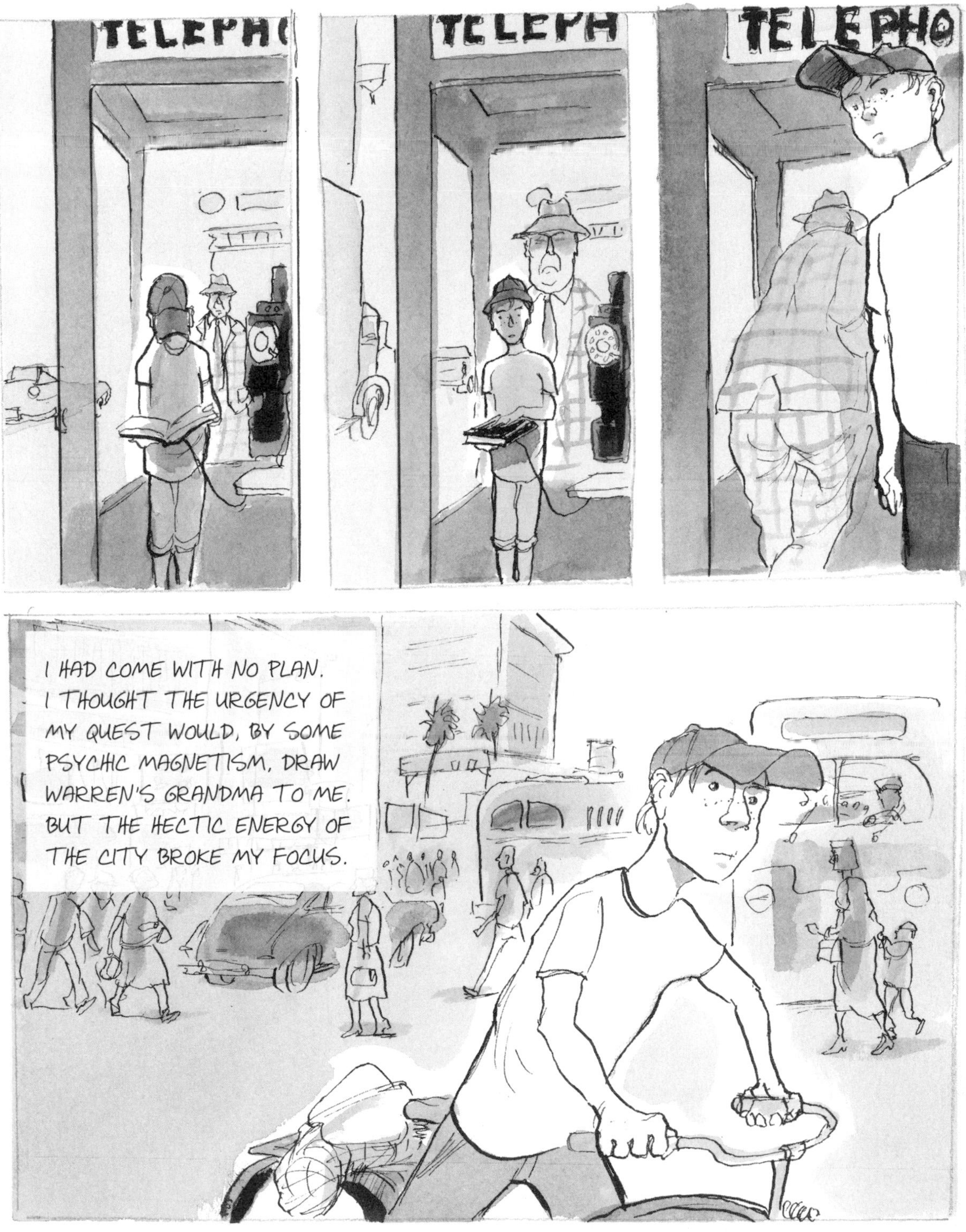
TELEPHO
TELEPH
TELEPHO
I HAD COME WITH NO PLAN. I THOUGHT THE URGENCY OF MY QUEST WOULD, BY SOME PSYCHIC MAGNETISM, DRAW WARREN'S GRANDMA TO ME. BUT THE HECTIC ENERGY OF THE CITY BROKE MY FOCUS.

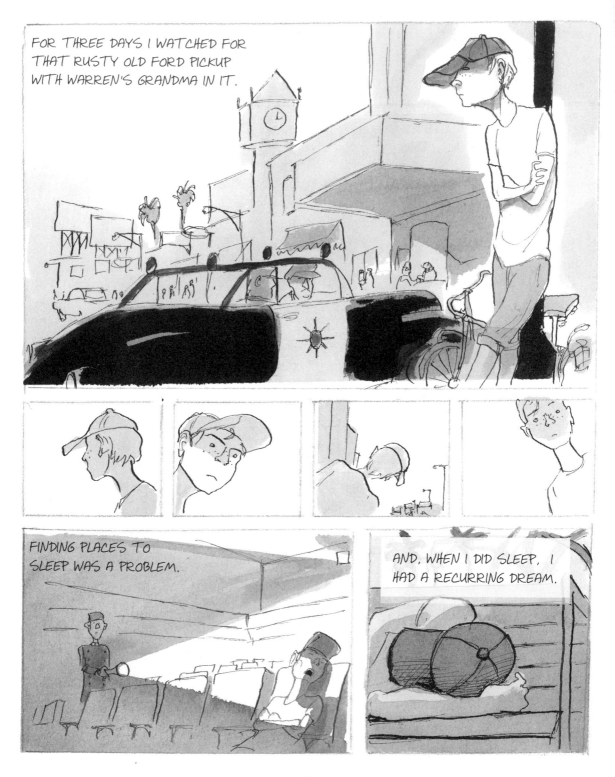

FOR THREE DAYS I WATCHED FOR THAT RUSTY OLD FORD PICKUP WITH WARREN'S GRANDMA IN IT.

FINDING PLACES TO SLEEP WAS A PROBLEM.

AND, WHEN I DID SLEEP, I HAD A RECURRING DREAM.

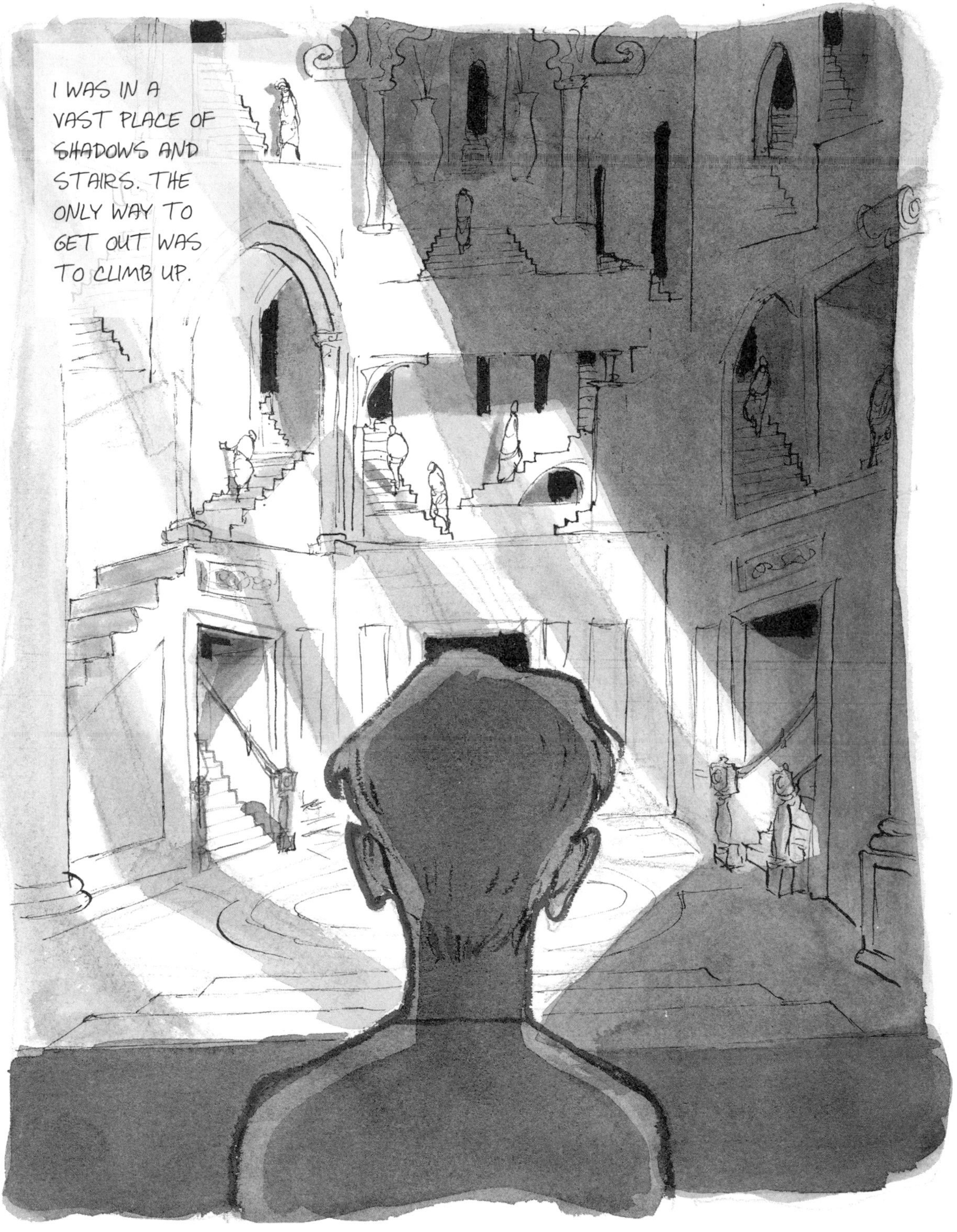
I WAS IN A VAST PLACE OF SHADOWS AND STAIRS. THE ONLY WAY TO GET OUT WAS TO CLIMB UP.

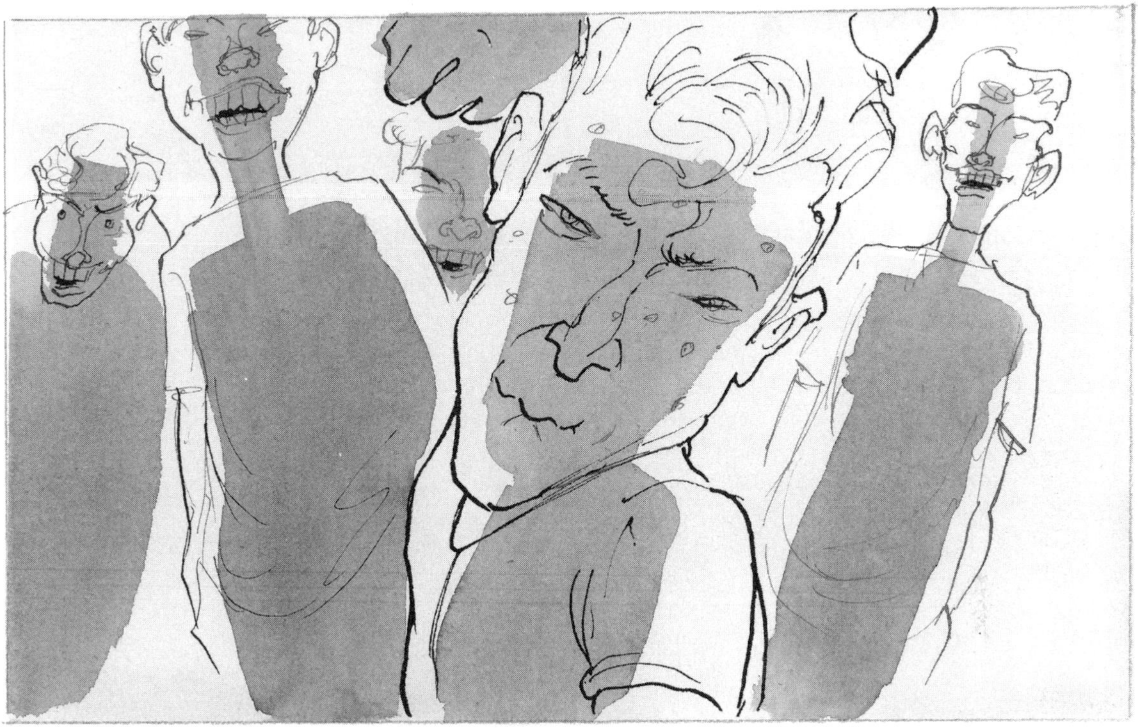

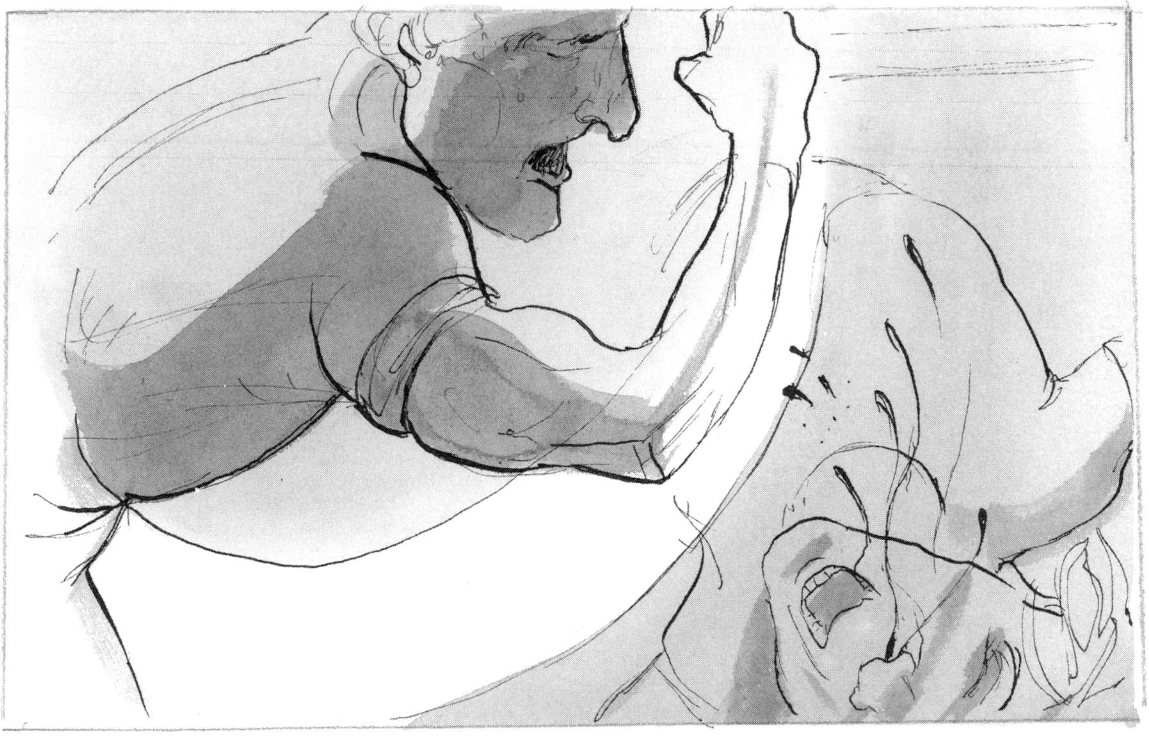

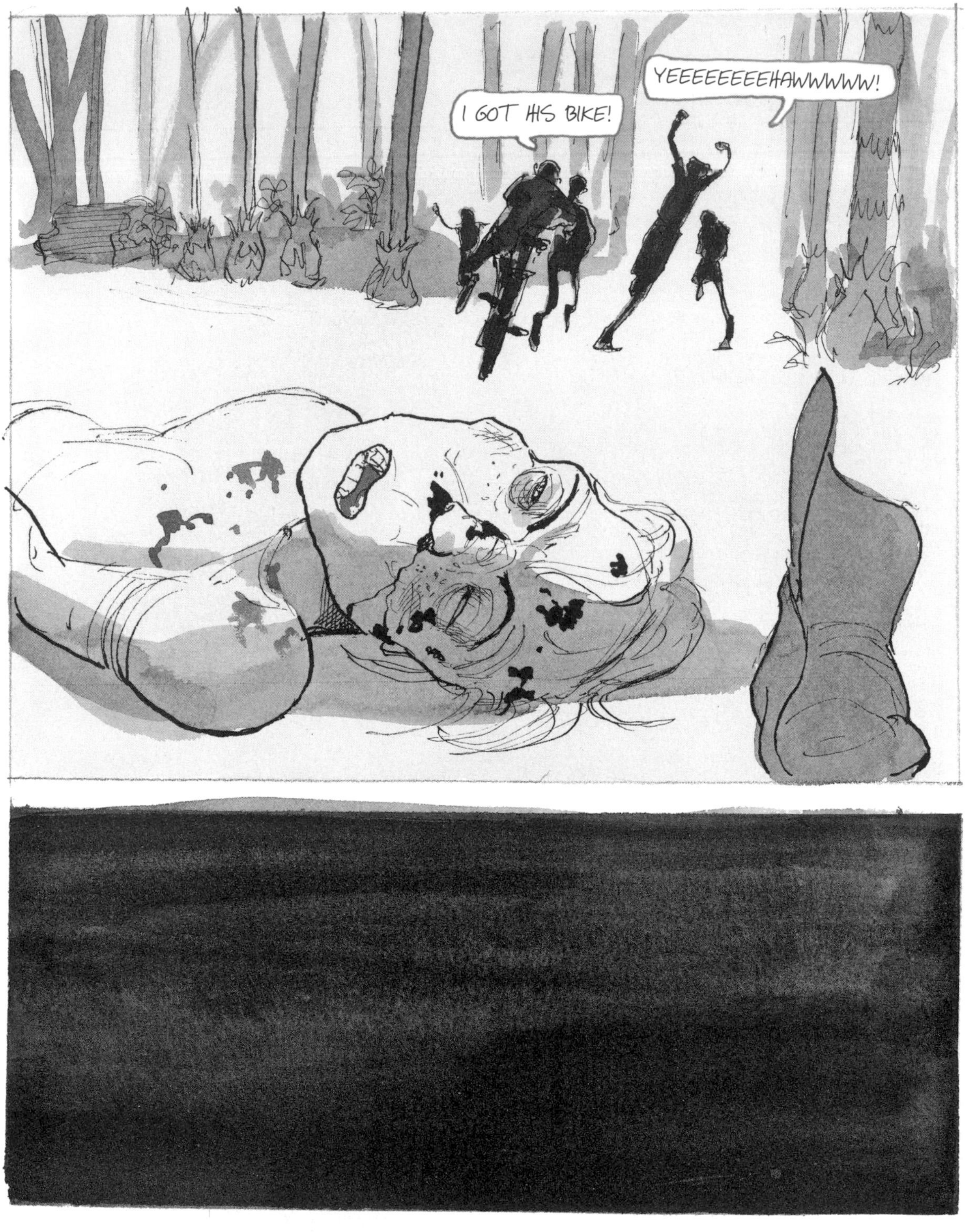
I GOT HIS BIKE!
YEEEEEEEEEHAWWWWW!

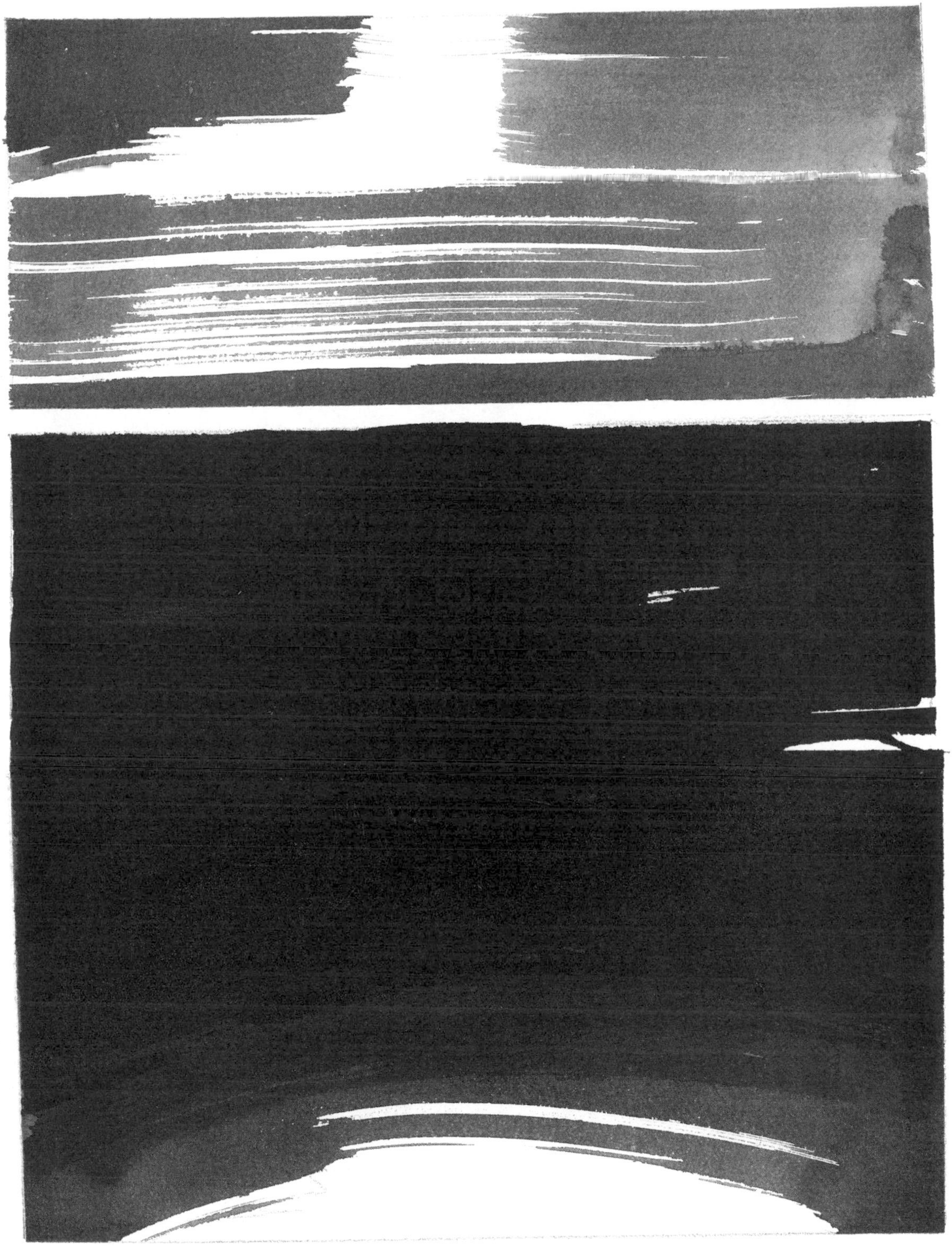

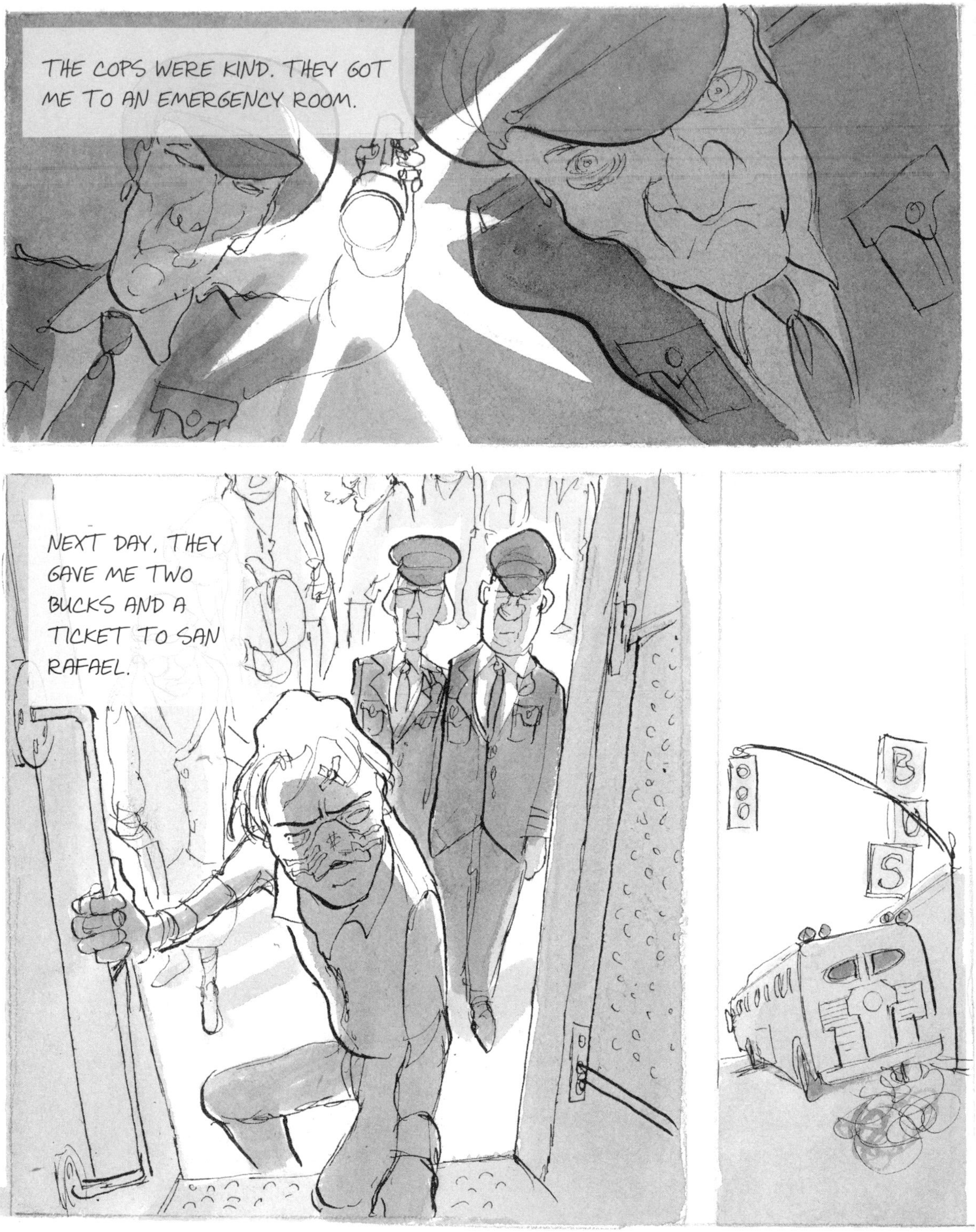
THE COPS WERE KIND. THEY GOT ME TO AN EMERGENCY ROOM.
NEXT DAY, THEY GAVE ME TWO BUCKS AND A TICKET TO SAN RAFAEL.
BUS

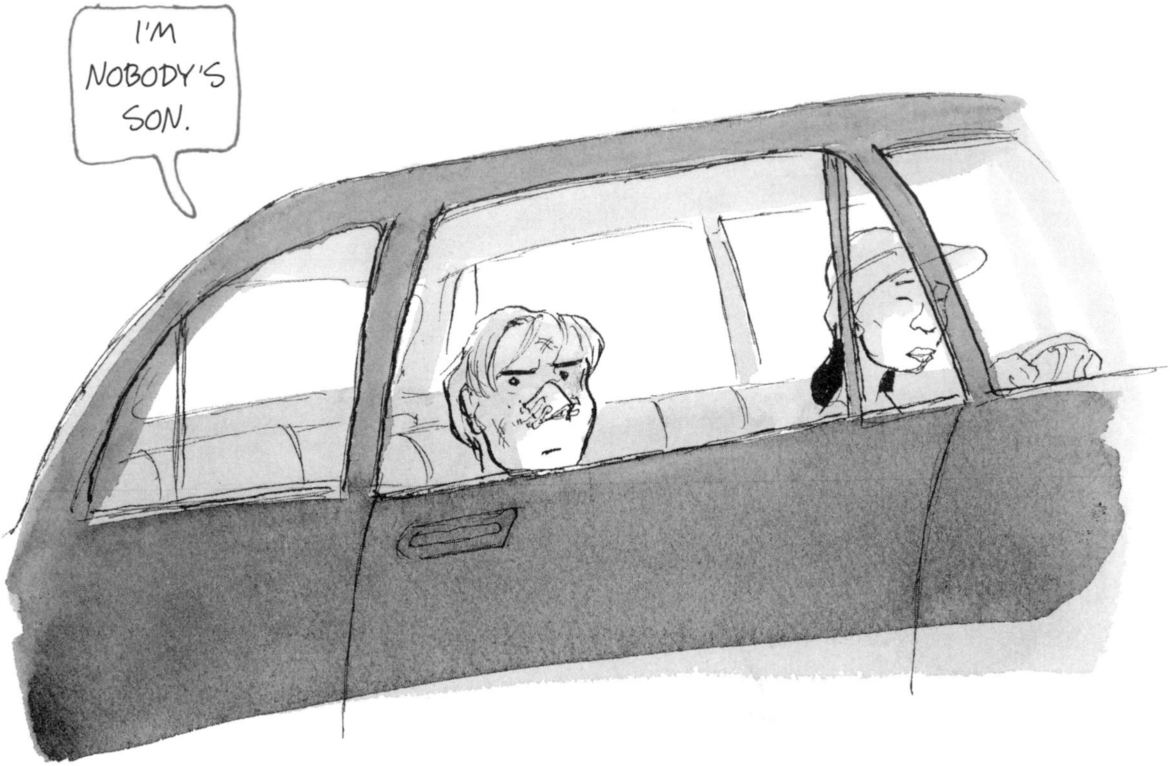
I'M NOBODY'S SON.

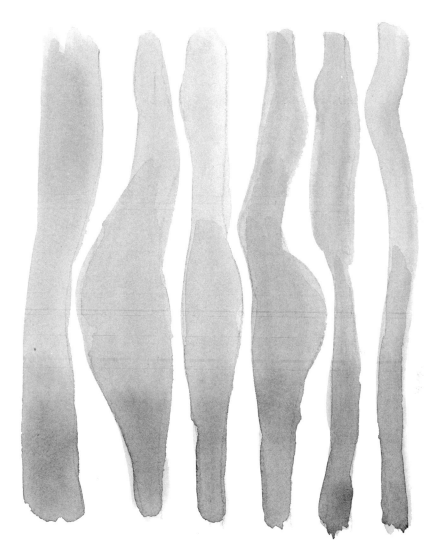

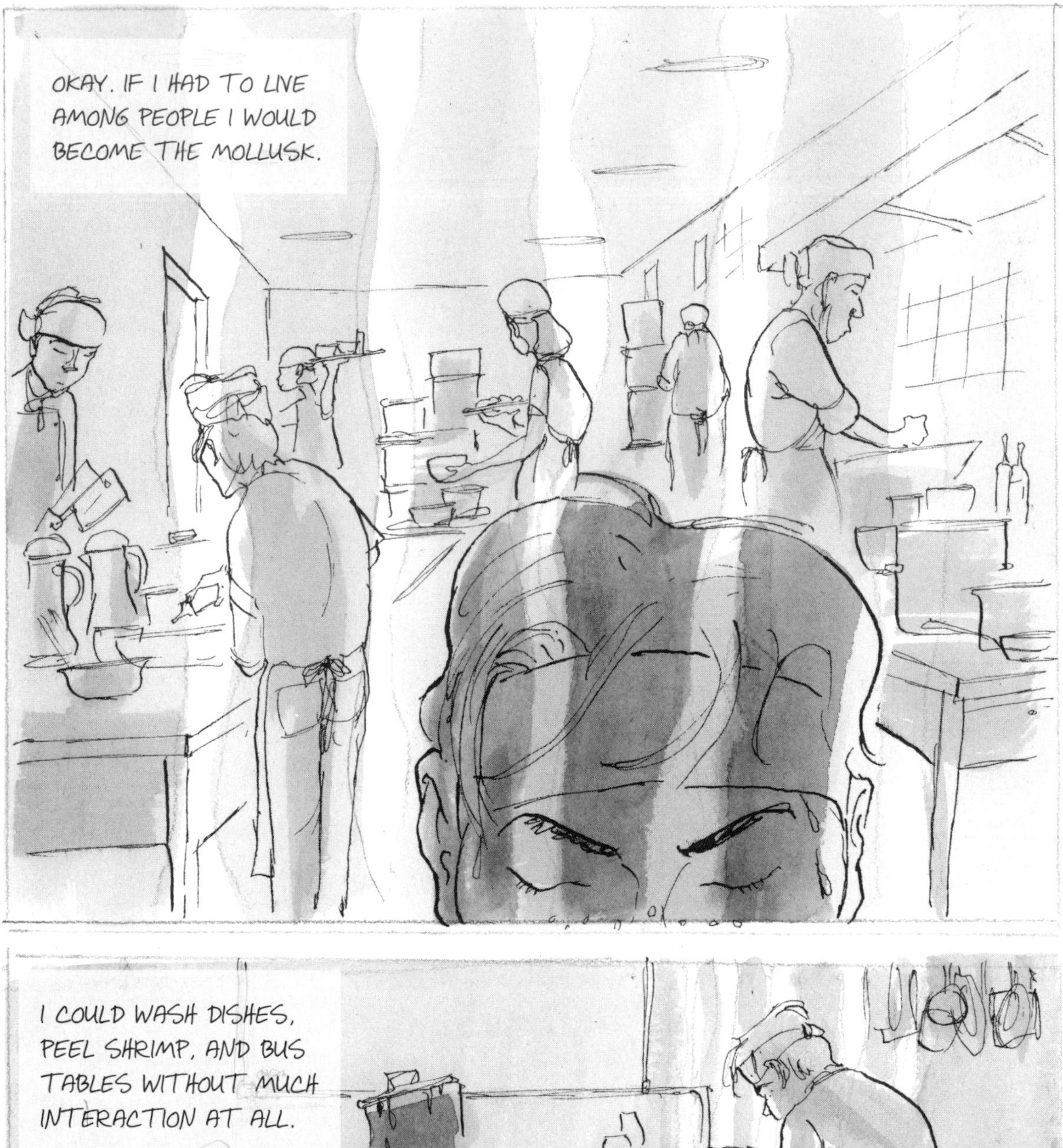
OKAY. IF I HAD TO LIVE AMONG PEOPLE I WOULD BECOME THE MOLLUSK.

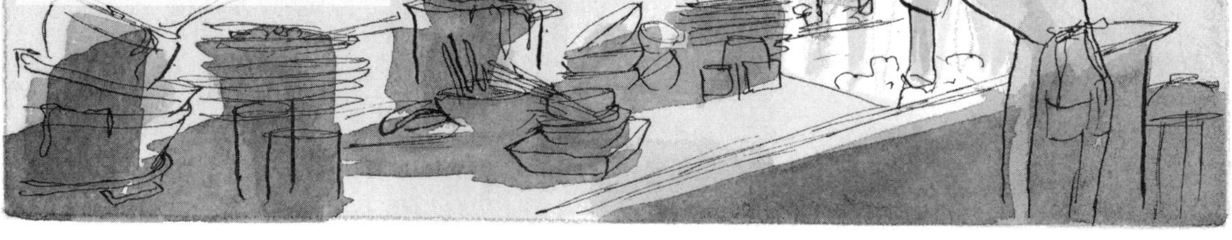
I COULD WASH DISHES, PEEL SHRIMP, AND BUS TABLES WITHOUT MUCH INTERACTION AT ALL.

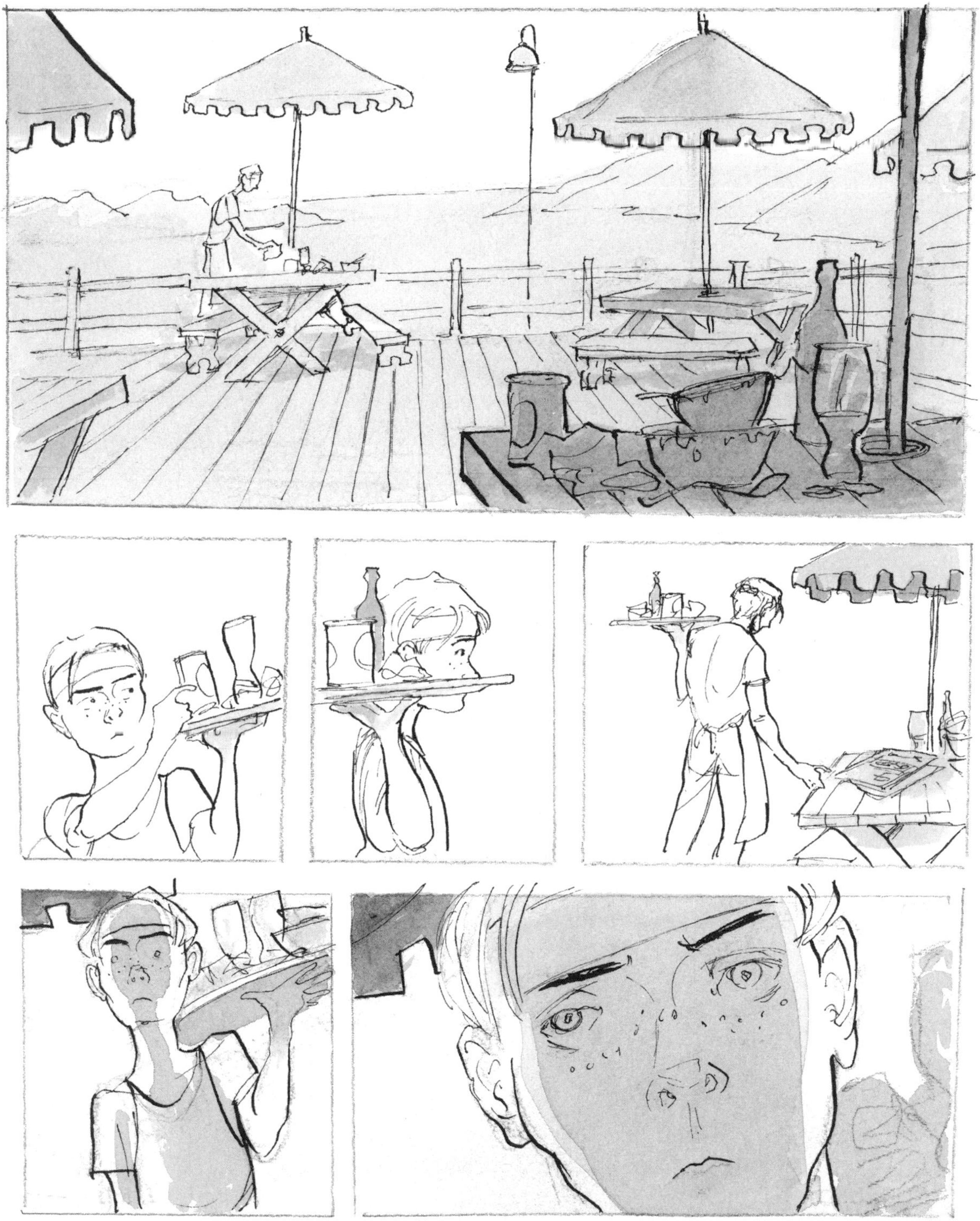

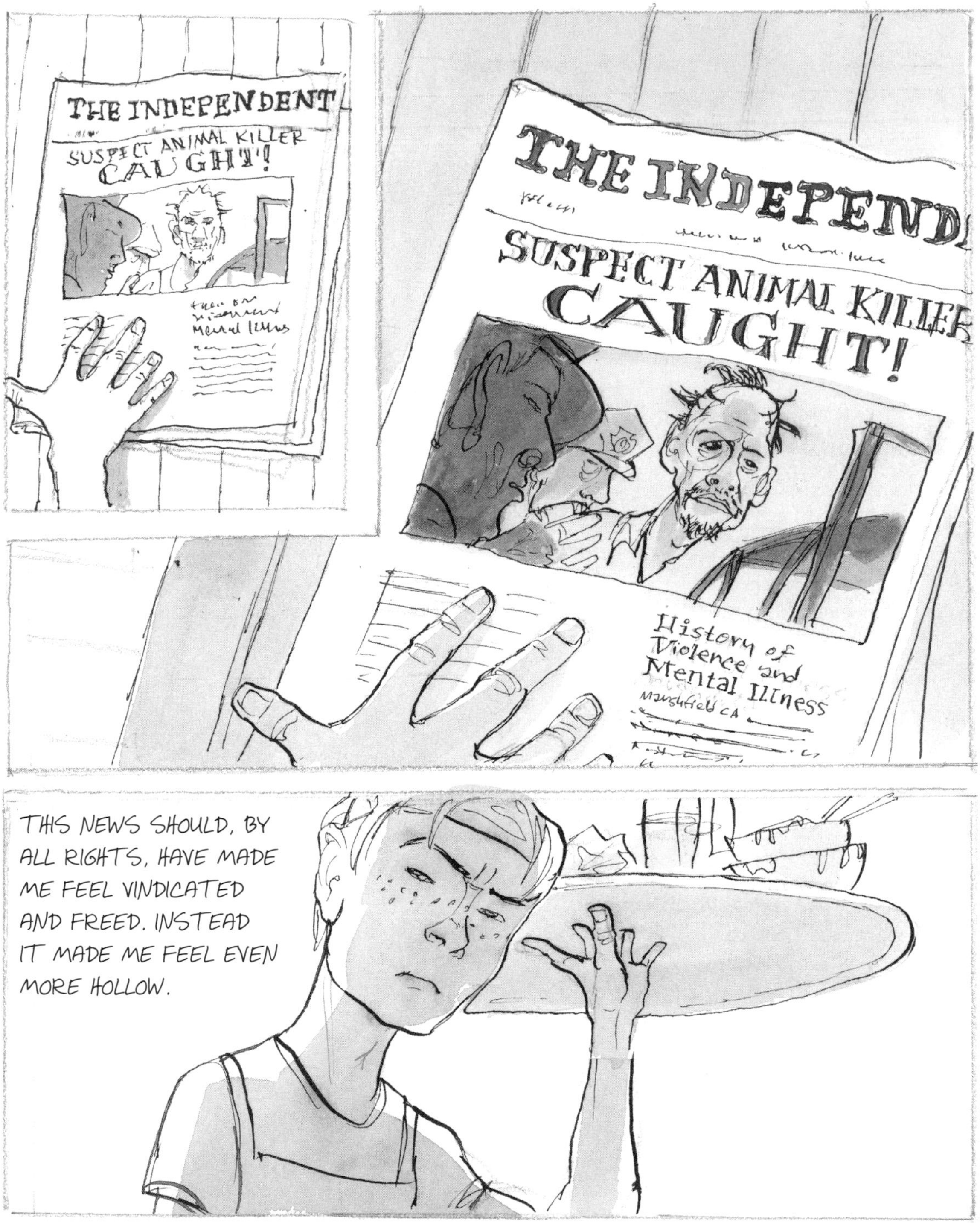
THE INDEPENDENT
SUSPECT ANIMAL KILLER CAUGHT!
SUSPECT ANIMAL KILLER CAUGHT!
History of Violence and Mental Illness
THIS NEWS SHOULD, BY ALL RIGHTS, HAVE MADE ME FEEL VINDICATED AND FREED. INSTEAD IT MADE ME FEEL EVEN MORE HOLLOW.

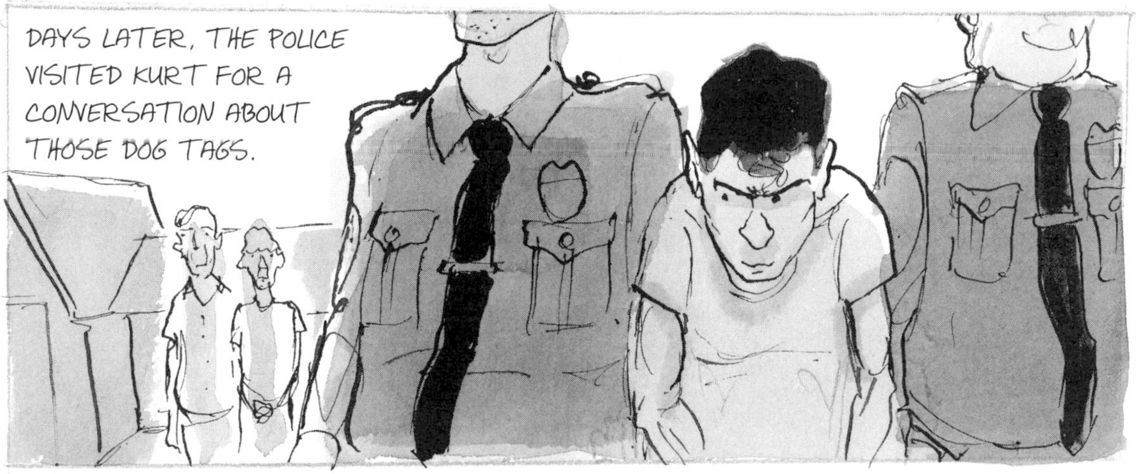
DAYS LATER, THE POLICE VISITED KURT FOR A CONVERSATION ABOUT THOSE DOG TAGS.

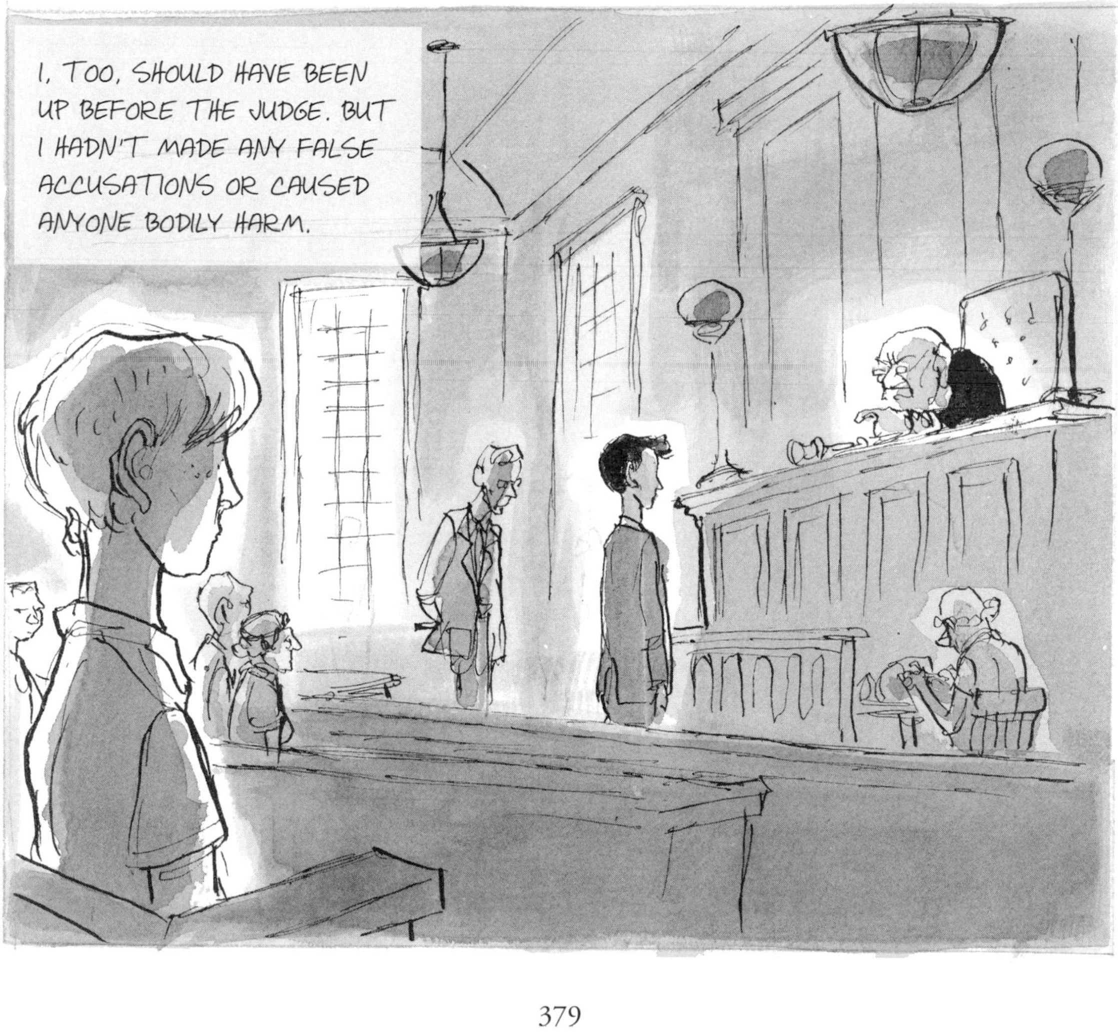
I, TOO, SHOULD HAVE BEEN UP BEFORE THE JUDGE. BUT I HADN'T MADE ANY FALSE ACCUSATIONS OR CAUSED ANYONE BODILY HARM.

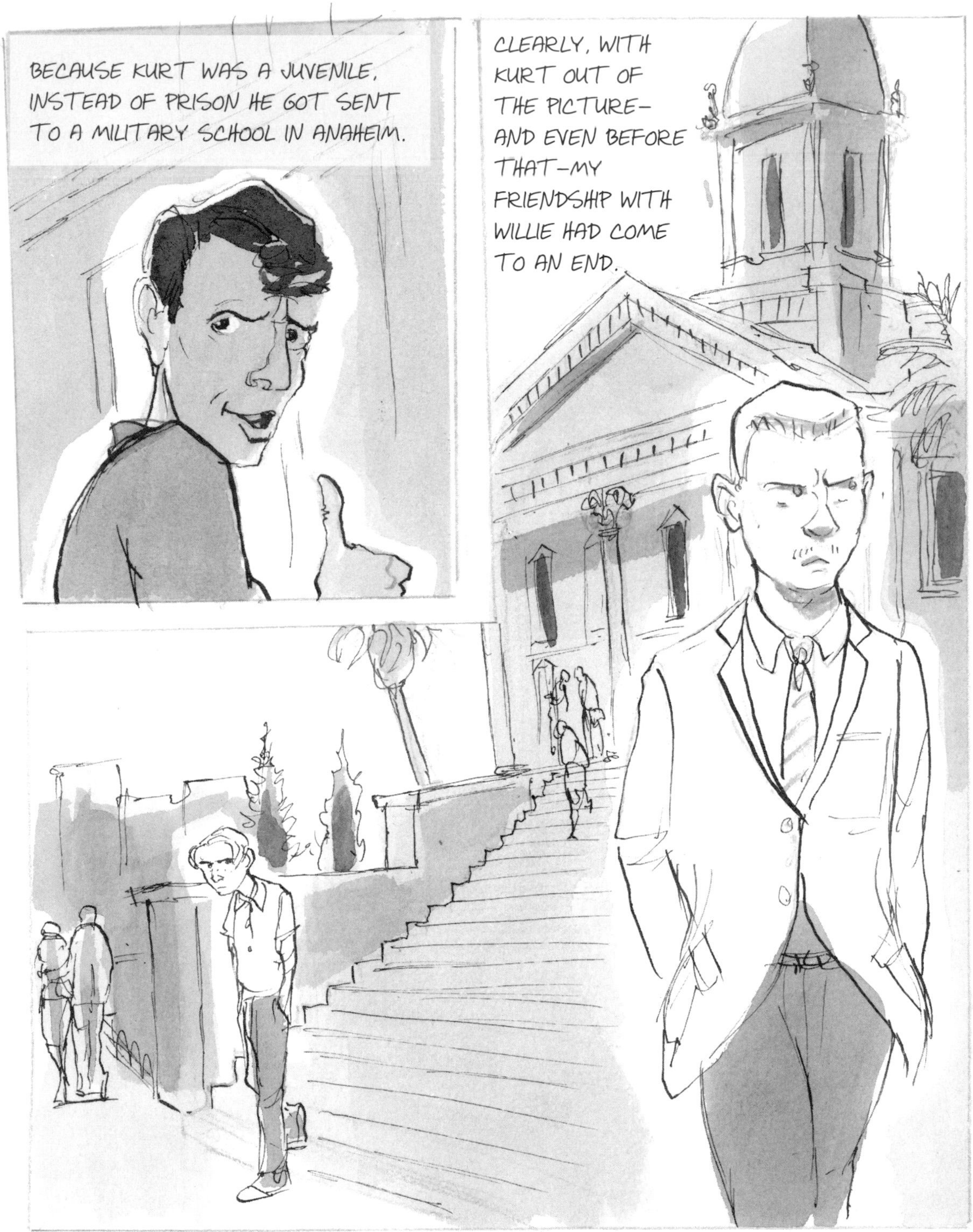
BECAUSE KURT WAS A JUVENILE, INSTEAD OF PRISON HE GOT SENT TO A MILITARY SCHOOL IN ANAHEIM.
CLEARLY, WITH KURT OUT OF THE PICTURE— AND EVEN BEFORE THAT—MY FRIENDSHIP WITH WILLIE HAD COME TO AN END.

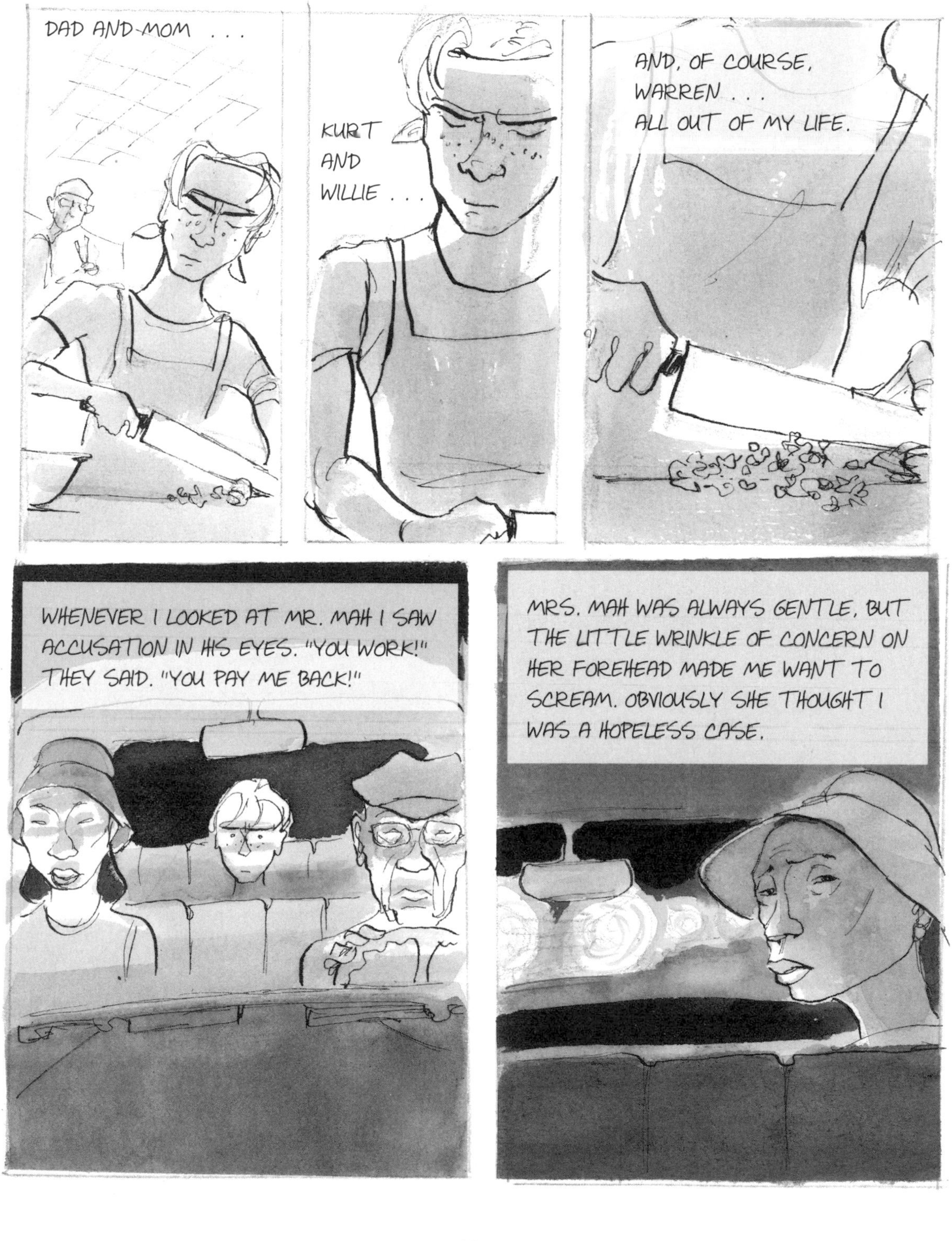

DAD AND MOM . . .
KURT AND WILLIE . . .
AND, OF COURSE, WARREN . . . ALL OUT OF MY LIFE.
WHENEVER I LOOKED AT MR. MAH I SAW ACCUSATION IN HIS EYES. "YOU WORK!" THEY SAID. "YOU PAY ME BACK!"
MRS. MAH WAS ALWAYS GENTLE, BUT THE LITTLE WRINKLE OF CONCERN ON HER FOREHEAD MADE ME WANT TO SCREAM. OBVIOUSLY SHE THOUGHT I WAS A HOPELESS CASE.

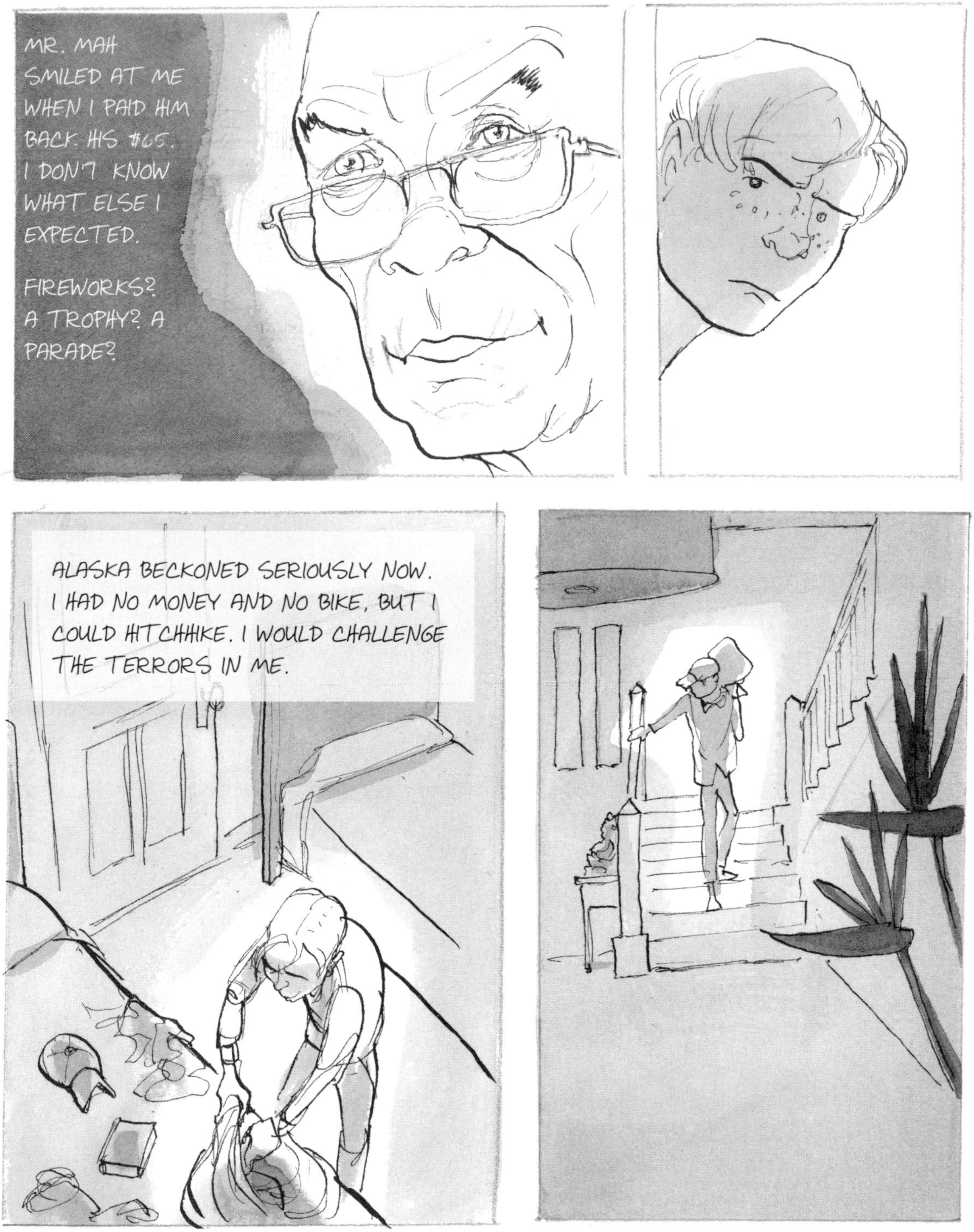
MR. MAH SMILED AT ME WHEN I PAID HIM BACK HIS $65. I DON'T KNOW WHAT ELSE I EXPECTED.
FIREWORKS? A TROPHY? A PARADE?
ALASKA BECKONED SERIOUSLY NOW. I HAD NO MONEY AND NO BIKE, BUT I COULD HITCHHIKE. I WOULD CHALLENGE THE TERRORS IN ME.

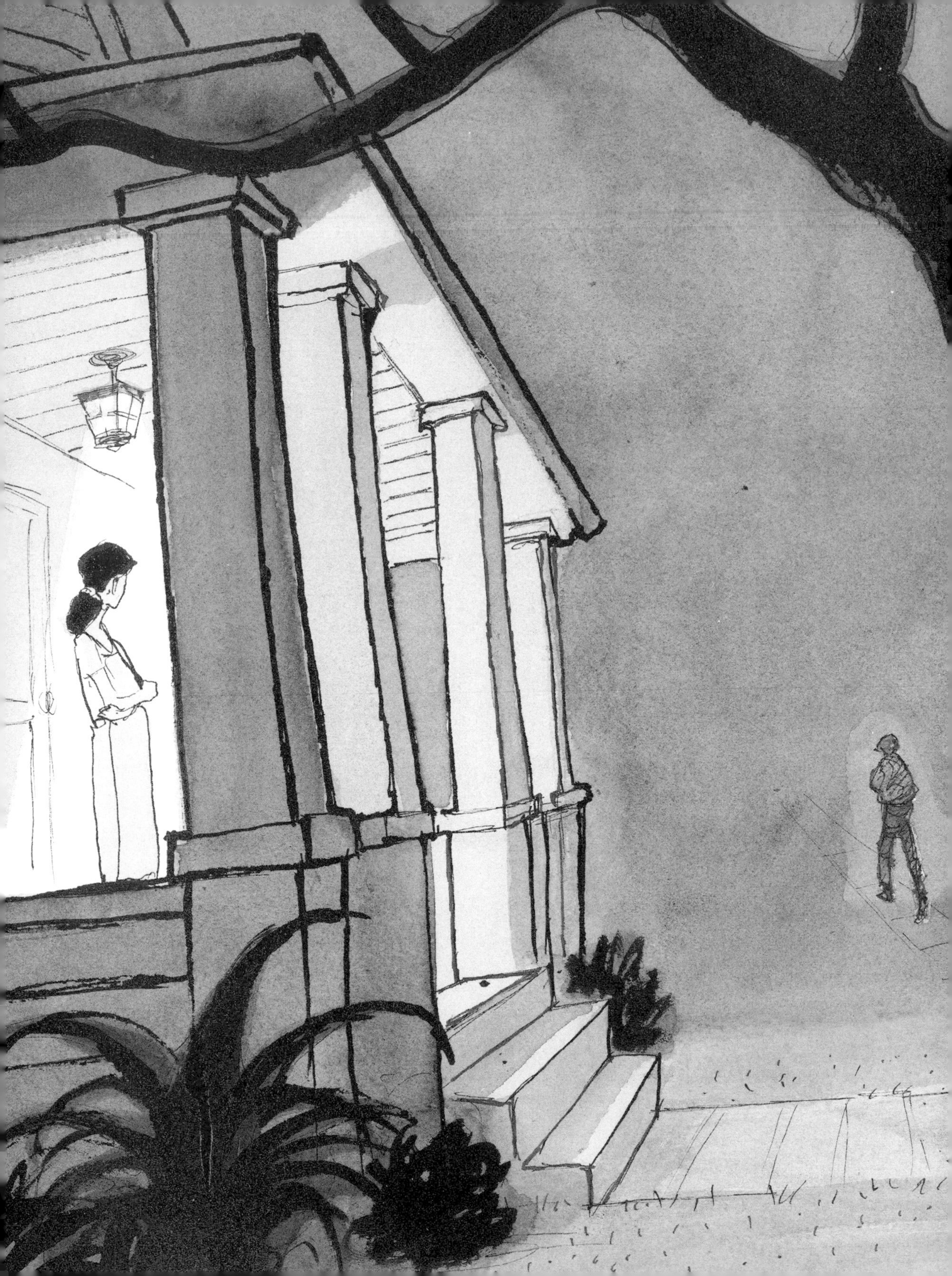

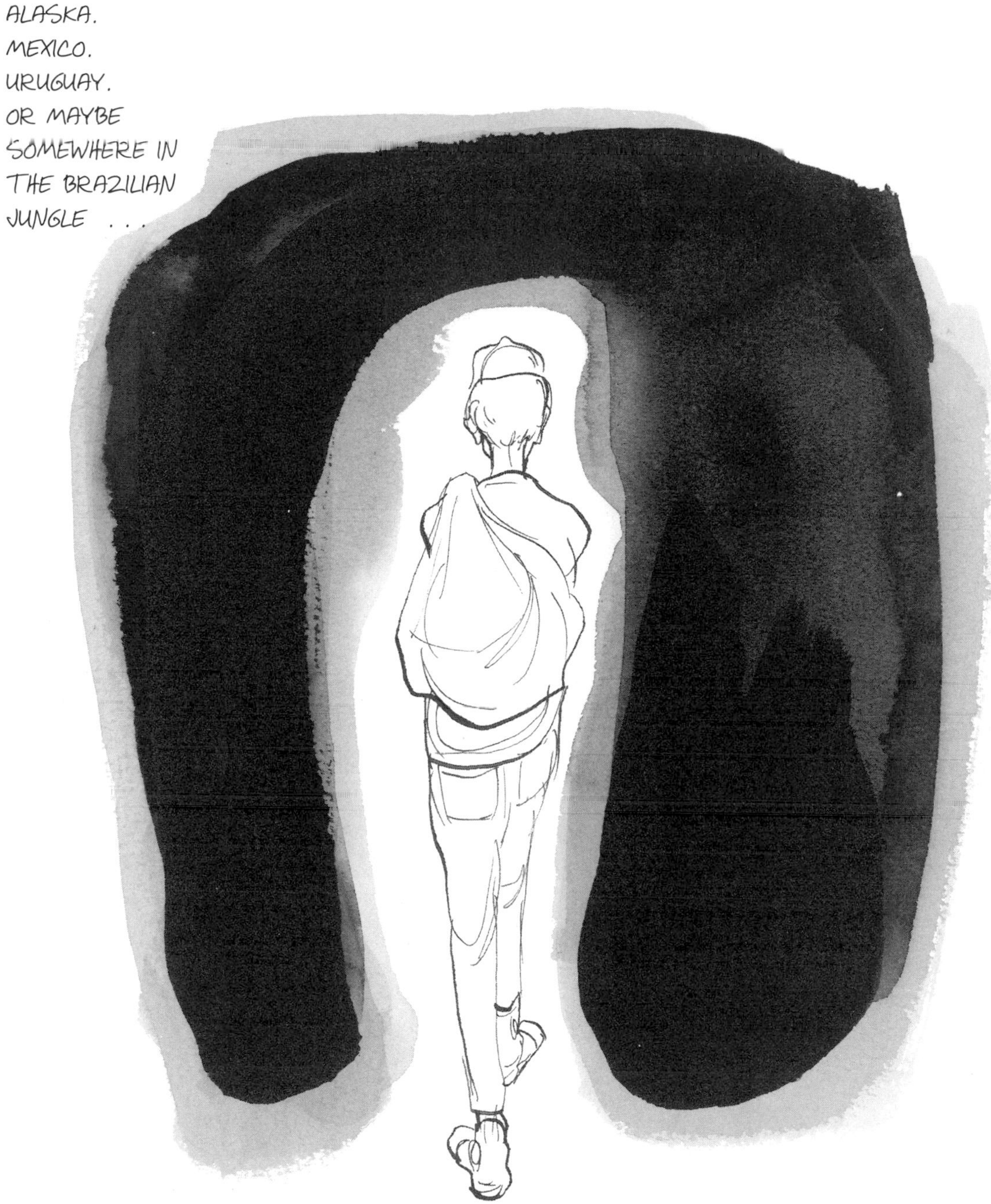
ALASKA.
MEXICO.
URUGUAY.
OR MAYBE
SOMEWHERE IN
THE BRAZILIAN
JUNGLE . . .

CHAPTER SEVENTEEN

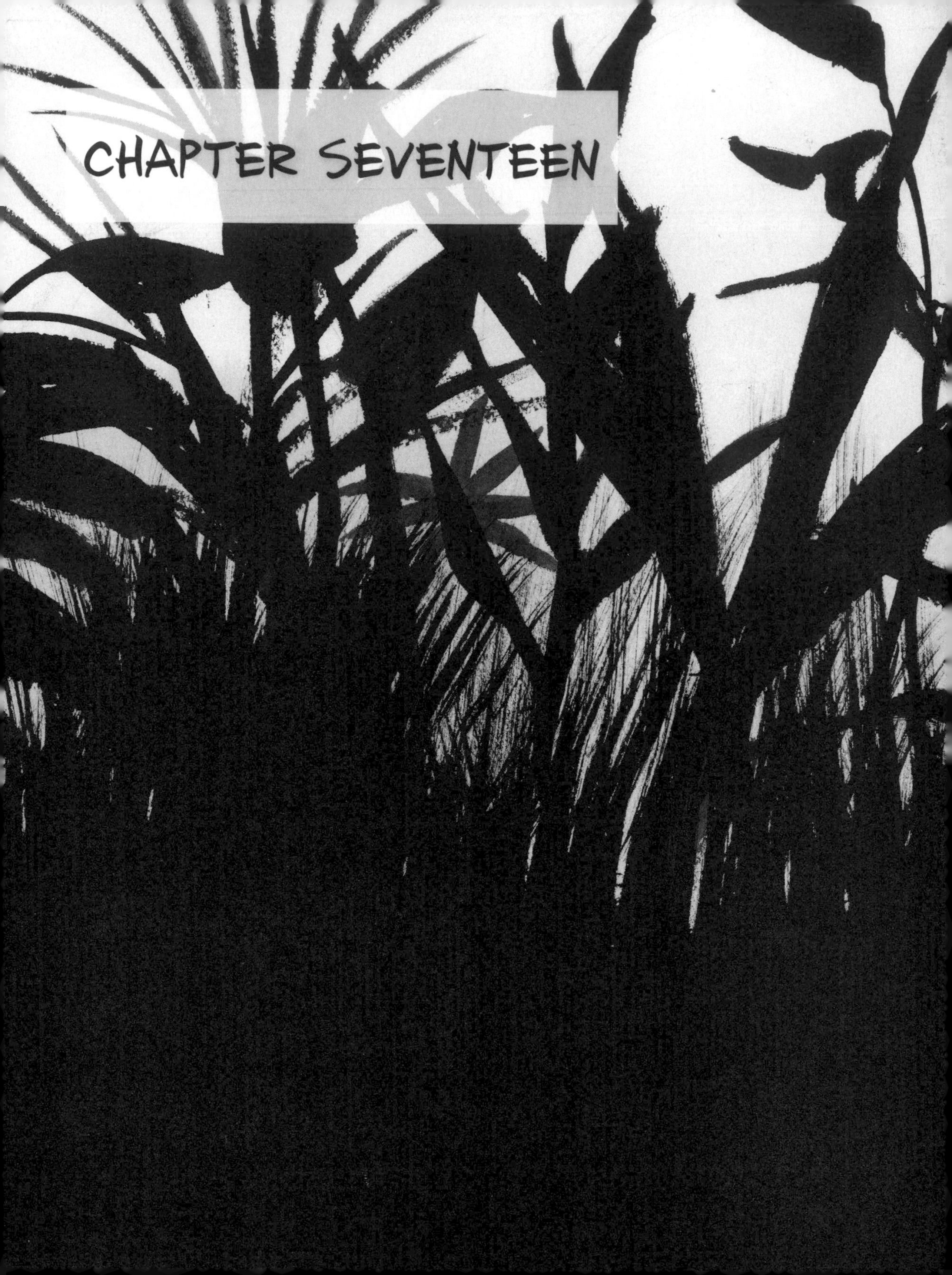

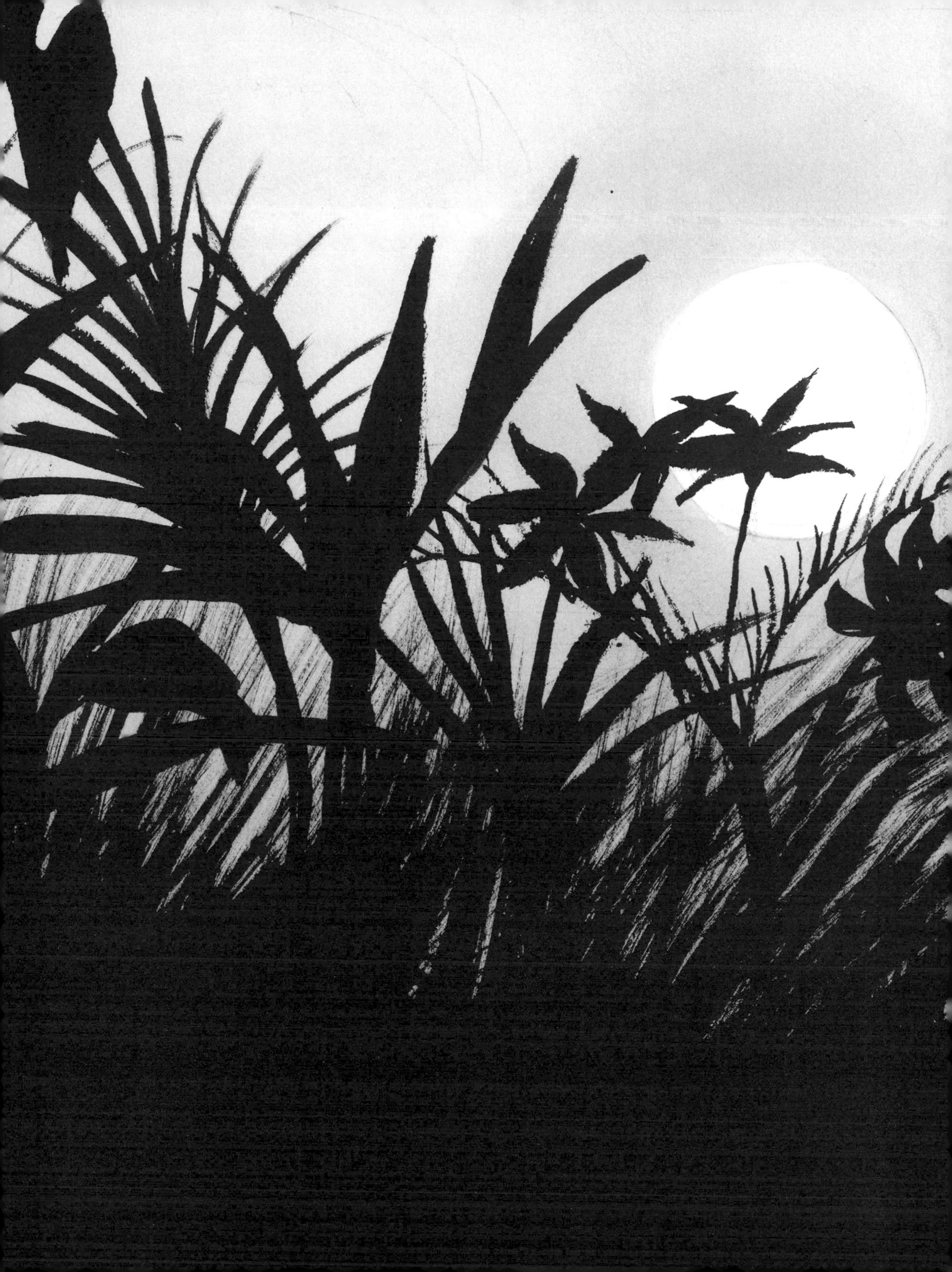

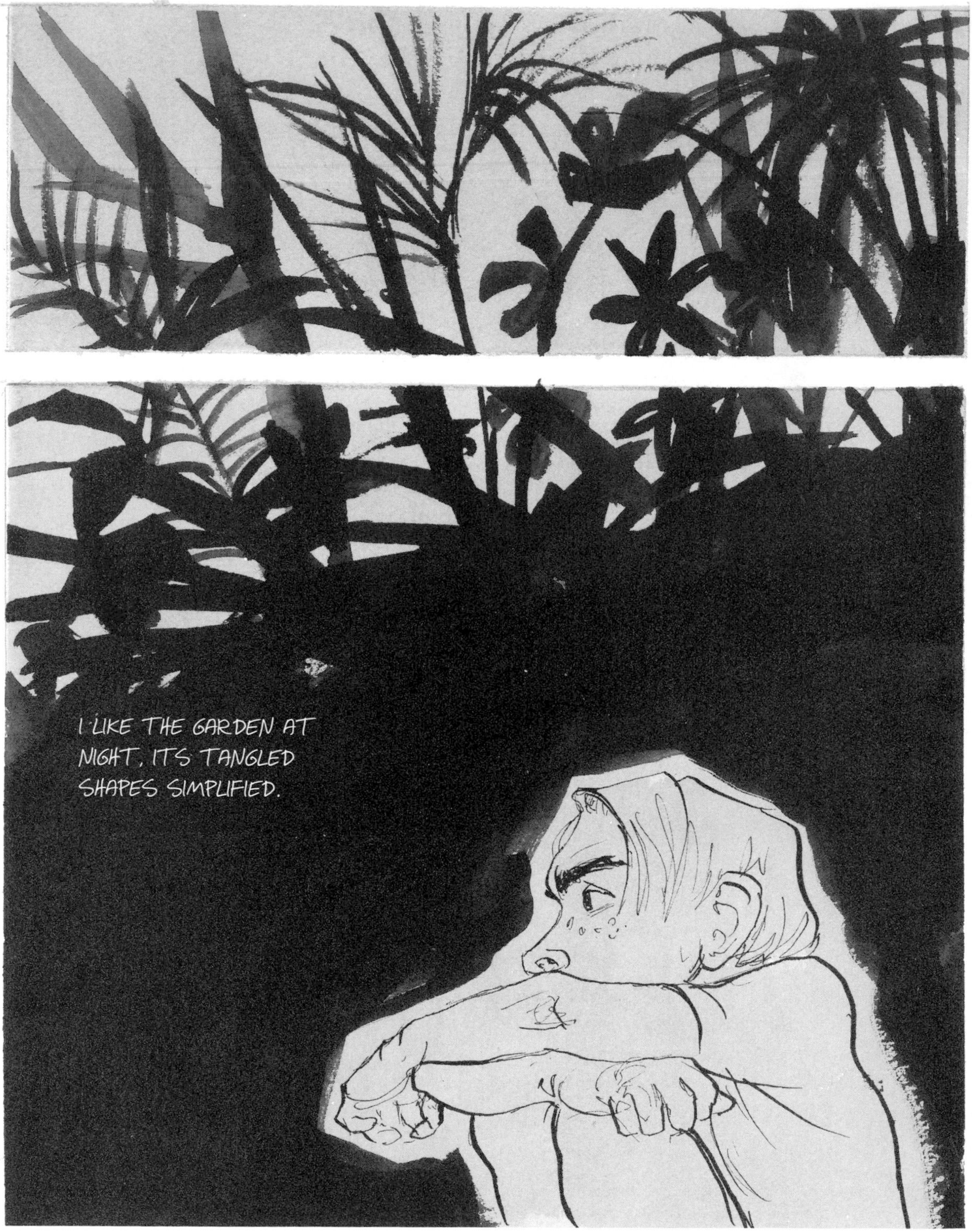
I LIKE THE GARDEN AT NIGHT, ITS TANGLED SHAPES SIMPLIFIED.

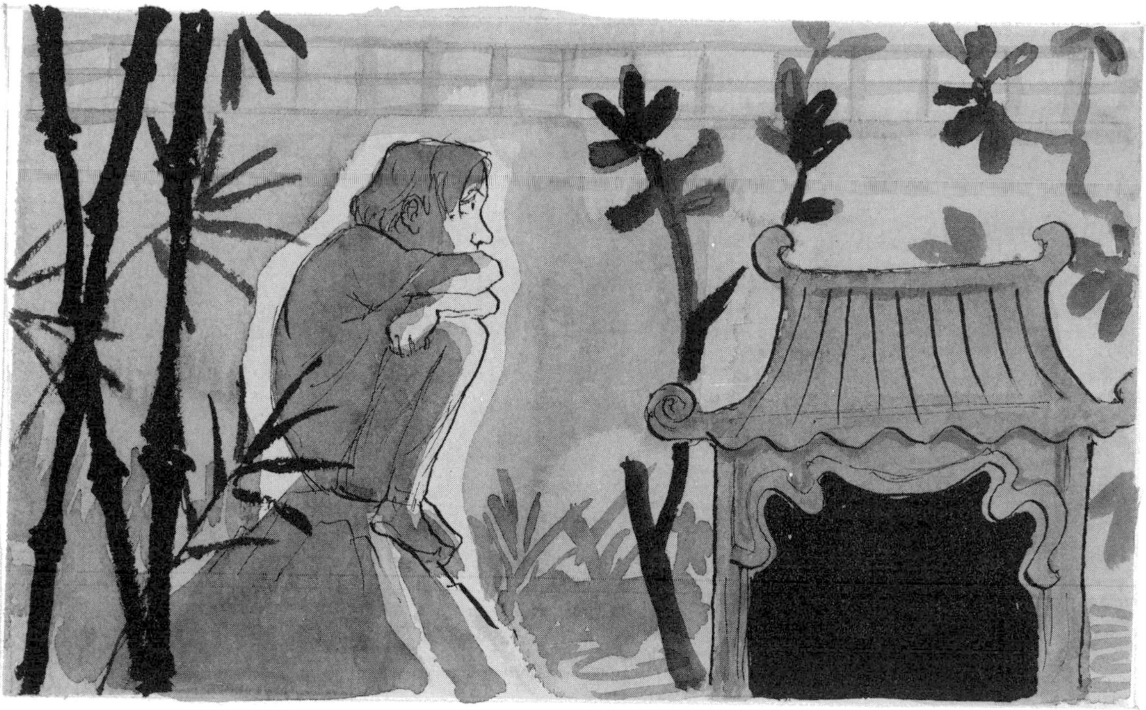

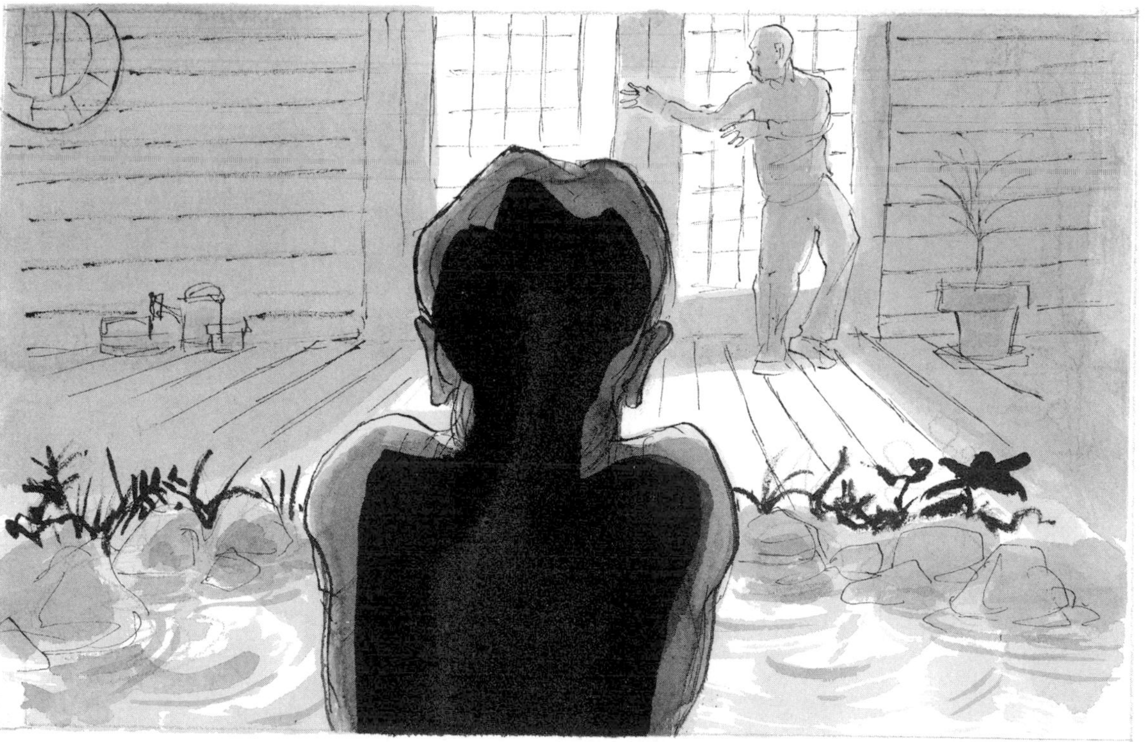

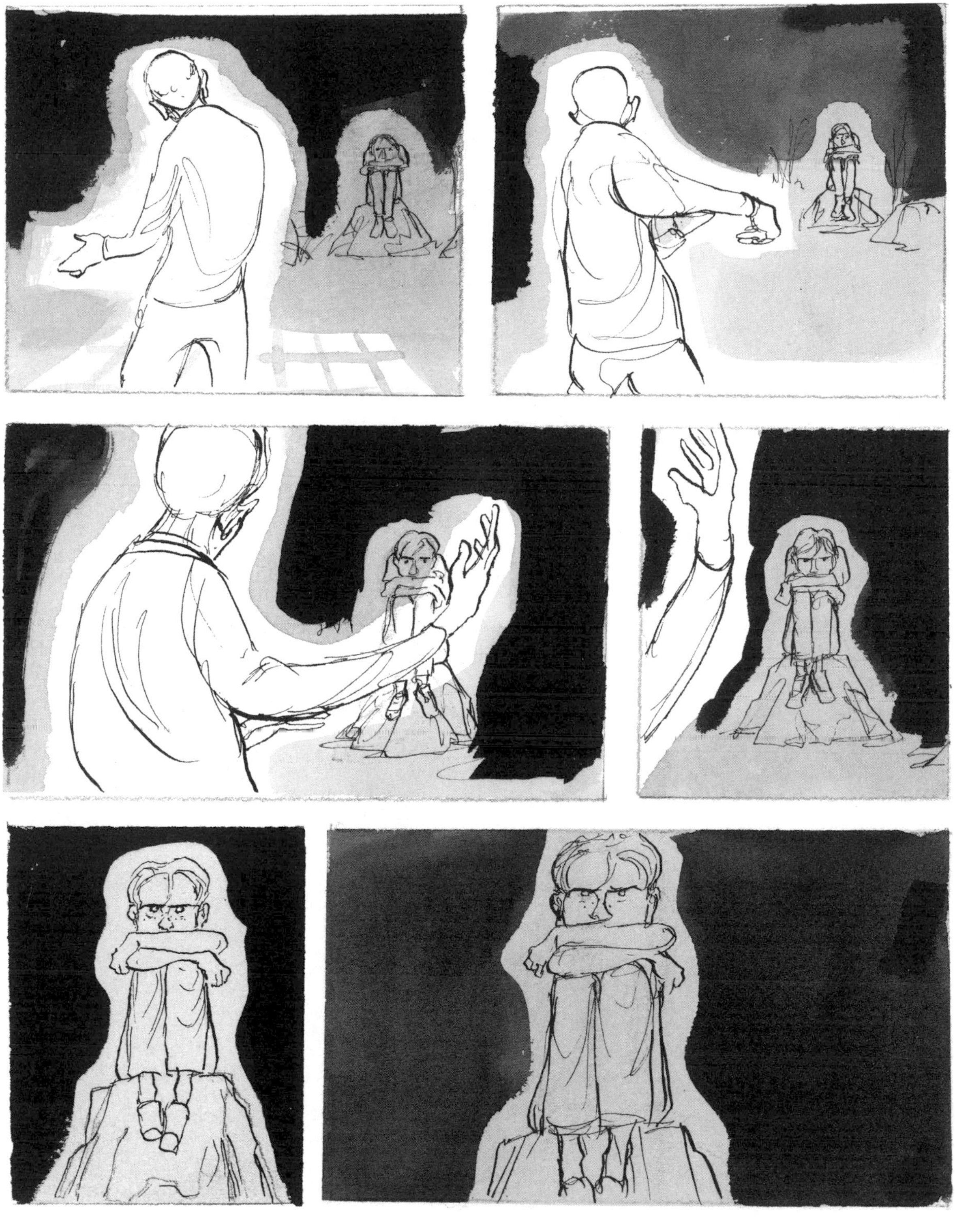

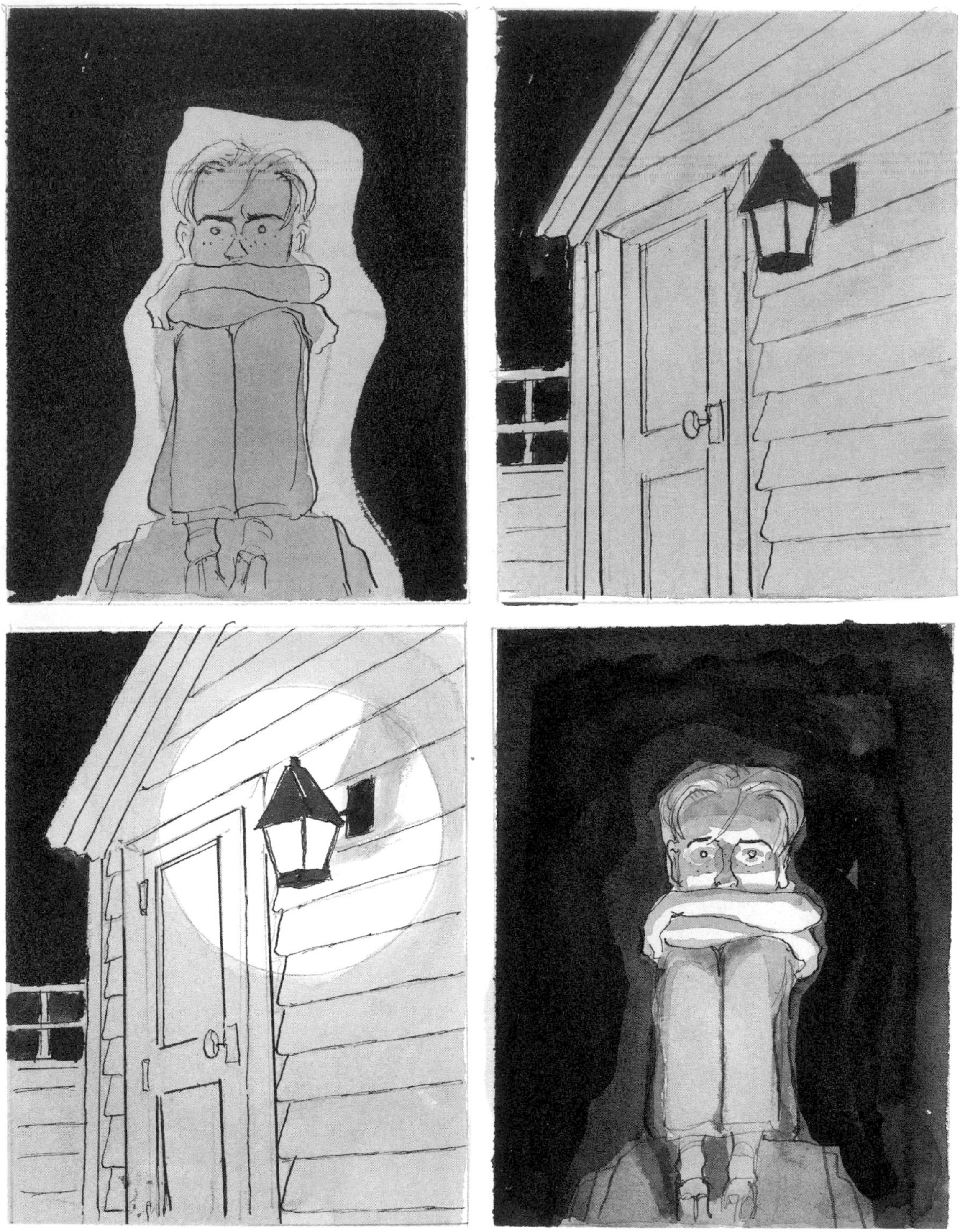

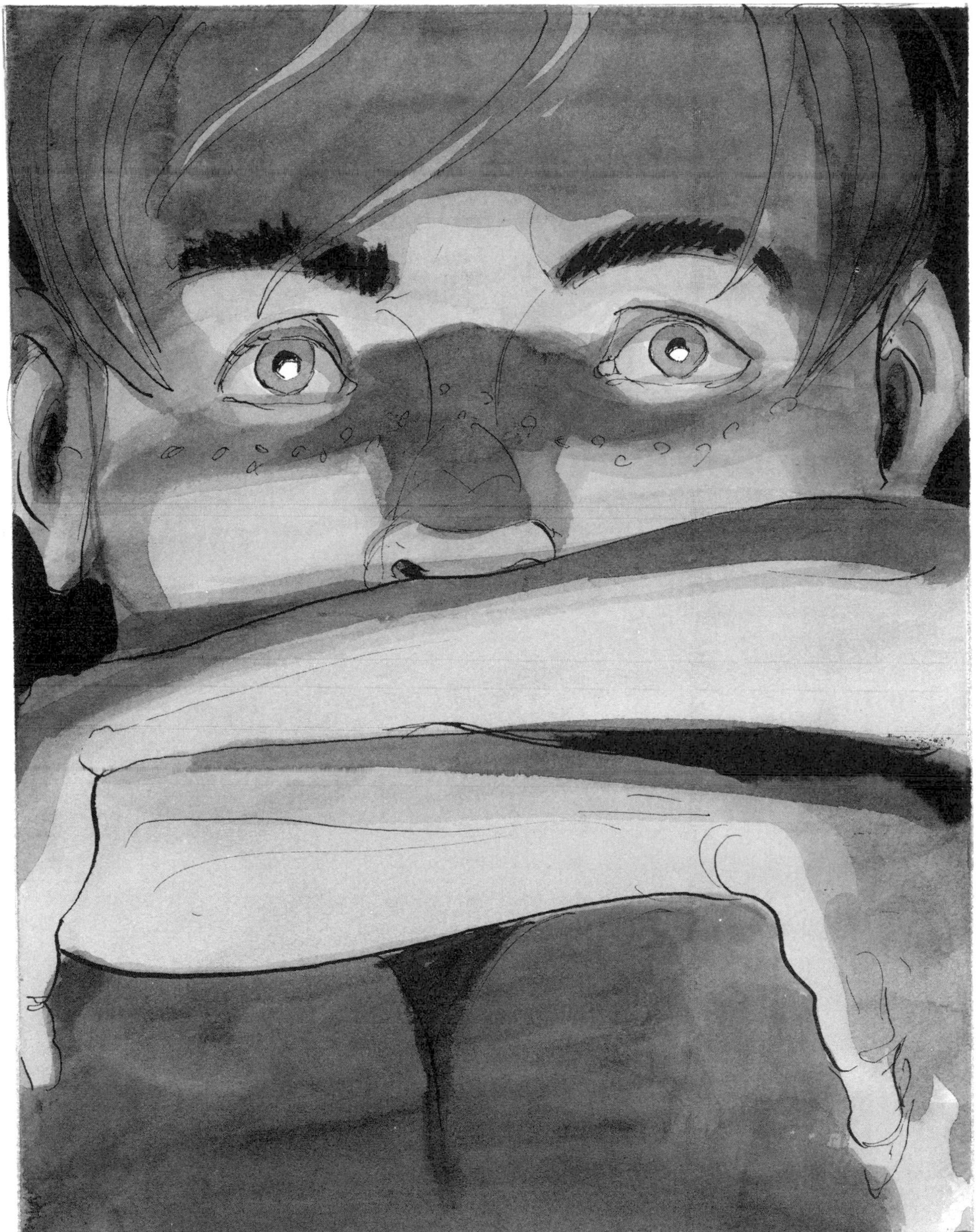

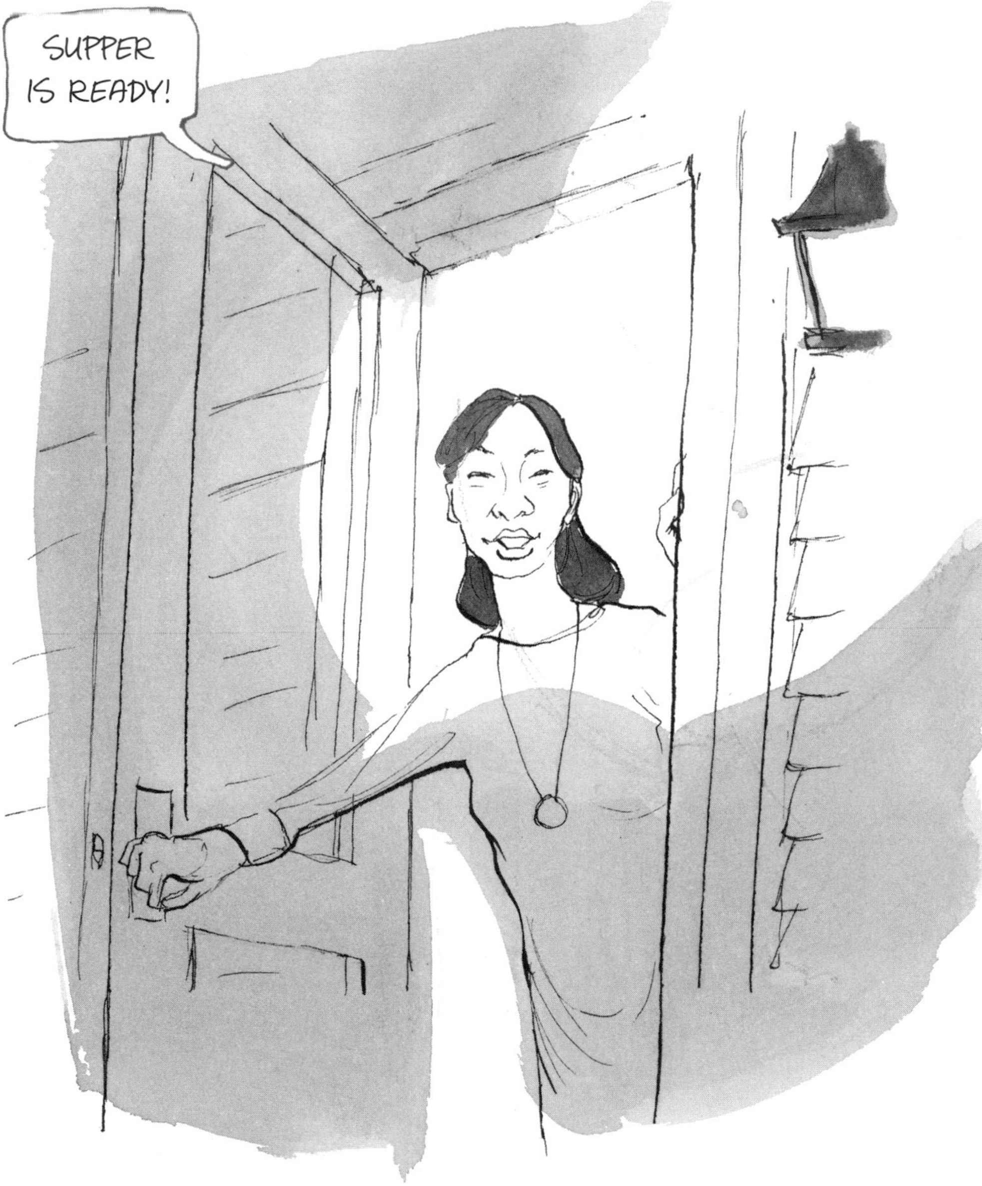
SUPPER IS READY!

ACKNOWLEDGMENTS

To Mike Kleimo, whose wicked-keen recollections of his youth were the catalyst for this story; to Kevin Brady, Mark Guin, and Brad Zellar—all brothers of my heart—who gave freely of their memories of adolescent chaos and middle-school brutality; to my agent, Holly McGhee, for her support and sharp editorial comments through the many different versions of this book; to my editor, Bob Weil, whose generosity, enthusiasm, and good counsel never flagged for three years, despite numerous stalls and setbacks; to Marie Pantojan, Bob's steady, discerning assistant; to Anna Oler, the best art director an artist could ever wish for; to Steve Attardo, whose amazing design skills and acute editorial sense produced a bounty of great jacket comps, so hard to choose from; to Joe Lops and Nat Kent, who did most of the behind-the-scenes heavy lifting on this project; to Peter Miller, to Nick Curley, and to my old friend Kate Kubert, who made all the publicity and marketing cogs and wheels run with seeming ease; to my *homies* Robert and Bill Trenary, who were with me on this ride from the start, who leaned with the sharpest curves and held on through the skids and near-collisions, always with forbearance and good humor; and, lastly, to Anita Chong for her penetrating and granular editorial advice, and—during one wintry week in Toronto—for lifting me up and setting me back on my creative feet when I needed it most.

ABOUT THE AUTHOR

David Small started his illustration career as an editorial artist for national publications such as *The New Yorker*, the *New York Times*, the *Washington Post*, *Esquire*, and *Playboy*. As the author and illustrator of numerous picture books for children, his books have been translated into several languages, made into animated films and musicals, and have won many of the top awards accorded to illustration, including the 2001 Caldecott Medal, two Caldecott Honor Awards, the Society for Illustrators' Gold Medal, and, twice, the Christopher Medal. In 2009 Small's illustration career took a dramatic turn with the publication of his graphic memoir, *Stitches*, which became a *New York Times* bestseller, a National Book Award Finalist, and received the American Library Association's Alex Award. To date, *Stitches* has been translated into ten foreign languages.

Small and his wife, the writer Sarah Stewart, make their home in an 1833 manor house on a bend of the St. Joseph River in Michigan.